VIZ GRAPHIC NOVEL

MAISON IKKOKU™ VOLUME TEN

DOGGED PURSUIT

STORY AND ART BY
RUMIKO TAKAHASHI

CONTENTS

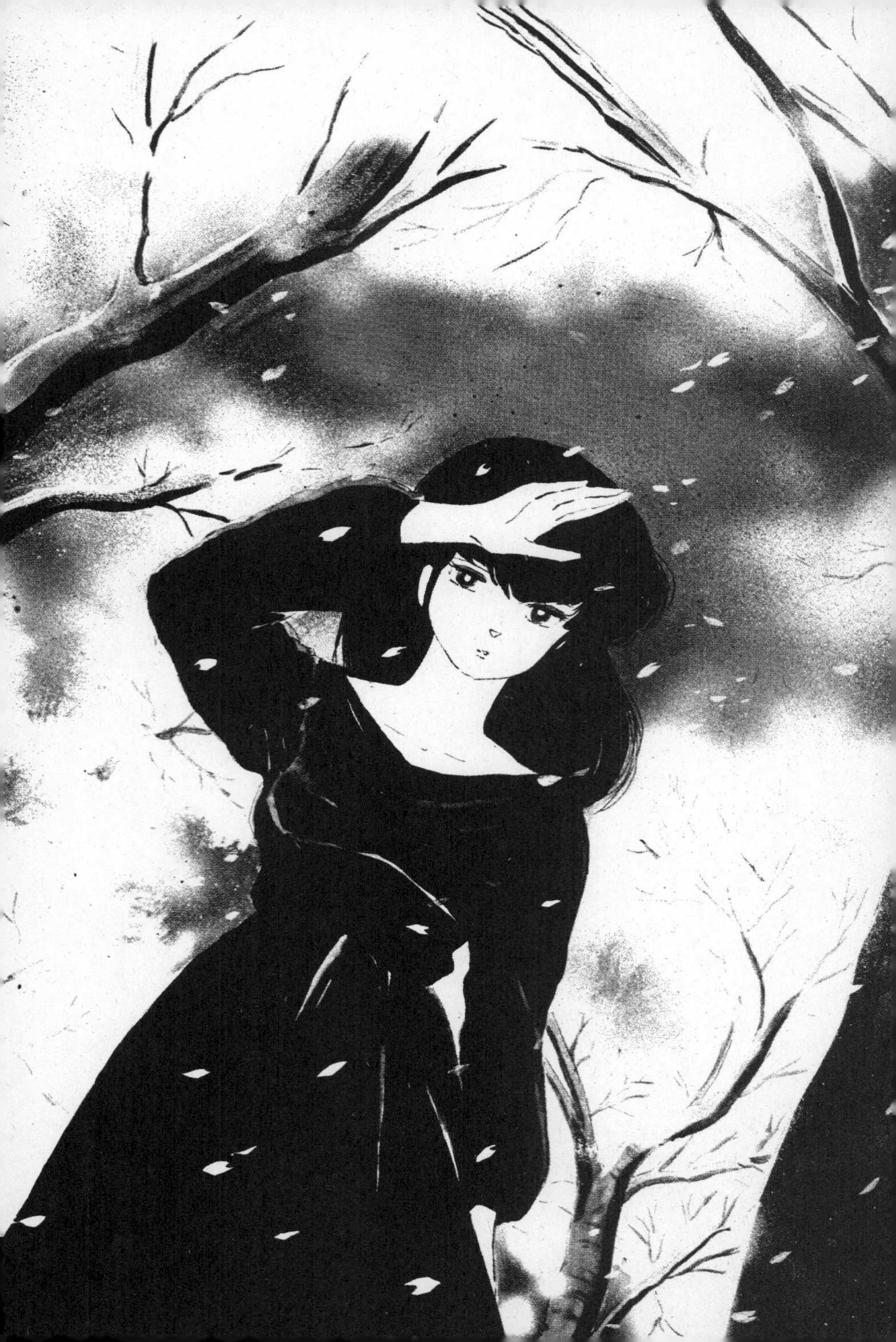

PART 1
LOST IN THE BLOSSOMS

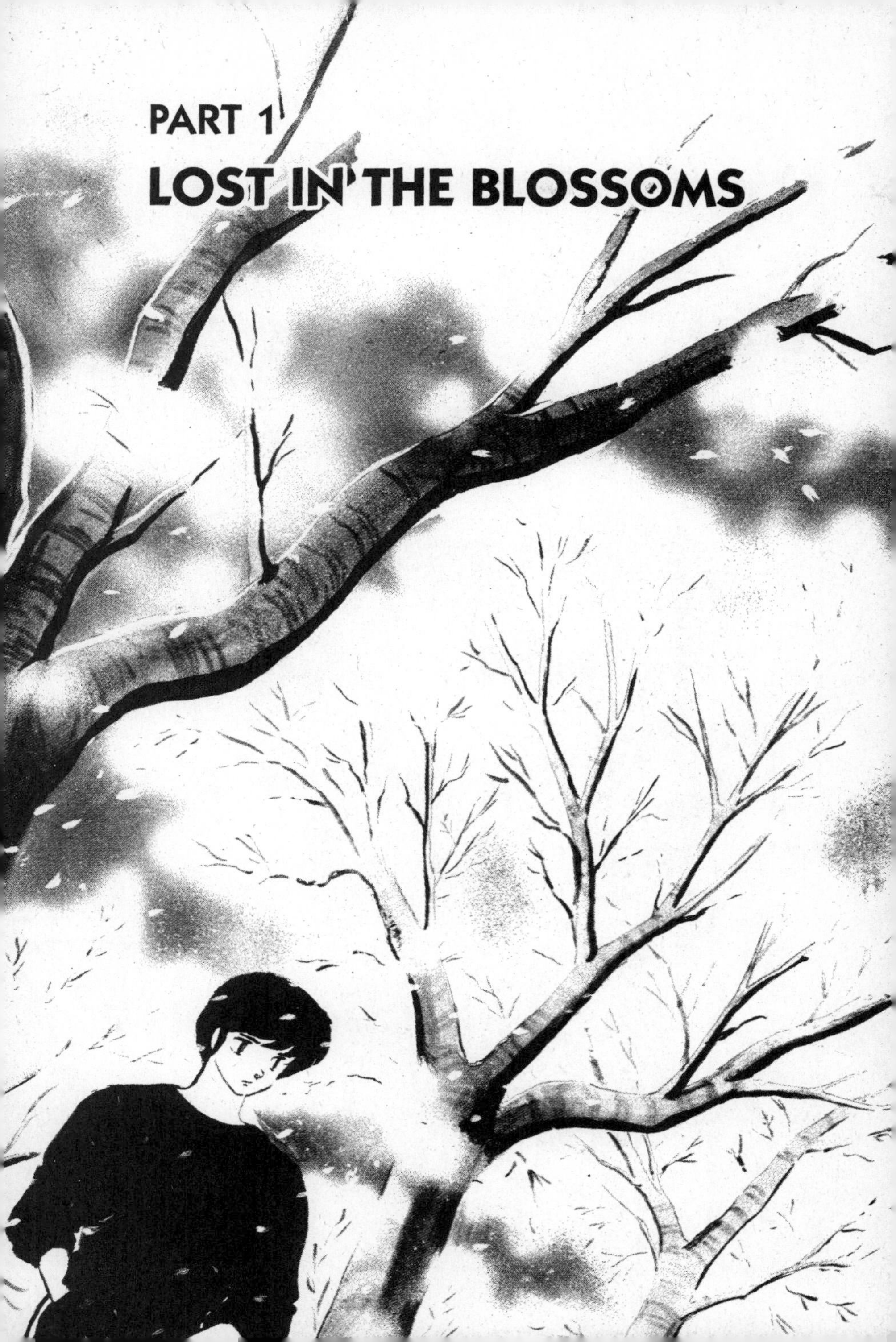

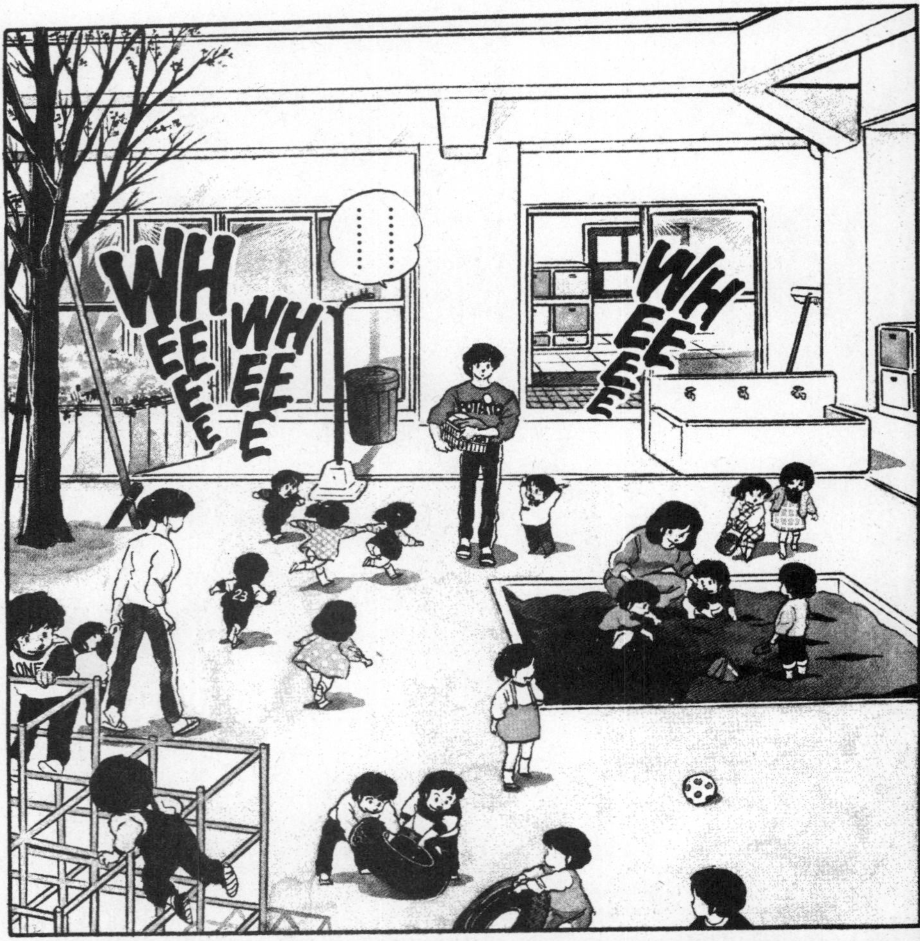
WHEEEE
WHEEEE
......
WHEEEE

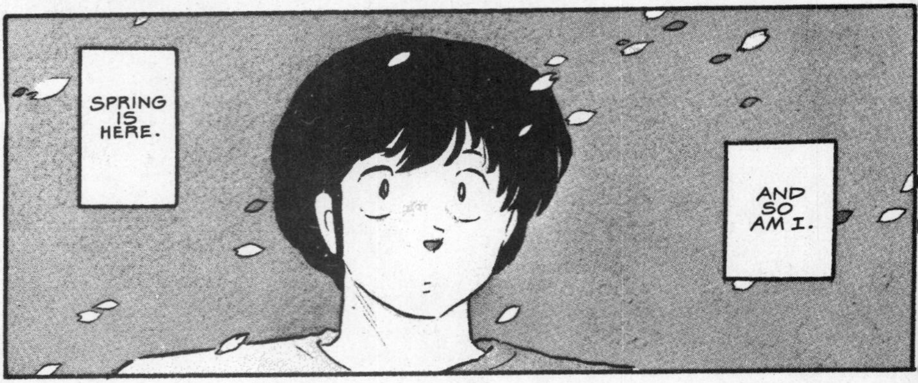
SPRING IS HERE.
AND SO AM I.

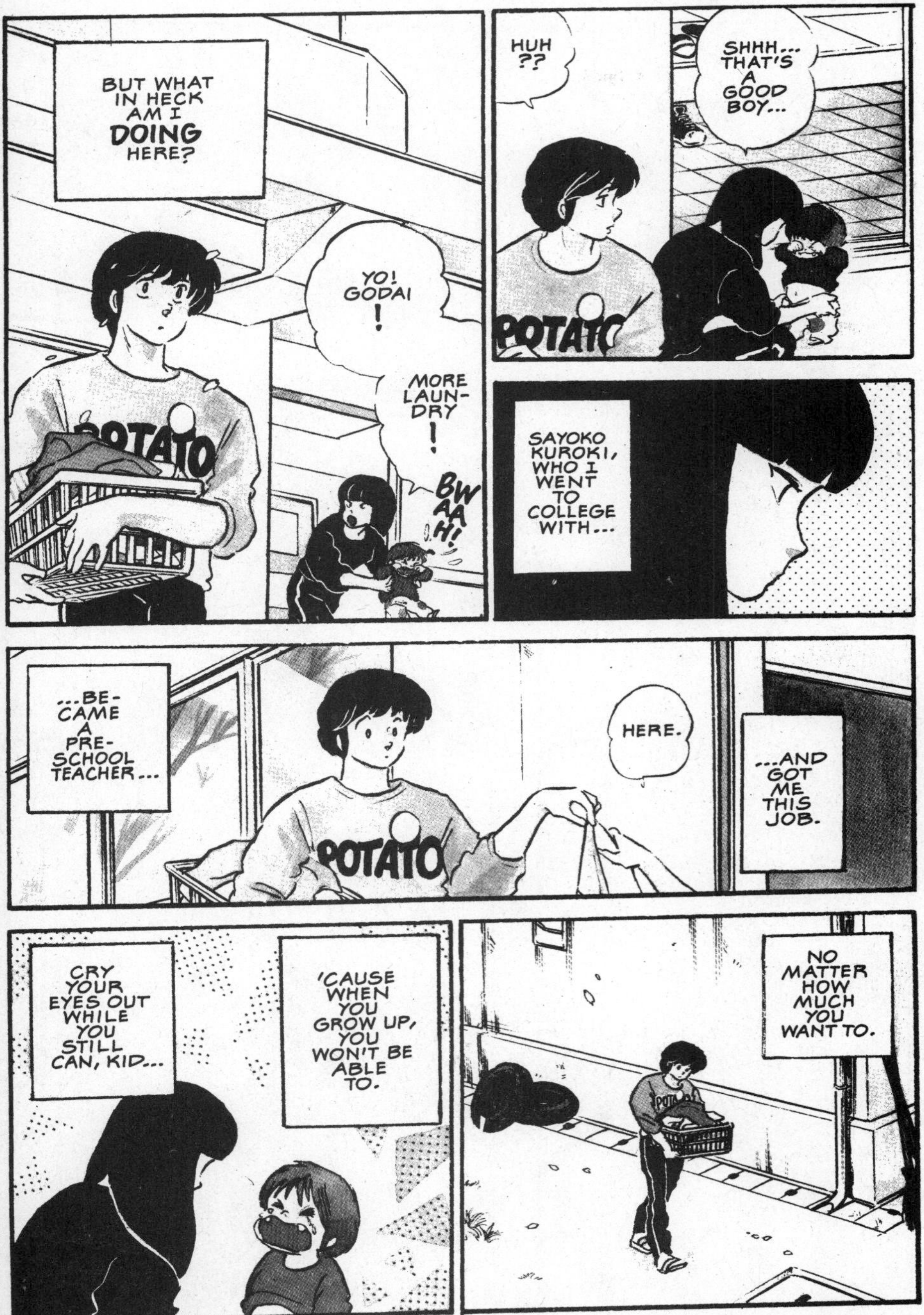
BUT WHAT IN HECK AM I DOING HERE?
YO! GODAI!
MORE LAUN-DRY!
BWAAH!
HUH??
SHHH... THAT'S A GOOD BOY...
SAYOKO KUROKI, WHO I WENT TO COLLEGE WITH...
...BE-CAME A PRE-SCHOOL TEACHER...
HERE.
...AND GOT ME THIS JOB.
CRY YOUR EYES OUT WHILE YOU STILL CAN, KID...
'CAUSE WHEN YOU GROW UP, YOU WON'T BE ABLE TO.
NO MATTER HOW MUCH YOU WANT TO.

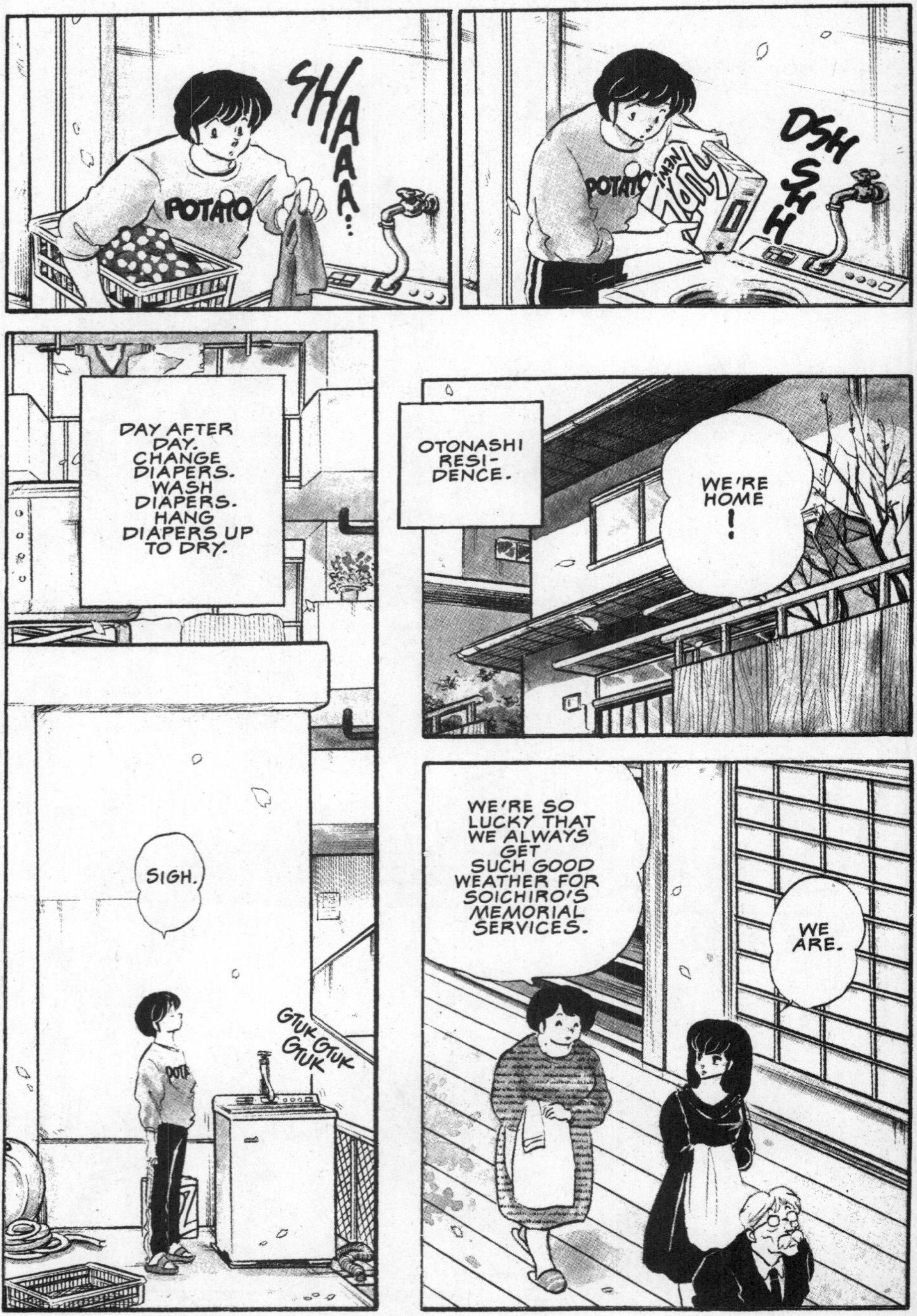
SHAAAA..
DSH SHH
DAY AFTER DAY. CHANGE DIAPERS. WASH DIAPERS. HANG DIAPERS UP TO DRY.
SIGH.
GTUK GTUK GTUK
OTONASHI RESI-DENCE.
WE'RE HOME!
WE'RE SO LUCKY THAT WE ALWAYS GET SUCH GOOD WEATHER FOR SOICHIRO'S MEMORIAL SERVICES.
WE ARE.

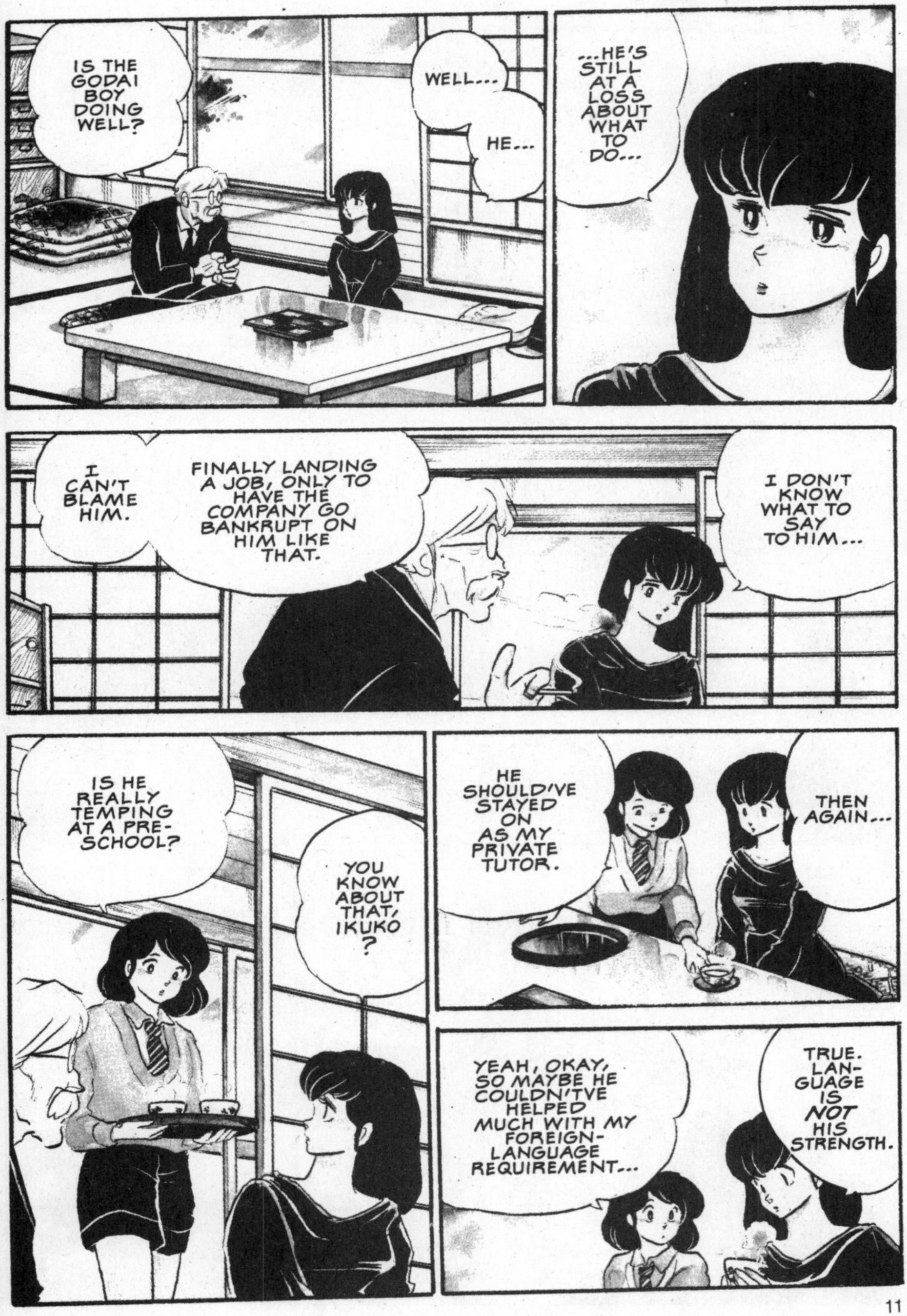
IS THE GODAI BOY DOING WELL?
WELL...
HE...
...HE'S STILL AT A LOSS ABOUT WHAT TO DO...
I CAN'T BLAME HIM.
FINALLY LANDING A JOB, ONLY TO HAVE THE COMPANY GO BANKRUPT ON HIM LIKE THAT.
I DON'T KNOW WHAT TO SAY TO HIM...
IS HE REALLY TEMPING AT A PRE-SCHOOL?
YOU KNOW ABOUT THAT, IKUKO?
HE SHOULD'VE STAYED ON AS MY PRIVATE TUTOR.
THEN AGAIN...
YEAH, OKAY, SO MAYBE HE COULDN'TVE HELPED MUCH WITH MY FOREIGN-LANGUAGE REQUIREMENT...
TRUE. LAN-GUAGE IS *NOT* HIS STRENGTH.

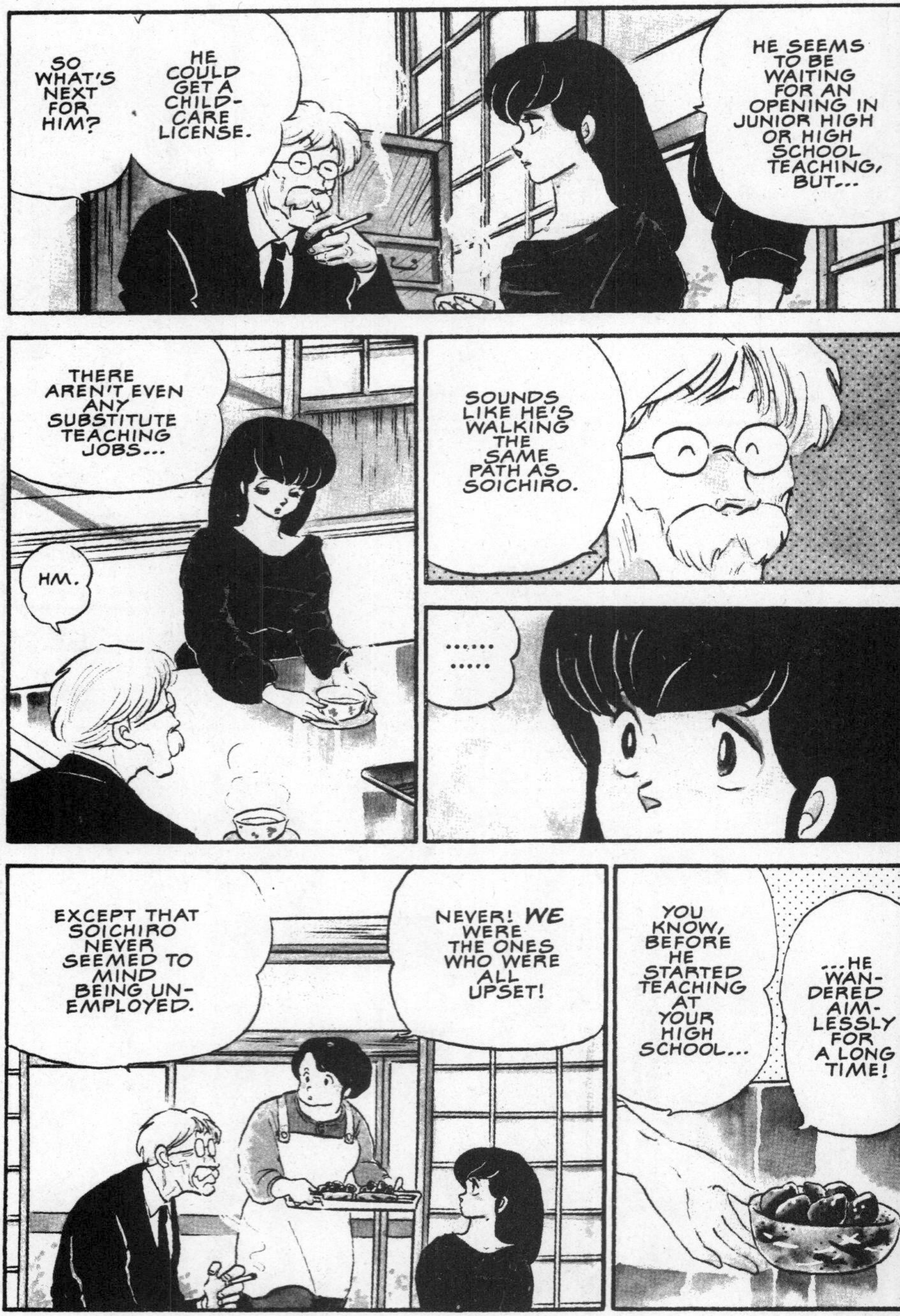
SO WHAT'S NEXT FOR HIM?
HE COULD GET A CHILD-CARE LICENSE.
HE SEEMS TO BE WAITING FOR AN OPENING IN JUNIOR HIGH OR HIGH SCHOOL TEACHING, BUT...
THERE AREN'T EVEN ANY SUBSTITUTE TEACHING JOBS...
HM.
SOUNDS LIKE HE'S WALKING THE SAME PATH AS SOICHIRO.
....
EXCEPT THAT SOICHIRO NEVER SEEMED TO MIND BEING UN-EMPLOYED.
NEVER! *WE* WERE THE ONES WHO WERE ALL UPSET!
YOU KNOW, BEFORE HE STARTED TEACHING AT YOUR HIGH SCHOOL...
...HE WANDERED AIMLESSLY FOR A LONG TIME!

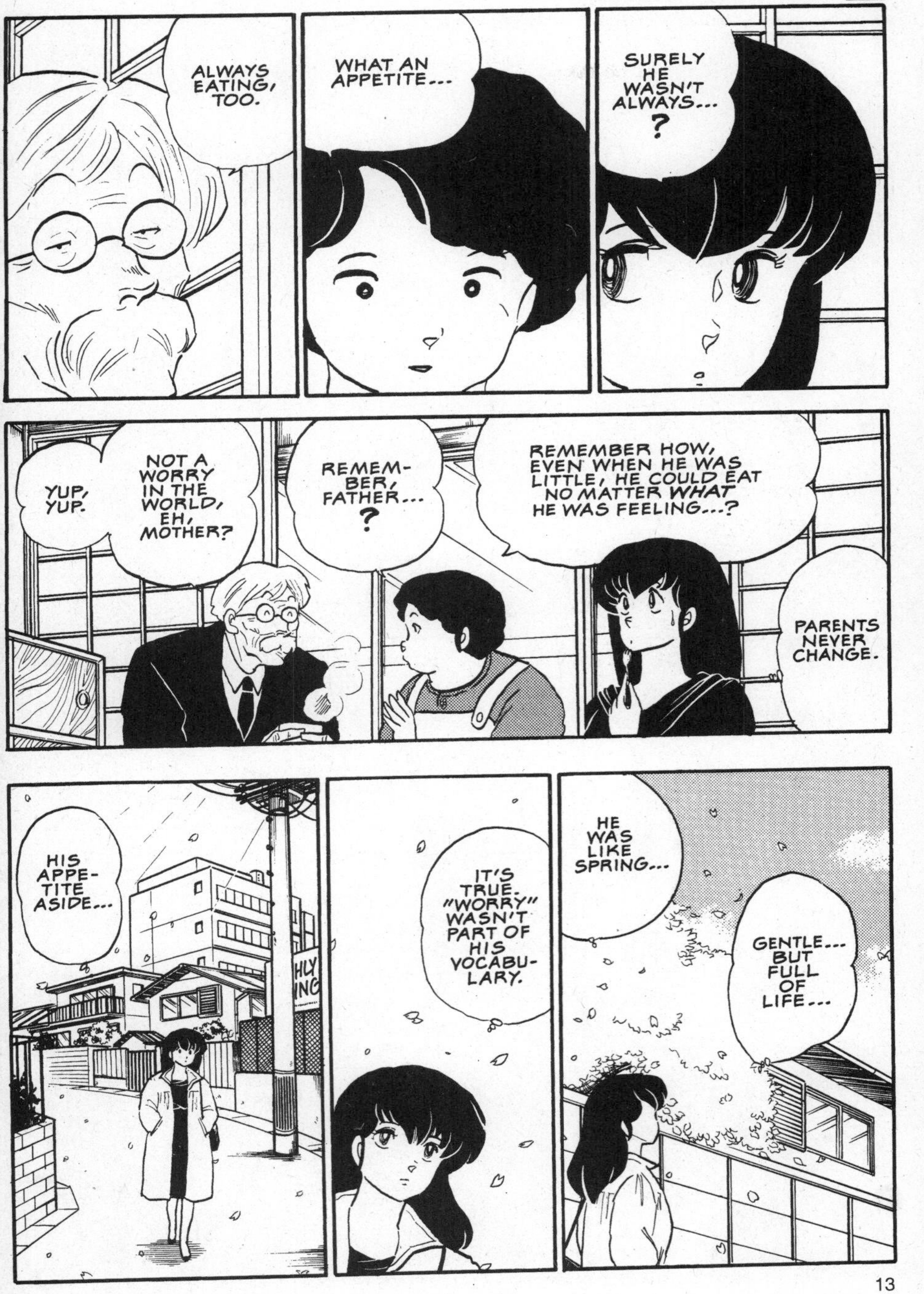
ALWAYS EATING, TOO.
WHAT AN APPETITE...
SURELY HE WASN'T ALWAYS... ?
YUP, YUP.
NOT A WORRY IN THE WORLD, EH, MOTHER?
REMEMBER, FATHER... ?
REMEMBER HOW, EVEN WHEN HE WAS LITTLE, HE COULD EAT NO MATTER *WHAT* HE WAS FEELING...?
PARENTS NEVER CHANGE.
HIS APPETITE ASIDE...
IT'S TRUE. "WORRY" WASN'T PART OF HIS VOCABULARY.
HE WAS LIKE SPRING...
GENTLE... BUT FULL OF LIFE...

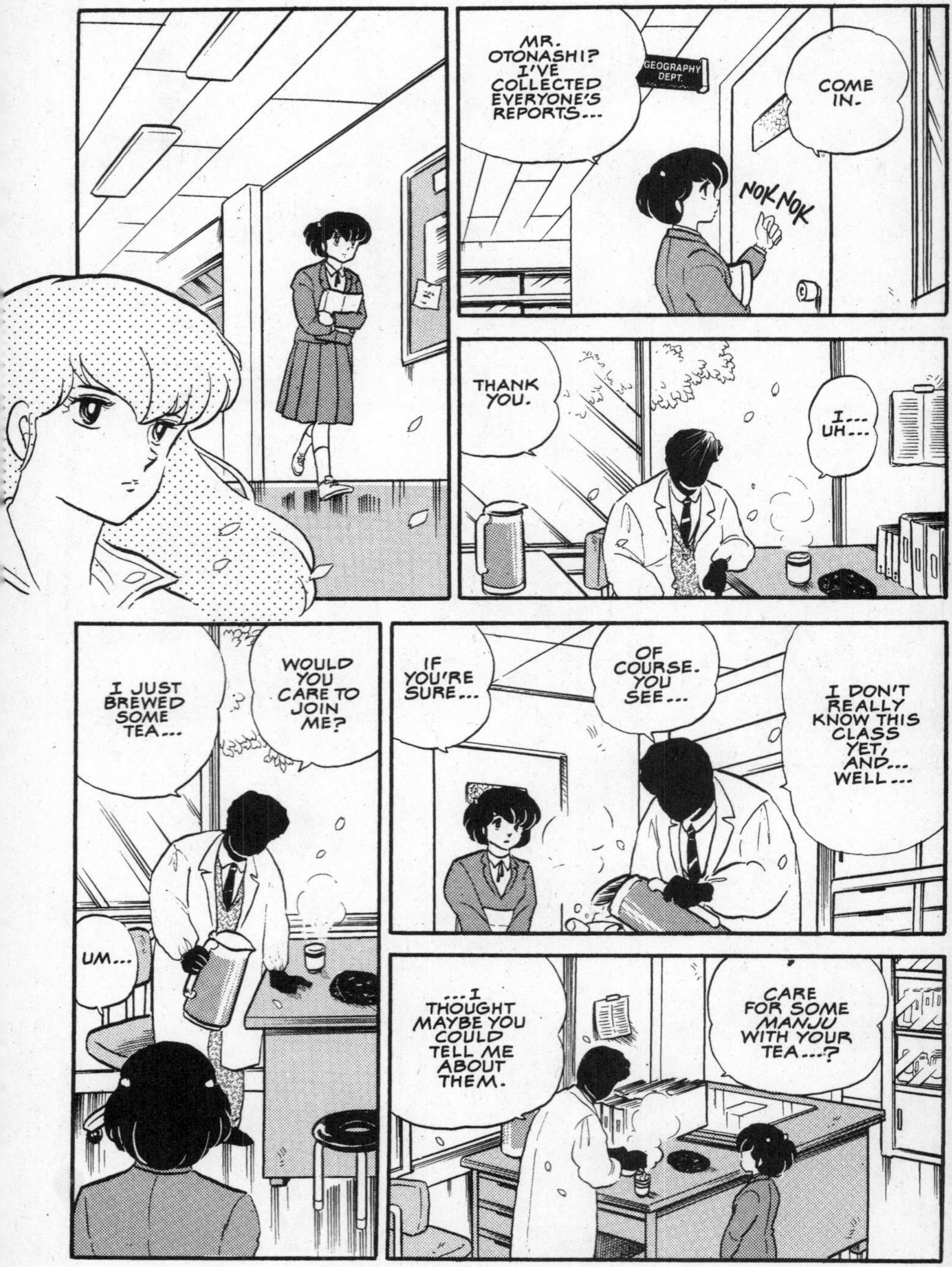
MR. OTONASHI? I'VE COLLECTED EVERYONE'S REPORTS...
GEOGRAPHY DEPT.
COME IN.
NOK NOK
THANK YOU.
I... UH...
I JUST BREWED SOME TEA...
WOULD YOU CARE TO JOIN ME?
UM...
IF YOU'RE SURE...
OF COURSE. YOU SEE...
I DON'T REALLY KNOW THIS CLASS YET, AND... WELL...
...I THOUGHT MAYBE YOU COULD TELL ME ABOUT THEM.
CARE FOR SOME MANJU WITH YOUR TEA...?

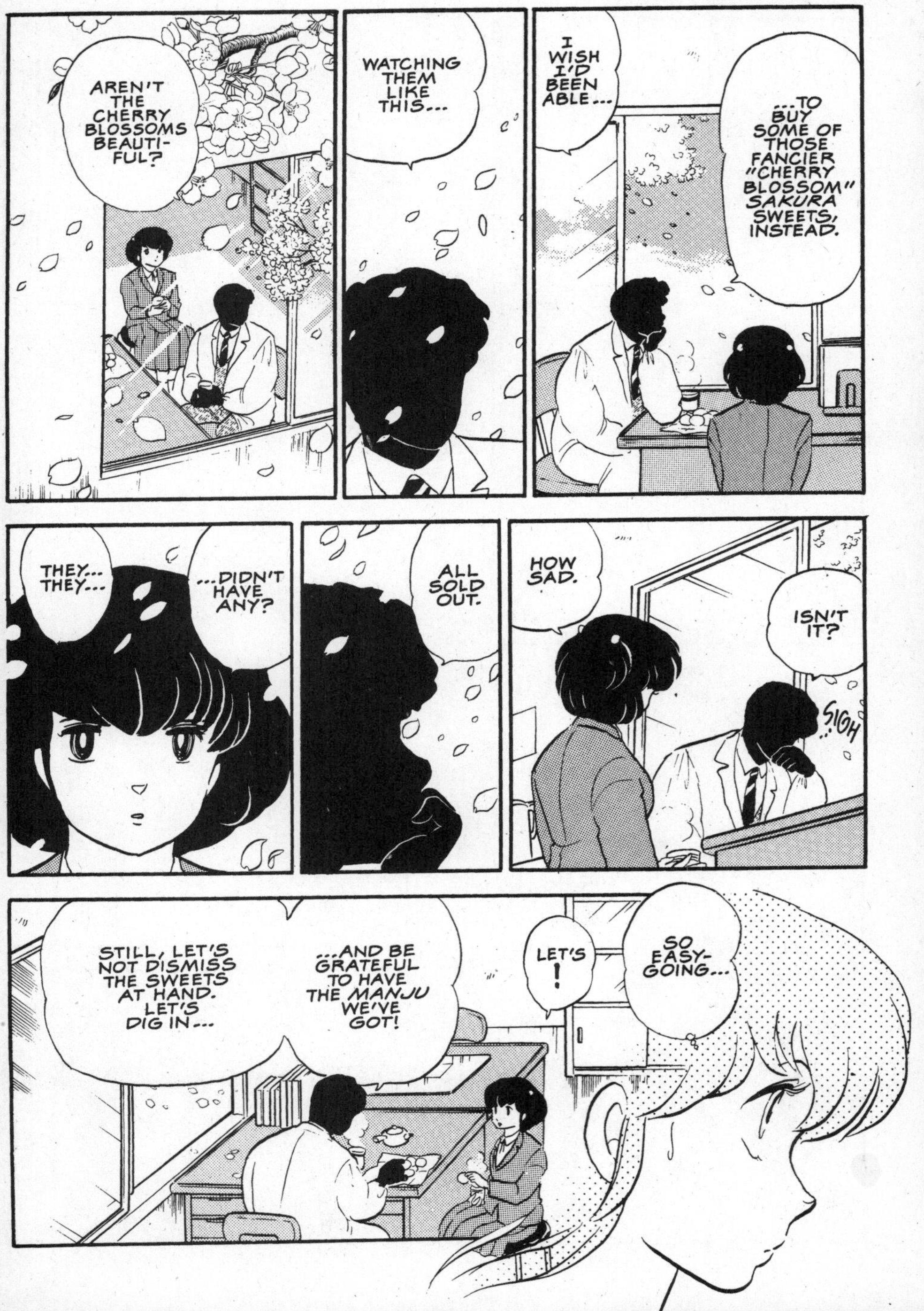
AREN'T THE CHERRY BLOSSOMS BEAUTIFUL?
WATCHING THEM LIKE THIS...
I WISH I'D BEEN ABLE...
...TO BUY SOME OF THOSE FANCIER "CHERRY BLOSSOM" SAKURA SWEETS, INSTEAD.
THEY... THEY...
...DIDN'T HAVE ANY?
ALL SOLD OUT.
HOW SAD.
ISN'T IT?
SIGH
STILL, LET'S NOT DISMISS THE SWEETS AT HAND. LET'S DIG IN...
...AND BE GRATEFUL TO HAVE THE MANJU WE'VE GOT!
LET'S
!
SO EASY-GOING...

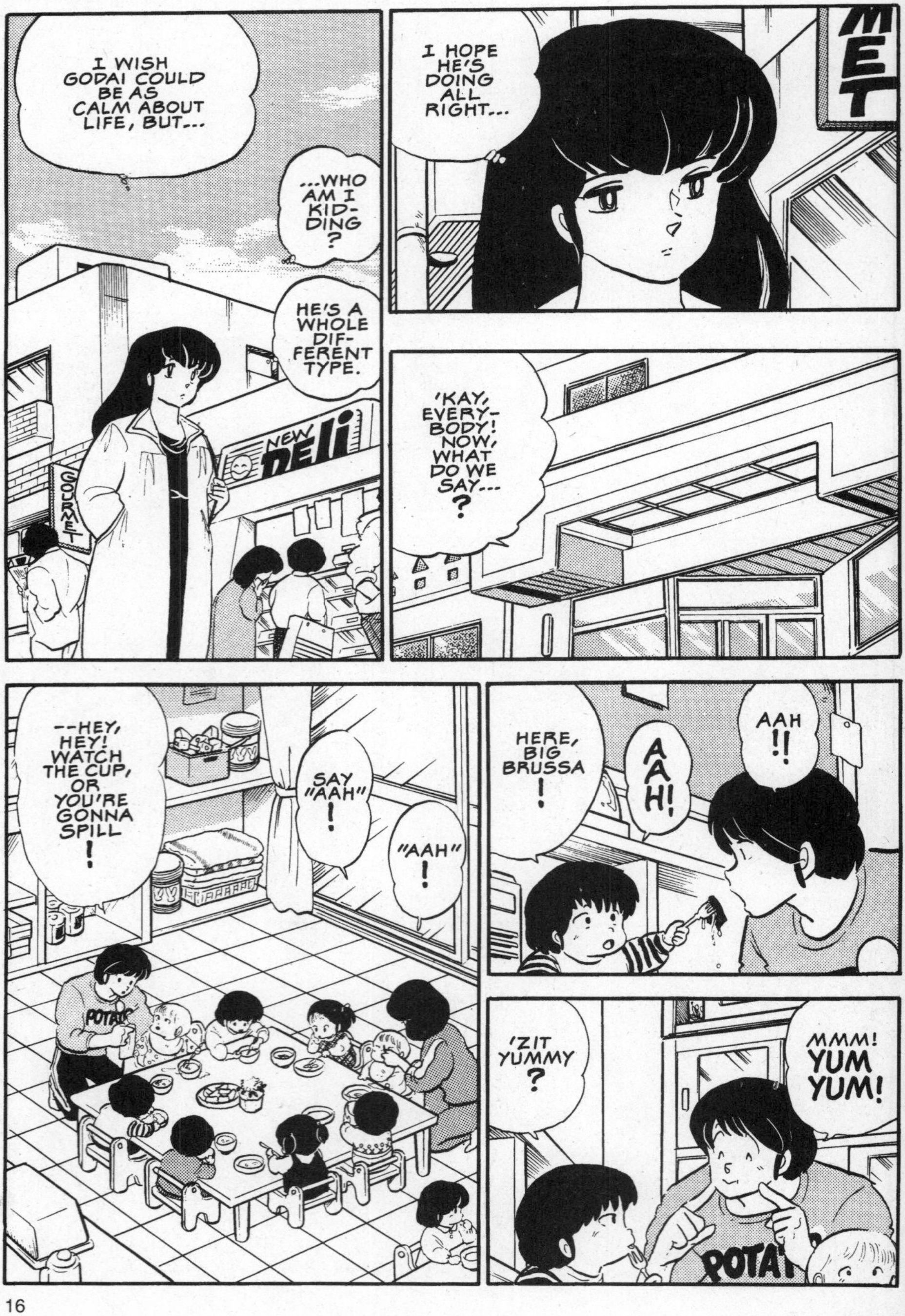
I WISH GODAI COULD BE AS CALM ABOUT LIFE, BUT...
...WHO AM I KID-DING?
HE'S A WHOLE DIF-FERENT TYPE.
NEW DELI
GOURMET
I HOPE HE'S DOING ALL RIGHT...
MET
'KAY, EVERY-BODY! NOW, WHAT DO WE SAY...?
--HEY, HEY! WATCH THE CUP, OR YOU'RE GONNA SPILL!
SAY "AAH"!
"AAH"!
HERE, BIG BRUSSA!
AAH!
AAH!!
'ZIT YUMMY?
MMM! YUM YUM!

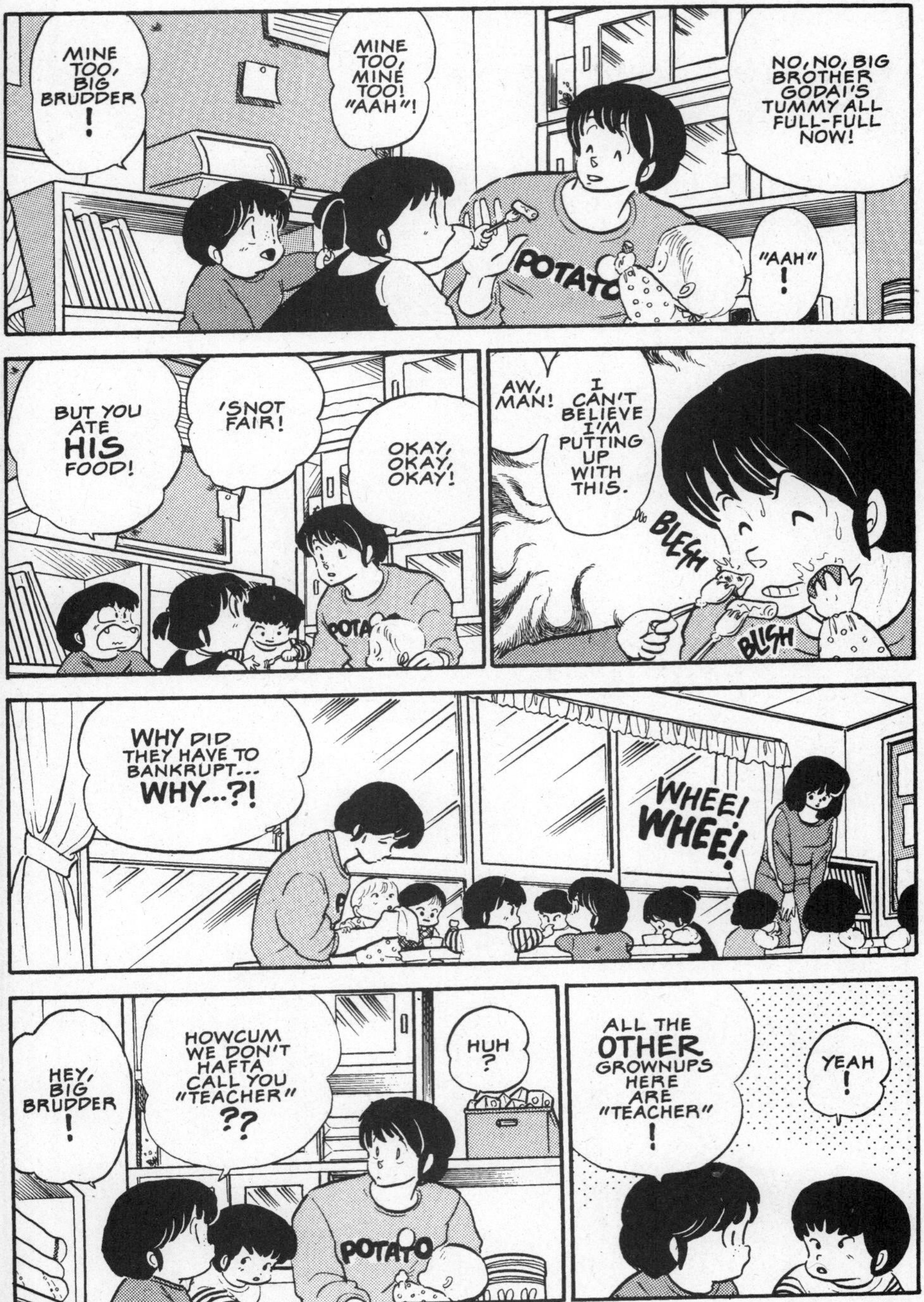
MINE TOO, BIG BRUDDER!
MINE TOO, MINE TOO! "AAH"!
NO, NO, BIG BROTHER GODAI'S TUMMY ALL FULL-FULL NOW!
POTATO
"AAH"!
BUT YOU ATE HIS FOOD!
'SNOT FAIR!
OKAY, OKAY, OKAY!
POTA
AW, MAN!
I CAN'T BELIEVE I'M PUTTING UP WITH THIS.
BLESH
BLESH
WHY DID THEY HAVE TO BANKRUPT... WHY...?!
WHEE! WHEE!
HEY, BIG BRUDDER!
HOWCUM WE DON'T HAFTA CALL YOU "TEACHER"??
HUH?
POTATO
ALL THE OTHER GROWNUPS HERE ARE "TEACHER"!
YEAH!

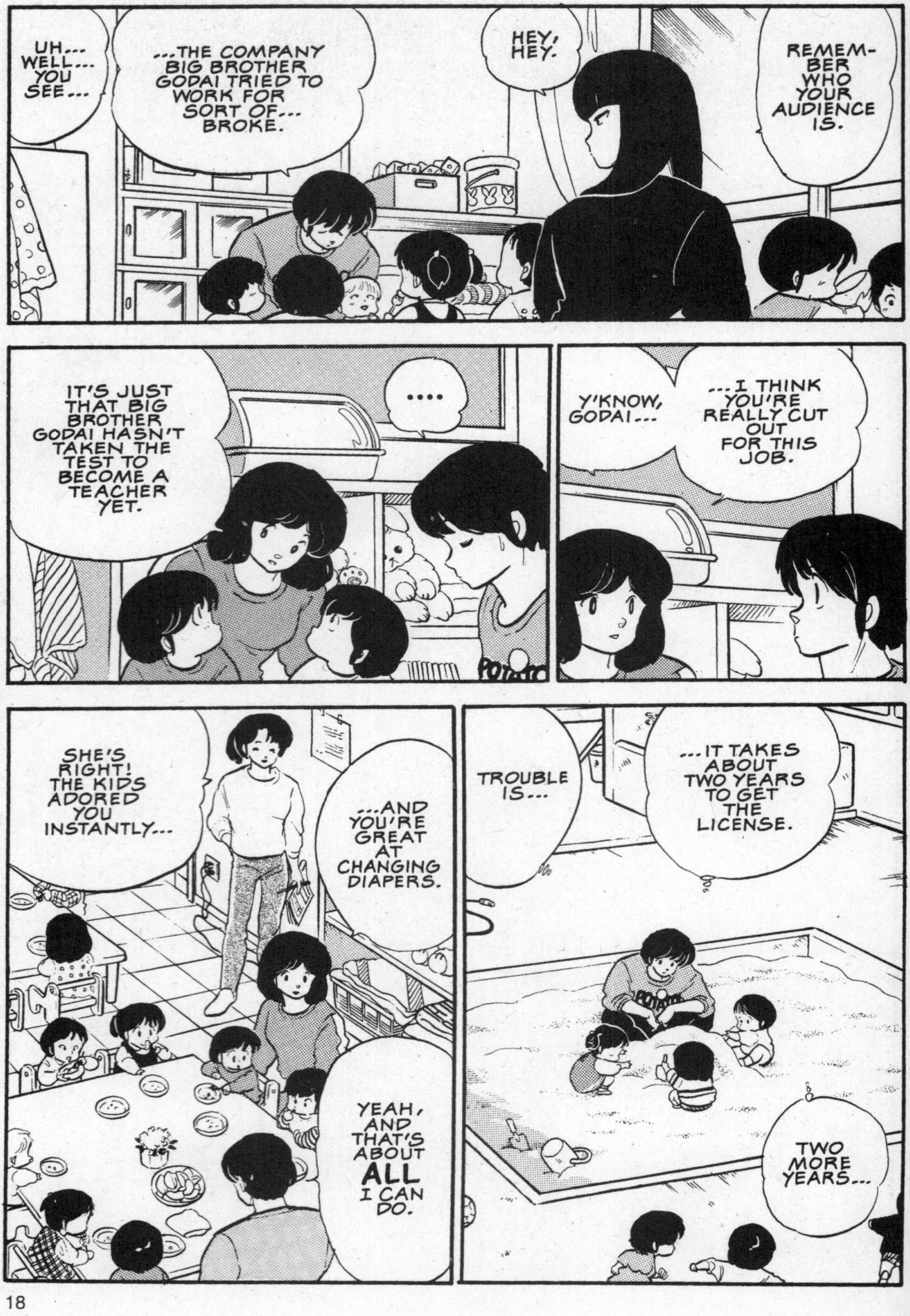
UH... WELL... YOU SEE...
...THE COMPANY BIG BROTHER GODAI TRIED TO WORK FOR SORT OF... BROKE.
HEY, HEY.
REMEMBER WHO YOUR AUDIENCE IS.
IT'S JUST THAT BIG BROTHER GODAI HASN'T TAKEN THE TEST TO BECOME A TEACHER YET.
....
Y'KNOW, GODAI...
...I THINK YOU'RE REALLY CUT OUT FOR THIS JOB.
SHE'S RIGHT! THE KIDS ADORED YOU INSTANTLY...
...AND YOU'RE GREAT AT CHANGING DIAPERS.
YEAH, AND THAT'S ABOUT ALL I CAN DO.
TROUBLE IS...
...IT TAKES ABOUT TWO YEARS TO GET THE LICENSE.
TWO MORE YEARS...

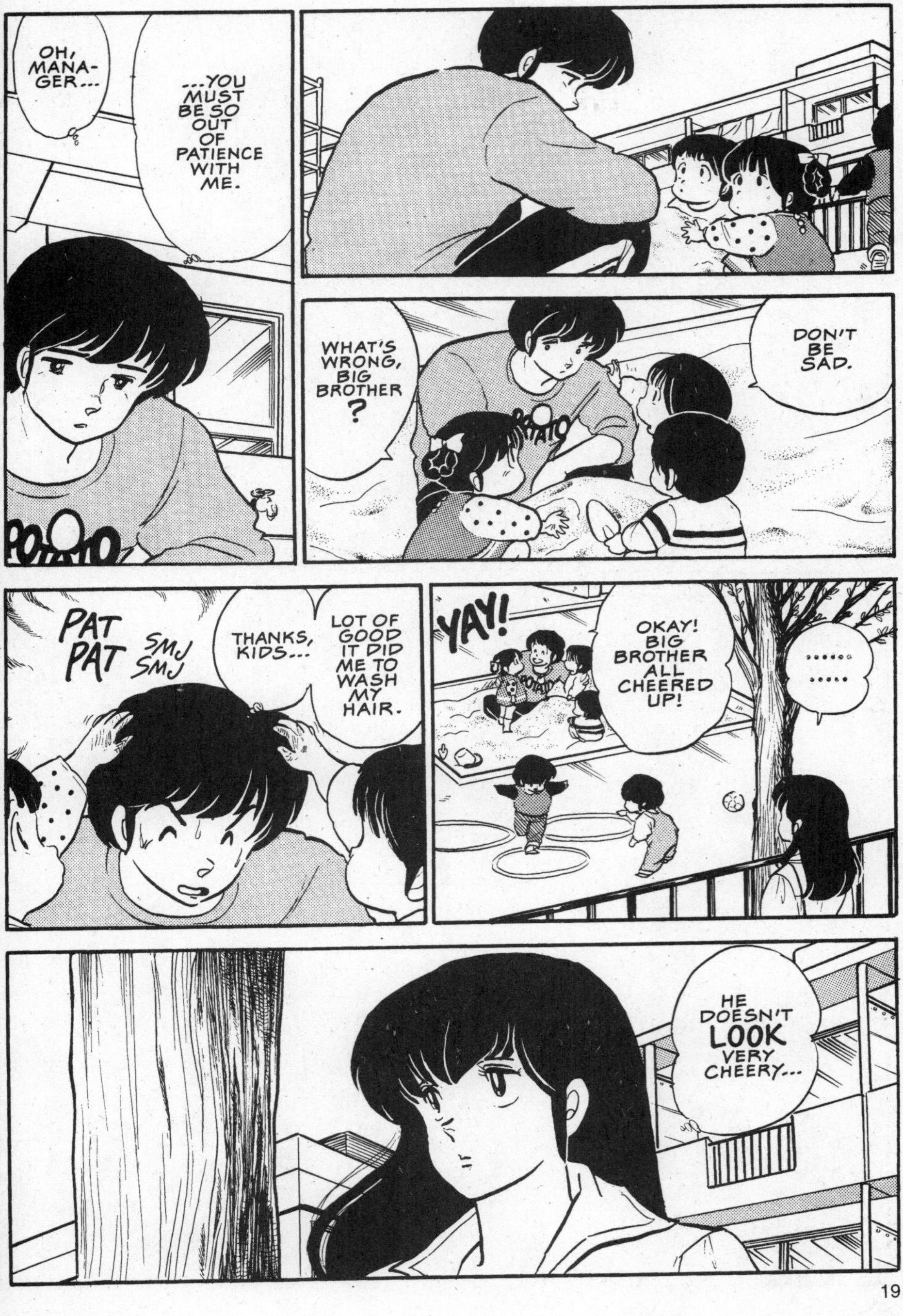
OH, MANA-GER...
...YOU MUST BE SO OUT OF PATIENCE WITH ME.
WHAT'S WRONG, BIG BROTHER?
DON'T BE SAD.
PAT PAT
SMJ SMJ
THANKS, KIDS...
LOT OF GOOD IT DID ME TO WASH MY HAIR.
YAY!
OKAY! BIG BROTHER ALL CHEERED UP!
......
.....
HE DOESN'T LOOK VERY CHEERY...

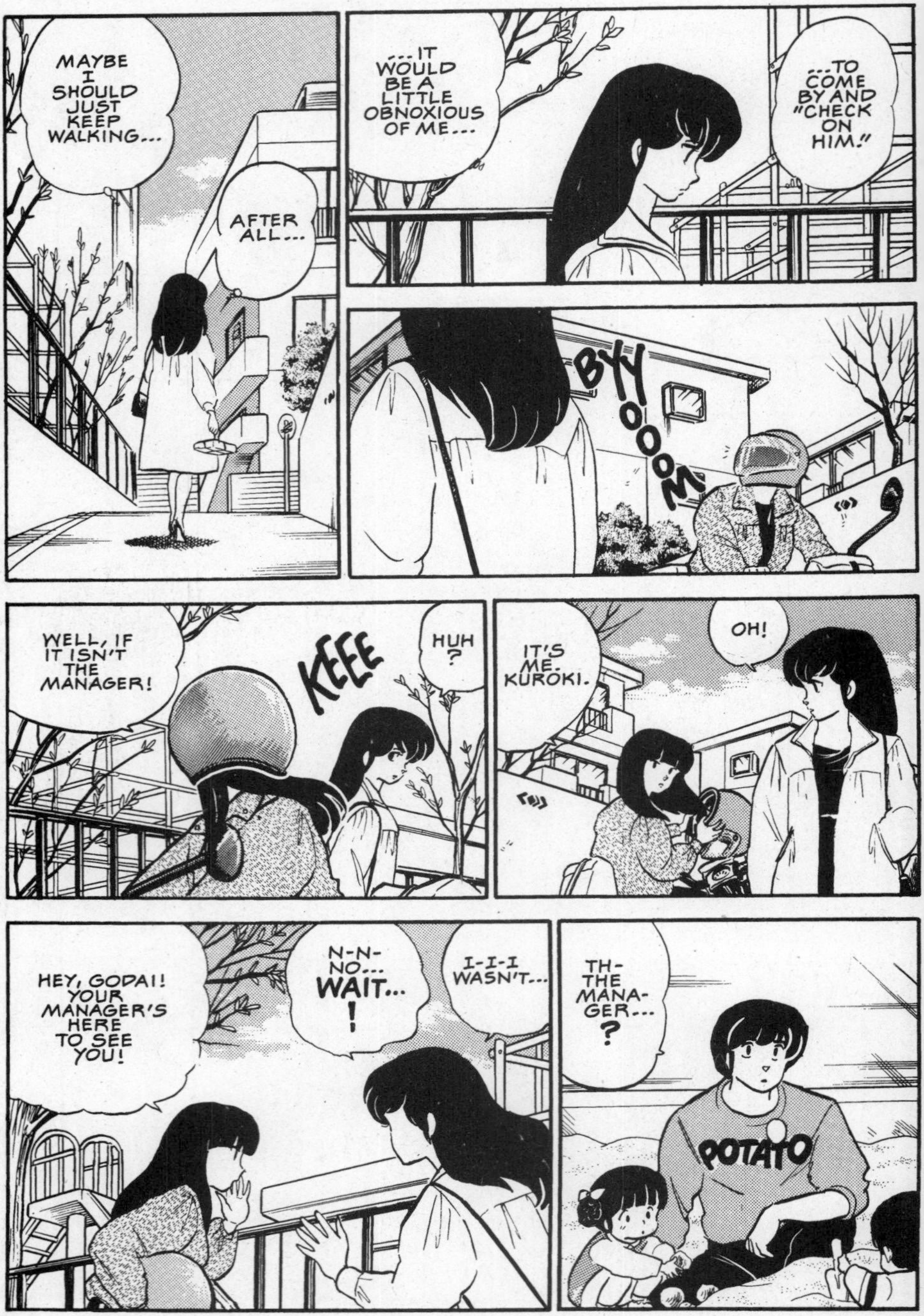
MAYBE I SHOULD JUST KEEP WALKING...
AFTER ALL...
...IT WOULD BE A LITTLE OBNOXIOUS OF ME...
...TO COME BY AND "CHECK ON HIM."
BYYOOOM
WELL, IF IT ISN'T THE MANAGER!
KEEE
HUH?
IT'S ME. KUROKI.
OH!
HEY, GODAI! YOUR MANAGER'S HERE TO SEE YOU!
N-N-NO... WAIT...!
I-I-I WASN'T...
TH-THE MANA-GER...?
POTATO

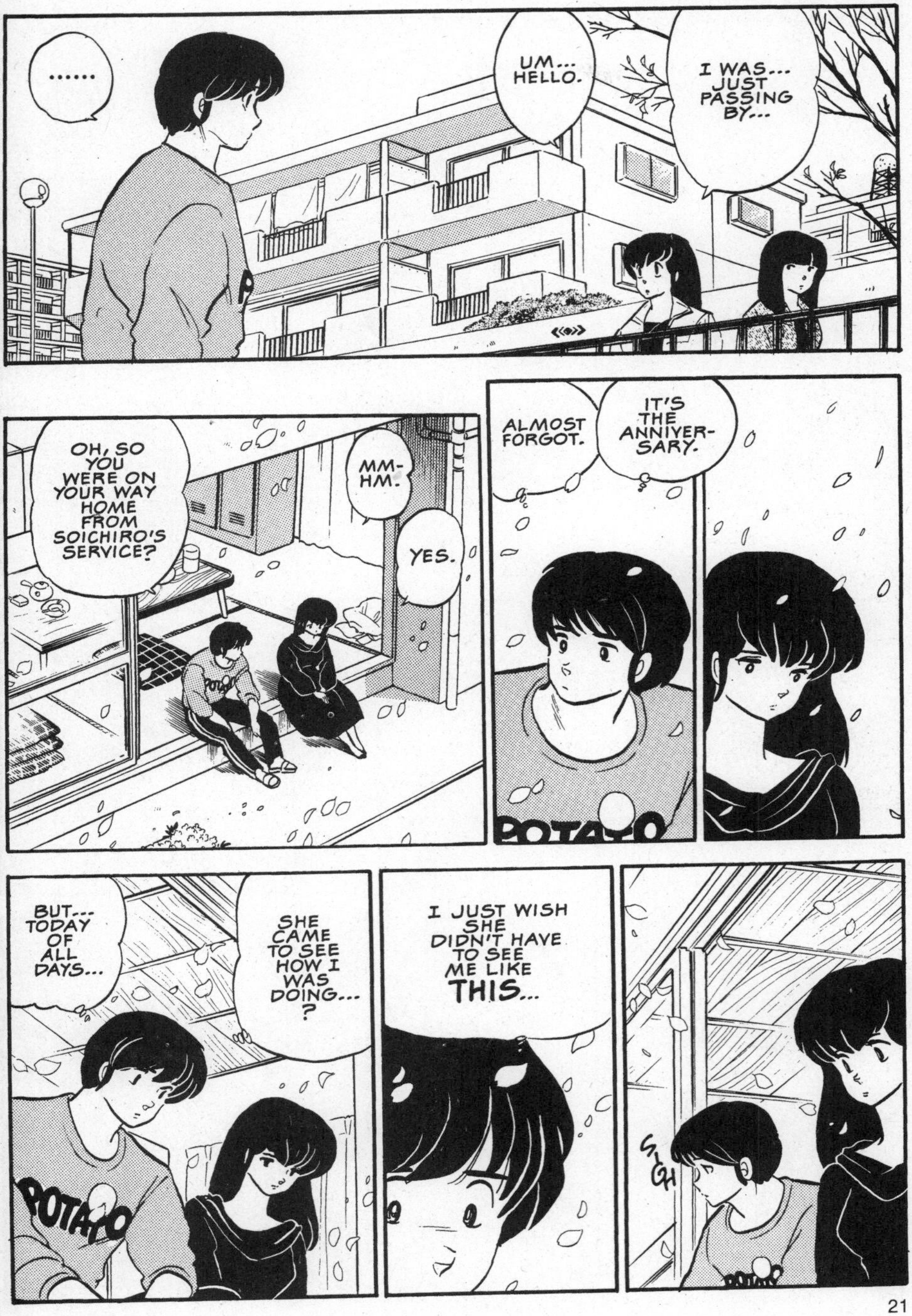
......
UM... HELLO.
I WAS... JUST PASSING BY...
OH, SO YOU WERE ON YOUR WAY HOME FROM SOICHIRO'S SERVICE?
MM-HM.
YES.
ALMOST FORGOT.
IT'S THE ANNIVER-SARY.
POTATO
BUT... TODAY OF ALL DAYS...
SHE CAME TO SEE HOW I WAS DOING...?
POTATO
I JUST WISH SHE DIDN'T HAVE TO SEE ME LIKE THIS...
SIGH

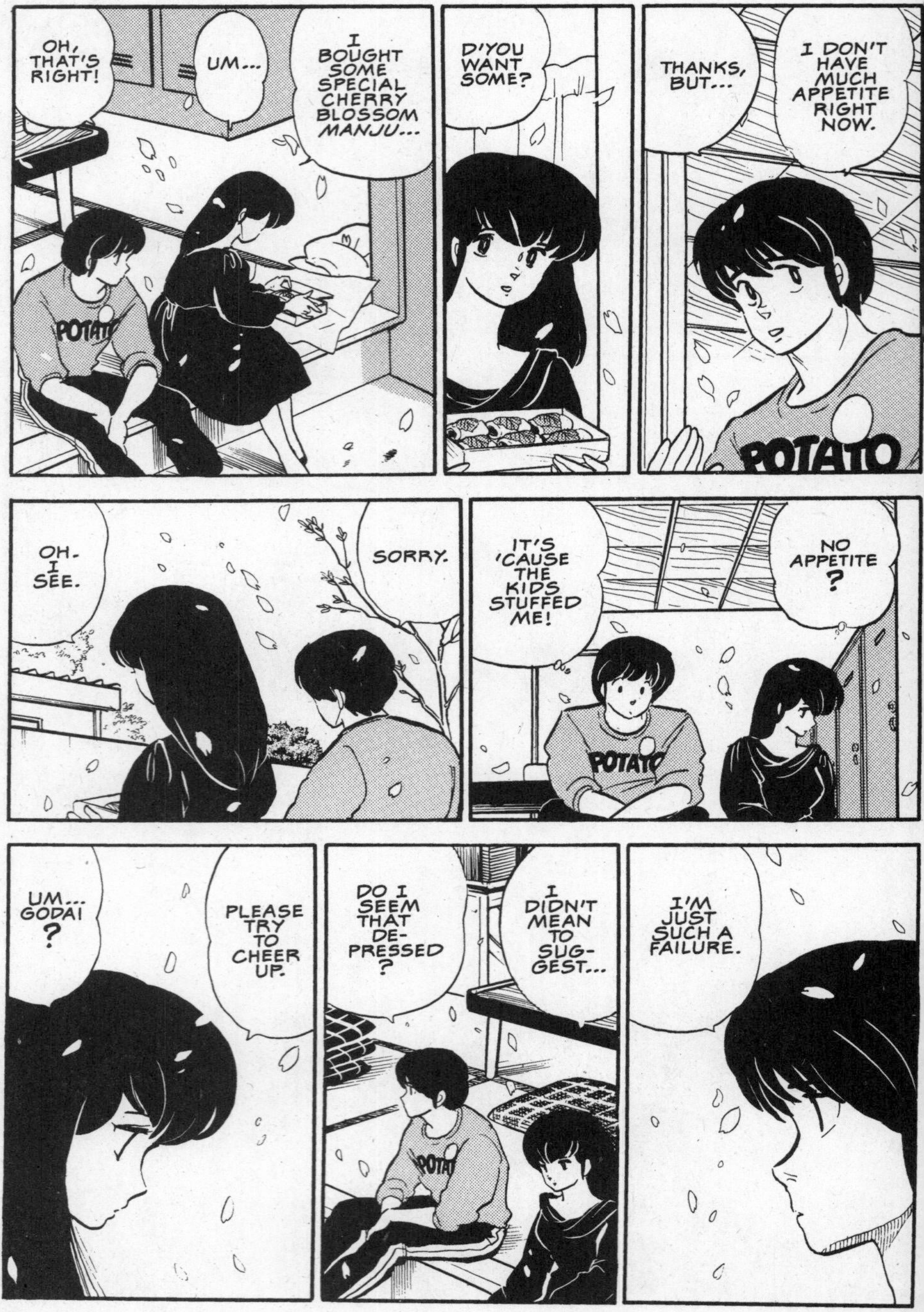
OH, THAT'S RIGHT!
UM...
I BOUGHT SOME SPECIAL CHERRY BLOSSOM MANJU...
D'YOU WANT SOME?
THANKS, BUT...
I DON'T HAVE MUCH APPETITE RIGHT NOW.
OH. I SEE.
SORRY.
IT'S 'CAUSE THE KIDS STUFFED ME!
NO APPETITE?
UM... GODAI?
PLEASE TRY TO CHEER UP.
DO I SEEM THAT DE-PRESSED?
I DIDN'T MEAN TO SUG-GEST...
I'M JUST SUCH A FAILURE.

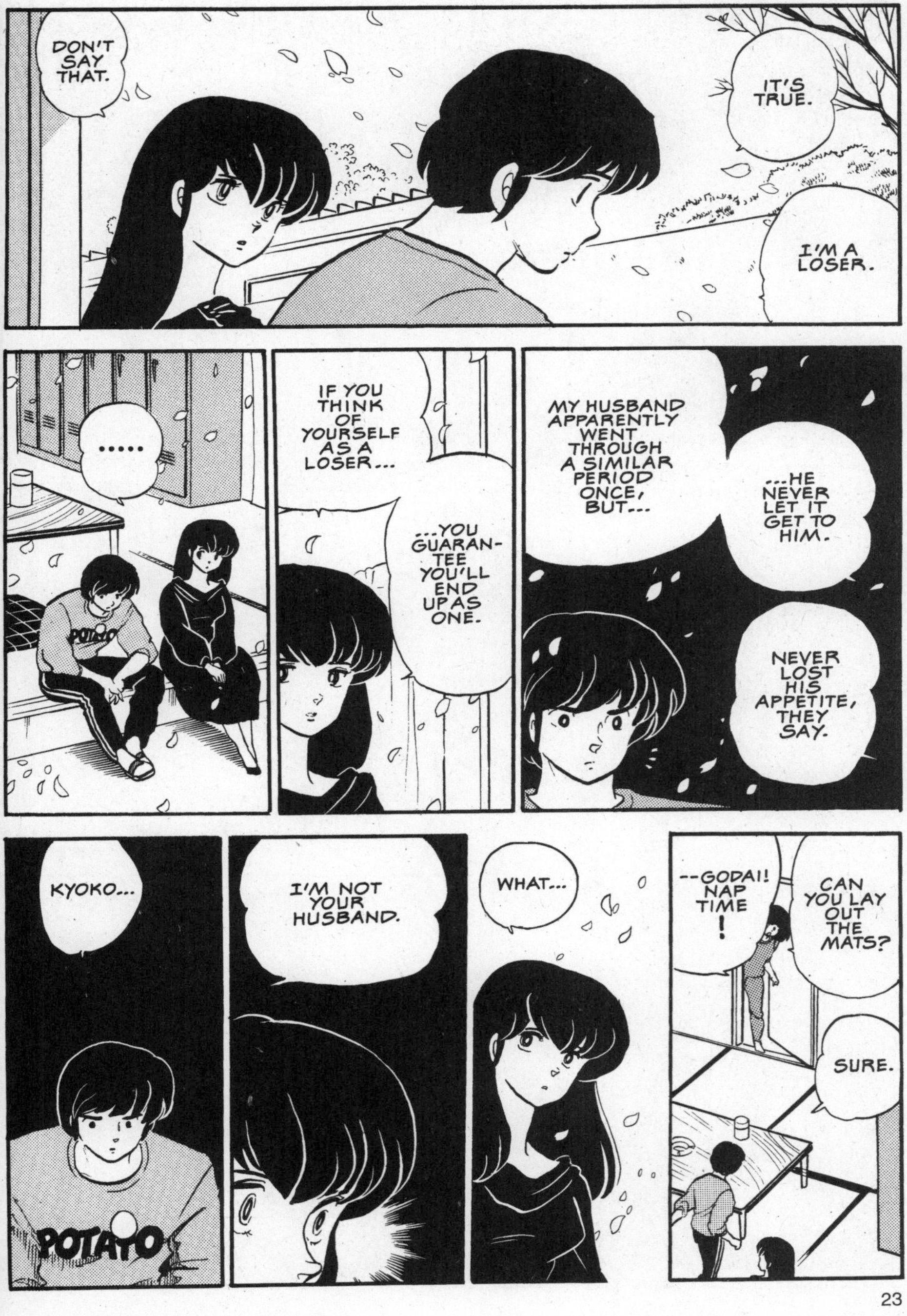
DON'T SAY THAT.
IT'S TRUE.
I'M A LOSER.
.....
IF YOU THINK OF YOURSELF AS A LOSER...
...YOU GUARANTEE YOU'LL END UPAS ONE.
MY HUSBAND APPARENTLY WENT THROUGH A SIMILAR PERIOD ONCE, BUT...
...HE NEVER LET IT GET TO HIM.
NEVER LOST HIS APPETITE, THEY SAY.
KYOKO...
I'M NOT YOUR HUSBAND.
WHAT...
--GODAI! NAP TIME !
CAN YOU LAY OUT THE MATS?
SURE.

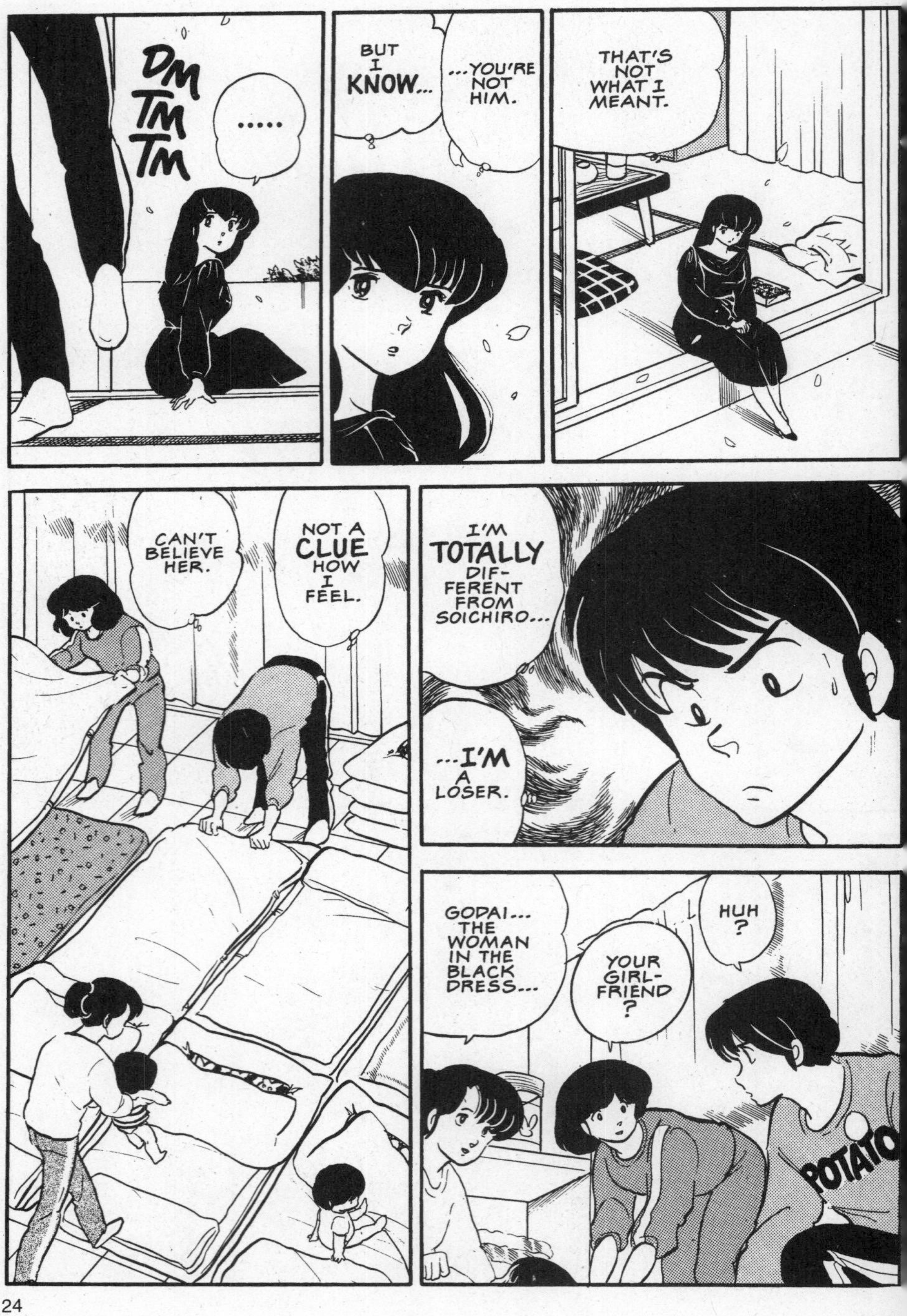
DM TM TM
......
BUT I KNOW...
...YOU'RE NOT HIM.
THAT'S NOT WHAT I MEANT.
CAN'T BELIEVE HER.
NOT A CLUE HOW I FEEL.
I'M TOTALLY DIF-FERENT FROM SOICHIRO...
...I'M A LOSER.
GODAI... THE WOMAN IN THE BLACK DRESS...
HUH?
YOUR GIRL-FRIEND?
POTATO

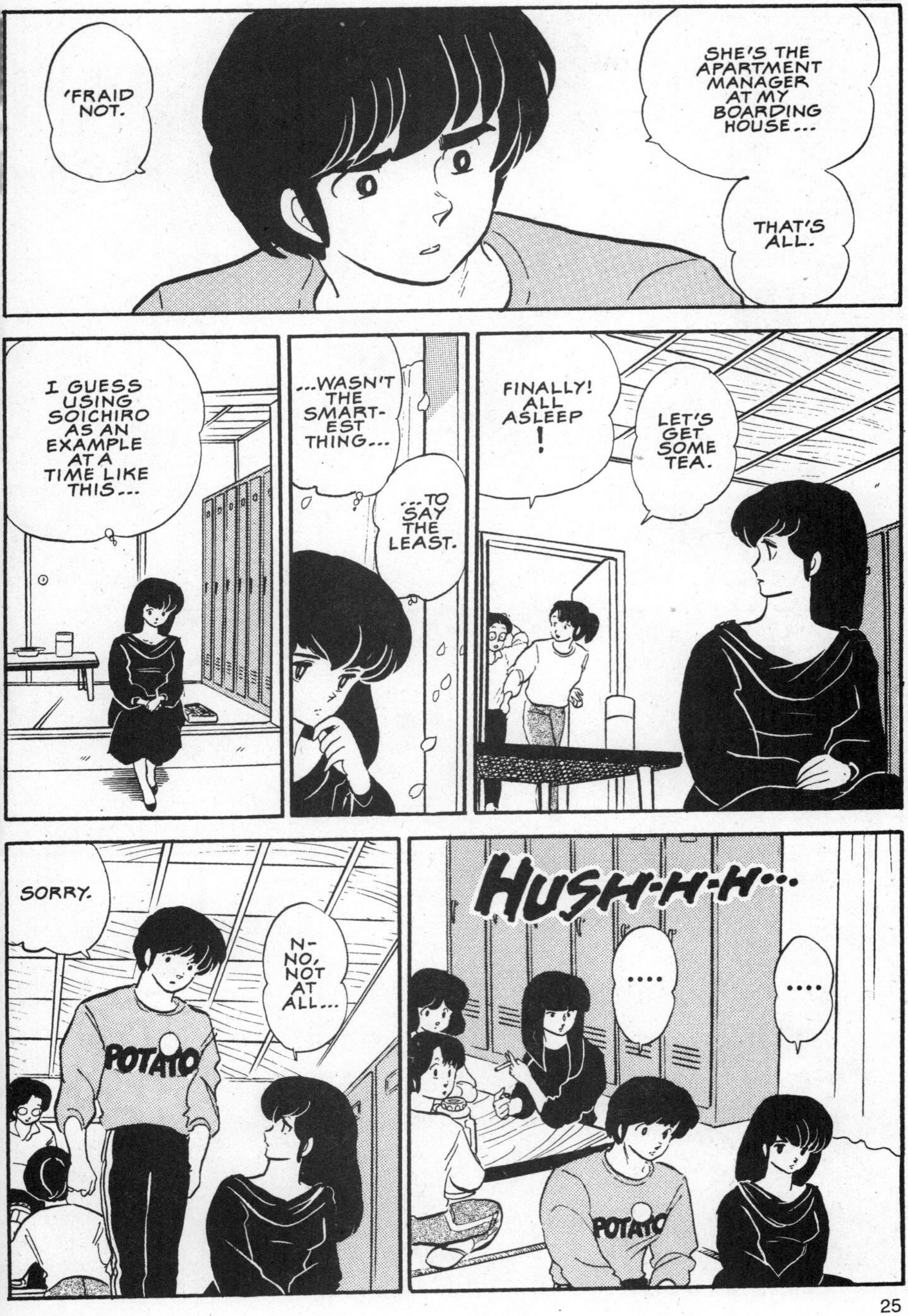
'FRAID NOT.
SHE'S THE APARTMENT MANAGER AT MY BOARDING HOUSE...
THAT'S ALL.
I GUESS USING SOICHIRO AS AN EXAMPLE AT A TIME LIKE THIS...
...WASN'T THE SMART-EST THING...
...TO SAY THE LEAST.
FINALLY! ALL ASLEEP!
LET'S GET SOME TEA.
SORRY.
N-NO, NOT AT ALL...
HUSH-H-H...
....
....

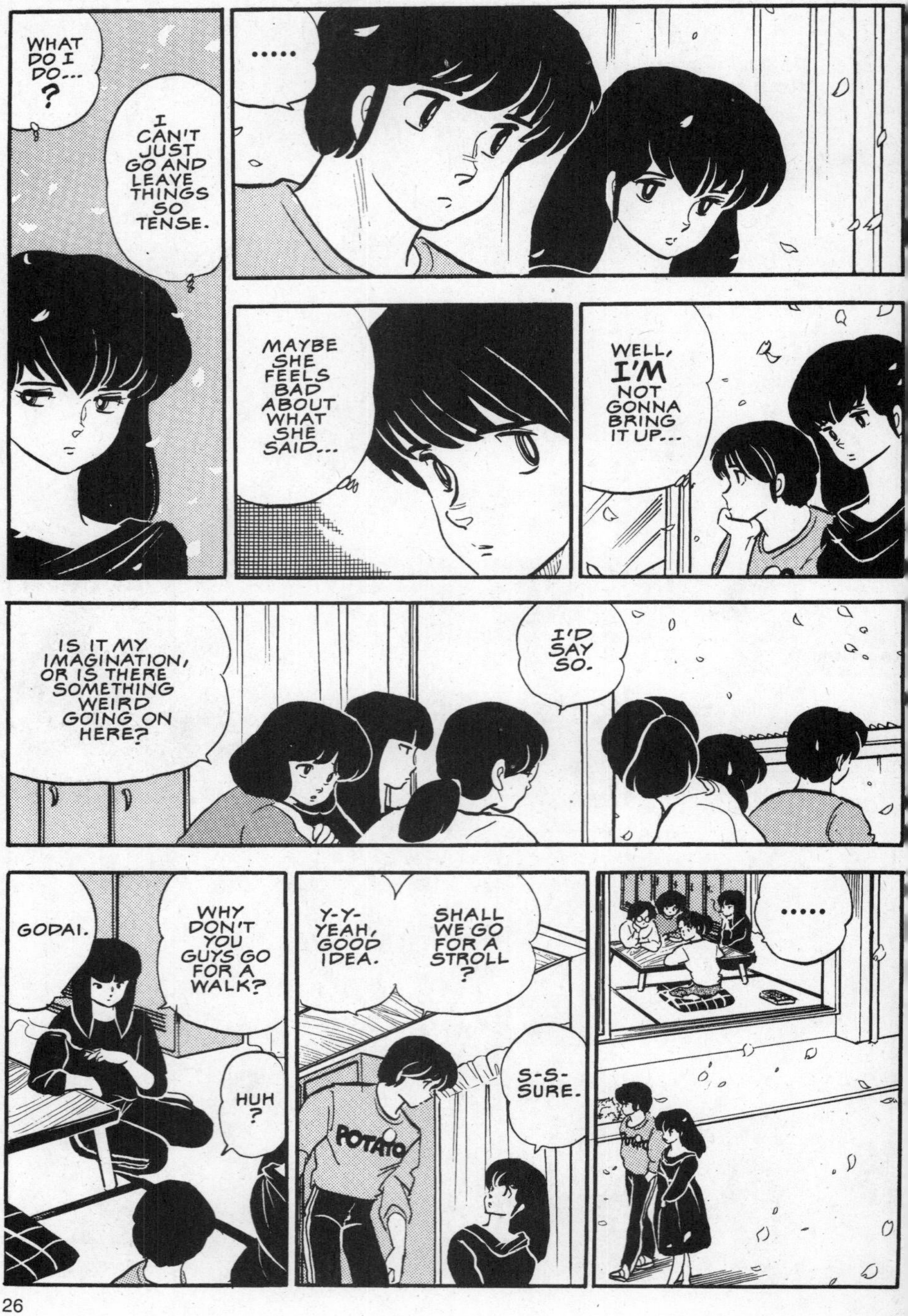
WHAT DO I DO...?
I CAN'T JUST GO AND LEAVE THINGS SO TENSE.
.....
MAYBE SHE FEELS BAD ABOUT WHAT SHE SAID...
WELL, I'M NOT GONNA BRING IT UP...
IS IT MY IMAGINATION, OR IS THERE SOMETHING WEIRD GOING ON HERE?
I'D SAY SO.
GODAI.
WHY DON'T YOU GUYS GO FOR A WALK?
HUH?
Y-Y-YEAH, GOOD IDEA.
SHALL WE GO FOR A STROLL?
S-S-SURE.
POTATO
.....

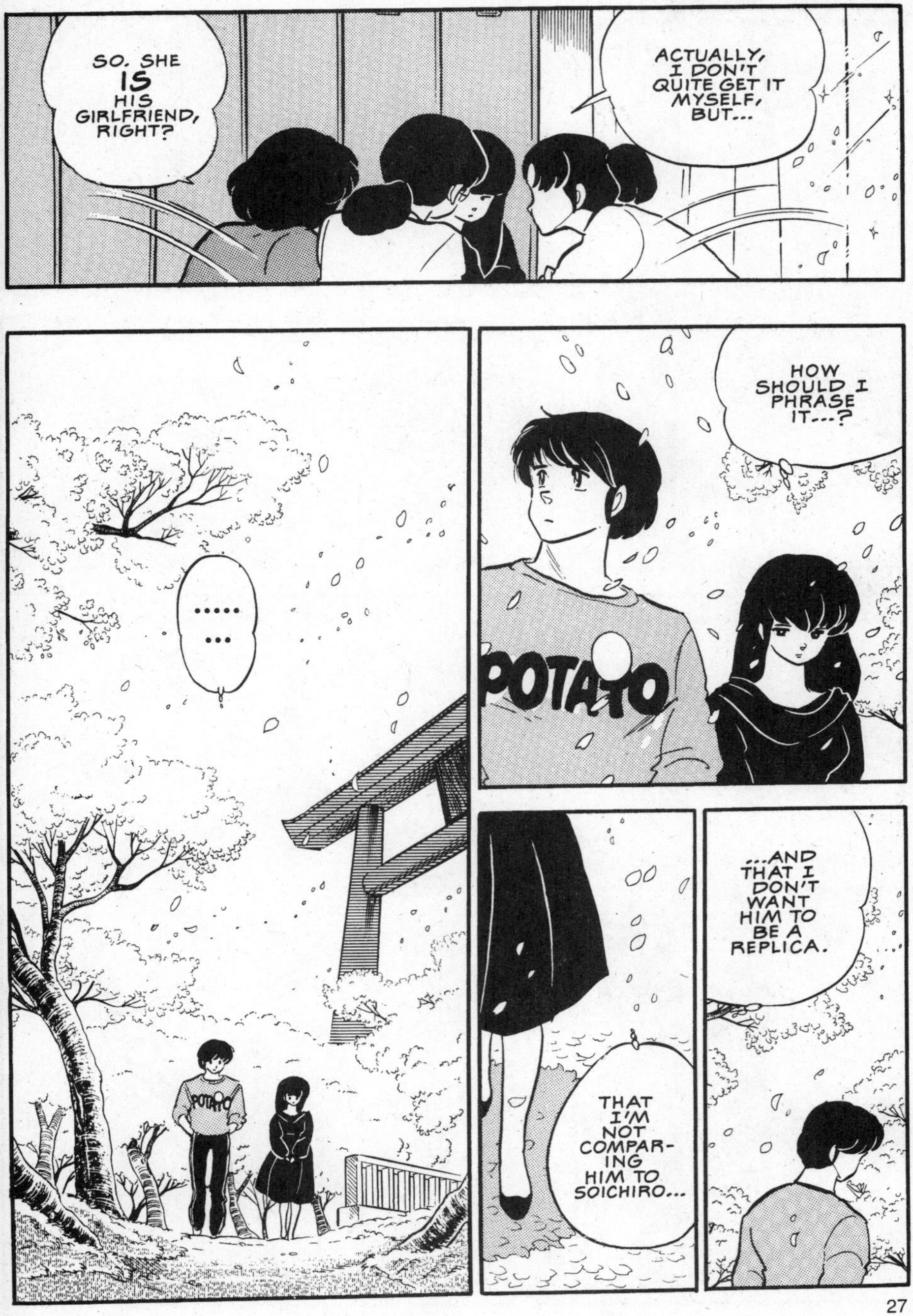
SO. SHE IS HIS GIRLFRIEND, RIGHT?
ACTUALLY, I DON'T QUITE GET IT MYSELF, BUT...
......
HOW SHOULD I PHRASE IT...?
THAT I'M NOT COMPARING HIM TO SOICHIRO...
...AND THAT I DON'T WANT HIM TO BE A REPLICA.

THEY **ARE** DIFFER- ENT.

TWO VERY DIFFER- ENT MEN.

WHAT IF---

...WHAT IF SHE'D MET SOICHIRO WHILE HE WAS UN- EMPLOYED?

WOULD SHE STILL HAVE FALLEN SO MADLY IN LOVE WITH HIM---?

COME ON... OF COURSE NOT.

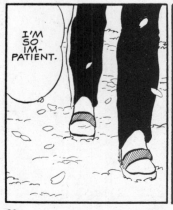

I'M SO IM- PATIENT.

I WANT TO MAKE HER HAPPY SO BLASTED **FAST**...

AT THIS RATE...

HHH-SHH

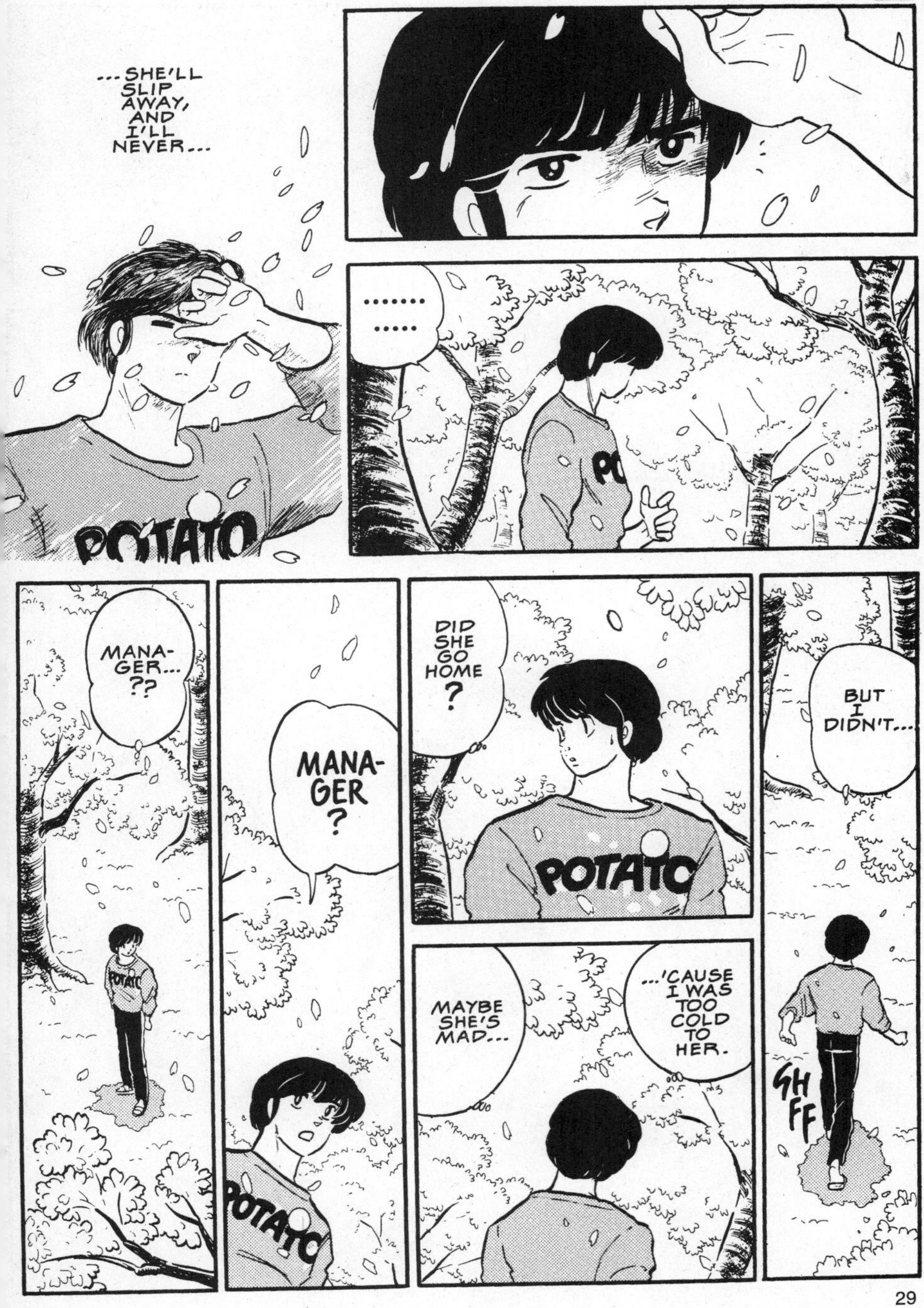
...SHE'LL SLIP AWAY, AND I'LL NEVER...
....
.....
MANAGER...??
MANAGER?
DID SHE GO HOME?
BUT I DIDN'T...
MAYBE SHE'S MAD...
...'CAUSE I WAS TOO COLD TO HER.
SHFF

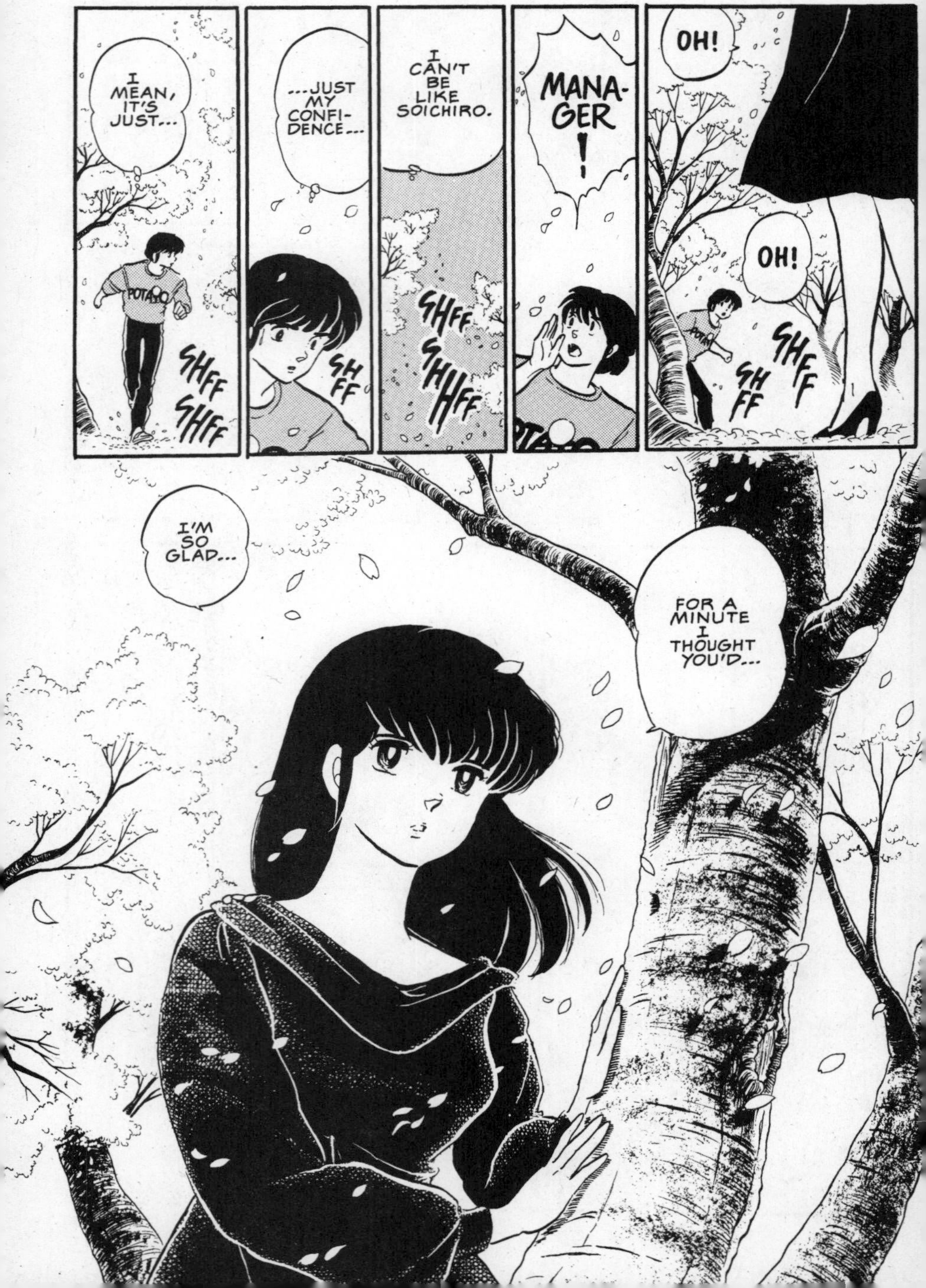
I MEAN, IT'S JUST...
SHFF SHFF
...JUST MY CONFIDENCE...
SHFF
I CAN'T BE LIKE SOICHIRO.
SHFF SHHFF
MANAGER!
OH!
OH!
SHFF SHFF
I'M SO GLAD...
FOR A MINUTE I THOUGHT YOU'D...

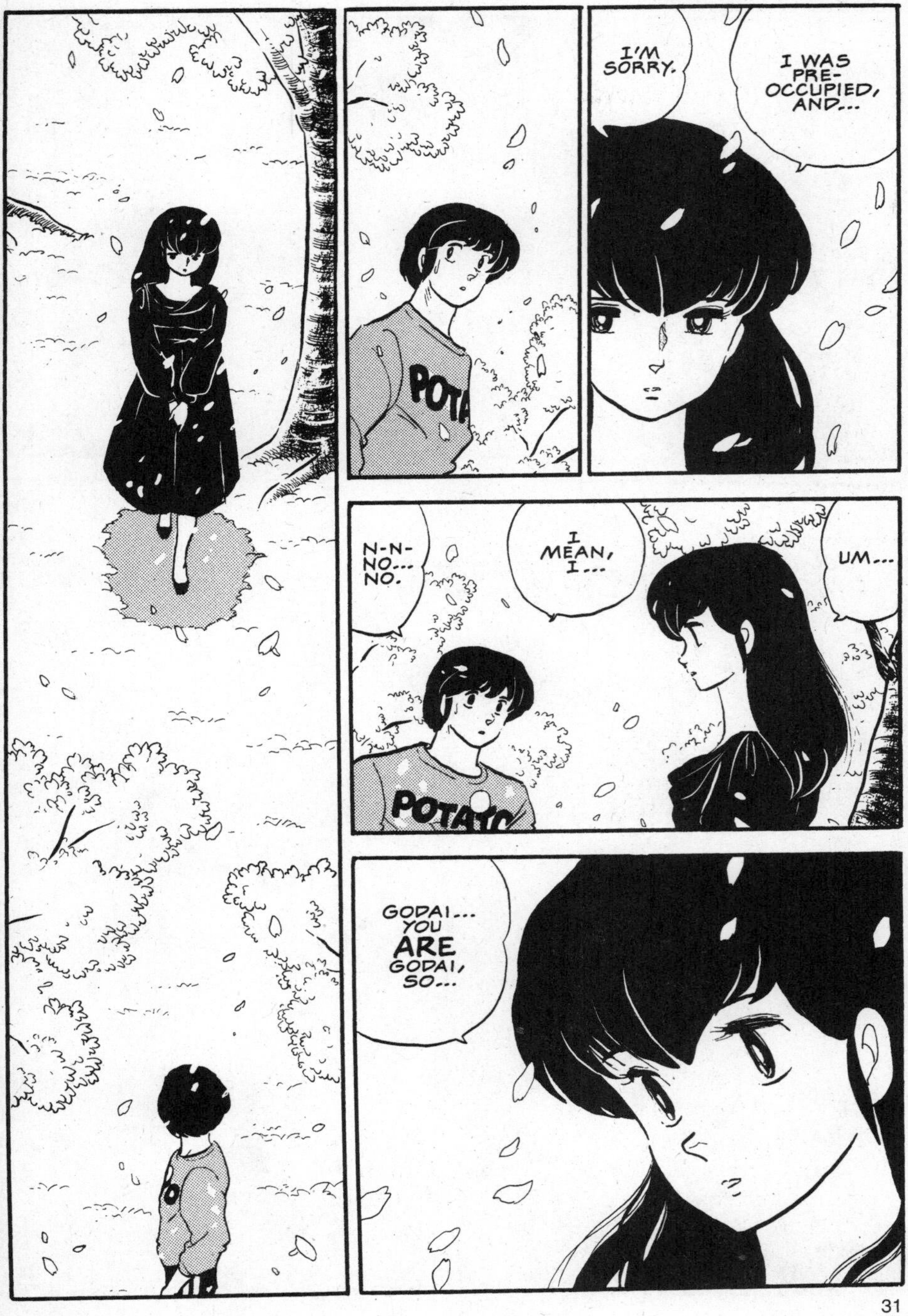
I'M SORRY.
I WAS PRE-OCCUPIED, AND...
N-N-NO... NO.
I MEAN, I...
UM...
GODAI... YOU **ARE** GODAI, SO...

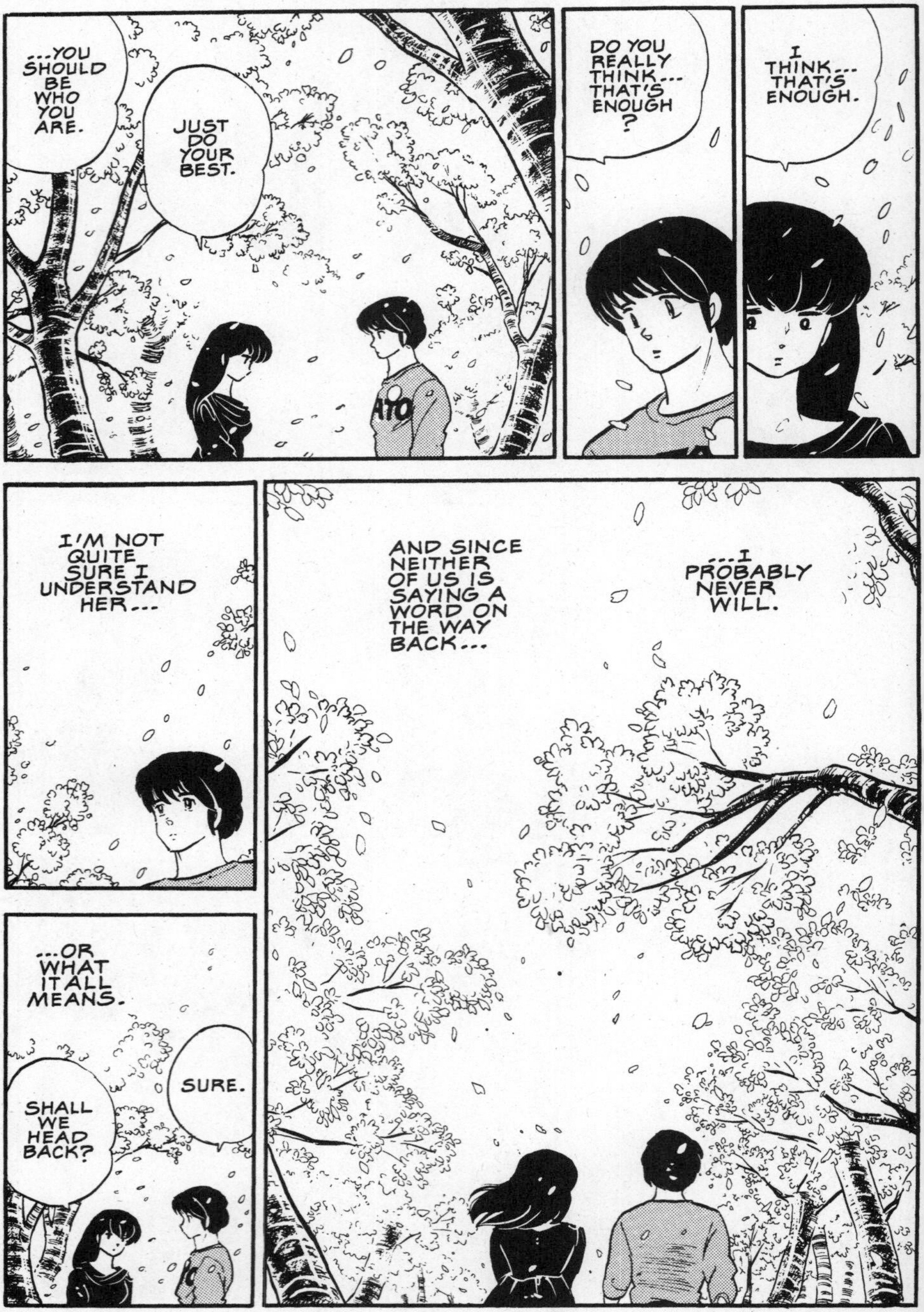
...YOU SHOULD BE WHO YOU ARE.
JUST DO YOUR BEST.
DO YOU REALLY THINK... THAT'S ENOUGH ?
I THINK... THAT'S ENOUGH.
I'M NOT QUITE SURE I UNDERSTAND HER...
...OR WHAT IT ALL MEANS.
SHALL WE HEAD BACK?
SURE.
AND SINCE NEITHER OF US IS SAYING A WORD ON THE WAY BACK...
...I PROBABLY NEVER WILL.

PART 2
LUCKY DAY

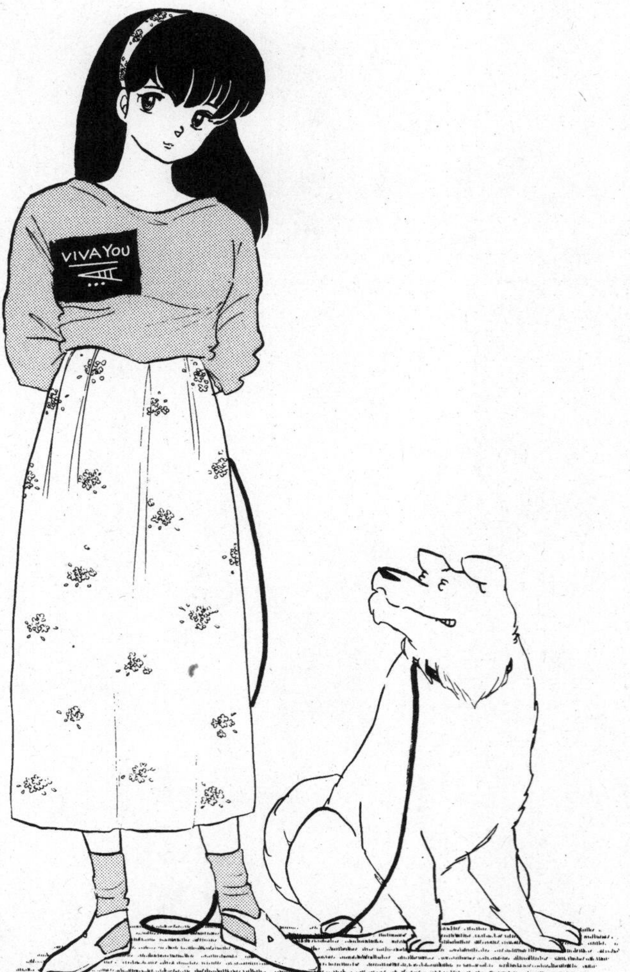
VIVA YOU

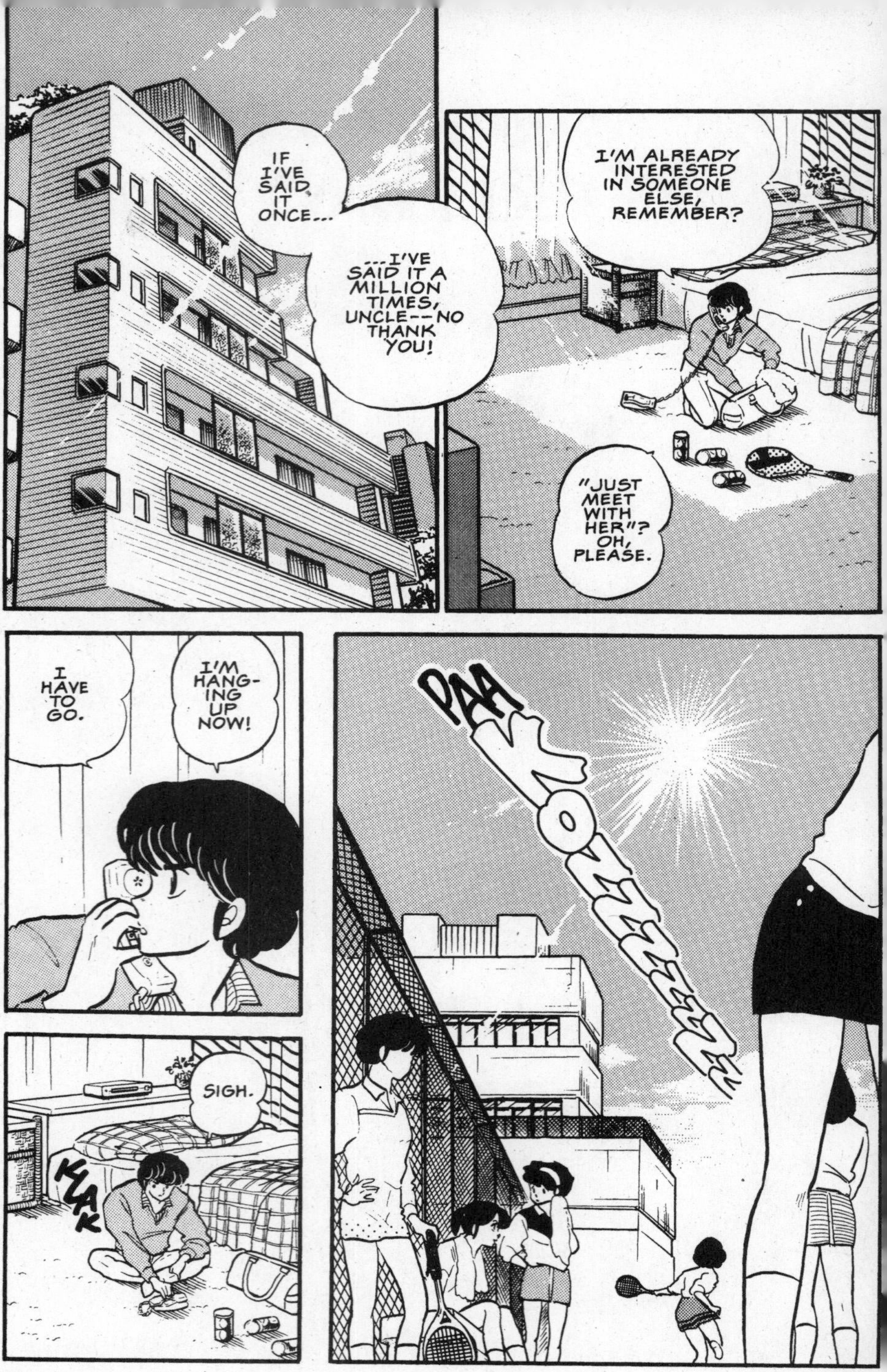
IF I'VE SAID IT ONCE...
...I'VE SAID IT A MILLION TIMES, UNCLE--NO THANK YOU!
I'M ALREADY INTERESTED IN SOMEONE ELSE, REMEMBER?
"JUST MEET WITH HER"? OH, PLEASE.
I HAVE TO GO.
I'M HANGING UP NOW!
SIGH.
KLAK
PAAKOOOOOONNNN

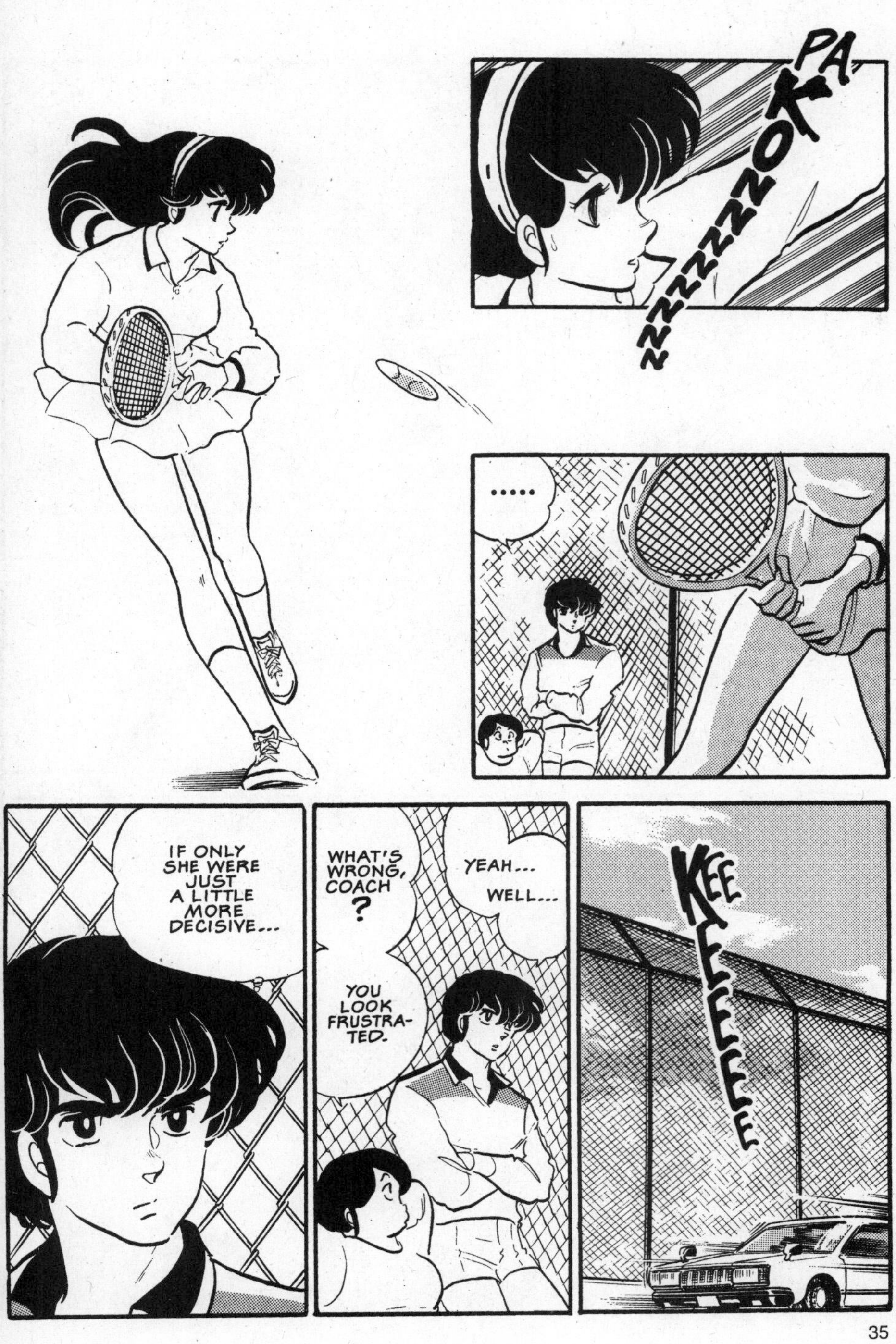
PAKOONNNNNNNNNN
......
IF ONLY SHE WERE JUST A LITTLE MORE DECISIVE...
WHAT'S WRONG, COACH?
YEAH... WELL...
YOU LOOK FRUSTRA-TED.
KEEEEEEE

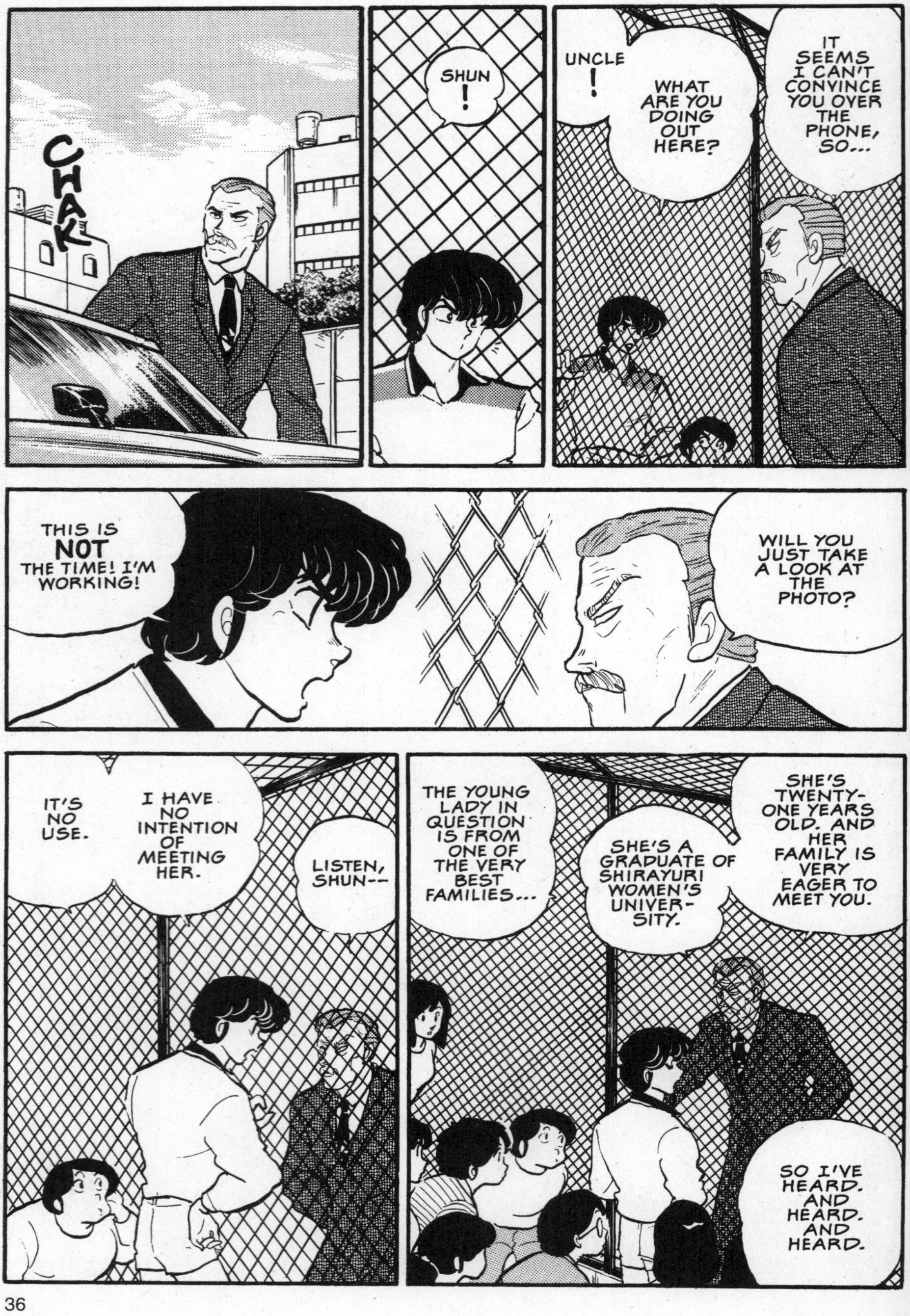
CHAK
SHUN!
UNCLE!
WHAT ARE YOU DOING OUT HERE?
IT SEEMS I CAN'T CONVINCE YOU OVER THE PHONE, SO...
THIS IS NOT THE TIME! I'M WORKING!
WILL YOU JUST TAKE A LOOK AT THE PHOTO?
IT'S NO USE.
I HAVE NO INTENTION OF MEETING HER.
LISTEN, SHUN--
THE YOUNG LADY IN QUESTION IS FROM ONE OF THE VERY BEST FAMILIES...
SHE'S A GRADUATE OF SHIRAYURI WOMEN'S UNIVERSITY.
SHE'S TWENTY-ONE YEARS OLD. AND HER FAMILY IS VERY EAGER TO MEET YOU.
SO I'VE HEARD. AND HEARD. AND HEARD.

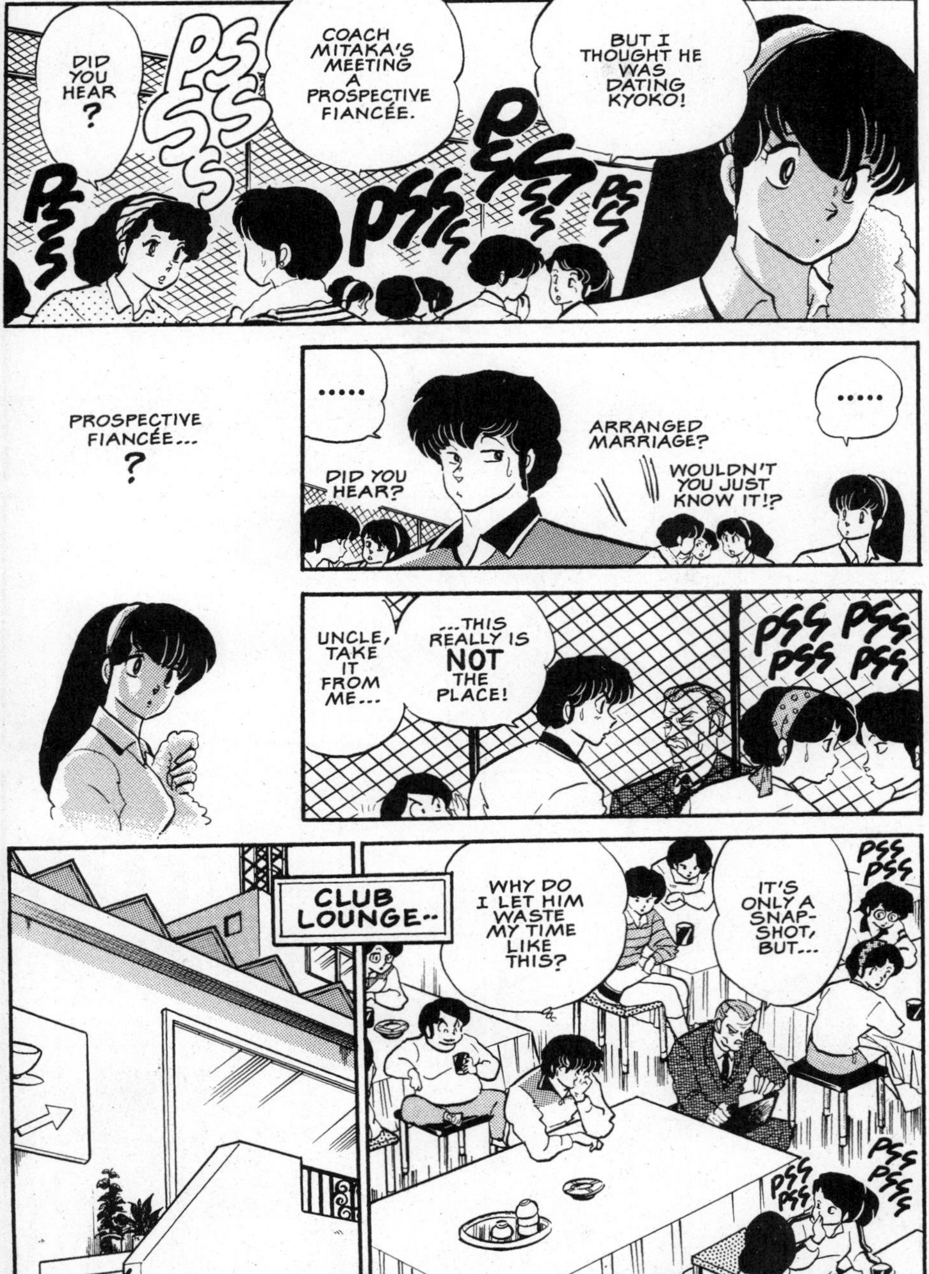
DID YOU HEAR?
PSSS
COACH MITAKA'S MEETING A PROSPECTIVE FIANCÉE.
PSS PSSS PSSS PSS
BUT I THOUGHT HE WAS DATING KYOKO!
PROSPECTIVE FIANCÉE...?
.....
DID YOU HEAR?
ARRANGED MARRIAGE?
WOULDN'T YOU JUST KNOW IT!?
.....
UNCLE, TAKE IT FROM ME...
...THIS REALLY IS NOT THE PLACE!
PSS PSS PSS PSS
CLUB LOUNGE..
WHY DO I LET HIM WASTE MY TIME LIKE THIS?
IT'S ONLY A SNAPSHOT, BUT...
PSS PSS
PSS PSS PSS PSS

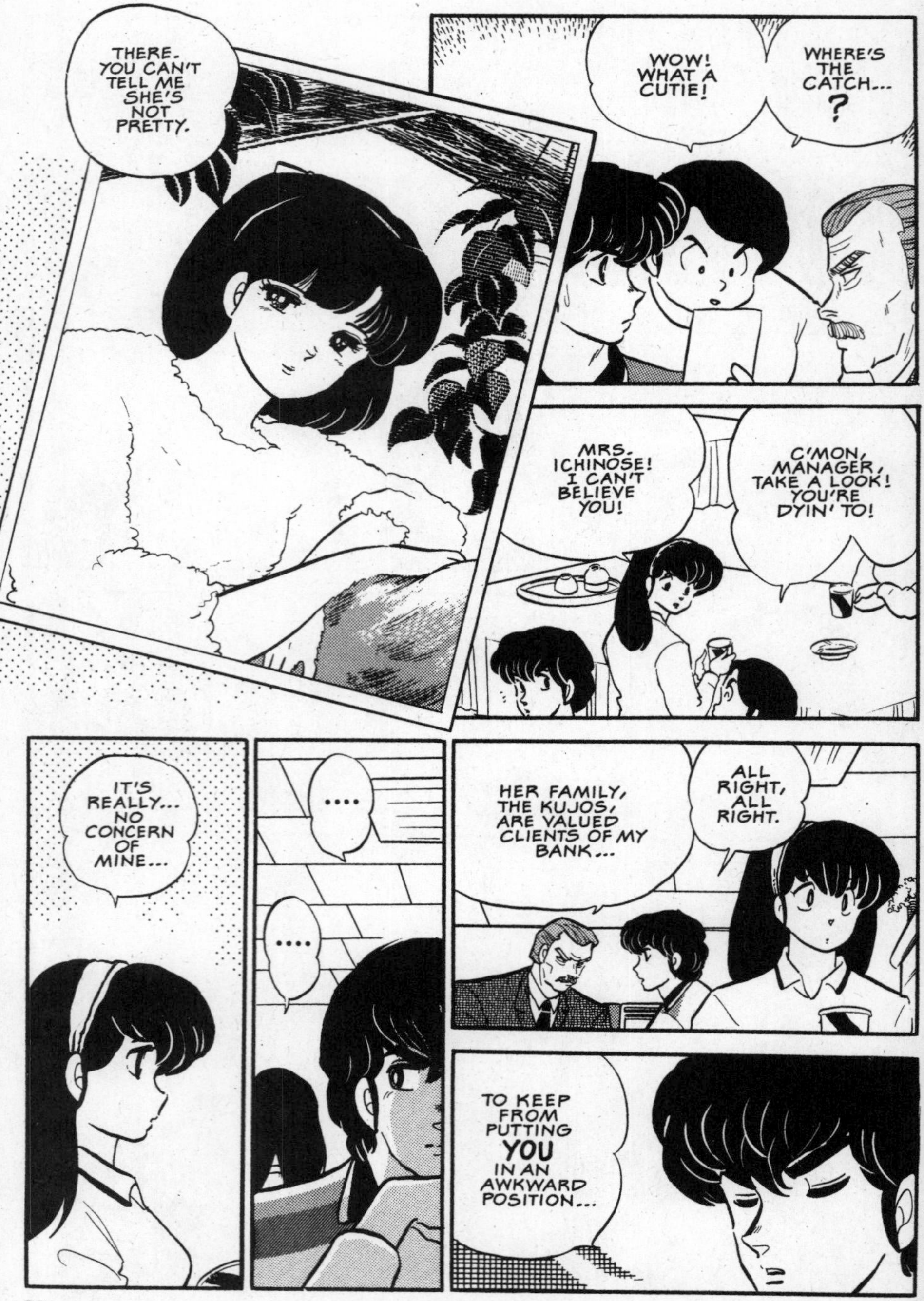
THERE. YOU CAN'T TELL ME SHE'S NOT PRETTY.
WOW! WHAT A CUTIE!
WHERE'S THE CATCH...?
MRS. ICHINOSE! I CAN'T BELIEVE YOU!
C'MON, MANAGER, TAKE A LOOK! YOU'RE DYIN' TO!
IT'S REALLY... NO CONCERN OF MINE...
....
....
HER FAMILY, THE KUJOS, ARE VALUED CLIENTS OF MY BANK...
ALL RIGHT, ALL RIGHT.
TO KEEP FROM PUTTING YOU IN AN AWKWARD POSITION...

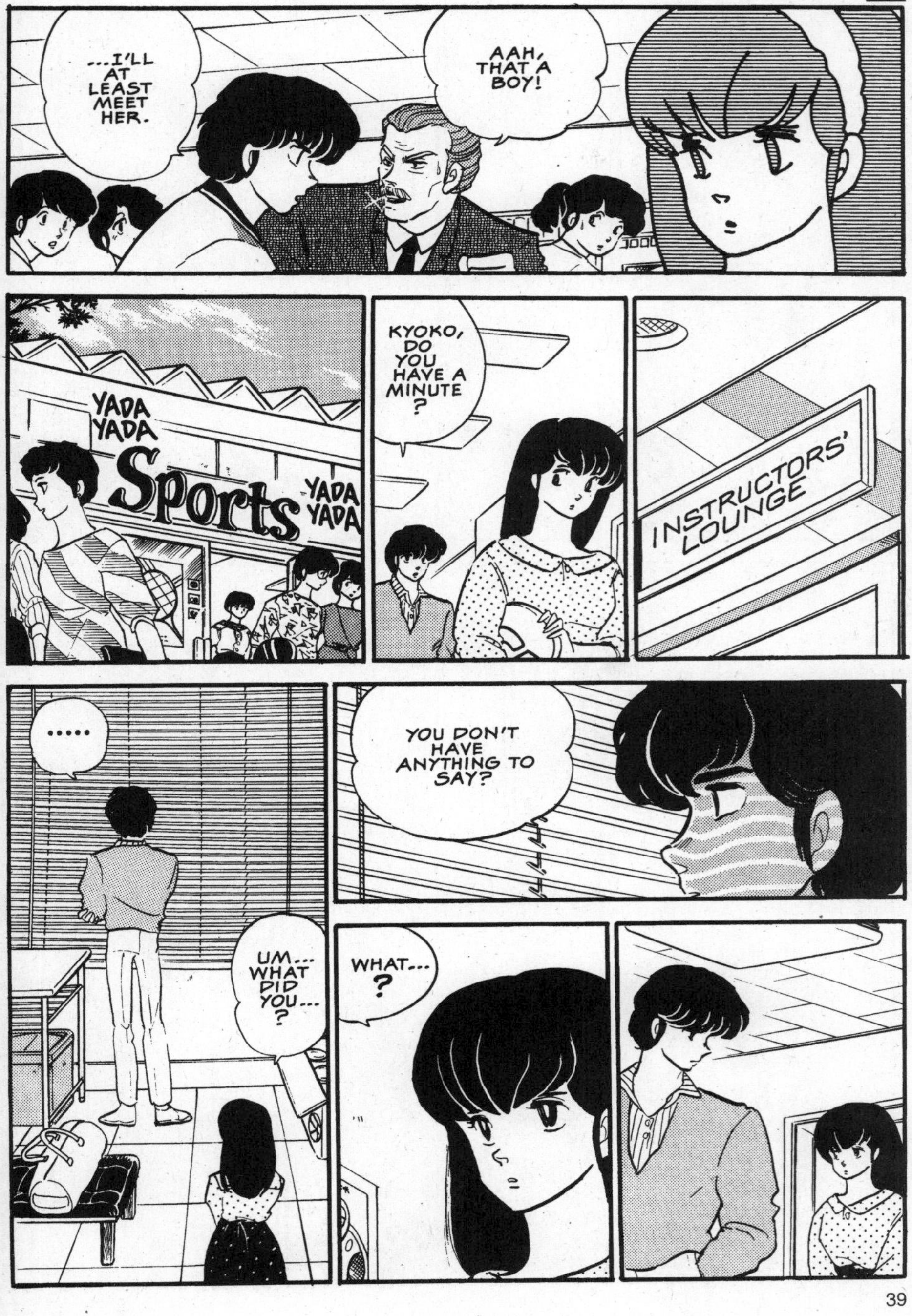
...I'LL AT LEAST MEET HER.
AAH, THAT A BOY!
YADA YADA
Sports
YADA YADA
KYOKO, DO YOU HAVE A MINUTE?
INSTRUCTORS' LOUNGE
.....
YOU DON'T HAVE ANYTHING TO SAY?
UM... WHAT DID YOU...?
WHAT...?

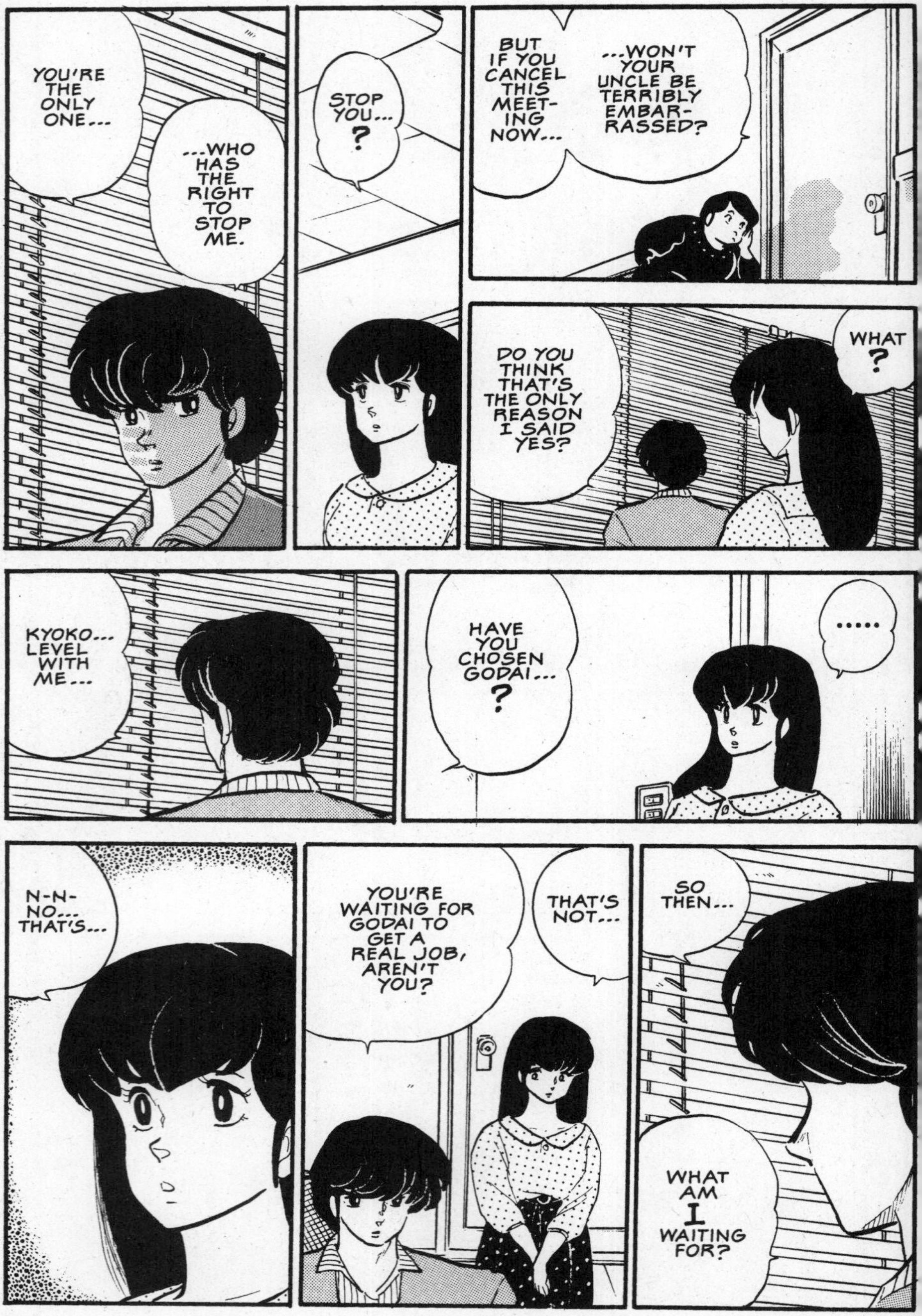

YOU'RE THE ONLY ONE...
...WHO HAS THE RIGHT TO STOP ME.
STOP YOU...?
BUT IF YOU CANCEL THIS MEET-ING NOW...
...WON'T YOUR UNCLE BE TERRIBLY EMBAR-RASSED?
DO YOU THINK THAT'S THE ONLY REASON I SAID YES?
WHAT?
KYOKO... LEVEL WITH ME...
HAVE YOU CHOSEN GODAI...?
.....
N-N-NO... THAT'S...
YOU'RE WAITING FOR GODAI TO GET A REAL JOB, AREN'T YOU?
THAT'S NOT...
SO THEN...
WHAT AM I WAITING FOR?

THEN YOU'RE... CONSIDERING MARRY- ING...?

IT'S UP TO YOU.

FWIP

WELL, KYOKO...?

ARE YOU GOING TO WAIT FOREVER FOR GODAI TO FIND SOMETHING?

WELL, I...I...

...I DON'T THINK SO.

YOU MEAN THAT, KYOKO?

I-I THINK SO...

SKWEE

YOU DON'T KNOW HOW HAPPY YOU'VE MADE ME!

MAN, OH MAN...

RUCTORS' UNGE

AND I THOUGHT GODAI WAS THE WISHY-WASHY ONE IN THAT RELATION-SHIP.

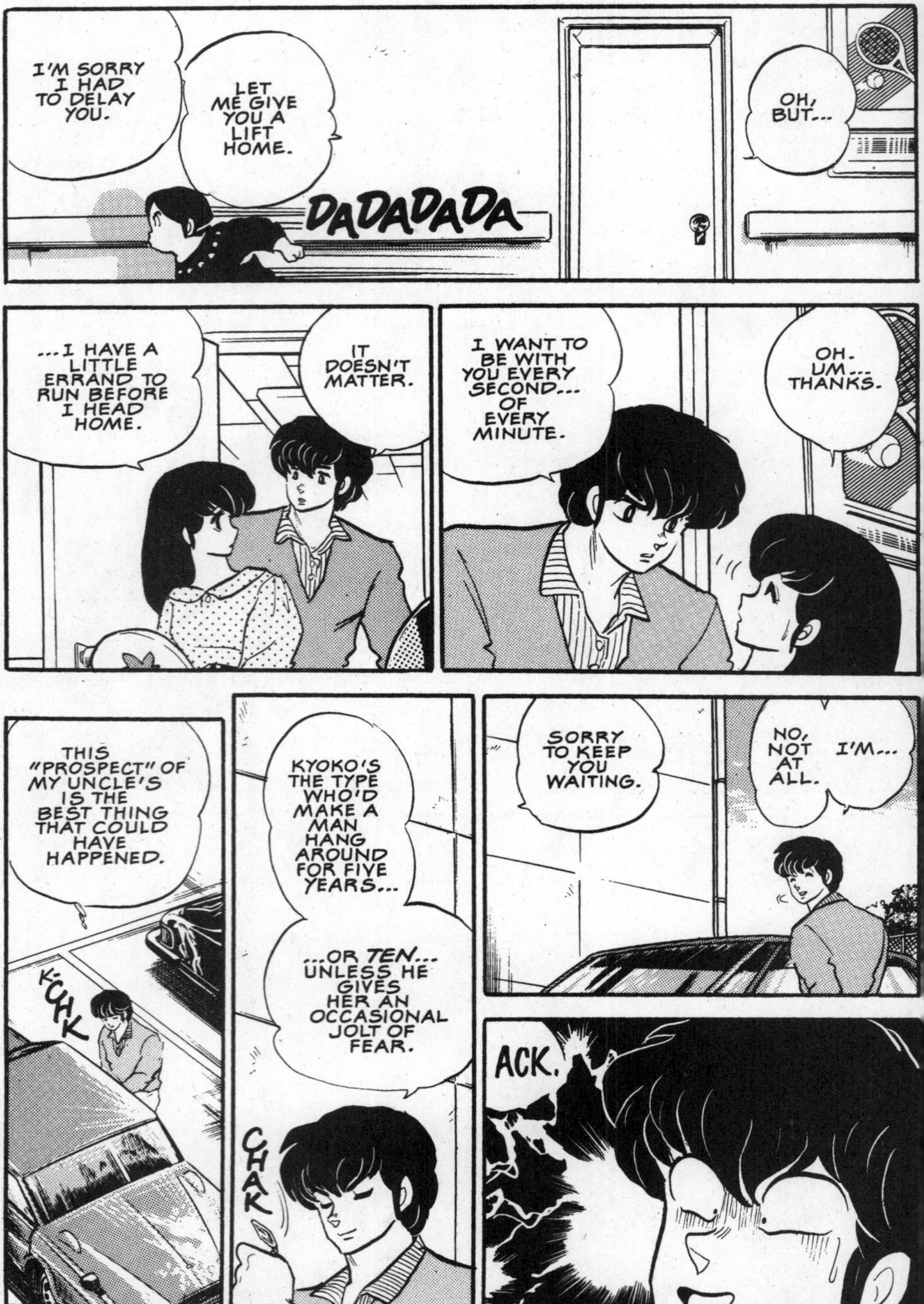
I'M SORRY I HAD TO DELAY YOU.
LET ME GIVE YOU A LIFT HOME.
DADADADA
OH, BUT...
...I HAVE A LITTLE ERRAND TO RUN BEFORE I HEAD HOME.
IT DOESN'T MATTER.
I WANT TO BE WITH YOU EVERY SECOND... OF EVERY MINUTE.
OH. UM... THANKS.
THIS "PROSPECT" OF MY UNCLE'S IS THE BEST THING THAT COULD HAVE HAPPENED.
K-CHK
KYOKO'S THE TYPE WHO'D MAKE A MAN HANG AROUND FOR FIVE YEARS...
...OR *TEN*... UNLESS HE GIVES HER AN OCCASIONAL JOLT OF FEAR.
CHAK
SORRY TO KEEP YOU WAITING.
NO, NOT AT ALL.
I'M...
ACK.

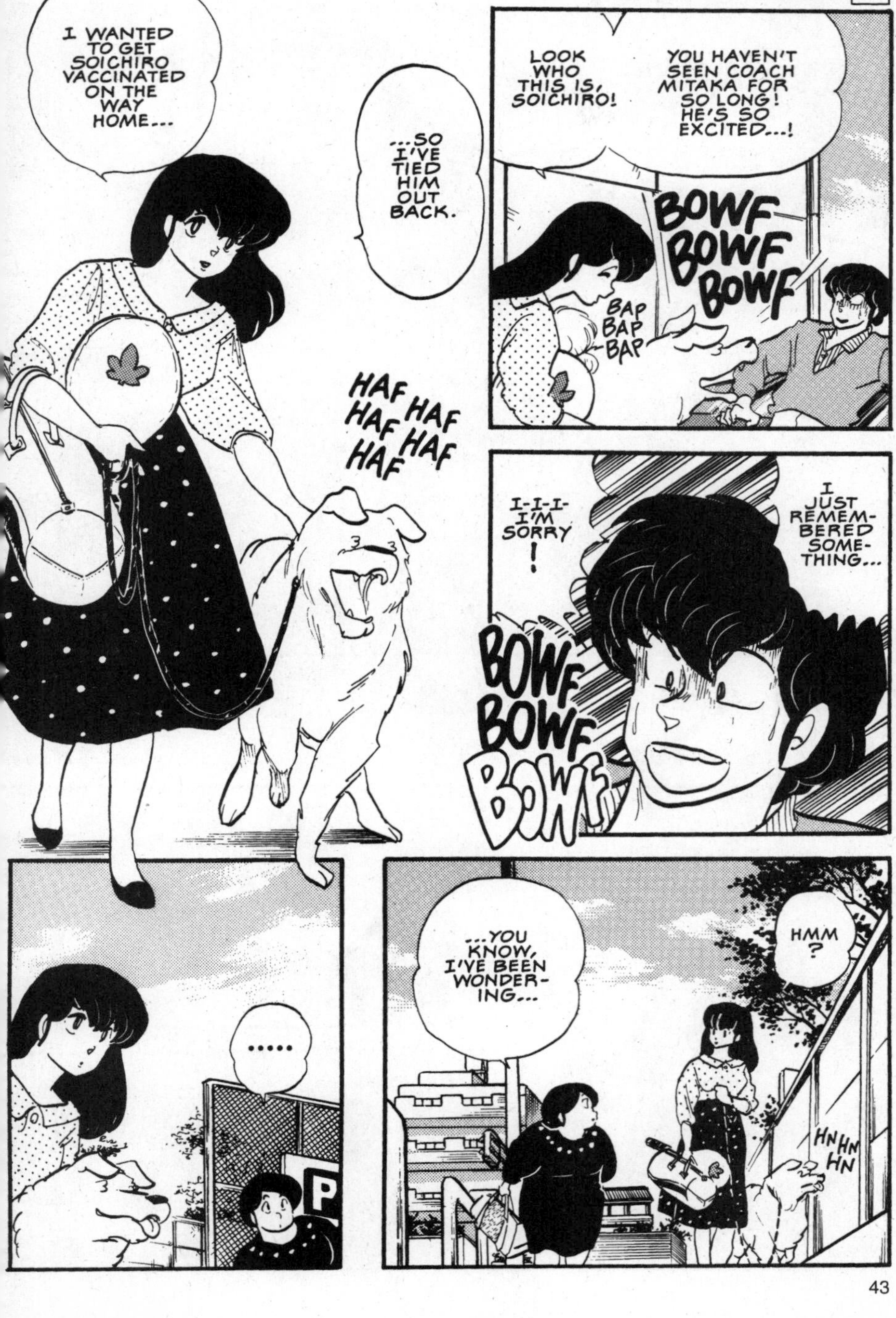
I WANTED TO GET SOICHIRO VACCINATED ON THE WAY HOME...
...SO I'VE TIED HIM OUT BACK.
HAF HAF HAF HAF HAF
LOOK WHO THIS IS, SOICHIRO!
YOU HAVEN'T SEEN COACH MITAKA FOR SO LONG! HE'S SO EXCITED...!
BOWF BOWF BOWF
BAP BAP BAP
I-I-I-I'M SORRY!
I JUST REMEM-BERED SOME-THING...
BOWF BOWF BOWF
......
...YOU KNOW, I'VE BEEN WONDER-ING...
HMM?
HN HN HN

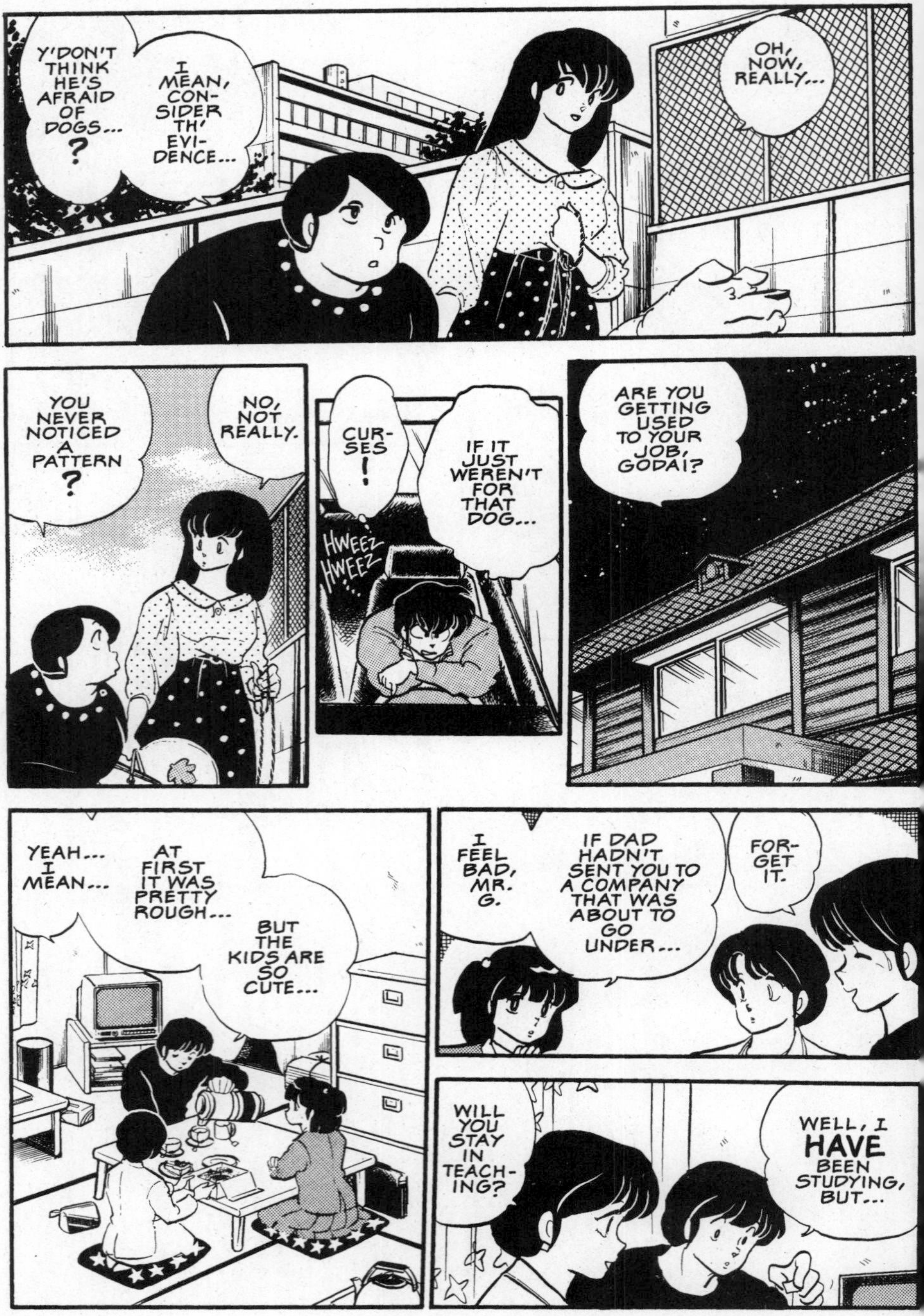
Y'DON'T THINK HE'S AFRAID OF DOGS...?
I MEAN, CONSIDER TH' EVIDENCE...
OH, NOW, REALLY...
YOU NEVER NOTICED A PATTERN?
NO, NOT REALLY.
CURSES!
IF IT JUST WEREN'T FOR THAT DOG...
HWEEZ HWEEZ
ARE YOU GETTING USED TO YOUR JOB, GODAI?
YEAH... I MEAN...
AT FIRST IT WAS PRETTY ROUGH...
BUT THE KIDS ARE SO CUTE...
I FEEL BAD, MR. G.
IF DAD HADN'T SENT YOU TO A COMPANY THAT WAS ABOUT TO GO UNDER...
FORGET IT.
WILL YOU STAY IN TEACHING?
WELL, I HAVE BEEN STUDYING, BUT...

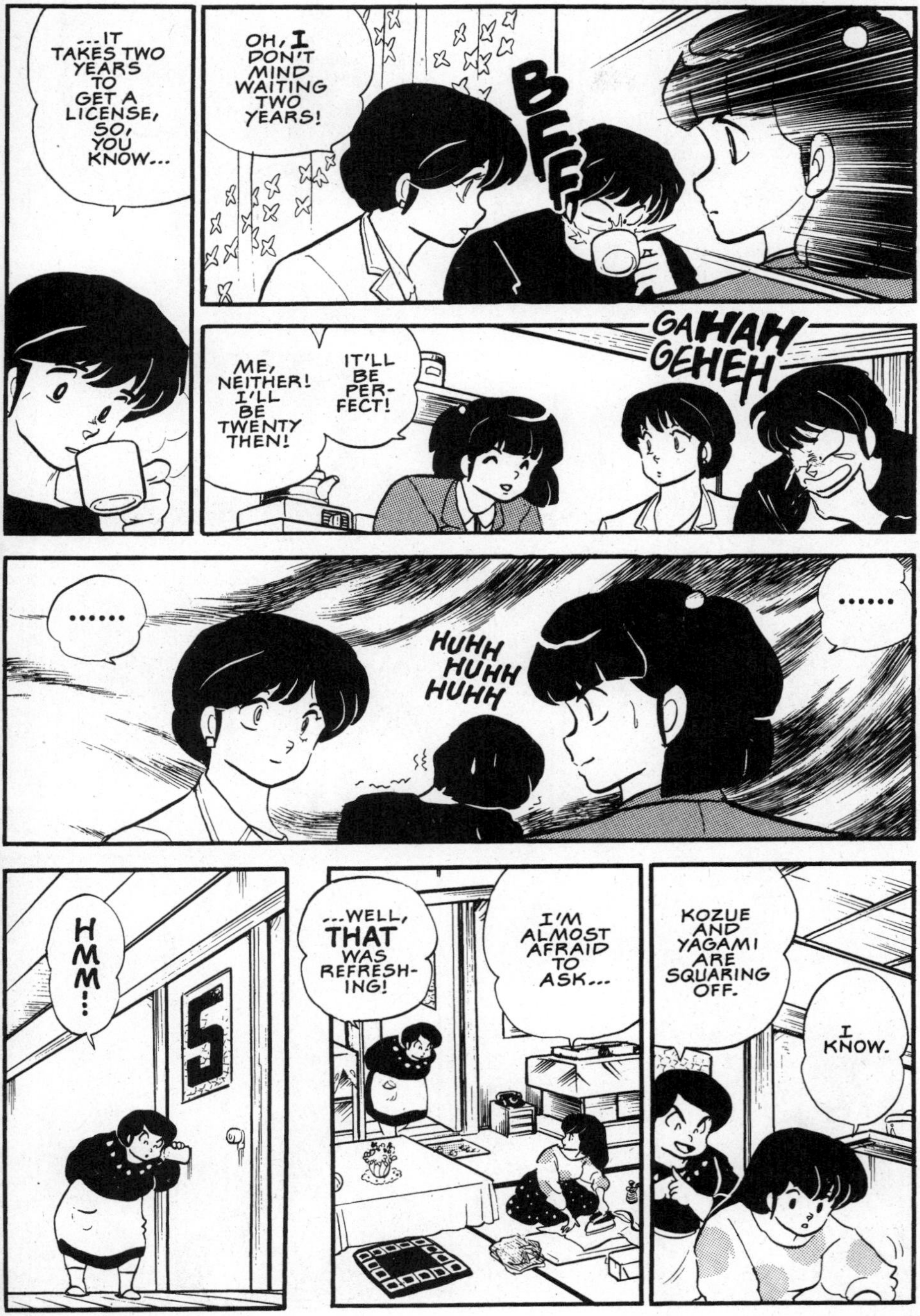
...IT TAKES TWO YEARS TO GET A LICENSE, SO, YOU KNOW...
OH, I DON'T MIND WAITING TWO YEARS!
BFF
ME, NEITHER! I'LL BE TWENTY THEN!
IT'LL BE PER-FECT!
GAHAH GEHEH
......
HUHH HUHH HUHH
......
HMM...
...WELL, THAT WAS REFRESH-ING!
I'M ALMOST AFRAID TO ASK...
KOZUE AND YAGAMI ARE SQUARING OFF.
I KNOW.

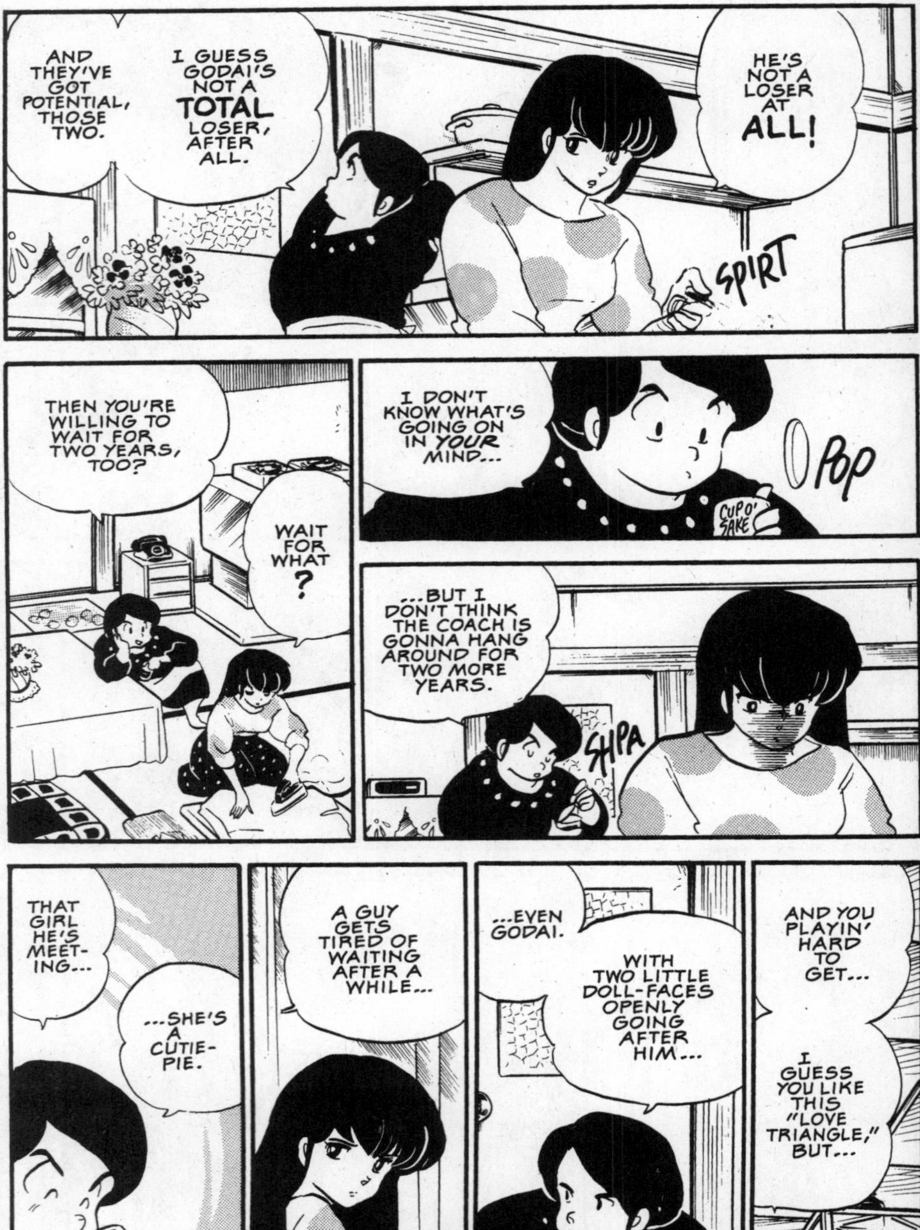
AND THEY'VE GOT POTENTIAL, THOSE TWO.
I GUESS GODAI'S NOT A TOTAL LOSER, AFTER ALL.
HE'S NOT A LOSER AT ALL!
SPIRT
THEN YOU'RE WILLING TO WAIT FOR TWO YEARS, TOO?
WAIT FOR WHAT?
I DON'T KNOW WHAT'S GOING ON IN YOUR MIND...
POP
CUP O' SAKE
...BUT I DON'T THINK THE COACH IS GONNA HANG AROUND FOR TWO MORE YEARS.
SHPA
THAT GIRL HE'S MEET-ING...
...SHE'S A CUTIE-PIE.
CUP O' SAKE
A GUY GETS TIRED OF WAITING AFTER A WHILE...
...EVEN GODAI.
WITH TWO LITTLE DOLL-FACES OPENLY GOING AFTER HIM...
AND YOU PLAYIN' HARD TO GET...
I GUESS YOU LIKE THIS "LOVE TRIANGLE," BUT...

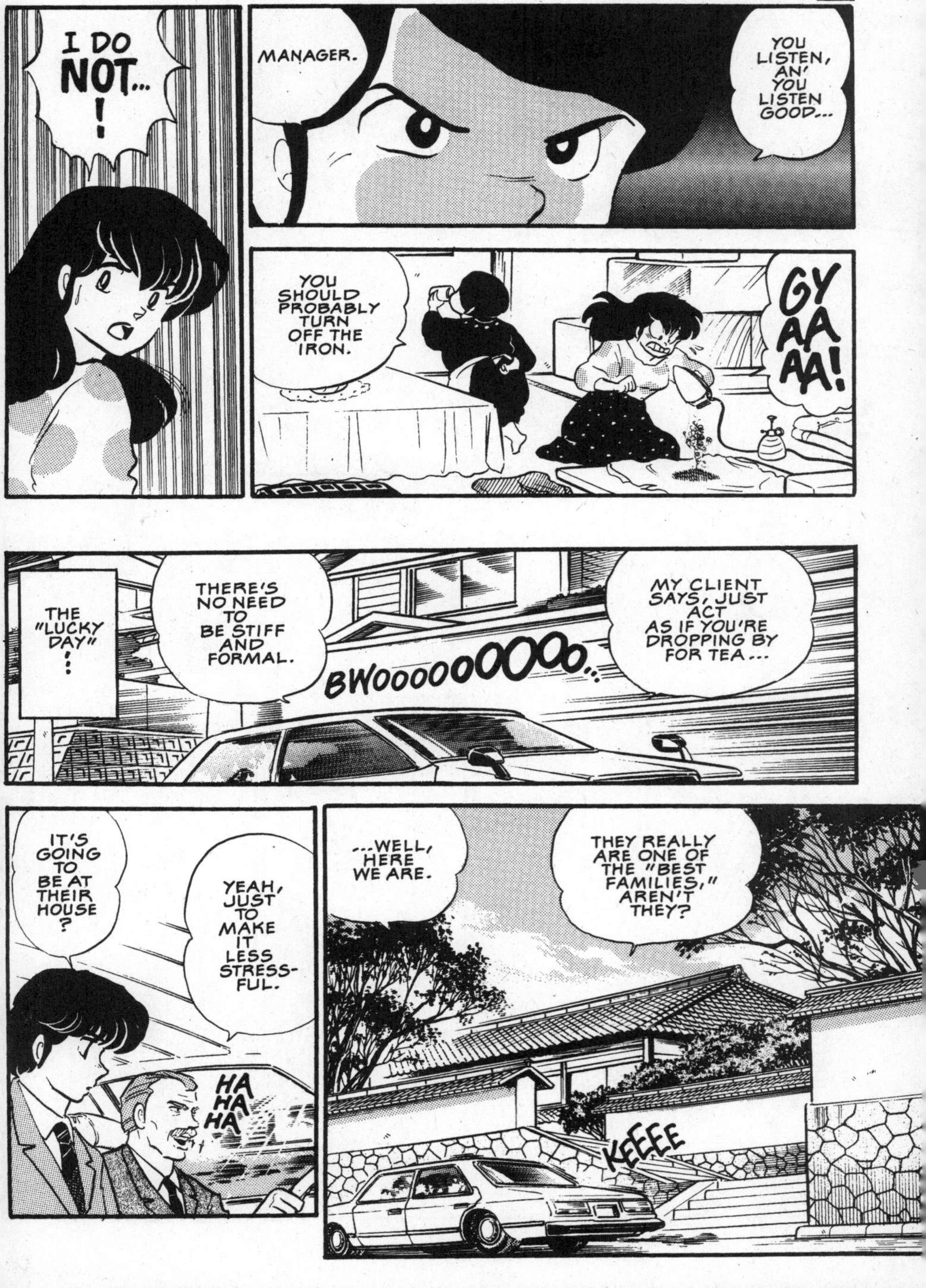
I DO NOT... !
MANAGER.
YOU LISTEN, AN' YOU LISTEN GOOD...
YOU SHOULD PROBABLY TURN OFF THE IRON.
GYAAAAA!
THE "LUCKY DAY" :
THERE'S NO NEED TO BE STIFF AND FORMAL.
BWOOOOOOOOOo...
MY CLIENT SAYS, JUST ACT AS IF YOU'RE DROPPING BY FOR TEA...
IT'S GOING TO BE AT THEIR HOUSE?
YEAH, JUST TO MAKE IT LESS STRESSFUL.
HA HA HA
...WELL, HERE WE ARE.
THEY REALLY ARE ONE OF THE "BEST FAMILIES," AREN'T THEY?
KEEEE

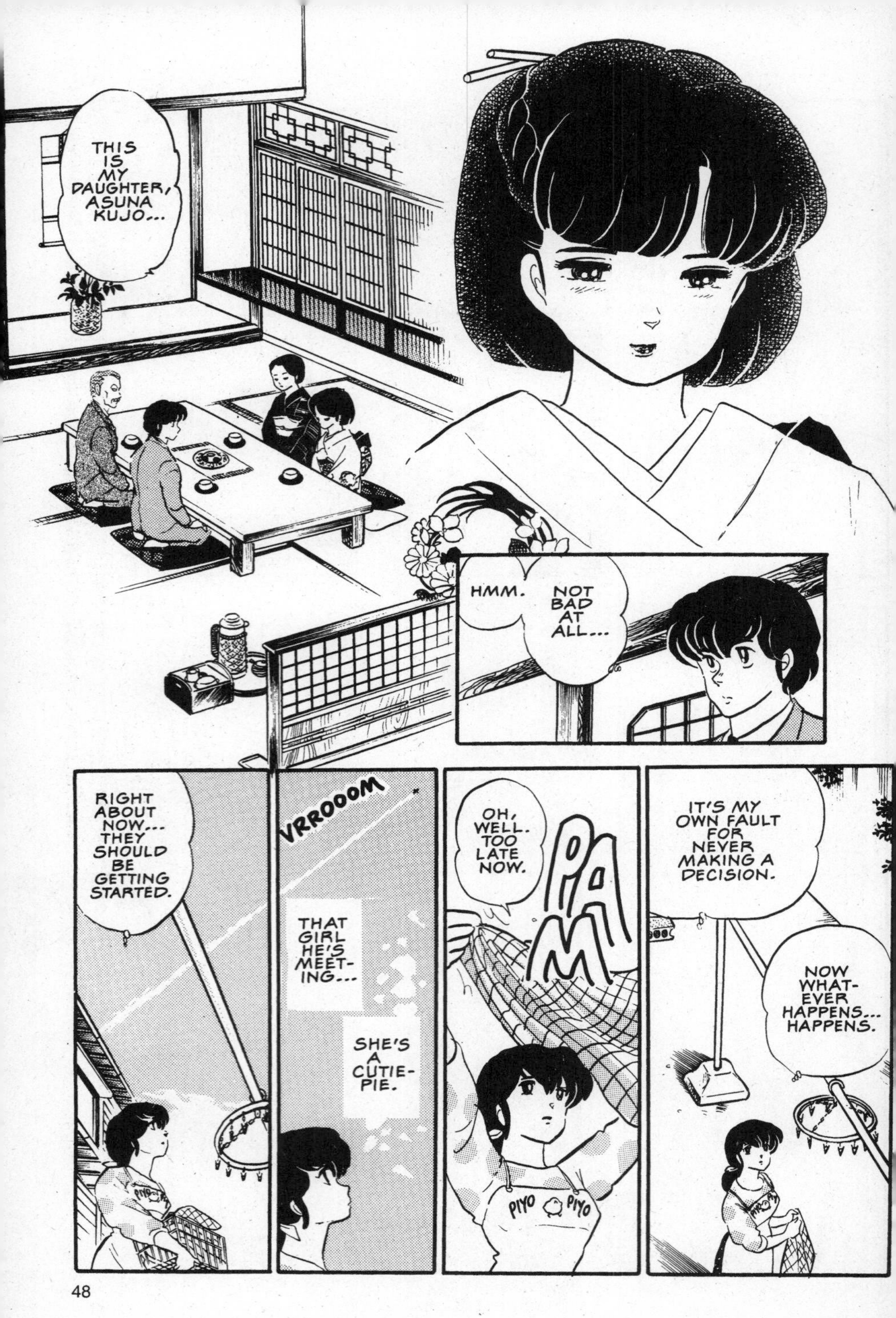
THIS IS MY DAUGHTER, ASUNA KUJO...
HMM.
NOT BAD AT ALL...
RIGHT ABOUT NOW... THEY SHOULD BE GETTING STARTED.
VRROOOM
THAT GIRL HE'S MEETING...
SHE'S A CUTIE-PIE.
OH, WELL. TOO LATE NOW.
PAM
PIYO PIYO
IT'S MY OWN FAULT FOR NEVER MAKING A DECISION.
NOW WHATEVER HAPPENS... HAPPENS.

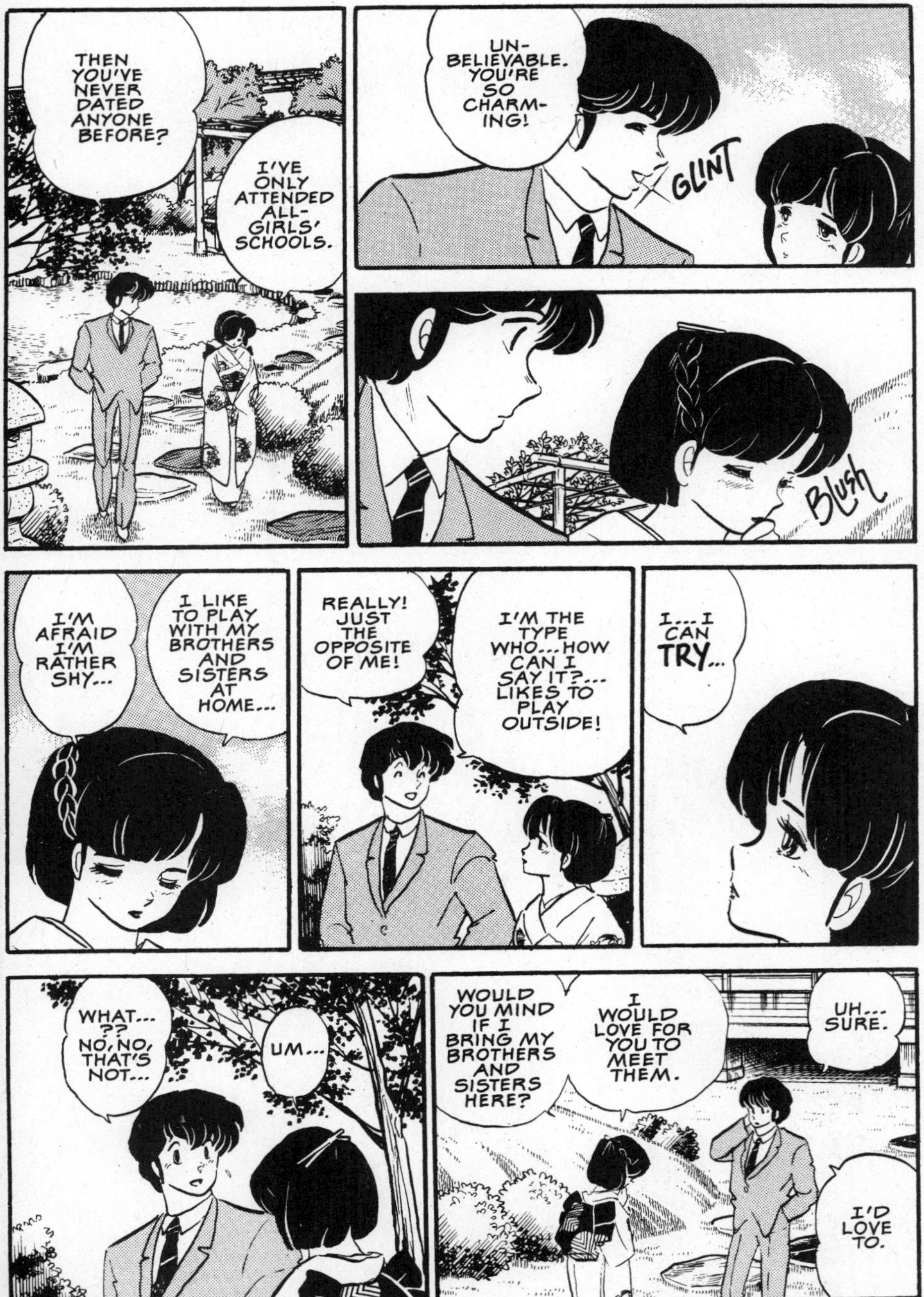
THEN YOU'VE NEVER DATED ANYONE BEFORE?
I'VE ONLY ATTENDED ALL-GIRLS' SCHOOLS.
UN-BELIEVABLE. YOU'RE SO CHARMING!
GLINT
BLUSH
I'M AFRAID I'M RATHER SHY...
I LIKE TO PLAY WITH MY BROTHERS AND SISTERS AT HOME...
REALLY! JUST THE OPPOSITE OF ME!
I'M THE TYPE WHO...HOW CAN I SAY IT?...LIKES TO PLAY OUTSIDE!
I...I CAN TRY...
WHAT...??
NO, NO, THAT'S NOT...
UM...
WOULD YOU MIND IF I BRING MY BROTHERS AND SISTERS HERE?
I WOULD LOVE FOR YOU TO MEET THEM.
UH...SURE.
I'D LOVE TO.

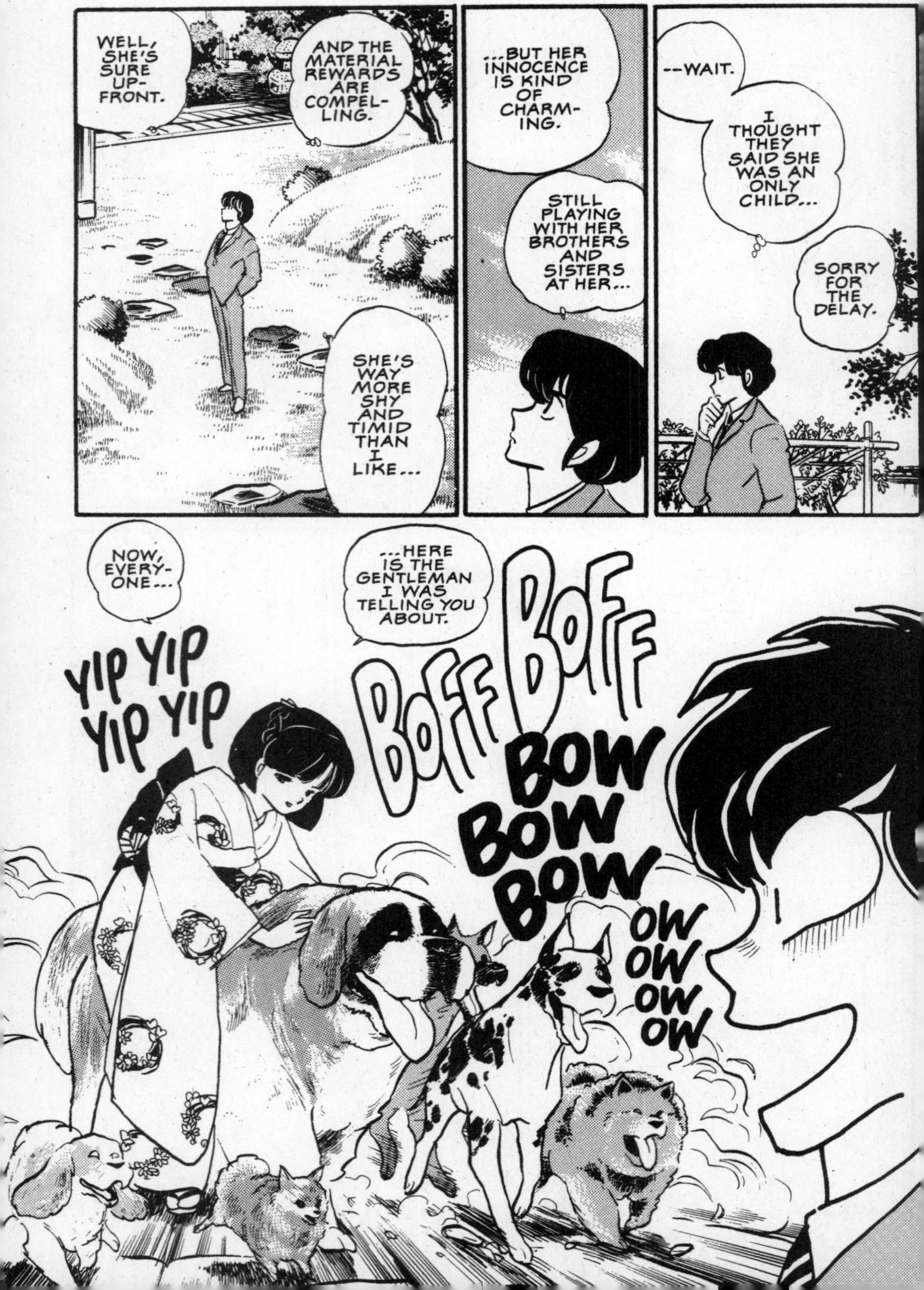
WELL, SHE'S SURE UP-FRONT.
AND THE MATERIAL REWARDS ARE COMPEL-LING.
SHE'S WAY MORE SHY AND TIMID THAN I LIKE...
...BUT HER INNOCENCE IS KIND OF CHARM-ING.
STILL PLAYING WITH HER BROTHERS AND SISTERS AT HER...
--WAIT.
I THOUGHT THEY SAID SHE WAS AN ONLY CHILD...
SORRY FOR THE DELAY.
NOW, EVERY-ONE...
...HERE IS THE GENTLEMAN I WAS TELLING YOU ABOUT.
YIP YIP YIP YIP
BOFF BOFF
BOW BOW BOW
OW OW OW OW

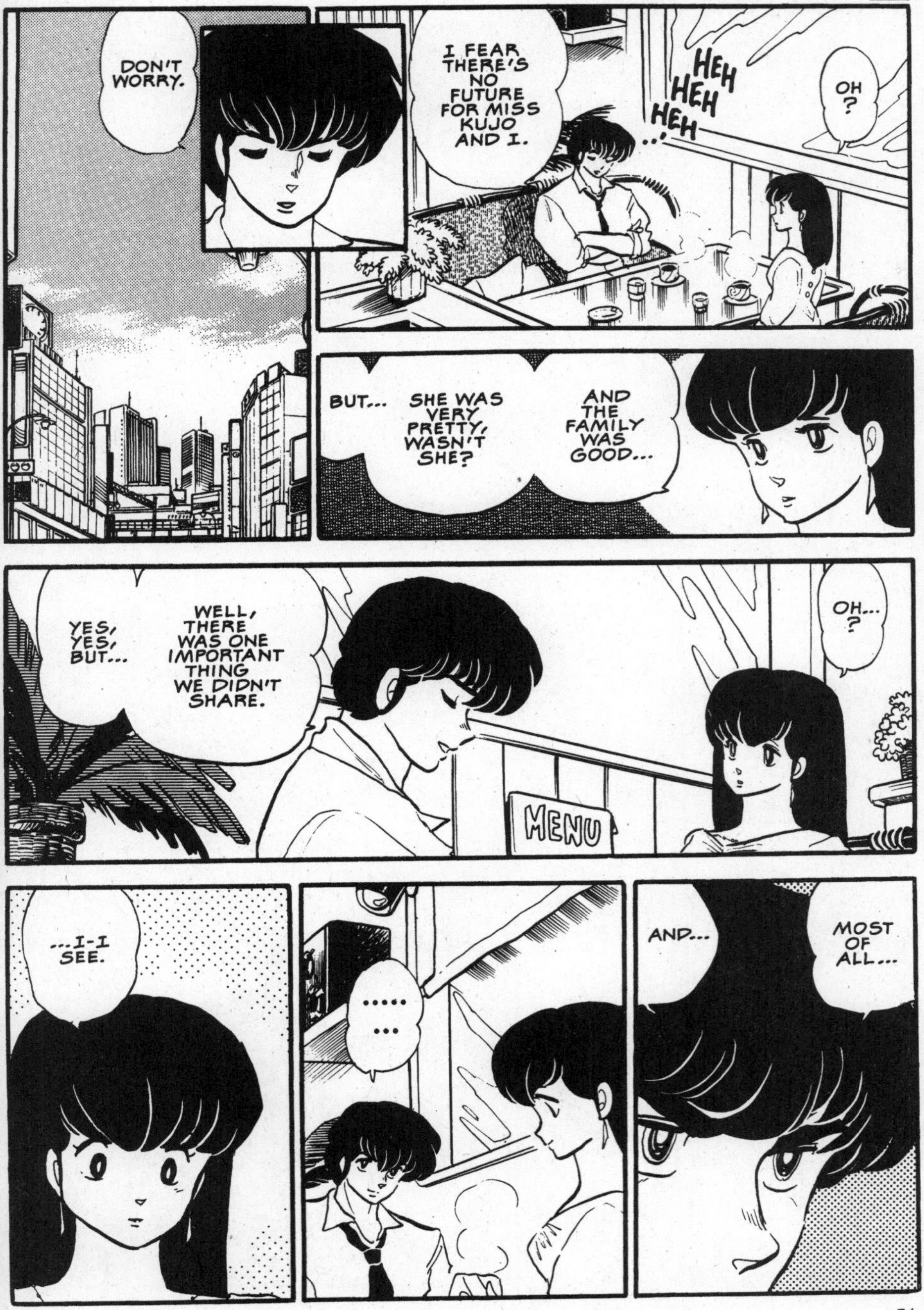
DON'T WORRY.
I FEAR THERE'S NO FUTURE FOR MISS KUJO AND I.
HEH HEH HEH...
OH?
BUT...
SHE WAS VERY PRETTY, WASN'T SHE?
AND THE FAMILY WAS GOOD...
YES, YES, BUT...
WELL, THERE WAS ONE IMPORTANT THING WE DIDN'T SHARE.
OH...?
MENU
...I-I SEE.
....
AND...
MOST OF ALL...

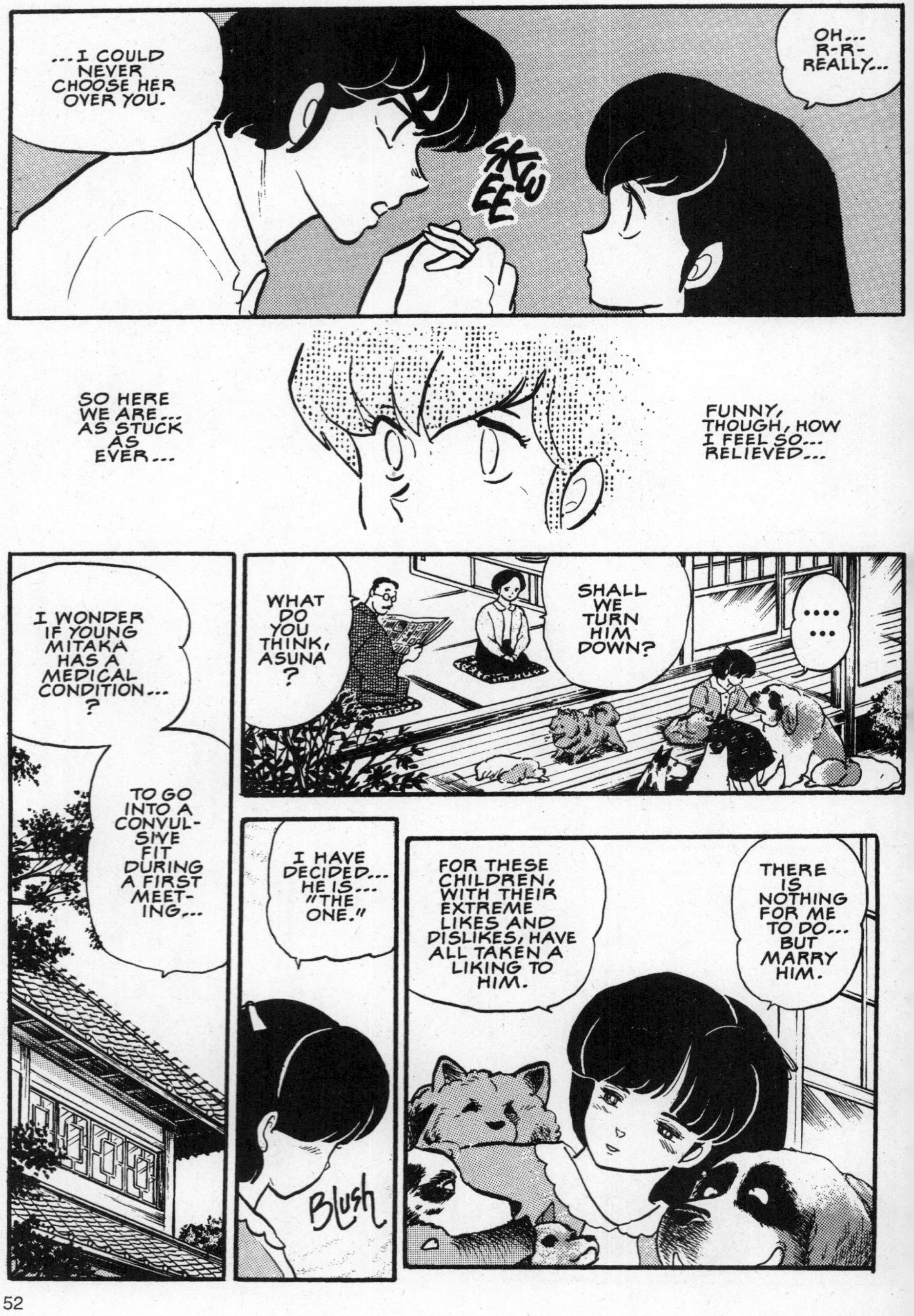
...I COULD NEVER CHOOSE HER OVER YOU.
SKWEE
OH... R-R-REALLY...
SO HERE WE ARE... AS STUCK AS EVER...
FUNNY, THOUGH, HOW I FEEL SO... RELIEVED...
I WONDER IF YOUNG MITAKA HAS A MEDICAL CONDITION...?
TO GO INTO A CONVUL-SIVE FIT DURING A FIRST MEET-ING...
WHAT DO YOU THINK, ASUNA?
SHALL WE TURN HIM DOWN?
....
...
I HAVE DECIDED... HE IS... "THE ONE."
Blush
FOR THESE CHILDREN, WITH THEIR EXTREME LIKES AND DISLIKES, HAVE ALL TAKEN A LIKING TO HIM.
THERE IS NOTHING FOR ME TO DO... BUT MARRY HIM.

PART 3
"I LOVE DOGS" • 1

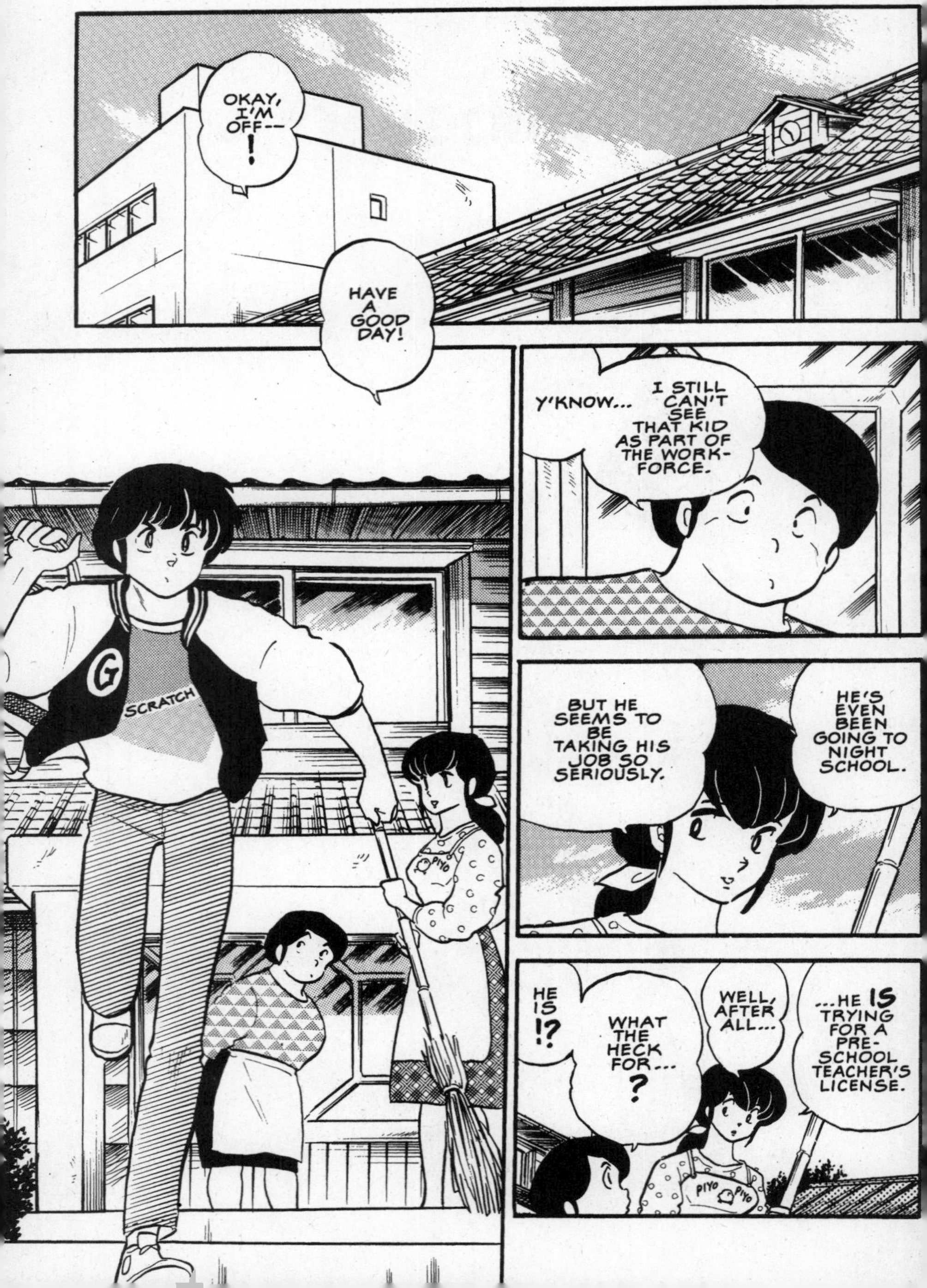
OKAY, I'M OFF--!
HAVE A GOOD DAY!
SCRATCH
Y'KNOW...
I STILL CAN'T SEE THAT KID AS PART OF THE WORK-FORCE.
BUT HE SEEMS TO BE TAKING HIS JOB SO SERIOUSLY.
HE'S EVEN BEEN GOING TO NIGHT SCHOOL.
HE IS!?
WHAT THE HECK FOR...?
WELL, AFTER ALL...
...HE IS TRYING FOR A PRE-SCHOOL TEACHER'S LICENSE.

IT **IS** DIFFERENT NOW...

...FROM HIS STUDENT DAYS.

HE LEAVES SO EARLY AND GETS HOME SO LATE...

...AND HE EVEN SEEMS BUSY ON HIS DAYS OFF.

NOW THAT I THINK ABOUT IT...

...THE ONLY TIMES I SEE HIM ANYMORE ARE OUR GOODBYES AND HELLOS...

THIS IS RIDICULOUS, UNCLE.

THAT MARRIAGE ARRANGEMENT WAS SUPPOSED TO BE BROKEN OFF...

SO **YOU** THINK.

MR. KUJO'S DAUGHTER IS COMPLETELY BESOTTED WITH YOU.

SHE HAS EXPRESSED A DESIRE TO ENTER A FORMAL RELATIONSHIP.

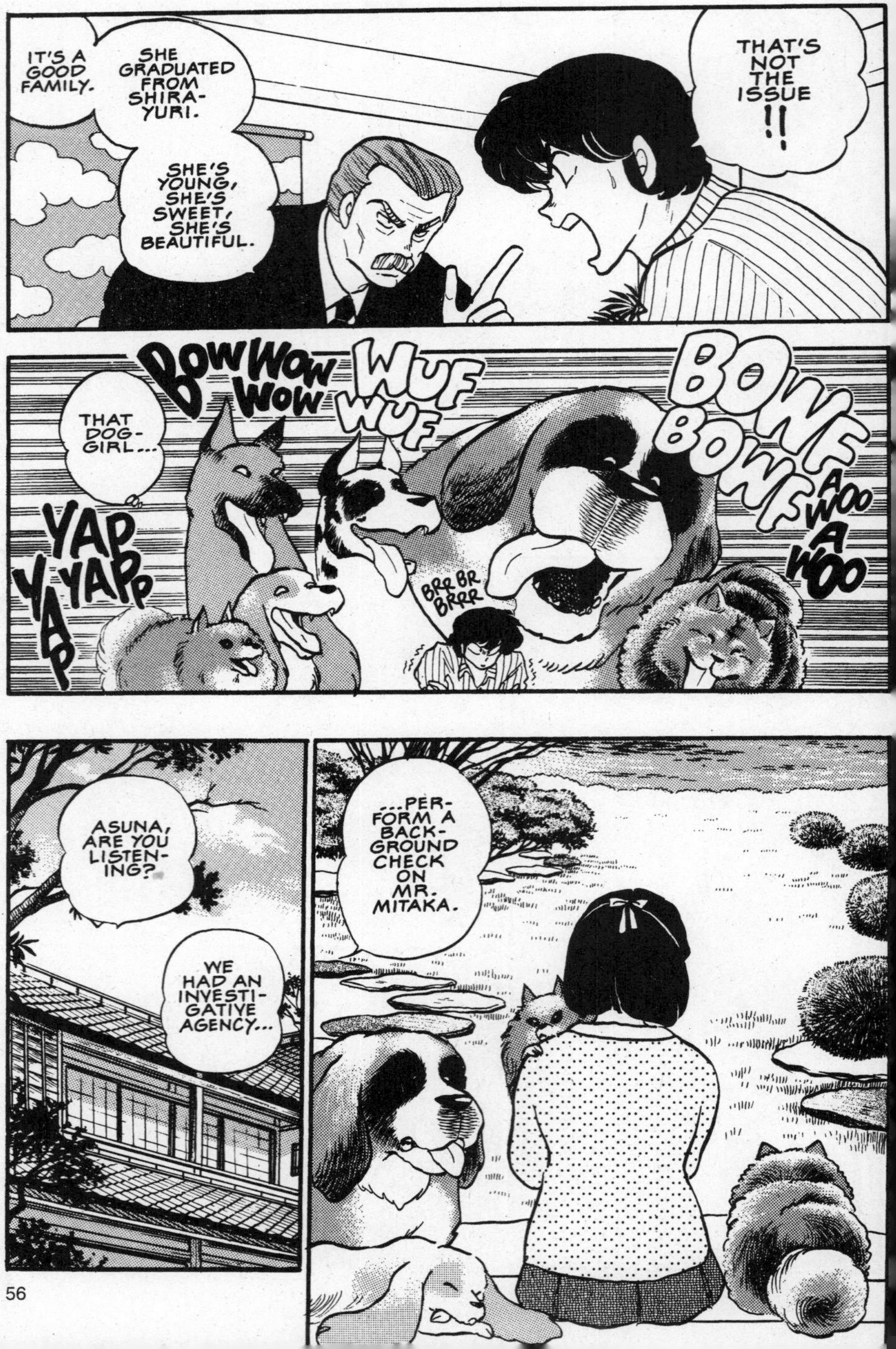
IT'S A GOOD FAMILY.
SHE GRADUATED FROM SHIRA-YURI.
SHE'S YOUNG, SHE'S SWEET, SHE'S BEAUTIFUL.
THAT'S NOT THE ISSUE !!
BOW WOW WOW
WUF WUF
BOWF BOWF
AWOO AWOO
THAT DOG-GIRL...
YAP YAPP YAP
BRR BR BRRR
ASUNA, ARE YOU LISTEN-ING?
WE HAD AN INVESTI-GATIVE AGENCY...
...PER-FORM A BACK-GROUND CHECK ON MR. MITAKA.

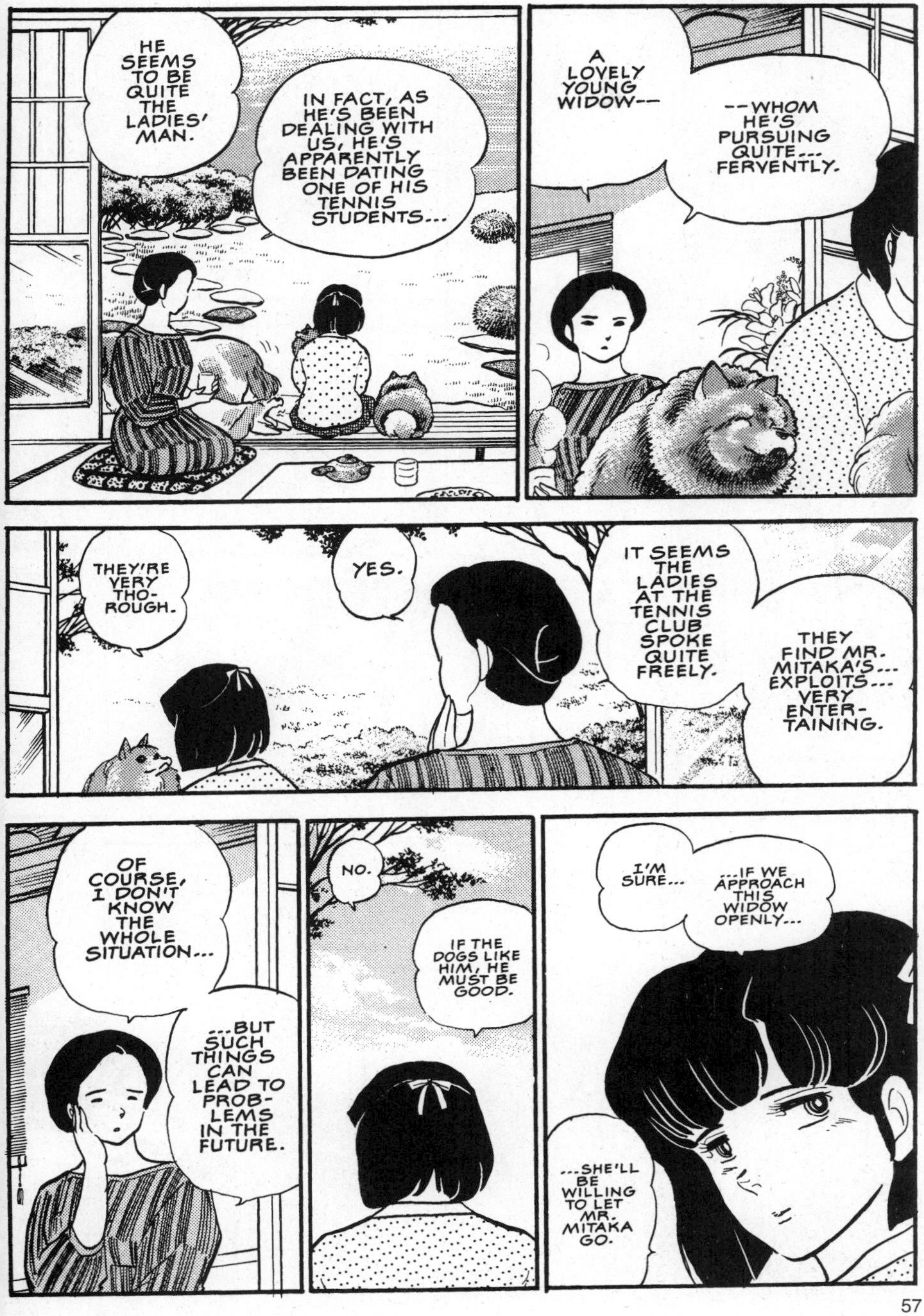
HE SEEMS TO BE QUITE THE LADIES' MAN.
IN FACT, AS HE'S BEEN DEALING WITH US, HE'S APPARENTLY BEEN DATING ONE OF HIS TENNIS STUDENTS...
A LOVELY YOUNG WIDOW--
--WHOM HE'S PURSUING QUITE... FERVENTLY.
THEY'RE VERY THO-ROUGH.
YES.
IT SEEMS THE LADIES AT THE TENNIS CLUB SPOKE QUITE FREELY.
THEY FIND MR. MITAKA'S... EXPLOITS... VERY ENTER-TAINING.
OF COURSE, I DON'T KNOW THE WHOLE SITUATION...
...BUT SUCH THINGS CAN LEAD TO PROB-LEMS IN THE FUTURE.
NO.
IF THE DOGS LIKE HIM, HE MUST BE GOOD.
I'M SURE...
...IF WE APPROACH THIS WIDOW OPENLY...
...SHE'LL BE WILLING TO LET MR. MITAKA GO.

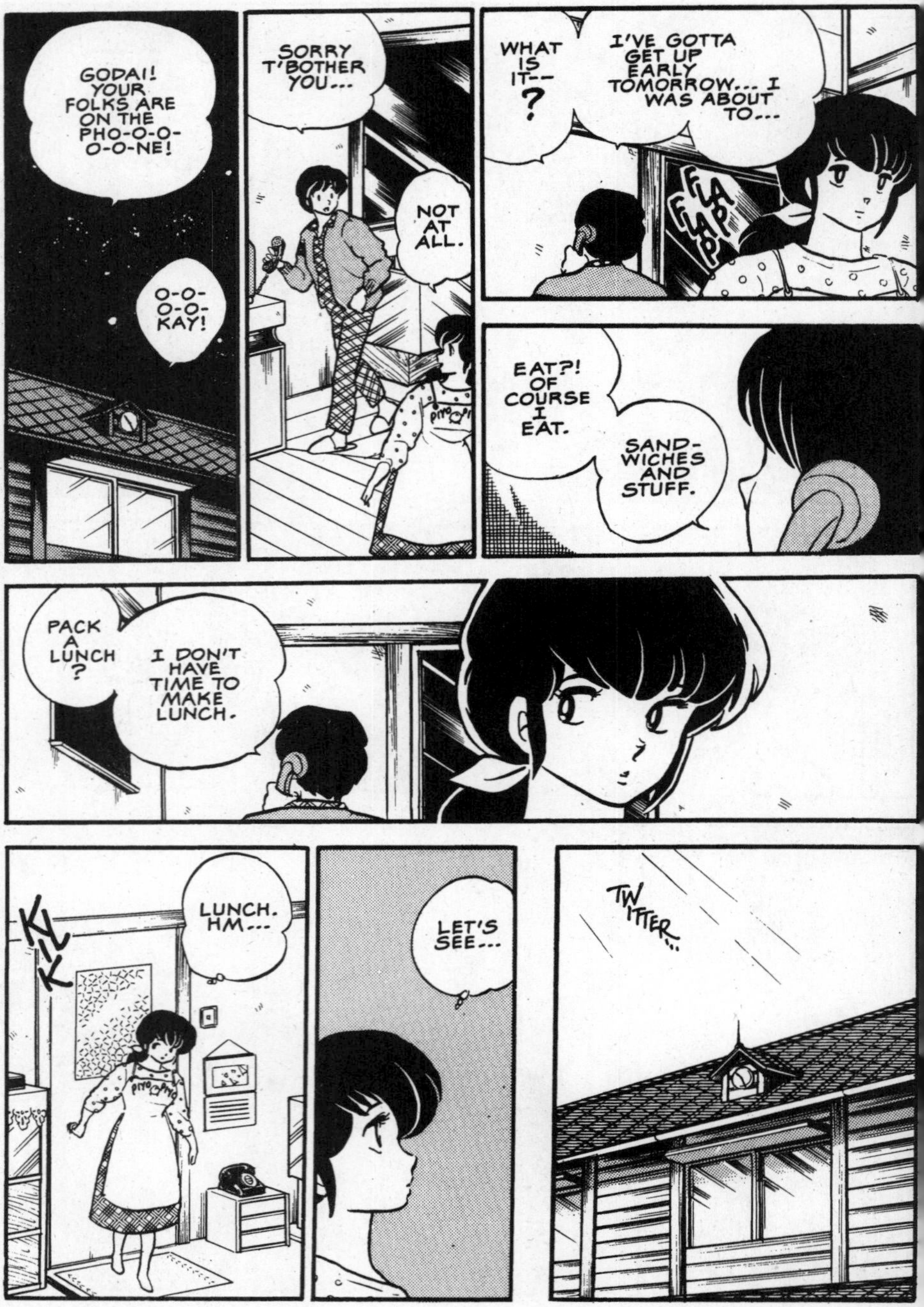
GODAI! YOUR FOLKS ARE ON THE PHO-O-O-O-O-NE!
O-O-O-O-KAY!
SORRY T'BOTHER YOU...
NOT AT ALL.
WHAT IS IT--?
I'VE GOTTA GET UP EARLY TOMORROW... I WAS ABOUT TO...
FLAP FLAP
EAT?! OF COURSE I EAT.
SANDWICHES AND STUFF.
PACK A LUNCH?
I DON'T HAVE TIME TO MAKE LUNCH.
KLIK
LUNCH. HM...
LET'S SEE...
TWITTER...

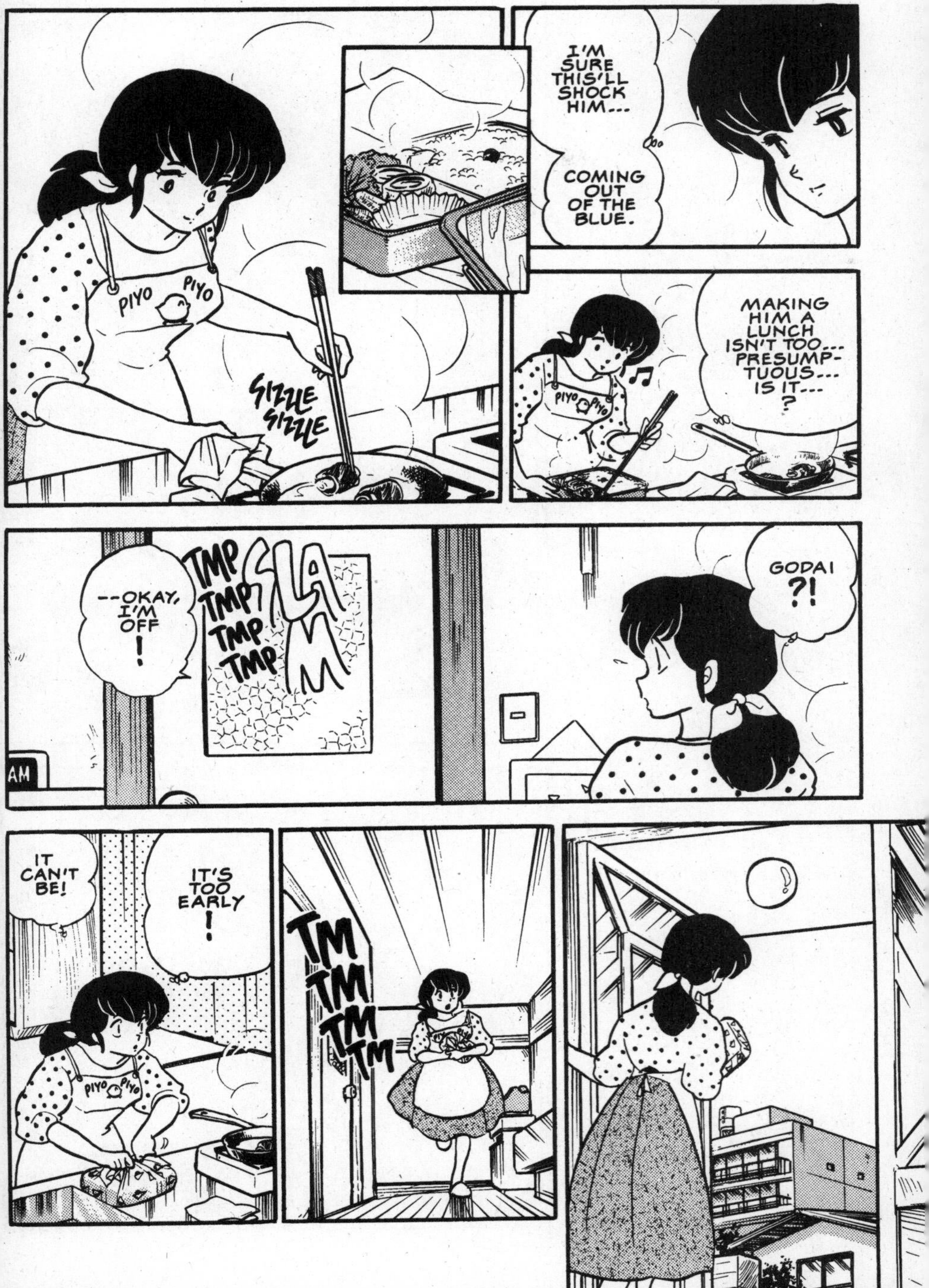
PIYO PIYO
SIZZLE SIZZLE
I'M SURE THIS'LL SHOCK HIM...
COMING OUT OF THE BLUE.
MAKING HIM A LUNCH ISN'T TOO... PRESUMPTUOUS... IS IT...?
PIYO PIYO
--OKAY, I'M OFF!
TMP TMP TMP TMP
SLAM
AM
GODAI ?!
IT CAN'T BE!
IT'S TOO EARLY!
PIYO PIYO
TM TM TM TM

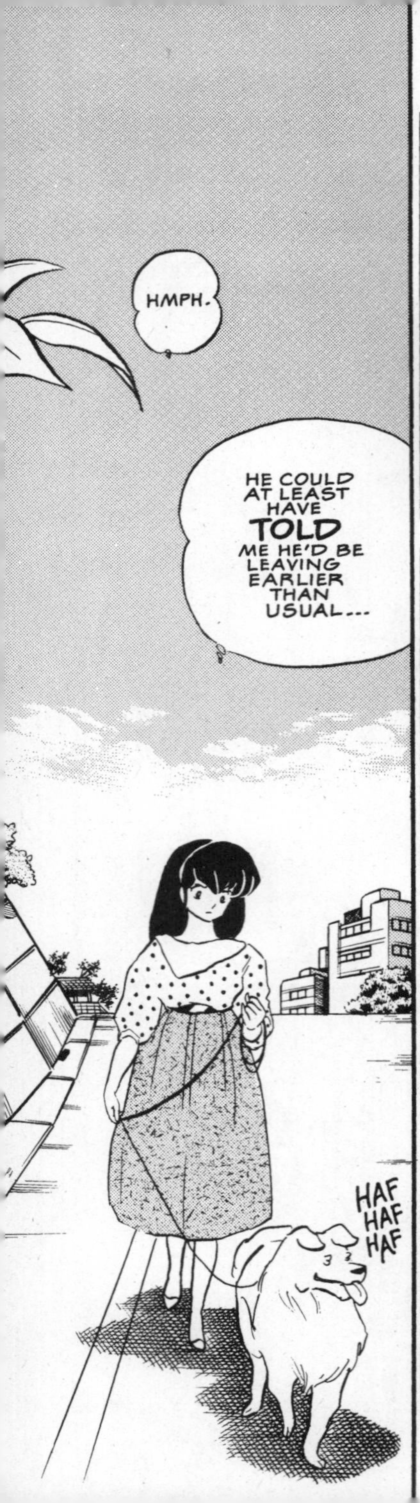
HMPH.
HE COULD AT LEAST HAVE TOLD ME HE'D BE LEAVING EARLIER THAN USUAL...
HAF HAF HAF

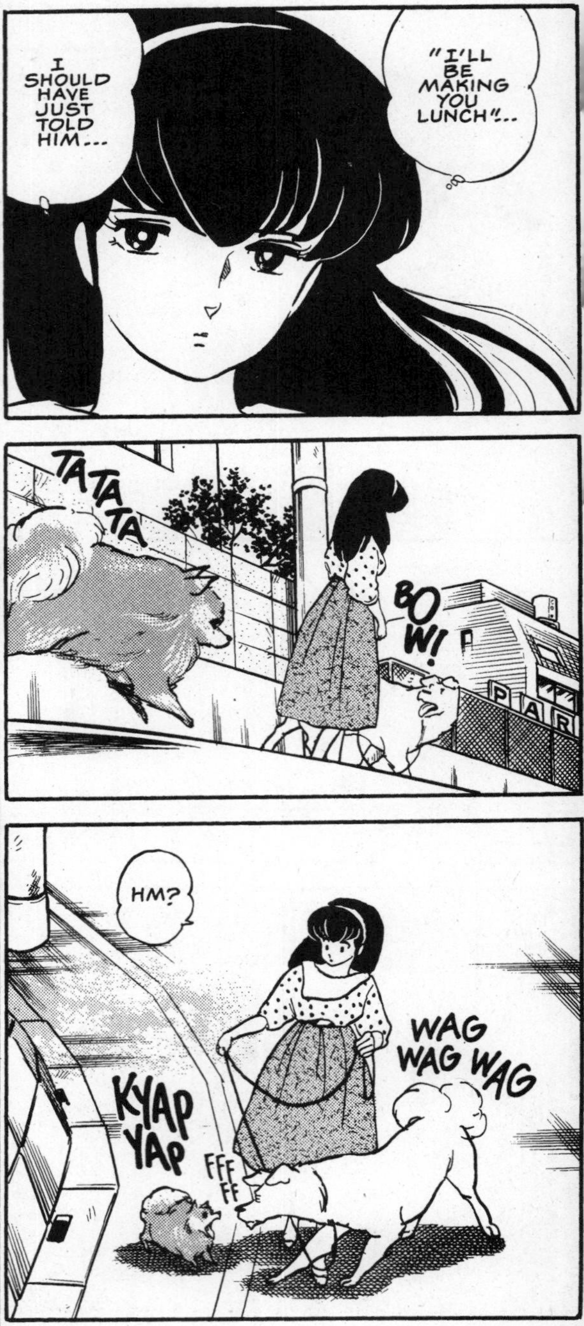
I SHOULD HAVE JUST TOLD HIM...
"I'LL BE MAKING YOU LUNCH"...
TATATA
BOW!
PAR
HM?
KYAP YAP
FFF FF
WAG WAG WAG

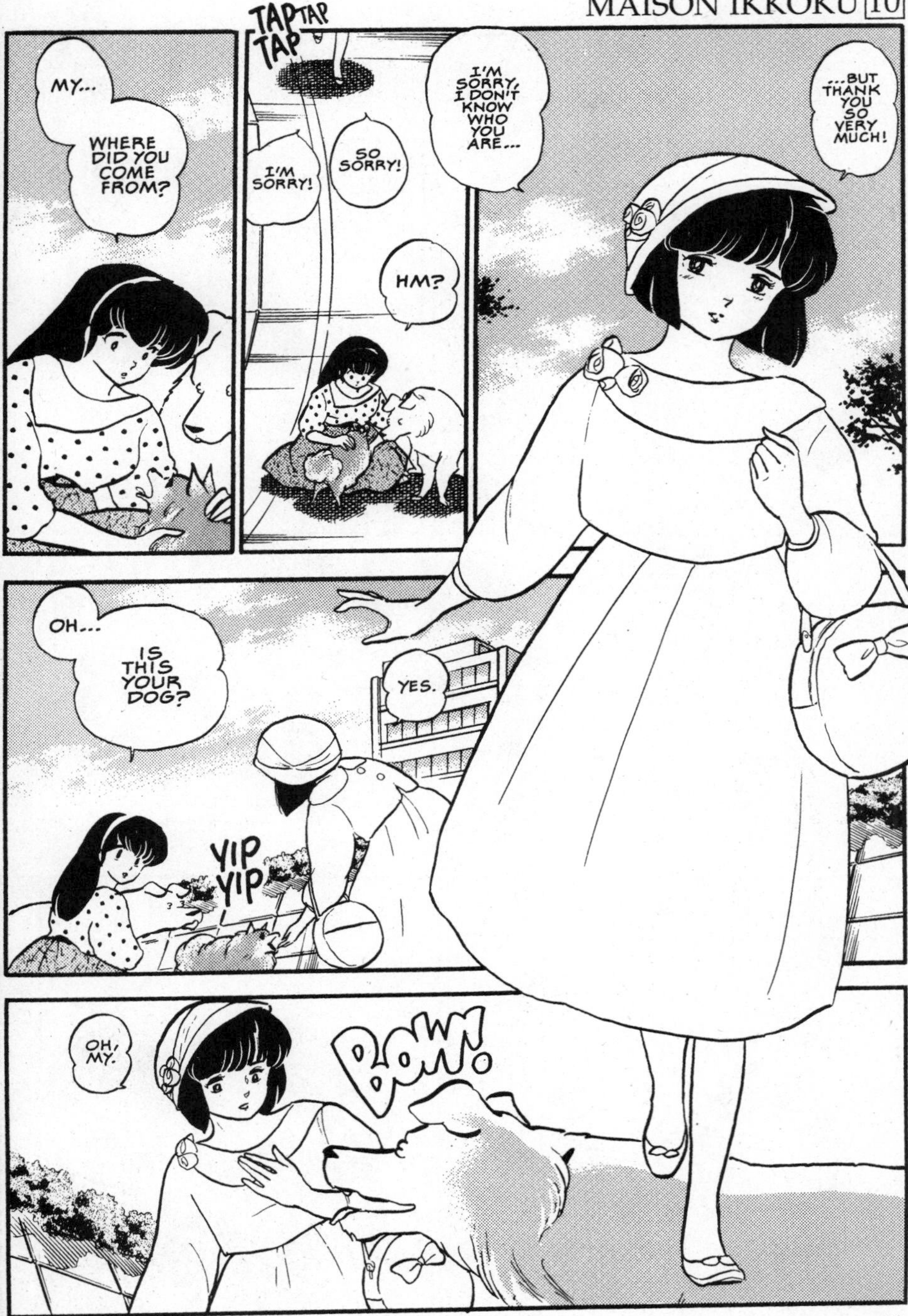
MY...
WHERE DID YOU COME FROM?
TAP TAP TAP
I'M SORRY!
SO SORRY!
HM?
I'M SORRY, I DON'T KNOW WHO YOU ARE...
...BUT THANK YOU SO VERY MUCH!
OH...
IS THIS YOUR DOG?
YES.
YIP YIP
OH, MY.
BOW!

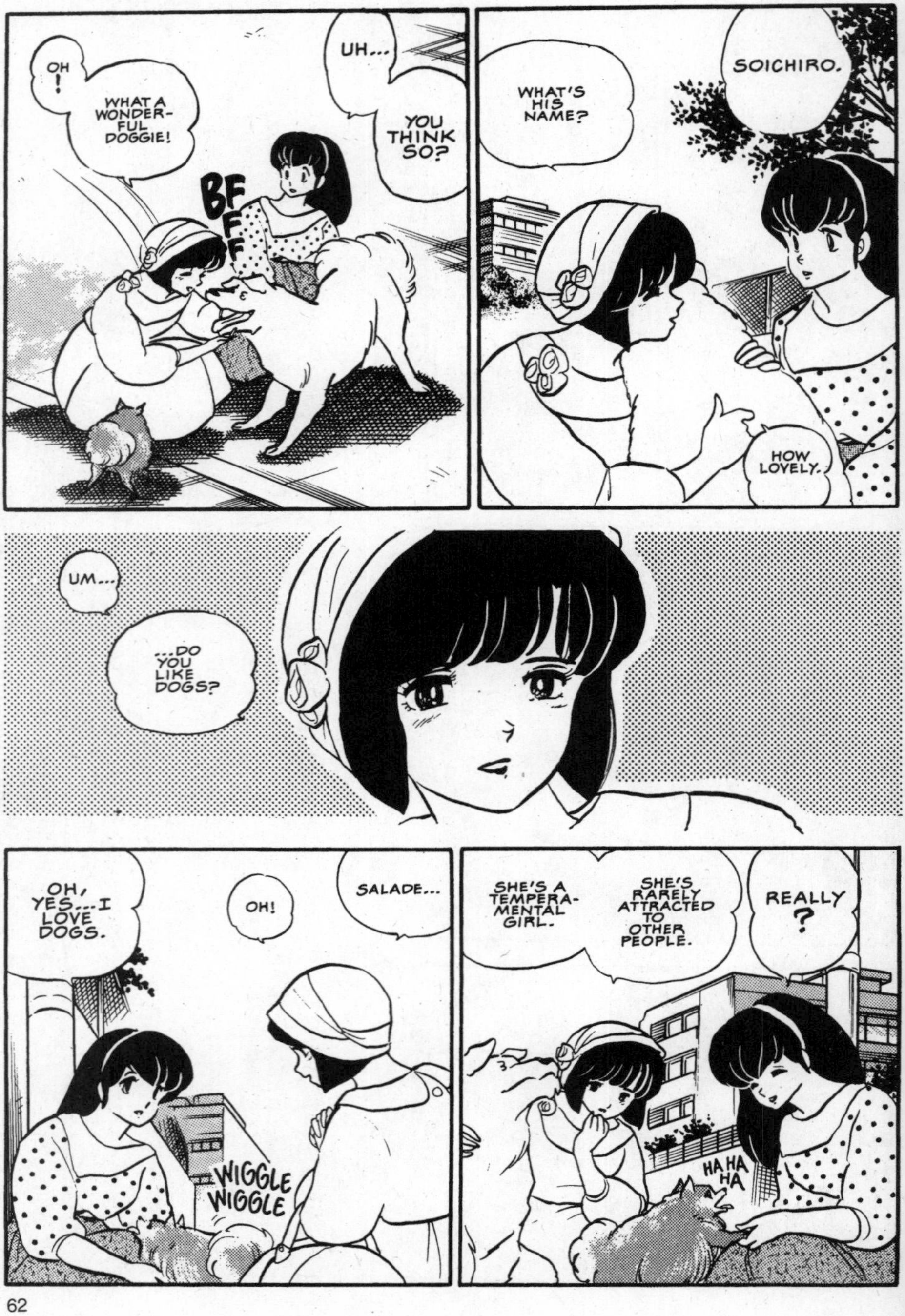
OH!
WHAT A WONDERFUL DOGGIE!
UH...
YOU THINK SO?
BFFF
WHAT'S HIS NAME?
SOICHIRO.
HOW LOVELY.
UM...
...DO YOU LIKE DOGS?
OH, YES... I LOVE DOGS.
OH!
SALADE...
WIGGLE WIGGLE
SHE'S A TEMPERAMENTAL GIRL.
SHE'S RARELY ATTRACTED TO OTHER PEOPLE.
REALLY?
HA HA HA

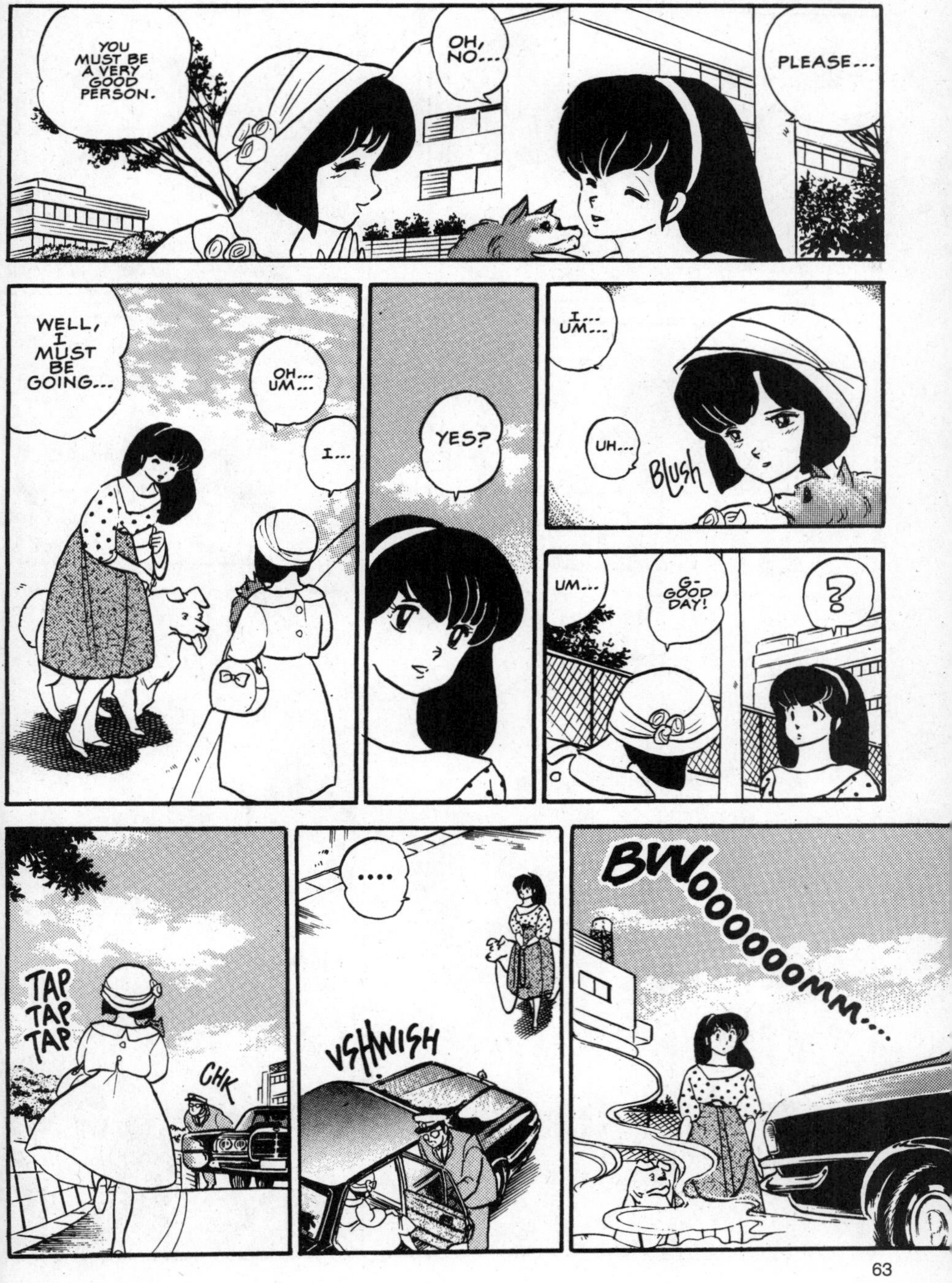

YOU MUST BE A VERY GOOD PERSON.
OH, NO...
PLEASE...
WELL, I MUST BE GOING...
OH... UM...
I...
YES?
I... UM...
UH...
BLUSH
UM...
G-GOOD DAY!
?
TAP TAP TAP
CHK
....
VSHWISH
BWOOOOOOOMM...

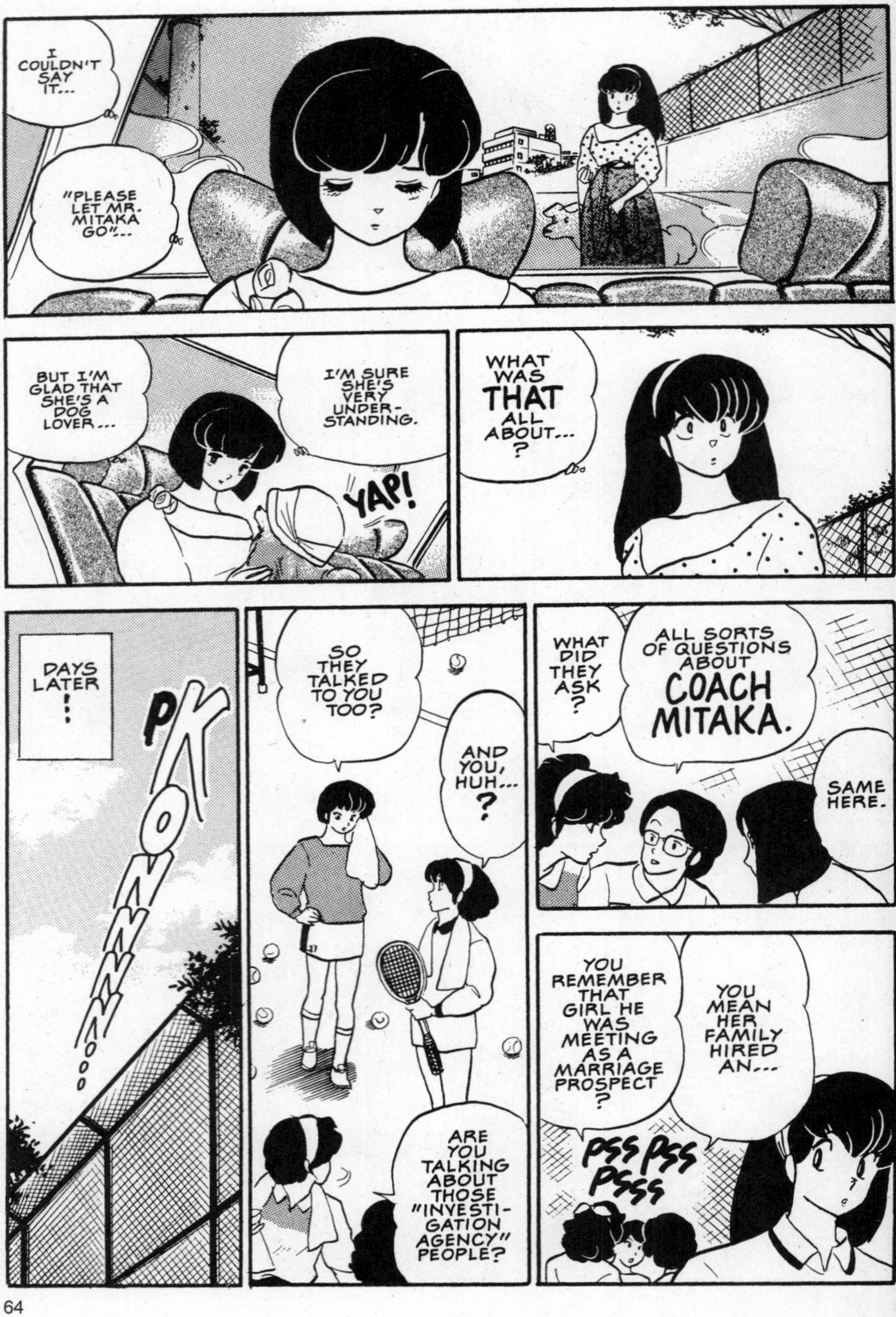
I COULDN'T SAY IT...
"PLEASE LET MR. MITAKA GO"...
BUT I'M GLAD THAT SHE'S A DOG LOVER...
I'M SURE SHE'S VERY UNDER-STANDING.
YAP!
WHAT WAS THAT ALL ABOUT...?
DAYS LATER...
PKONNNNNNooo
SO THEY TALKED TO YOU TOO?
AND YOU, HUH...?
ARE YOU TALKING ABOUT THOSE "INVESTI-GATION AGENCY" PEOPLE?
WHAT DID THEY ASK?
ALL SORTS OF QUESTIONS ABOUT COACH MITAKA.
SAME HERE.
YOU REMEMBER THAT GIRL HE WAS MEETING AS A MARRIAGE PROSPECT?
YOU MEAN HER FAMILY HIRED AN...
PSS PSS PSSS

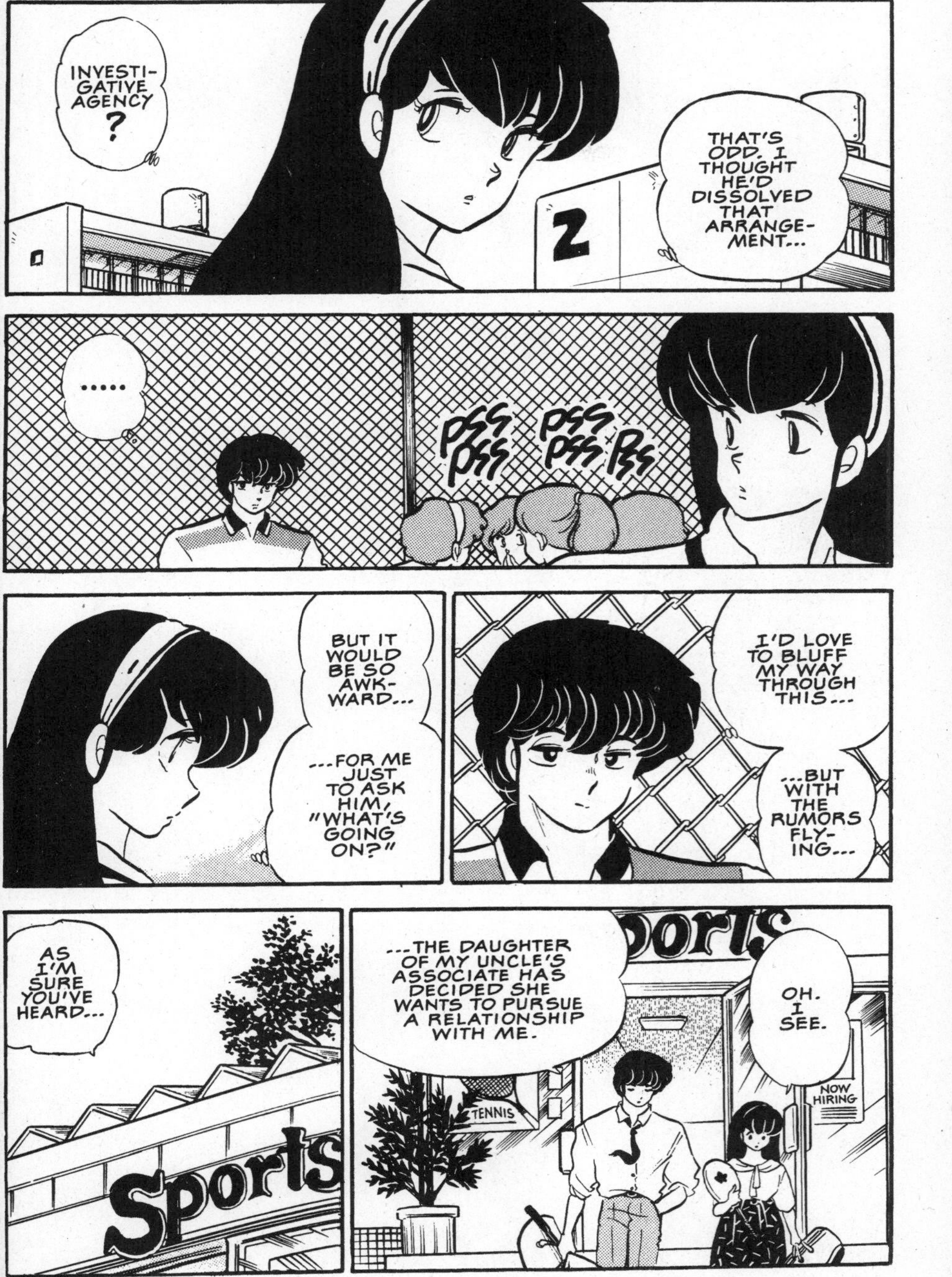
INVESTI-GATIVE AGENCY ?
2
THAT'S ODD. I THOUGHT HE'D DISSOLVED THAT ARRANGE-MENT...
......
PSS PSS PSS PSS PSS
BUT IT WOULD BE SO AWK-WARD...
...FOR ME JUST TO ASK HIM, "WHAT'S GOING ON?"
I'D LOVE TO BLUFF MY WAY THROUGH THIS...
...BUT WITH THE RUMORS FLY-ING...
AS I'M SURE YOU'VE HEARD...
Sports
...THE DAUGHTER OF MY UNCLE'S ASSOCIATE HAS DECIDED SHE WANTS TO PURSUE A RELATIONSHIP WITH ME.
OH. I SEE.
TENNIS
NOW HIRING

THIS MR. KUJO IS AN IMPORTANT CLIENT OF MY UNCLE'S FIRM...

...WHICH MAKES IT AWKWARD FOR ME JUST TO SAY NO...

....

...I'D LIKE TO HAVE YOUR DECISION WITHIN A WEEK.

KYOKO...

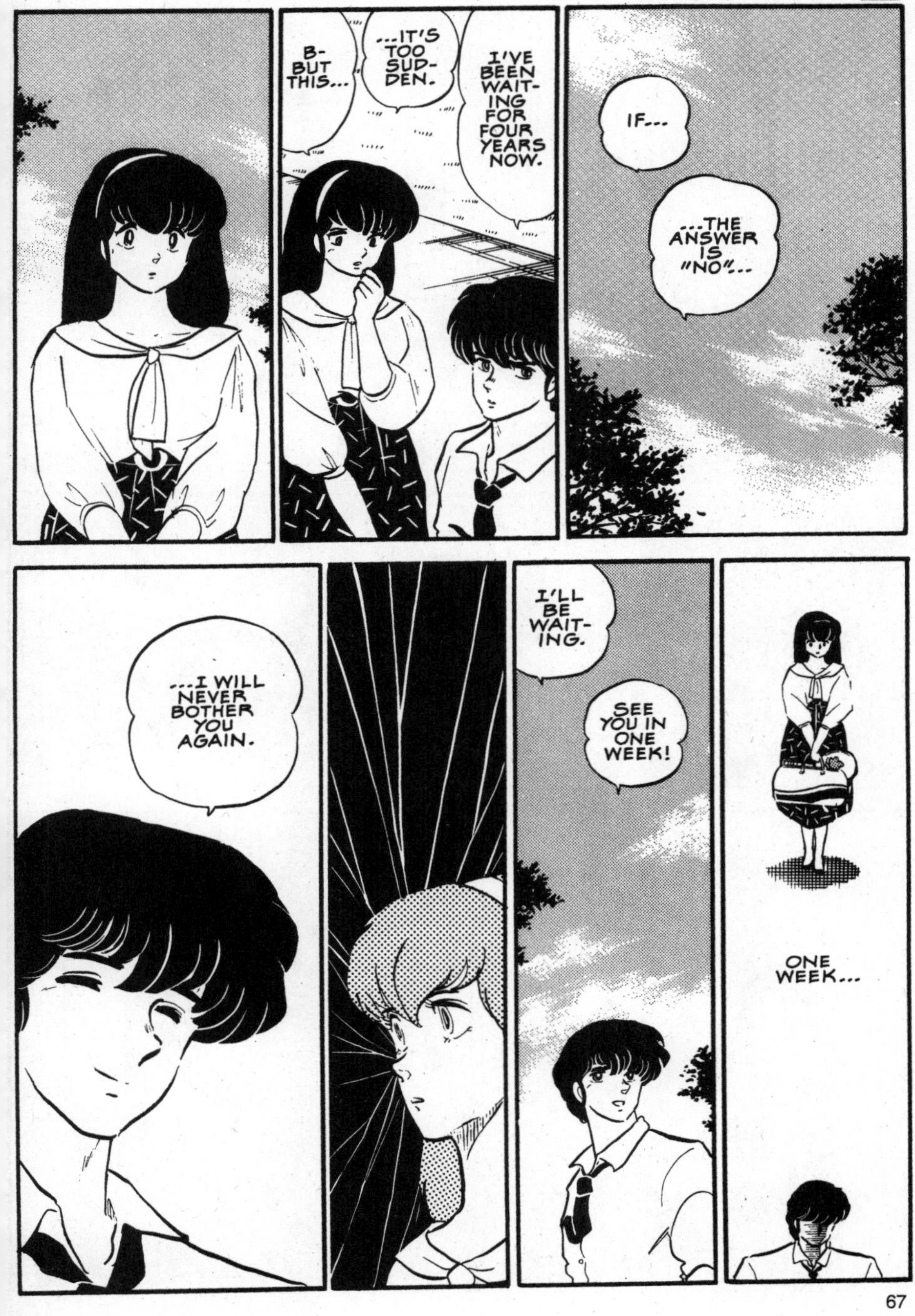
B-BUT THIS...
...IT'S TOO SUDDEN.
I'VE BEEN WAITING FOR FOUR YEARS NOW.
IF...
...THE ANSWER IS "NO"...
...I WILL NEVER BOTHER YOU AGAIN.
I'LL BE WAITING.
SEE YOU IN ONE WEEK!
ONE WEEK...

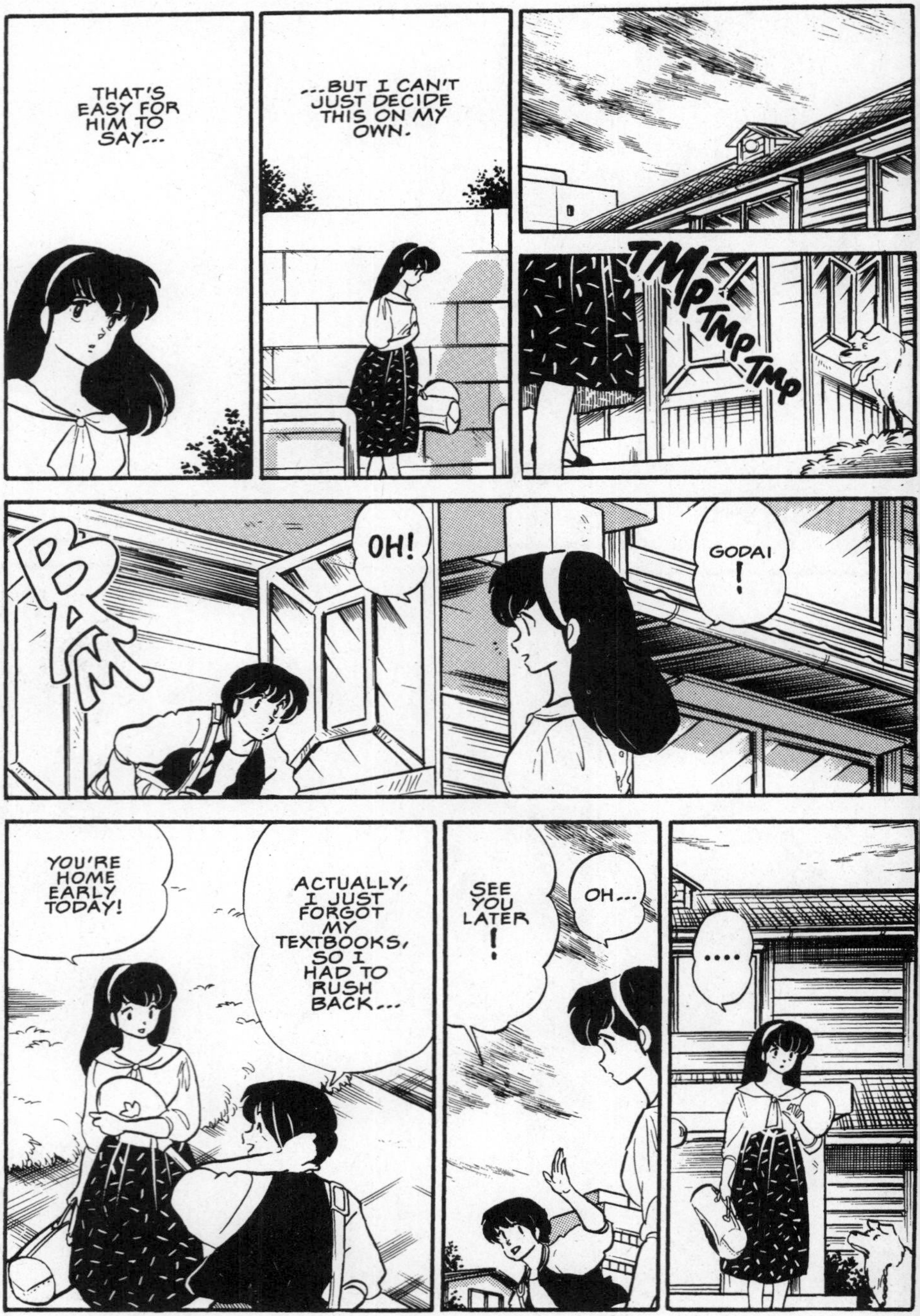
THAT'S EASY FOR HIM TO SAY...
...BUT I CAN'T JUST DECIDE THIS ON MY OWN.
TMP TMP TMP TMP
BAM
OH!
GODAI!
YOU'RE HOME EARLY TODAY!
ACTUALLY, I JUST FORGOT MY TEXTBOOKS, SO I HAD TO RUSH BACK...
OH...
SEE YOU LATER!
.....

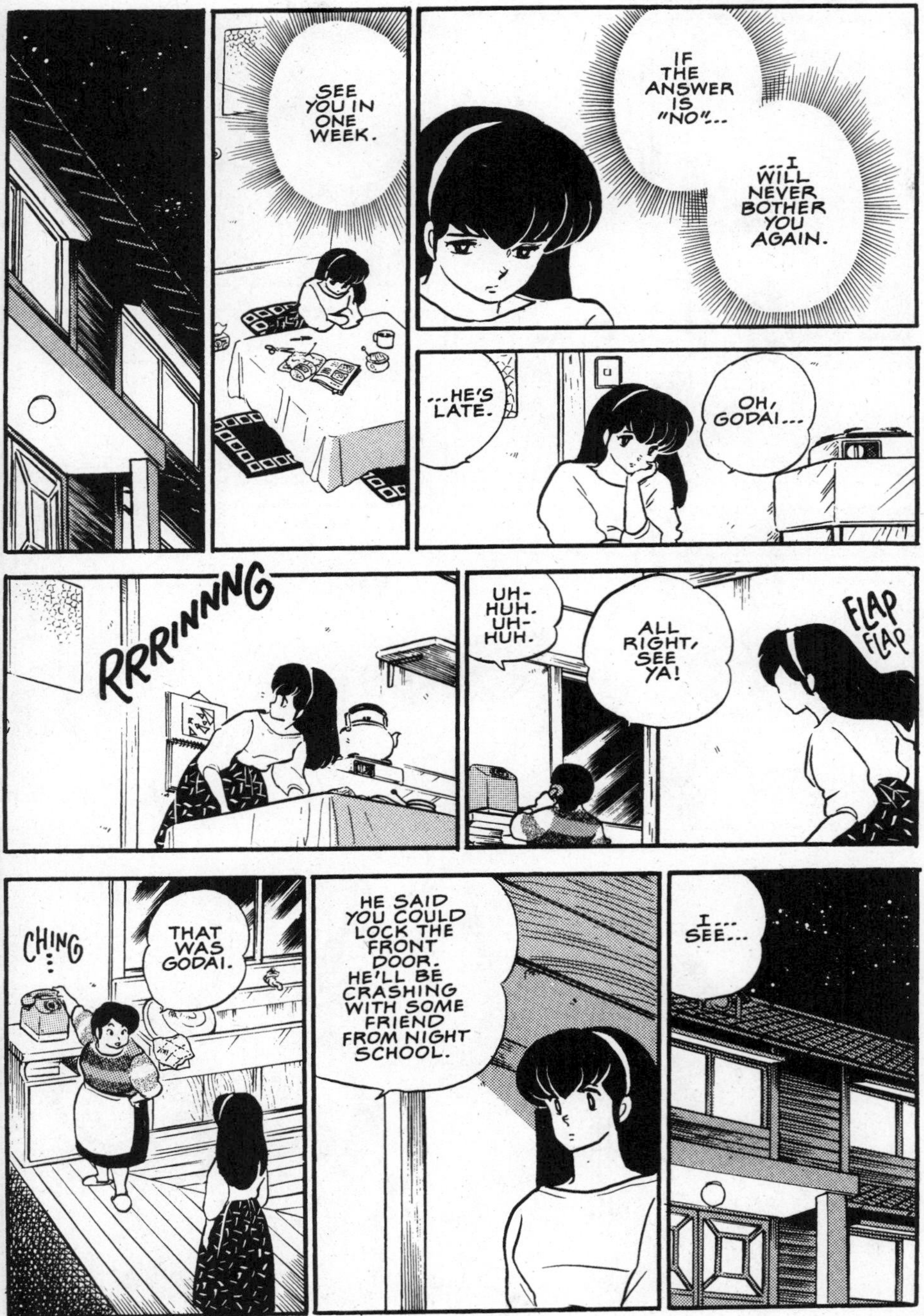
SEE YOU IN ONE WEEK.
IF THE ANSWER IS "NO"...
...I WILL NEVER BOTHER YOU AGAIN.
...HE'S LATE.
OH, GODAI...
RRRINNNG
UH-HUH. UH-HUH.
ALL RIGHT, SEE YA!
FLAP FLAP
CHING
THAT WAS GODAI.
HE SAID YOU COULD LOCK THE FRONT DOOR. HE'LL BE CRASHING WITH SOME FRIEND FROM NIGHT SCHOOL.
I... SEE...

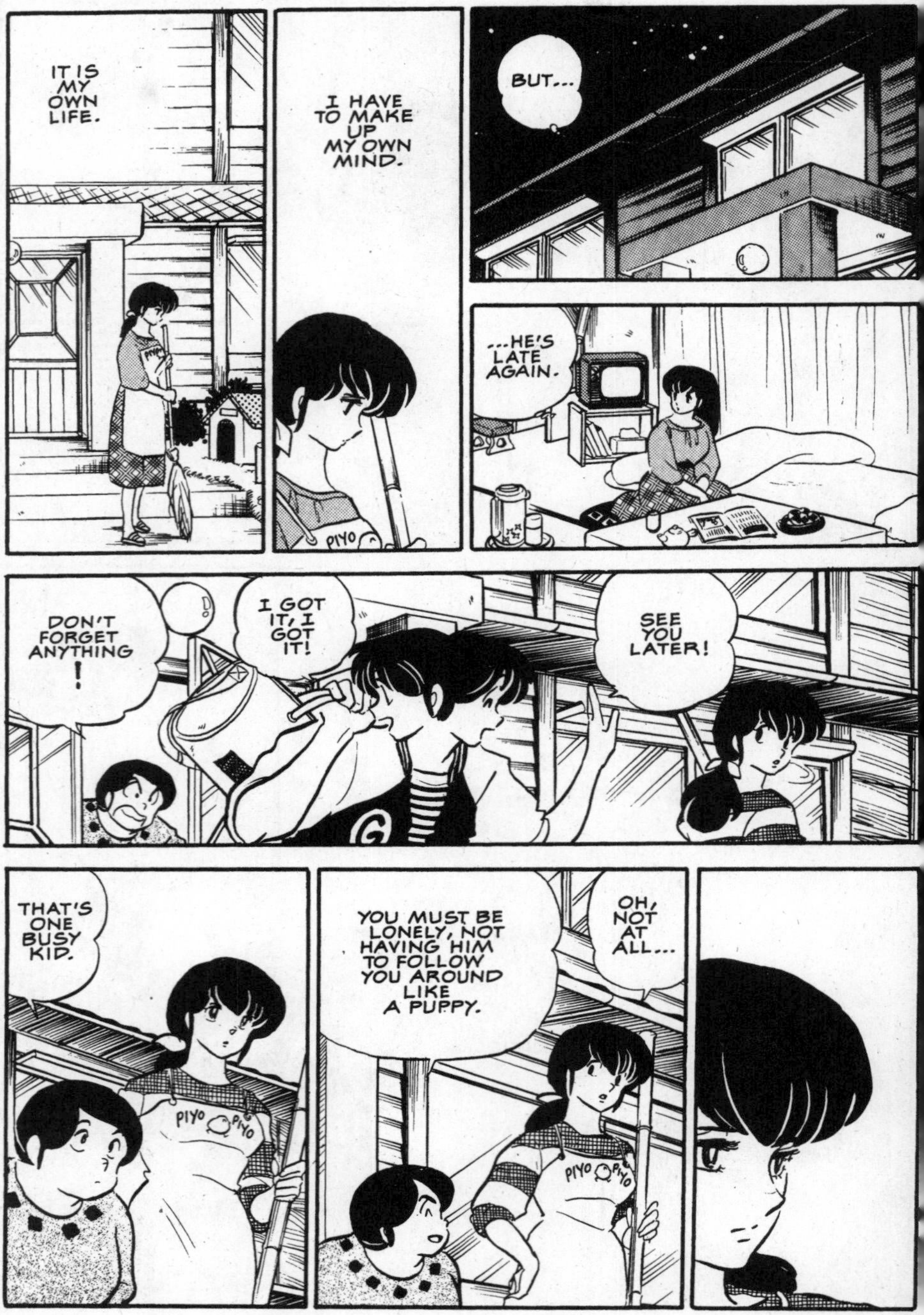
IT IS MY OWN LIFE.
I HAVE TO MAKE UP MY OWN MIND.
BUT...
...HE'S LATE AGAIN.
DON'T FORGET ANYTHING!
I GOT IT, I GOT IT!
SEE YOU LATER!
THAT'S ONE BUSY KID.
YOU MUST BE LONELY, NOT HAVING HIM TO FOLLOW YOU AROUND LIKE A PUPPY.
OH, NOT AT ALL...

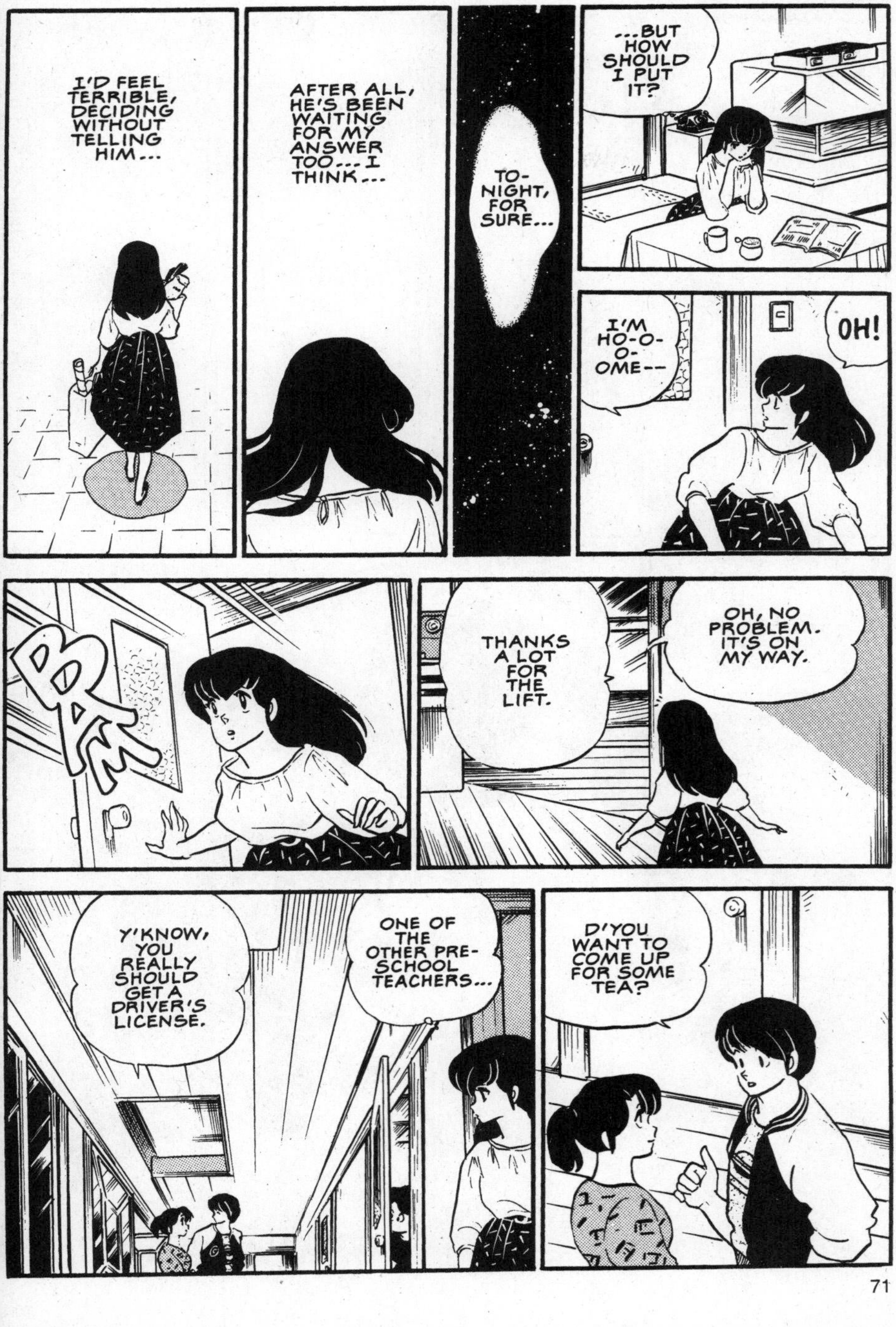
I'D FEEL TERRIBLE, DECIDING WITHOUT TELLING HIM...
AFTER ALL, HE'S BEEN WAITING FOR MY ANSWER TOO... I THINK...
TO-NIGHT, FOR SURE...
...BUT HOW SHOULD I PUT IT?
I'M HO-O-O-OME--
OH!
THANKS A LOT FOR THE LIFT.
OH, NO PROBLEM. IT'S ON MY WAY.
Y'KNOW, YOU REALLY SHOULD GET A DRIVER'S LICENSE.
ONE OF THE OTHER PRE-SCHOOL TEACHERS...
D'YOU WANT TO COME UP FOR SOME TEA?

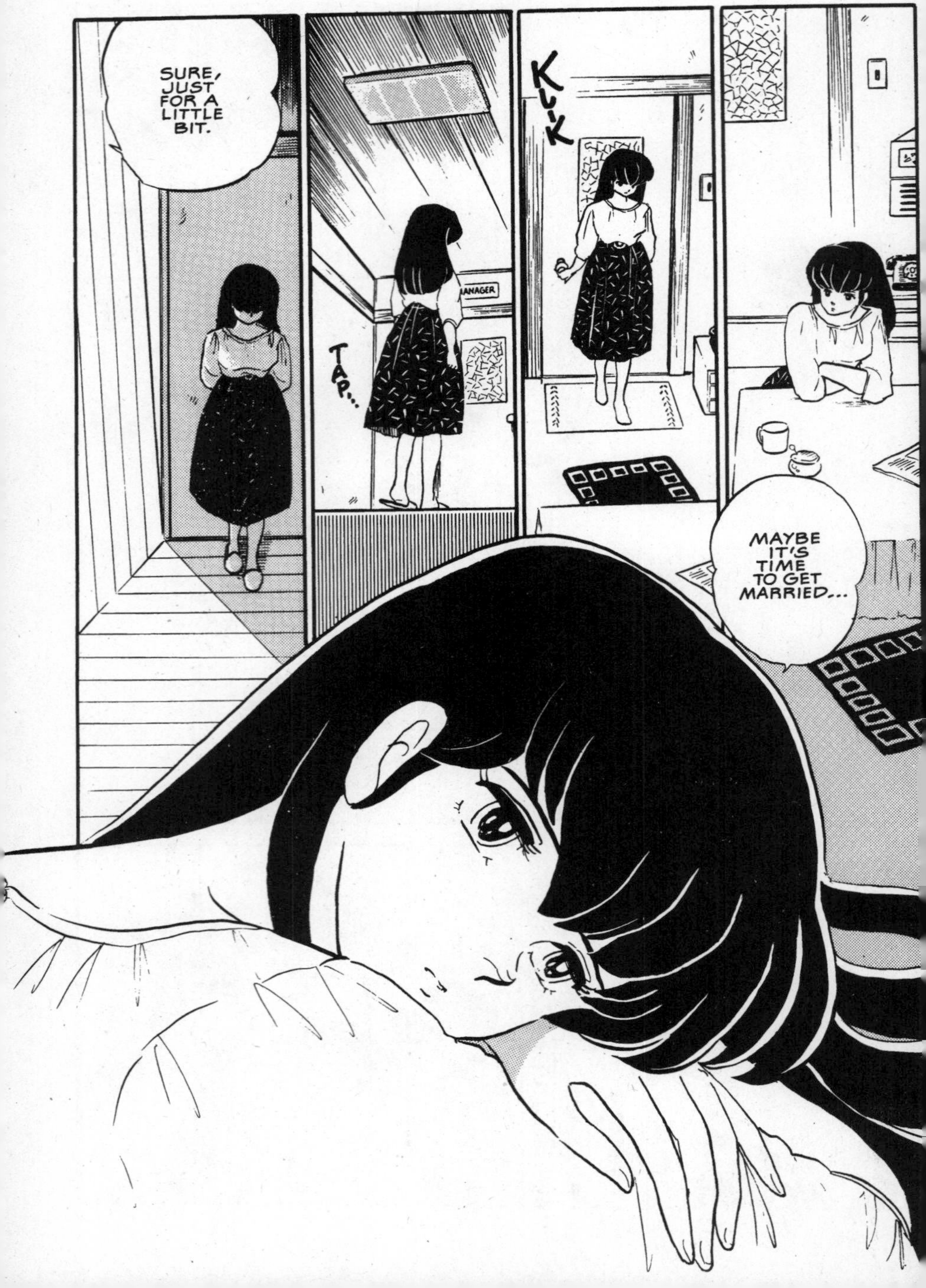
SURE, JUST FOR A LITTLE BIT.
TAP...
MANAGER
KLIK
MAYBE IT'S TIME TO GET MARRIED...

PART 4
"I LOVE DOGS" • II

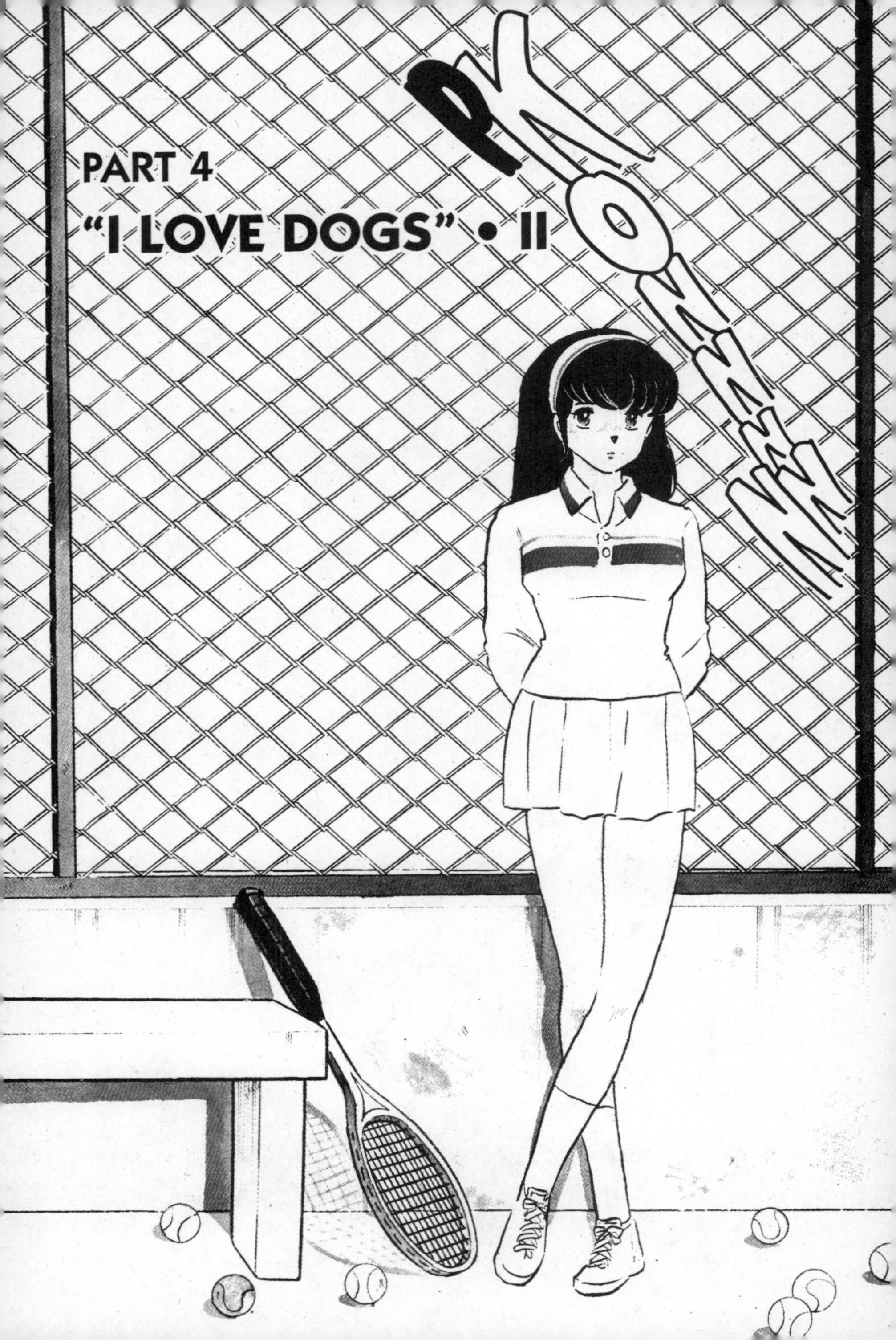

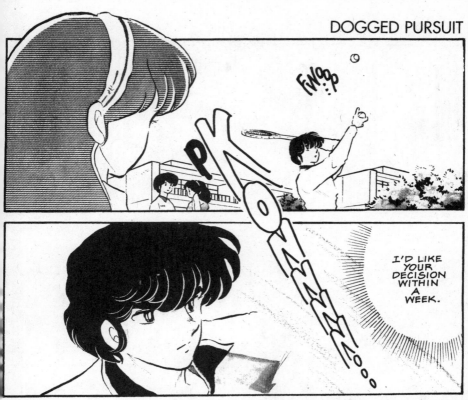

FWOOP...!?

PKOMMMMOOO

I'D LIKE YOUR DECISION WITHIN A WEEK.

IF THE ANSWER IS "NO"...

...I WILL NEVER BOTHER YOU AGAIN.

PKOMMMMOOO

TENNIS SCHOOL

ADVANCED LESSONS

75

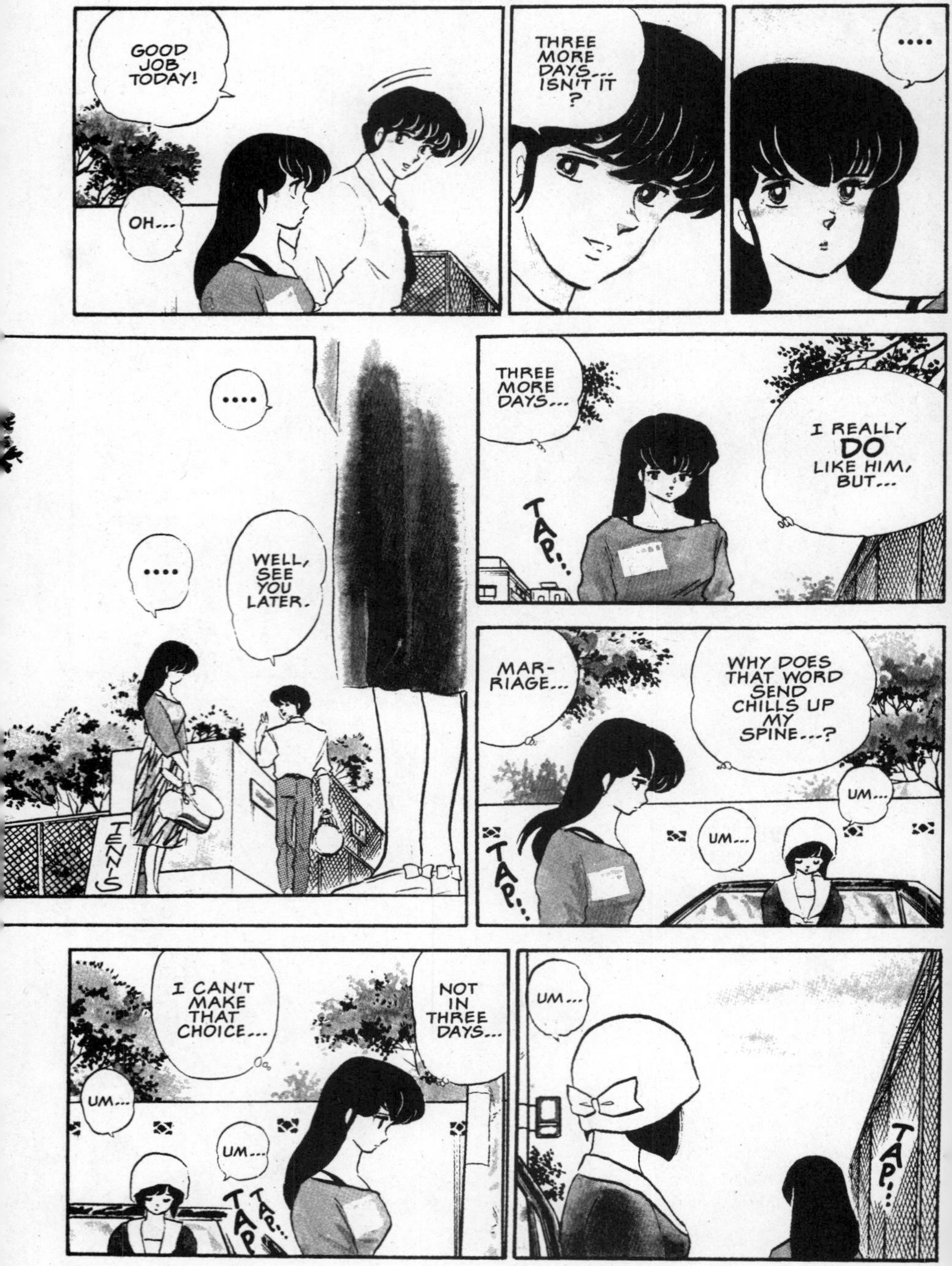
GOOD JOB TODAY!
OH...
THREE MORE DAYS... ISN'T IT ?
....
....
....
WELL, SEE YOU LATER.
TENNIS
THREE MORE DAYS...
I REALLY DO LIKE HIM, BUT...
TAP...
MAR-RIAGE...
WHY DOES THAT WORD SEND CHILLS UP MY SPINE...?
UM...
UM...
TAP...
I CAN'T MAKE THAT CHOICE...
NOT IN THREE DAYS...
UM...
UM...
TAP TAP...
UM...
TAP...

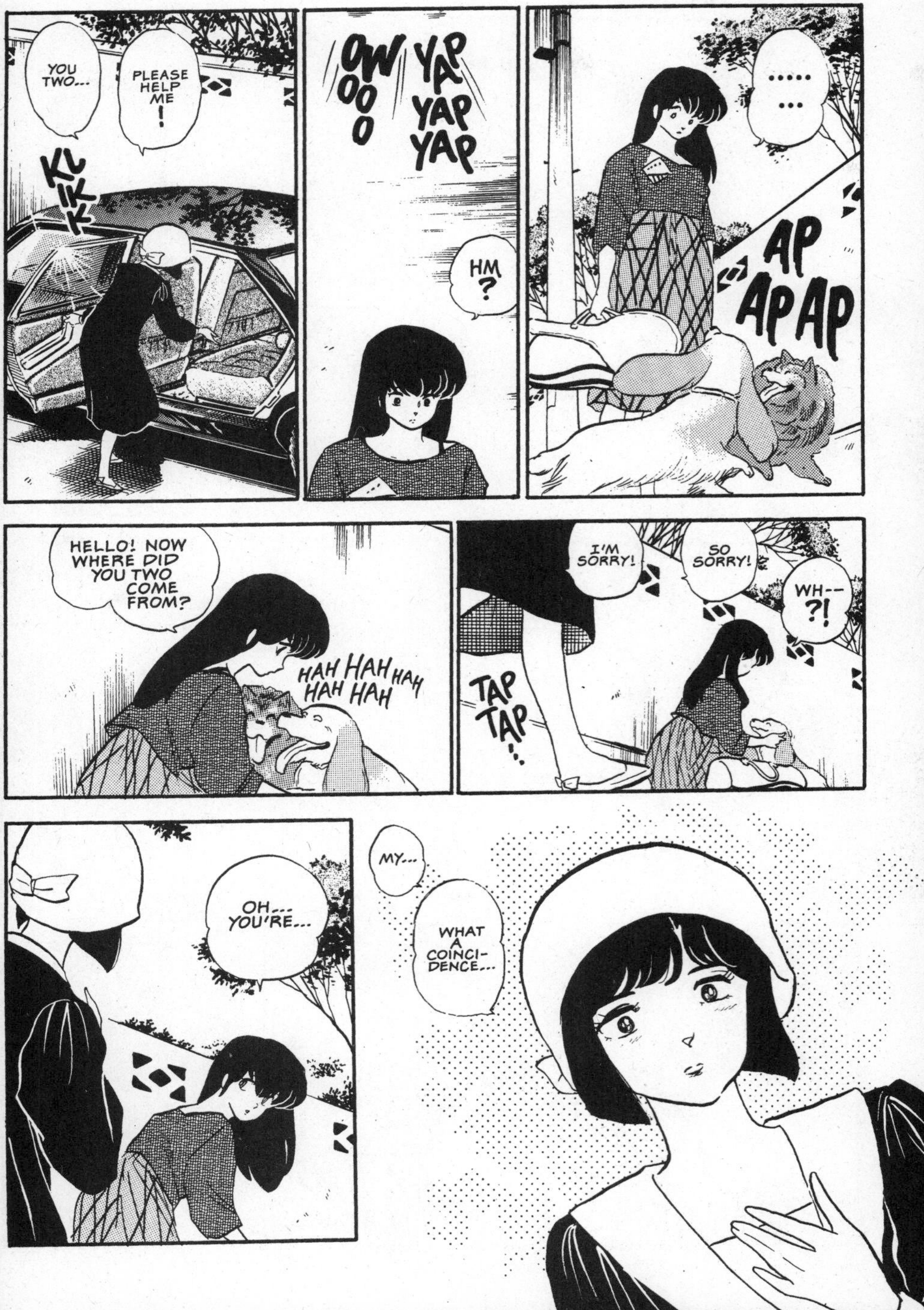
YOU TWO...
PLEASE HELP ME!
KLIKK
OWOOO
YAP YAP YAP
HM?
......
...
AP AP AP
HELLO! NOW WHERE DID YOU TWO COME FROM?
HAH HAH HAH HAH HAH
I'M SORRY!
SO SORRY!
WH--?!
TAP TAP...
OH... YOU'RE...
MY...
WHAT A COINCIDENCE...

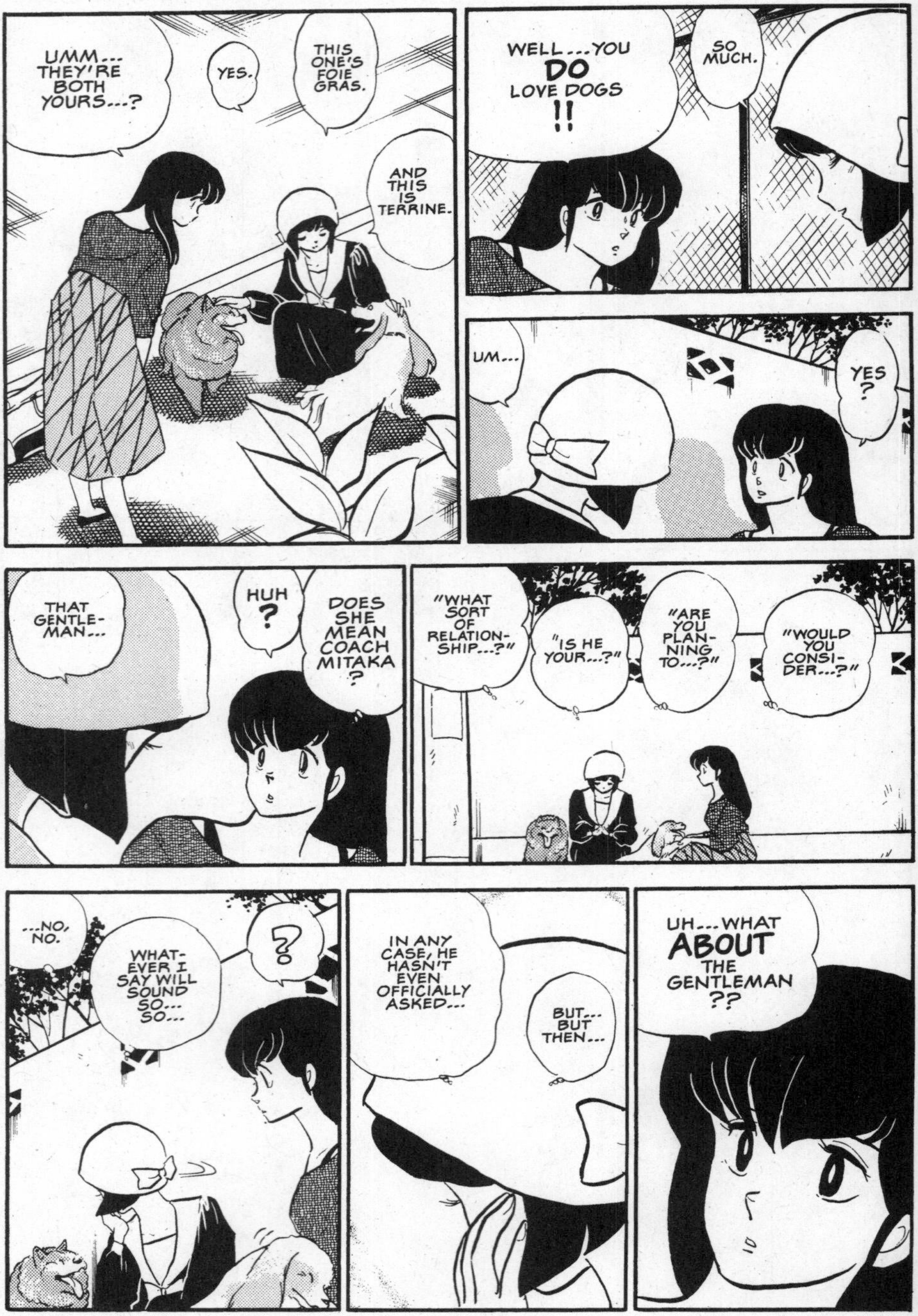
UMM... THEY'RE BOTH YOURS...?
YES.
THIS ONE'S FOIE GRAS.
AND THIS IS TERRINE.
WELL...YOU DO LOVE DOGS !!
SO MUCH.
UM...
YES ?
THAT GENTLE-MAN...
HUH ?
DOES SHE MEAN COACH MITAKA ?
"WHAT SORT OF RELATION-SHIP...?"
"IS HE YOUR...?"
"ARE YOU PLAN-NING TO...?"
"WOULD YOU CONSI-DER...?"
...NO, NO.
WHAT-EVER I SAY WILL SOUND SO... SO...
?
IN ANY CASE, HE HASN'T EVEN OFFICIALLY ASKED...
BUT... BUT THEN...
UH...WHAT ABOUT THE GENTLEMAN ??

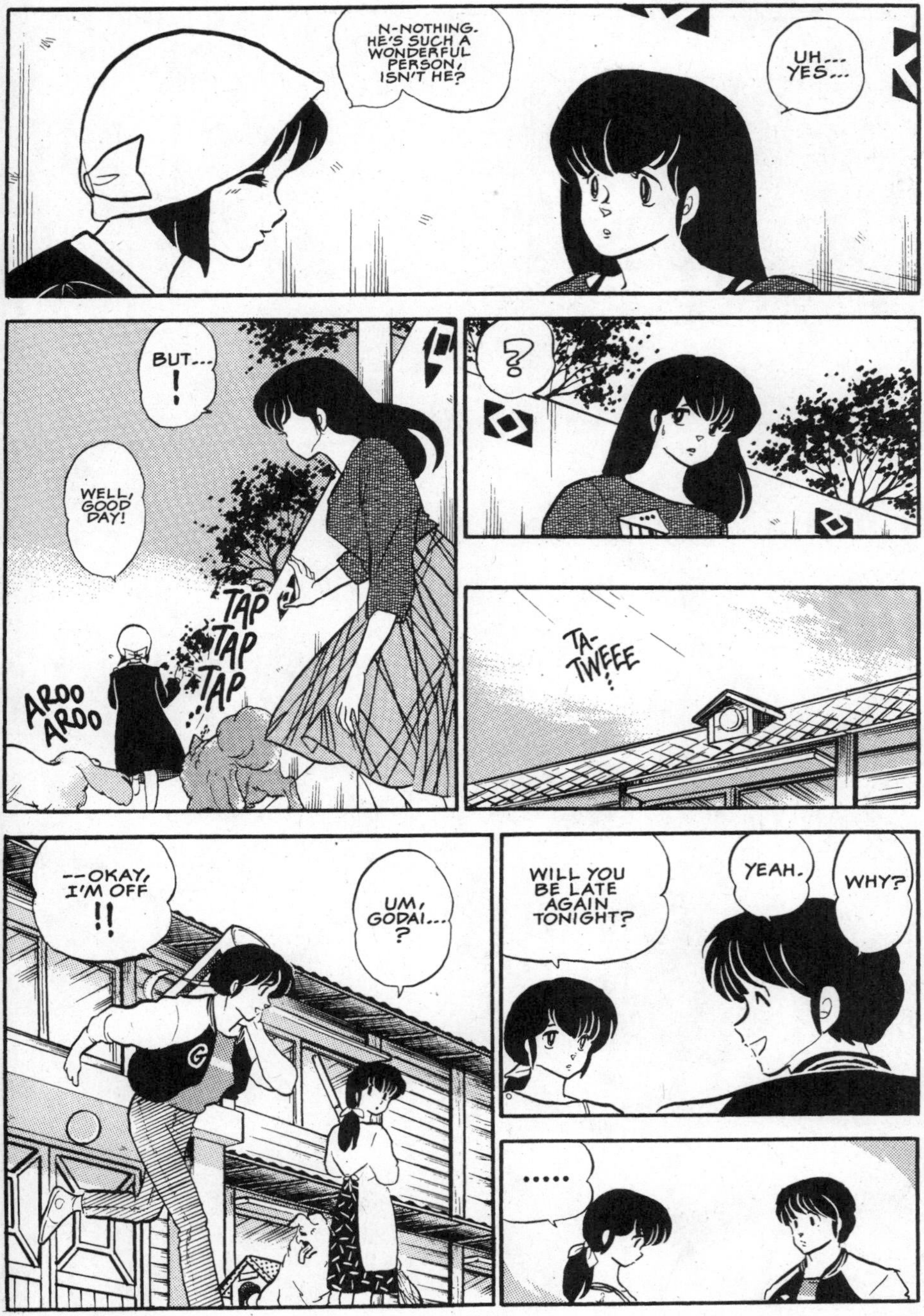
N-NOTHING. HE'S SUCH A WONDERFUL PERSON, ISN'T HE?
UH... YES...
BUT... !
WELL, GOOD DAY!
TAP TAP TAP
AROO AROO
?
TA-TWEEE
--OKAY, I'M OFF !!
UM, GODAI... ?
WILL YOU BE LATE AGAIN TONIGHT?
YEAH.
WHY?
.....

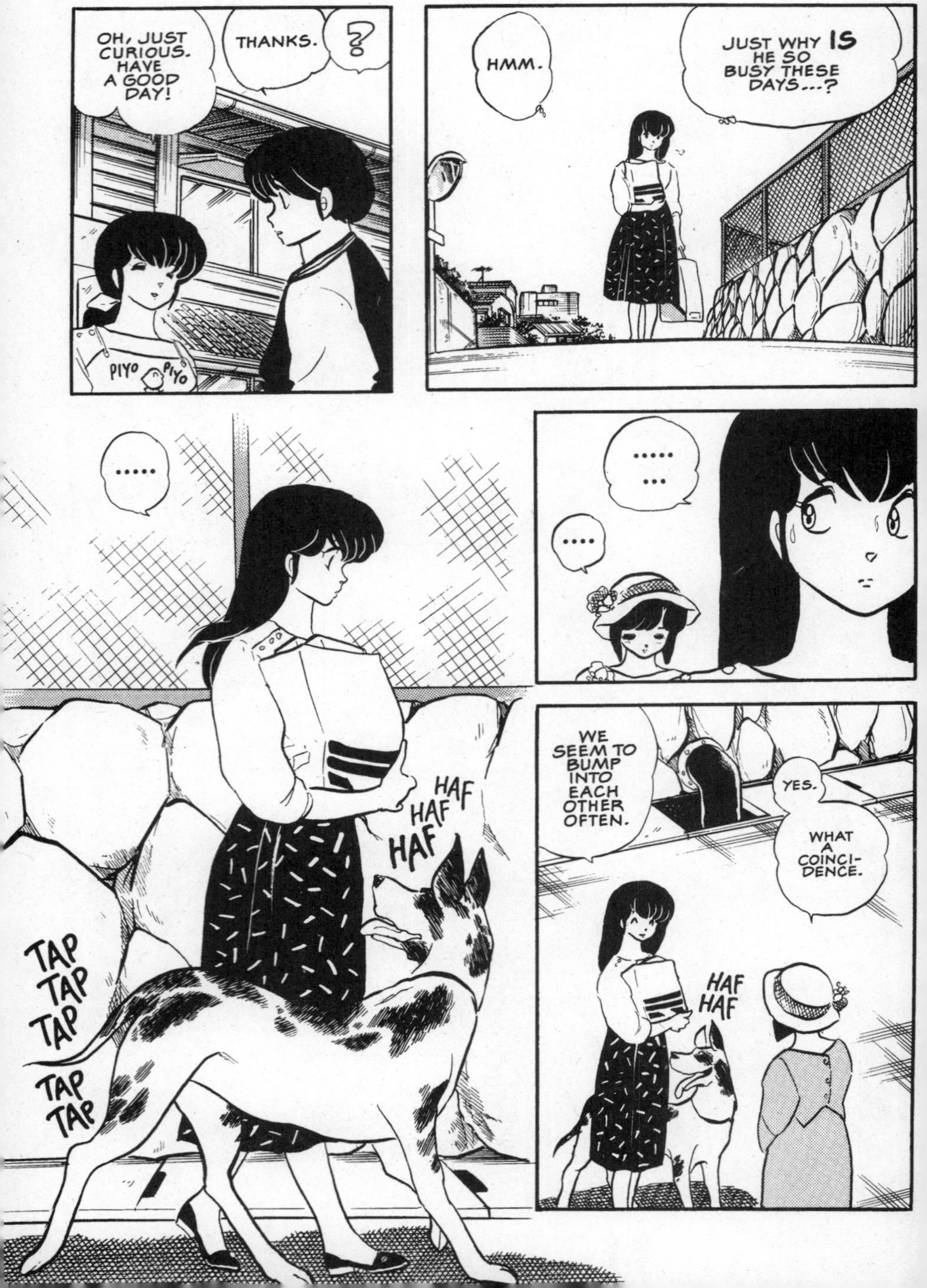
OH, JUST CURIOUS. HAVE A GOOD DAY!
THANKS.
?
PIYO PIYO
HMM.
JUST WHY IS HE SO BUSY THESE DAYS...?
......
HAF HAF HAF
TAP TAP TAP
TAP TAP
.....
...
....
WE SEEM TO BUMP INTO EACH OTHER OFTEN.
YES.
WHAT A COINCIDENCE.
HAF HAF

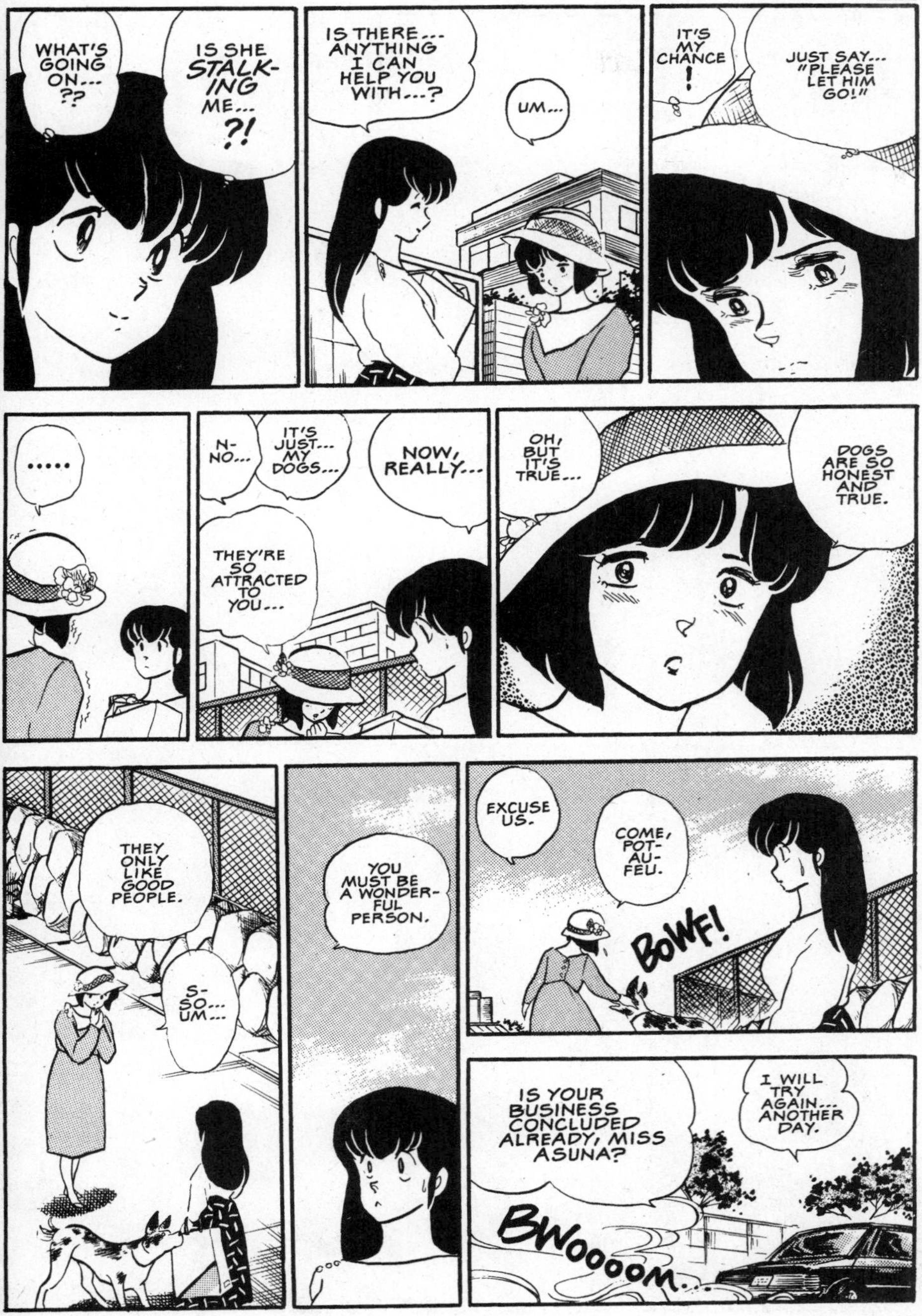
WHAT'S GOING ON... ??
IS SHE STALKING ME... ?!
IS THERE... ANYTHING I CAN HELP YOU WITH...?
UM...
IT'S MY CHANCE !
JUST SAY... "PLEASE LET HIM GO!"
......
N-NO...
IT'S JUST... MY DOGS...
NOW, REALLY...
THEY'RE SO ATTRACTED TO YOU...
OH, BUT IT'S TRUE...
DOGS ARE SO HONEST AND TRUE.
THEY ONLY LIKE GOOD PEOPLE.
S-SO... UM...
YOU MUST BE A WONDERFUL PERSON.
EXCUSE US.
COME, POT-AU-FEU.
BOWF!
IS YOUR BUSINESS CONCLUDED ALREADY, MISS ASUNA?
I WILL TRY AGAIN... ANOTHER DAY.
BWOOOOM...

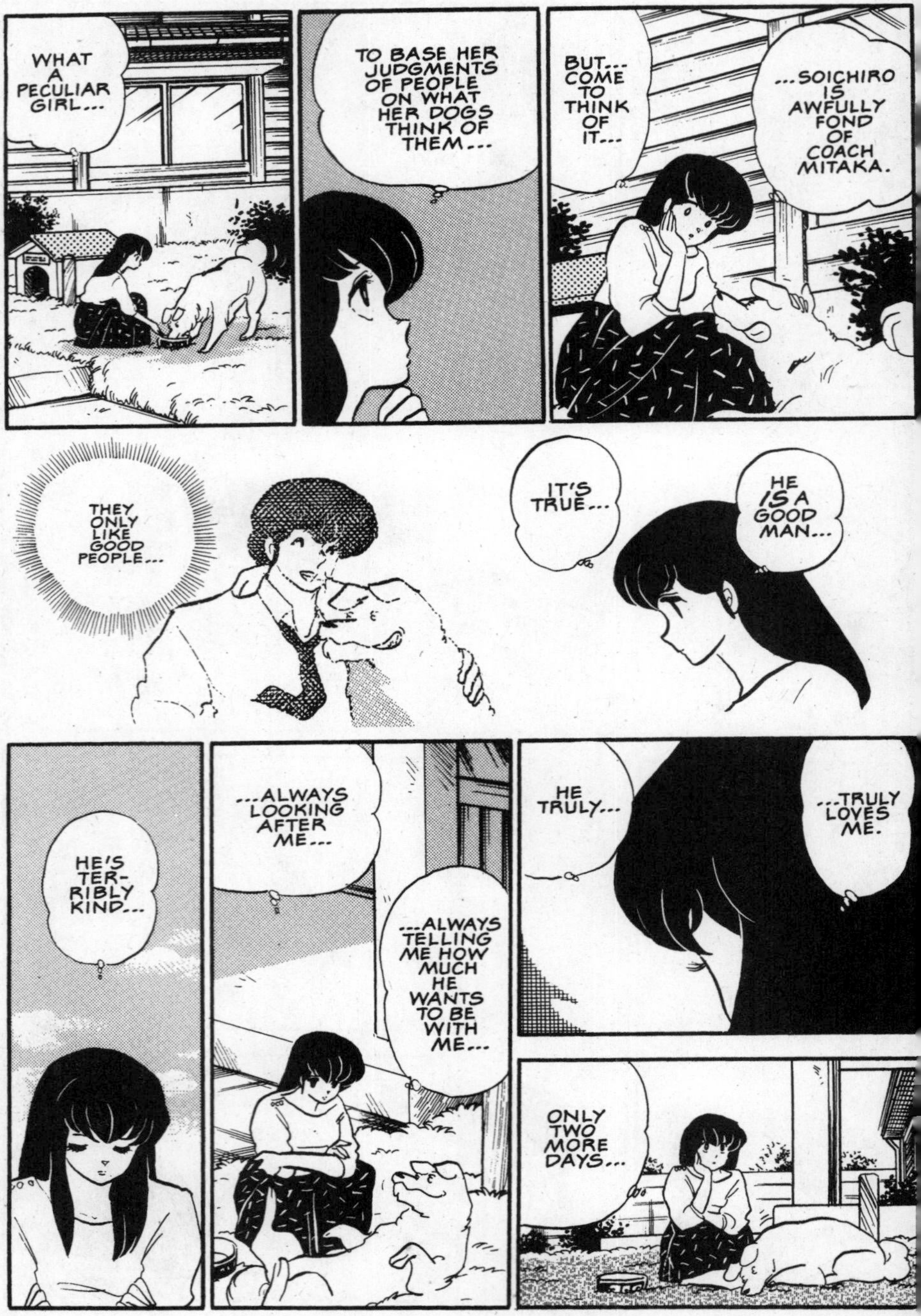
WHAT A PECULIAR GIRL...
TO BASE HER JUDGMENTS OF PEOPLE ON WHAT HER DOGS THINK OF THEM...
BUT... COME TO THINK OF IT...
...SOICHIRO IS AWFULLY FOND OF COACH MITAKA.
THEY ONLY LIKE GOOD PEOPLE...
IT'S TRUE...
HE IS A GOOD MAN...
HE'S TER-RIBLY KIND...
...ALWAYS LOOKING AFTER ME...
...ALWAYS TELLING ME HOW MUCH HE WANTS TO BE WITH ME...
HE TRULY...
...TRULY LOVES ME.
ONLY TWO MORE DAYS...

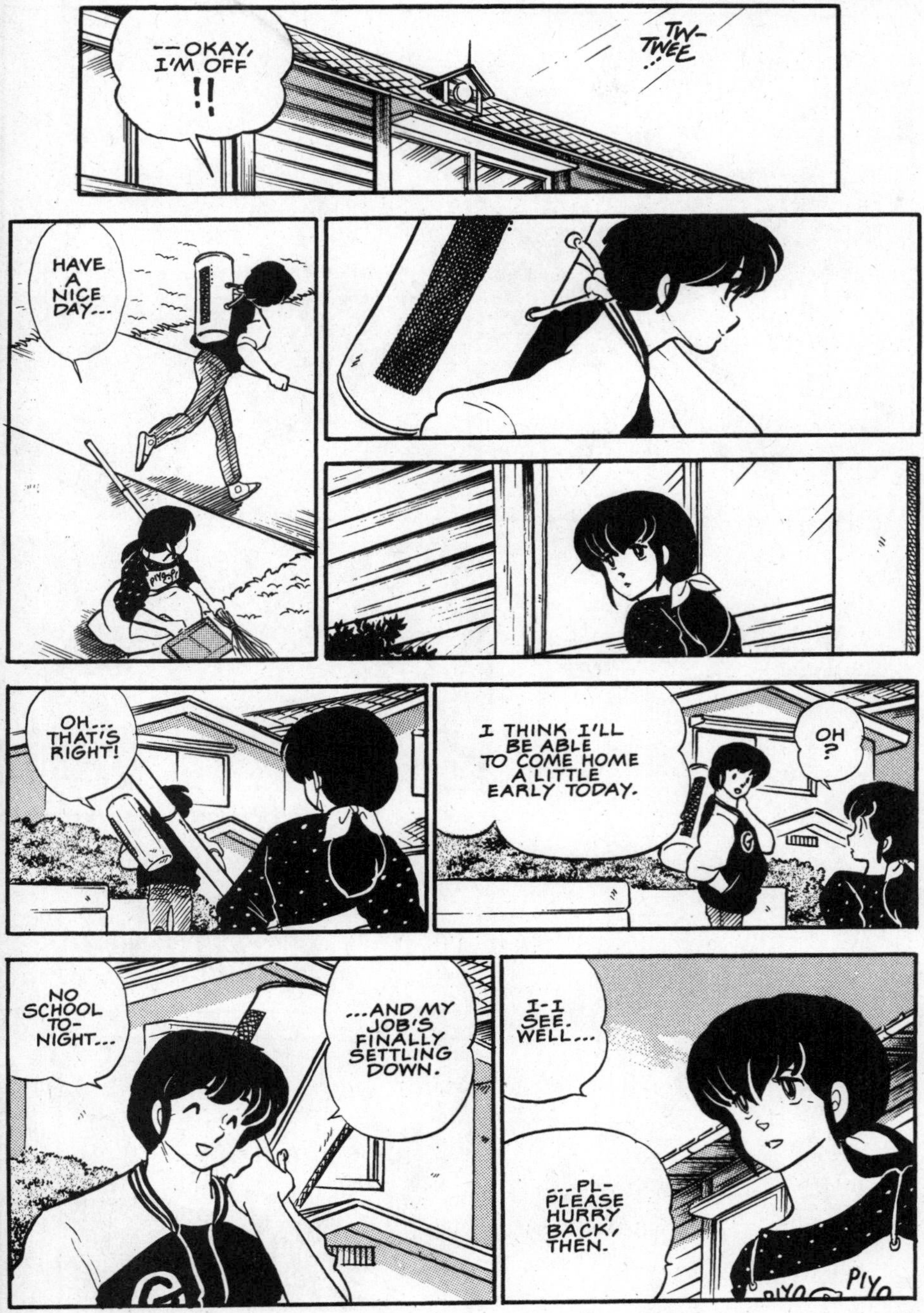
--OKAY, I'M OFF !!
TW-TWEE...
HAVE A NICE DAY...
PIYO PIYO
OH... THAT'S RIGHT!
I THINK I'LL BE ABLE TO COME HOME A LITTLE EARLY TODAY.
OH?
NO SCHOOL TO-NIGHT...
...AND MY JOB'S FINALLY SETTLING DOWN.
I-I SEE. WELL...
...PL-PLEASE HURRY BACK, THEN.
PIYO PIYO

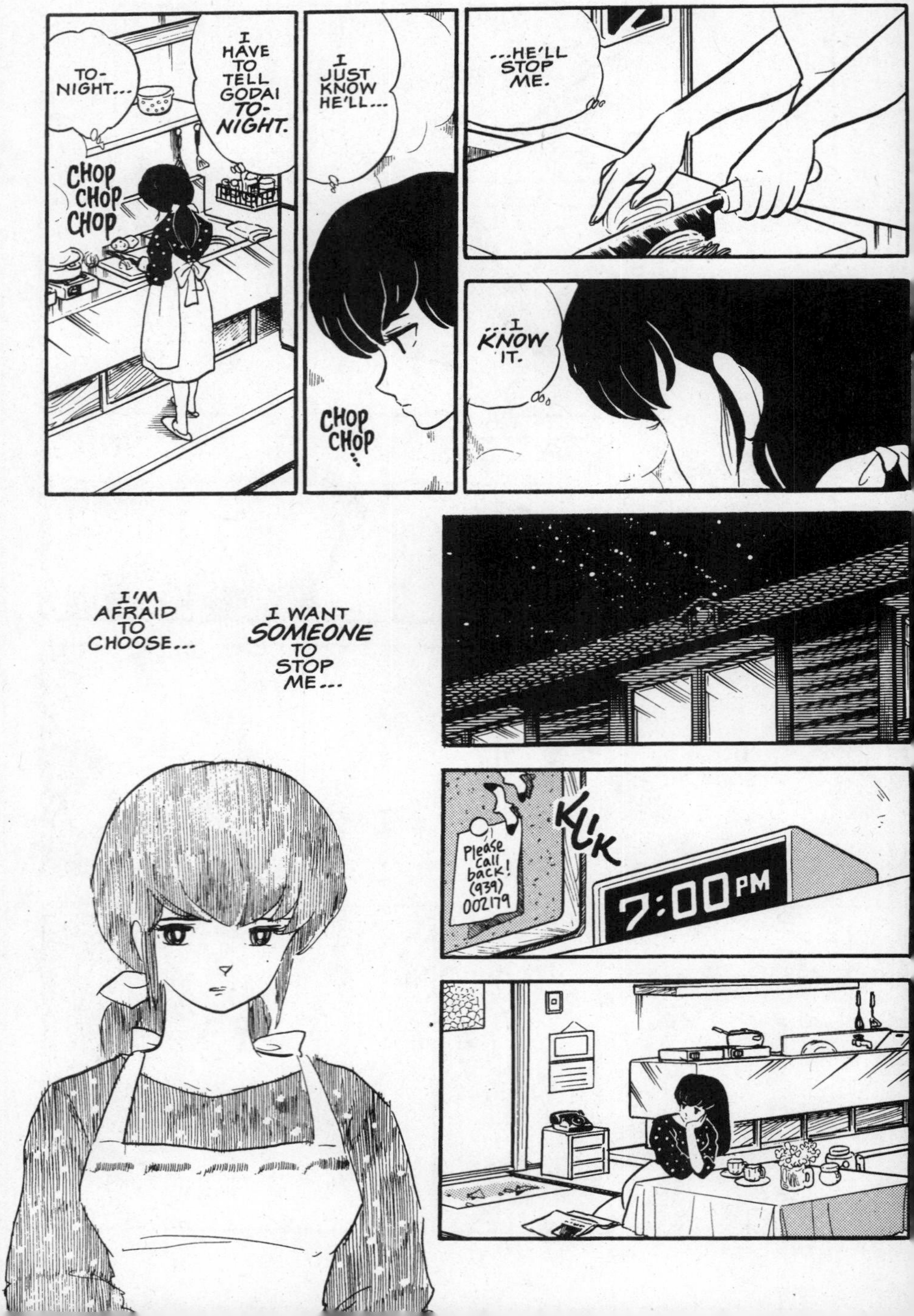
TO-NIGHT...
I HAVE TO TELL GODAI TO-NIGHT.
CHOP CHOP CHOP
I JUST KNOW HE'LL...
CHOP CHOP...
...HE'LL STOP ME.
...I KNOW IT.
I'M AFRAID TO CHOOSE...
I WANT SOMEONE TO STOP ME...
KLIK
Please call back! (939) 002179
7:00PM

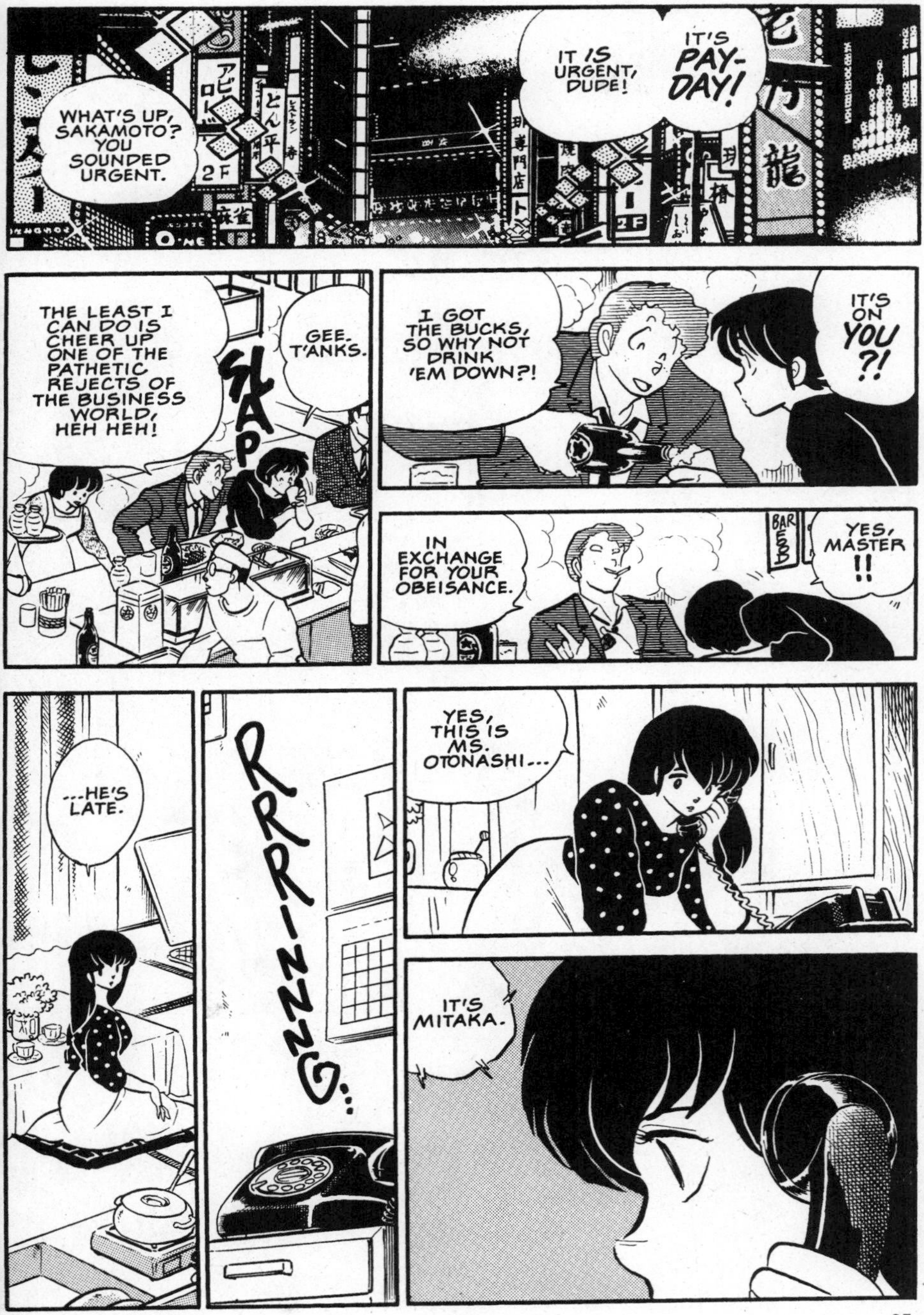
WHAT'S UP, SAKAMOTO? YOU SOUNDED URGENT.
IT IS URGENT, DUDE!
IT'S PAY-DAY!
THE LEAST I CAN DO IS CHEER UP ONE OF THE PATHETIC REJECTS OF THE BUSINESS WORLD, HEH HEH!
SLAP
GEE. T'ANKS.
I GOT THE BUCKS, SO WHY NOT DRINK 'EM DOWN?!
IT'S ON YOU?!
IN EXCHANGE FOR YOUR OBEISANCE.
YES, MASTER!!
...HE'S LATE.
RRRINNNG...
YES, THIS IS MS. OTONASHI...
IT'S MITAKA.

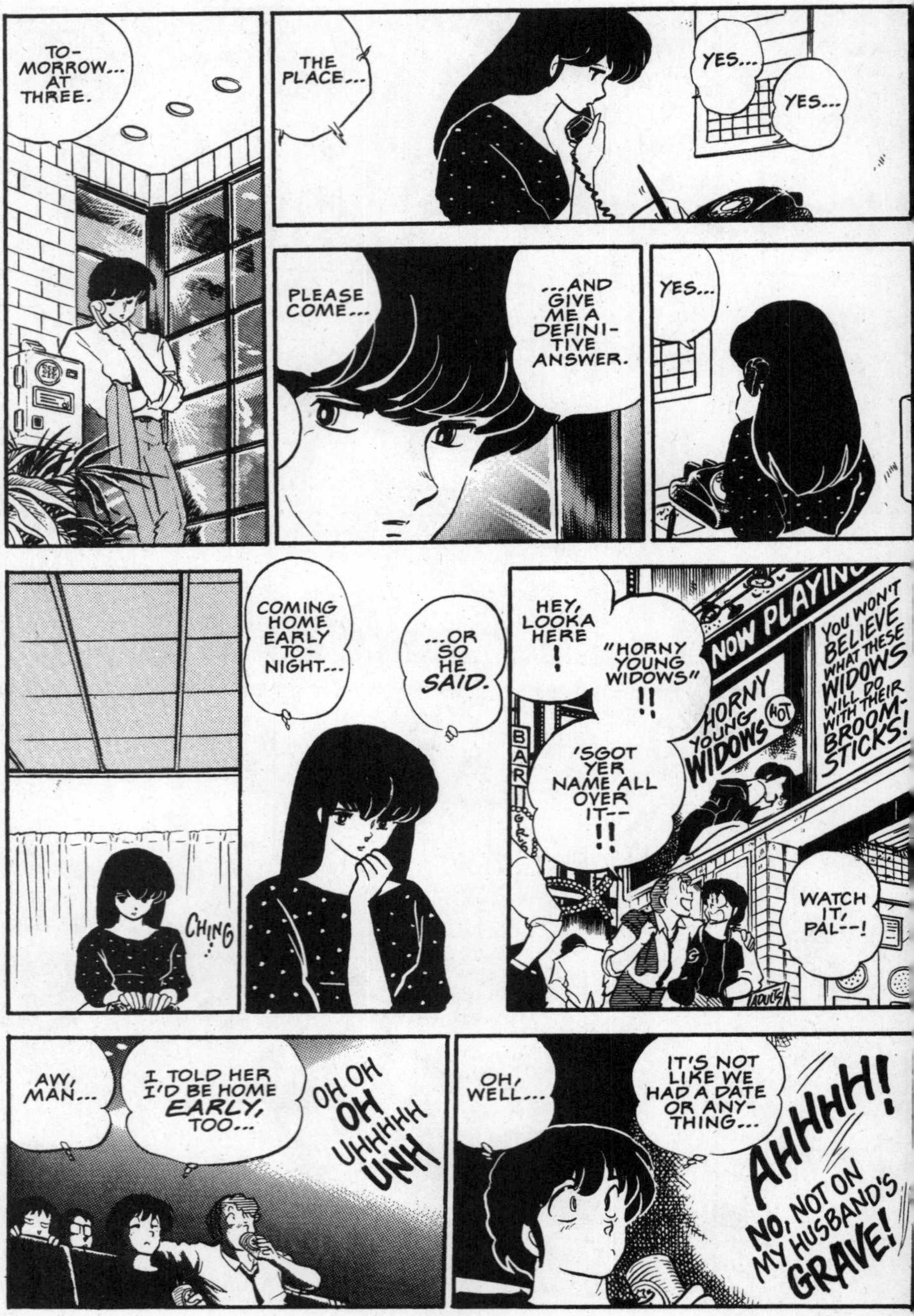
TO-MORROW... AT THREE.
THE PLACE...
YES...
YES...
PLEASE COME...
...AND GIVE ME A DEFINITIVE ANSWER.
YES...
CHING
COMING HOME EARLY TO-NIGHT...
...OR SO HE SAID.
HEY, LOOKA HERE!
"HORNY YOUNG WIDOWS"!!
NOW PLAYING
HORNY YOUNG WIDOWS HOT
YOU WON'T BELIEVE WHAT THESE WIDOWS WILL DO WITH THEIR BROOM-STICKS!
BAR
'SGOT YER NAME ALL OVER IT--!!
WATCH IT, PAL--!
ADULTS
AW, MAN...
I TOLD HER I'D BE HOME EARLY, TOO...
OH OH OH UHHHHH UNH
OH, WELL...
IT'S NOT LIKE WE HAD A DATE OR ANY-THING...
AHHHH!
NO, NOT ON MY HUSBAND'S GRAVE!

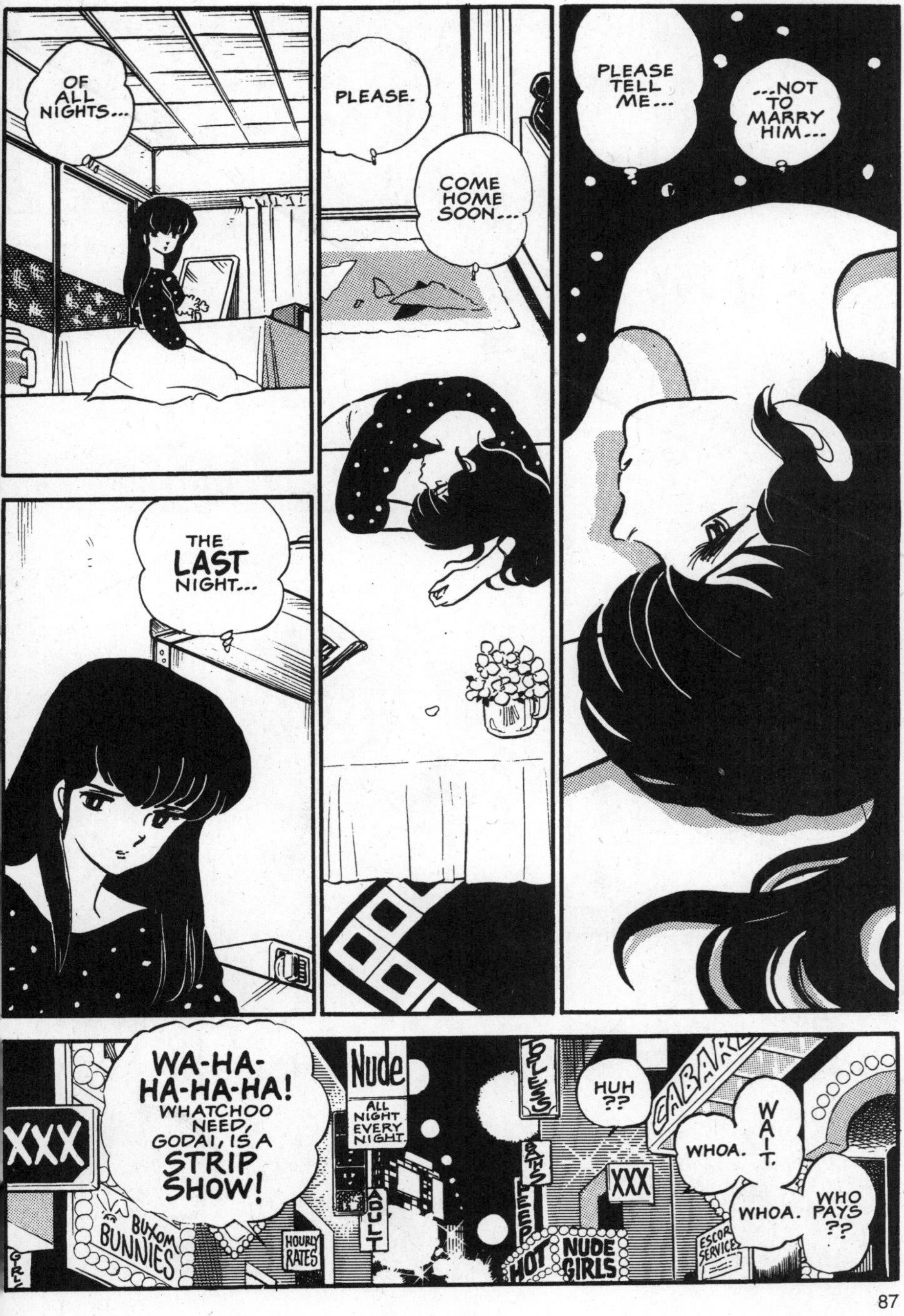
OF ALL NIGHTS...
THE LAST NIGHT...
PLEASE.
COME HOME SOON...
PLEASE TELL ME...
...NOT TO MARRY HIM...
WA-HA-HA-HA-HA! WHATCHOO NEED, GODAI, IS A STRIP SHOW!
XXX
BUXOM BUNNIES
Nude
ALL NIGHT EVERY NIGHT
ADULT
HOURLY RATES
TOPLESS
BATHS
PEEP
HOT
NUDE GIRLS
XXX
HUH ??
WAIT.
WHOA.
WHOA.
WHO PAYS ??

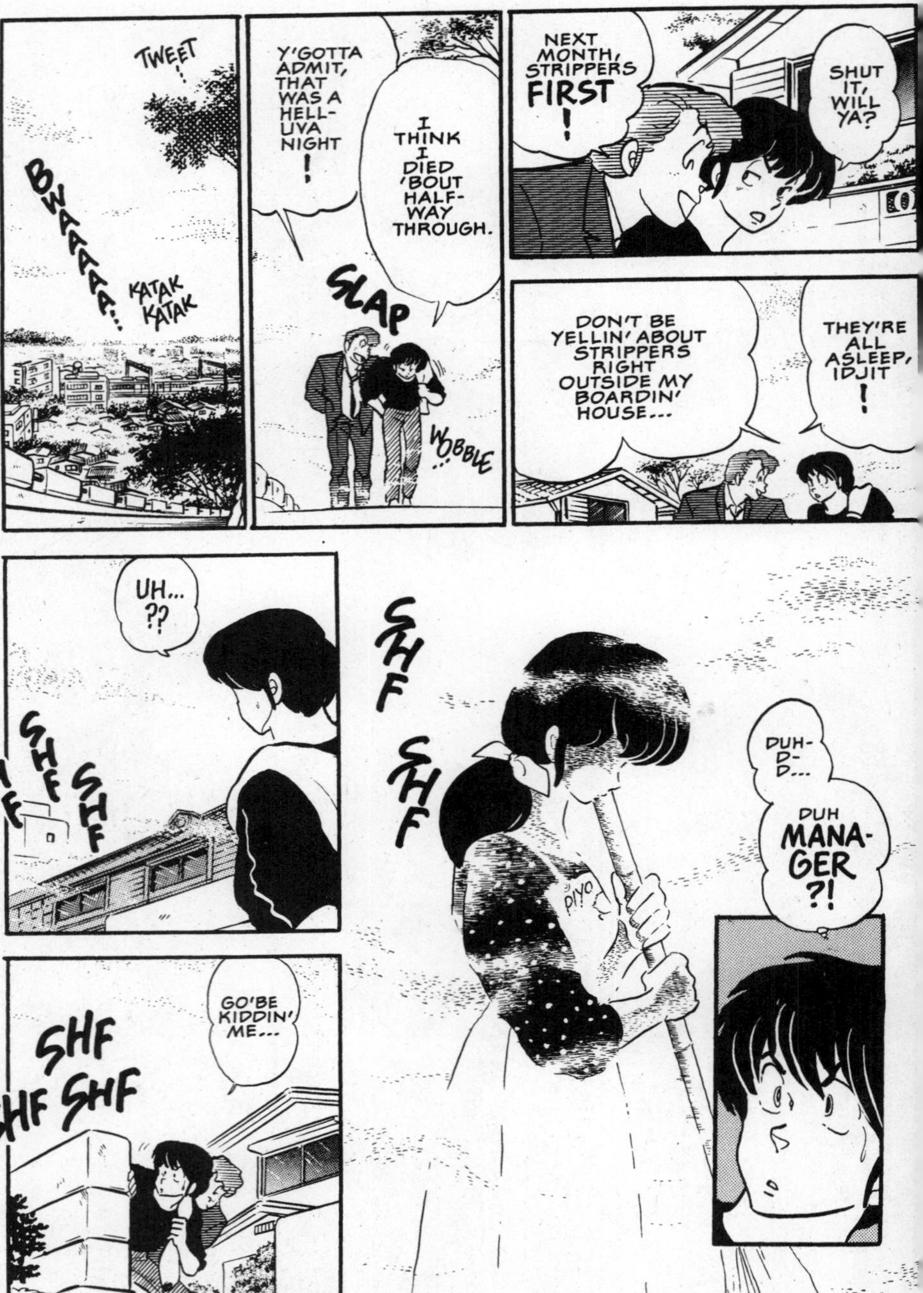
TWEET
BWAAAAA...
KATAK KATAK
Y'GOTTA ADMIT, THAT WAS A HELL-UVA NIGHT!
I THINK I DIED 'BOUT HALF-WAY THROUGH.
SLAP
WOBBLE
NEXT MONTH, STRIPPERS FIRST!
SHUT IT, WILL YA?
DON'T BE YELLIN' ABOUT STRIPPERS RIGHT OUTSIDE MY BOARDIN' HOUSE...
THEY'RE ALL ASLEEP, IDJIT!
UH... ??
SHF SHF SHF SHF
GO'BE KIDDIN' ME...
SHF SHF SHF
SHF SHF
PIYO
DUH-D-D...
DUH MANA-GER?!

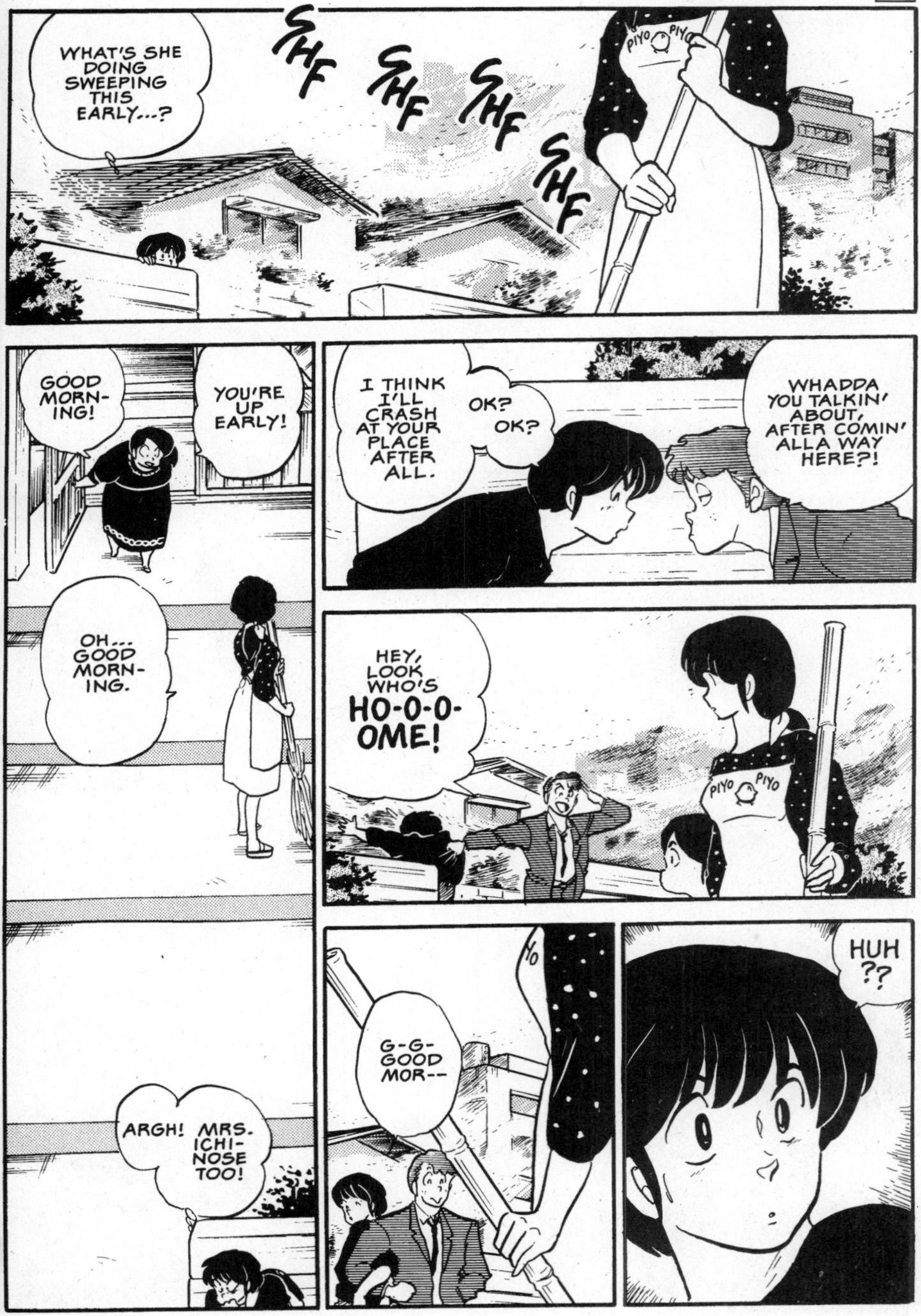
WHAT'S SHE DOING SWEEPING THIS EARLY...?
SHF SHF SHF SHF
PIYO PIYO
GOOD MORN-ING!
YOU'RE UP EARLY!
I THINK I'LL CRASH AT YOUR PLACE AFTER ALL.
OK? OK?
WHADDA YOU TALKIN' ABOUT, AFTER COMIN' ALLA WAY HERE?!
OH... GOOD MORN-ING.
HEY, LOOK WHO'S HO-O-O-OME!
PIYO PIYO
ARGH! MRS. ICHI-NOSE TOO!
HO
G-G-GOOD MOR--
HUH ??

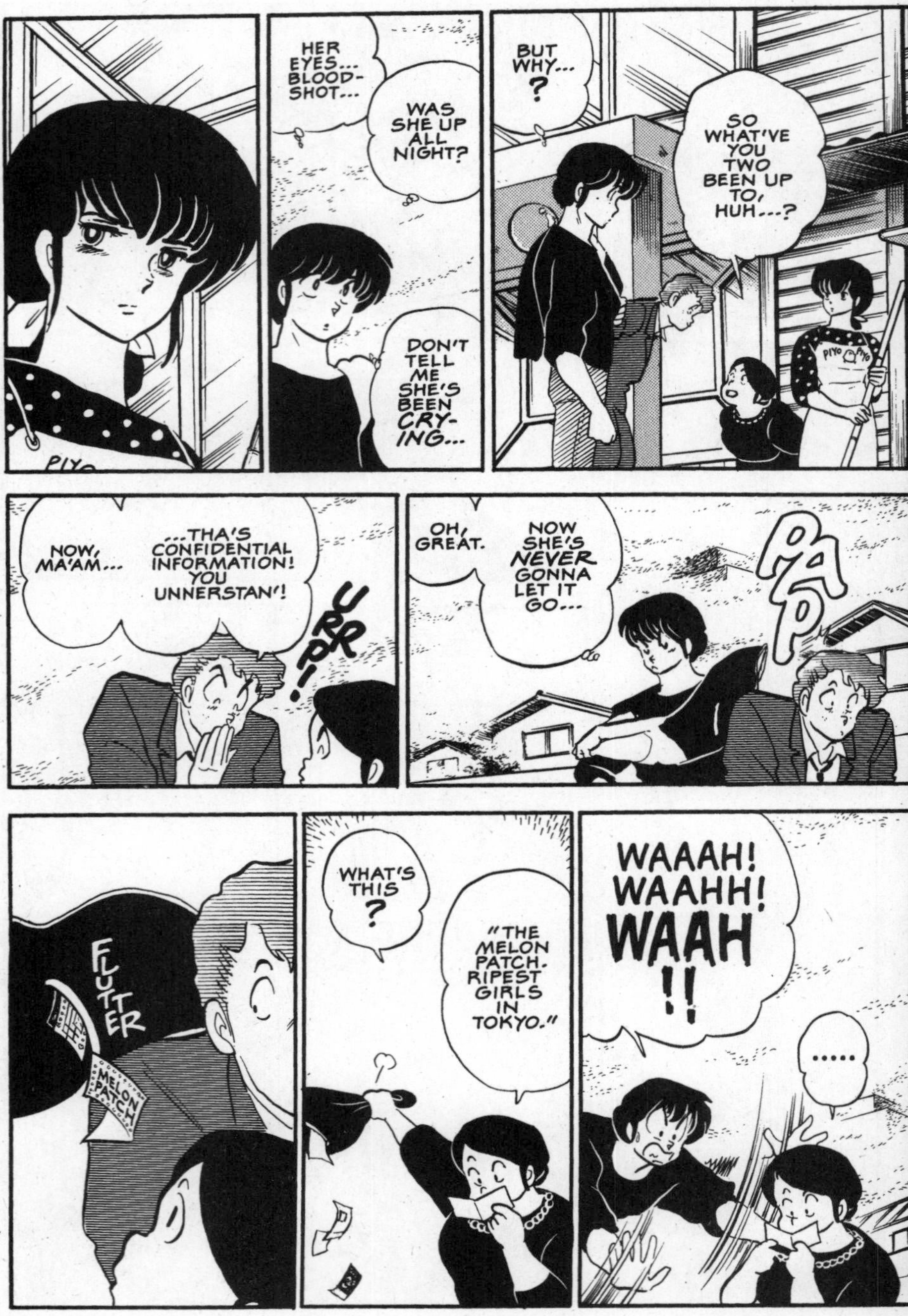
PIYO
HER EYES... BLOOD-SHOT...
WAS SHE UP ALL NIGHT?
DON'T TELL ME SHE'S BEEN CRY-ING...
BUT WHY... ?
SO WHAT'VE YOU TWO BEEN UP TO, HUH...?
PIYO PIYO
NOW, MA'AM...
...THA'S CONFIDENTIAL INFORMATION! YOU UNNERSTAN'!
URRP!
OH, GREAT.
NOW SHE'S NEVER GONNA LET IT GO...
PAP
FLUTTER
MELON PATCH
WHAT'S THIS ?
"THE MELON PATCH. RIPEST GIRLS IN TOKYO."
WAAAH! WAAHH! WAAH !!
......

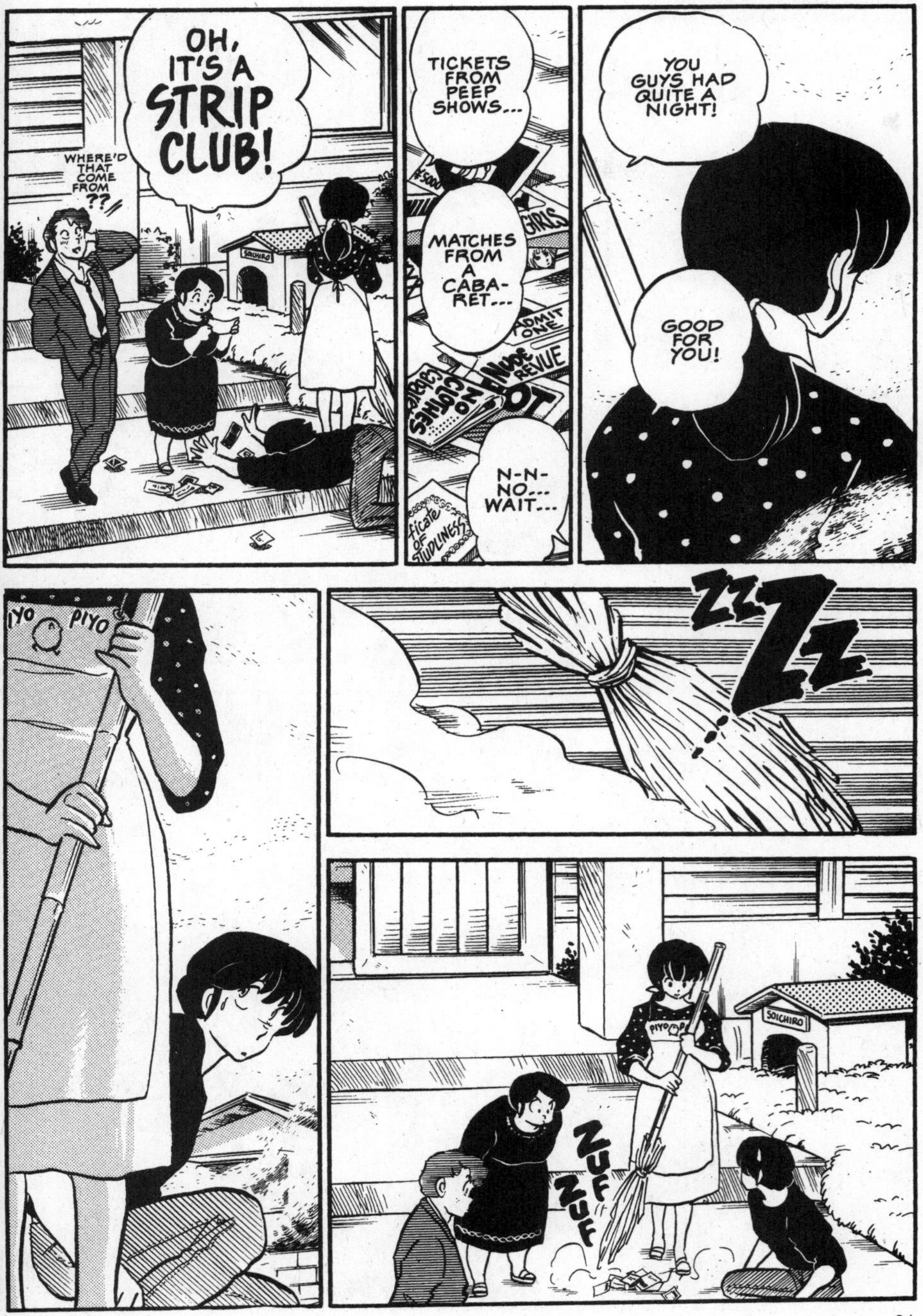
OH, IT'S A STRIP CLUB!
WHERE'D THAT COME FROM ??
SOICHIRO
TICKETS FROM PEEP SHOWS...
MATCHES FROM A CABA-RET...
GIRLS
ADMIT ONE
NUDE REVUE
NO CLOTHES
N-N-NO... WAIT...
ficate OF STUDLINESS
YOU GUYS HAD QUITE A NIGHT!
GOOD FOR YOU!
PIYO PIYO
ZZZ
SOICHIRO
PIYO
ZUF ZUF ZUF

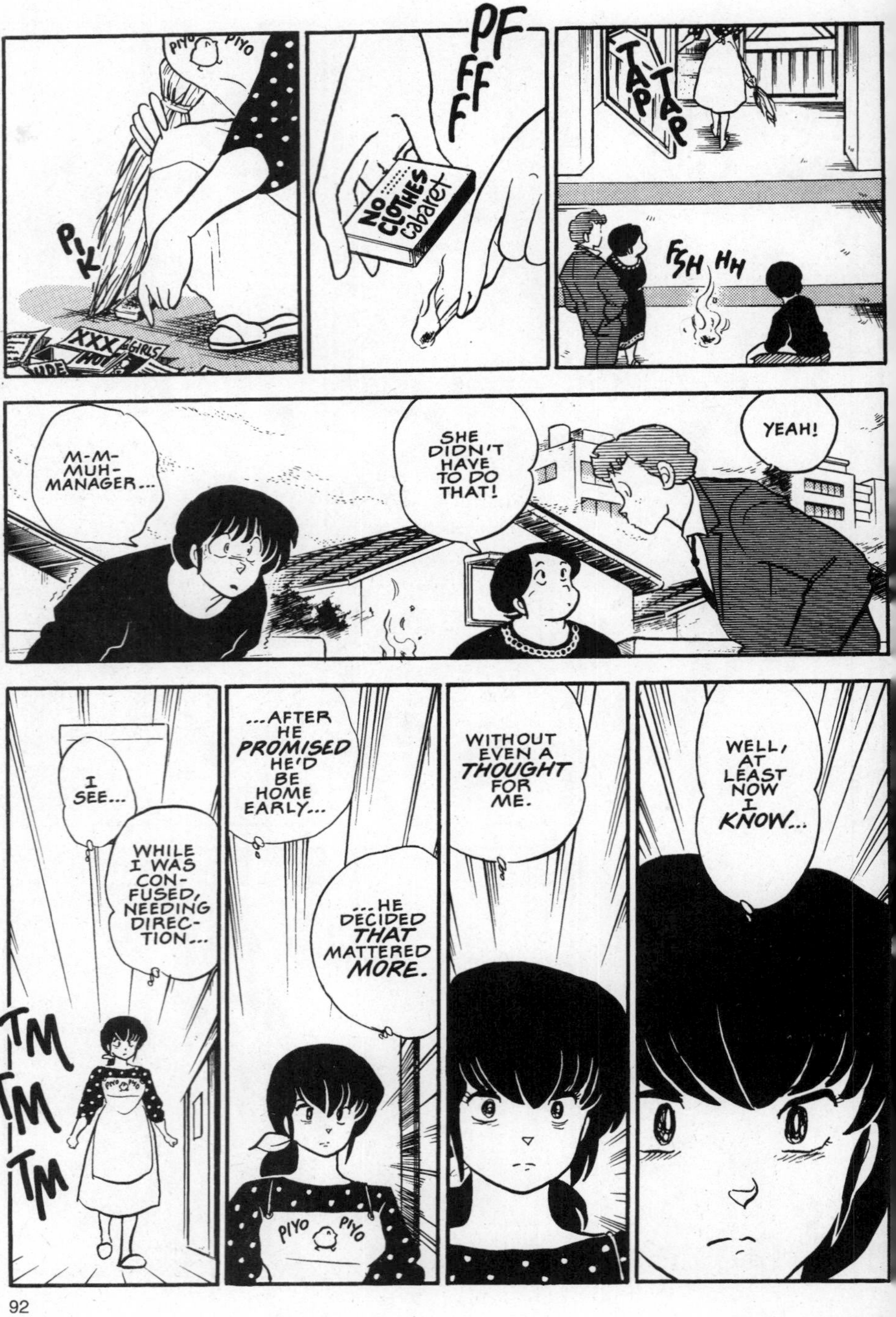
PIYO PIYO
PIK
XXX
GIRLS
HOT
PFFFFF
NO CLOTHES cabaret
TAP TAP
FSHHH
M-M-MUH-MANAGER...
SHE DIDN'T HAVE TO DO THAT!
YEAH!
I SEE...
WHILE I WAS CONFUSED, NEEDING DIRECTION...
TM TM TM
...AFTER HE *PROMISED* HE'D BE HOME EARLY...
...HE DECIDED *THAT* MATTERED *MORE*.
PIYO PIYO
WITHOUT EVEN A *THOUGHT* FOR ME.
WELL, AT LEAST NOW I *KNOW*...

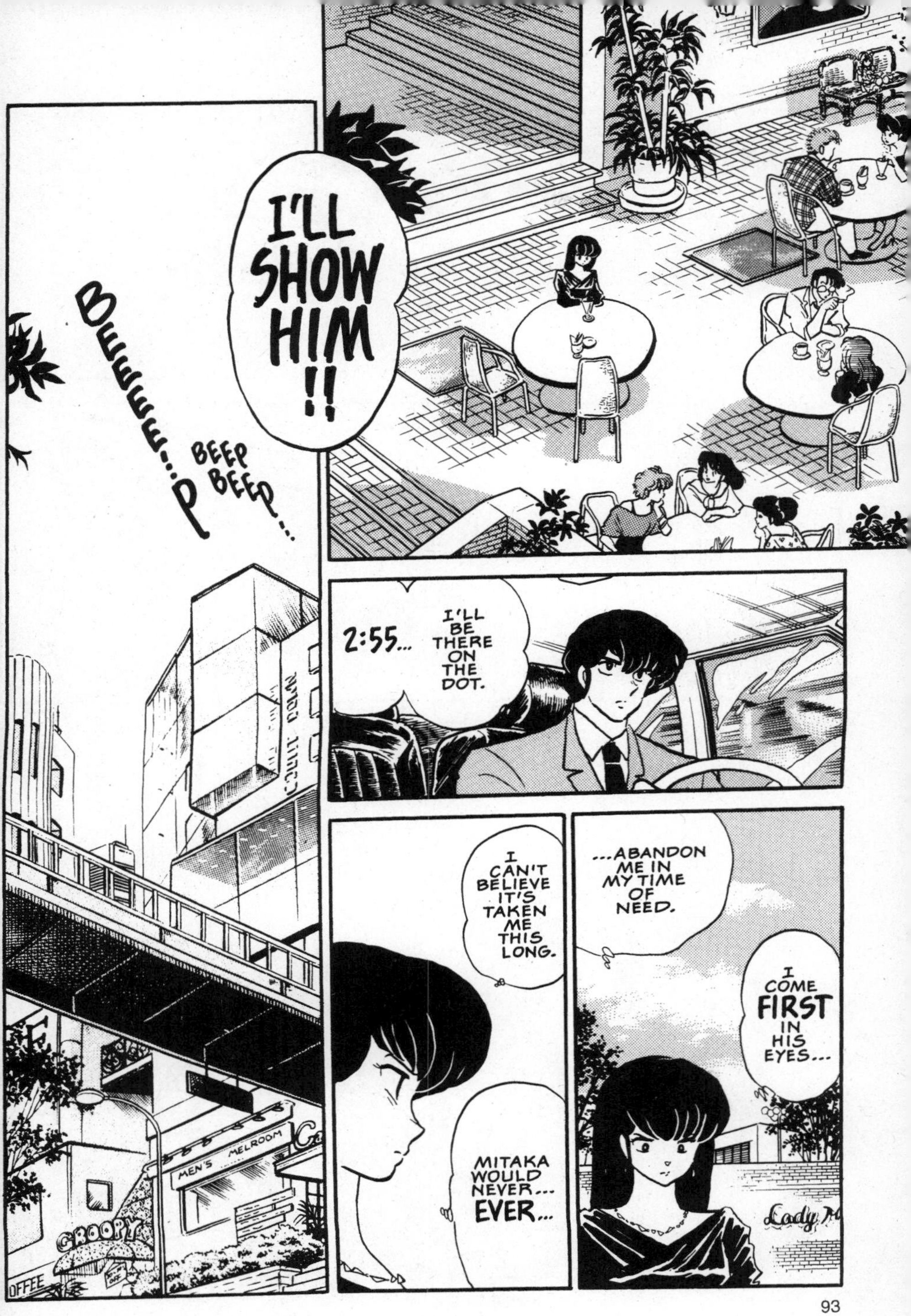

I'LL SHOW HIM!!
BEEEEE...P
BEEP BEEP...
MEN'S MELROOM
GROOPY
2:55...
I'LL BE THERE ON THE DOT.
I CAN'T BELIEVE IT'S TAKEN ME THIS LONG.
MITAKA WOULD NEVER... EVER...
...ABANDON ME IN MY TIME OF NEED.
I COME FIRST IN HIS EYES...

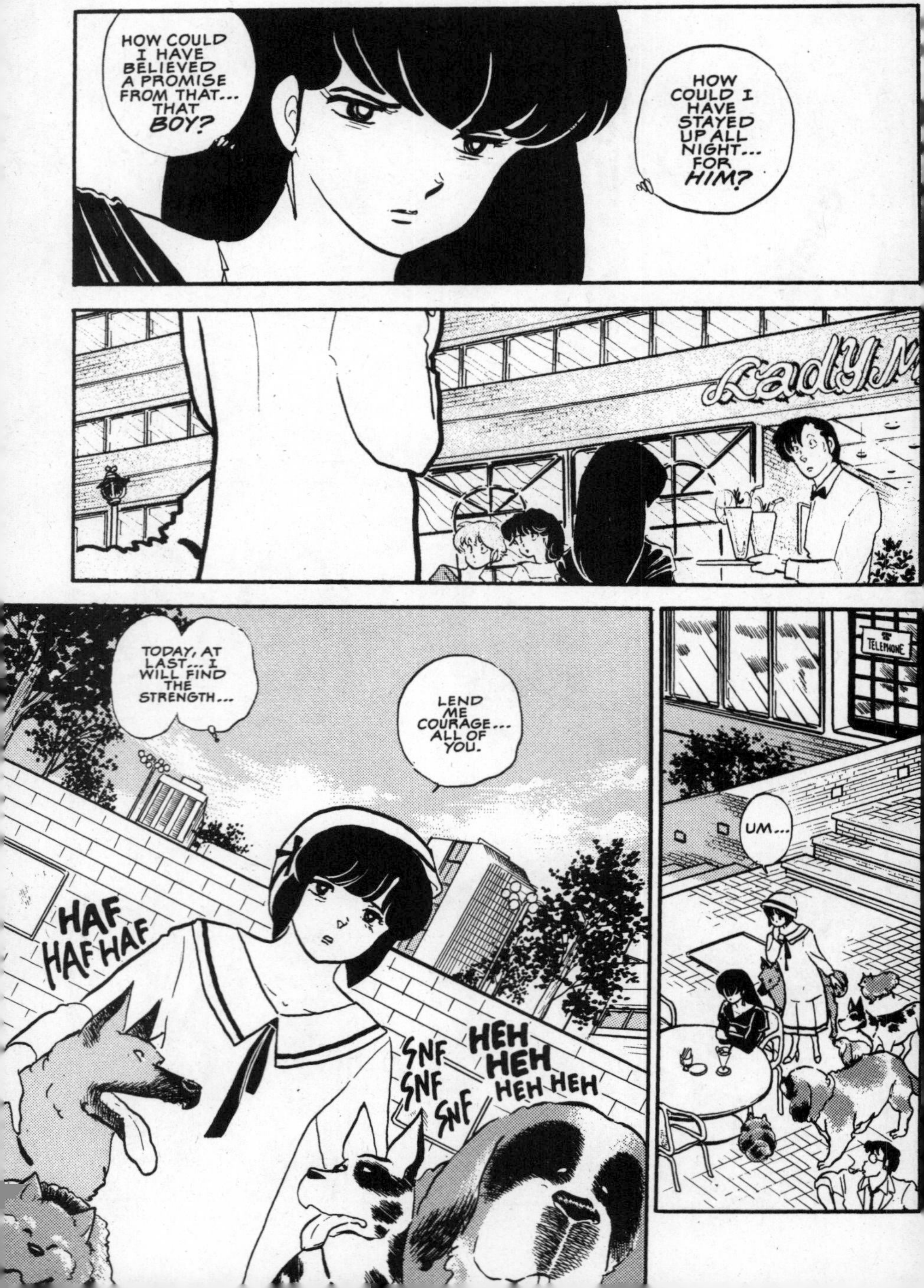
HOW COULD I HAVE BELIEVED A PROMISE FROM THAT... THAT BOY?
HOW COULD I HAVE STAYED UP ALL NIGHT... FOR HIM?
TODAY, AT LAST... I WILL FIND THE STRENGTH...
LEND ME COURAGE... ALL OF YOU.
HAF HAF HAF
SNF SNF SNF
HEH HEH HEH HEH
TELEPHONE
UM...

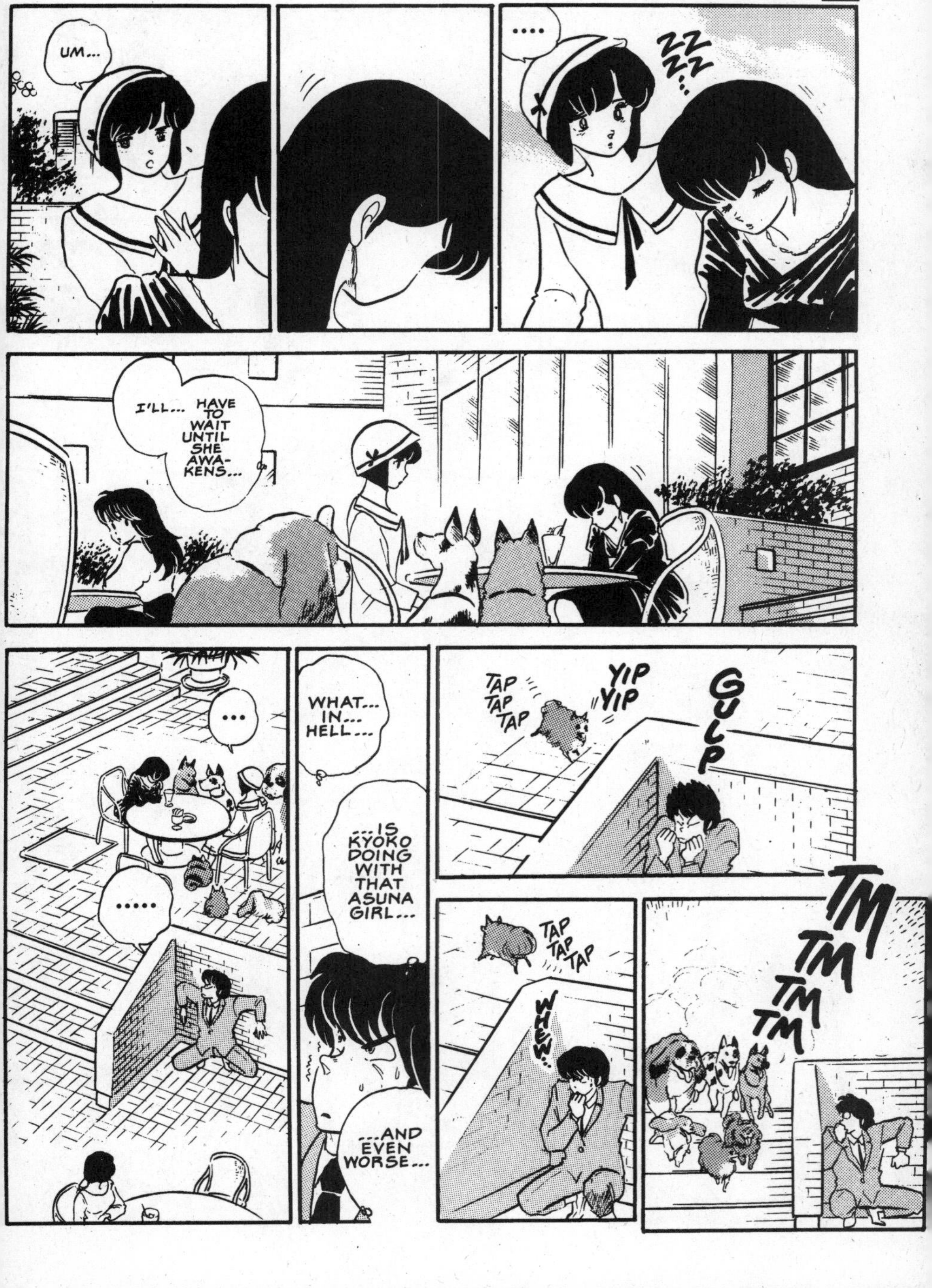
UM...
.....
ZZZZ...
I'LL... HAVE TO WAIT UNTIL SHE AWA-KENS...
...
.....
WHAT... IN... HELL...
...IS KYOKO DOING WITH THAT ASUNA GIRL...
...AND EVEN WORSE...
TAP TAP TAP
YIP YIP
GULP
TAP TAP TAP
WHEW...
TM TM TM TM

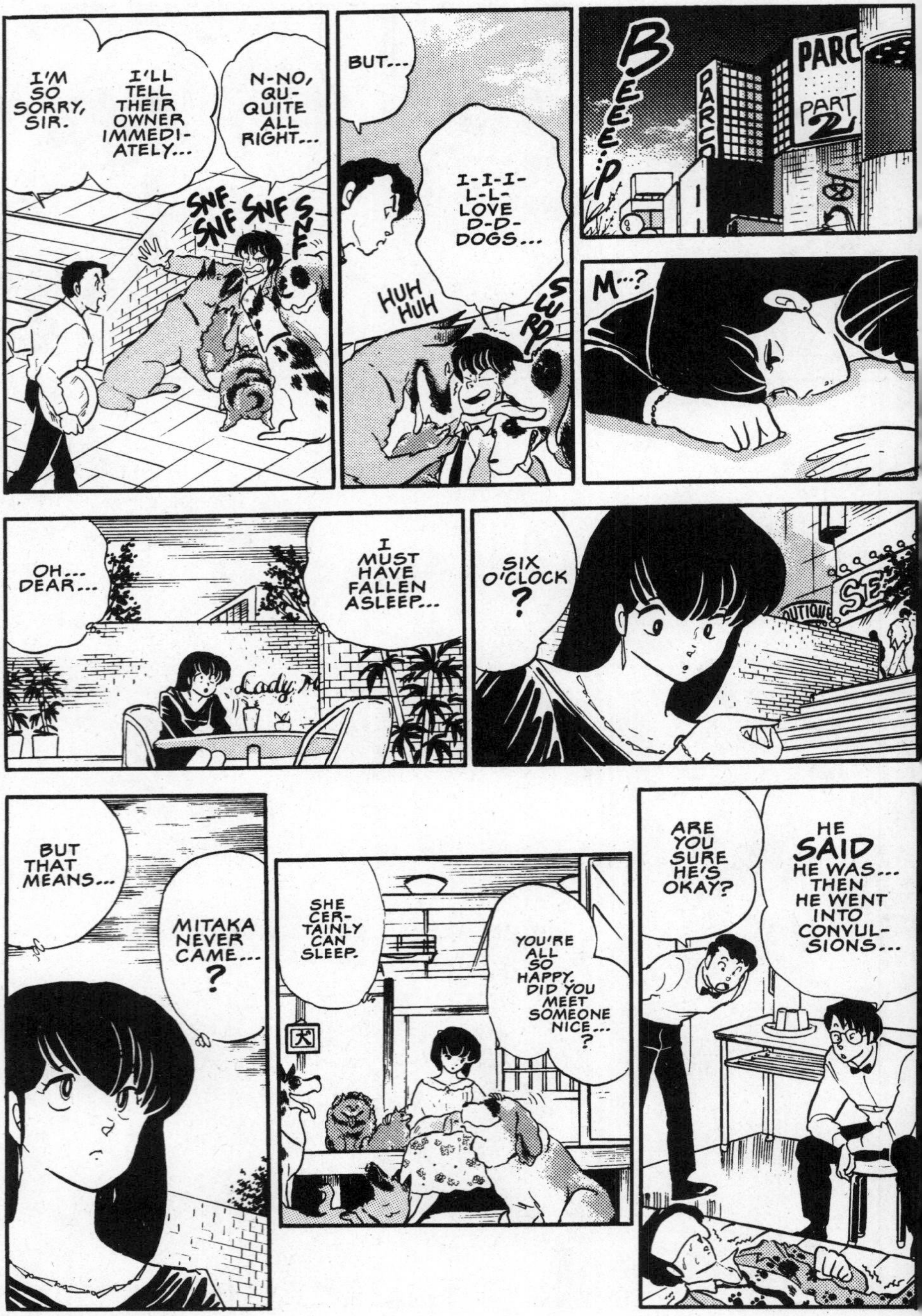
I'M SO SORRY, SIR.
I'LL TELL THEIR OWNER IMMEDI-ATELY...
N-NO, QU-QUITE ALL RIGHT...
SNF SNF SNF SNF SNF SNF
BUT...
I-I-I- L-L-LOVE D-D-DOGS...
HUH HUH
SWRP
BEEEP
PARCO
PARCO
PART 2
M...?
OH... DEAR...
I MUST HAVE FALLEN ASLEEP...
SIX O'CLOCK ?
BUT THAT MEANS...
MITAKA NEVER CAME... ?
SHE CER-TAINLY CAN SLEEP.
YOU'RE ALL SO HAPPY. DID YOU MEET SOMEONE NICE... ?
ARE YOU SURE HE'S OKAY?
HE SAID HE WAS... THEN HE WENT INTO CONVUL-SIONS...

PART 5
LOVE YOU LOTS

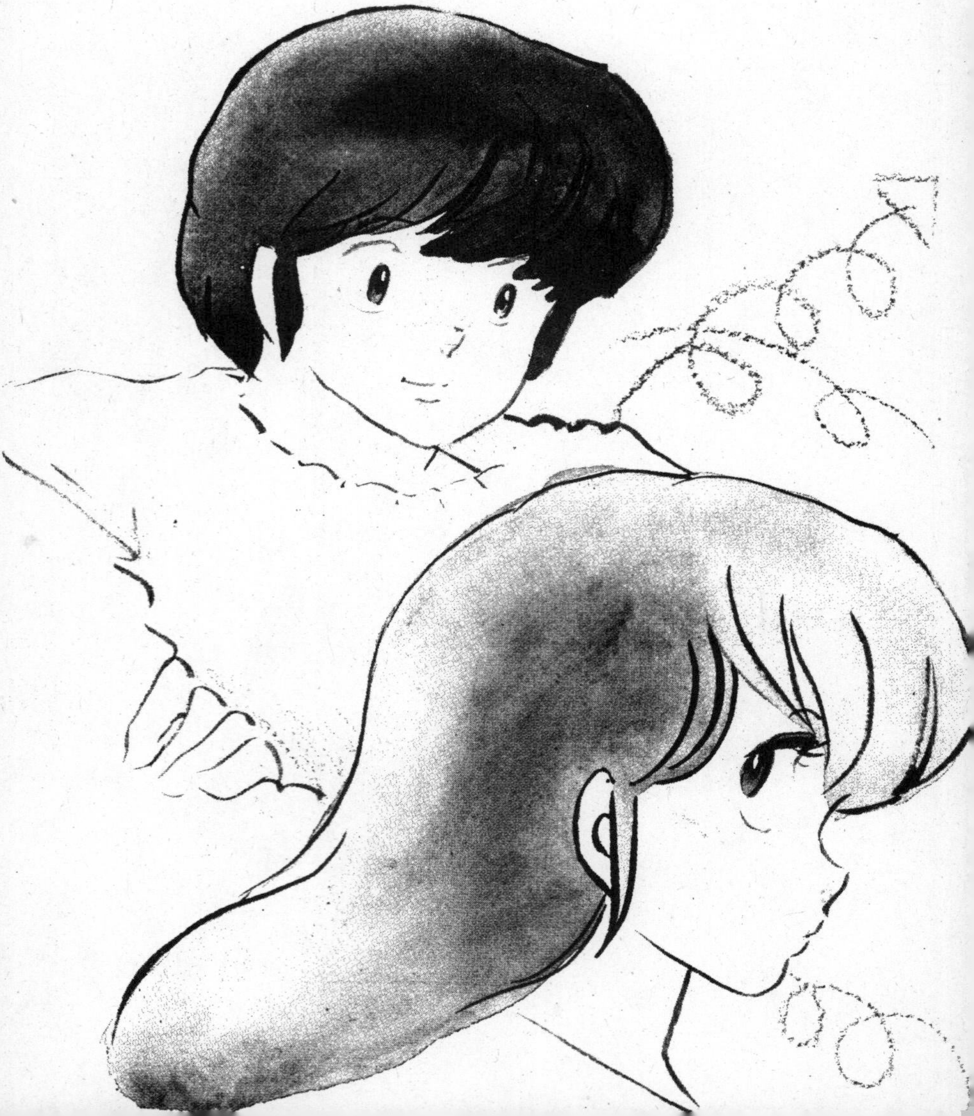

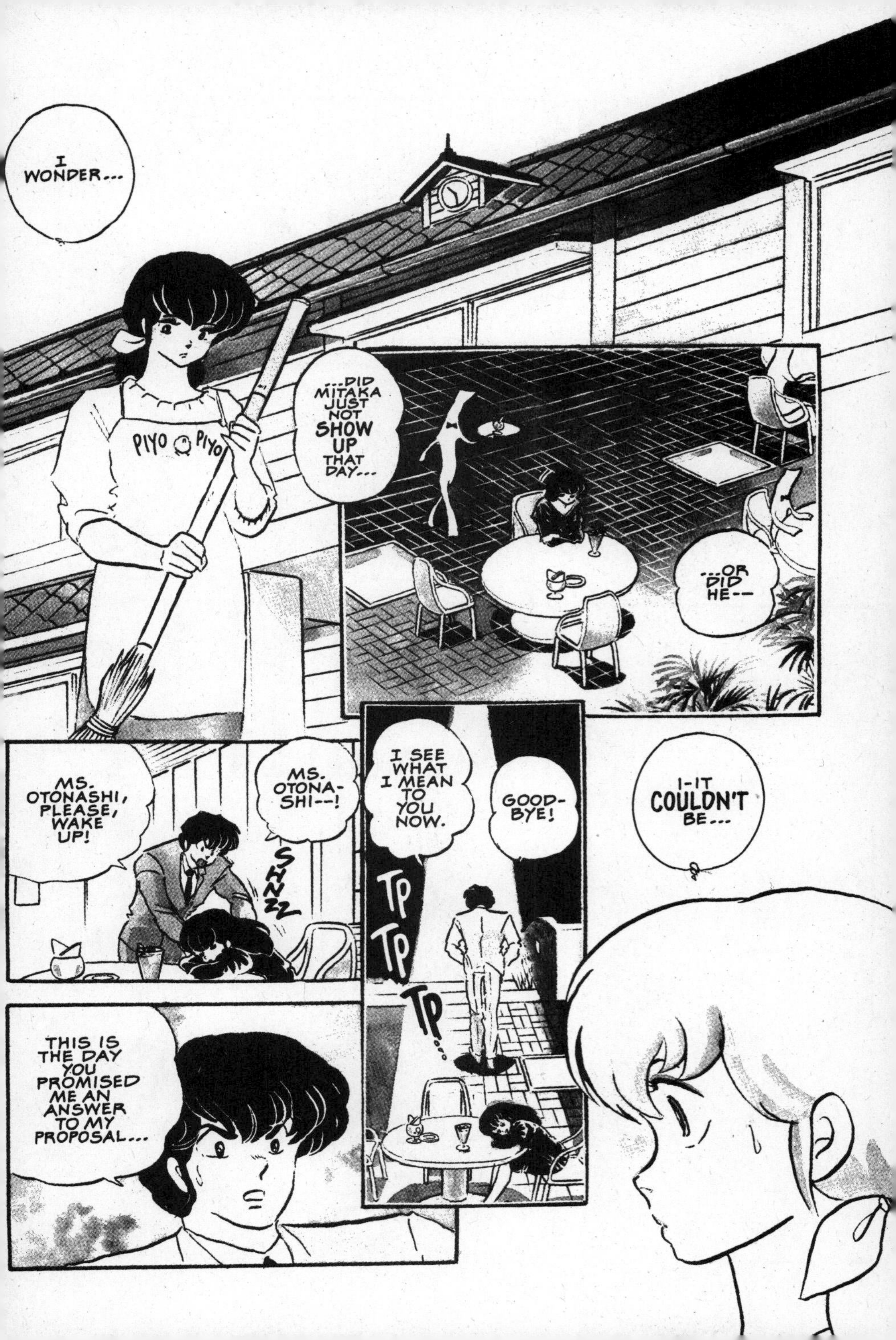
I WONDER...
...DID MITAKA JUST NOT SHOW UP THAT DAY...
...OR DID HE--
MS. OTONASHI, PLEASE, WAKE UP!
MS. OTONASHI--!
SHNZZ
I SEE WHAT I MEAN TO YOU NOW.
GOOD-BYE!
TP TP TP...
I-IT COULDN'T BE...
THIS IS THE DAY YOU PROMISED ME AN ANSWER TO MY PROPOSAL...
PIYO PIYO

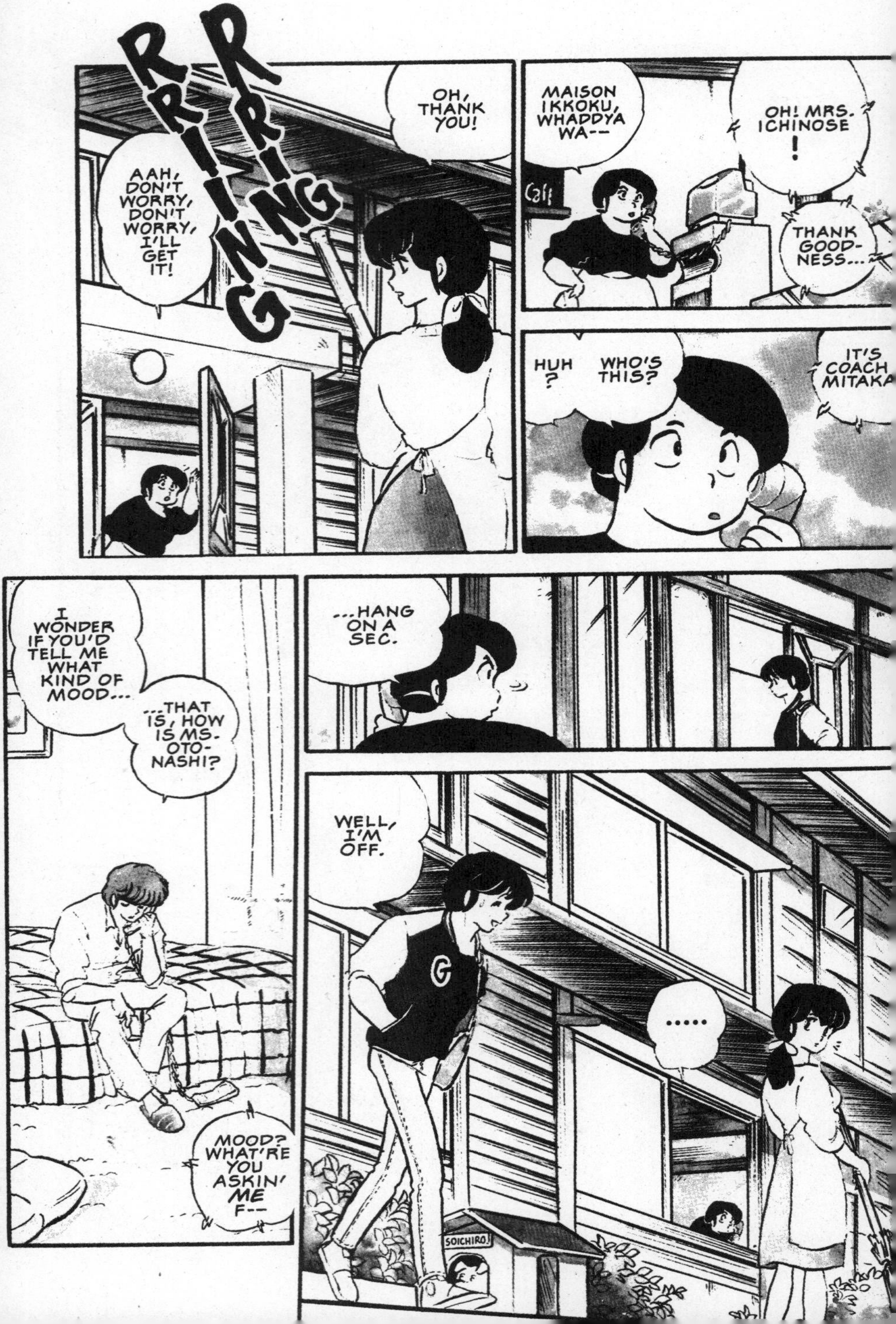
RRRIIINNNG
AAH, DON'T WORRY, DON'T WORRY, I'LL GET IT!
OH, THANK YOU!
MAISON IKKOKU, WHADDYA WA--
OH! MRS. ICHINOSE!
THANK GOODNESS...
HUH?
WHO'S THIS?
IT'S COACH MITAKA
I WONDER IF YOU'D TELL ME WHAT KIND OF MOOD...
...THAT IS, HOW IS MS. OTONASHI?
MOOD? WHAT'RE YOU ASKIN' ME F--
...HANG ON A SEC.
WELL, I'M OFF.
......
SOICHIRO

.....

.....

MRS. ICHINOSE? WHAT'S HAPPENING?

WELL...

I GUESS SHE'S, UH....

I'D HAFTA SAY SHE SEEMS PRETTY P.O.'ED.

WHAT?!?

NO, NO, NOT AT YOU OR ANYTHING.

IS THERE... ANY REASON SHE SHOULD BE...?

ONLY THAT... UH....

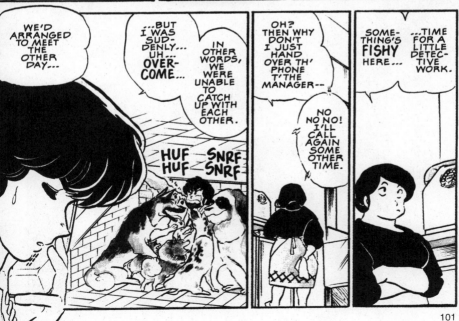

WE'D ARRANGED TO MEET THE OTHER DAY...

...BUT I WAS SUDDENLY... UH... OVERCOME...

IN OTHER WORDS, WE WERE UNABLE TO CATCH UP WITH EACH OTHER.

HUF HUF SNRF SNRF

OH? THEN WHY DON'T I JUST HAND OVER TH' PHONE T'THE MANAGER--

NO NO NO! I'LL CALL AGAIN SOME OTHER TIME.

SOMETHING'S FISHY HERE...

...TIME FOR A LITTLE DETECTIVE WORK.

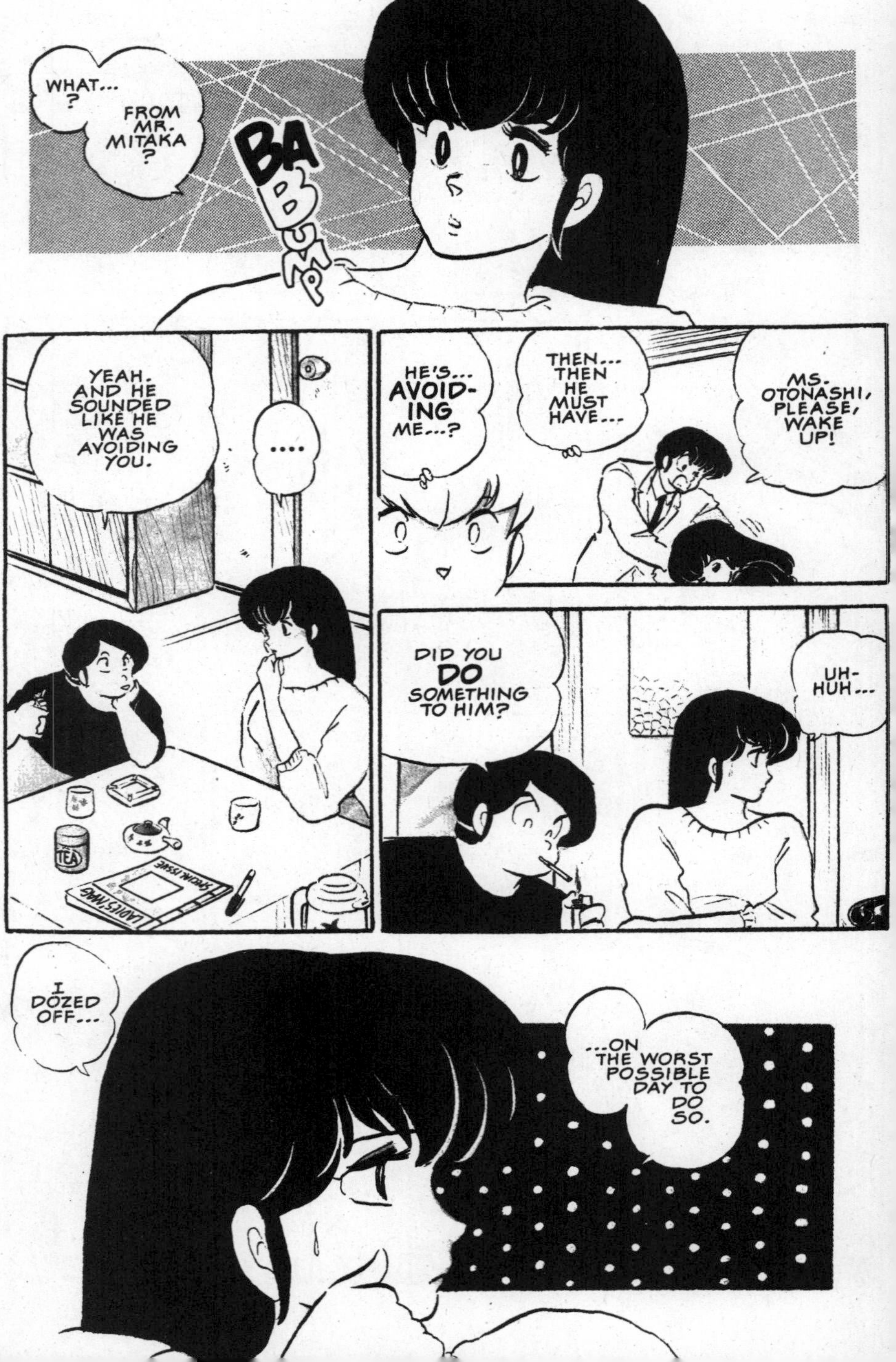
WHAT...?
FROM MR. MITAKA?
BA BUMP
YEAH. AND HE SOUNDED LIKE HE WAS AVOIDING YOU.
....
TEA
LADIES' MAG
SPECIAL ISSUE
HE'S... AVOIDING ME...?
THEN... THEN HE MUST HAVE...
MS. OTONASHI, PLEASE, WAKE UP!
DID YOU DO SOMETHING TO HIM?
UH-HUH...
I DOZED OFF...
...ON THE WORST POSSIBLE DAY TO DO SO.

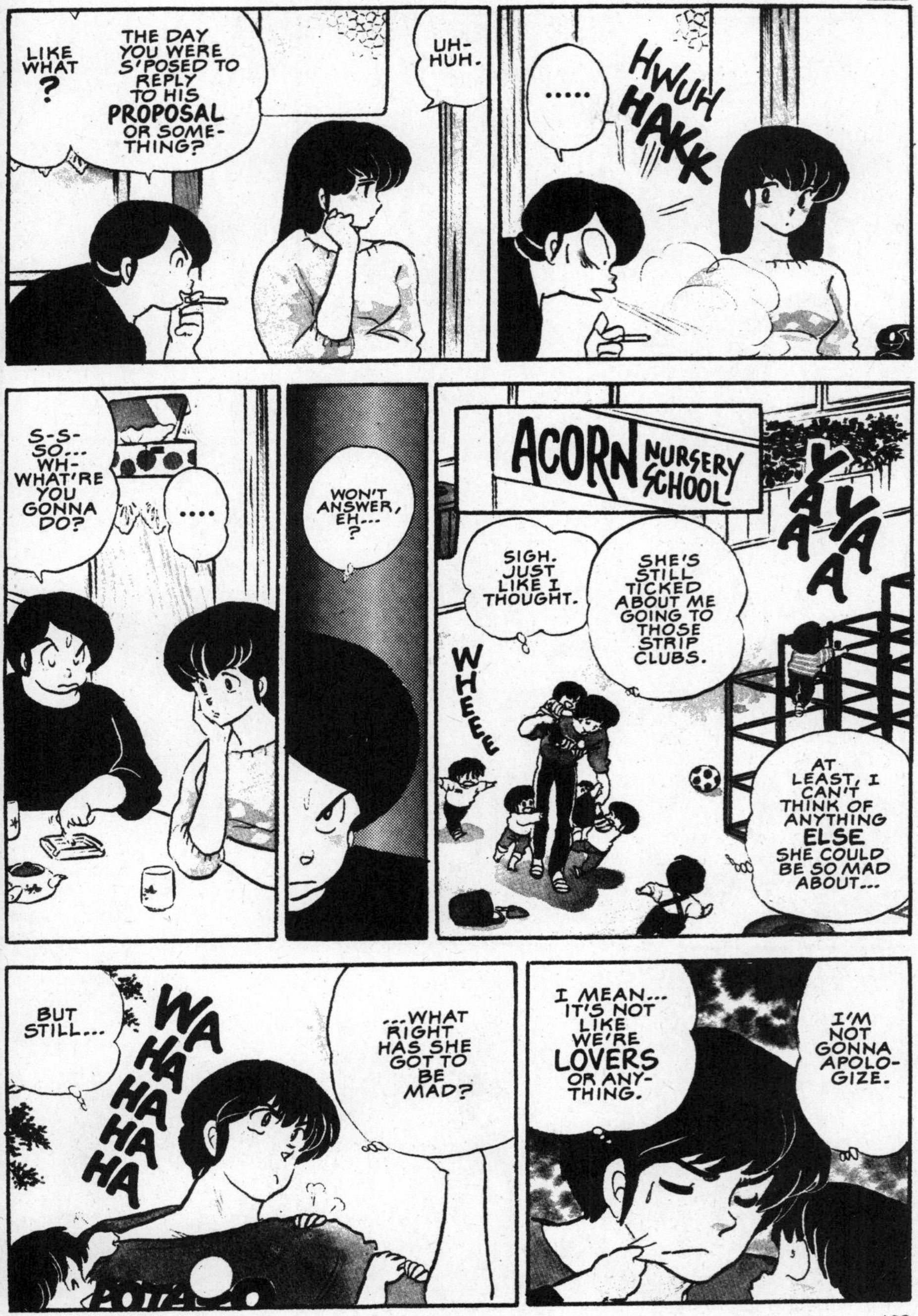
LIKE WHAT?
THE DAY YOU WERE S'POSED TO REPLY TO HIS **PROPOSAL** OR SOMETHING?
UH-HUH.
.....
HWUH HAKK
S-S-SO... WH-WHAT'RE YOU GONNA DO?
....
WON'T ANSWER, EH...?
ACORN NURSERY SCHOOL
YAA YAAA
SIGH. JUST LIKE I THOUGHT.
SHE'S STILL TICKED ABOUT ME GOING TO THOSE STRIP CLUBS.
WHEEEE
AT LEAST, I CAN'T THINK OF ANYTHING **ELSE** SHE COULD BE SO MAD ABOUT...
BUT STILL...
WA HA HA HA HA HA
...WHAT RIGHT HAS SHE GOT TO BE MAD?
I MEAN... IT'S NOT LIKE WE'RE **LOVERS** OR ANYTHING.
I'M NOT GONNA APOLOGIZE.

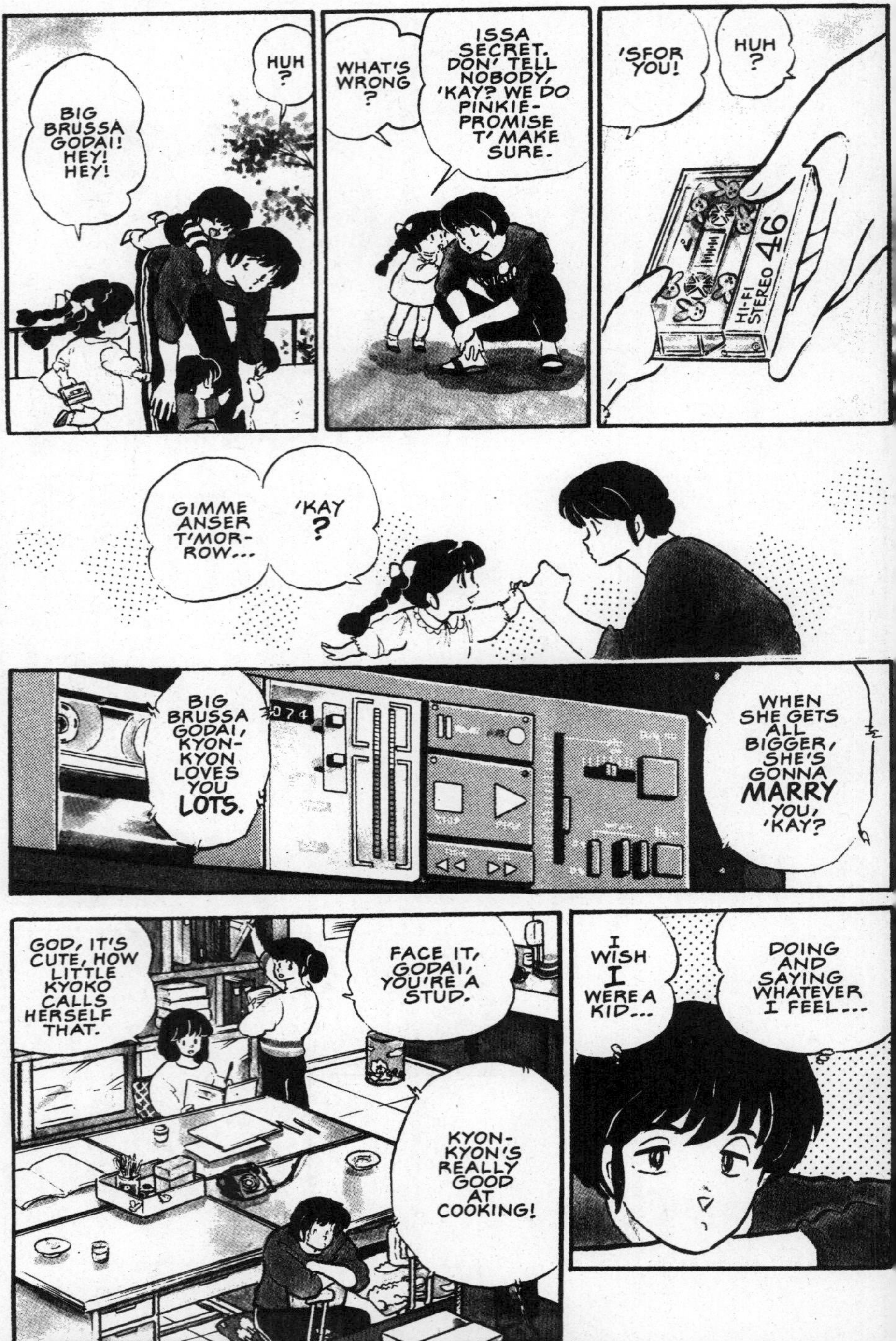

BIG BRUSSA GODAI! HEY! HEY!
HUH?
WHAT'S WRONG?
ISSA SECRET. DON' TELL NOBODY, 'KAY? WE DO PINKIE-PROMISE T' MAKE SURE.
'SFOR YOU!
HUH?
HI-FI STEREO 46
GIMME ANSER T'MOR-ROW...
'KAY?
BIG BRUSSA GODAI, KYON-KYON LOVES YOU LOTS.
WHEN SHE GETS ALL BIGGER, SHE'S GONNA MARRY YOU, 'KAY?
GOD, IT'S CUTE, HOW LITTLE KYOKO CALLS HERSELF THAT.
FACE IT, GODAI, YOU'RE A STUD.
KYON-KYON'S REALLY GOOD AT COOKING!
I WISH I WERE A KID...
DOING AND SAYING WHATEVER I FEEL...

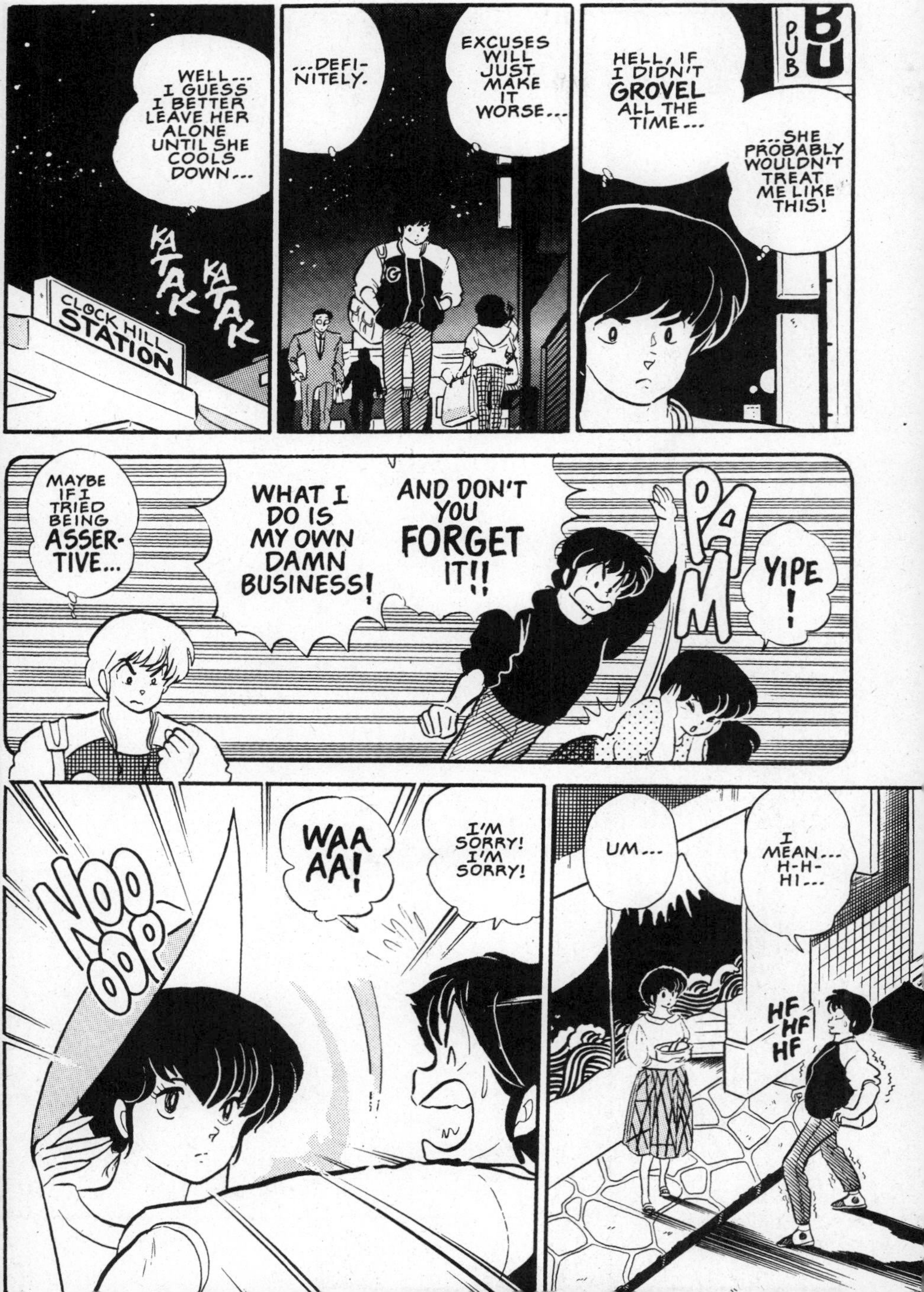
WELL... I GUESS I BETTER LEAVE HER ALONE UNTIL SHE COOLS DOWN...
KATAK KATAK
CLOCK HILL STATION
...DEFINITELY.
EXCUSES WILL JUST MAKE IT WORSE...
PUB BU
HELL, IF I DIDN'T GROVEL ALL THE TIME...
...SHE PROBABLY WOULDN'T TREAT ME LIKE THIS!
MAYBE IF I TRIED BEING ASSERTIVE...
WHAT I DO IS MY OWN DAMN BUSINESS!
AND DON'T YOU FORGET IT!!
PAM
YIPE!
NOOOOP
WAA AA!
I'M SORRY! I'M SORRY!
UM...
I MEAN... H-H-HI...
HF HF HF

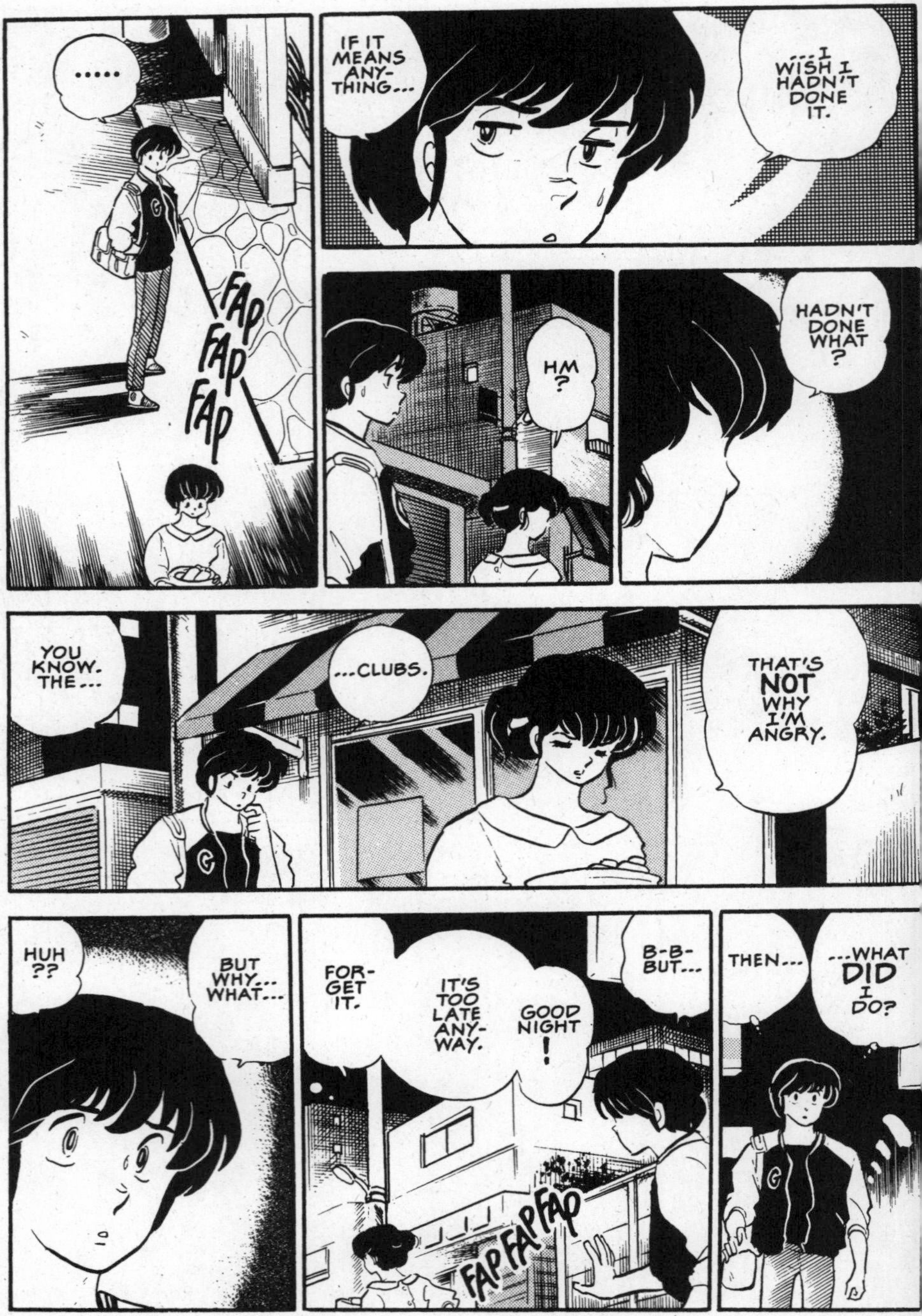

......
FAP FAP FAP FAP
IF IT MEANS ANYTHING...
...I WISH I HADN'T DONE IT.
HM?
HADN'T DONE WHAT?
YOU KNOW. THE...
...CLUBS.
THAT'S NOT WHY I'M ANGRY.
HUH??
BUT WHY... WHAT...
FORGET IT.
IT'S TOO LATE ANYWAY.
GOOD NIGHT!
B-B-BUT...
FAP FAP FAP
THEN...
...WHAT DID I DO?

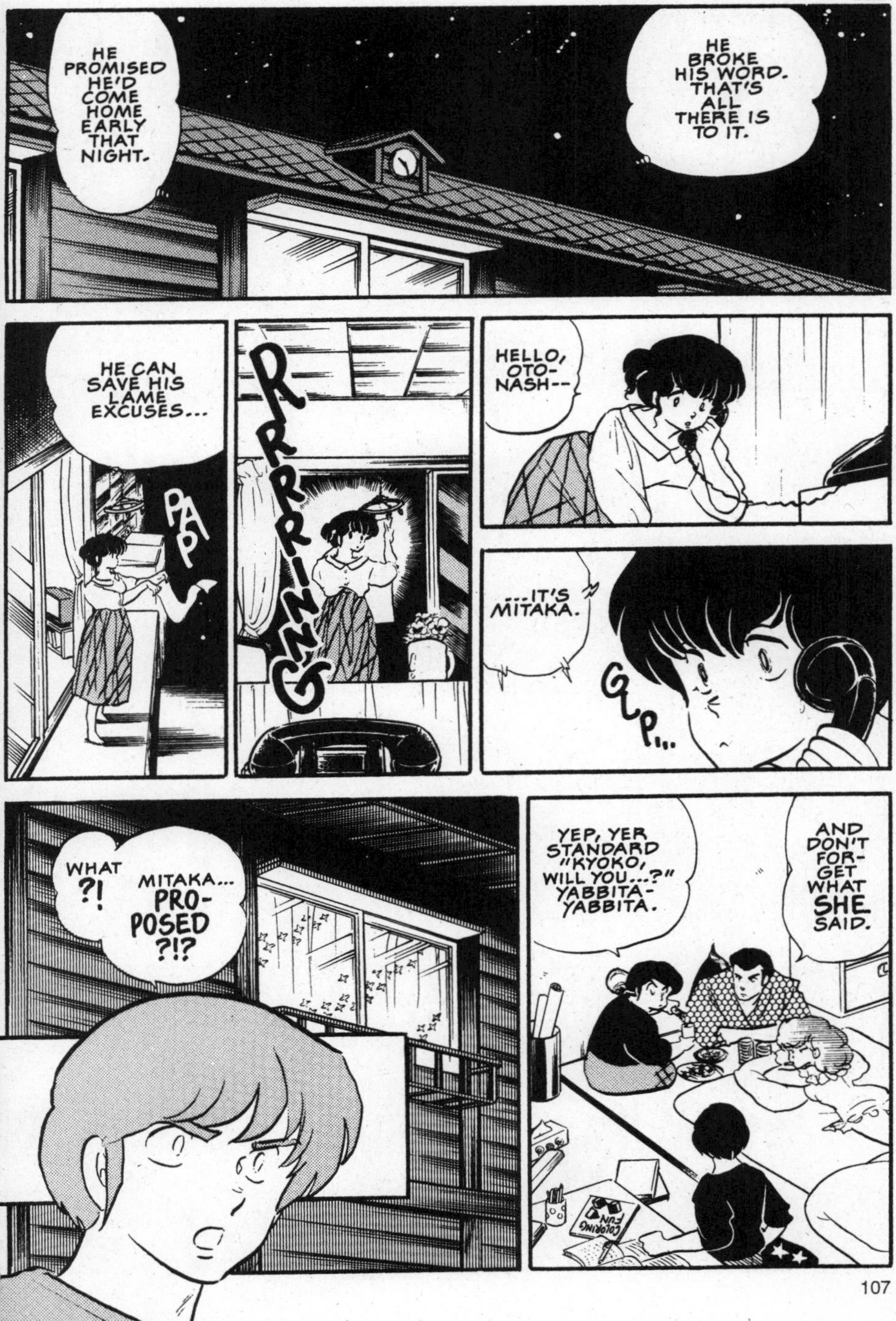
HE PROMISED HE'D COME HOME EARLY THAT NIGHT.
HE BROKE HIS WORD. THAT'S ALL THERE IS TO IT.
HE CAN SAVE HIS LAME EXCUSES...
PAP
RRRRRINNG
HELLO, OTO-NASH--
...IT'S MITAKA.
GLP...
WHAT ?!
MITAKA... PRO-POSED ?!?
YEP, YER STANDARD "KYOKO, WILL YOU...?" YABBITA-YABBITA.
AND DON'T FOR-GET WHAT SHE SAID.
COLORING FUN

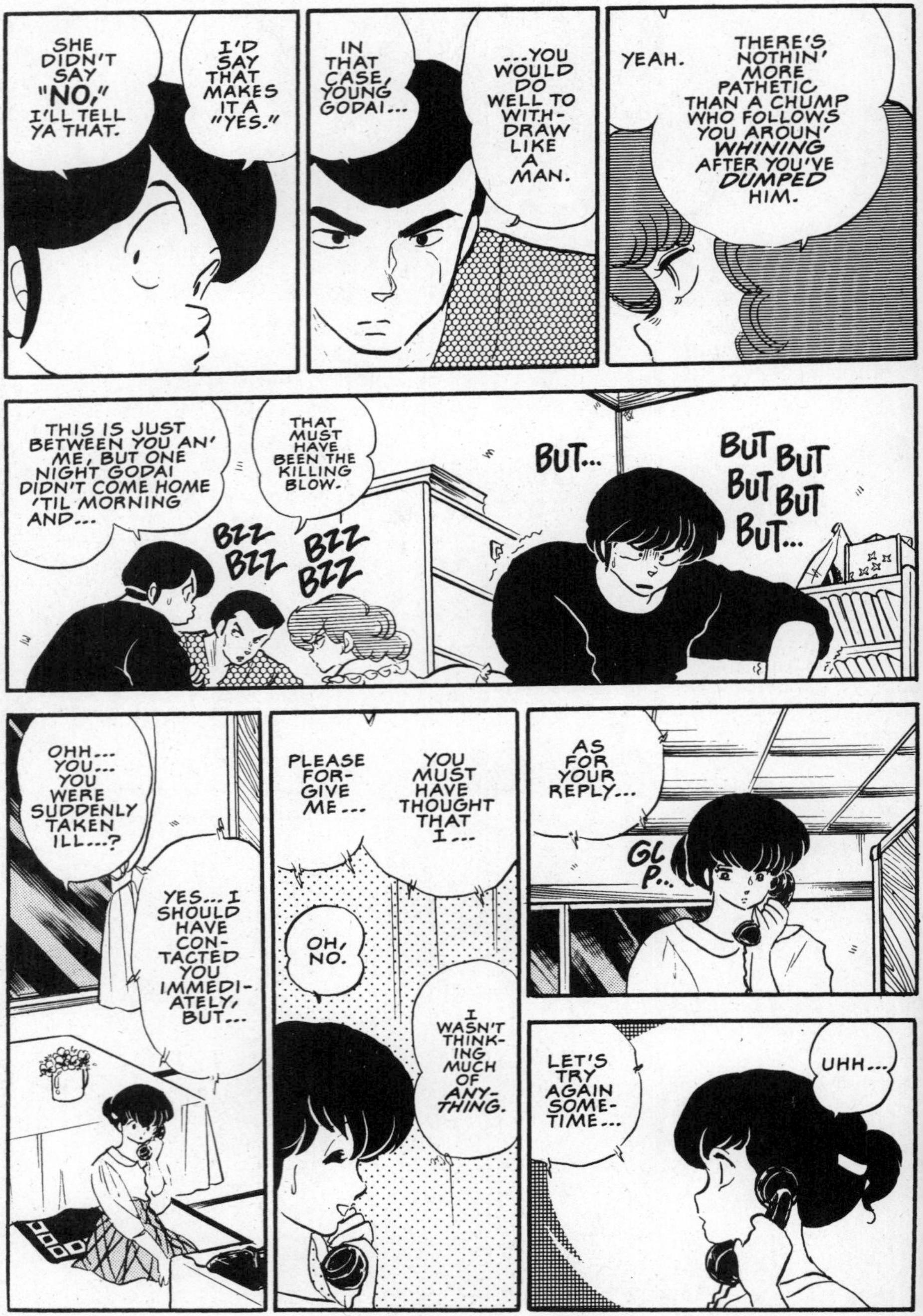
SHE DIDN'T SAY "NO," I'LL TELL YA THAT.
I'D SAY THAT MAKES IT A "YES."
IN THAT CASE, YOUNG GODAI...
...YOU WOULD DO WELL TO WITH-DRAW LIKE A MAN.
YEAH.
THERE'S NOTHIN' MORE PATHETIC THAN A CHUMP WHO FOLLOWS YOU AROUN' *WHINING* AFTER YOU'VE *DUMPED* HIM.
THIS IS JUST BETWEEN YOU AN' ME, BUT ONE NIGHT GODAI DIDN'T COME HOME 'TIL MORNING AND...
THAT MUST HAVE BEEN THE KILLING BLOW.
BZZ BZZ
BZZ BZZ
BUT...
BUT BUT BUT BUT BUT...
OHH... YOU... YOU WERE SUDDENLY TAKEN ILL...?
YES... I SHOULD HAVE CON-TACTED YOU IMMEDI-ATELY, BUT...
PLEASE FOR-GIVE ME...
YOU MUST HAVE THOUGHT THAT I...
OH, NO.
I WASN'T THINK-ING MUCH OF *ANY-THING*.
AS FOR YOUR REPLY...
GLP...
LET'S TRY AGAIN SOME-TIME...
UHH...

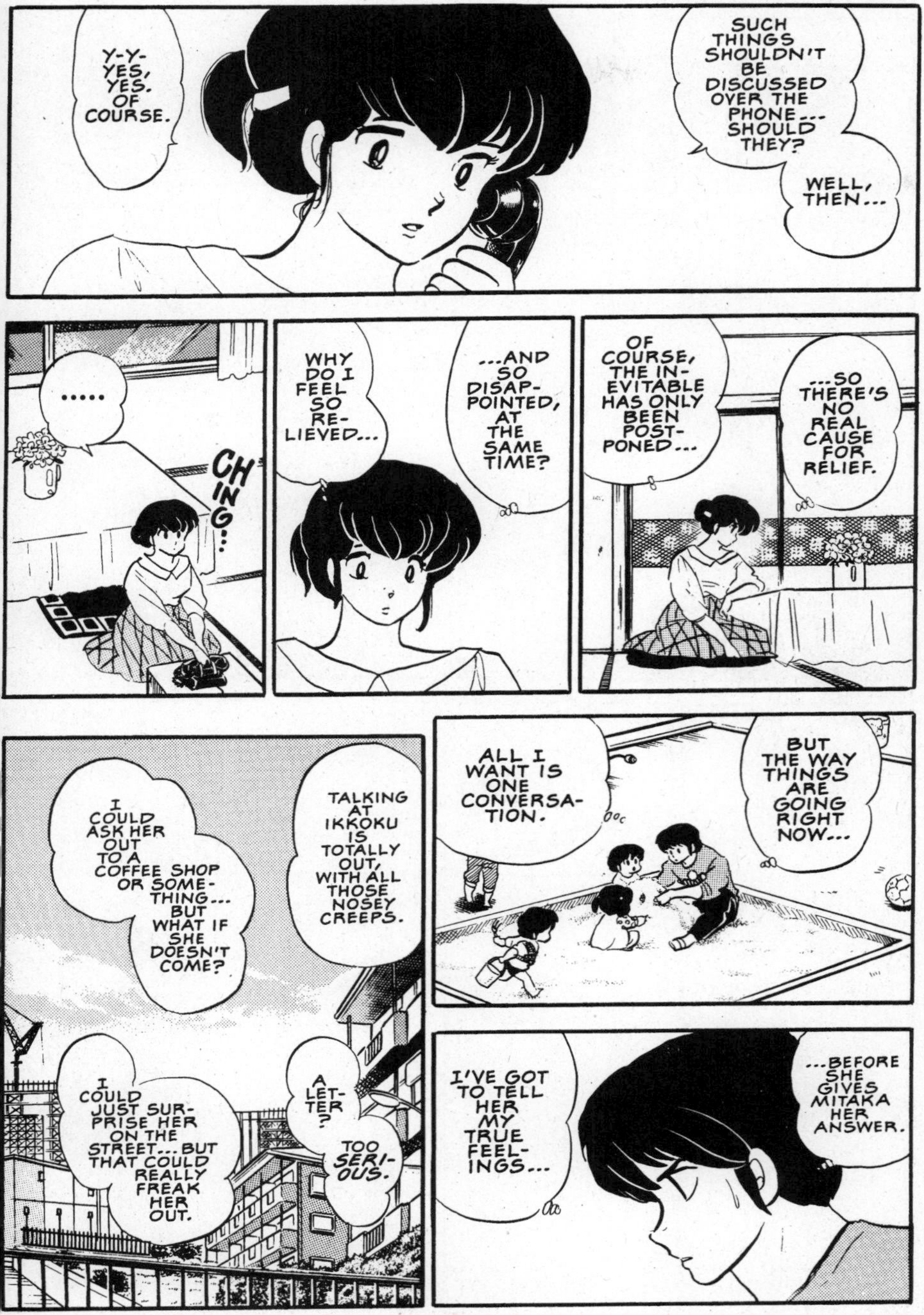
Y-Y-YES, YES. OF COURSE.
SUCH THINGS SHOULDN'T BE DISCUSSED OVER THE PHONE... SHOULD THEY?
WELL, THEN...
......
CHING
WHY DO I FEEL SO RELIEVED...
...AND SO DISAPPOINTED, AT THE SAME TIME?
OF COURSE, THE INEVITABLE HAS ONLY BEEN POSTPONED...
...SO THERE'S NO REAL CAUSE FOR RELIEF.
I COULD ASK HER OUT TO A COFFEE SHOP OR SOMETHING... BUT WHAT IF SHE DOESN'T COME?
TALKING AT IKKOKU IS TOTALLY OUT, WITH ALL THOSE NOSEY CREEPS.
I COULD JUST SURPRISE HER ON THE STREET... BUT THAT COULD REALLY FREAK HER OUT.
A LETTER?
TOO SERIOUS.
ALL I WANT IS ONE CONVERSATION.
BUT THE WAY THINGS ARE GOING RIGHT NOW...
I'VE GOT TO TELL HER MY TRUE FEELINGS...
...BEFORE SHE GIVES MITAKA HER ANSWER.

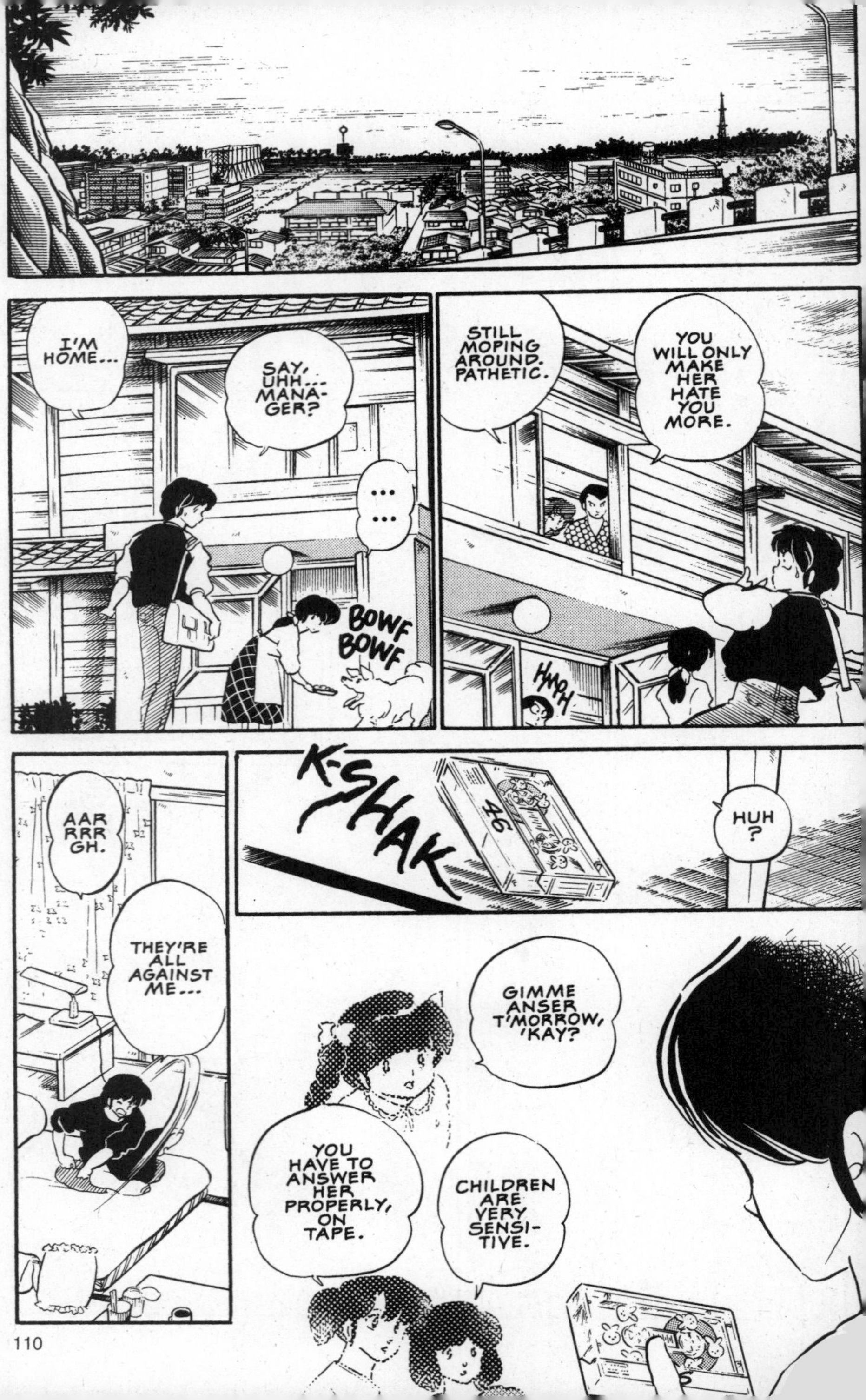
I'M HOME...
SAY, UHH... MANAGER?
...
...
BOWF BOWF
STILL MOPING AROUND. PATHETIC.
YOU WILL ONLY MAKE HER HATE YOU MORE.
HMPH
AARRRRGH.
THEY'RE ALL AGAINST ME...
K-SHAK
46
HUH?
GIMME ANSER T'MORROW, 'KAY?
YOU HAVE TO ANSWER HER PROPERLY, ON TAPE.
CHILDREN ARE VERY SENSITIVE.

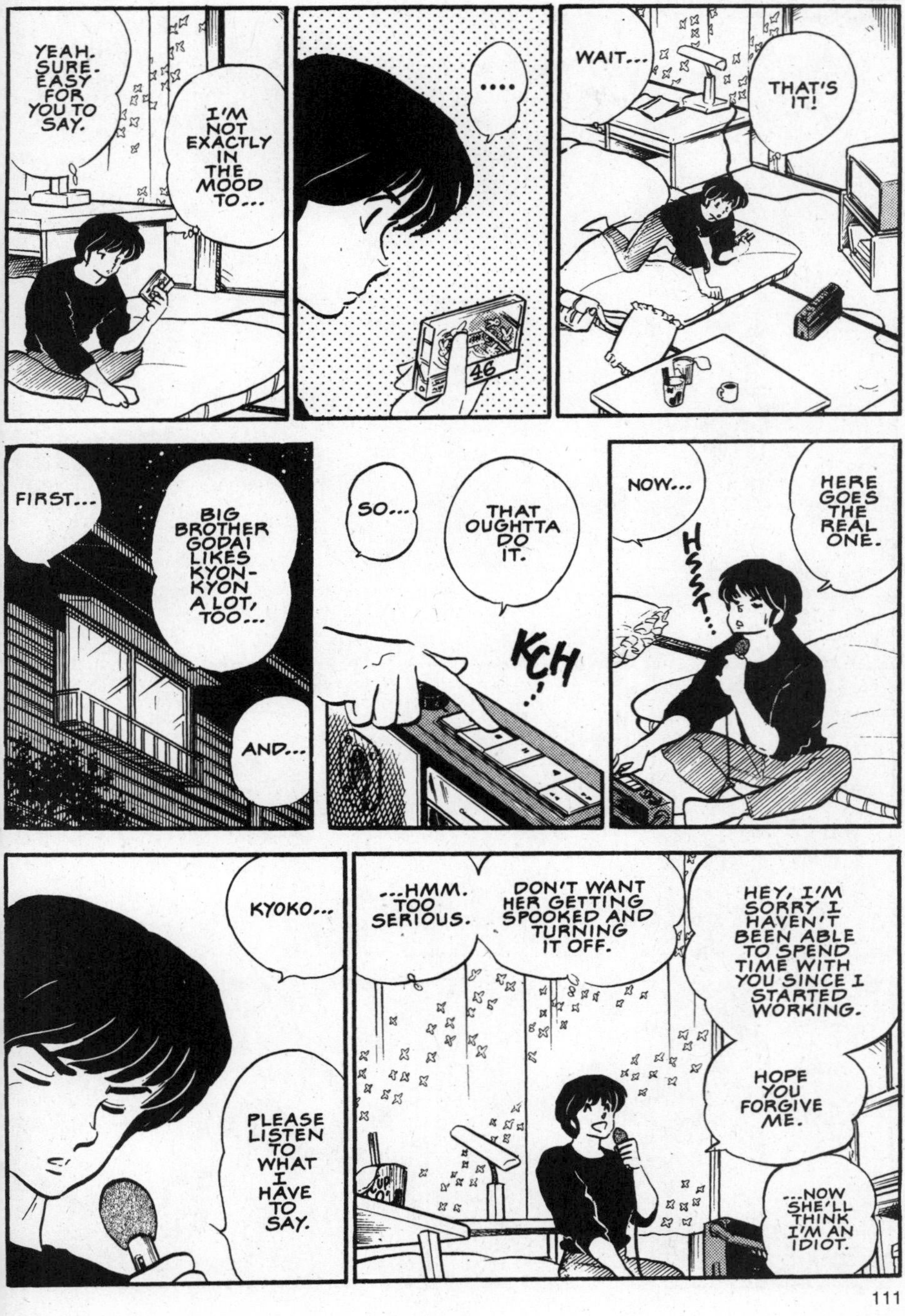
YEAH. SURE. EASY FOR YOU TO SAY.
I'M NOT EXACTLY IN THE MOOD TO...
....
WAIT...
THAT'S IT!
FIRST...
BIG BROTHER GODAI LIKES KYON-KYON A LOT, TOO...
AND...
SO...
THAT OUGHTTA DO IT.
KCH
NOW...
HSST...
HERE GOES THE REAL ONE.
KYOKO...
PLEASE LISTEN TO WHAT I HAVE TO SAY.
...HMM. TOO SERIOUS.
DON'T WANT HER GETTING SPOOKED AND TURNING IT OFF.
HEY, I'M SORRY I HAVEN'T BEEN ABLE TO SPEND TIME WITH YOU SINCE I STARTED WORKING.
HOPE YOU FORGIVE ME.
...NOW SHE'LL THINK I'M AN IDIOT.

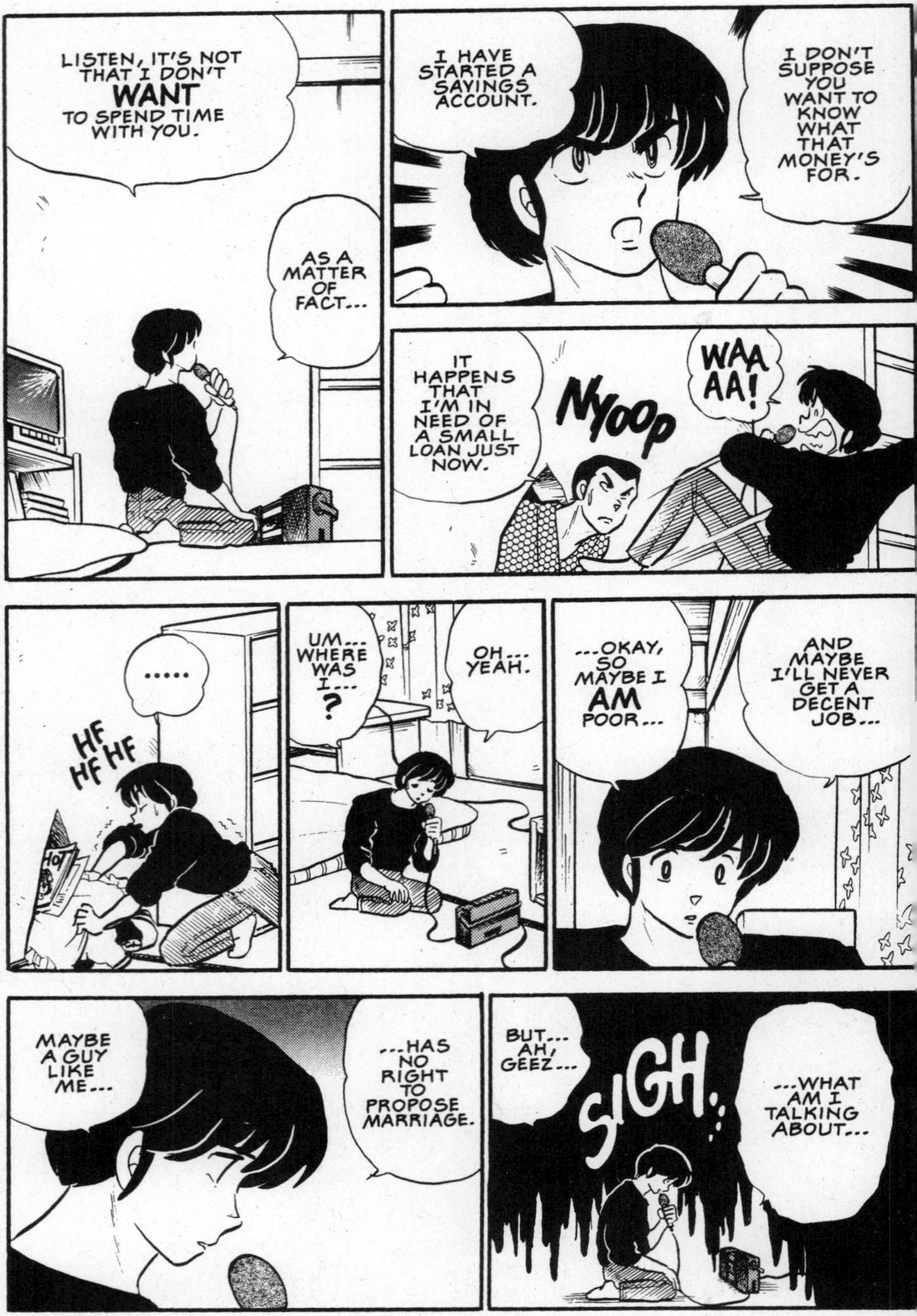
LISTEN, IT'S NOT THAT I DON'T **WANT** TO SPEND TIME WITH YOU.
AS A MATTER OF FACT...
I HAVE STARTED A SAVINGS ACCOUNT.
I DON'T SUPPOSE YOU WANT TO KNOW WHAT THAT MONEY'S FOR.
IT HAPPENS THAT I'M IN NEED OF A SMALL LOAN JUST NOW.
NYOOP
WAAAA!
......
HF HF HF
HOT
UM... WHERE WAS I...?
OH... YEAH.
...OKAY, SO MAYBE I **AM** POOR...
AND MAYBE I'LL NEVER GET A DECENT JOB...
MAYBE A GUY LIKE ME...
...HAS NO RIGHT TO PROPOSE MARRIAGE.
BUT... AH, GEEZ...
SIGH...
...WHAT AM I TALKING ABOUT...

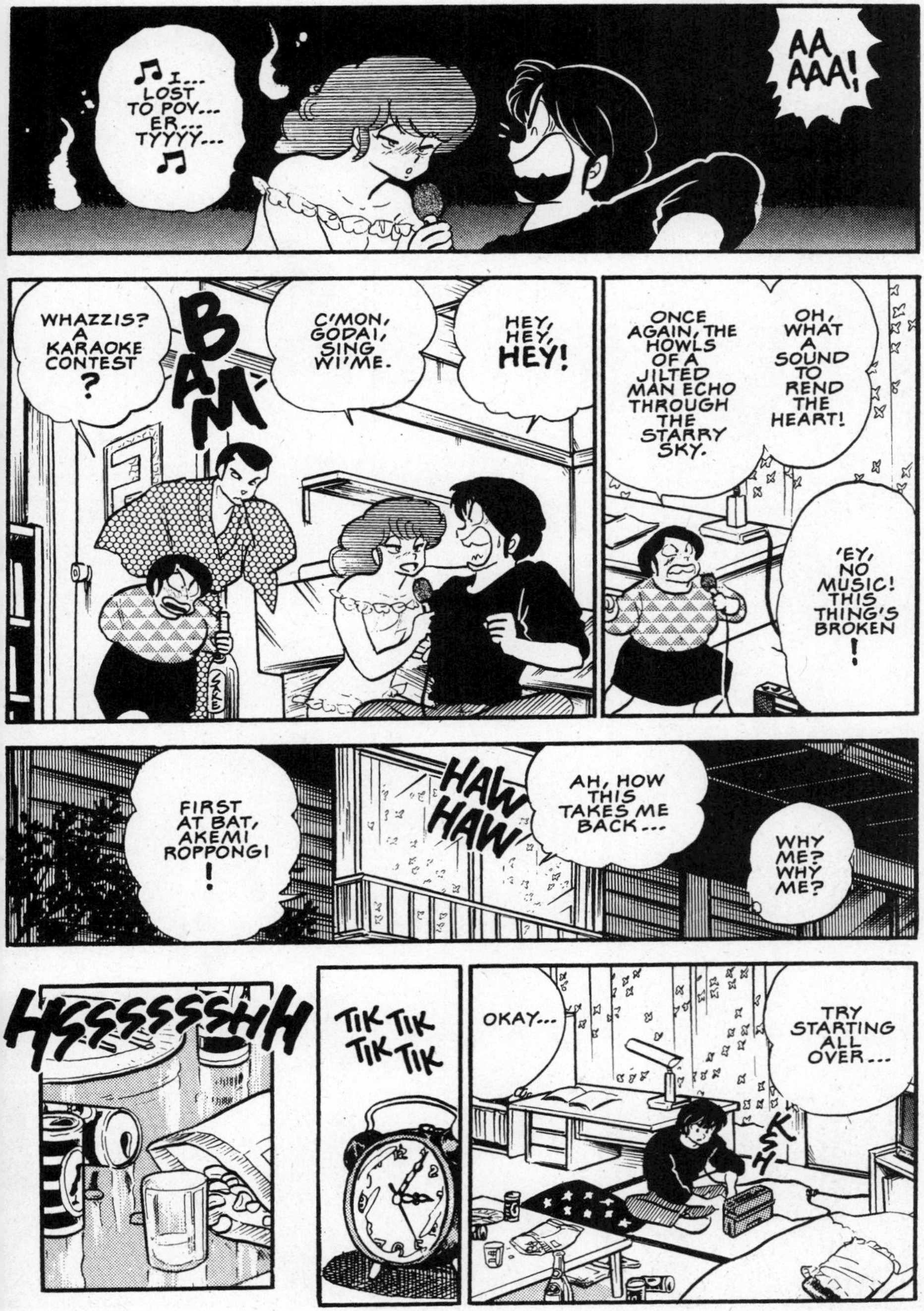
♫ I... LOST TO POV... ER... TYYYY... ♫
AA AAA!
WHAZZIS? A KARAOKE CONTEST?
BAM
C'MON, GODAI, SING WI'ME.
HEY, HEY, HEY!
ONCE AGAIN, THE HOWLS OF A JILTED MAN ECHO THROUGH THE STARRY SKY.
OH, WHAT A SOUND TO REND THE HEART!
'EY, NO MUSIC! THIS THING'S BROKEN!
FIRST AT BAT, AKEMI ROPPONGI!
HAW HAW
AH, HOW THIS TAKES ME BACK...
WHY ME? WHY ME?
HSSSSSSHH
TIK TIK TIK TIK
OKAY...
TRY STARTING ALL OVER...
KSH

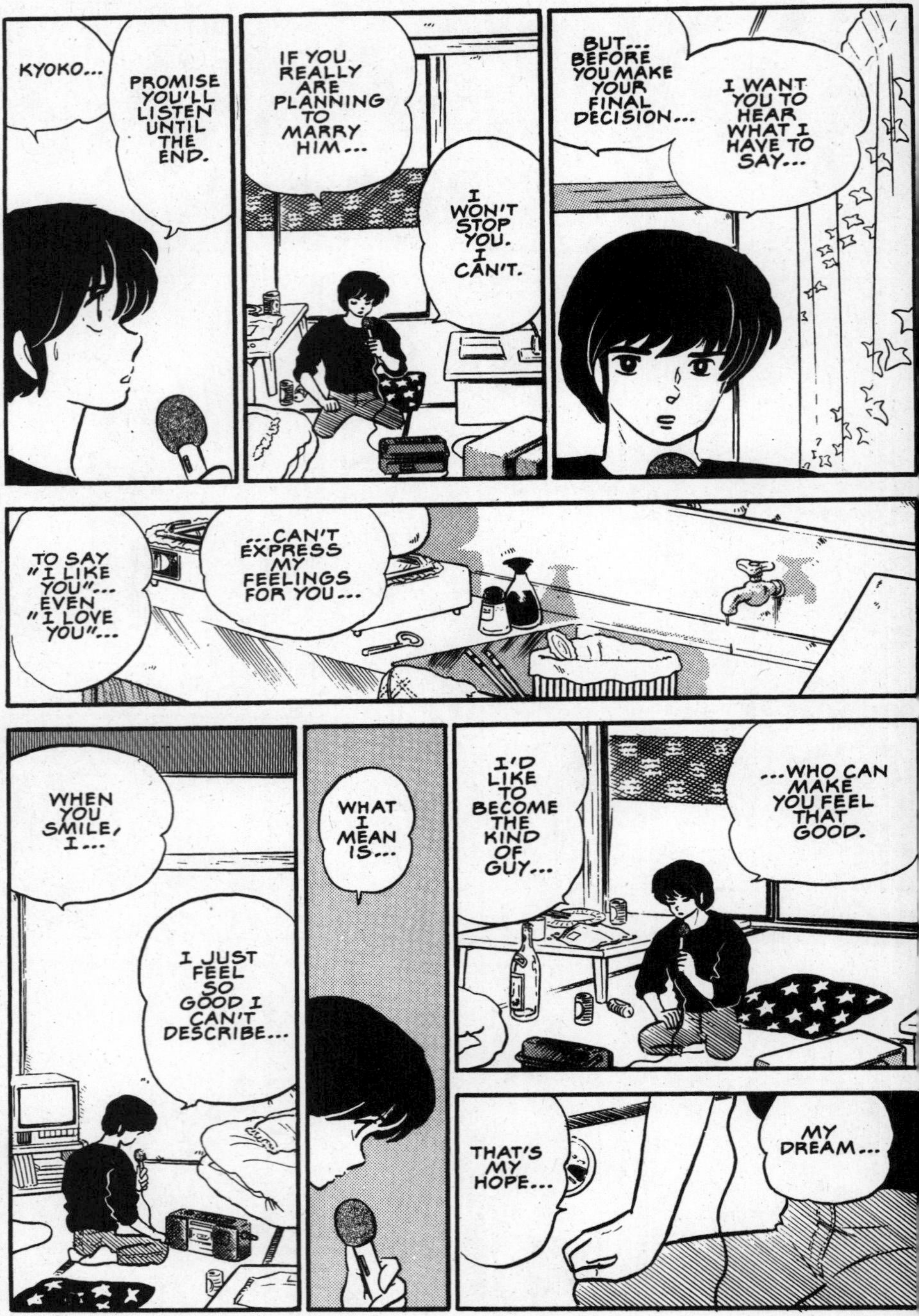
KYOKO...
PROMISE YOU'LL LISTEN UNTIL THE END.
IF YOU REALLY ARE PLANNING TO MARRY HIM...
I WON'T STOP YOU. I CAN'T.
BUT... BEFORE YOU MAKE YOUR FINAL DECISION...
I WANT YOU TO HEAR WHAT I HAVE TO SAY...
TO SAY "I LIKE YOU"... EVEN "I LOVE YOU"...
...CAN'T EXPRESS MY FEELINGS FOR YOU...
WHEN YOU SMILE, I...
I JUST FEEL SO GOOD I CAN'T DESCRIBE...
WHAT I MEAN IS...
I'D LIKE TO BECOME THE KIND OF GUY...
...WHO CAN MAKE YOU FEEL THAT GOOD.
THAT'S MY HOPE...
MY DREAM...

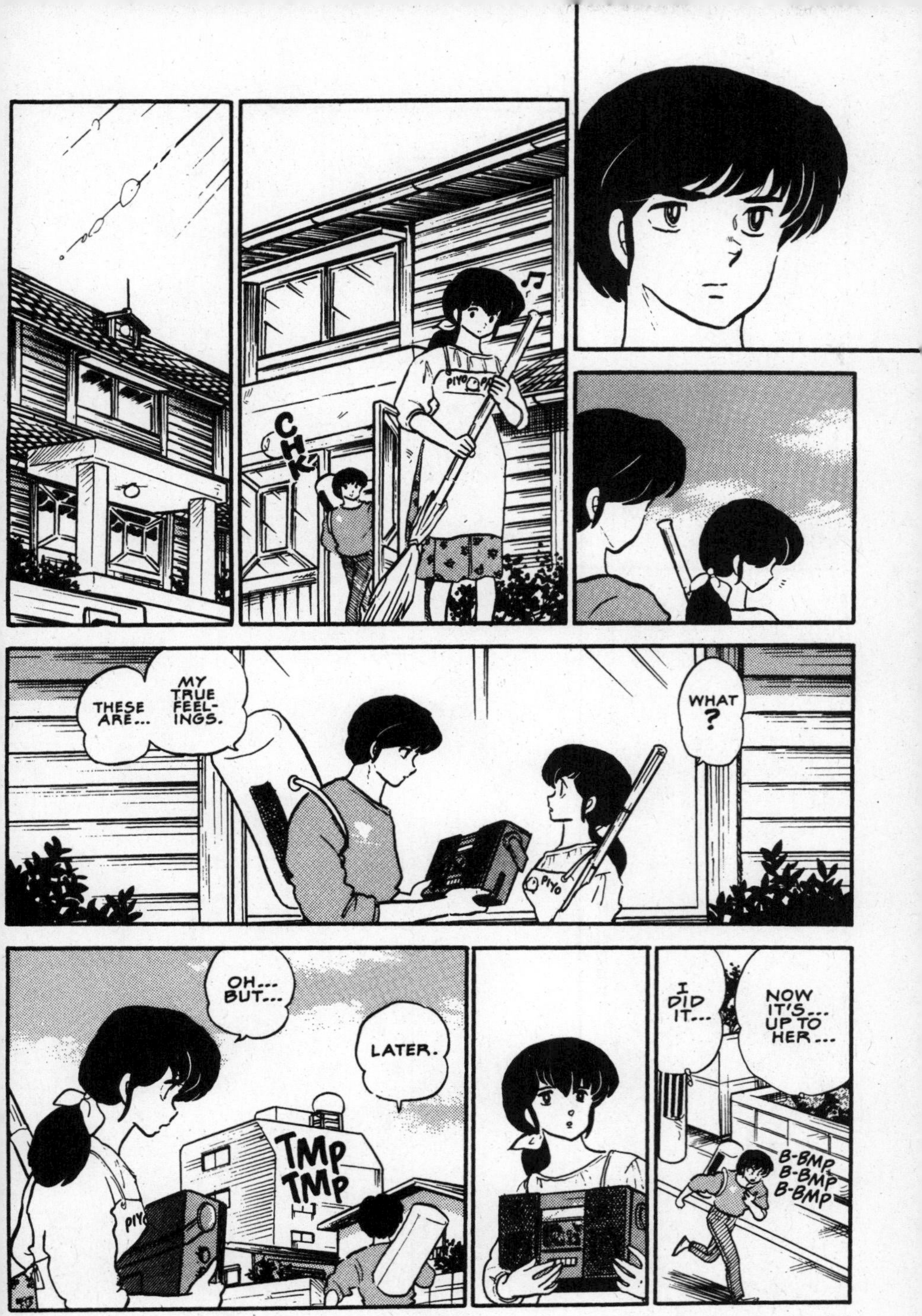
CHK
THESE ARE... MY TRUE FEELINGS.
WHAT?
OH... BUT...
LATER.
TMP TMP
I DID IT...
NOW IT'S... UP TO HER...
B-BMP B-BMP B-BMP

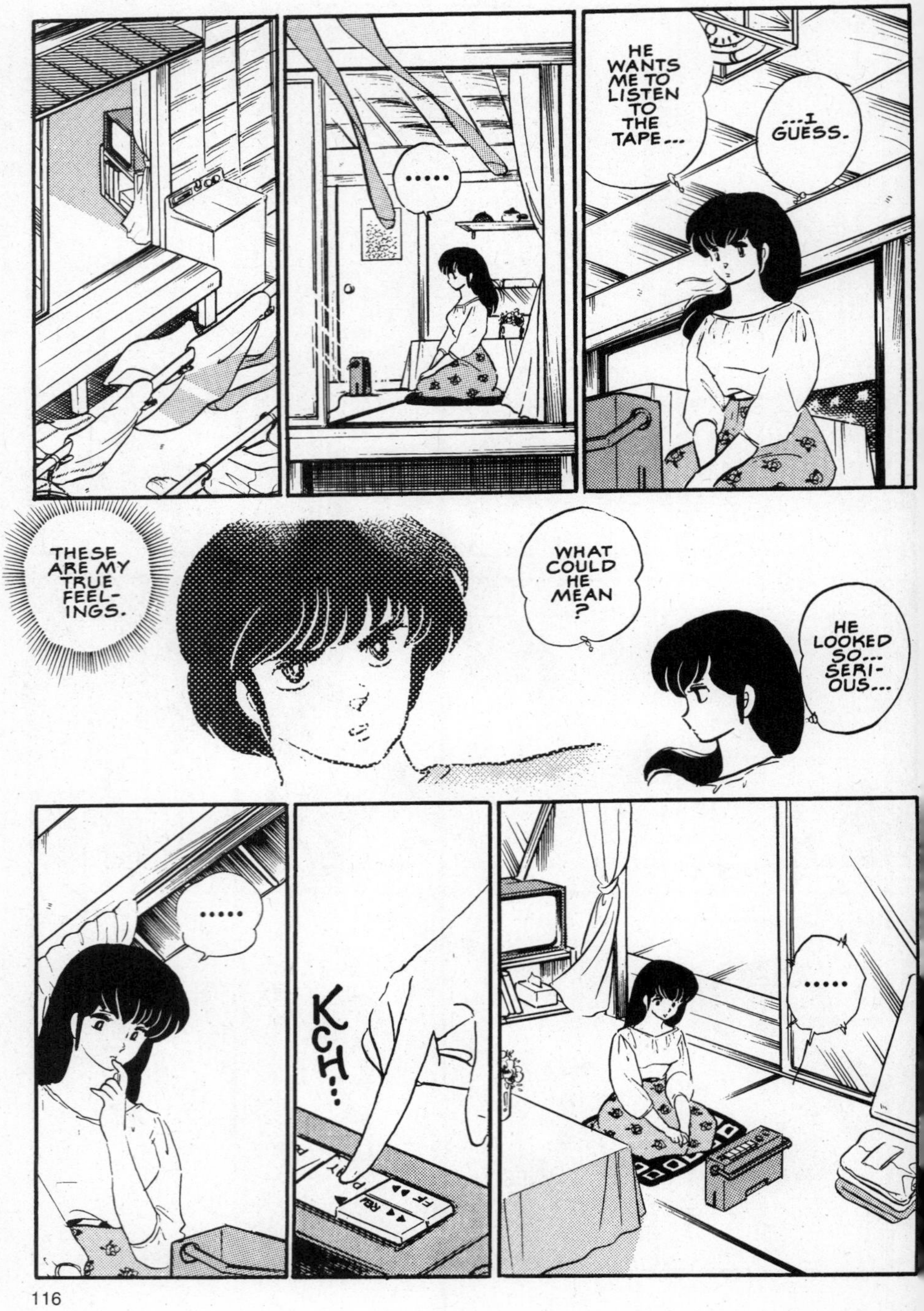
HE WANTS ME TO LISTEN TO THE TAPE...
...I GUESS.
......
WHAT COULD HE MEAN?
HE LOOKED SO... SERI-OUS...
THESE ARE MY TRUE FEEL-INGS.
......
KCH...
......

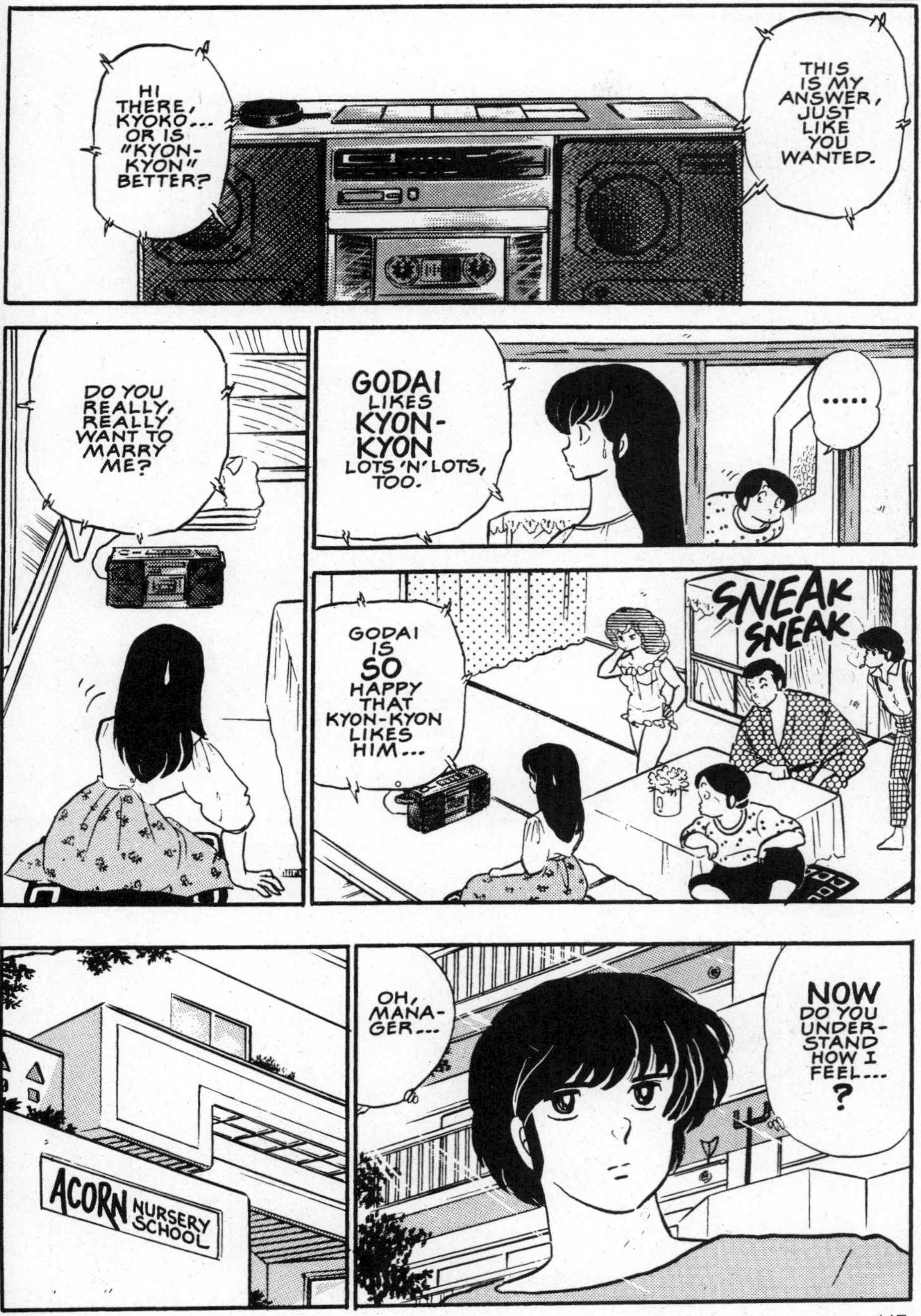
HI THERE, KYOKO... OR IS "KYON-KYON" BETTER?
THIS IS MY ANSWER, JUST LIKE YOU WANTED.
DO YOU REALLY, REALLY WANT TO MARRY ME?
GODAI LIKES KYON-KYON LOTS 'N' LOTS, TOO.
.....
GODAI IS SO HAPPY THAT KYON-KYON LIKES HIM...
SNEAK SNEAK
ACORN NURSERY SCHOOL
OH, MANA-GER...
NOW DO YOU UNDER-STAND HOW I FEEL...?

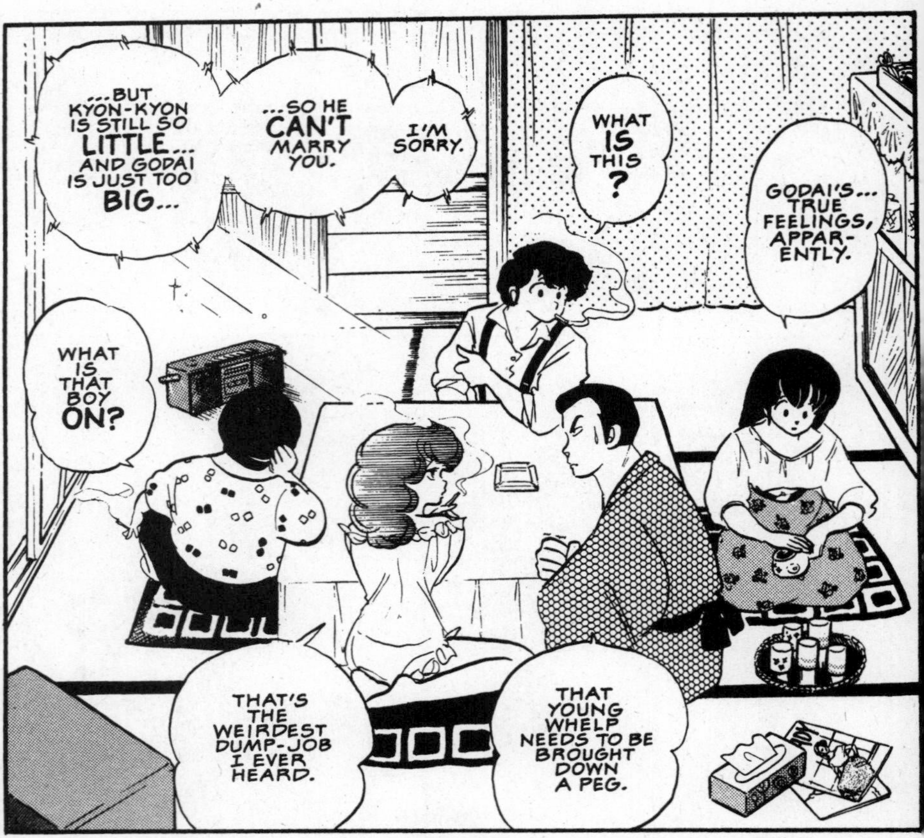
...BUT KYON-KYON IS STILL SO LITTLE... AND GODAI IS JUST TOO BIG...
...SO HE CAN'T MARRY YOU.
I'M SORRY.
WHAT IS THIS?
GODAI'S... TRUE FEELINGS, APPARENTLY.
WHAT IS THAT BOY ON?
THAT'S THE WEIRDEST DUMP-JOB I EVER HEARD.
THAT YOUNG WHELP NEEDS TO BE BROUGHT DOWN A PEG.
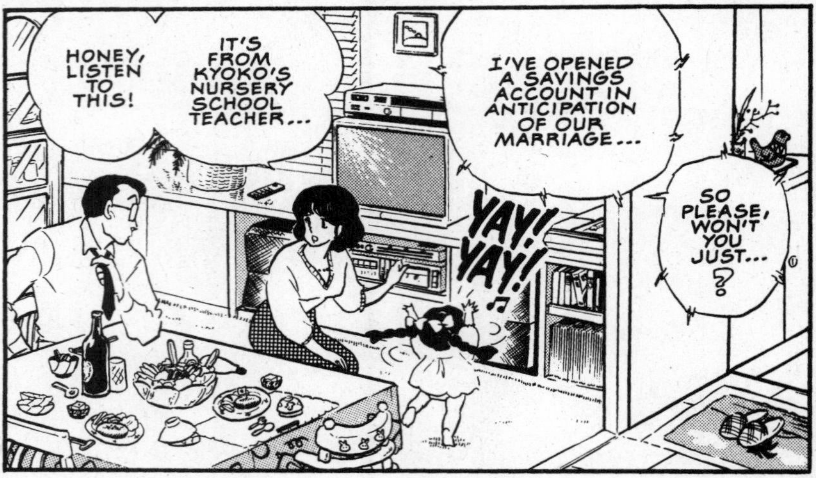
HONEY, LISTEN TO THIS!
IT'S FROM KYOKO'S NURSERY SCHOOL TEACHER...
I'VE OPENED A SAVINGS ACCOUNT IN ANTICIPATION OF OUR MARRIAGE...
YAY! YAY!
SO PLEASE, WON'T YOU JUST...?

PART 6

SEND IN THE HOUNDS

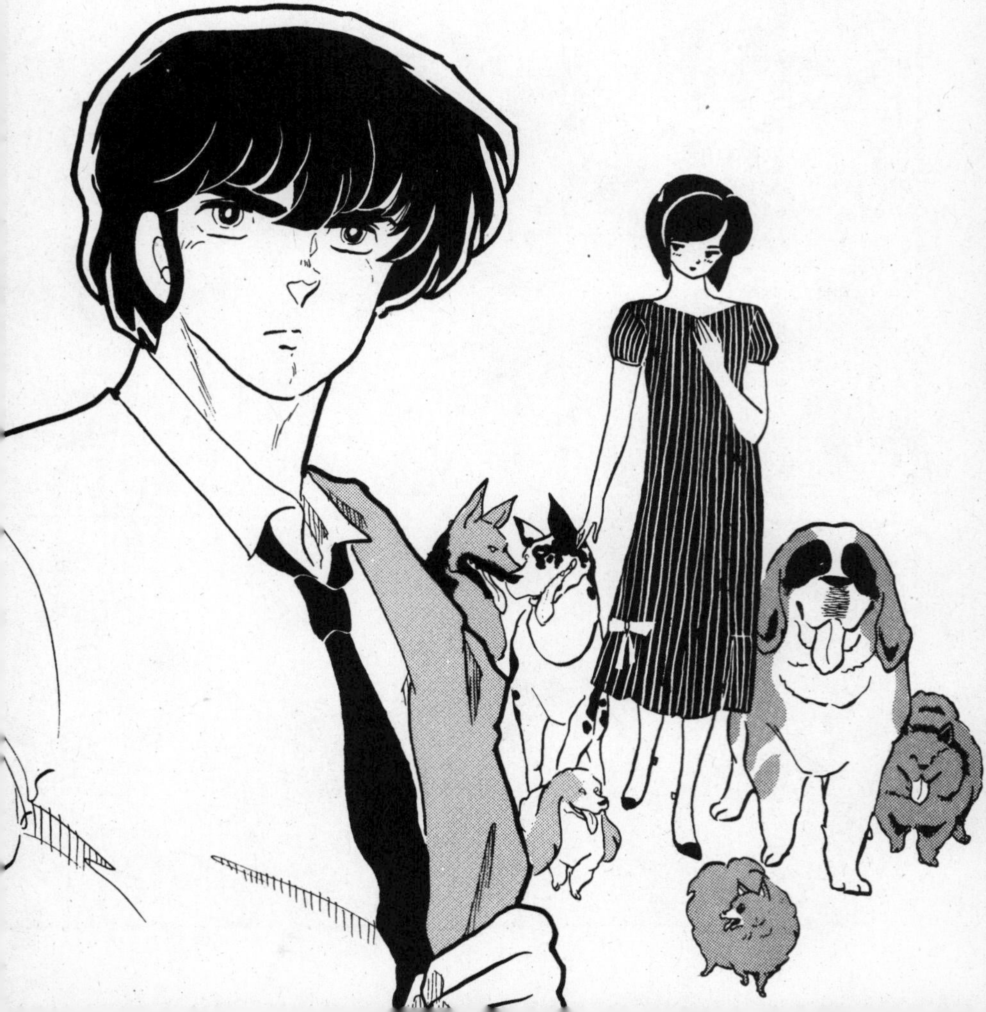

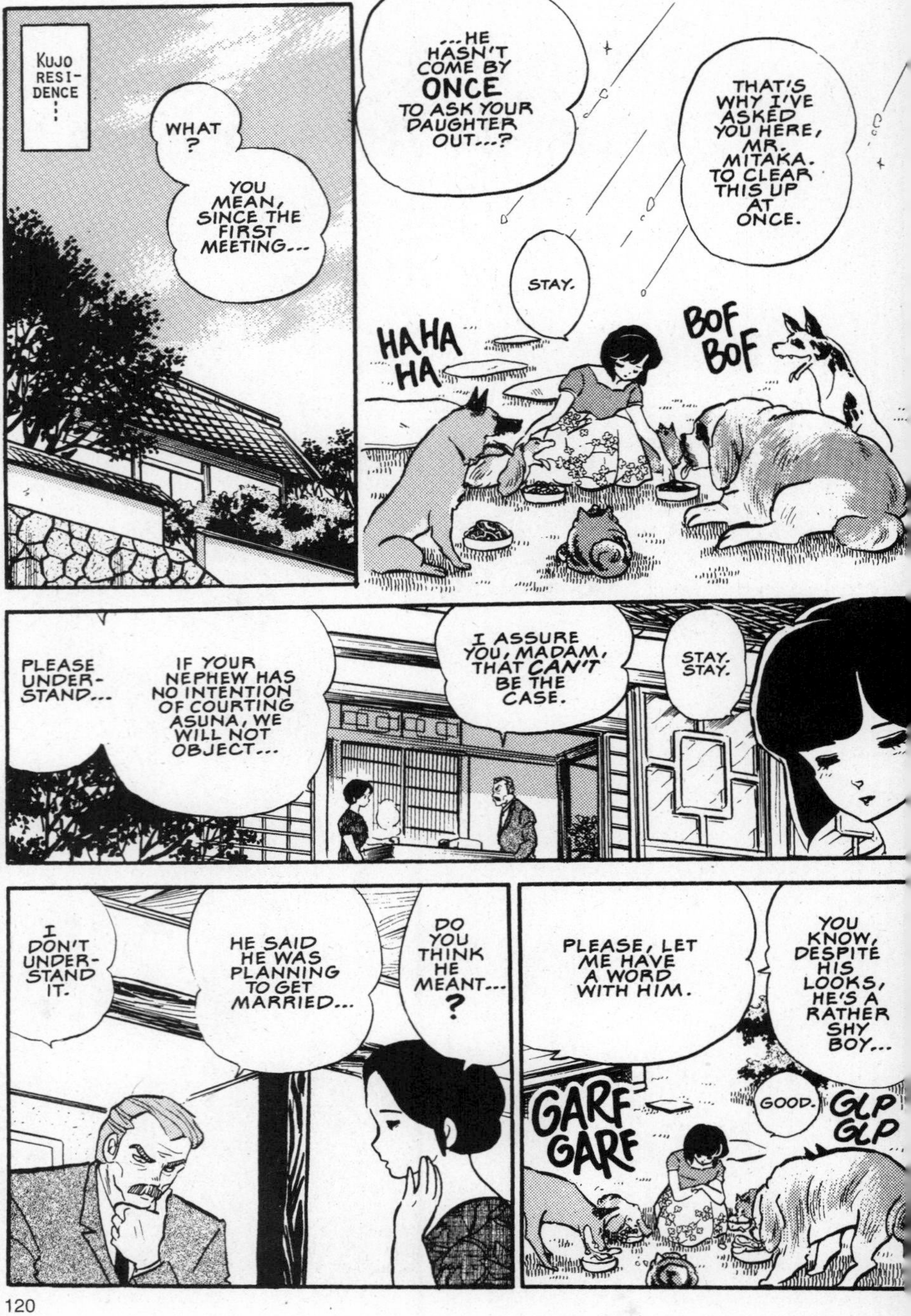

KUJO RESI-DENCE...
WHAT?
YOU MEAN, SINCE THE FIRST MEETING...
...HE HASN'T COME BY ONCE TO ASK YOUR DAUGHTER OUT...?
THAT'S WHY I'VE ASKED YOU HERE, MR. MITAKA. TO CLEAR THIS UP AT ONCE.
STAY.
HA HA HA
BOF BOF
PLEASE UNDER-STAND...
IF YOUR NEPHEW HAS NO INTENTION OF COURTING ASUNA, WE WILL NOT OBJECT...
I ASSURE YOU, MADAM, THAT CAN'T BE THE CASE.
STAY. STAY.
I DON'T UNDER-STAND IT.
HE SAID HE WAS PLANNING TO GET MARRIED...
DO YOU THINK HE MEANT...?
PLEASE, LET ME HAVE A WORD WITH HIM.
YOU KNOW, DESPITE HIS LOOKS, HE'S A RATHER SHY BOY...
GARF GARF
GOOD.
GLP GLP

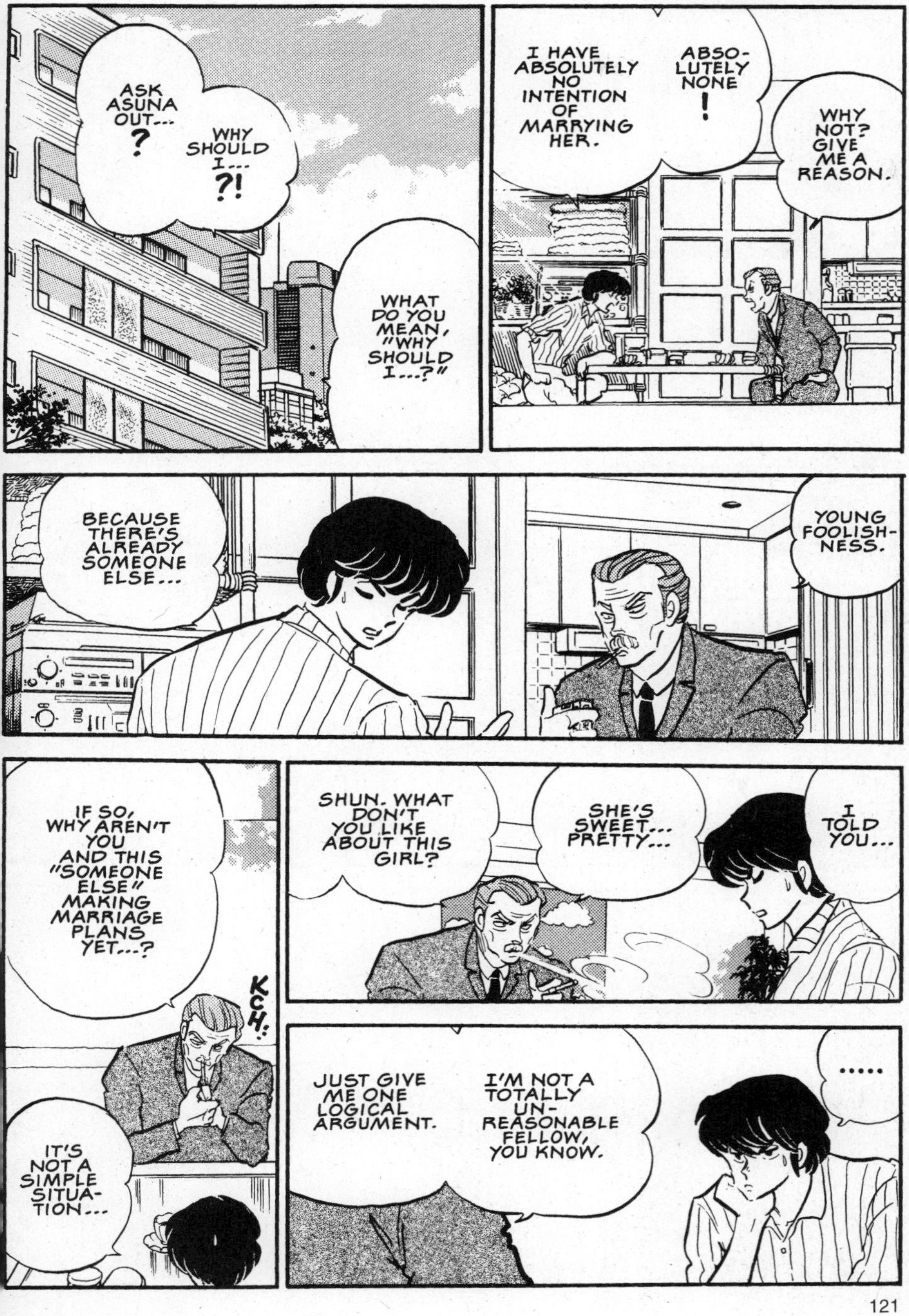
ASK ASUNA OUT...?
WHY SHOULD I...?!
WHAT DO YOU MEAN, "WHY SHOULD I...?"
I HAVE ABSOLUTELY NO INTENTION OF MARRYING HER.
ABSO-LUTELY NONE!
WHY NOT? GIVE ME A REASON.
BECAUSE THERE'S ALREADY SOMEONE ELSE...
YOUNG FOOLISH-NESS.
IF SO, WHY AREN'T YOU AND THIS "SOMEONE ELSE" MAKING MARRIAGE PLANS YET...?
KCH!!
IT'S NOT A SIMPLE SITUA-TION...
SHUN. WHAT DON'T YOU LIKE ABOUT THIS GIRL?
SHE'S SWEET... PRETTY...
I TOLD YOU...
JUST GIVE ME ONE LOGICAL ARGUMENT.
I'M NOT A TOTALLY UN-REASONABLE FELLOW, YOU KNOW.
.....

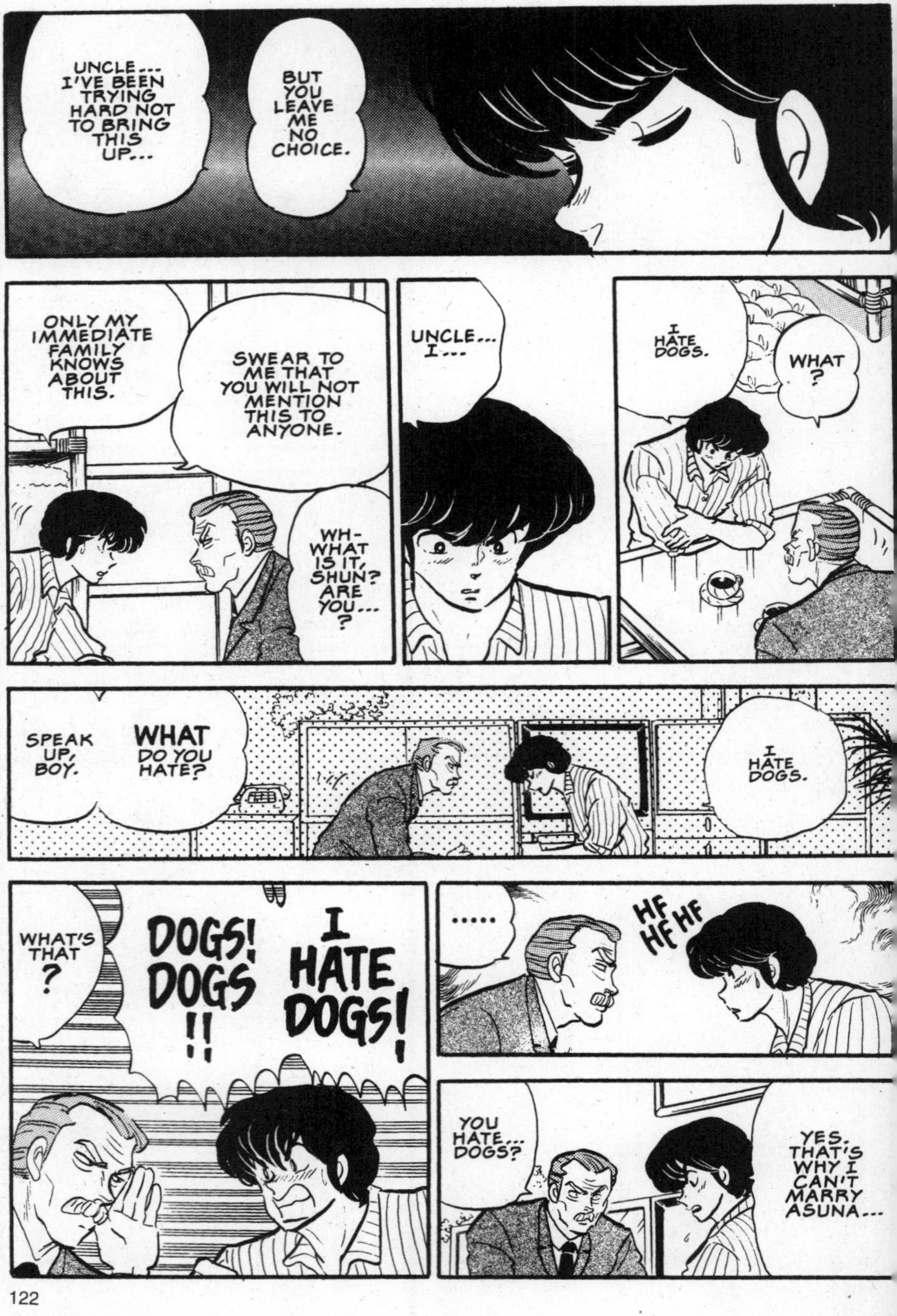
UNCLE... I'VE BEEN TRYING HARD NOT TO BRING THIS UP...
BUT YOU LEAVE ME NO CHOICE.
ONLY MY IMMEDIATE FAMILY KNOWS ABOUT THIS.
SWEAR TO ME THAT YOU WILL NOT MENTION THIS TO ANYONE.
WH-WHAT IS IT, SHUN? ARE YOU...?
UNCLE... I...
I HATE DOGS.
WHAT?
SPEAK UP, BOY.
WHAT DO YOU HATE?
I HATE DOGS.
WHAT'S THAT?
DOGS! DOGS!!
I HATE DOGS!
.....
HF HF HF
YOU HATE... DOGS?
YES. THAT'S WHY I CAN'T MARRY ASUNA...

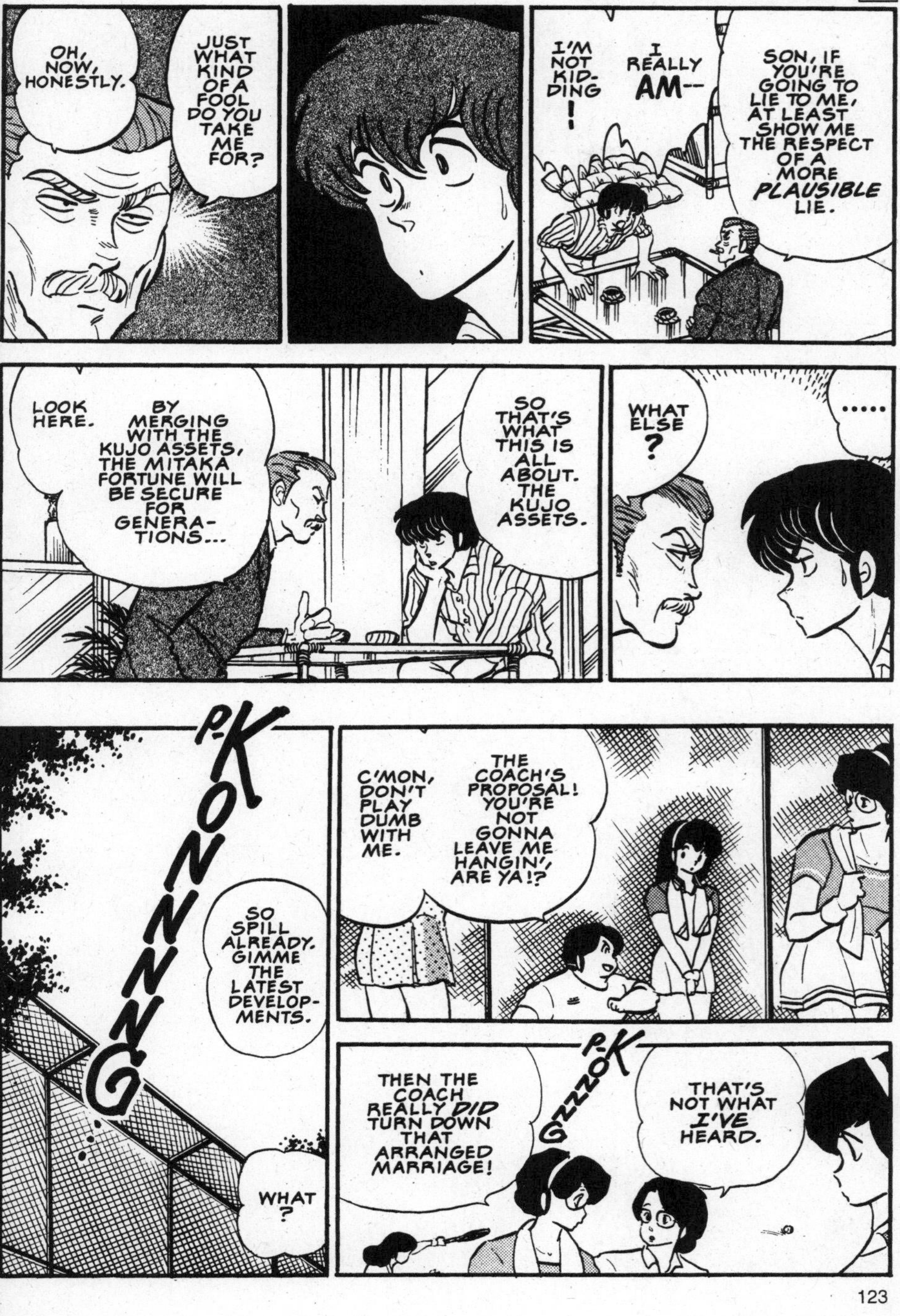
OH, NOW, HONESTLY.
JUST WHAT KIND OF A FOOL DO YOU TAKE ME FOR?
I'M NOT KID-DING!
I REALLY AM--
SON, IF YOU'RE GOING TO LIE TO ME, AT LEAST SHOW ME THE RESPECT OF A MORE *PLAUSIBLE* LIE.
LOOK HERE.
BY MERGING WITH THE KUJO ASSETS, THE MITAKA FORTUNE WILL BE SECURE FOR GENERA-TIONS...
SO THAT'S WHAT THIS IS ALL ABOUT. THE KUJO ASSETS.
WHAT ELSE?
.....
P-KONNNNG
SO SPILL ALREADY. GIMME THE LATEST DEVELOP-MENTS.
WHAT?
C'MON, DON'T PLAY DUMB WITH ME.
THE COACH'S PROPOSAL! YOU'RE NOT GONNA LEAVE ME HANGIN', ARE YA!?
P-K GZZZOK
THEN THE COACH REALLY *DID* TURN DOWN THAT ARRANGED MARRIAGE!
THAT'S NOT WHAT *I'VE* HEARD.

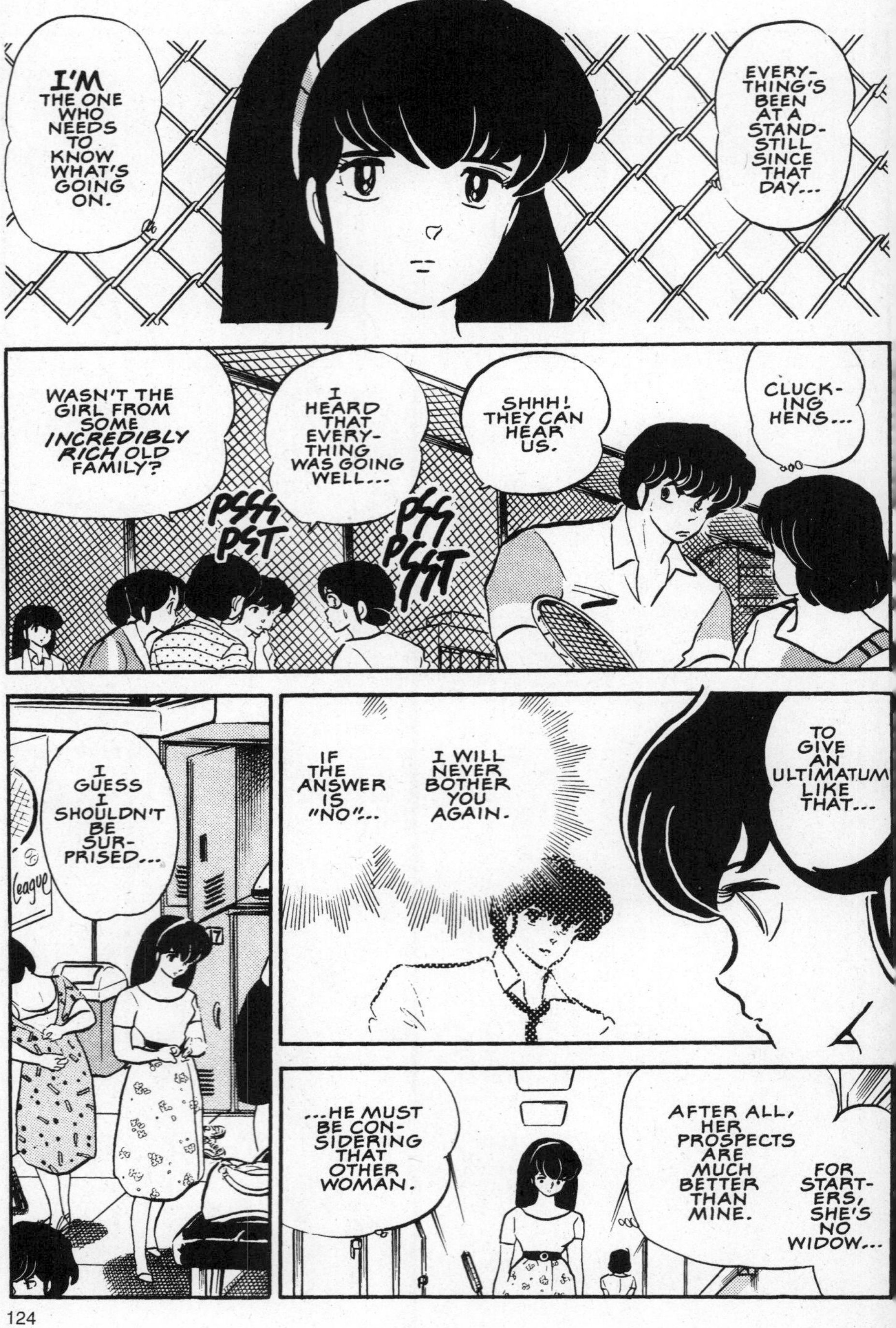
I'M THE ONE WHO NEEDS TO KNOW WHAT'S GOING ON.
EVERYTHING'S BEEN AT A STANDSTILL SINCE THAT DAY...
WASN'T THE GIRL FROM SOME INCREDIBLY RICH OLD FAMILY?
PSSS PST
I HEARD THAT EVERYTHING WAS GOING WELL...
PSS PSST
SHHH! THEY CAN HEAR US.
CLUCKING HENS...
I GUESS I SHOULDN'T BE SURPRISED...
League
IF THE ANSWER IS "NO"...
I WILL NEVER BOTHER YOU AGAIN.
TO GIVE AN ULTIMATUM LIKE THAT...
...HE MUST BE CONSIDERING THAT OTHER WOMAN.
AFTER ALL, HER PROSPECTS ARE MUCH BETTER THAN MINE.
FOR STARTERS, SHE'S NO WIDOW...

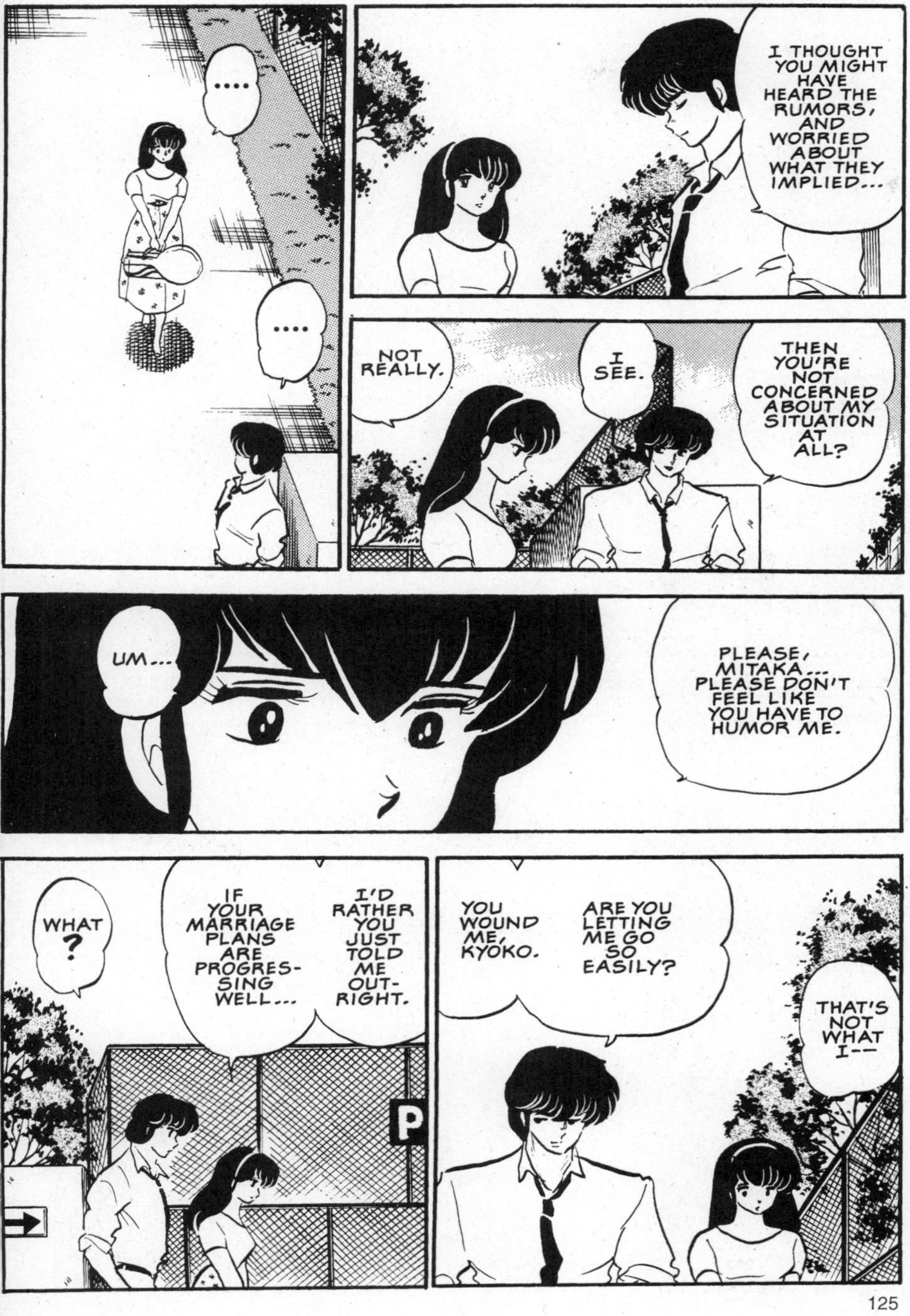
.....
.....
I THOUGHT YOU MIGHT HAVE HEARD THE RUMORS, AND WORRIED ABOUT WHAT THEY IMPLIED...
NOT REALLY.
I SEE.
THEN YOU'RE NOT CONCERNED ABOUT MY SITUATION AT ALL?
UM...
PLEASE, MITAKA... PLEASE DON'T FEEL LIKE YOU HAVE TO HUMOR ME.
WHAT?
IF YOUR MARRIAGE PLANS ARE PROGRES-SING WELL...
I'D RATHER YOU JUST TOLD ME OUT-RIGHT.
P
YOU WOUND ME, KYOKO.
ARE YOU LETTING ME GO SO EASILY?
THAT'S NOT WHAT I--

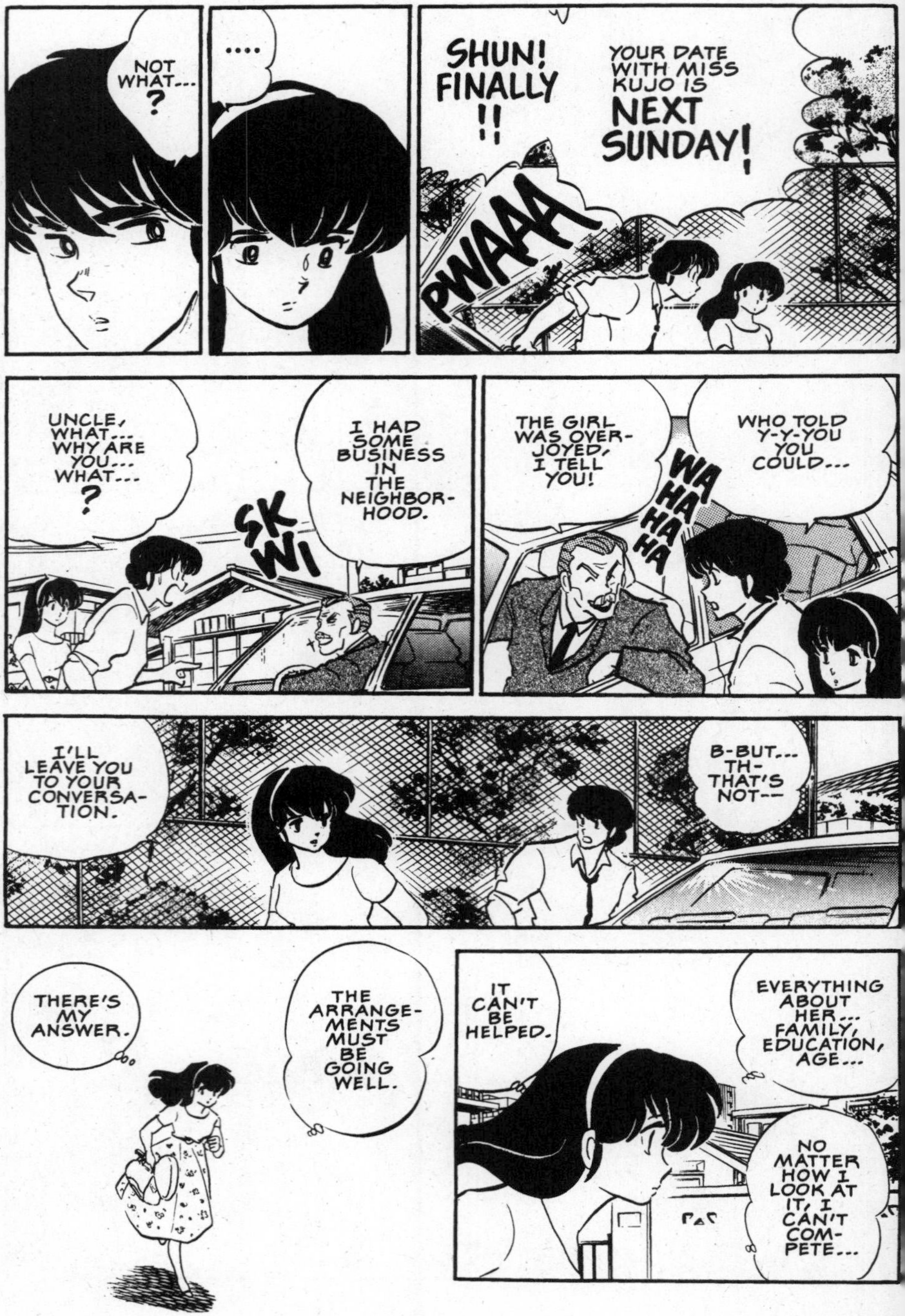
NOT WHAT...?
....
SHUN! FINALLY!!
YOUR DATE WITH MISS KUJO IS NEXT SUNDAY!
PWAAA
UNCLE, WHAT... WHY ARE YOU... WHAT...?
SK WI
I HAD SOME BUSINESS IN THE NEIGHBOR-HOOD.
THE GIRL WAS OVER-JOYED, I TELL YOU!
WA HA HA HA HA
WHO TOLD Y-Y-YOU YOU COULD...
I'LL LEAVE YOU TO YOUR CONVERSA-TION.
B-BUT... TH-THAT'S NOT--
THERE'S MY ANSWER.
THE ARRANGE-MENTS MUST BE GOING WELL.
IT CAN'T BE HELPED.
EVERYTHING ABOUT HER... FAMILY, EDUCATION, AGE...
NO MATTER HOW I LOOK AT IT, I CAN'T COM-PETE...

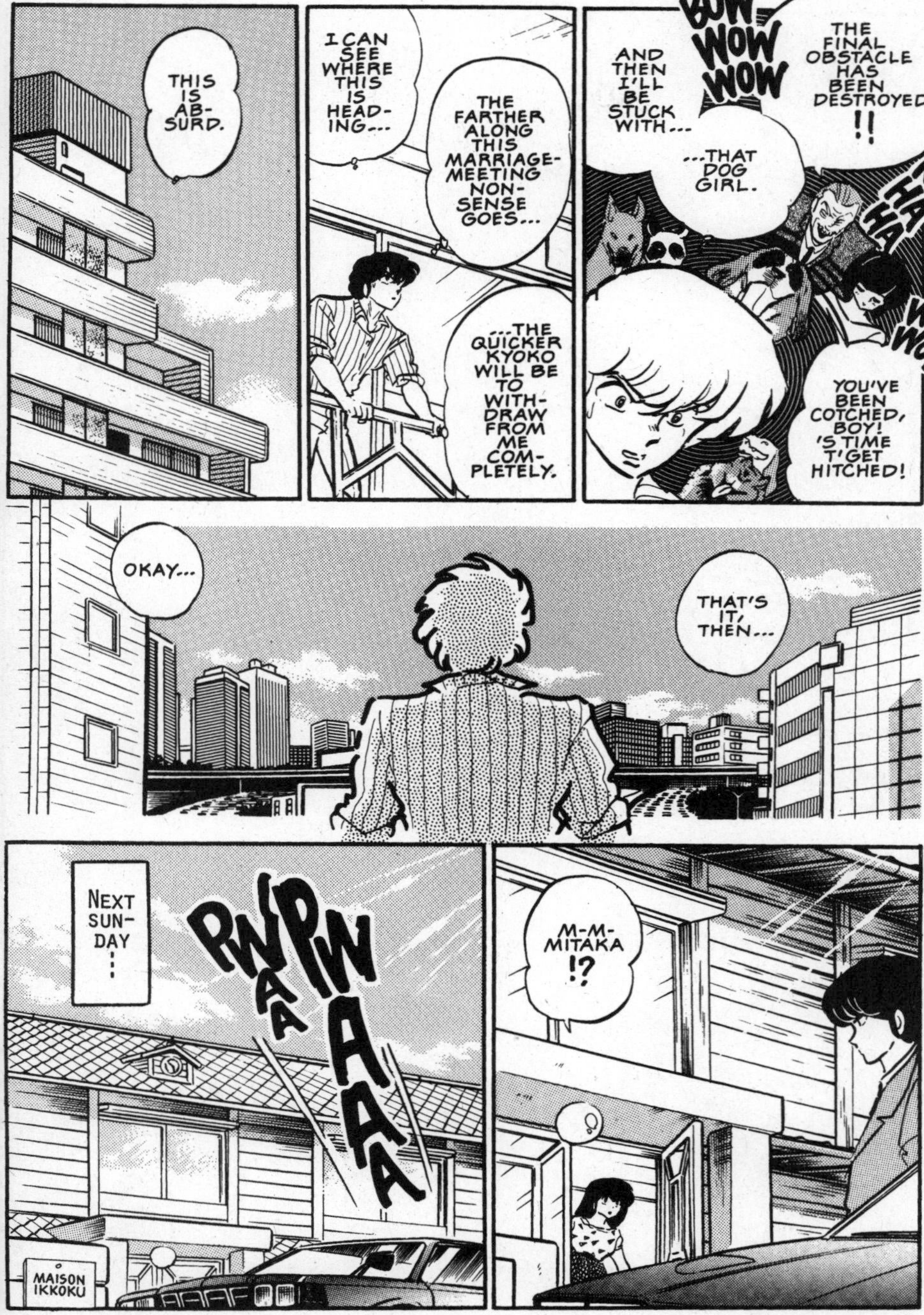

THIS IS AB-SURD.
I CAN SEE WHERE THIS IS HEAD-ING...
THE FARTHER ALONG THIS MARRIAGE-MEETING NON-SENSE GOES...
...THE QUICKER KYOKO WILL BE TO WITH-DRAW FROM ME COM-PLETELY.
AND THEN I'LL BE STUCK WITH...
...THAT DOG GIRL.
BOW WOW WOW
THE FINAL OBSTACLE HAS BEEN DESTROYED !!
NYA HA HA
WOW WOW
YOU'VE BEEN COTCHED, BOY! 'S TIME T'GET HITCHED!
OKAY...
THAT'S IT, THEN...
NEXT SUN-DAY...
PWAA
PWAAAA
MAISON IKKOKU
M-M-MITAKA !?

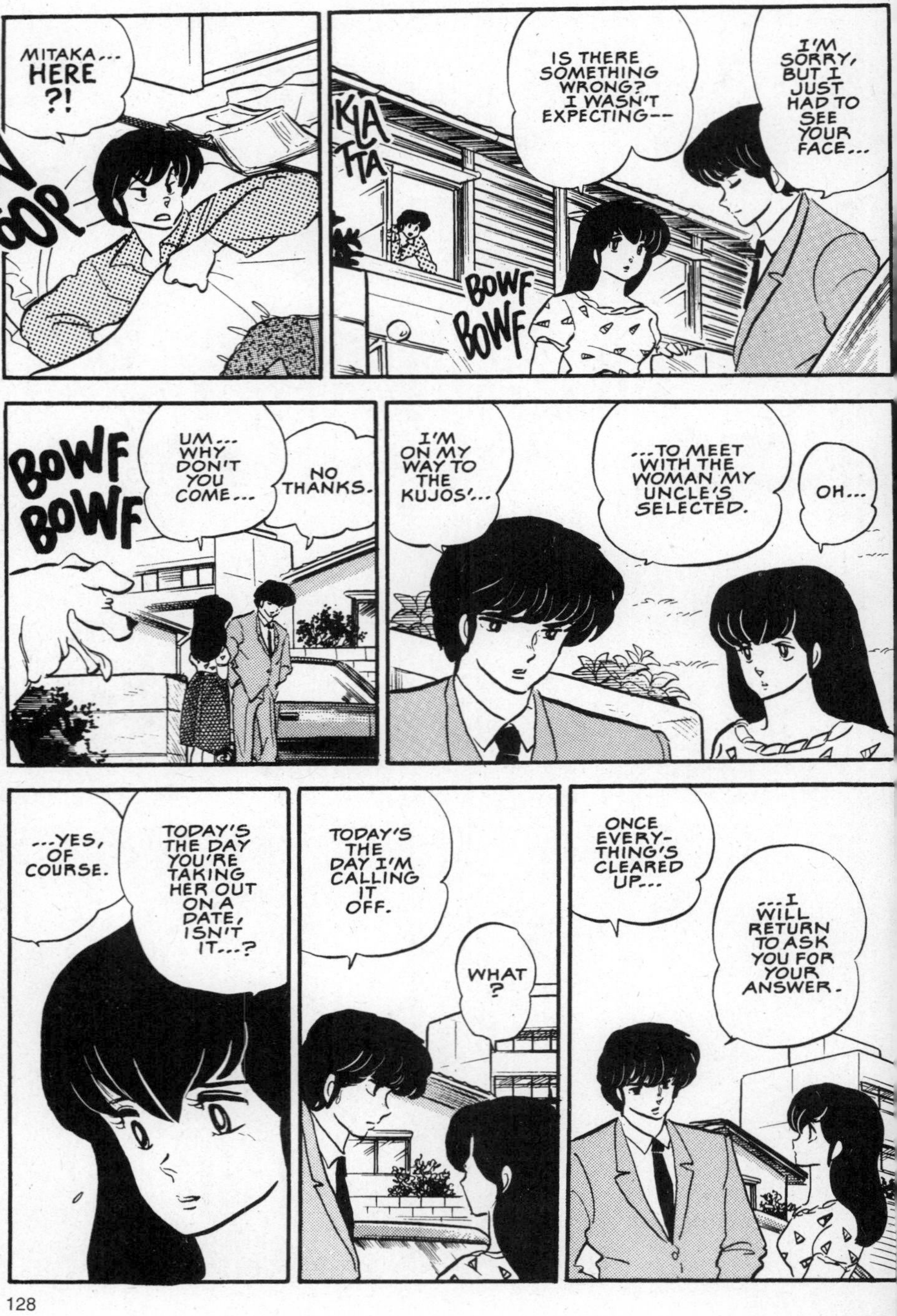

MITAKA... HERE ?!
KLATTA
IS THERE SOMETHING WRONG? I WASN'T EXPECTING--
I'M SORRY, BUT I JUST HAD TO SEE YOUR FACE...
BOWF BOWF
BOWF BOWF
UM... WHY DON'T YOU COME...
NO THANKS.
I'M ON MY WAY TO THE KUJOS'...
...TO MEET WITH THE WOMAN MY UNCLE'S SELECTED.
OH...
...YES, OF COURSE.
TODAY'S THE DAY YOU'RE TAKING HER OUT ON A DATE, ISN'T IT...?
TODAY'S THE DAY I'M CALLING IT OFF.
WHAT ?
ONCE EVERY-THING'S CLEARED UP...
...I WILL RETURN TO ASK YOU FOR YOUR ANSWER.

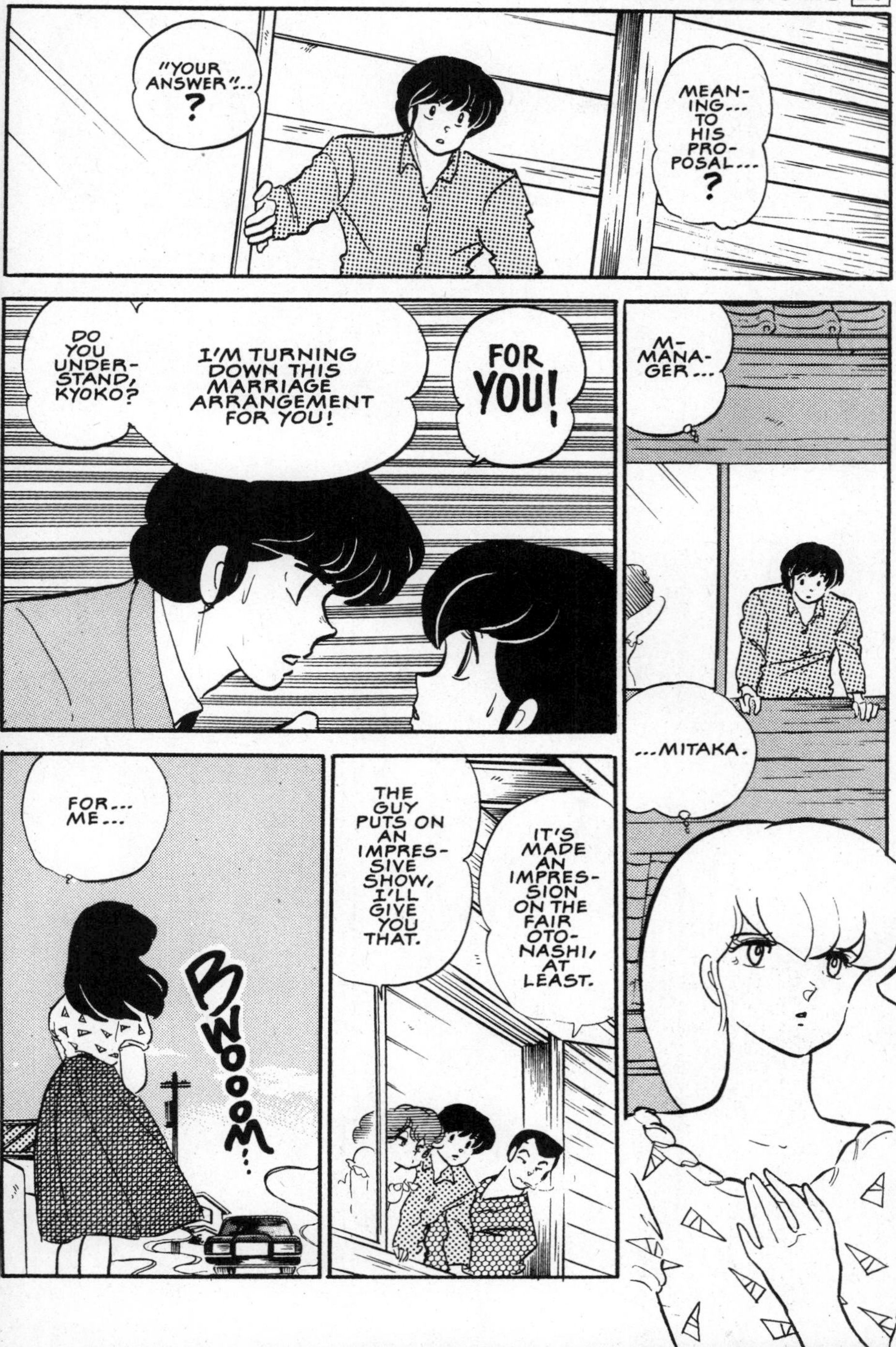
"YOUR ANSWER"... ?
MEANING... TO HIS PROPOSAL... ?
DO YOU UNDERSTAND, KYOKO?
I'M TURNING DOWN THIS MARRIAGE ARRANGEMENT FOR YOU!
FOR YOU!
M-MANAGER...
...MITAKA.
FOR... ME...
BWOOOOM..
THE GUY PUTS ON AN IMPRESSIVE SHOW, I'LL GIVE YOU THAT.
IT'S MADE AN IMPRESSION ON THE FAIR OTONASHI, AT LEAST.

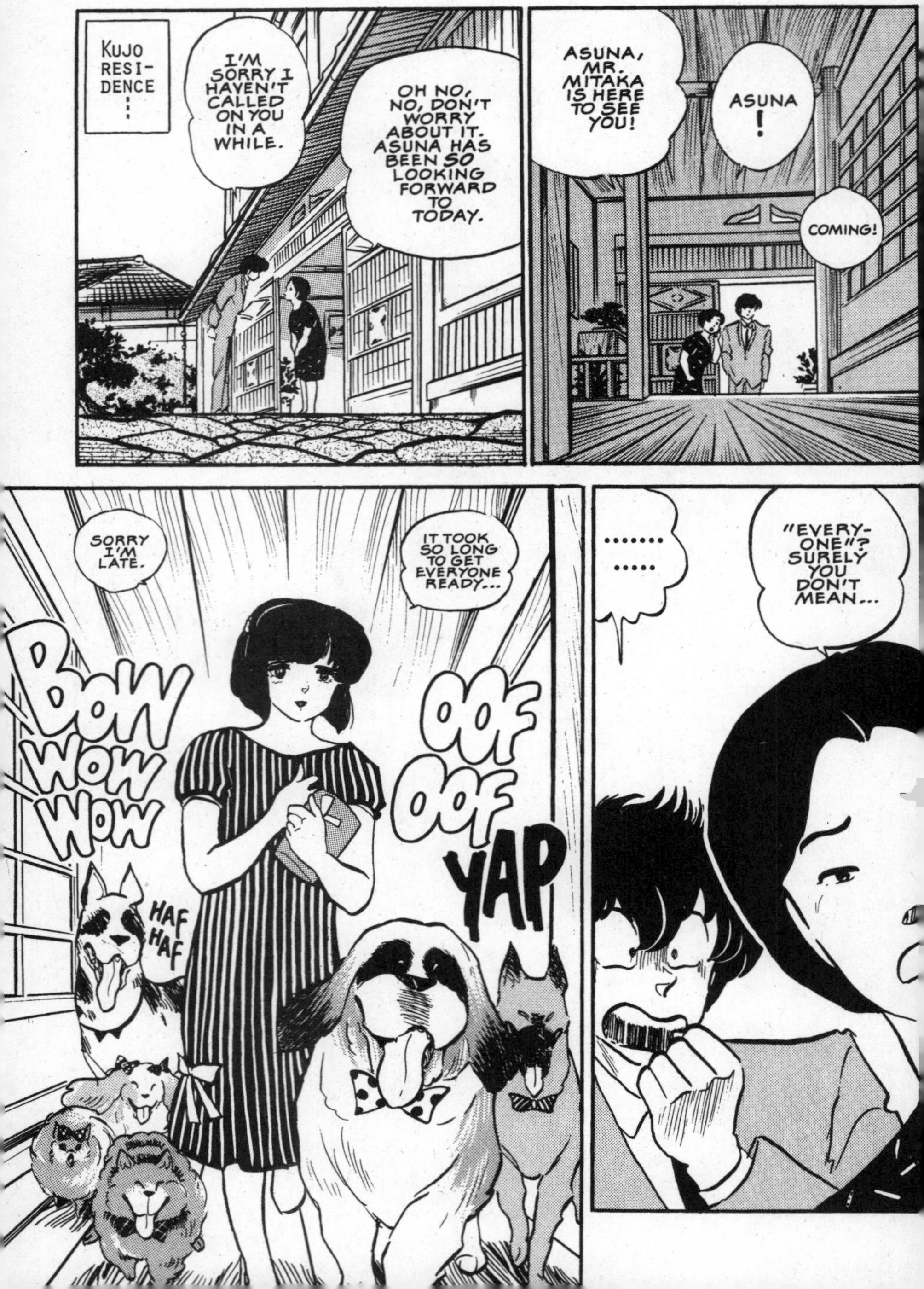
KUJO RESI-DENCE...
I'M SORRY I HAVEN'T CALLED ON YOU IN A WHILE.
OH NO, NO, DON'T WORRY ABOUT IT. ASUNA HAS BEEN SO LOOKING FORWARD TO TODAY.
ASUNA, MR. MITAKA IS HERE TO SEE YOU!
ASUNA!
COMING!
SORRY I'M LATE.
IT TOOK SO LONG TO GET EVERYONE READY...
BOW WOW WOW
OOF OOF
YAP
HAF HAF
....
.....
"EVERY-ONE"? SURELY YOU DON'T MEAN...

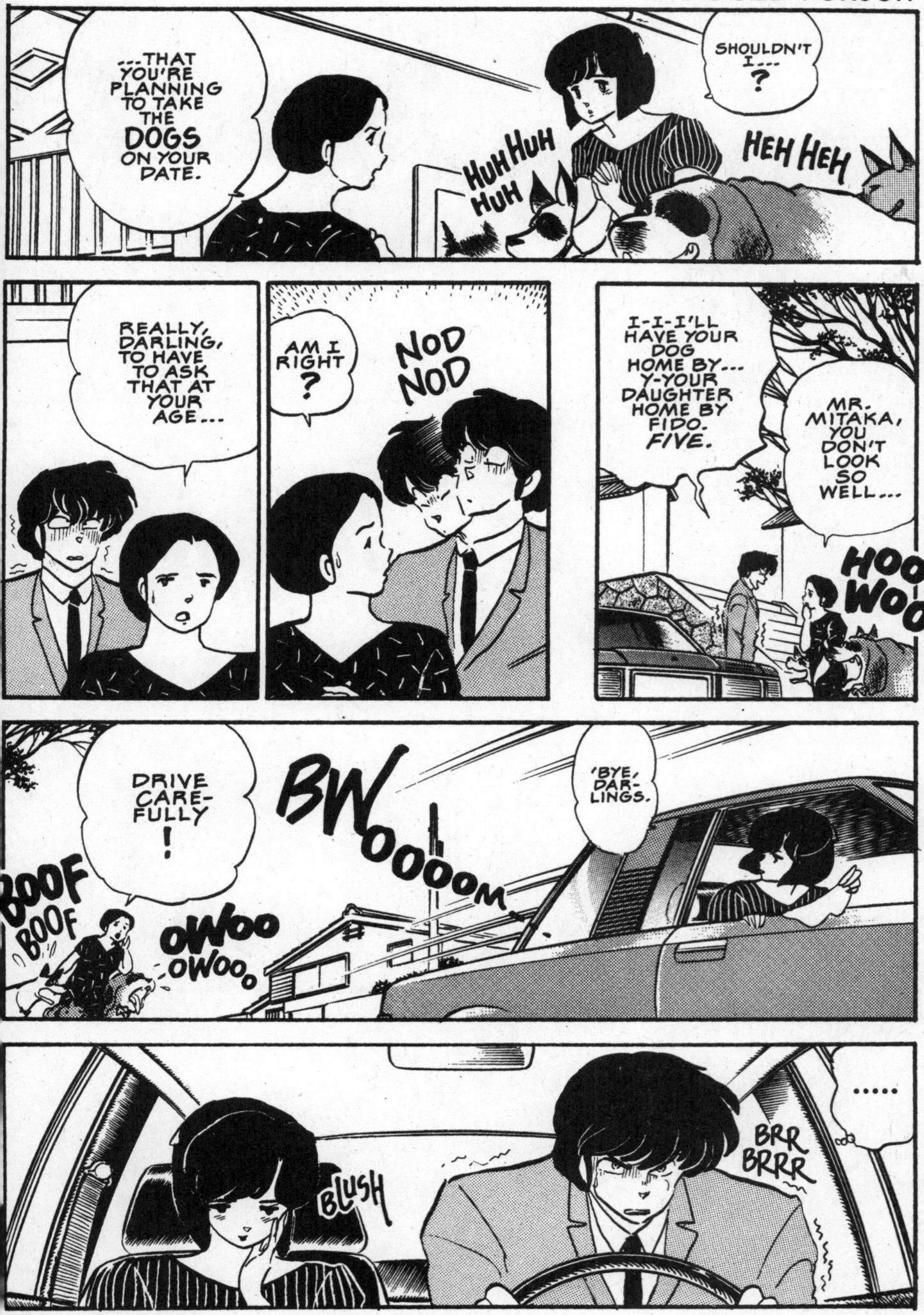
...THAT YOU'RE PLANNING TO TAKE THE DOGS ON YOUR DATE.
HUH HUH HUH
SHOULDN'T I...?
HEH HEH
REALLY, DARLING, TO HAVE TO ASK THAT AT YOUR AGE...
AM I RIGHT?
NOD NOD
I-I-I'LL HAVE YOUR DOG HOME BY... Y-YOUR DAUGHTER HOME BY FIDO. FIVE.
MR. MITAKA, YOU DON'T LOOK SO WELL...
HOO WOO
DRIVE CAREFULLY!
BOOF BOOF
OWOO OWOOO
BWOOOOOM
'BYE, DARLINGS.
BLUSH
BRR BRRR
.....

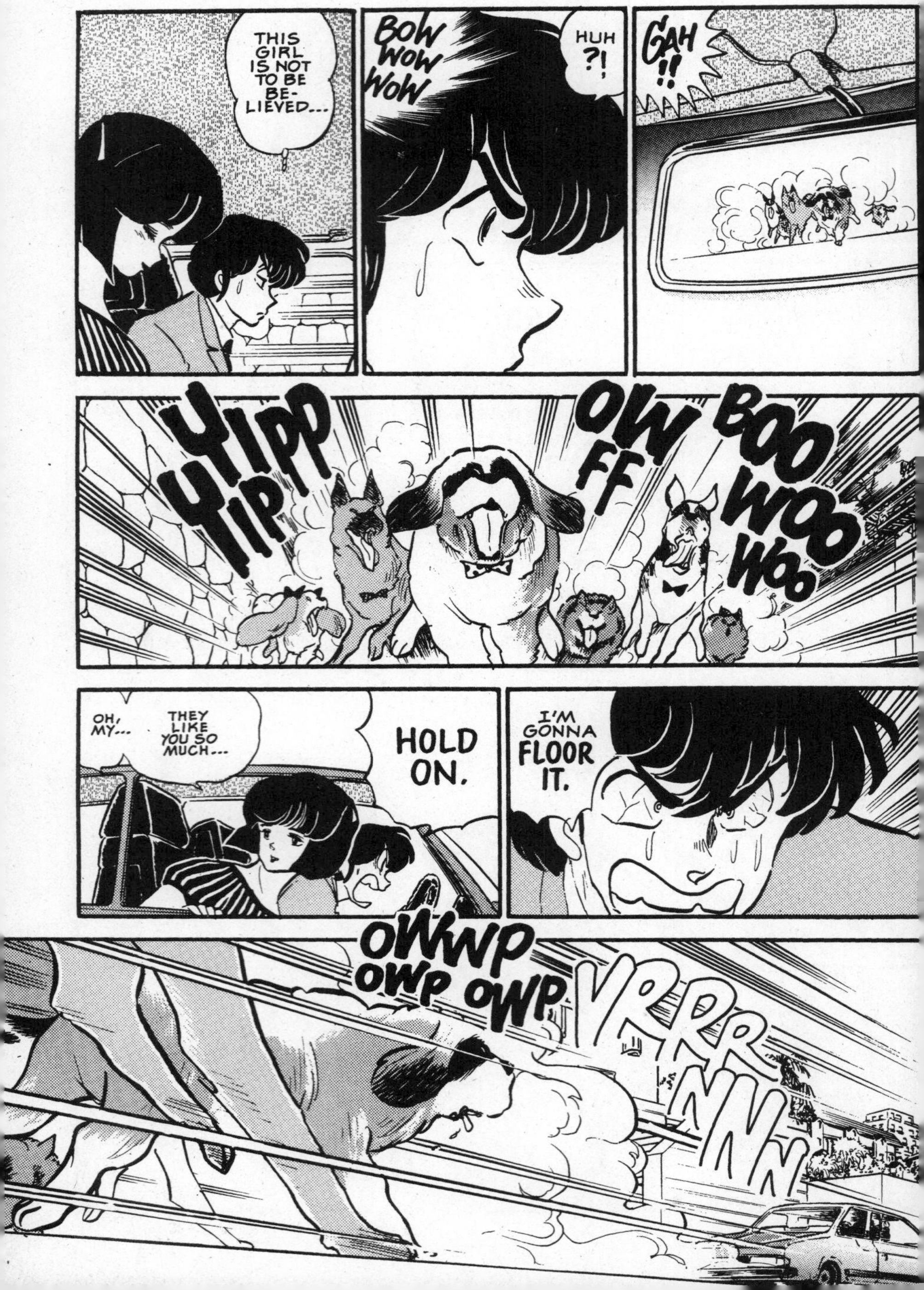

THIS GIRL IS NOT TO BE BE-LIEVED...
BOW WOW WOW
HUH ?!
GAH !!
YIPP YIP
OW FF
BOO WOO WOO
OH, MY...
THEY LIKE YOU SO MUCH...
HOLD ON.
I'M GONNA FLOOR IT.
OWWP OWP OWP
VRRRNNN

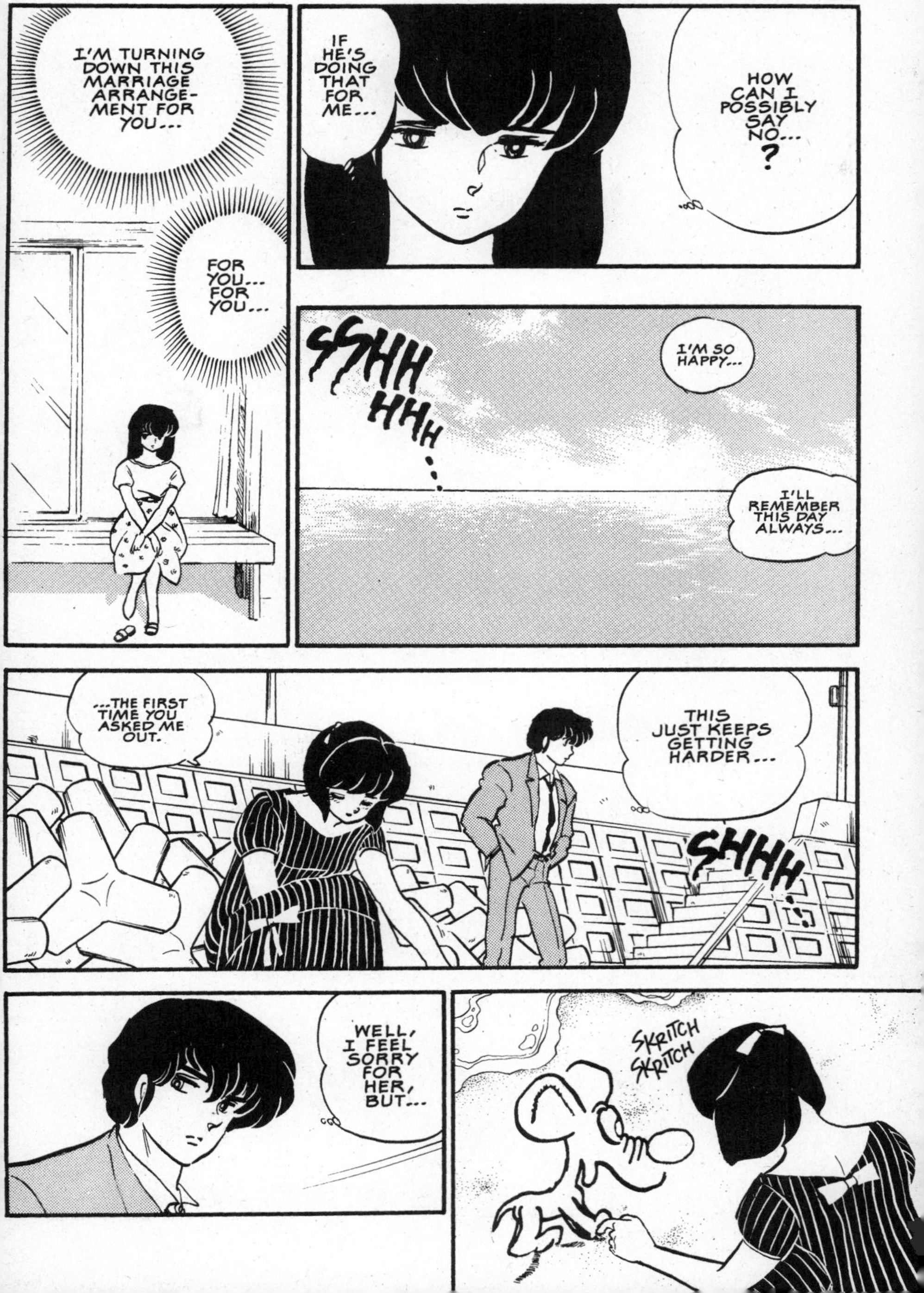
I'M TURNING DOWN THIS MARRIAGE ARRANGE-MENT FOR YOU...
FOR YOU... FOR YOU...
IF HE'S DOING THAT FOR ME...
HOW CAN I POSSIBLY SAY NO...?
SSHH HHH...
I'M SO HAPPY...
I'LL REMEMBER THIS DAY ALWAYS...
...THE FIRST TIME YOU ASKED ME OUT.
THIS JUST KEEPS GETTING HARDER...
SHHH...
WELL, I FEEL SORRY FOR HER, BUT...
SKRITCH SKRITCH

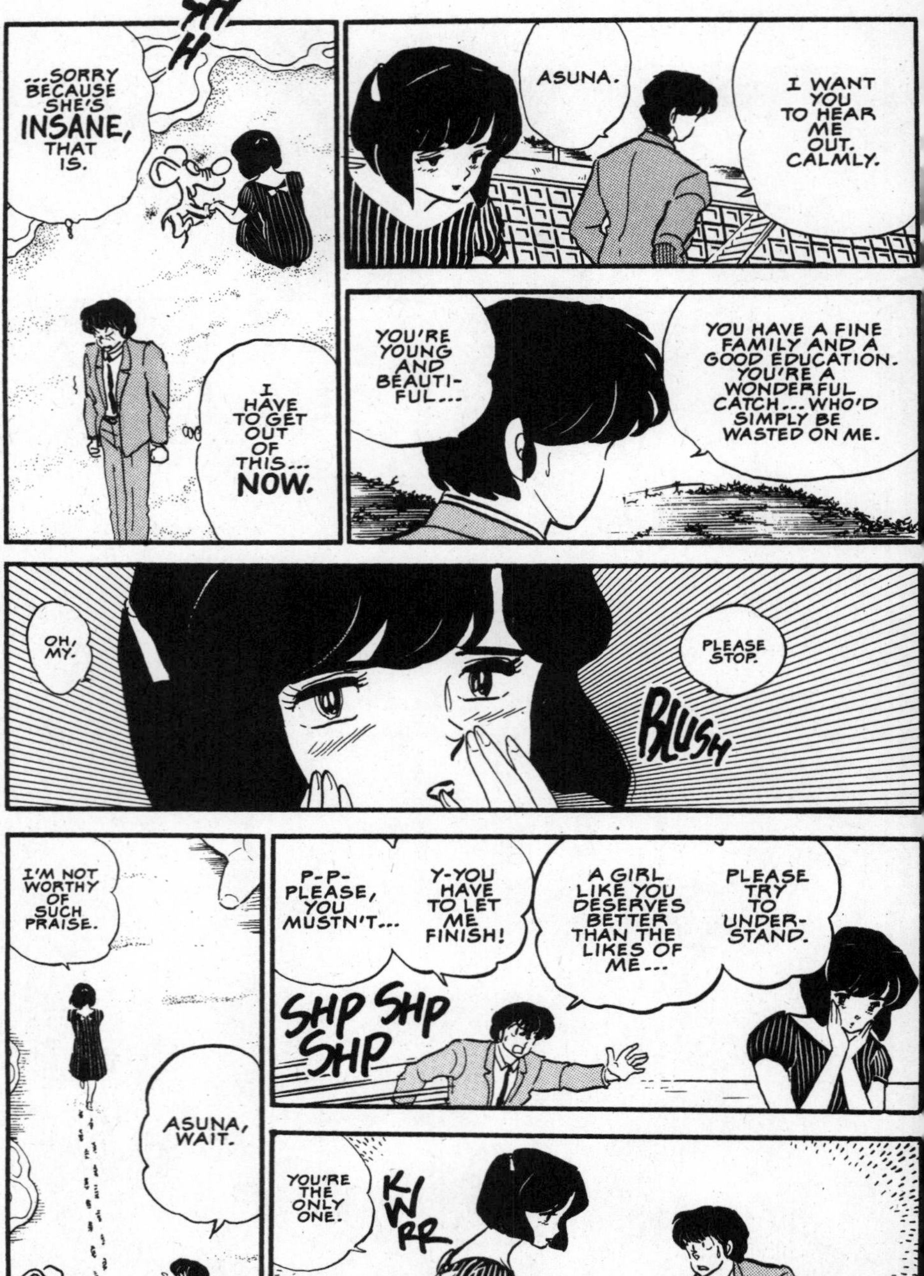
SH H
...SORRY BECAUSE SHE'S INSANE, THAT IS.
I HAVE TO GET OUT OF THIS... NOW.
ASUNA.
I WANT YOU TO HEAR ME OUT. CALMLY.
YOU'RE YOUNG AND BEAUTIFUL...
YOU HAVE A FINE FAMILY AND A GOOD EDUCATION. YOU'RE A WONDERFUL CATCH... WHO'D SIMPLY BE WASTED ON ME.
OH, MY.
PLEASE STOP.
BLUSH
I'M NOT WORTHY OF SUCH PRAISE.
ASUNA, WAIT.
P-P-PLEASE, YOU MUSTN'T...
Y-YOU HAVE TO LET ME FINISH!
A GIRL LIKE YOU DESERVES BETTER THAN THE LIKES OF ME...
PLEASE TRY TO UNDER-STAND.
SHP SHP SHP
YOU'RE THE ONLY ONE.
KWRR

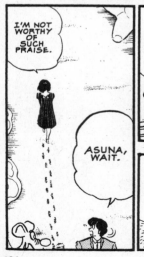

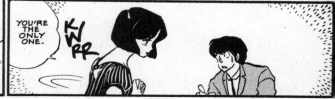

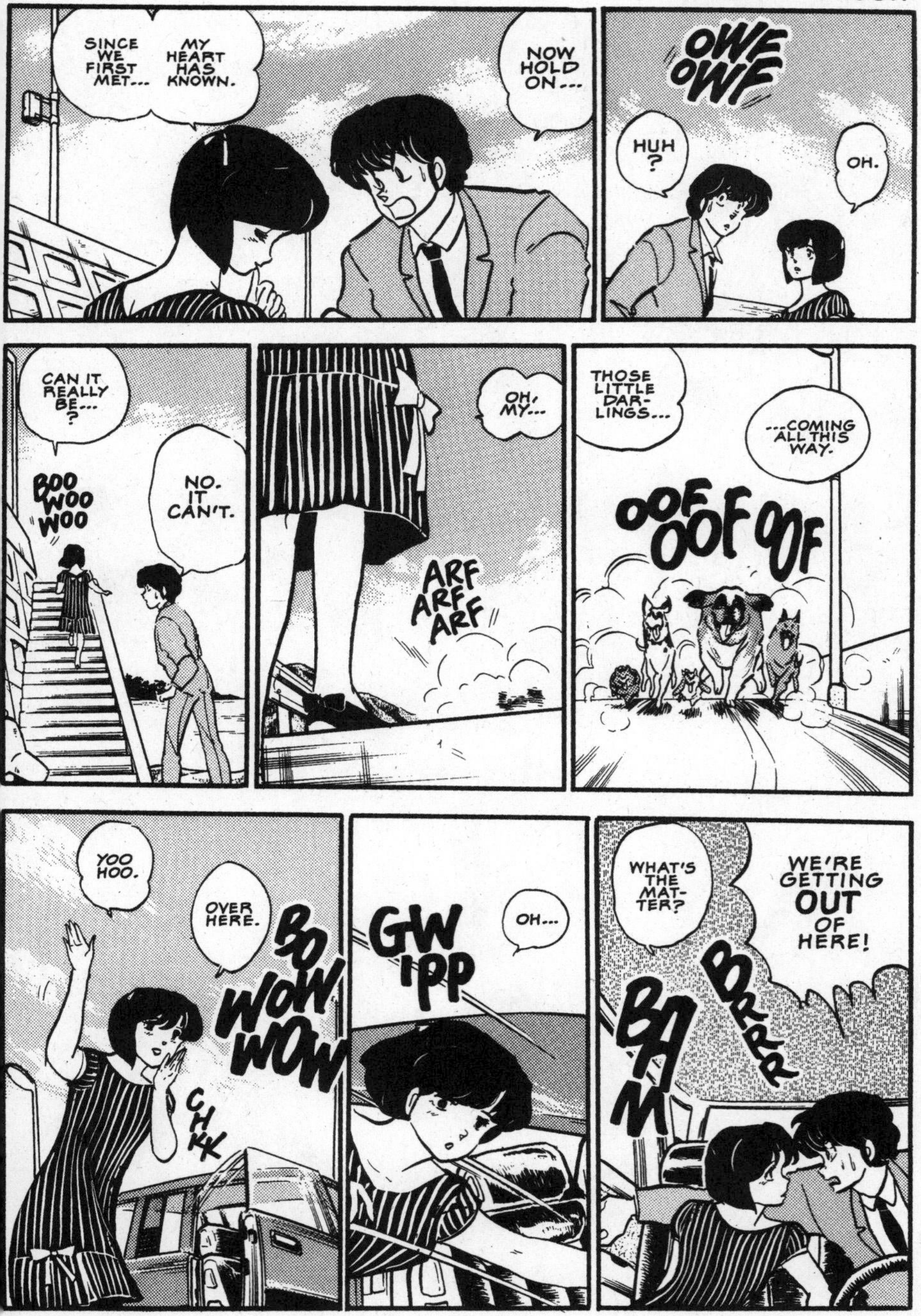
SINCE WE FIRST MET... MY HEART HAS KNOWN.
NOW HOLD ON...
OWF OWF
HUH?
OH.
CAN IT REALLY BE...?
BOO WOO WOO
NO. IT CAN'T.
OH, MY...
ARF ARF ARF
THOSE LITTLE DAR-LINGS...
...COMING ALL THIS WAY.
OOF OOF OOF
YOO HOO.
OVER HERE.
BO WOW WOW WOW
CHKK
GW IPP
OH...
WHAT'S THE MAT-TER?
WE'RE GETTING OUT OF HERE!
BAM
BDRRR

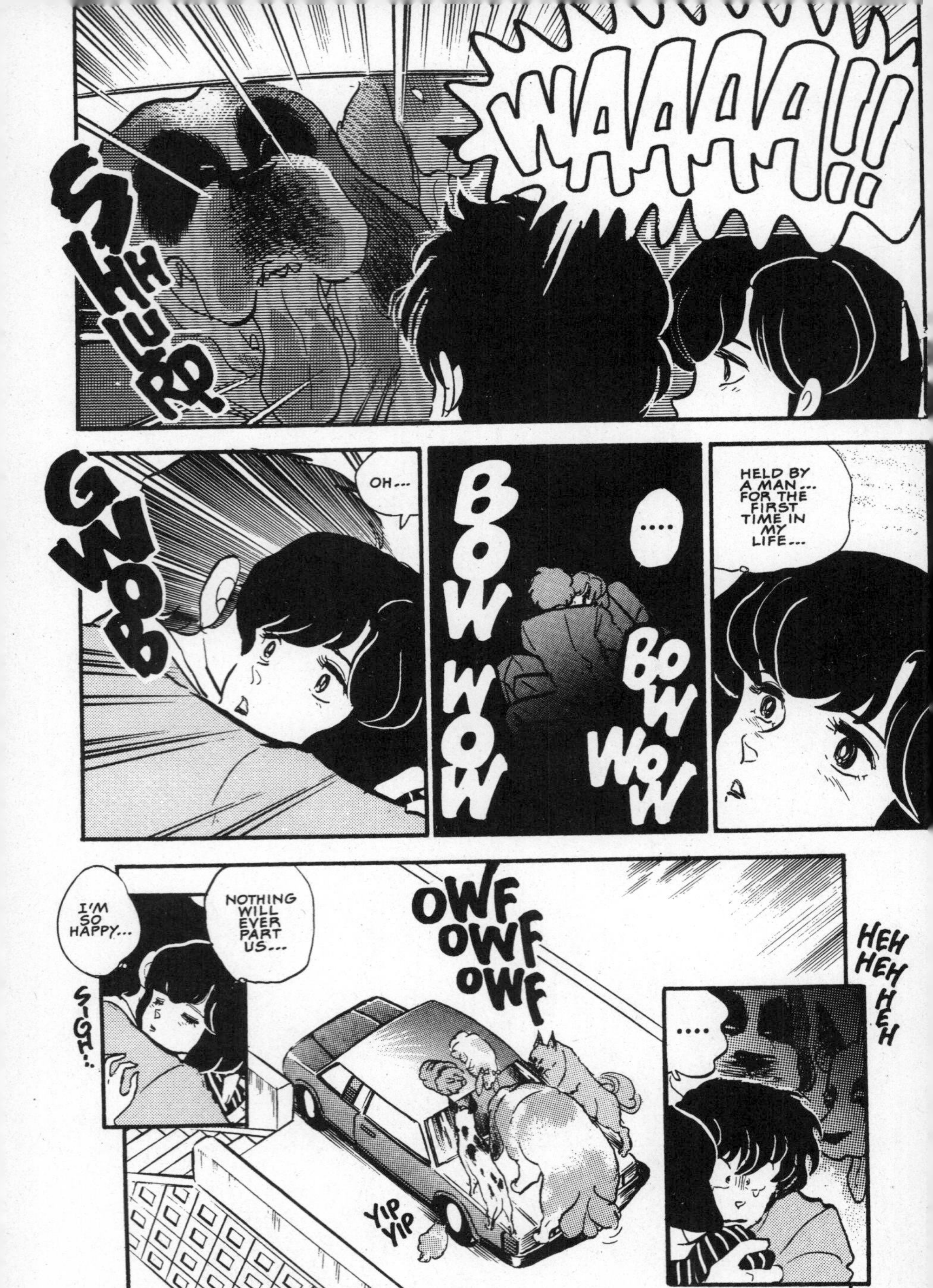
SHHLURP
WAAAA!!
GWOBB
OH...
BOW WOW WOW
.....
BOW WOW WOW
HELD BY A MAN... FOR THE FIRST TIME IN MY LIFE...
SIGH..
I'M SO HAPPY...
NOTHING WILL EVER PART US...
OWF OWF OWF
YIP YIP
.....
HEH HEH HEH HEH

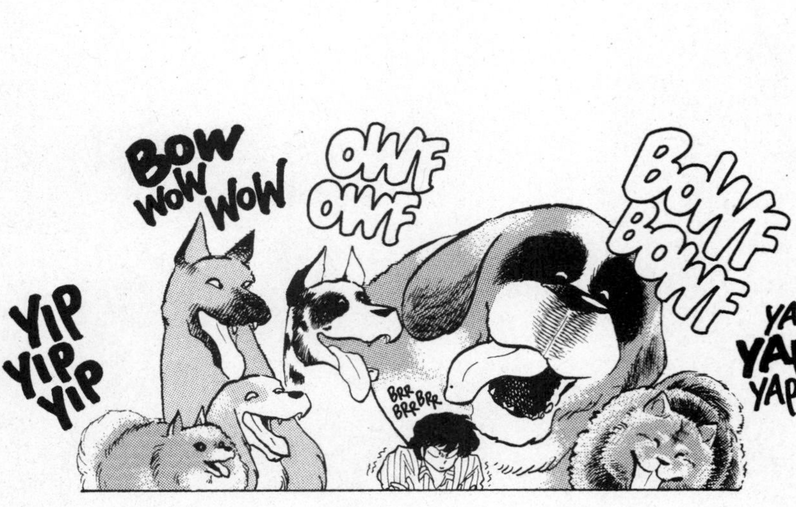

BOW WOW WOW
OWF OWF
BOWF BOWF
YIP YIP YIP
YAP YAP YAP
BRR BRR BRR

PART 7
THE DOOR'S STILL OPEN

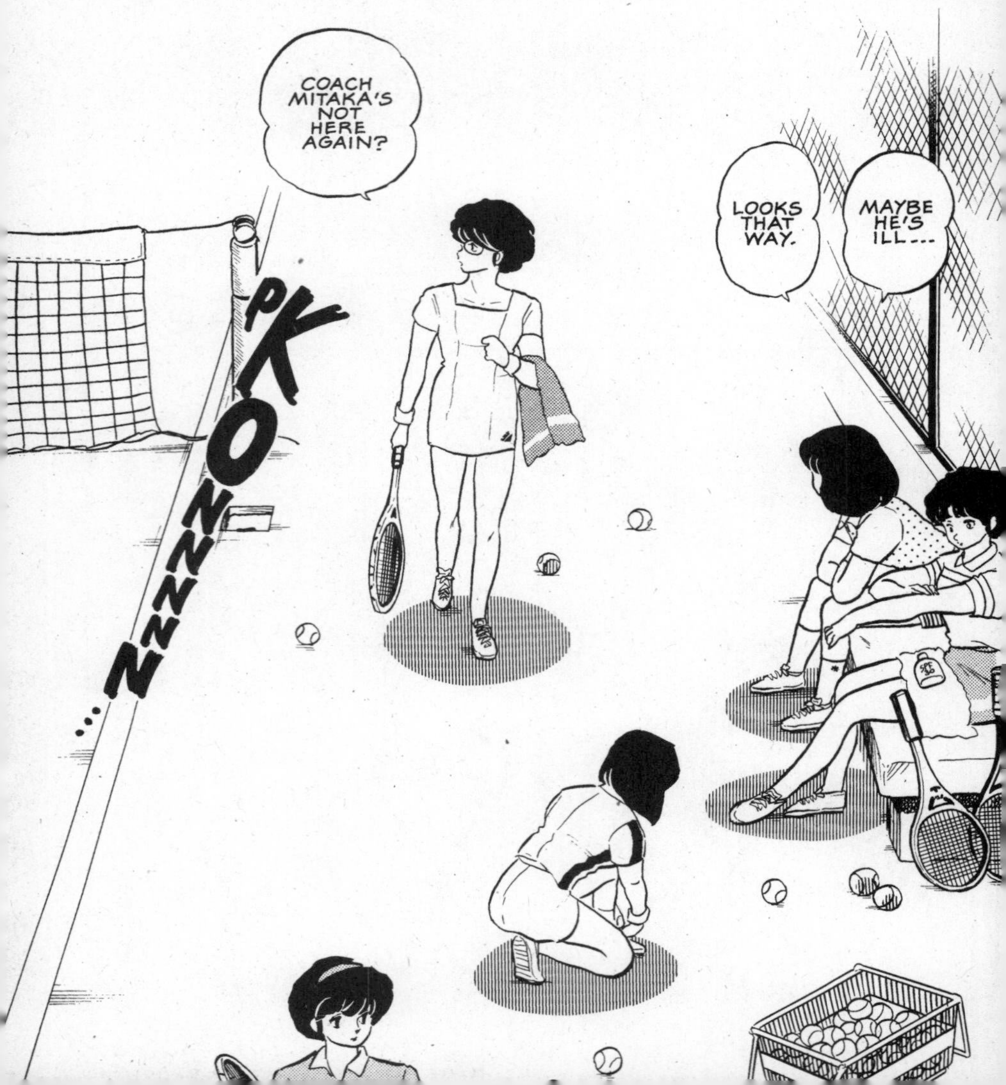

COACH MITAKA'S NOT HERE AGAIN?
LOOKS THAT WAY.
MAYBE HE'S ILL...
PKONNNNN...

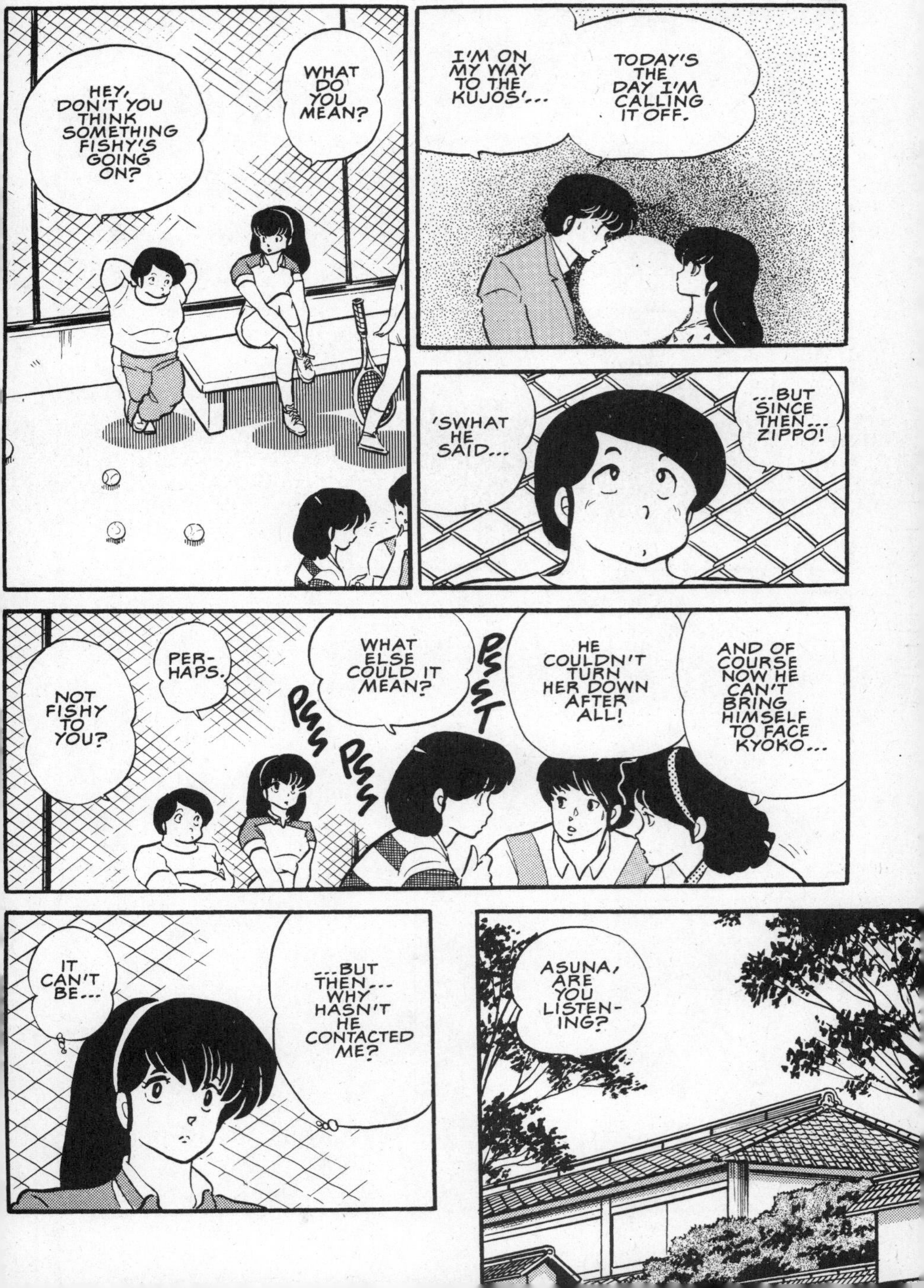
HEY, DON'T YOU THINK SOMETHING FISHY'S GOING ON?
WHAT DO YOU MEAN?
I'M ON MY WAY TO THE KUJOS'...
TODAY'S THE DAY I'M CALLING IT OFF.
'SWHAT HE SAID...
...BUT SINCE THEN... ZIPPO!
NOT FISHY TO YOU?
PER-HAPS.
WHAT ELSE COULD IT MEAN?
PSST
PSS PSS
HE COULDN'T TURN HER DOWN AFTER ALL!
AND OF COURSE NOW HE CAN'T BRING HIMSELF TO FACE KYOKO...
IT CAN'T BE...
...BUT THEN... WHY HASN'T HE CONTACTED ME?
ASUNA, ARE YOU LISTEN-ING?

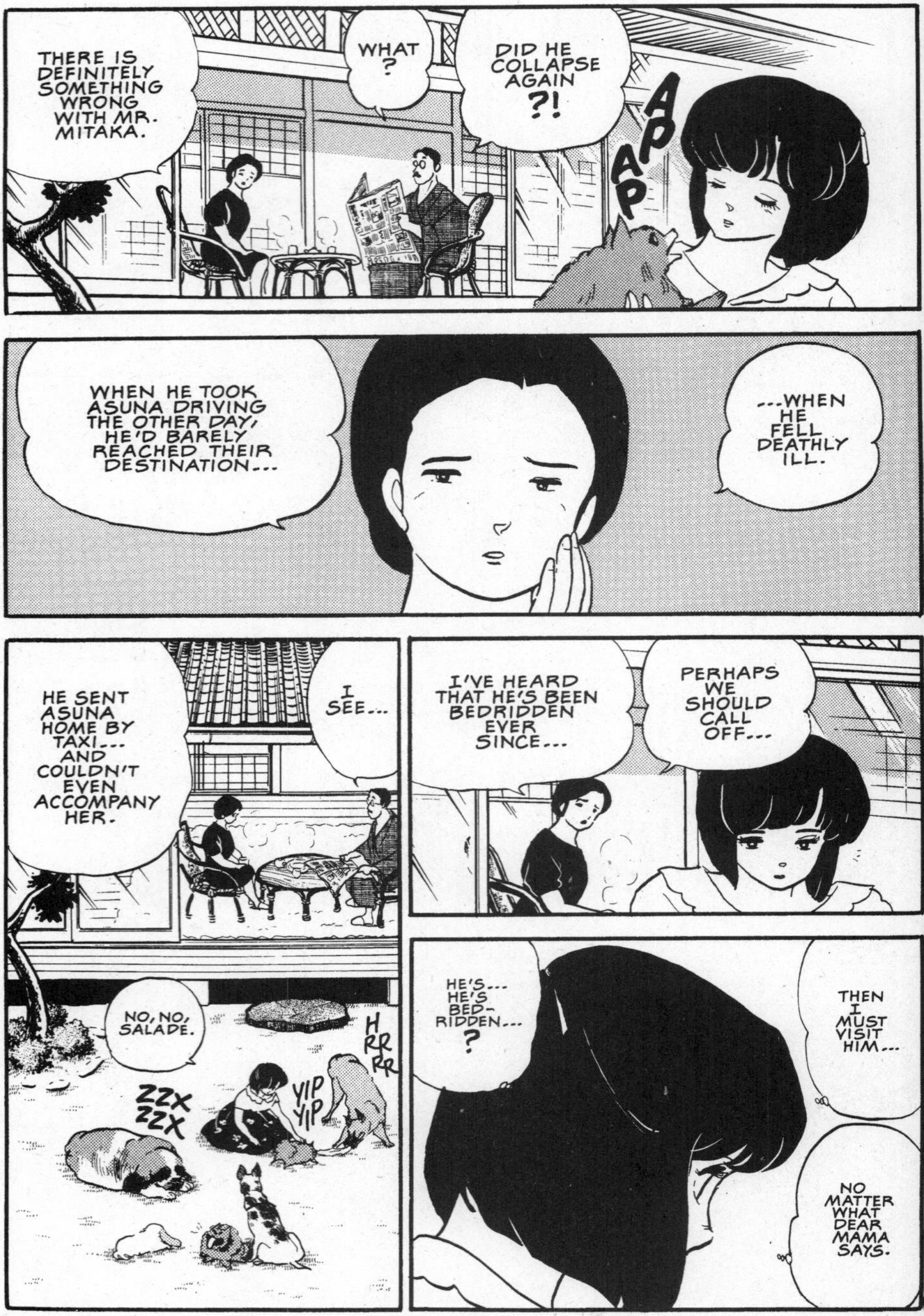
THERE IS DEFINITELY SOMETHING WRONG WITH MR. MITAKA.
WHAT?
DID HE COLLAPSE AGAIN?!
AP AP AP
WHEN HE TOOK ASUNA DRIVING THE OTHER DAY, HE'D BARELY REACHED THEIR DESTINATION...
---WHEN HE FELL DEATHLY ILL.
HE SENT ASUNA HOME BY TAXI... AND COULDN'T EVEN ACCOMPANY HER.
I SEE...
NO, NO, SALADE.
HRRRR
ZZX ZZX
YIP YIP
I'VE HEARD THAT HE'S BEEN BEDRIDDEN EVER SINCE...
PERHAPS WE SHOULD CALL OFF...
HE'S... HE'S BED-RIDDEN...?
THEN I MUST VISIT HIM...
NO MATTER WHAT DEAR MAMA SAYS.

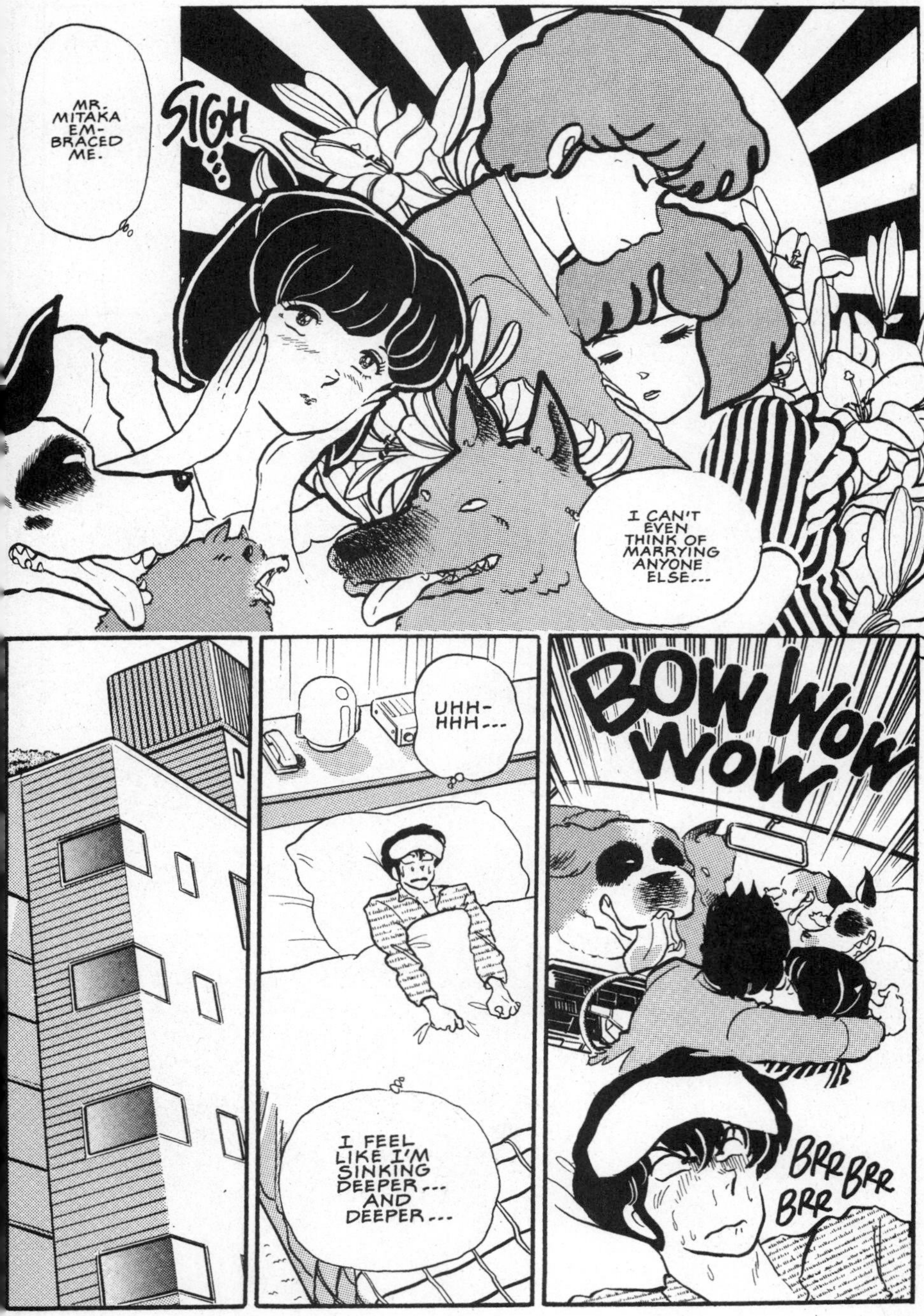
MR. MITAKA EM-BRACED ME.
SIGH...
I CAN'T EVEN THINK OF MARRYING ANYONE ELSE...
UHH-HHH...
I FEEL LIKE I'M SINKING DEEPER... AND DEEPER...
BOW WOW WOW
BRR BRR BRR

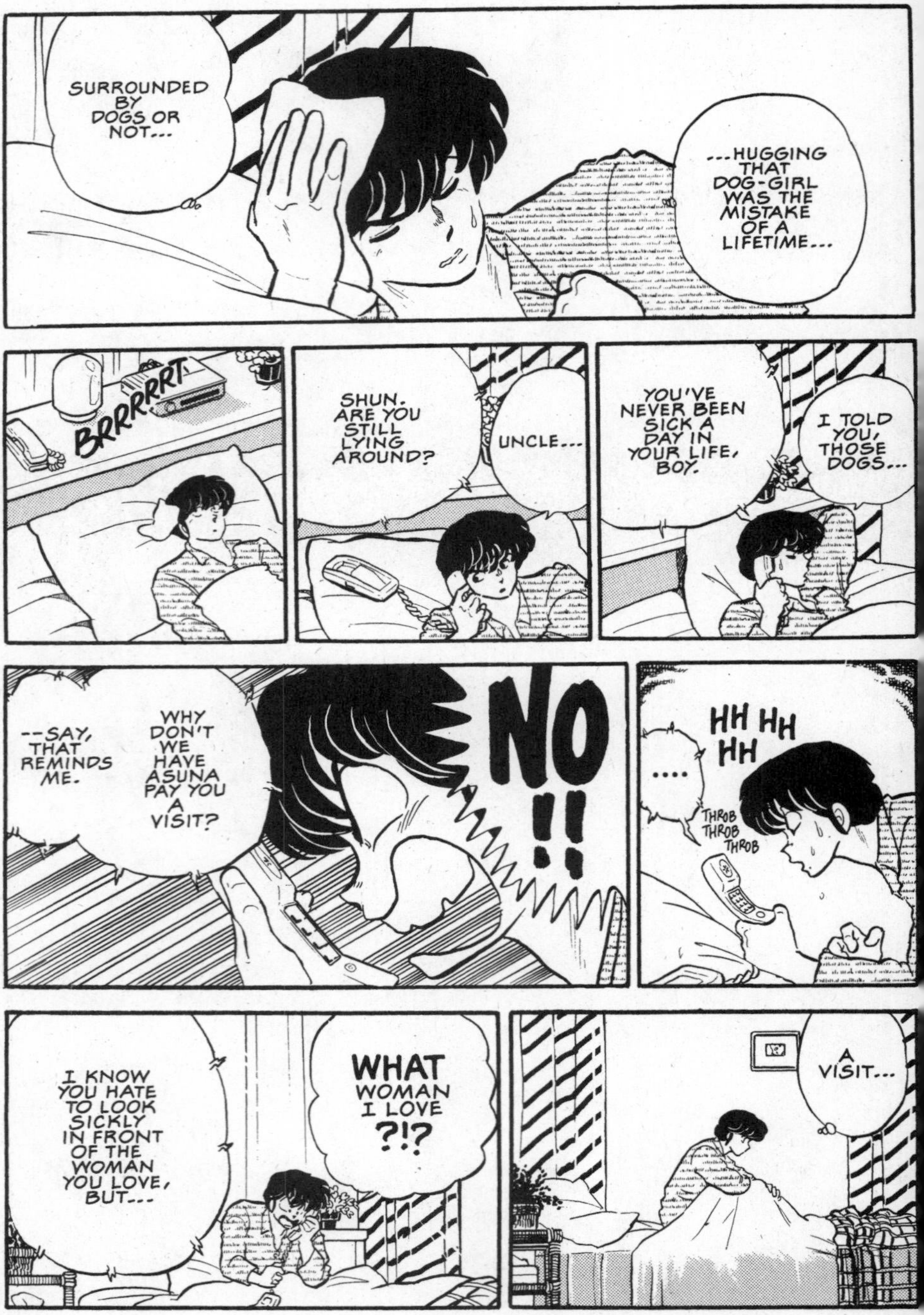
SURROUNDED BY DOGS OR NOT...
...HUGGING THAT DOG-GIRL WAS THE MISTAKE OF A LIFETIME...
BRRRRRT
SHUN. ARE YOU STILL LYING AROUND?
UNCLE...
YOU'VE NEVER BEEN SICK A DAY IN YOUR LIFE, BOY.
I TOLD YOU, THOSE DOGS...
--SAY, THAT REMINDS ME.
WHY DON'T WE HAVE ASUNA PAY YOU A VISIT?
NO!!
....
HH HH HH
THROB THROB THROB
I KNOW YOU HATE TO LOOK SICKLY IN FRONT OF THE WOMAN YOU LOVE, BUT...
WHAT WOMAN I LOVE ?!?
A VISIT...

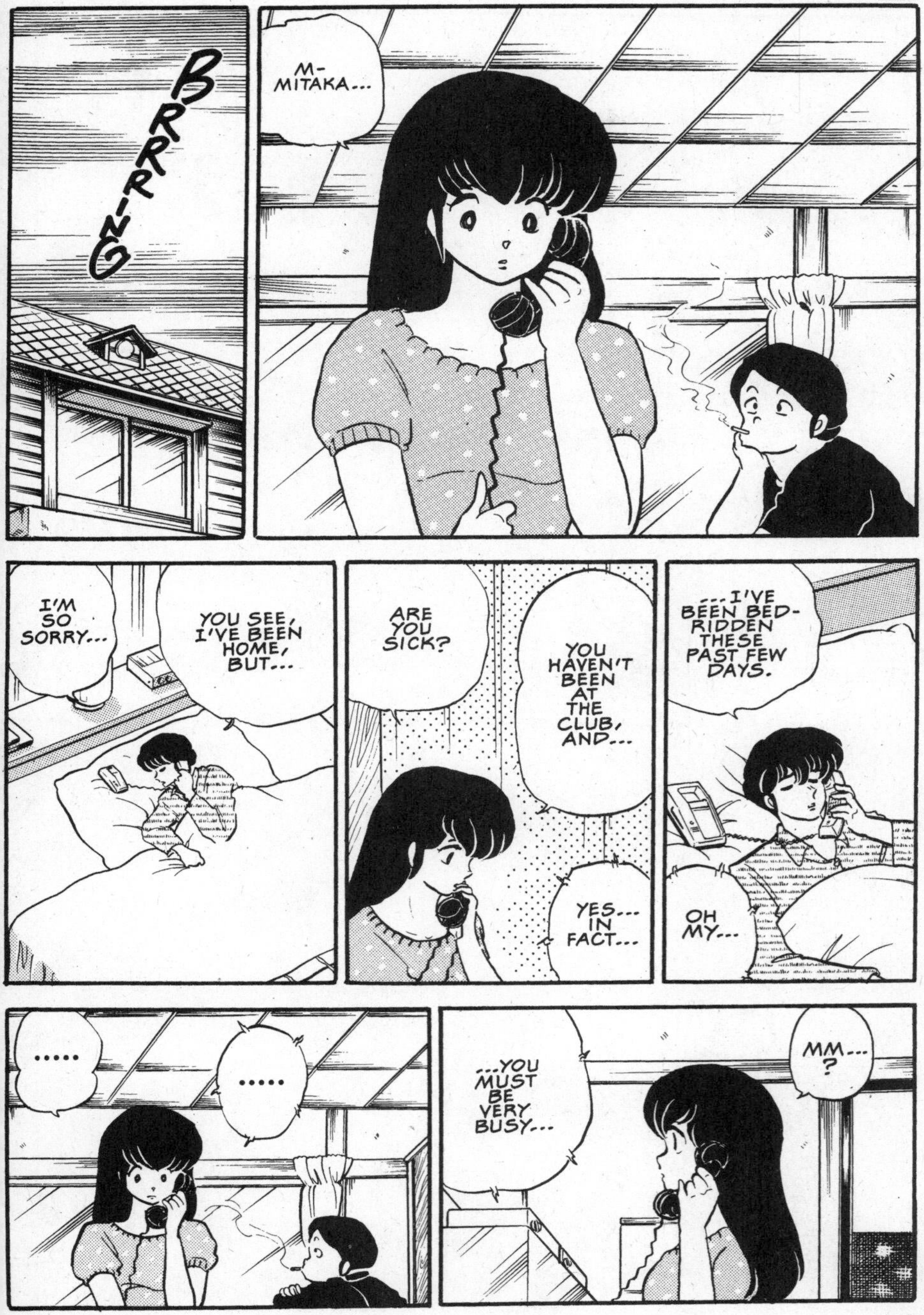
BRRRING
M-MITAKA...
I'M SO SORRY...
YOU SEE, I'VE BEEN HOME, BUT...
ARE YOU SICK?
YOU HAVEN'T BEEN AT THE CLUB, AND...
YES... IN FACT...
...I'VE BEEN BED-RIDDEN THESE PAST FEW DAYS.
OH MY...
.....
.....
...YOU MUST BE VERY BUSY...
MM...?

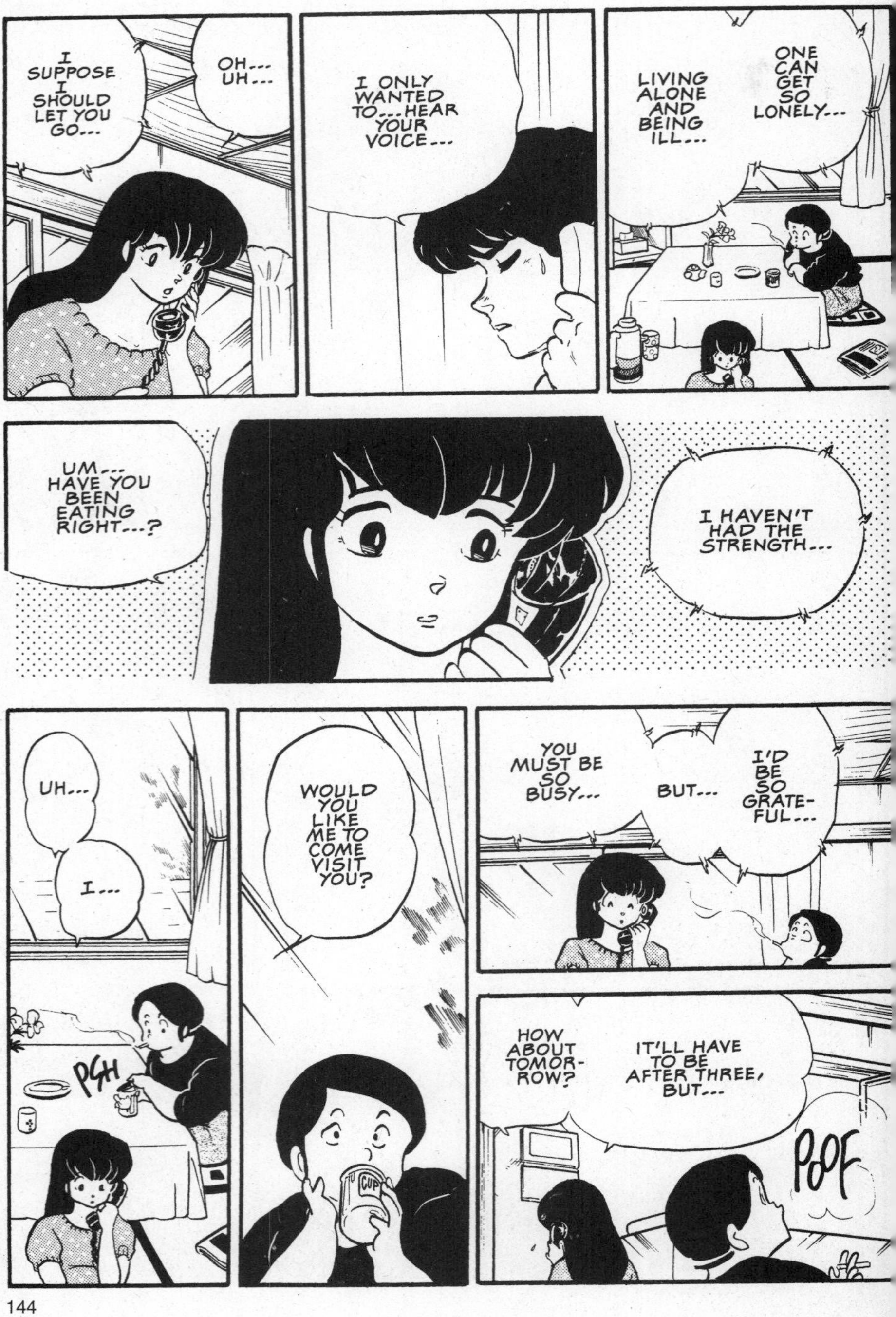
I SUPPOSE I SHOULD LET YOU GO...
OH... UH...
I ONLY WANTED TO... HEAR YOUR VOICE...
LIVING ALONE AND BEING ILL...
ONE CAN GET SO LONELY...
UM... HAVE YOU BEEN EATING RIGHT...?
I HAVEN'T HAD THE STRENGTH...
UH...
I...
PSH
WOULD YOU LIKE ME TO COME VISIT YOU?
CUP
YOU MUST BE SO BUSY...
BUT...
I'D BE SO GRATE-FUL...
HOW ABOUT TOMOR-ROW?
IT'LL HAVE TO BE AFTER THREE, BUT...
POOF

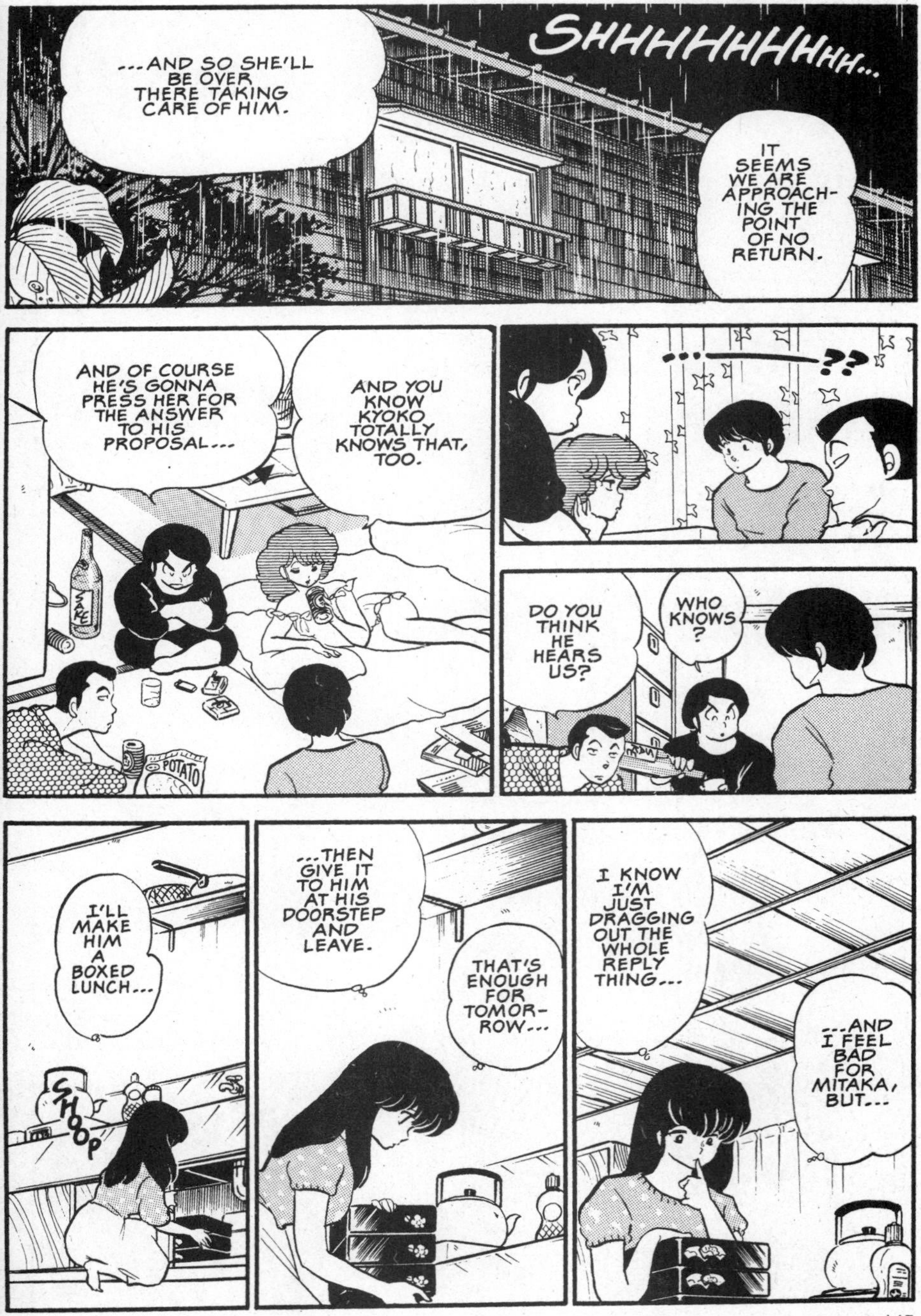
...AND SO SHE'LL BE OVER THERE TAKING CARE OF HIM.
SHHHHHHHHHH...
IT SEEMS WE ARE APPROACHING THE POINT OF NO RETURN.
AND OF COURSE HE'S GONNA PRESS HER FOR THE ANSWER TO HIS PROPOSAL...
AND YOU KNOW KYOKO TOTALLY KNOWS THAT, TOO.
SAKE
POTATO
...——??
DO YOU THINK HE HEARS US?
WHO KNOWS?
I'LL MAKE HIM A BOXED LUNCH...
SHOOP
...THEN GIVE IT TO HIM AT HIS DOORSTEP AND LEAVE.
THAT'S ENOUGH FOR TOMORROW...
I KNOW I'M JUST DRAGGING OUT THE WHOLE REPLY THING...
...AND I FEEL BAD FOR MITAKA, BUT...

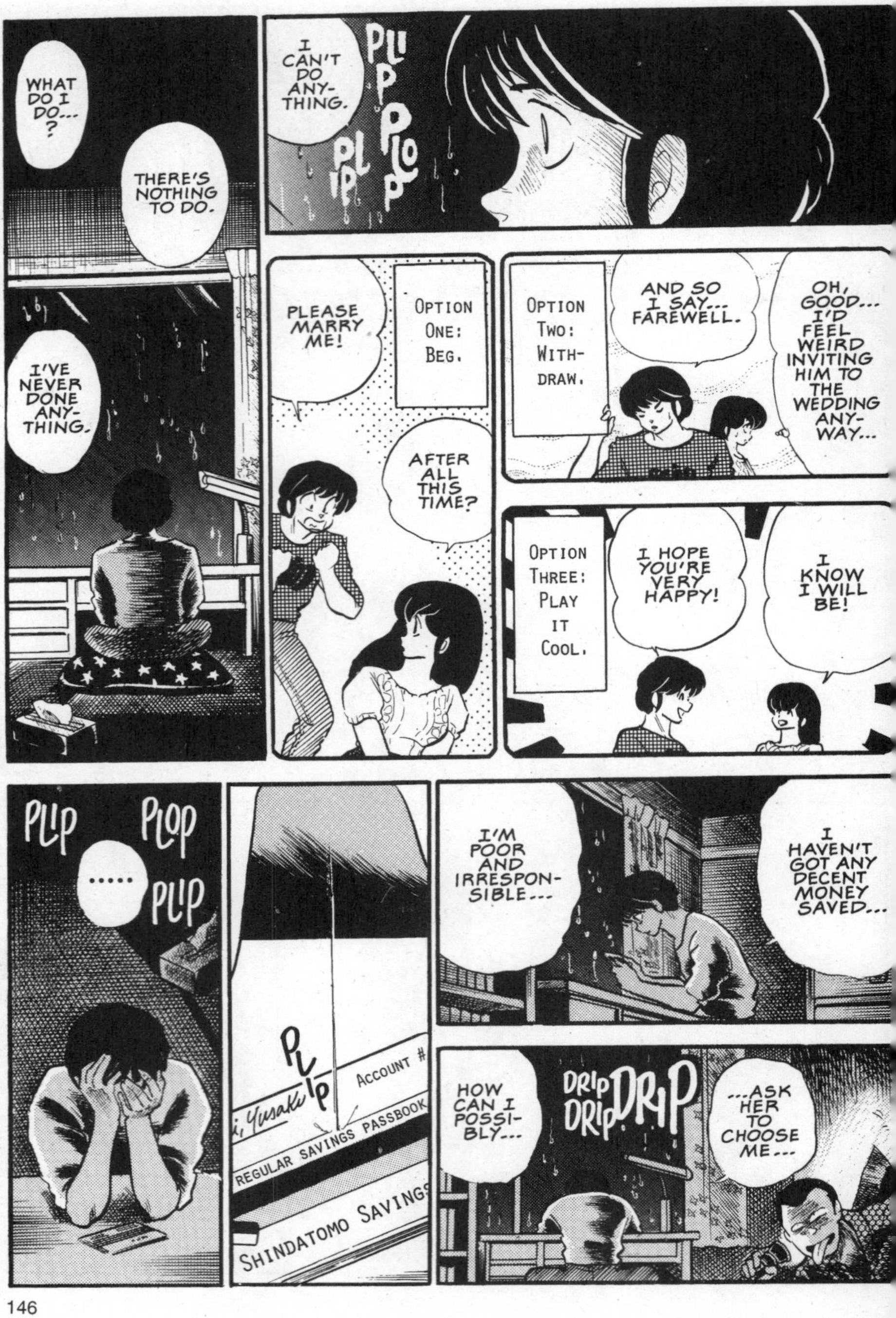
WHAT DO I DO...?
THERE'S NOTHING TO DO.
I'VE NEVER DONE ANYTHING.
I CAN'T DO ANYTHING.
PLIP PLIP PLIP PLOP
Option One: Beg.
PLEASE MARRY ME!
AFTER ALL THIS TIME?
Option Two: Withdraw.
AND SO I SAY... FAREWELL.
OH, GOOD... I'D FEEL WEIRD INVITING HIM TO THE WEDDING ANYWAY...
Option Three: Play it Cool.
I HOPE YOU'RE VERY HAPPY!
I KNOW I WILL BE!
PLIP PLOP
......
PLIP
PLIP
Account #
REGULAR SAVINGS PASSBOOK
SHINDATOMO SAVINGS
I'M POOR AND IRRESPONSIBLE...
I HAVEN'T GOT ANY DECENT MONEY SAVED...
HOW CAN I POSSIBLY...
DRIP DRIP DRIP
...ASK HER TO CHOOSE ME...

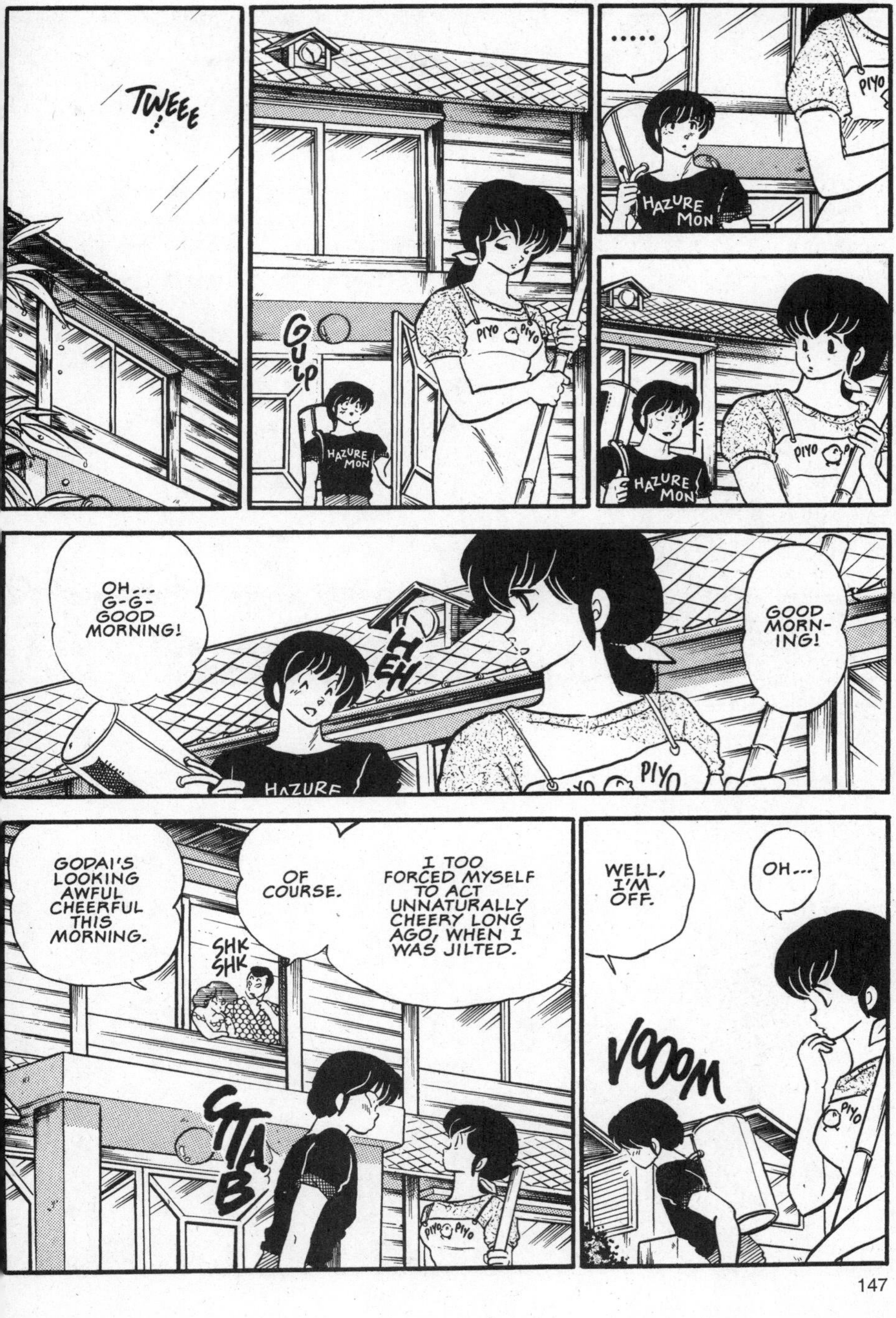
TWEEEE
GULP
HAZURE MON
PIYO PIYO
......
HAZURE MON
PIYO
HAZURE MON
PIYO
OH... G-G-GOOD MORNING!
HEH
GOOD MORNING!
HAZURE
PIYO
GODAI'S LOOKING AWFUL CHEERFUL THIS MORNING.
SHK SHK
OF COURSE.
I TOO FORCED MYSELF TO ACT UNNATURALLY CHEERY LONG AGO, WHEN I WAS JILTED.
STAB
PIYO PIYO
WELL, I'M OFF.
OH...
VOOOM
PIYO

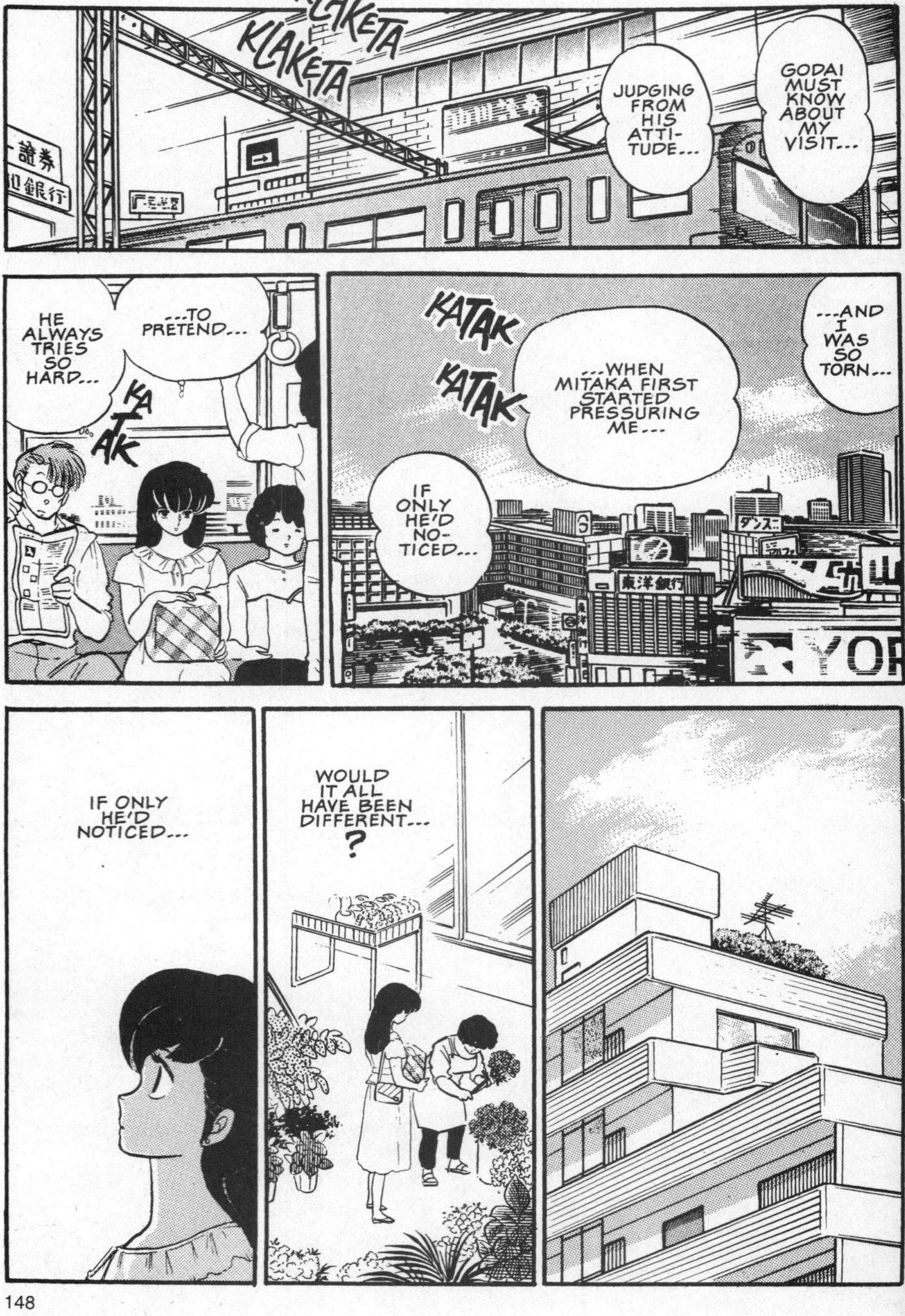

KLAKETA
KLAKETA
JUDGING FROM HIS ATTI-TUDE...
GODAI MUST KNOW ABOUT MY VISIT...
HE ALWAYS TRIES SO HARD...
...TO PRETEND...
KATAK
KATAK
KATAK
...WHEN MITAKA FIRST STARTED PRESSURING ME...
...AND I WAS SO TORN...
IF ONLY HE'D NO-TICED...
IF ONLY HE'D NOTICED...
WOULD IT ALL HAVE BEEN DIFFERENT...?

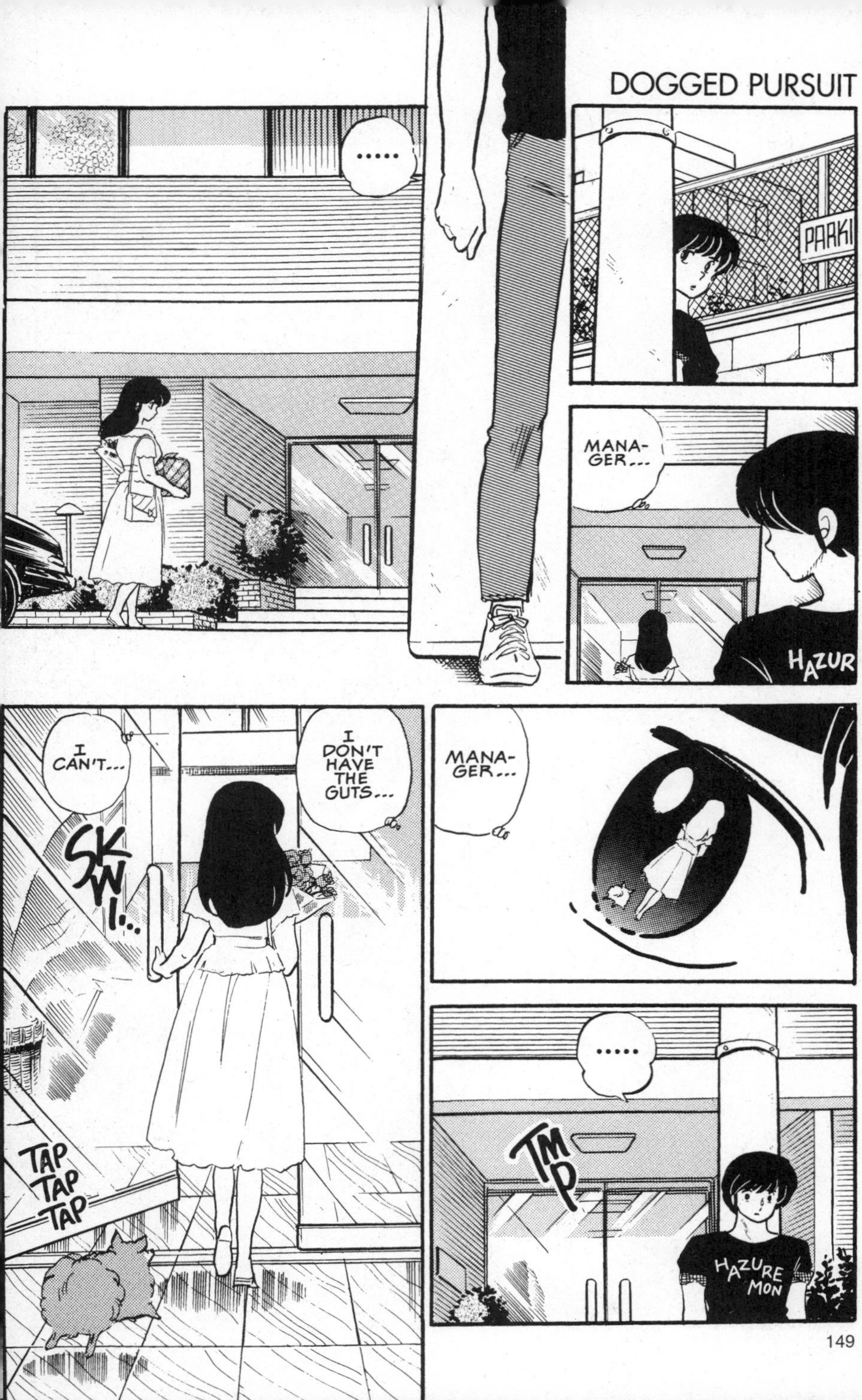
......
PARKI
MANA-GER...
HAZUR
I CAN'T...
I DON'T HAVE THE GUTS...
SKWI...
TAP TAP TAP
MANA-GER...
......
TMP
HAZURE MON

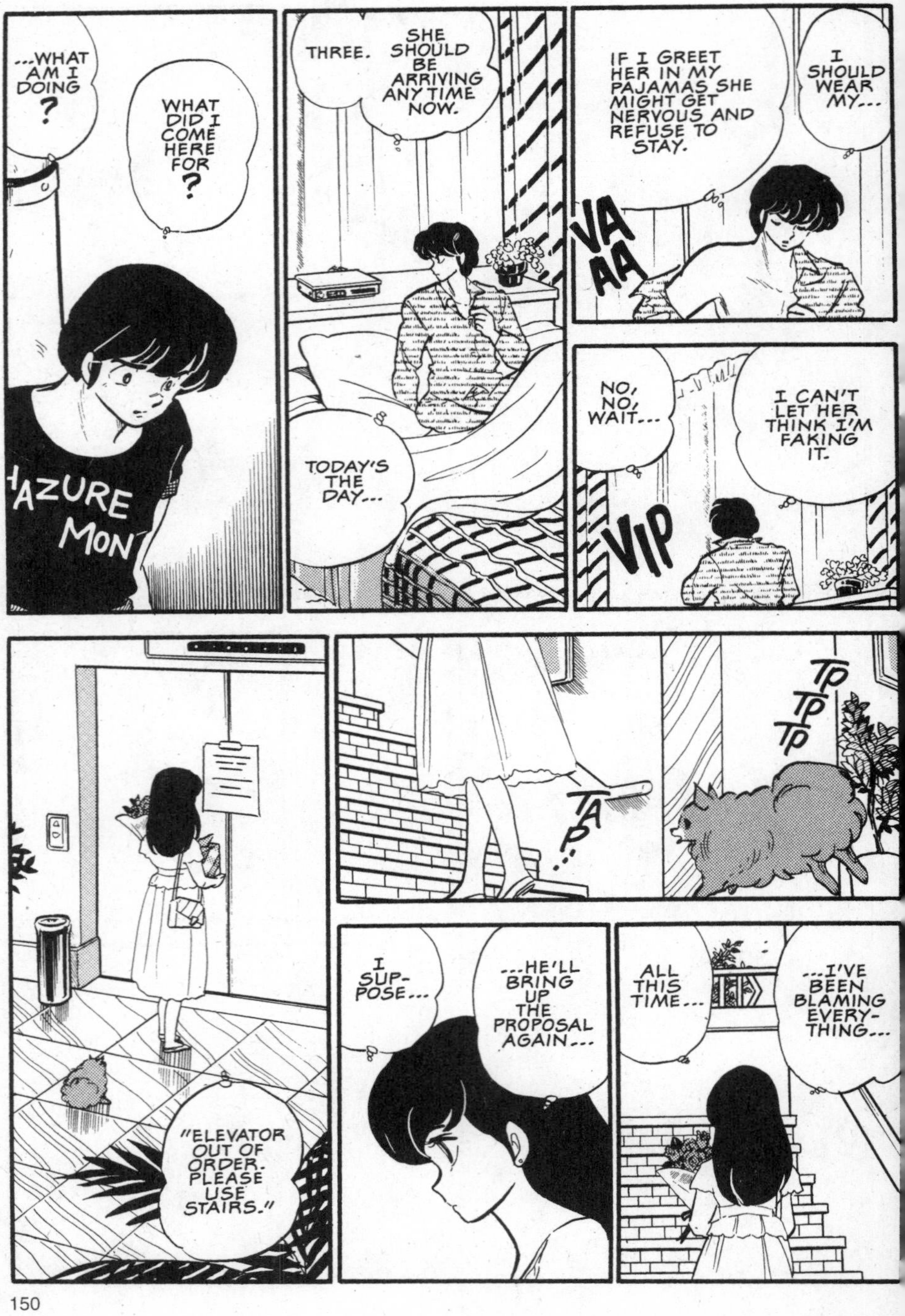
...WHAT AM I DOING?
WHAT DID I COME HERE FOR?
HAZURE MON
THREE. SHE SHOULD BE ARRIVING ANY TIME NOW.
TODAY'S THE DAY...
IF I GREET HER IN MY PAJAMAS SHE MIGHT GET NERVOUS AND REFUSE TO STAY.
I SHOULD WEAR MY...
VAAA
NO, NO, WAIT...
I CAN'T LET HER THINK I'M FAKING IT.
VIP
"ELEVATOR OUT OF ORDER. PLEASE USE STAIRS."
TAP...
TP TP TP
I SUPPOSE...
...HE'LL BRING UP THE PROPOSAL AGAIN...
ALL THIS TIME...
...I'VE BEEN BLAMING EVERYTHING...

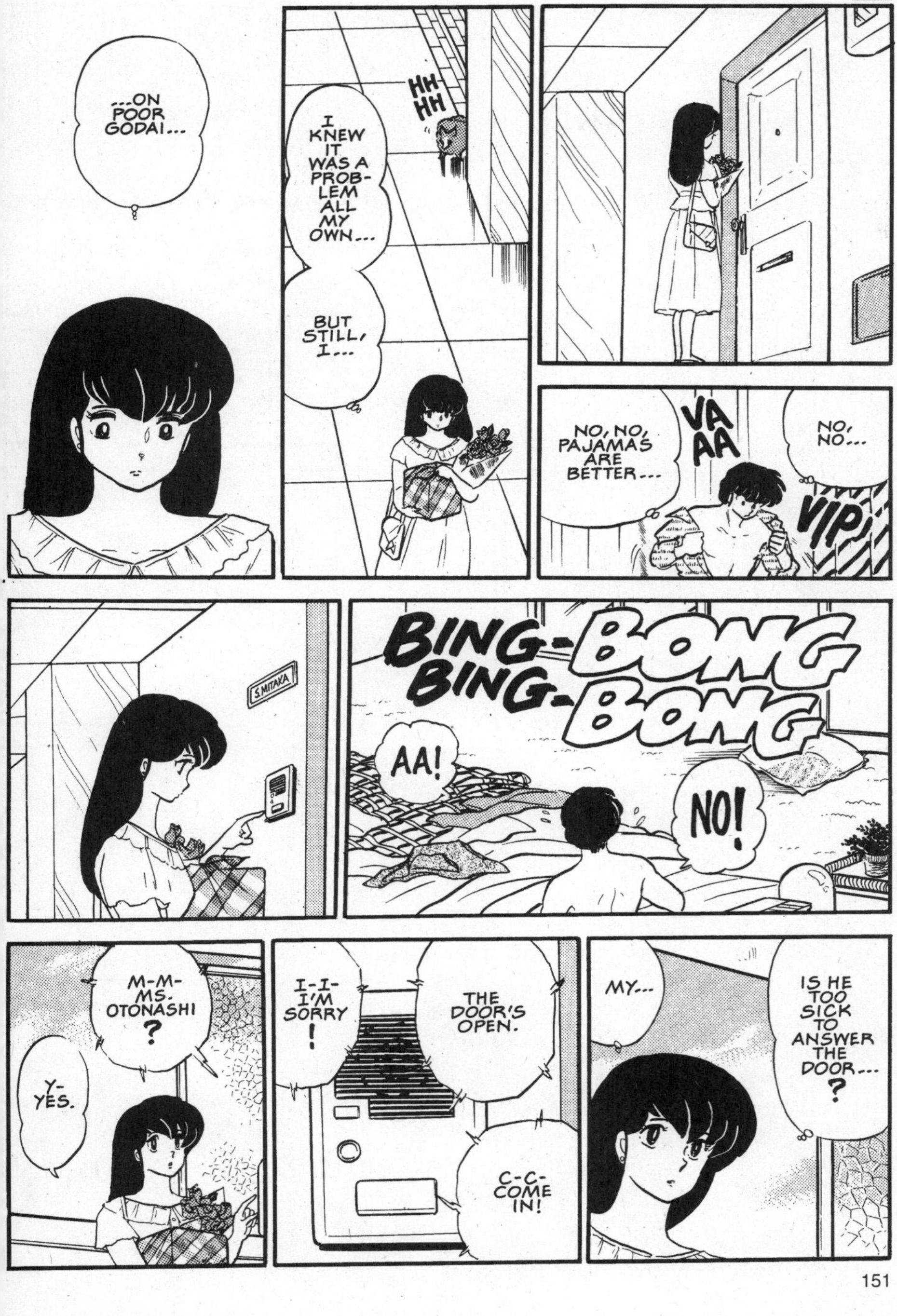
...ON POOR GODAI...
HH HH
I KNEW IT WAS A PROBLEM ALL MY OWN...
BUT STILL, I...
NO, NO, PAJAMAS ARE BETTER...
VA AA
NO, NO...
VIP
S. MITAKA
BING-BONG BING-BONG
AA!
NO!
M-M-MS. OTONASHI?
Y-YES.
I-I-I'M SORRY!
THE DOOR'S OPEN.
C-C-COME IN!
MY...
IS HE TOO SICK TO ANSWER THE DOOR...?

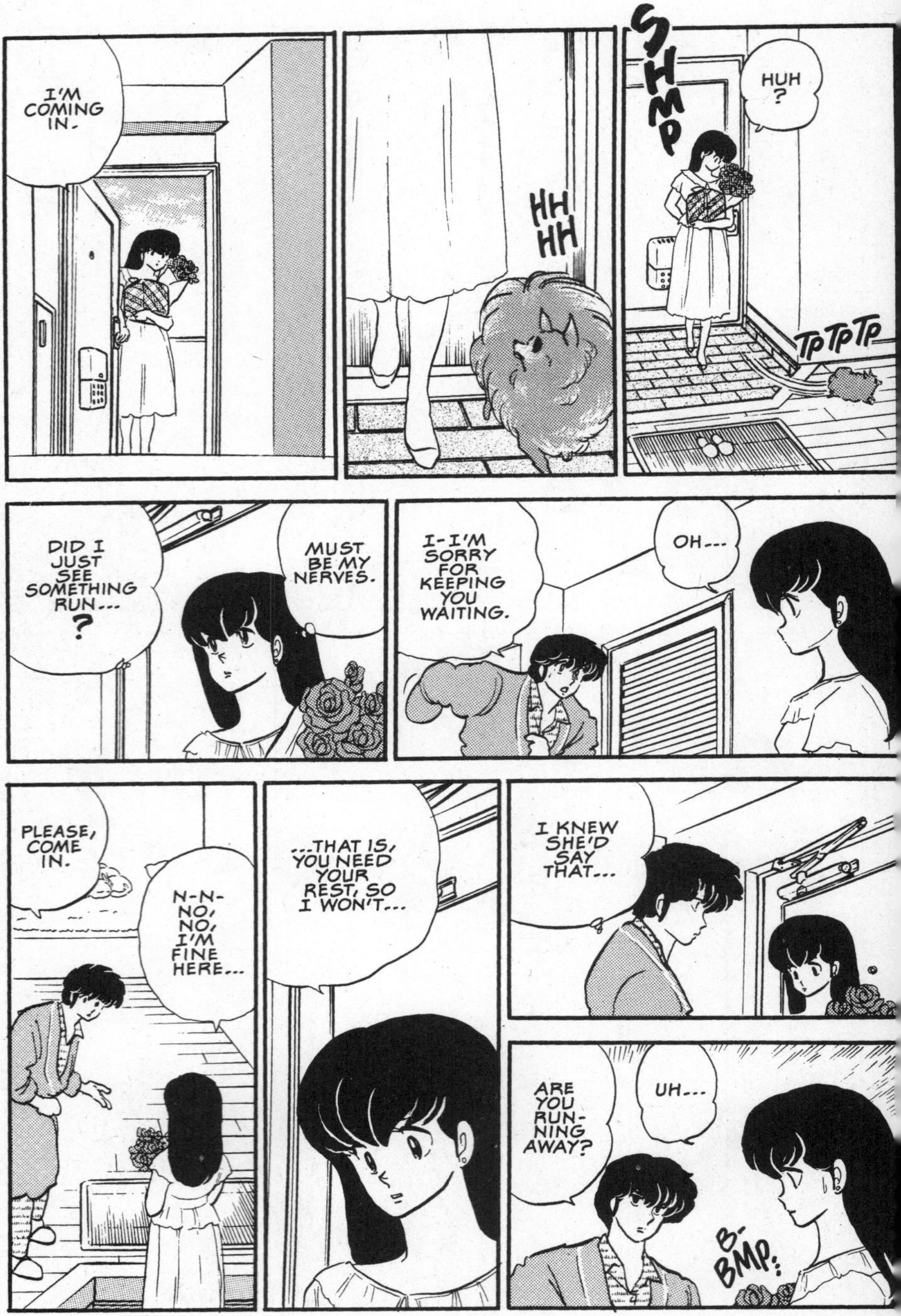
I'M COMING IN.
HH HH
SHMP
HUH?
TP TP TP
DID I JUST SEE SOMETHING RUN...?
MUST BE MY NERVES.
I-I'M SORRY FOR KEEPING YOU WAITING.
OH...
PLEASE, COME IN.
N-N-NO, NO, I'M FINE HERE...
...THAT IS, YOU NEED YOUR REST, SO I WON'T...
I KNEW SHE'D SAY THAT...
ARE YOU RUNNING AWAY?
UH...
B-BMP

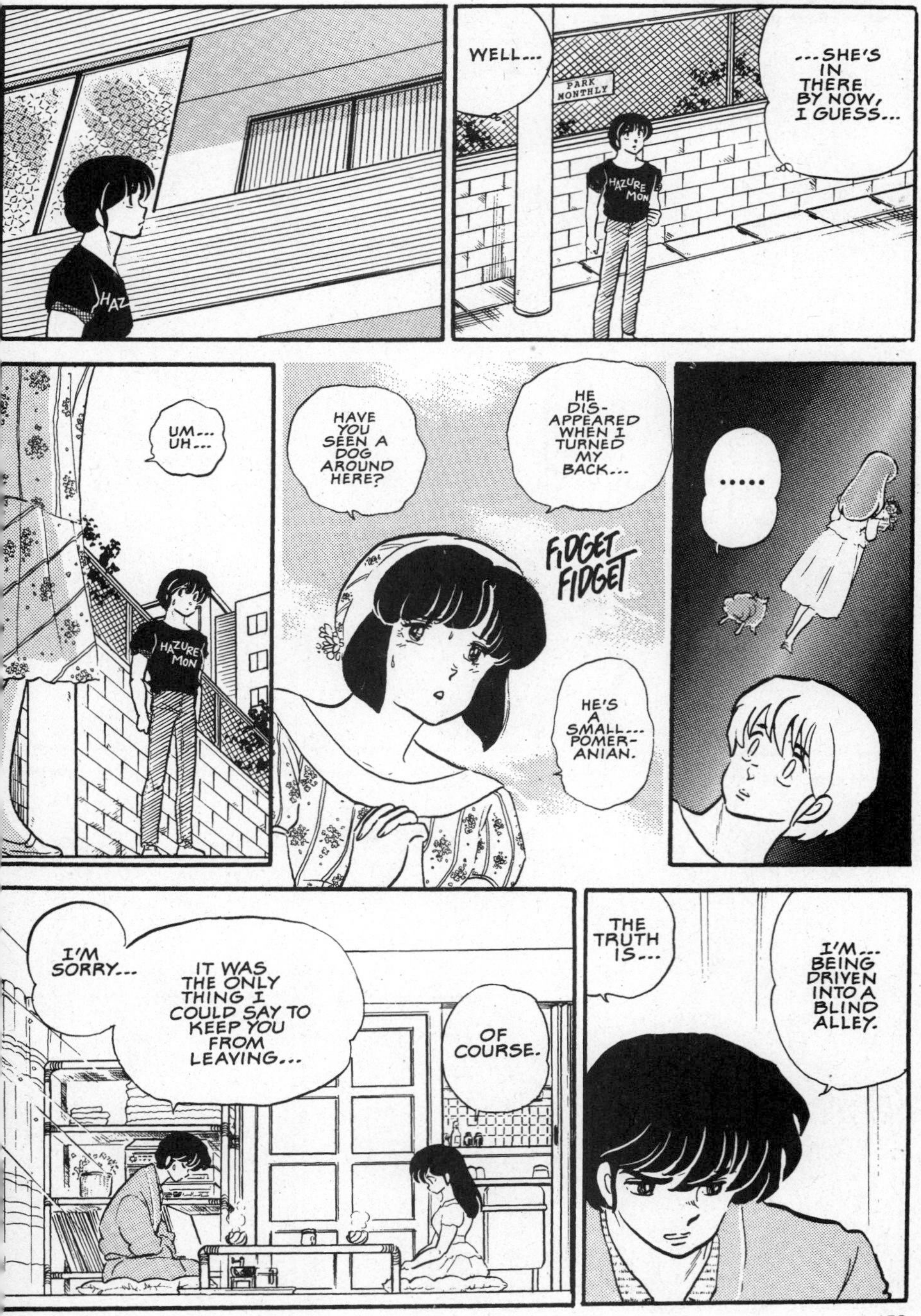
WELL...
PARK MONTHLY
...SHE'S IN THERE BY NOW, I GUESS...
UM... UH...
HAVE YOU SEEN A DOG AROUND HERE?
HE DIS-APPEARED WHEN I TURNED MY BACK...
FIDGET FIDGET
HE'S A SMALL... POMER-ANIAN.
.....
I'M SORRY...
IT WAS THE ONLY THING I COULD SAY TO KEEP YOU FROM LEAVING...
OF COURSE.
THE TRUTH IS...
I'M... BEING DRIVEN INTO A BLIND ALLEY.

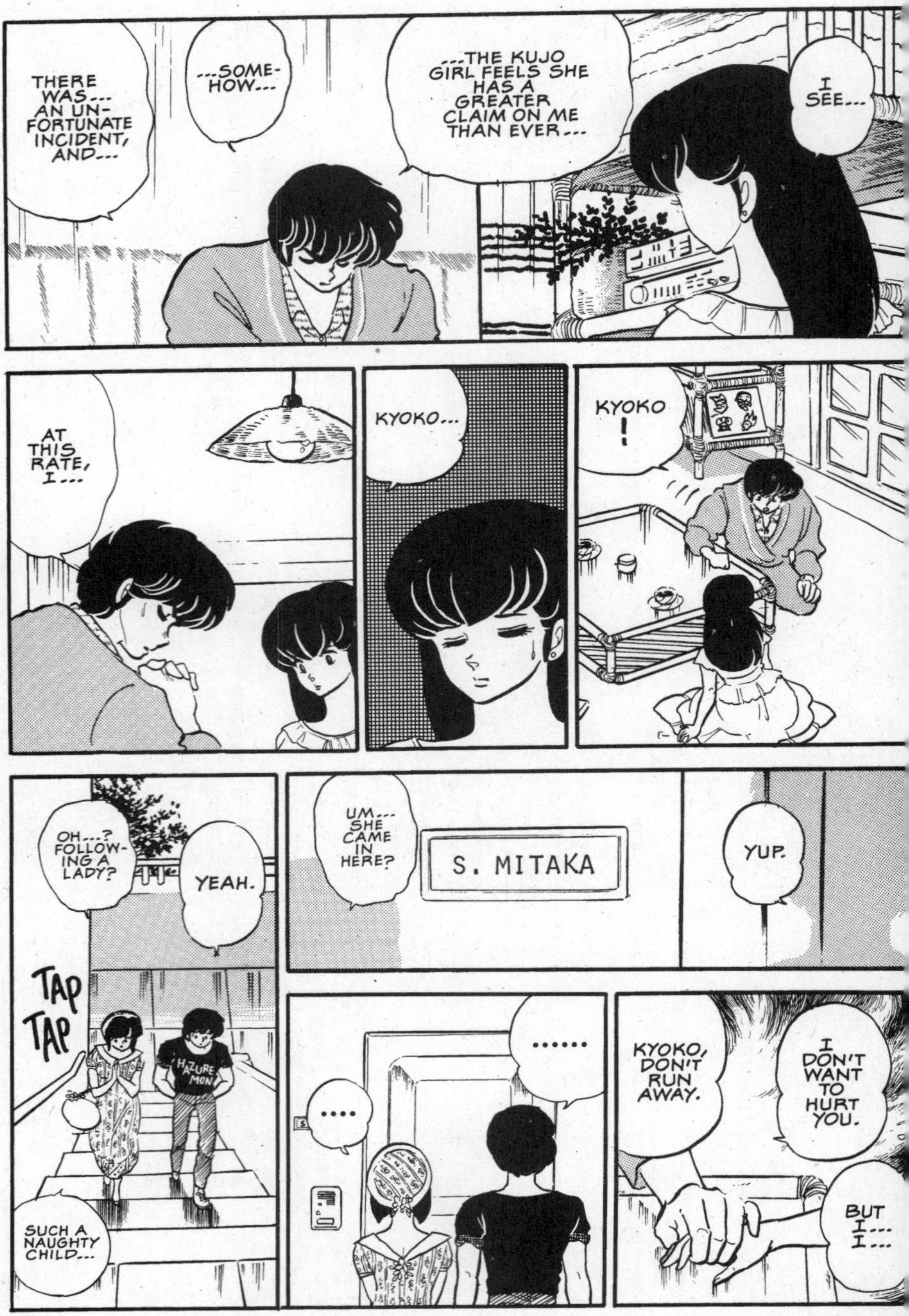
THERE WAS... AN UNFORTUNATE INCIDENT, AND...
...SOMEHOW...
...THE KUJO GIRL FEELS SHE HAS A GREATER CLAIM ON ME THAN EVER...
I SEE...
AT THIS RATE, I...
KYOKO...
KYOKO !
OH...? FOLLOWING A LADY?
YEAH.
TAP TAP
SUCH A NAUGHTY CHILD...
UM... SHE CAME IN HERE?
S. MITAKA
YUP.
....
......
KYOKO, DON'T RUN AWAY.
I DON'T WANT TO HURT YOU.
BUT I... I...

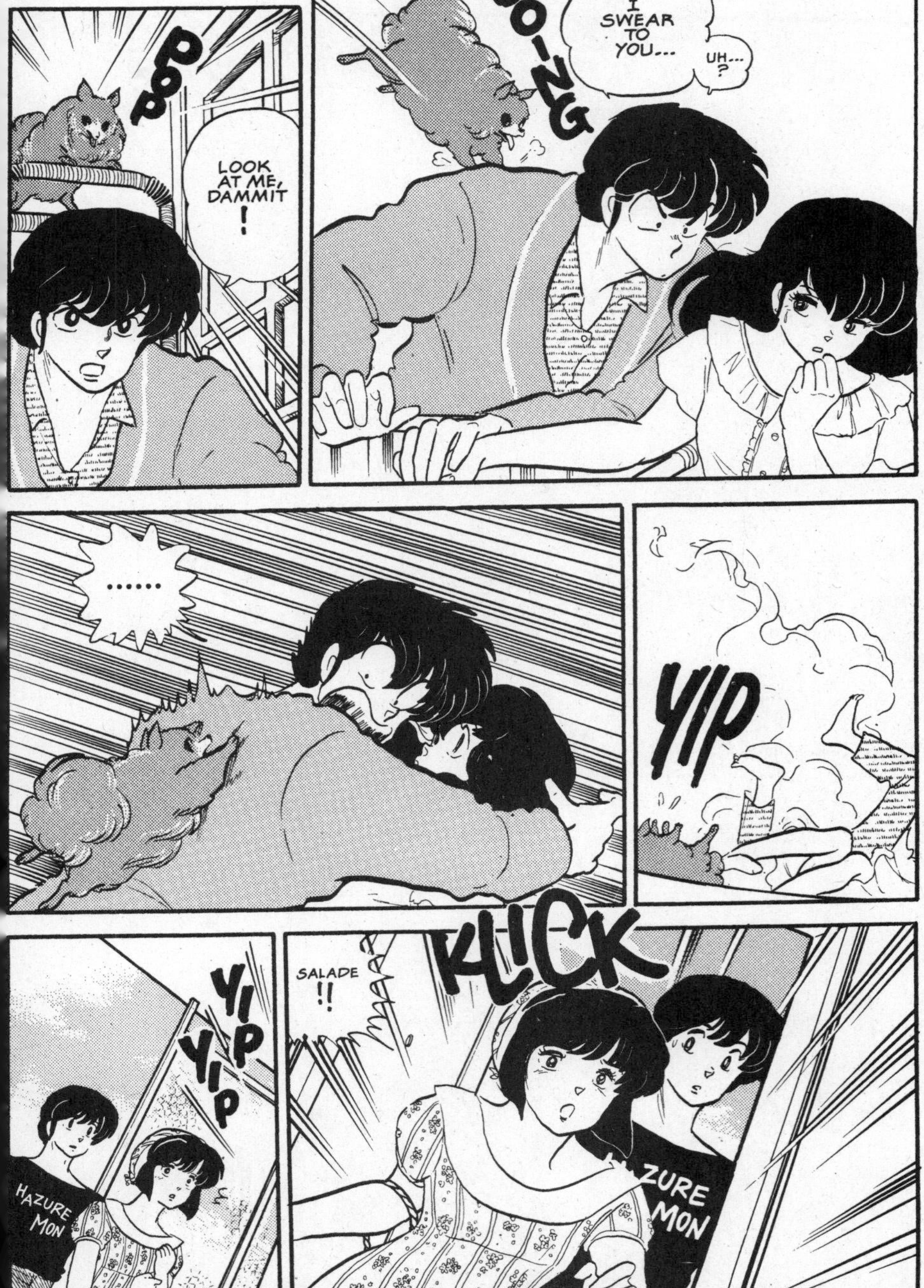
POP
LOOK AT ME, DAMMIT !
BOING
I SWEAR TO YOU...
UH... ?
......
YIP
YIP YIP YIP
HAZURE MON
KLICK
SALADE !!
ZURE MON

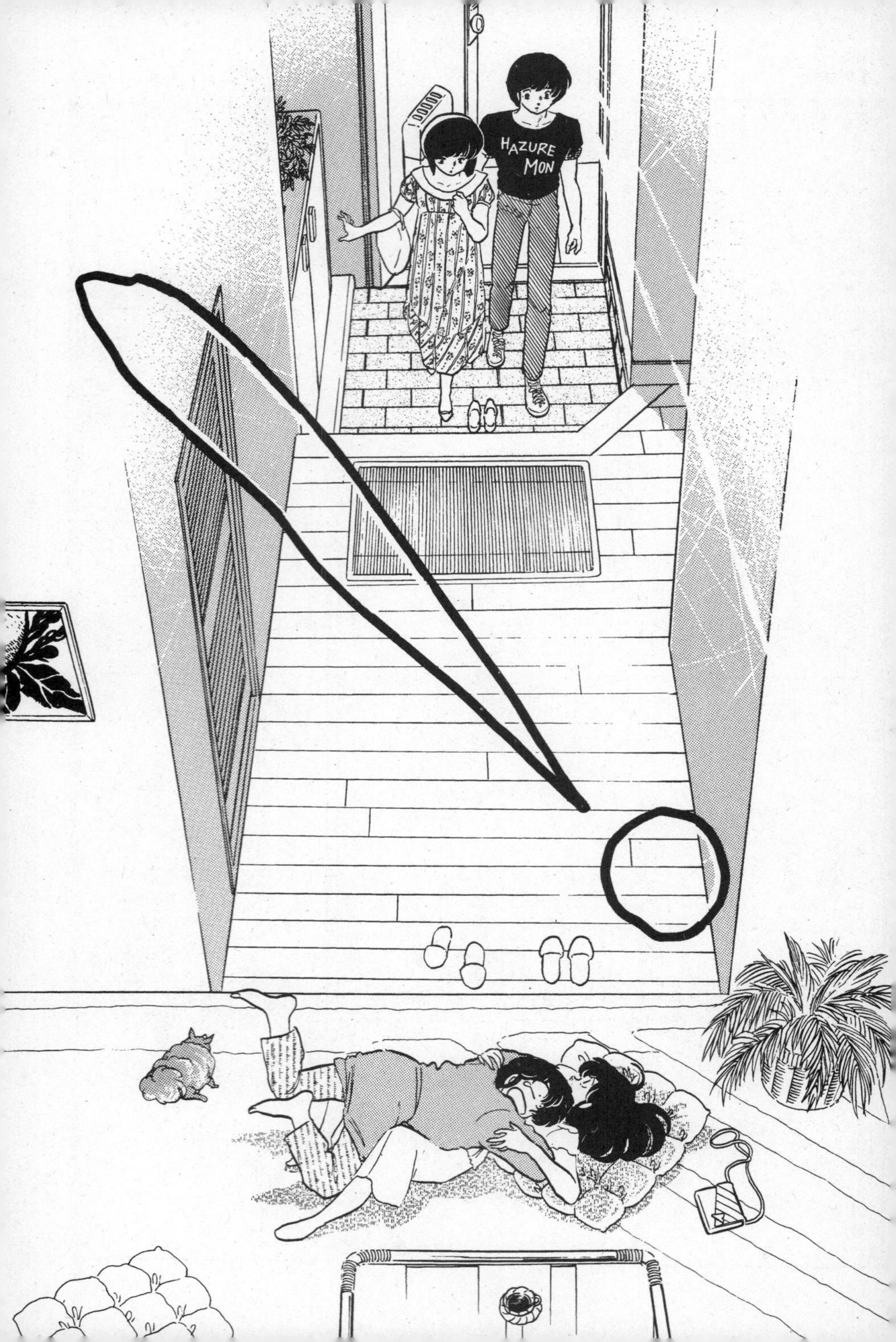
HAZURE
MON

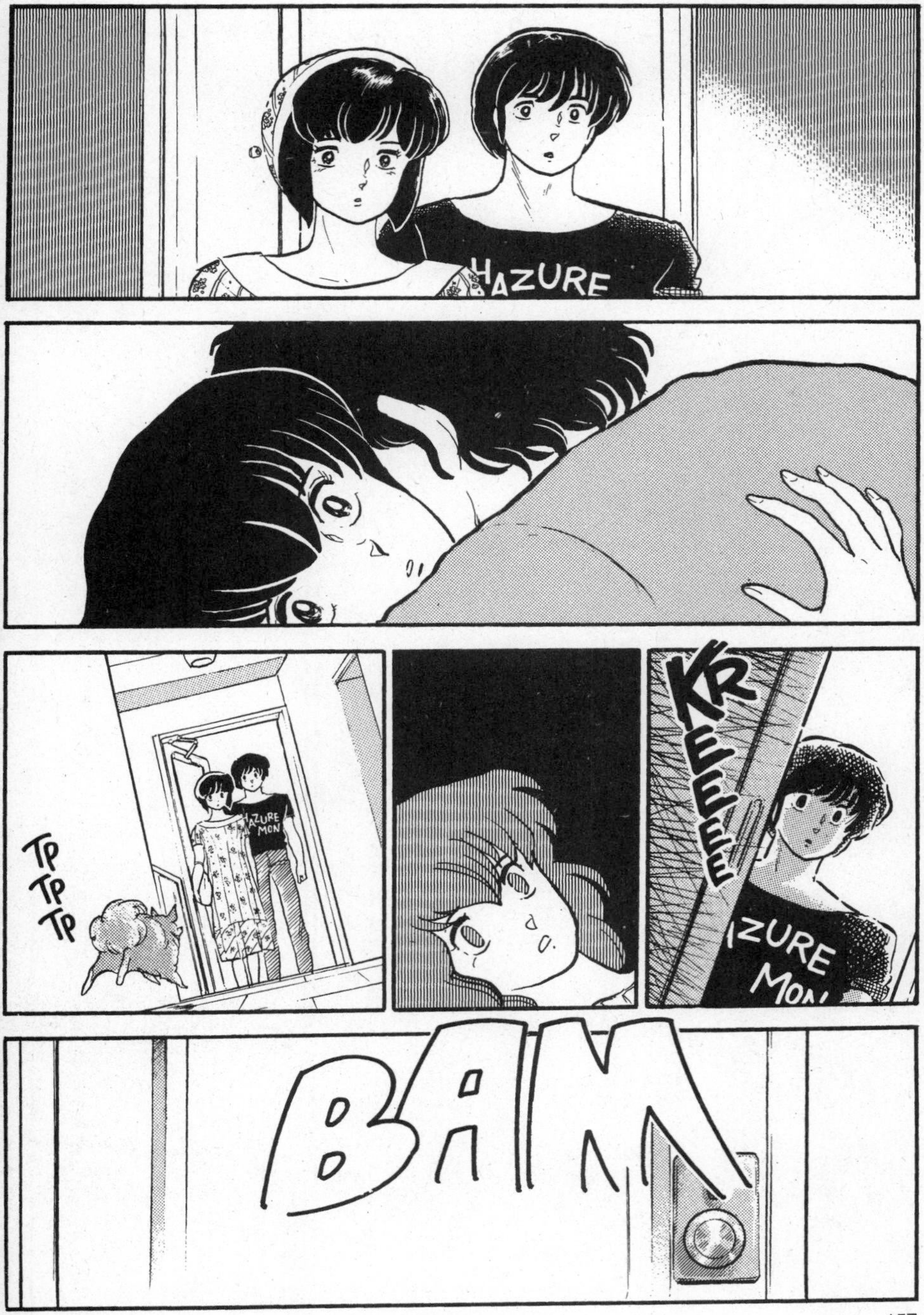
HAZURE
HAZURE MON
TP TP TP
KR EEEEE
IZURE MON
BAM

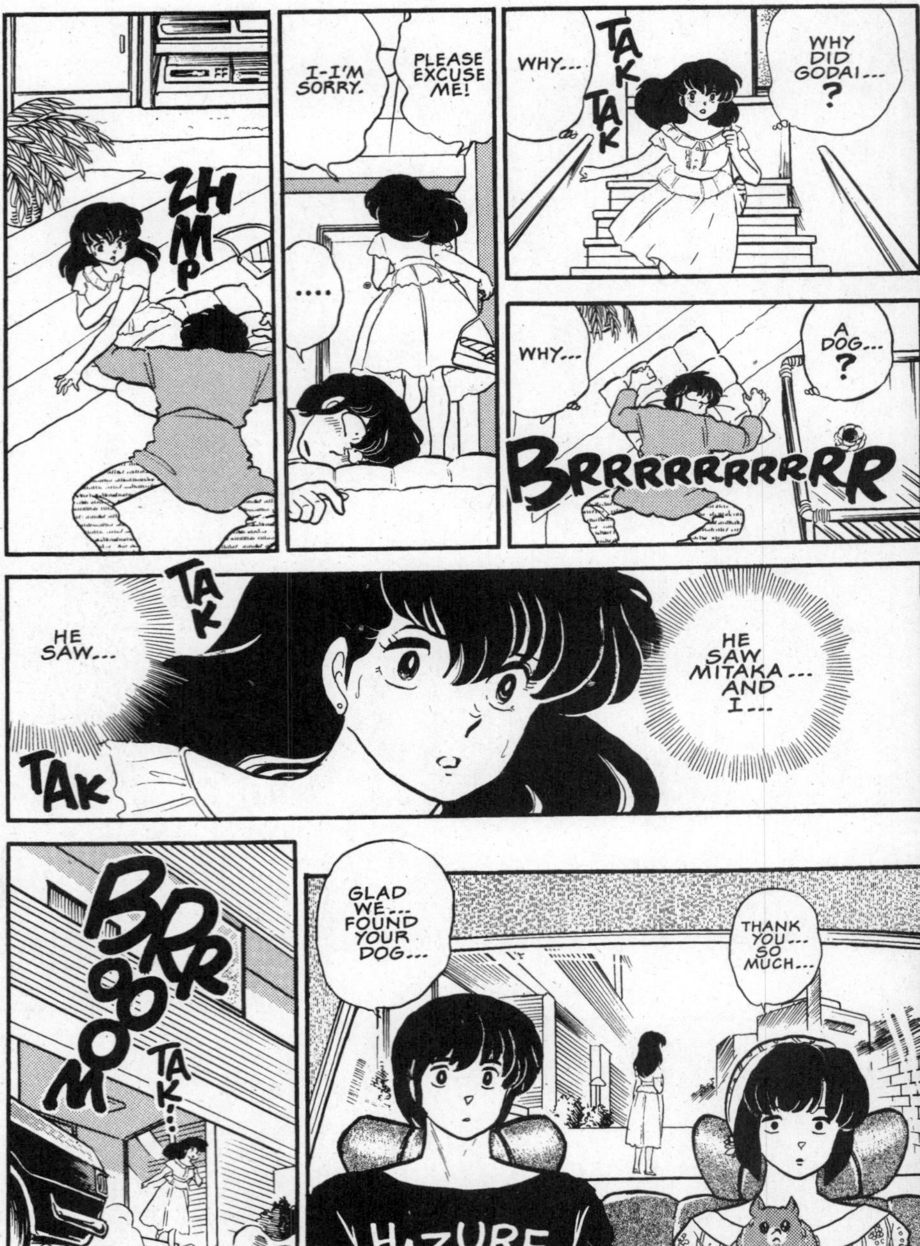

ZHMP
I-I'M SORRY.
PLEASE EXCUSE ME!
....
WHY...
TAK TAK TAK
WHY DID GODAI...?
WHY...
A DOG...?
BRRRRRRRRRR
HE SAW...
TAK
TAK
HE SAW MITAKA... AND I...
BRROOOM
TAK...
GLAD WE... FOUND YOUR DOG...
THANK YOU... SO MUCH...
HAZURE

PART 8

THE DOOR SLAMS

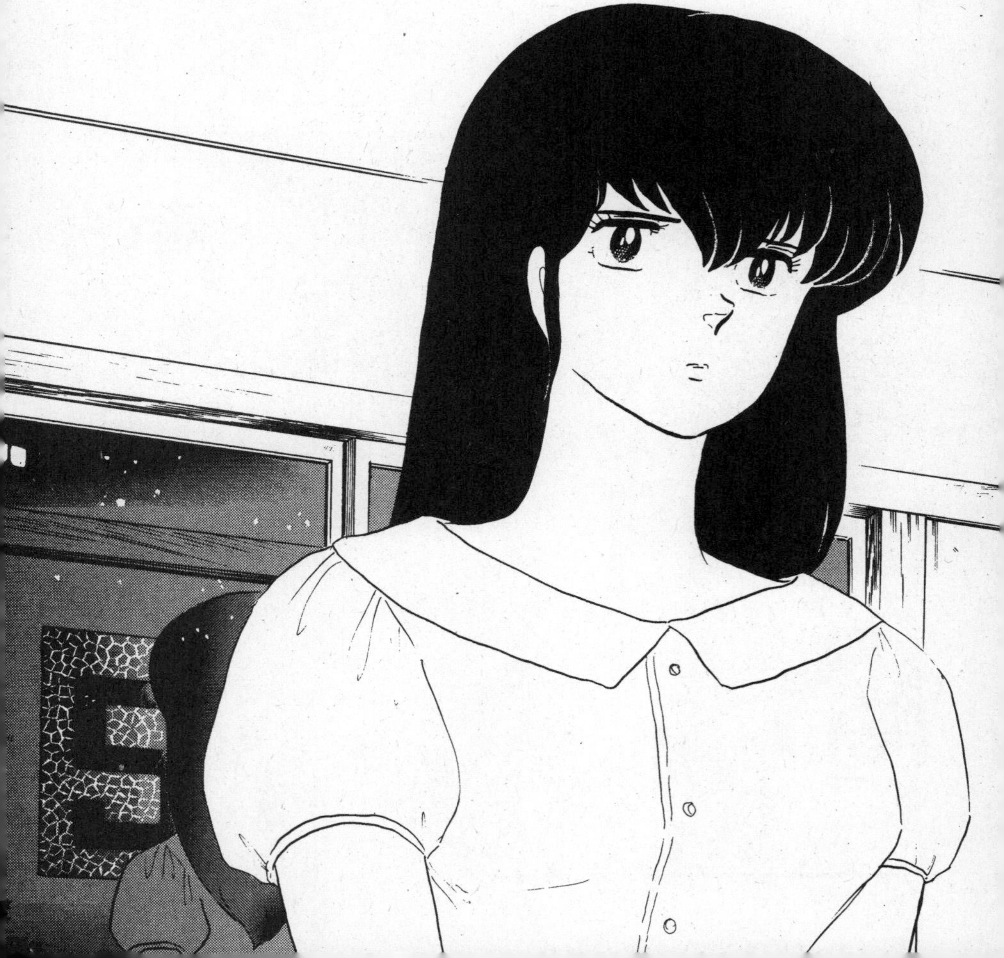

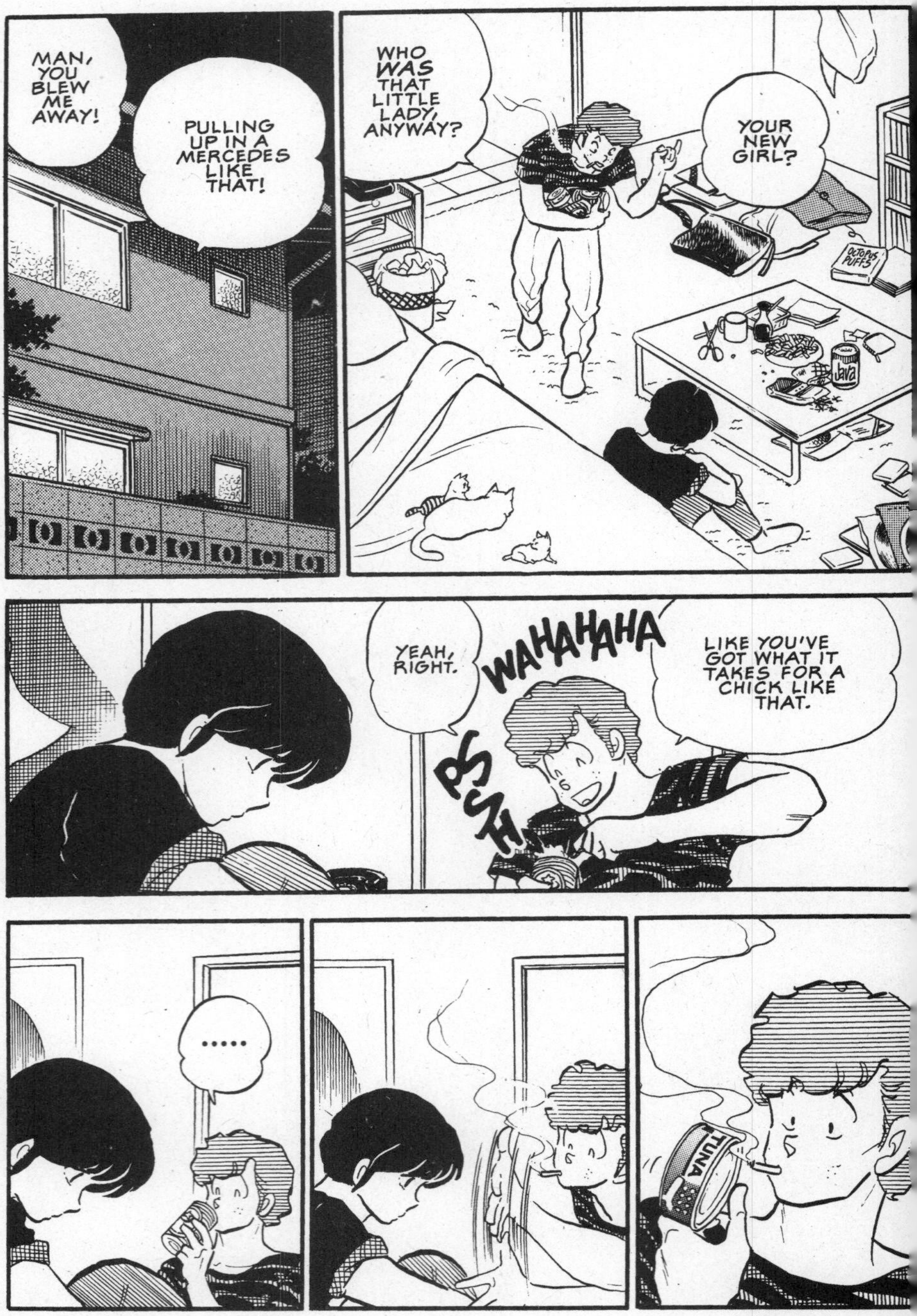
MAN, YOU BLEW ME AWAY!
PULLING UP IN A MERCEDES LIKE THAT!
WHO WAS THAT LITTLE LADY, ANYWAY?
YOUR NEW GIRL?
OCTOPUS PUFFS
JAVA
YEAH, RIGHT.
WAHAHAHA
LIKE YOU'VE GOT WHAT IT TAKES FOR A CHICK LIKE THAT.
PSSH
......
TUNA

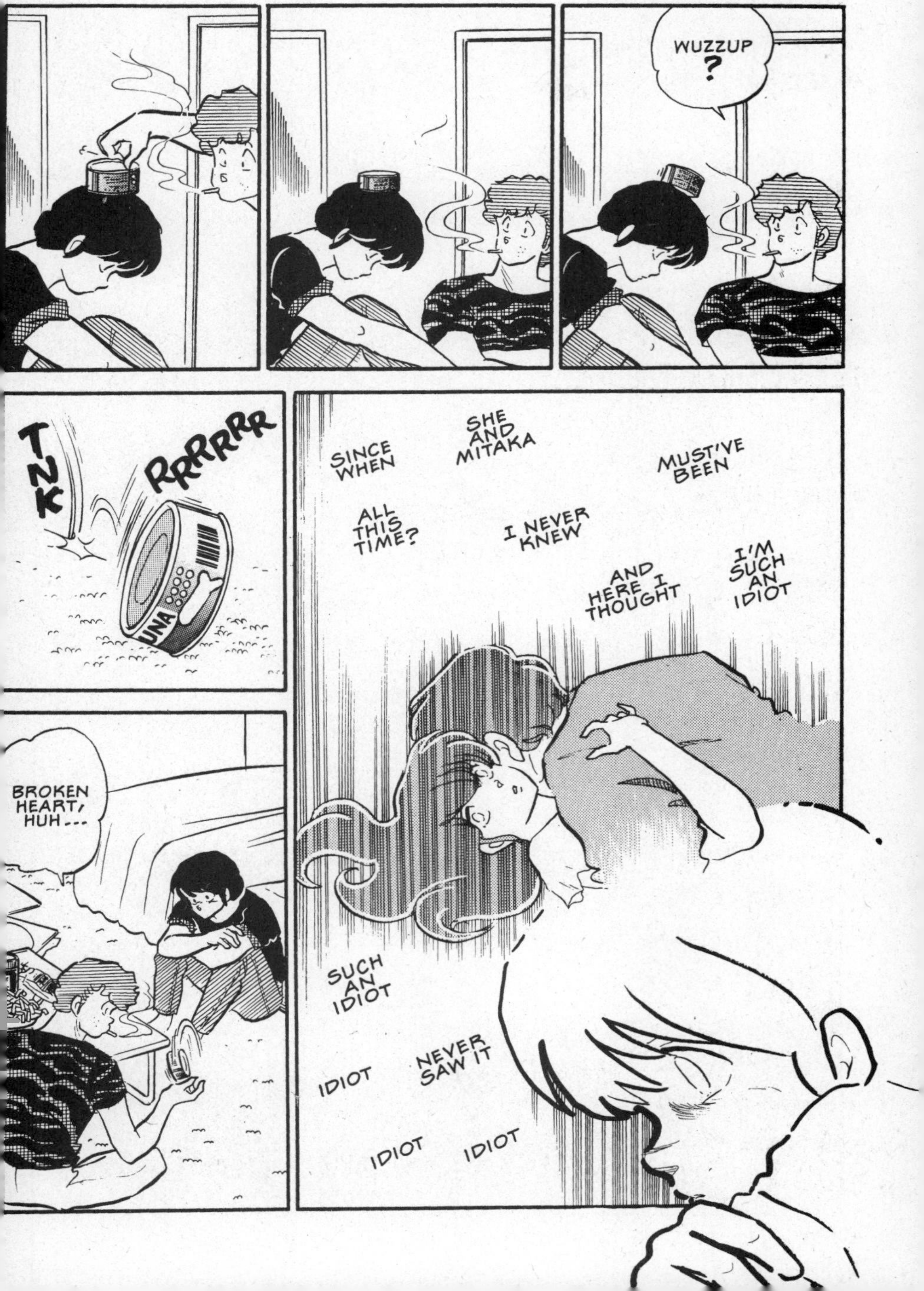
WUZZUP ?
TNK
RRRRRR
BROKEN HEART, HUH...
SINCE WHEN
SHE AND MITAKA
MUST'VE BEEN
ALL THIS TIME?
I NEVER KNEW
AND HERE I THOUGHT
I'M SUCH AN IDIOT
SUCH AN IDIOT
IDIOT
NEVER SAW IT
IDIOT
IDIOT

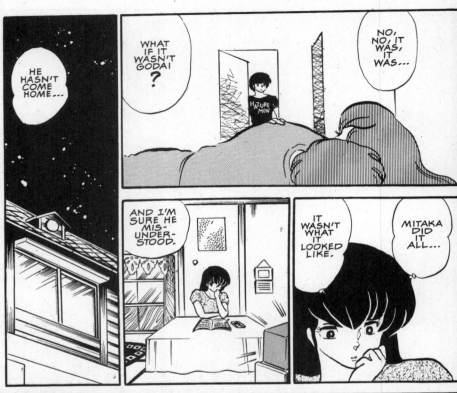

HE HASN'T COME HOME....

WHAT IF IT WASN'T GODAI?

NO, NO, IT WAS, IT WAS...

HAZURE MON

AND I'M SURE HE MIS-UNDER-STOOD.

IT WASN'T WHAT IT LOOKED LIKE.

MITAKA DID IT ALL...

I HAVE TO TELL HIM.

I'LL MAKE HIM UNDER-STAND.

I HAVE TO...

SHN3 SHN3

RB WR

MYEW

HAZURE

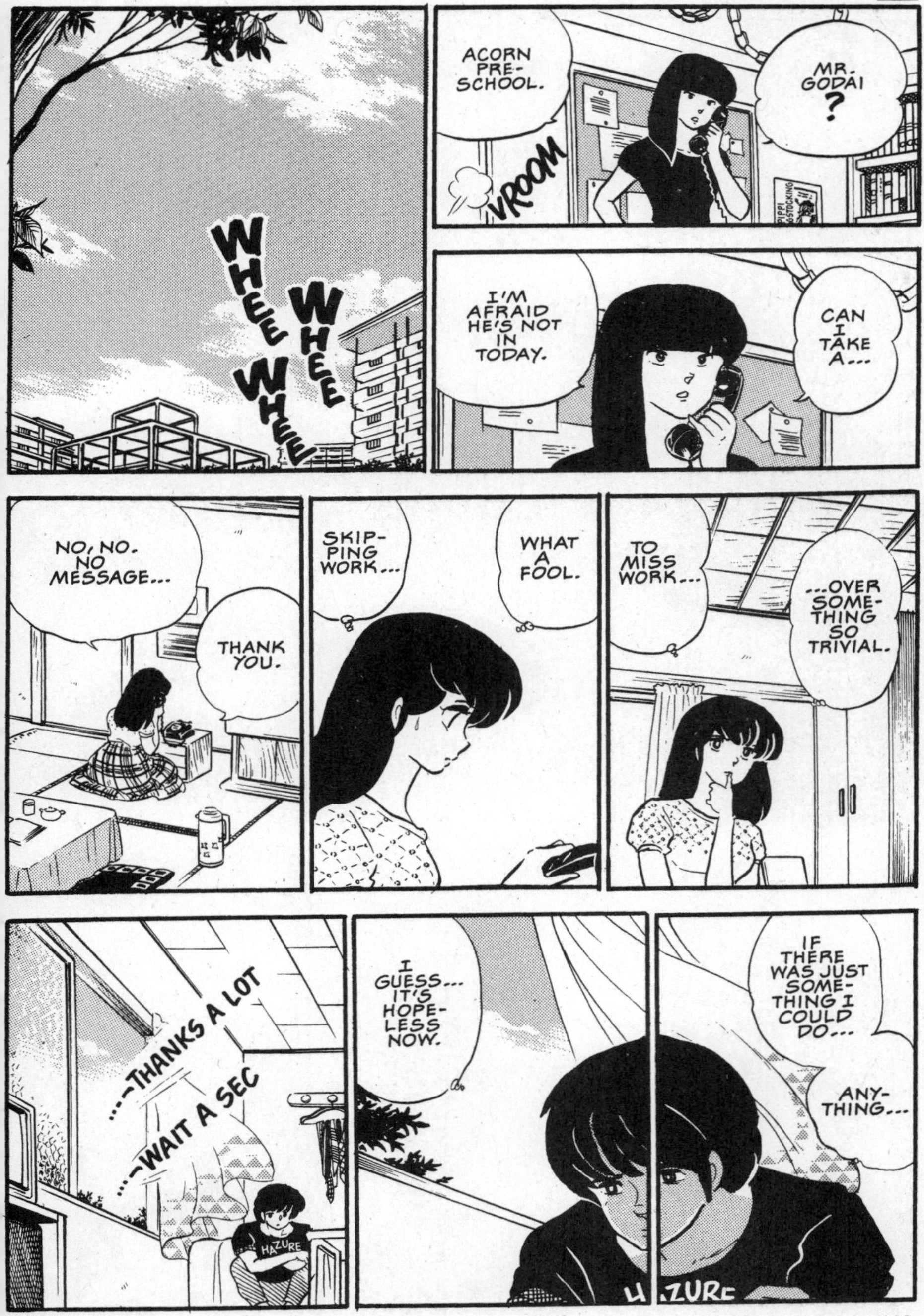
WHEE WHEE WHEE
ACORN PRE-SCHOOL.
VROOM
MR. GODAI ?
I'M AFRAID HE'S NOT IN TODAY.
CAN I TAKE A...
NO, NO. NO MESSAGE...
THANK YOU.
SKIP-PING WORK...
WHAT A FOOL.
TO MISS WORK...
...OVER SOME-THING SO TRIVIAL.
...THANKS A LOT
...WAIT A SEC
HAZURE
I GUESS... IT'S HOPE-LESS NOW.
IF THERE WAS JUST SOME-THING I COULD DO...
ANY-THING...
HAZURE

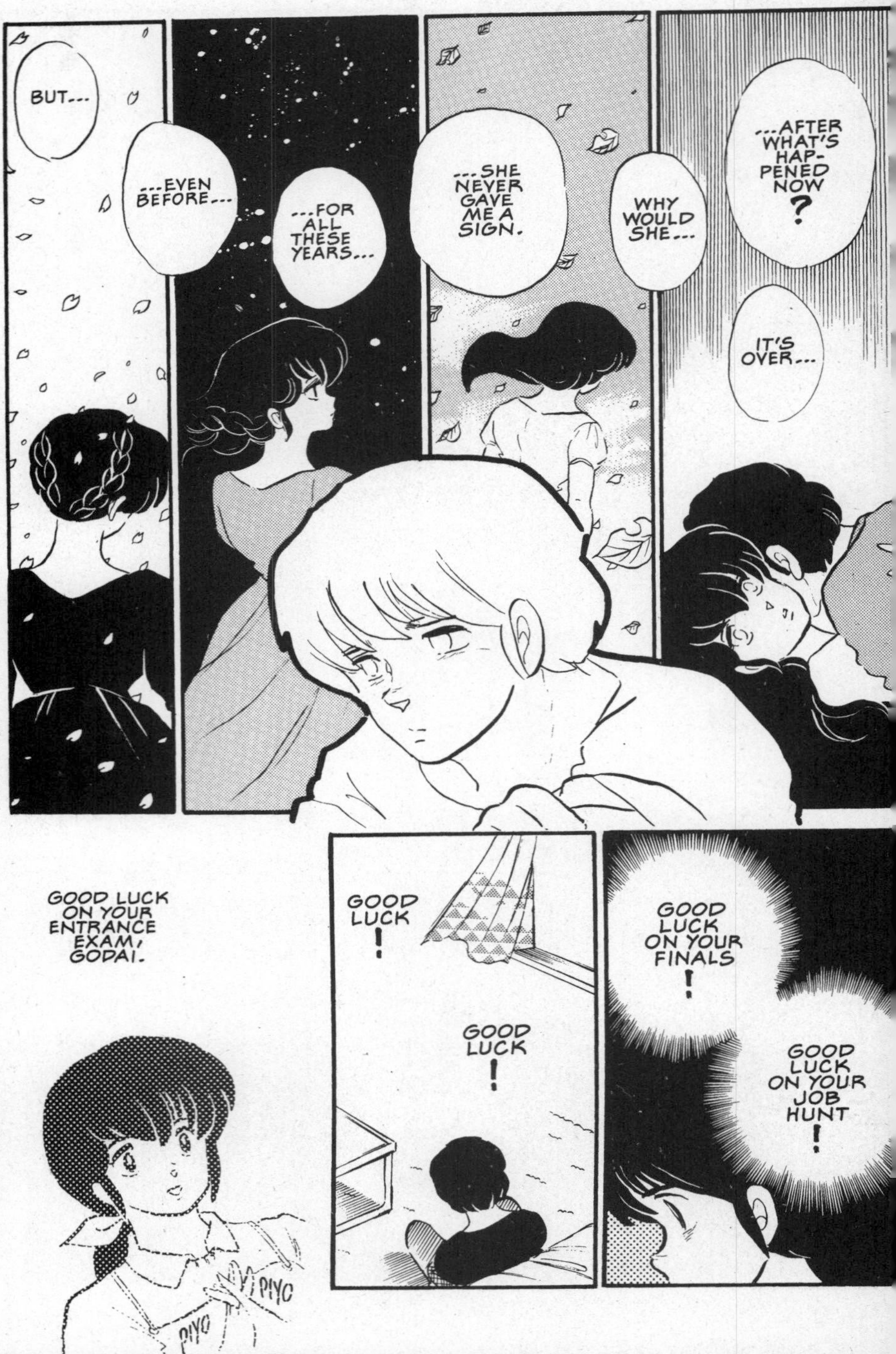
BUT...
...EVEN BEFORE...
...FOR ALL THESE YEARS...
...SHE NEVER GAVE ME A SIGN.
WHY WOULD SHE...
...AFTER WHAT'S HAP-PENED NOW?
IT'S OVER...
GOOD LUCK ON YOUR ENTRANCE EXAM, GODAI.
PIYO
PIYO
GOOD LUCK!
GOOD LUCK!
GOOD LUCK ON YOUR FINALS!
GOOD LUCK ON YOUR JOB HUNT!

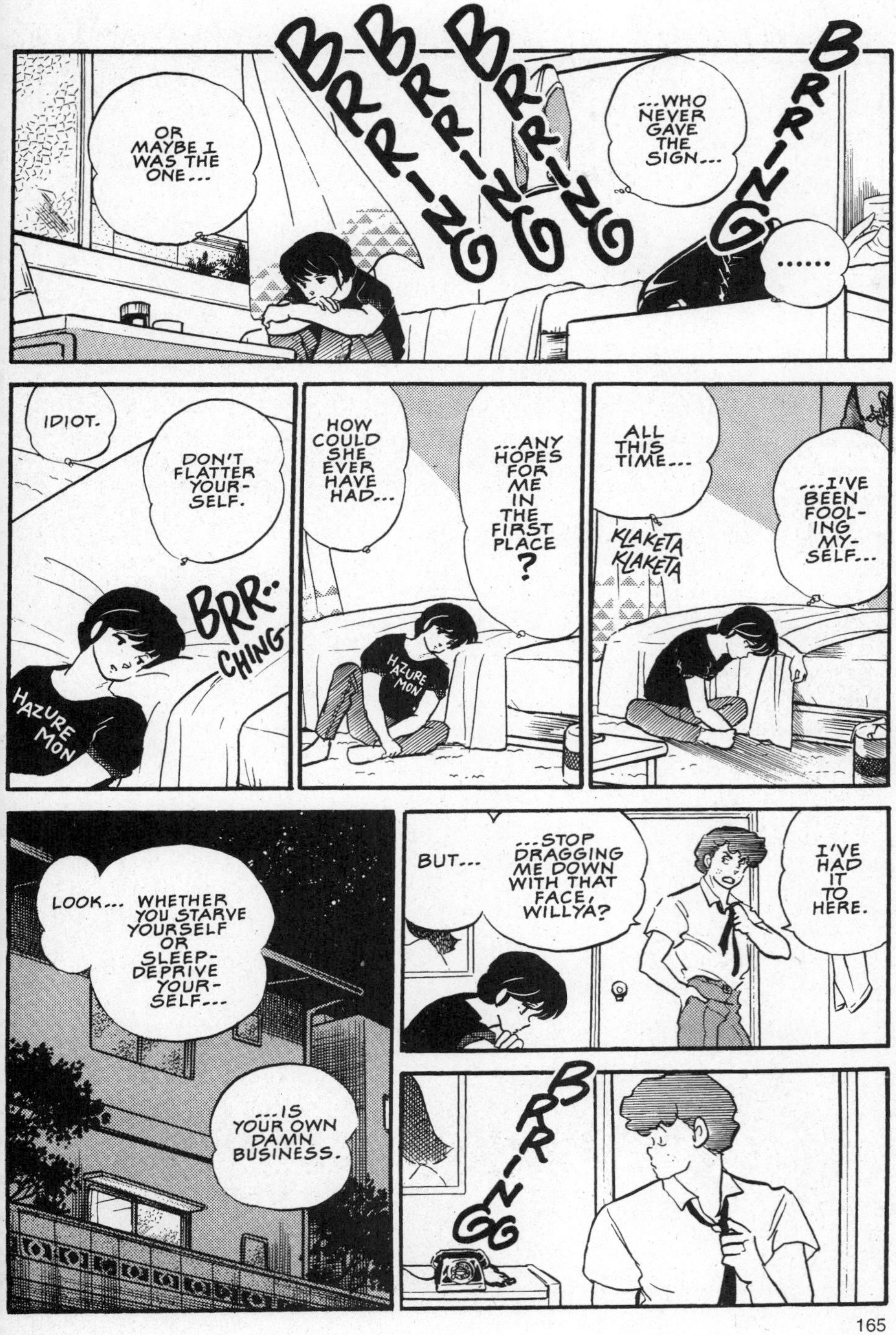
OR MAYBE I WAS THE ONE...
BRRRING
BRRRING
...WHO NEVER GAVE THE SIGN...
BRRING
......
IDIOT.
DON'T FLATTER YOURSELF.
BRR-CHING
HAZURE MON
HOW COULD SHE EVER HAVE HAD...
...ANY HOPES FOR ME IN THE FIRST PLACE?
HAZURE MON
ALL THIS TIME...
KLAKETA KLAKETA
...I'VE BEEN FOOLING MYSELF...
LOOK... WHETHER YOU STARVE YOURSELF OR SLEEP-DEPRIVE YOURSELF...
...IS YOUR OWN DAMN BUSINESS.
BUT...
...STOP DRAGGING ME DOWN WITH THAT FACE, WILLYA?
I'VE HAD IT TO HERE.
BRRRING

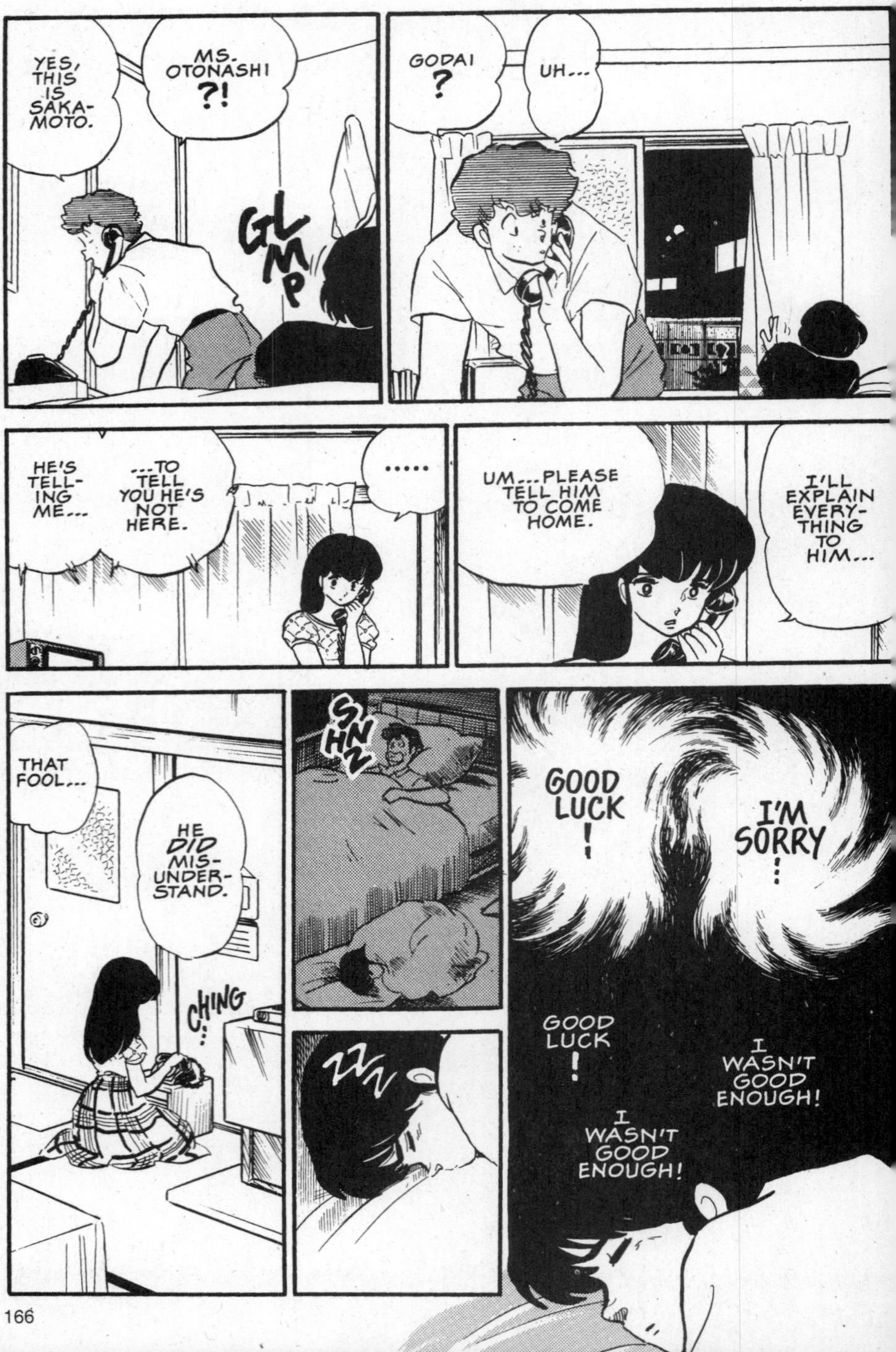
YES, THIS IS SAKAMOTO.
MS. OTONASHI ?!
GLMP
GODAI ?
UH...
HE'S TELLING ME...
...TO TELL YOU HE'S NOT HERE.
.....
UM...PLEASE TELL HIM TO COME HOME.
I'LL EXPLAIN EVERYTHING TO HIM...
THAT FOOL...
HE DID MISUNDERSTAND.
CHING...
ZZZ
GOOD LUCK!
I'M SORRY...
GOOD LUCK!
I WASN'T GOOD ENOUGH!
I WASN'T GOOD ENOUGH!

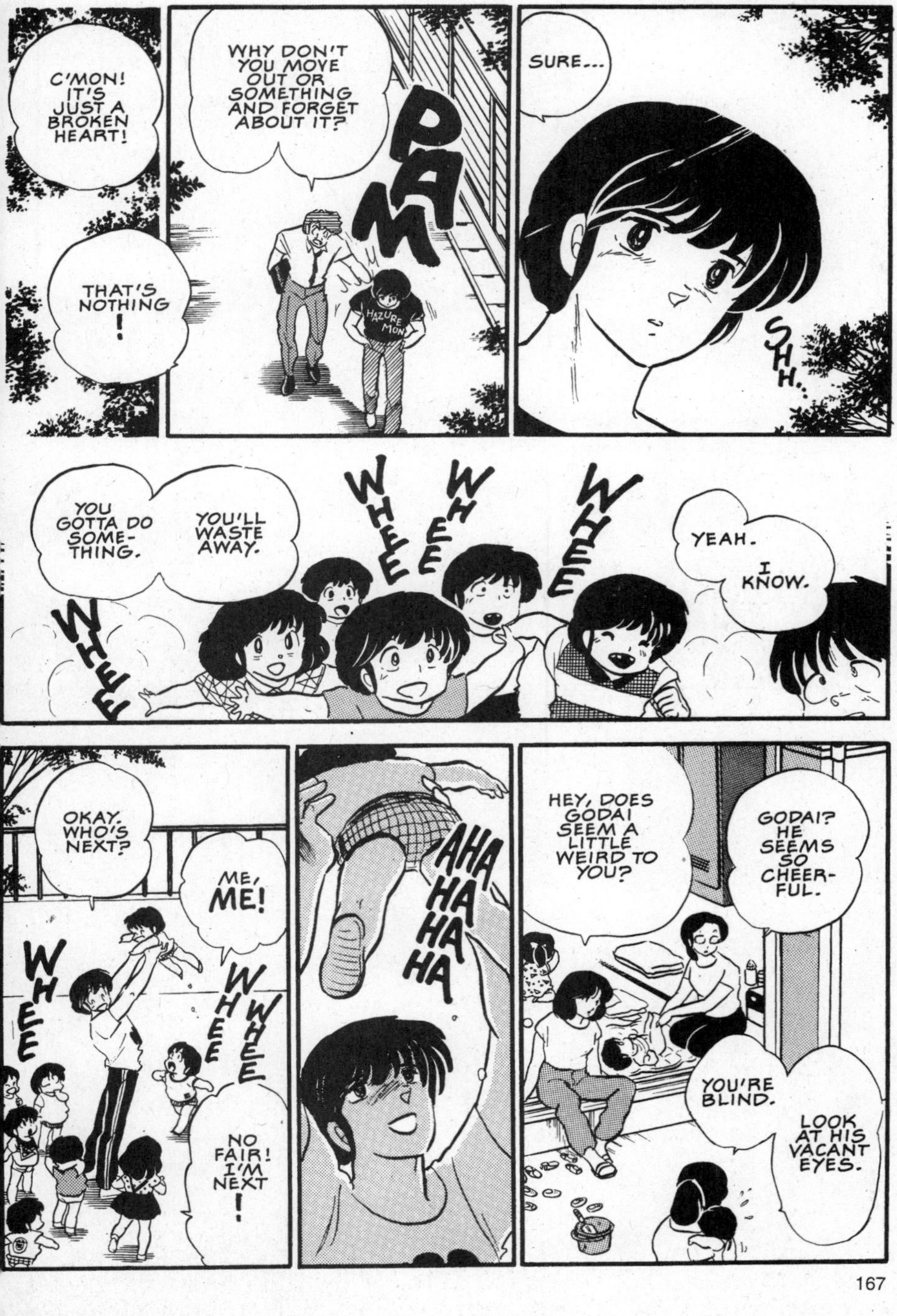
C'MON! IT'S JUST A BROKEN HEART!
THAT'S NOTHING!
WHY DON'T YOU MOVE OUT OR SOMETHING AND FORGET ABOUT IT?
PAM
HAZURE MON
SURE...
SHH..
YOU GOTTA DO SOME-THING.
YOU'LL WASTE AWAY.
WHEE
WHEE
WHEE
WHEE
YEAH.
I KNOW.
OKAY. WHO'S NEXT?
ME, ME!
WHEE
WHEE
WHEE
NO FAIR! I'M NEXT!
AHAHAHAHAHA
HEY, DOES GODAI SEEM A LITTLE WEIRD TO YOU?
GODAI? HE SEEMS SO CHEER-FUL.
YOU'RE BLIND.
LOOK AT HIS VACANT EYES.

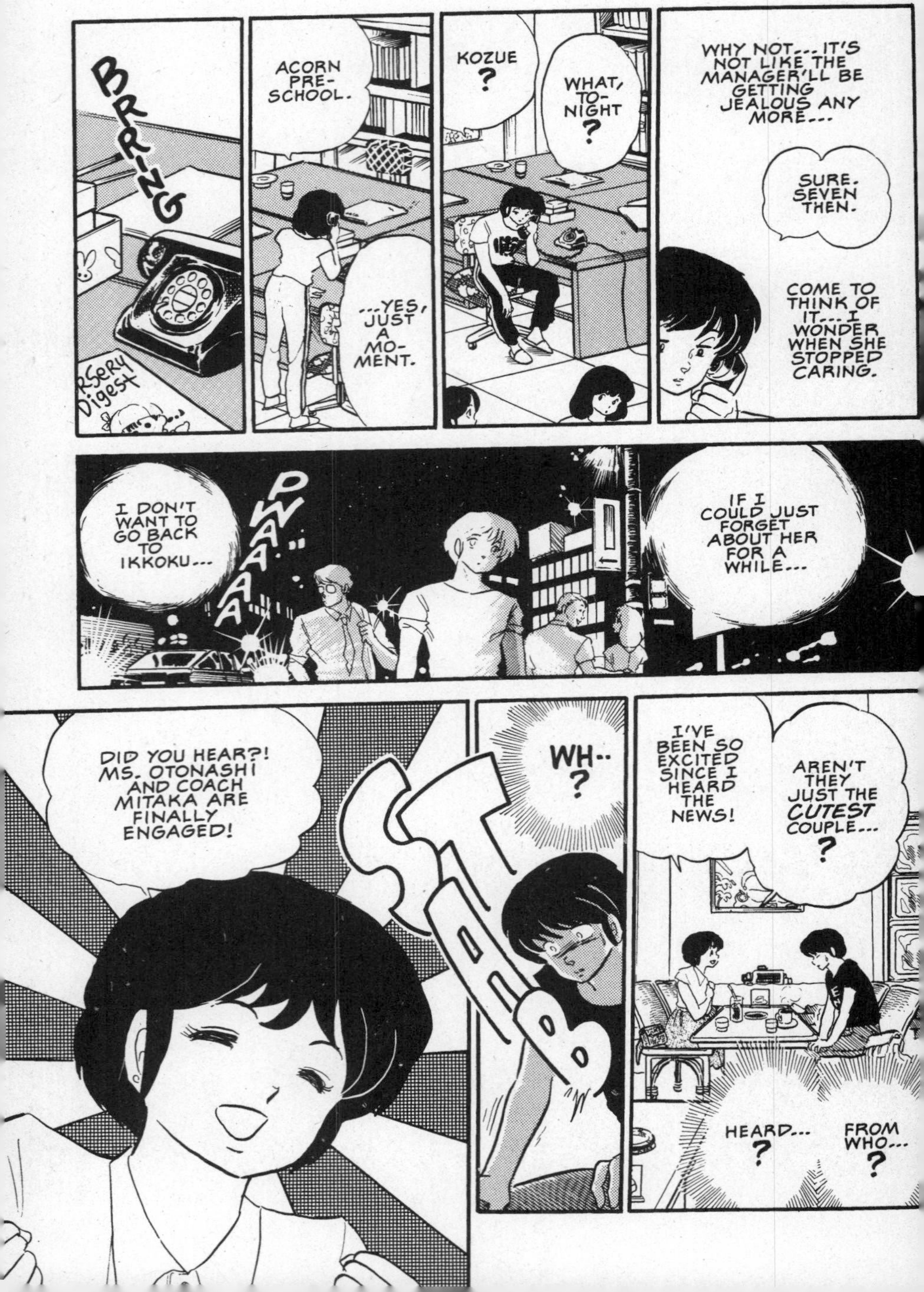
BRRRING
RSeRY Digest
ACORN PRE-SCHOOL.
...YES, JUST A MO-MENT.
KOZUE ?
WHAT, TO-NIGHT ?
WHY NOT... IT'S NOT LIKE THE MANAGER'LL BE GETTING JEALOUS ANY MORE...
SURE. SEVEN THEN.
COME TO THINK OF IT... I WONDER WHEN SHE STOPPED CARING.
I DON'T WANT TO GO BACK TO IKKOKU...
PWAAAA
IF I COULD JUST FORGET ABOUT HER FOR A WHILE...
DID YOU HEAR?! MS. OTONASHI AND COACH MITAKA ARE FINALLY ENGAGED!
WH.. ?
I'VE BEEN SO EXCITED SINCE I HEARD THE NEWS!
AREN'T THEY JUST THE *CUTEST* COUPLE... ?
HEARD... ?
FROM WHO... ?

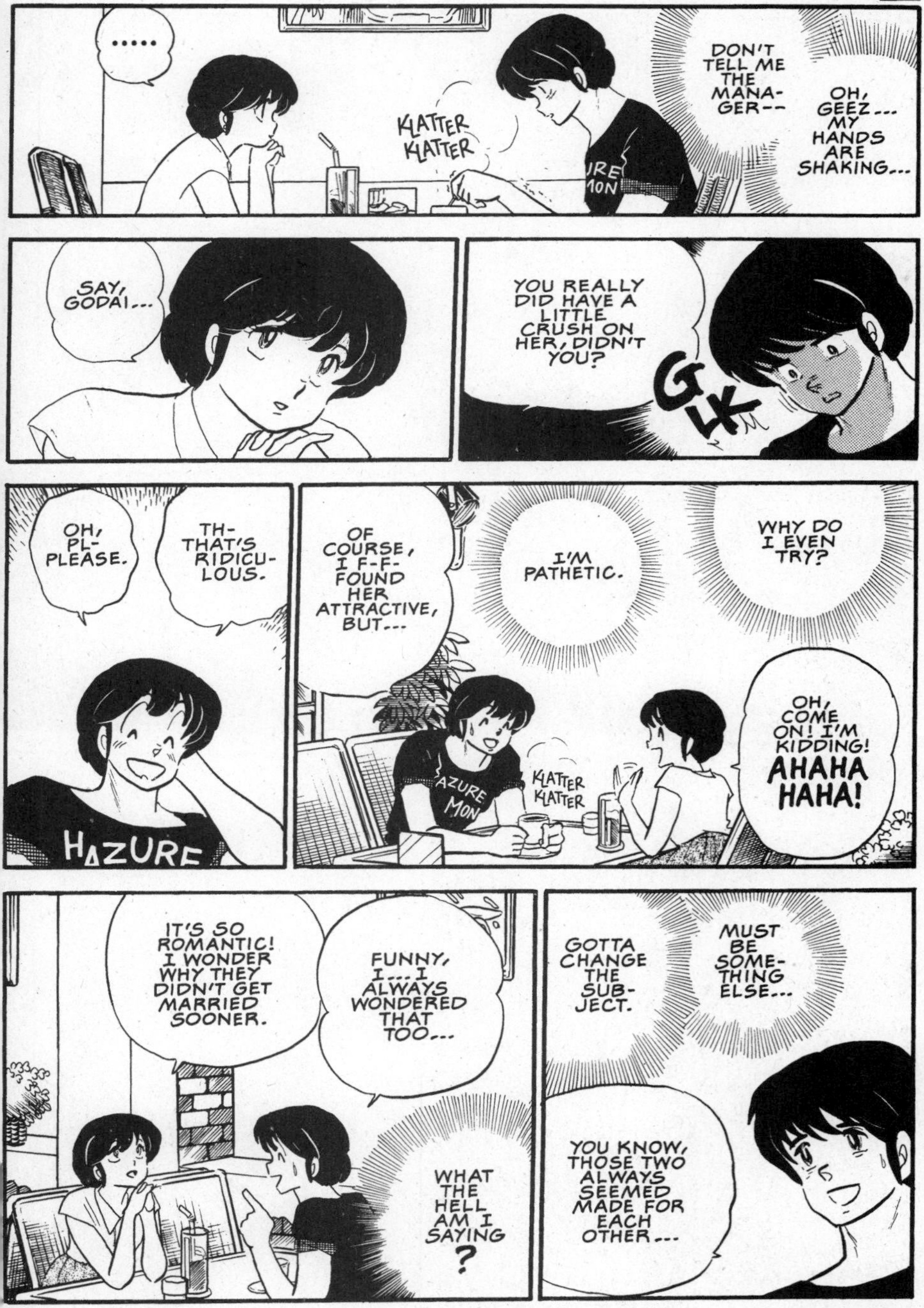
......
KLATTER KLATTER
DON'T TELL ME THE MANA-GER--
OH, GEEZ... MY HANDS ARE SHAKING...
SAY, GODAI...
YOU REALLY DID HAVE A LITTLE CRUSH ON HER, DIDN'T YOU?
GLK
OH, PL-PLEASE.
TH-THAT'S RIDICU-LOUS.
OF COURSE, I F-F-FOUND HER ATTRACTIVE, BUT...
I'M PATHETIC.
WHY DO I EVEN TRY?
KLATTER KLATTER
OH, COME ON! I'M KIDDING! AHAHA HAHA!
IT'S SO ROMANTIC! I WONDER WHY THEY DIDN'T GET MARRIED SOONER.
FUNNY, I... I ALWAYS WONDERED THAT TOO...
WHAT THE HELL AM I SAYING?
GOTTA CHANGE THE SUB-JECT.
MUST BE SOME-THING ELSE...
YOU KNOW, THOSE TWO ALWAYS SEEMED MADE FOR EACH OTHER...

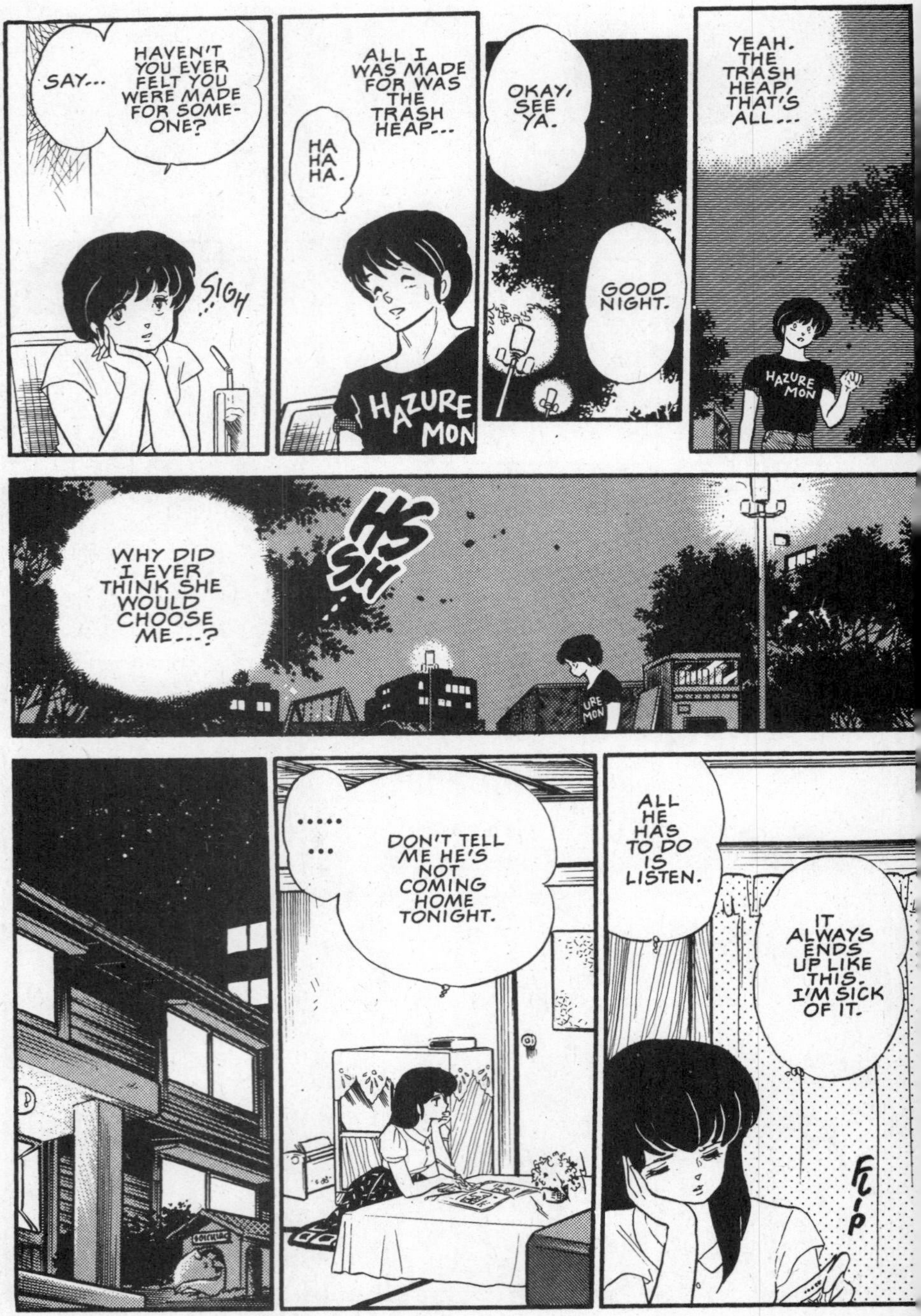
SAY...
HAVEN'T YOU EVER FELT YOU WERE MADE FOR SOME-ONE?
SIGH
ALL I WAS MADE FOR WAS THE TRASH HEAP...
HA HA HA.
HAZURE MON
OKAY, SEE YA.
GOOD NIGHT.
YEAH. THE TRASH HEAP, THAT'S ALL...
HAZURE MON
WHY DID I EVER THINK SHE WOULD CHOOSE ME...?
HSSH
.....
...
DON'T TELL ME HE'S NOT COMING HOME TONIGHT.
ALL HE HAS TO DO IS LISTEN.
IT ALWAYS ENDS UP LIKE THIS. I'M SICK OF IT.
FLIP

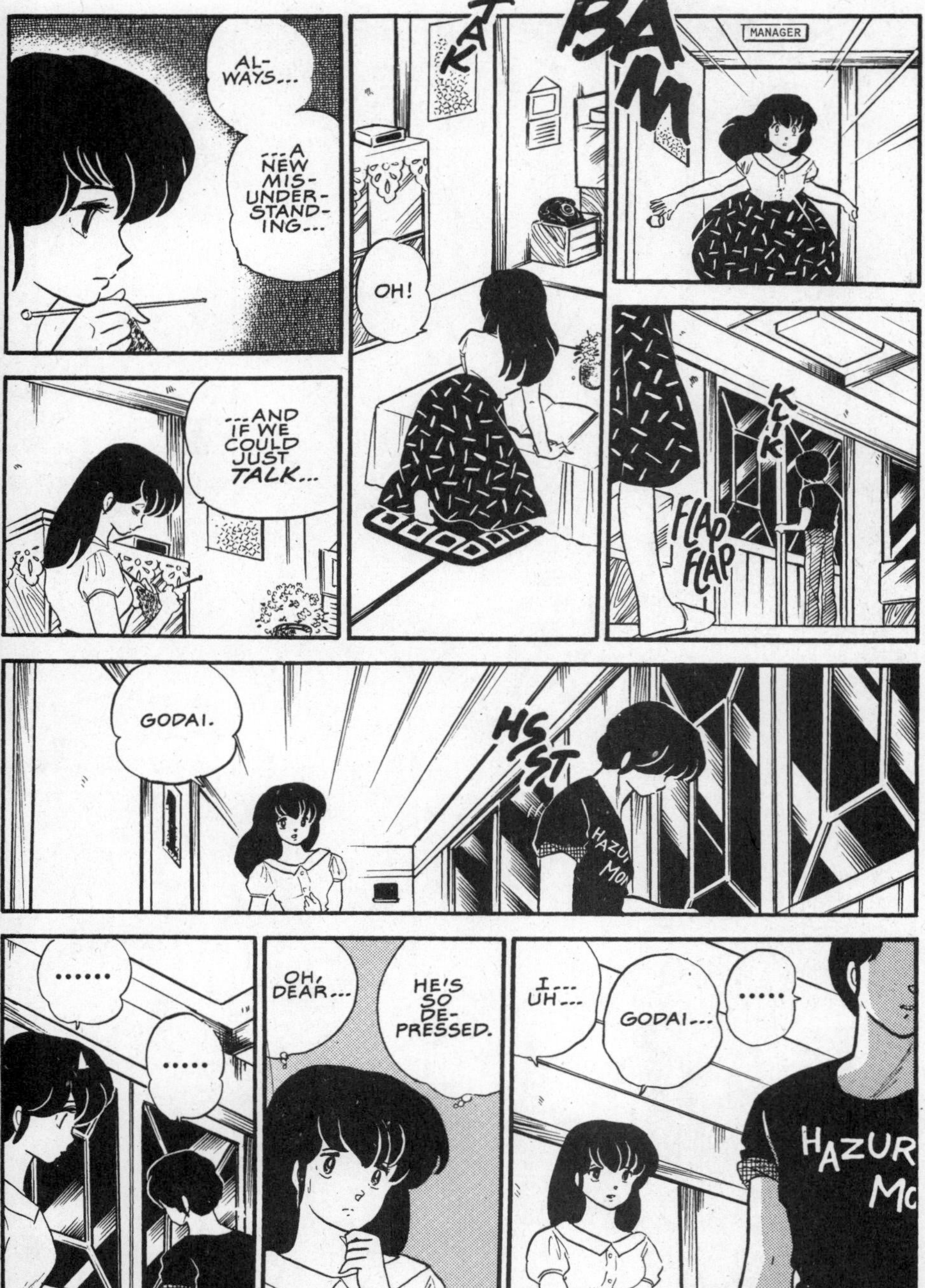
AL-WAYS...
...A NEW MIS-UNDER-STANDING...
OH!
TAK
BAM
MANAGER
...AND IF WE COULD JUST TALK...
KLIK
FLAP FLAP
GODAI.
HSST
HAZUR MO
......
.....
OH, DEAR...
HE'S SO DE-PRESSED.
I... UH...
GODAI...
.....
HAZUR MO

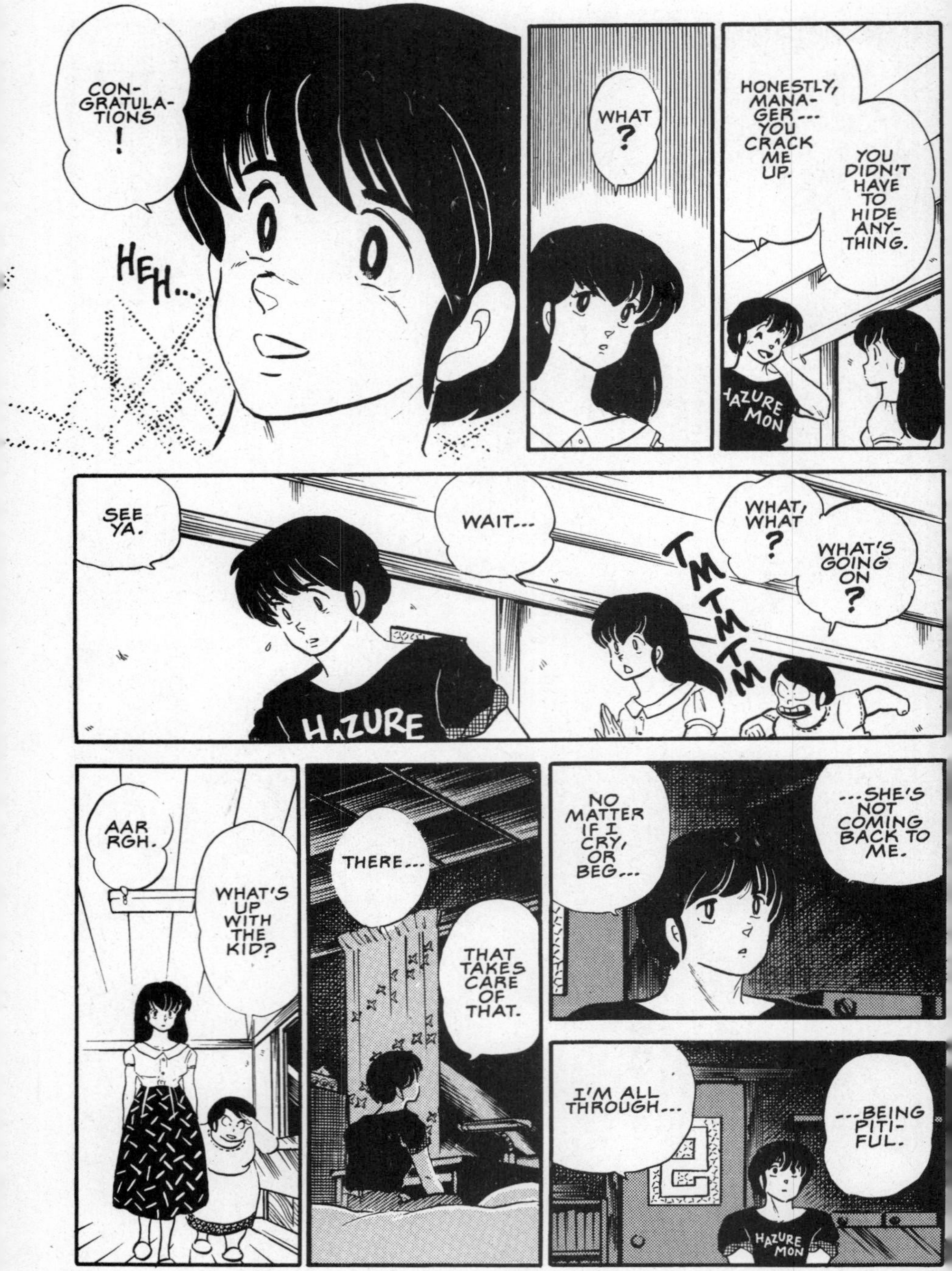
CONGRATULATIONS!
HEH...
WHAT?
HONESTLY, MANAGER--- YOU CRACK ME UP.
YOU DIDN'T HAVE TO HIDE ANYTHING.
HAZURE MON
SEE YA.
WAIT...
WHAT, WHAT?
WHAT'S GOING ON?
TMTMTM
HAZURE
AARRGH.
WHAT'S UP WITH THE KID?
THERE...
THAT TAKES CARE OF THAT.
NO MATTER IF I CRY, OR BEG...
...SHE'S NOT COMING BACK TO ME.
I'M ALL THROUGH...
...BEING PITIFUL.
HAZURE MON

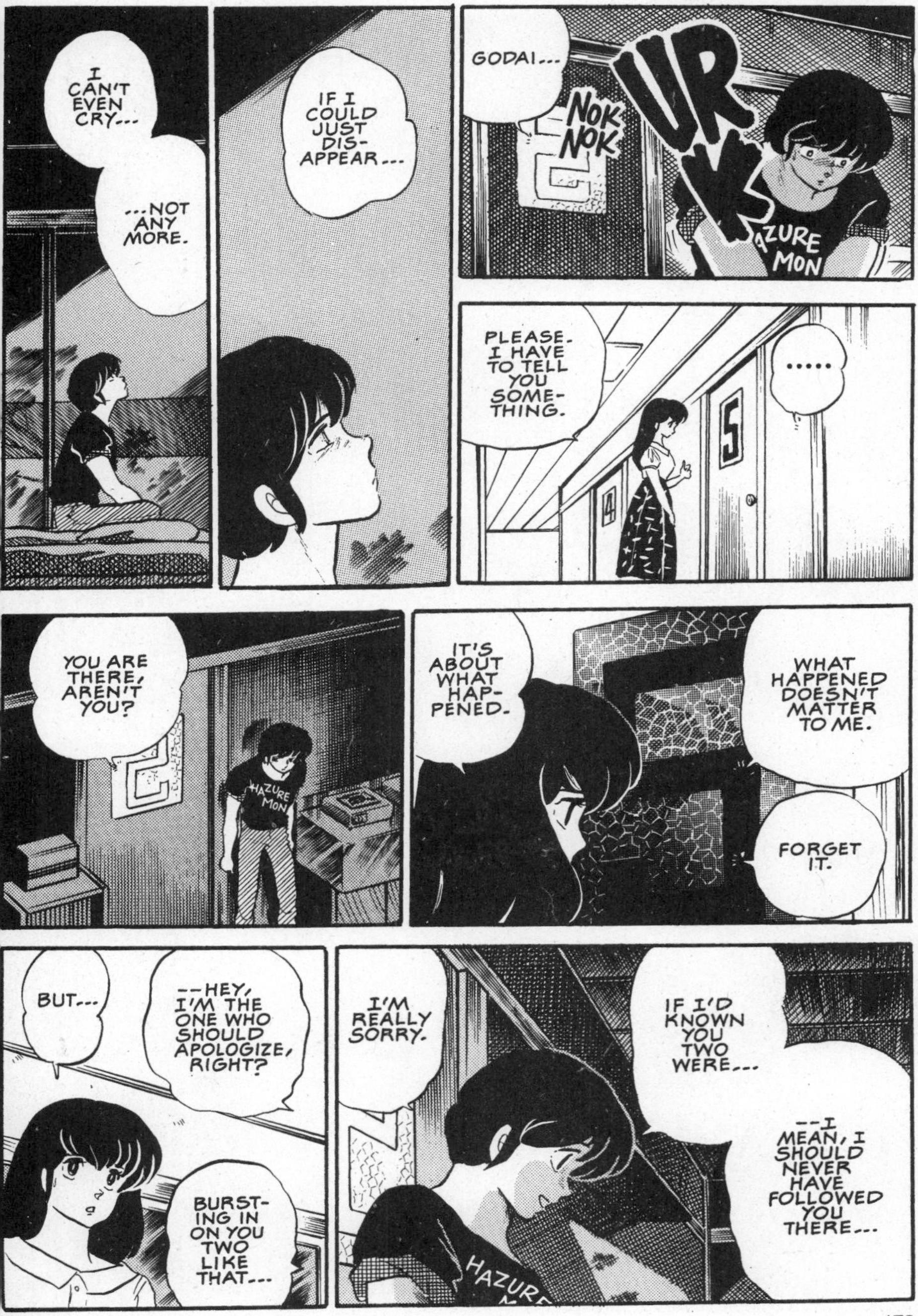
I CAN'T EVEN CRY...
...NOT ANY MORE.
IF I COULD JUST DIS-APPEAR...
GODAI...
NOK NOK
URK
HAZURE MON
PLEASE. I HAVE TO TELL YOU SOME-THING.
.....
YOU ARE THERE, AREN'T YOU?
HAZURE MON
IT'S ABOUT WHAT HAP-PENED.
WHAT HAPPENED DOESN'T MATTER TO ME.
FORGET IT.
BUT...
--HEY, I'M THE ONE WHO SHOULD APOLOGIZE, RIGHT?
BURST-ING IN ON YOU TWO LIKE THAT...
I'M REALLY SORRY.
IF I'D KNOWN YOU TWO WERE...
--I MEAN, I SHOULD NEVER HAVE FOLLOWED YOU THERE...

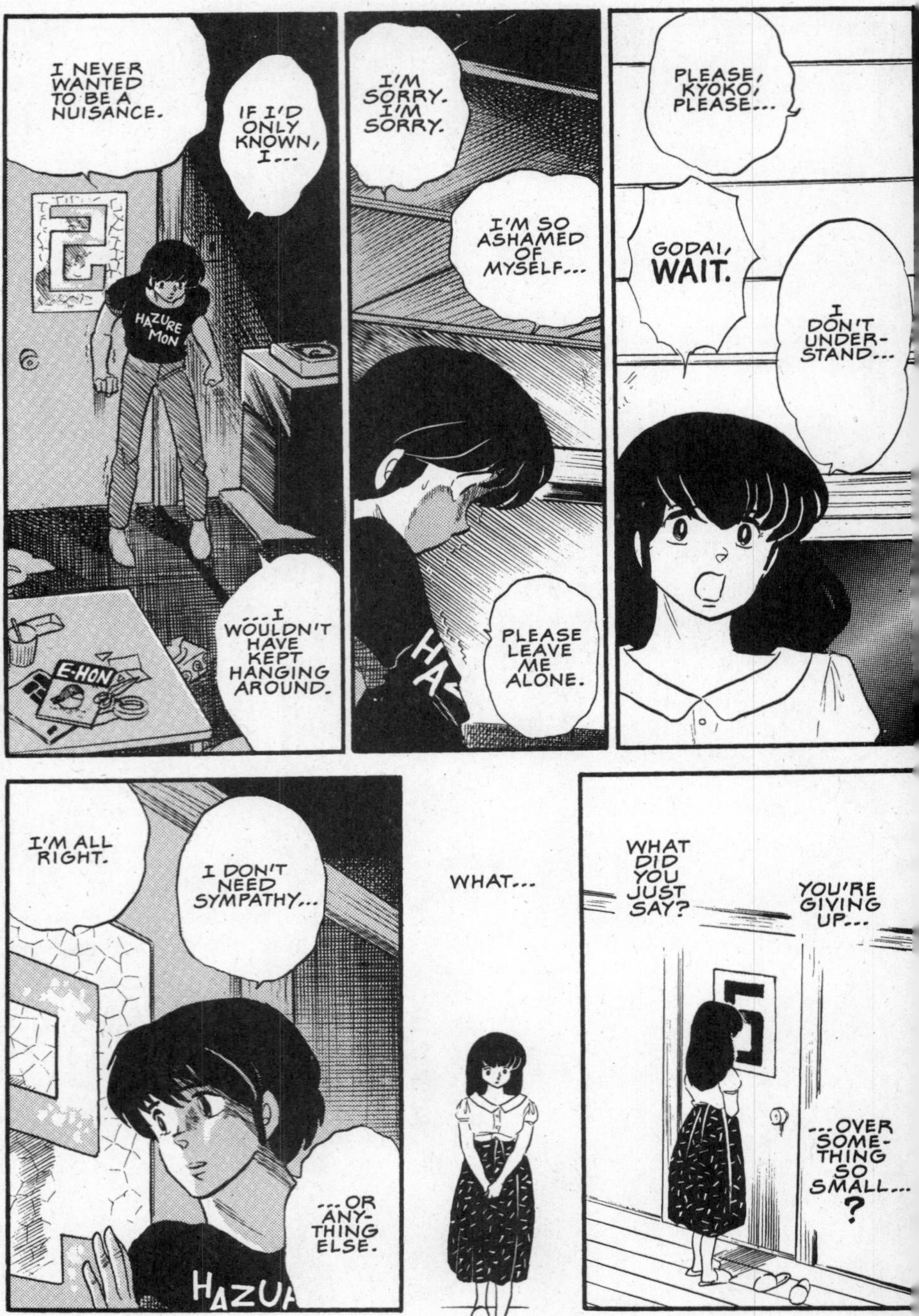
I NEVER WANTED TO BE A NUISANCE.
IF I'D ONLY KNOWN, I...
...I WOULDN'T HAVE KEPT HANGING AROUND.
HAZURE MON
E-HON
I'M SORRY. I'M SORRY.
I'M SO ASHAMED OF MYSELF...
PLEASE LEAVE ME ALONE.
PLEASE, KYOKO, PLEASE...
GODAI, WAIT.
I DON'T UNDERSTAND...
I'M ALL RIGHT.
I DON'T NEED SYMPATHY...
...OR ANYTHING ELSE.
WHAT...
WHAT DID YOU JUST SAY?
YOU'RE GIVING UP...
...OVER SOMETHING SO SMALL...?

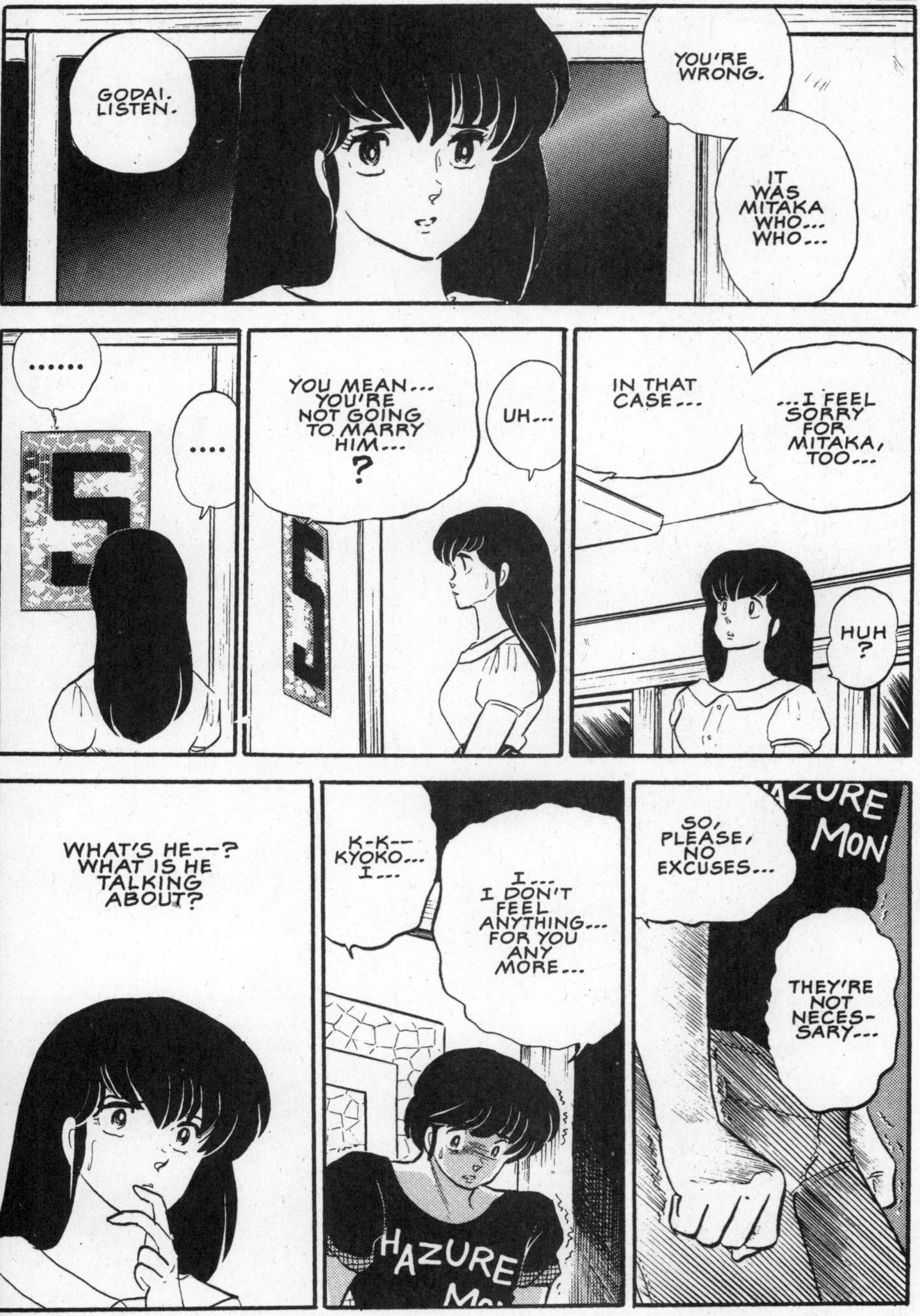
GODAI. LISTEN.
YOU'RE WRONG.
IT WAS MITAKA WHO... WHO...
......
....
YOU MEAN... YOU'RE NOT GOING TO MARRY HIM...?
UH...
IN THAT CASE...
...I FEEL SORRY FOR MITAKA, TOO...
HUH?
WHAT'S HE--? WHAT IS HE TALKING ABOUT?
K-K-- KYOKO... I...
I... I DON'T FEEL ANYTHING... FOR YOU ANY MORE...
HAZURE
SO, PLEASE, NO EXCUSES...
THEY'RE NOT NECES-SARY...
AZURE MON

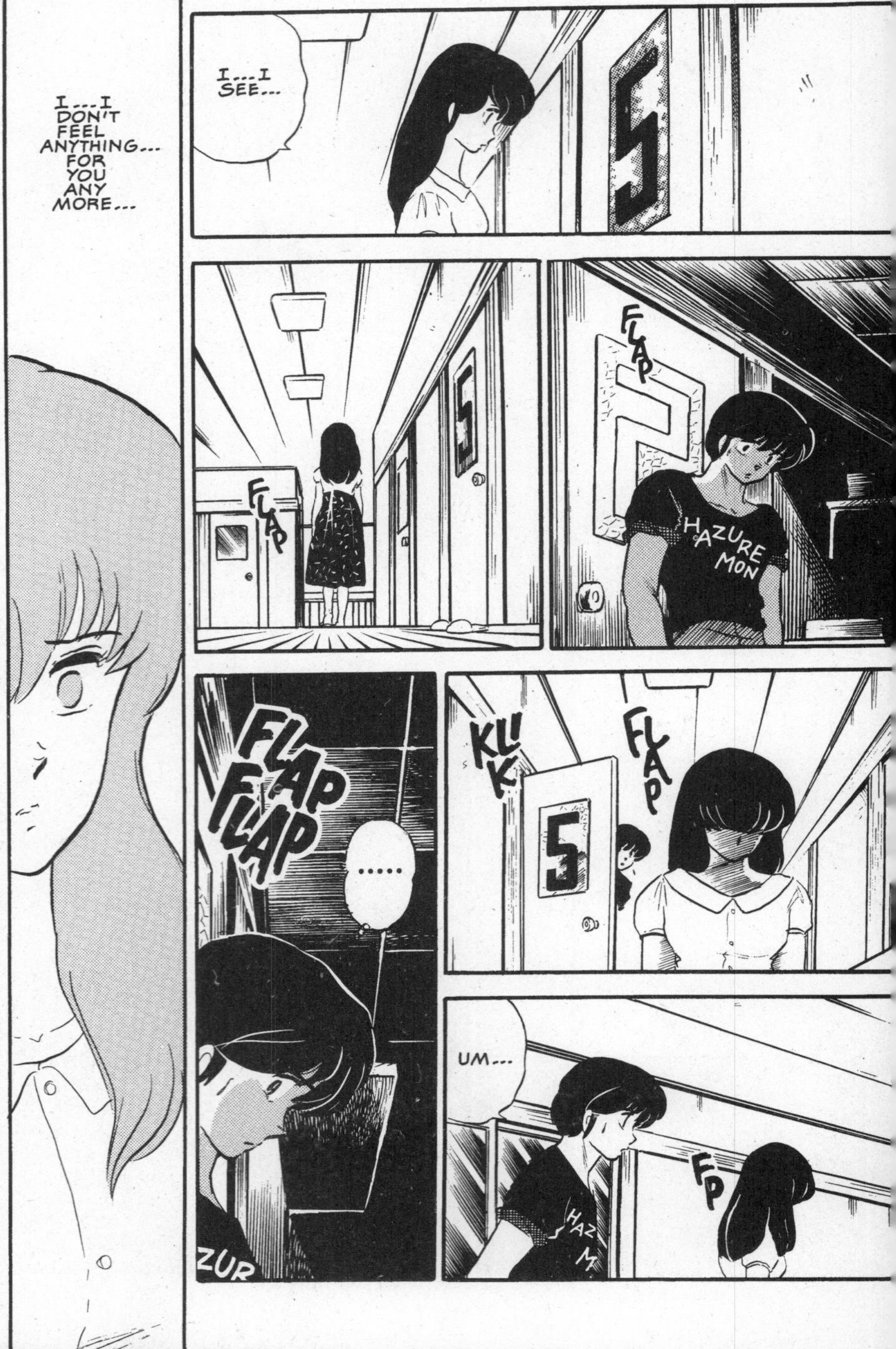
I...I DON'T FEEL ANYTHING... FOR YOU ANY MORE...
I...I SEE...
FLAP
FLAP
FLAP FLAP FLAP
......
ZUR
KLIK
FLAP
UM...
FP

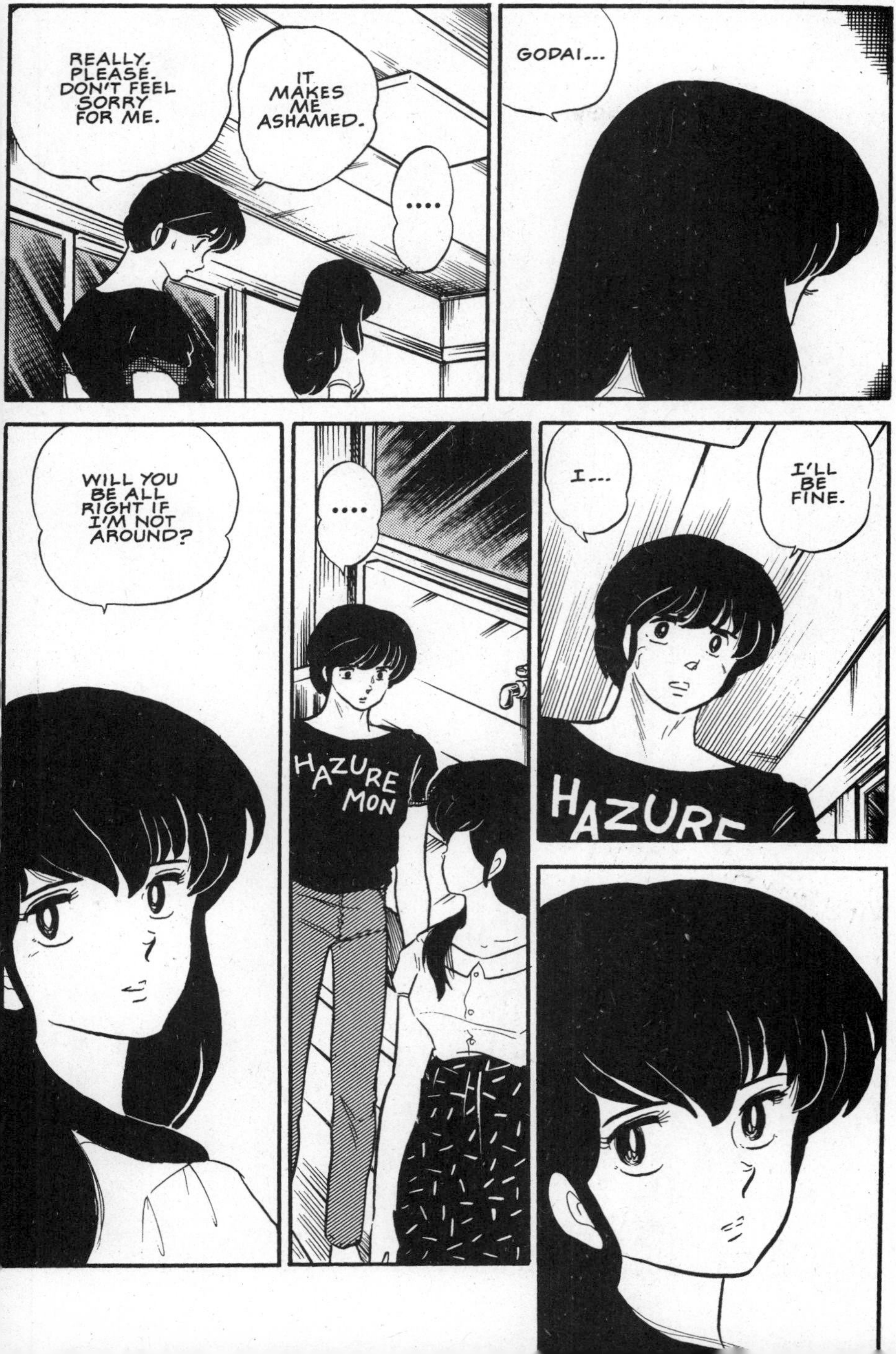
REALLY. PLEASE. DON'T FEEL SORRY FOR ME.
IT MAKES ME ASHAMED.
....
GODAI...
WILL YOU BE ALL RIGHT IF I'M NOT AROUND?
....
HAZURE MON
I...
I'LL BE FINE.
HAZURE

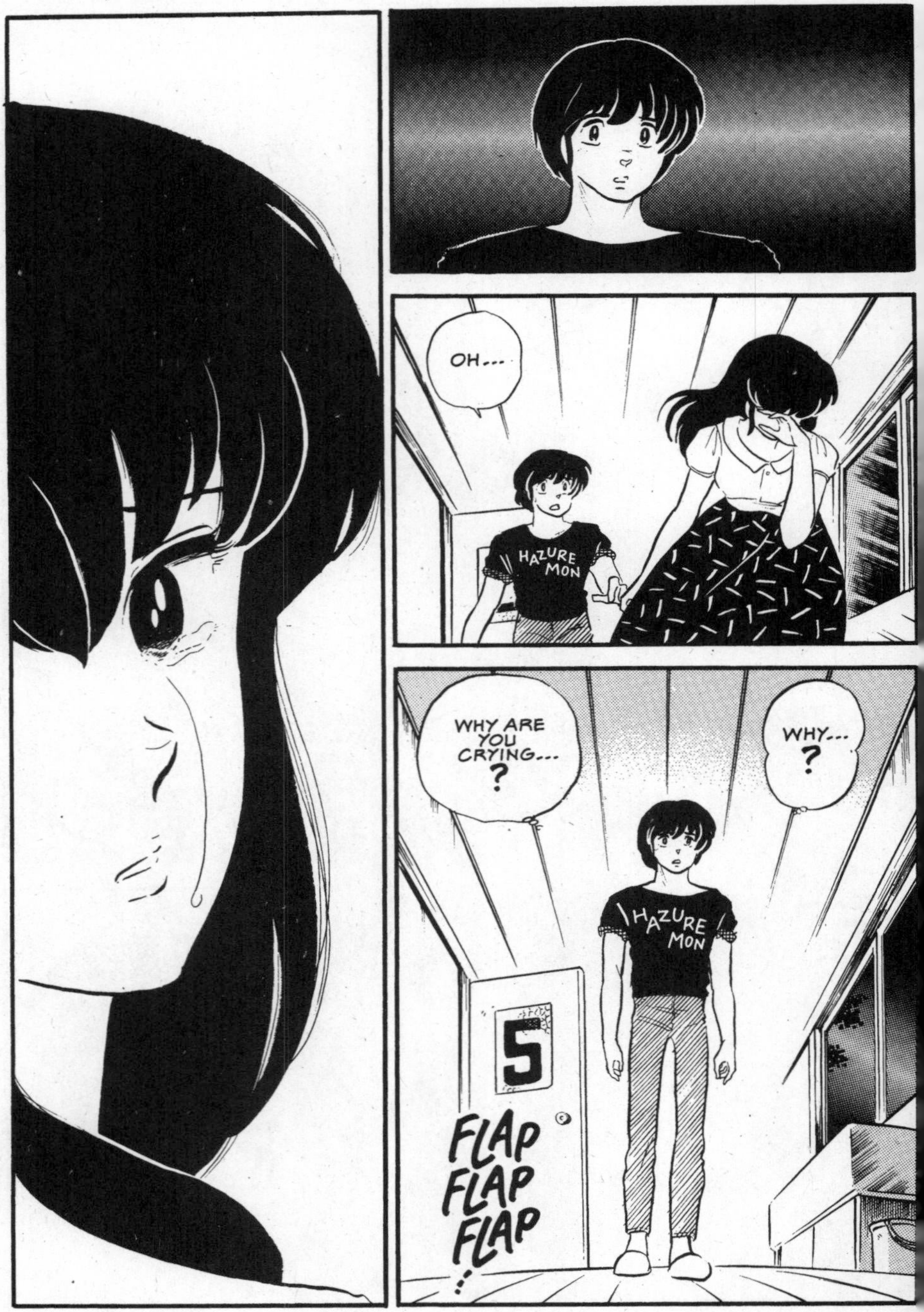
OH...
WHY ARE YOU CRYING...?
WHY...?
HAZURE MON
5
FLAP FLAP FLAP

PART 9
TWIN JOURNEYS

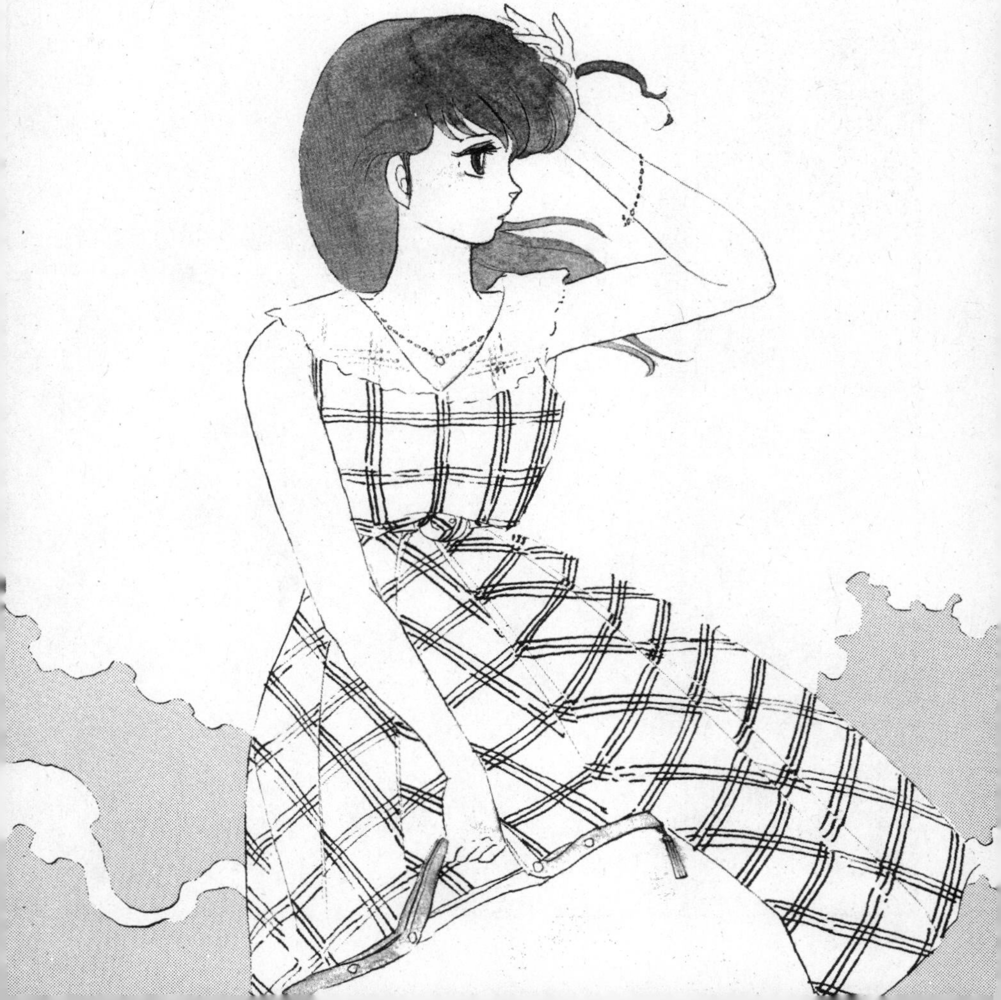

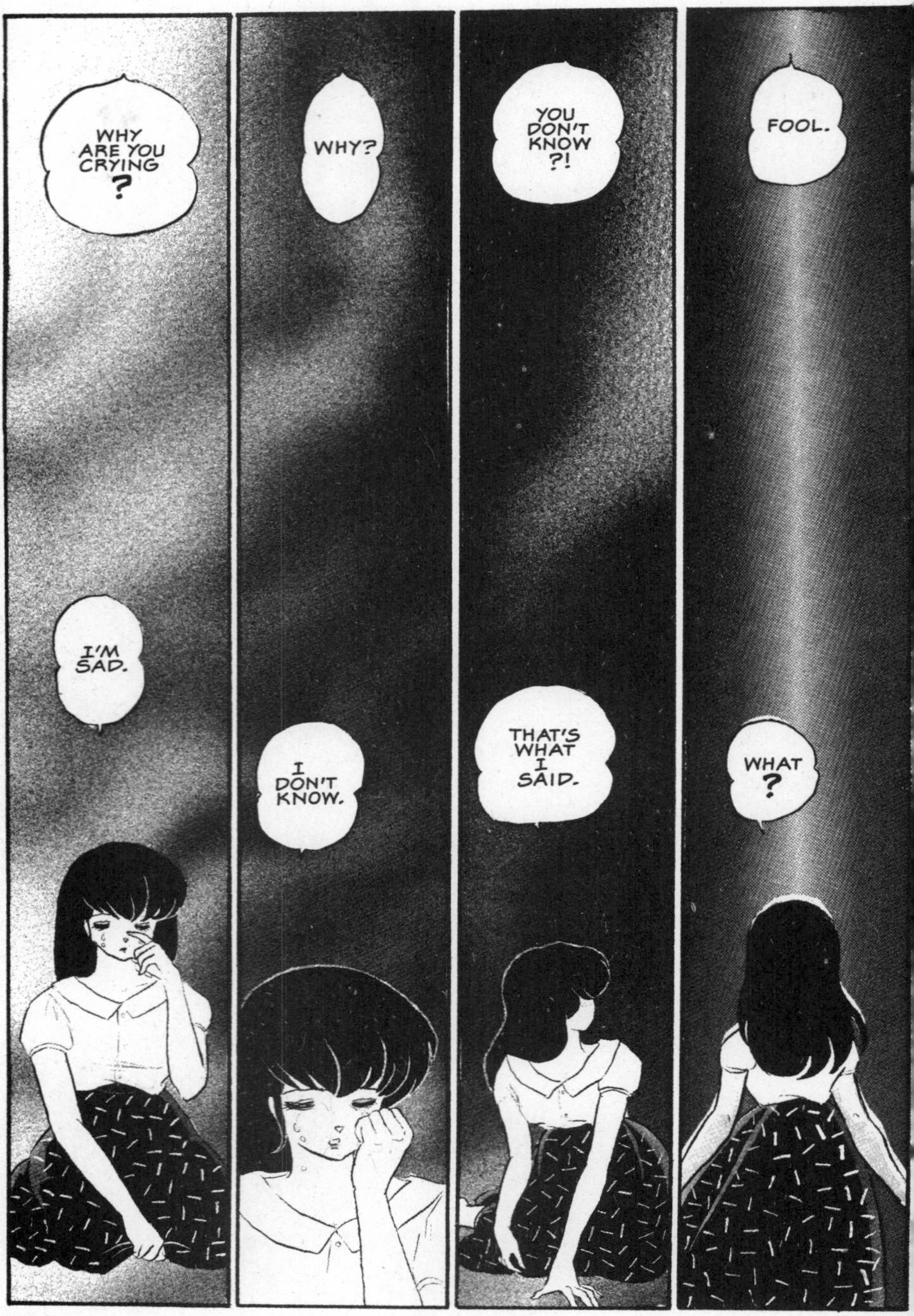
WHY ARE YOU CRYING?
I'M SAD.
WHY?
I DON'T KNOW.
YOU DON'T KNOW?!
THAT'S WHAT I SAID.
FOOL.
WHAT?

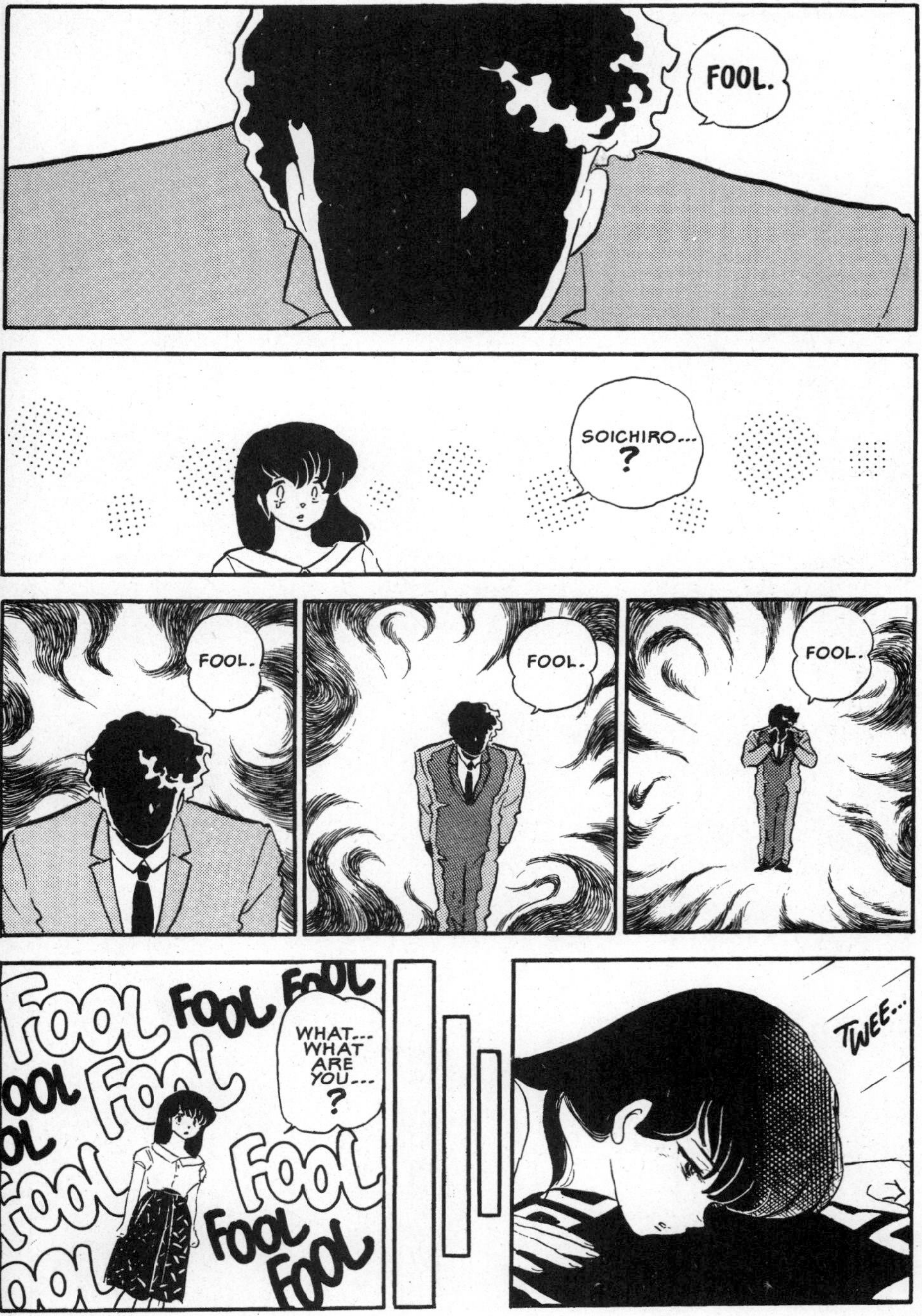
FOOL.
SOICHIRO...?
FOOL.
FOOL.
FOOL.
FOOL FOOL FOOL FOOL FOOL FOOL
WHAT... WHAT ARE YOU...?
TWEE...

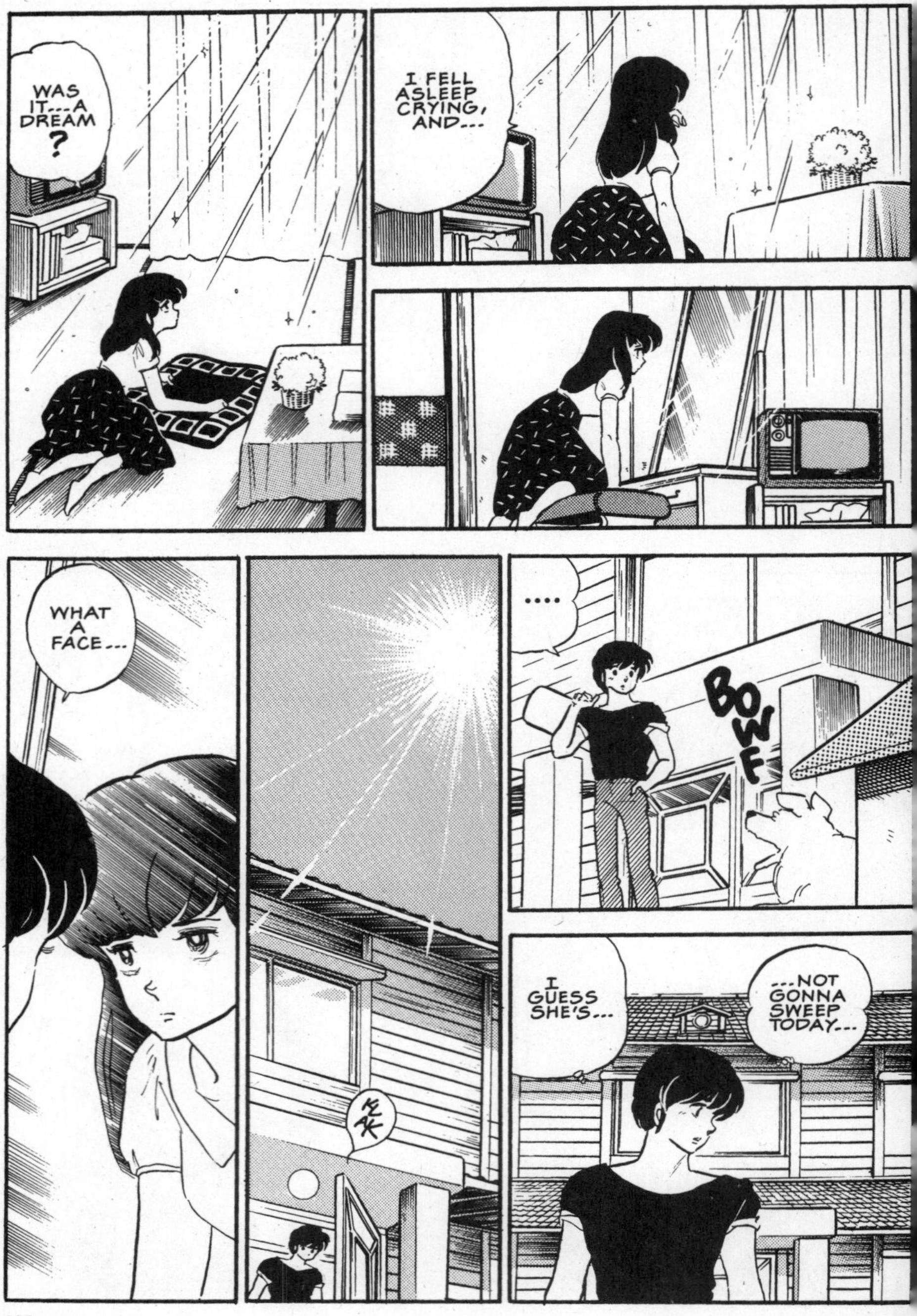
WAS IT...A DREAM?
I FELL ASLEEP CRYING, AND...
WHAT A FACE...
KLAK
....
BOWF
I GUESS SHE'S...
...NOT GONNA SWEEP TODAY...

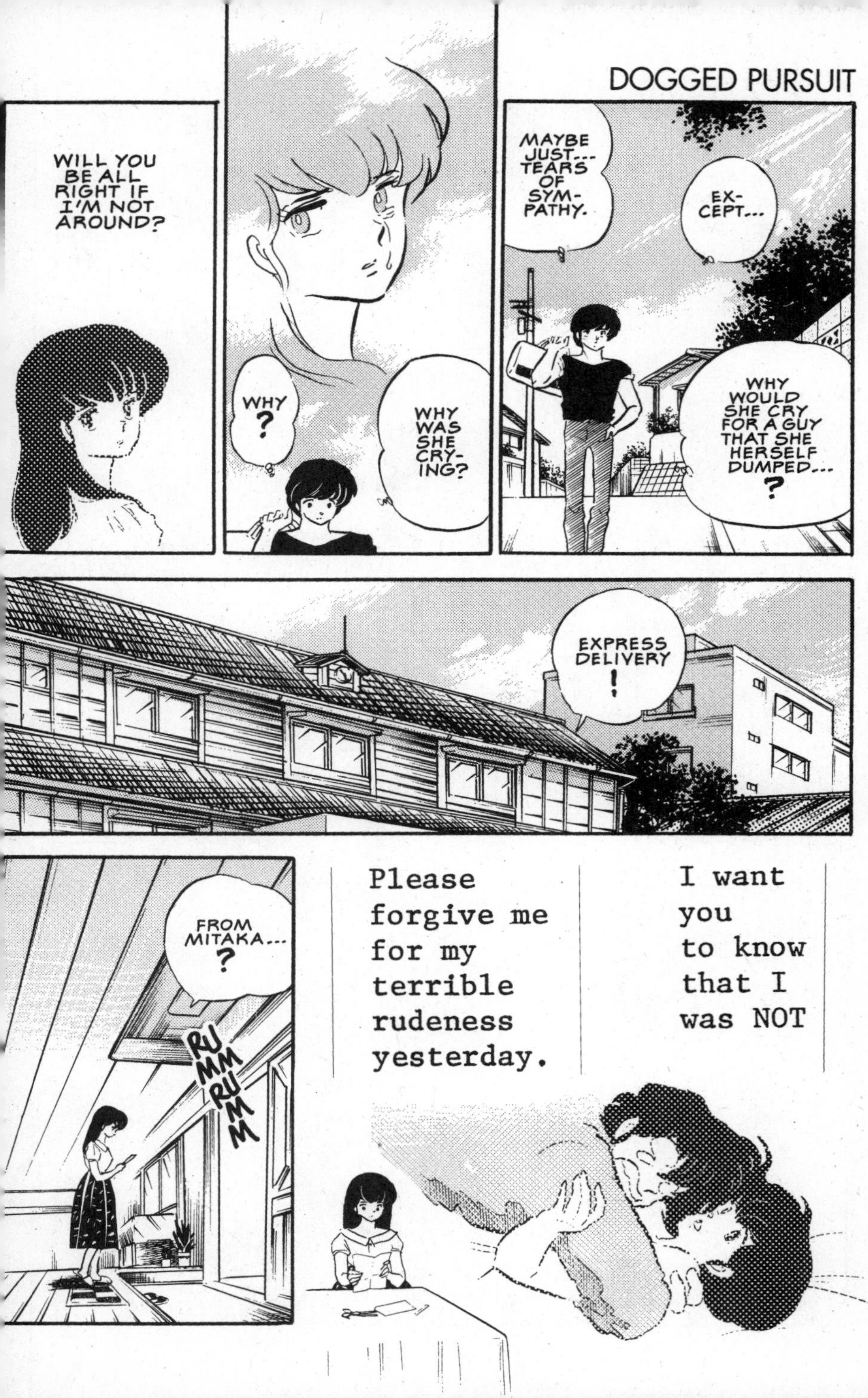
WILL YOU BE ALL RIGHT IF I'M NOT AROUND?
WHY?
WHY WAS SHE CRYING?
MAYBE JUST... TEARS OF SYMPATHY.
EXCEPT...
WHY WOULD SHE CRY FOR A GUY THAT SHE HERSELF DUMPED...?
EXPRESS DELIVERY!
FROM MITAKA...?
RUMMRUMM
Please forgive me for my terrible rudeness yesterday.
I want you to know that I was NOT

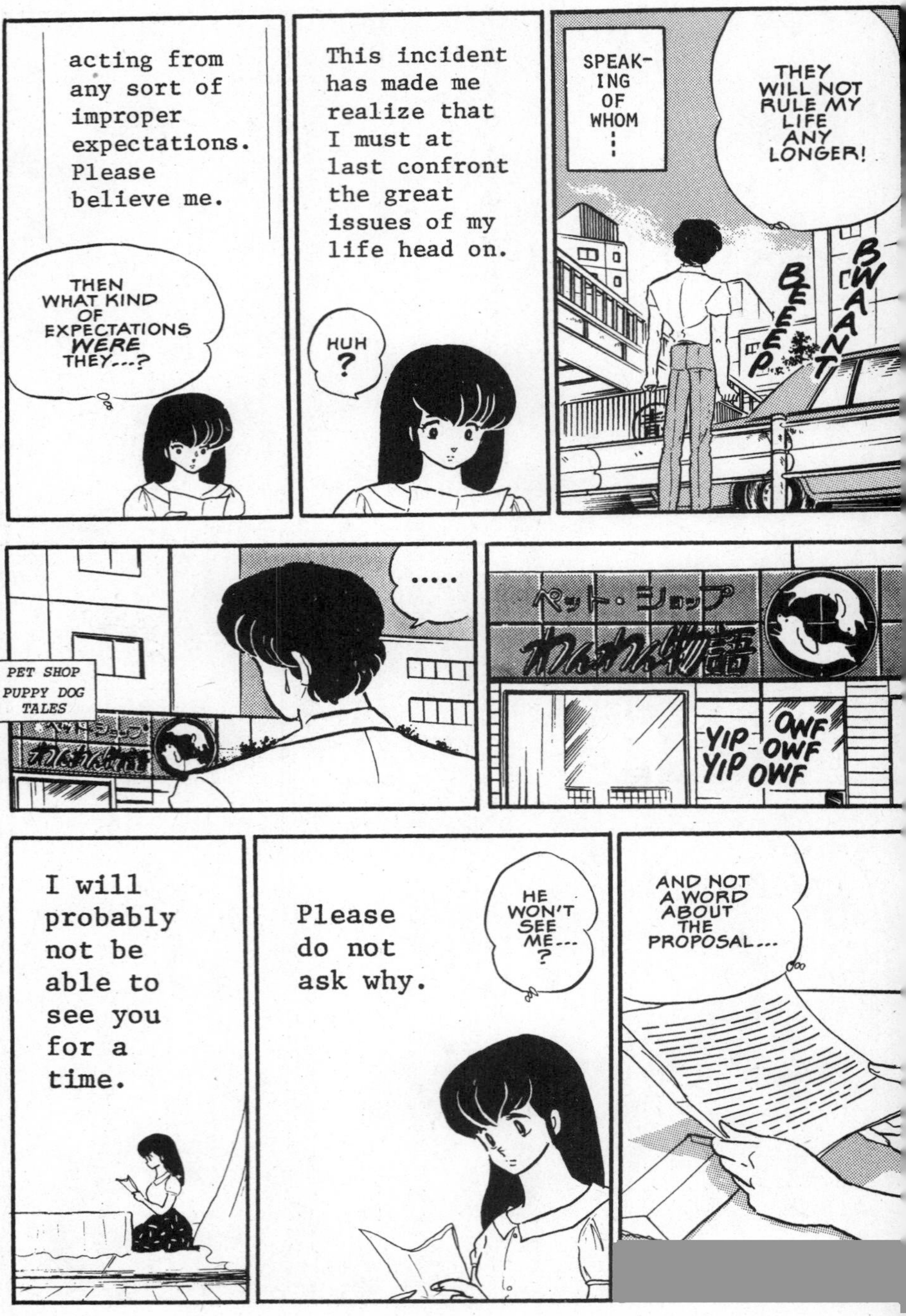

acting from any sort of improper expectations. Please believe me.
THEN WHAT KIND OF EXPECTATIONS WERE THEY...?
This incident has made me realize that I must at last confront the great issues of my life head on.
HUH ?
SPEAK-ING OF WHOM ...
THEY WILL NOT RULE MY LIFE ANY LONGER!
BEEEP
BWAANT
PET SHOP PUPPY DOG TALES
.....
ペット・ショップ
わんわん物語
YIP YIP
OWF OWF OWF
I will probably not be able to see you for a time.
Please do not ask why.
HE WON'T SEE ME...?
AND NOT A WORD ABOUT THE PROPOSAL...

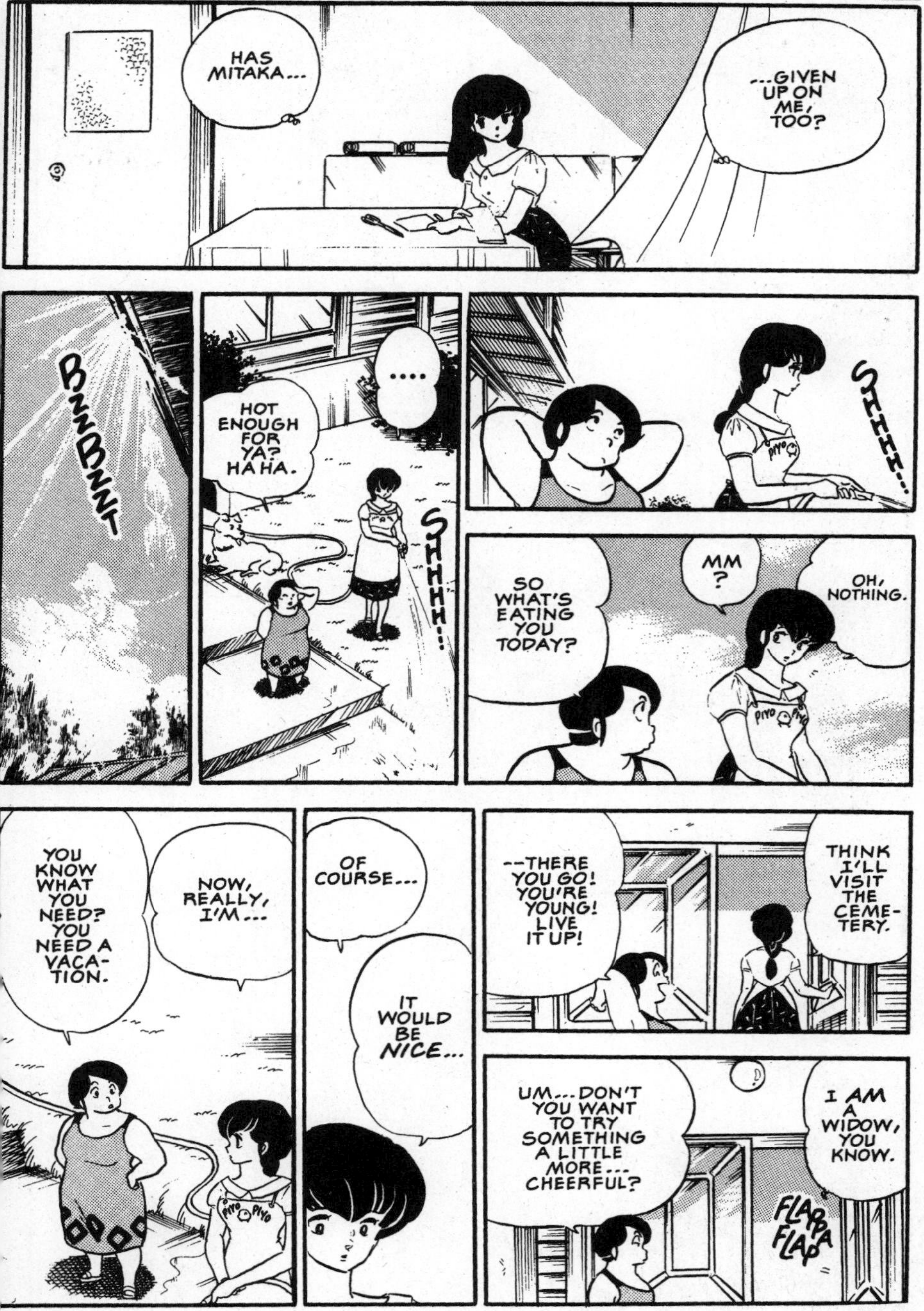
HAS MITAKA...
...GIVEN UP ON ME, TOO?
BZZBZZT
HOT ENOUGH FOR YA? HA HA.
....
SHHHH!!
SHHHH...
SO WHAT'S EATING YOU TODAY?
MM?
OH, NOTHING.
YOU KNOW WHAT YOU NEED? YOU NEED A VACATION.
NOW, REALLY, I'M...
OF COURSE...
IT WOULD BE NICE...
--THERE YOU GO! YOU'RE YOUNG! LIVE IT UP!
THINK I'LL VISIT THE CEMETERY.
UM... DON'T YOU WANT TO TRY SOMETHING A LITTLE MORE... CHEERFUL?
I AM A WIDOW, YOU KNOW.
FLAPPA FLAP

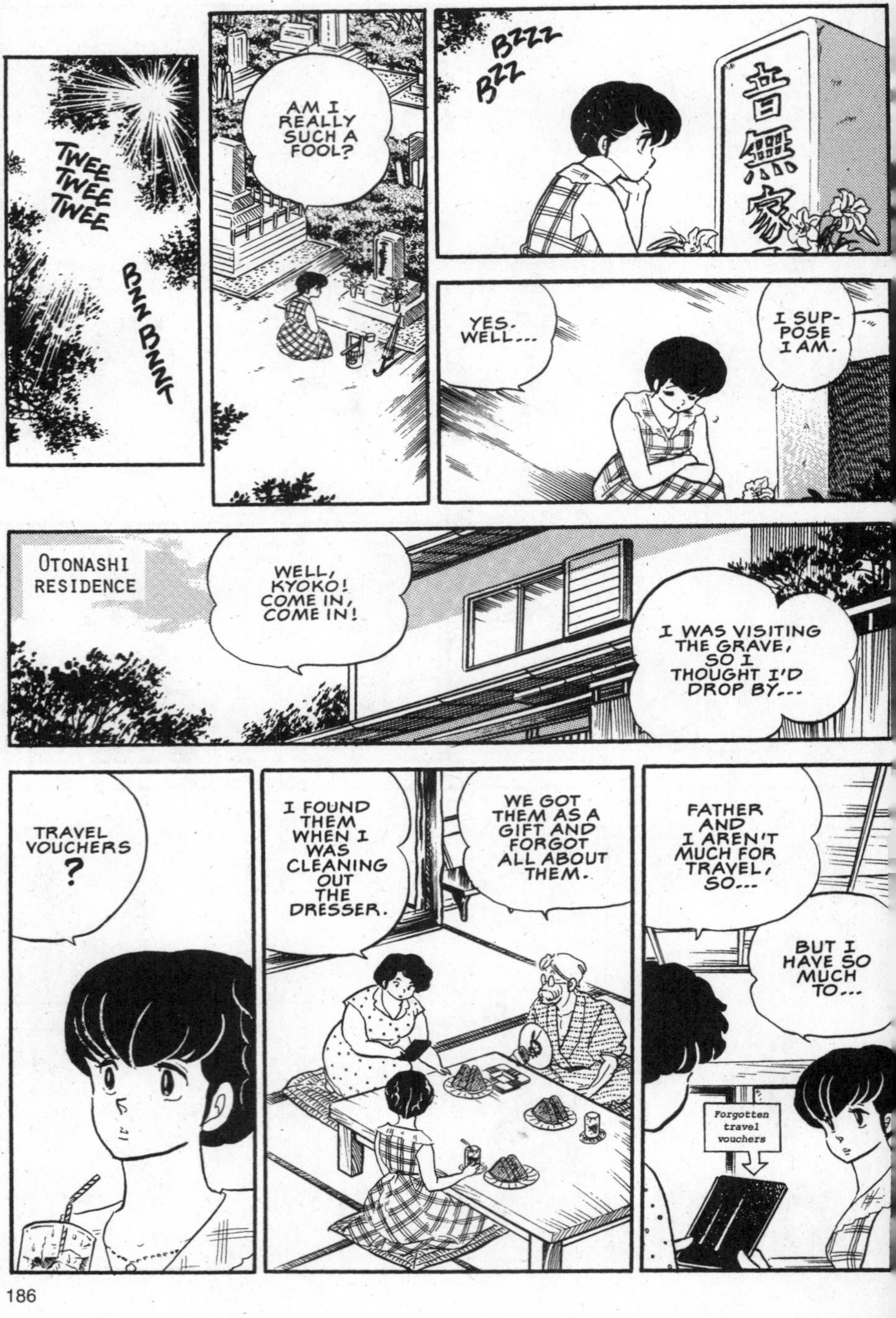
TWEE TWEE TWEE
BZZ BZZT
AM I REALLY SUCH A FOOL?
BZZZ BZZ
音無家
YES. WELL...
I SUP-POSE I AM.
OTONASHI RESIDENCE
WELL, KYOKO! COME IN, COME IN!
I WAS VISITING THE GRAVE, SO I THOUGHT I'D DROP BY...
TRAVEL VOUCHERS?
I FOUND THEM WHEN I WAS CLEANING OUT THE DRESSER.
WE GOT THEM AS A GIFT AND FORGOT ALL ABOUT THEM.
FATHER AND I AREN'T MUCH FOR TRAVEL, SO...
BUT I HAVE SO MUCH TO...
Forgotten travel vouchers

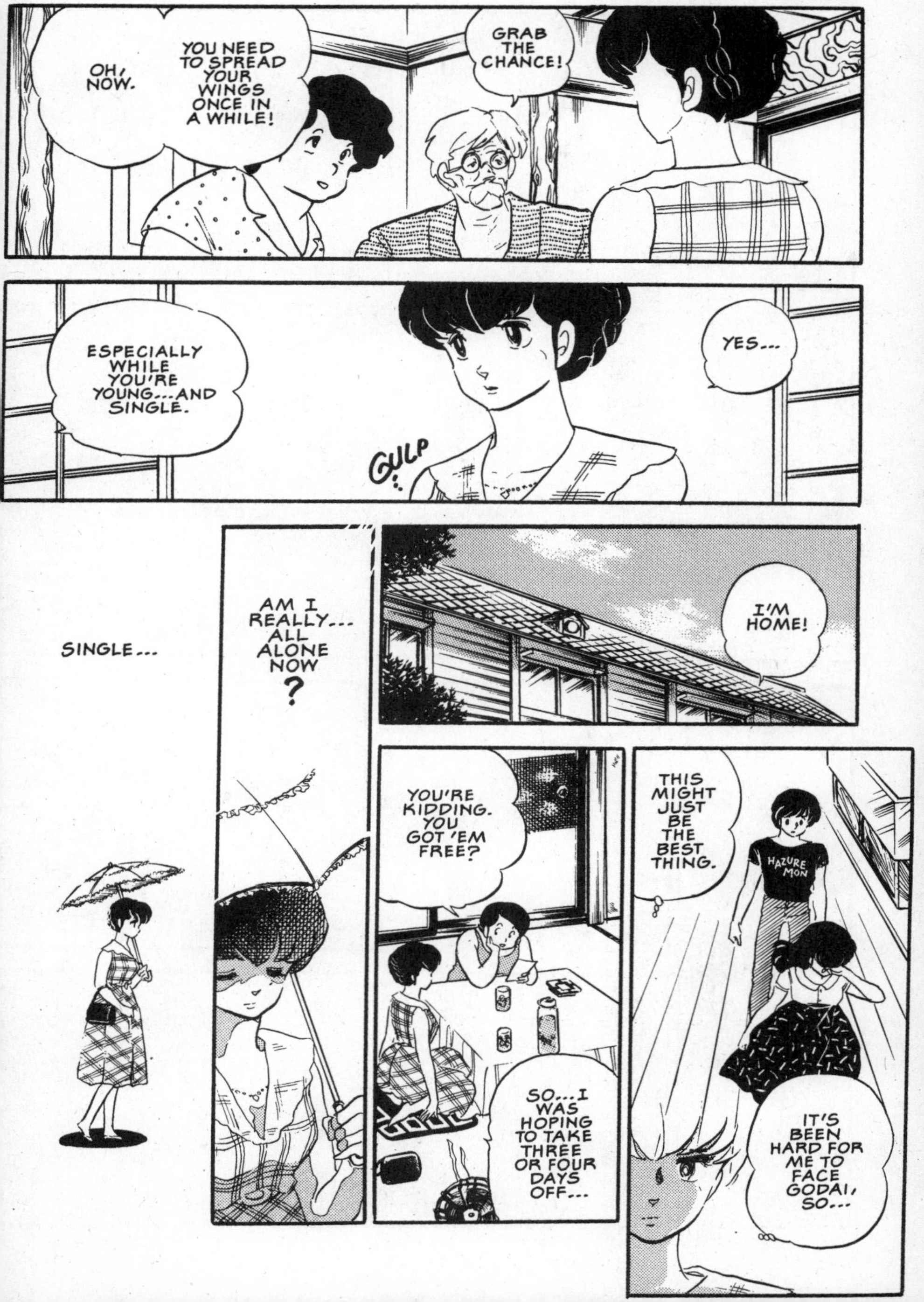
OH, NOW.
YOU NEED TO SPREAD YOUR WINGS ONCE IN A WHILE!
GRAB THE CHANCE!
ESPECIALLY WHILE YOU'RE YOUNG...AND SINGLE.
GULP
YES...
SINGLE...
AM I REALLY... ALL ALONE NOW?
I'M HOME!
YOU'RE KIDDING. YOU GOT 'EM FREE?
SO...I WAS HOPING TO TAKE THREE OR FOUR DAYS OFF...
THIS MIGHT JUST BE THE BEST THING.
HAZURE MON
IT'S BEEN HARD FOR ME TO FACE GODAI, SO...

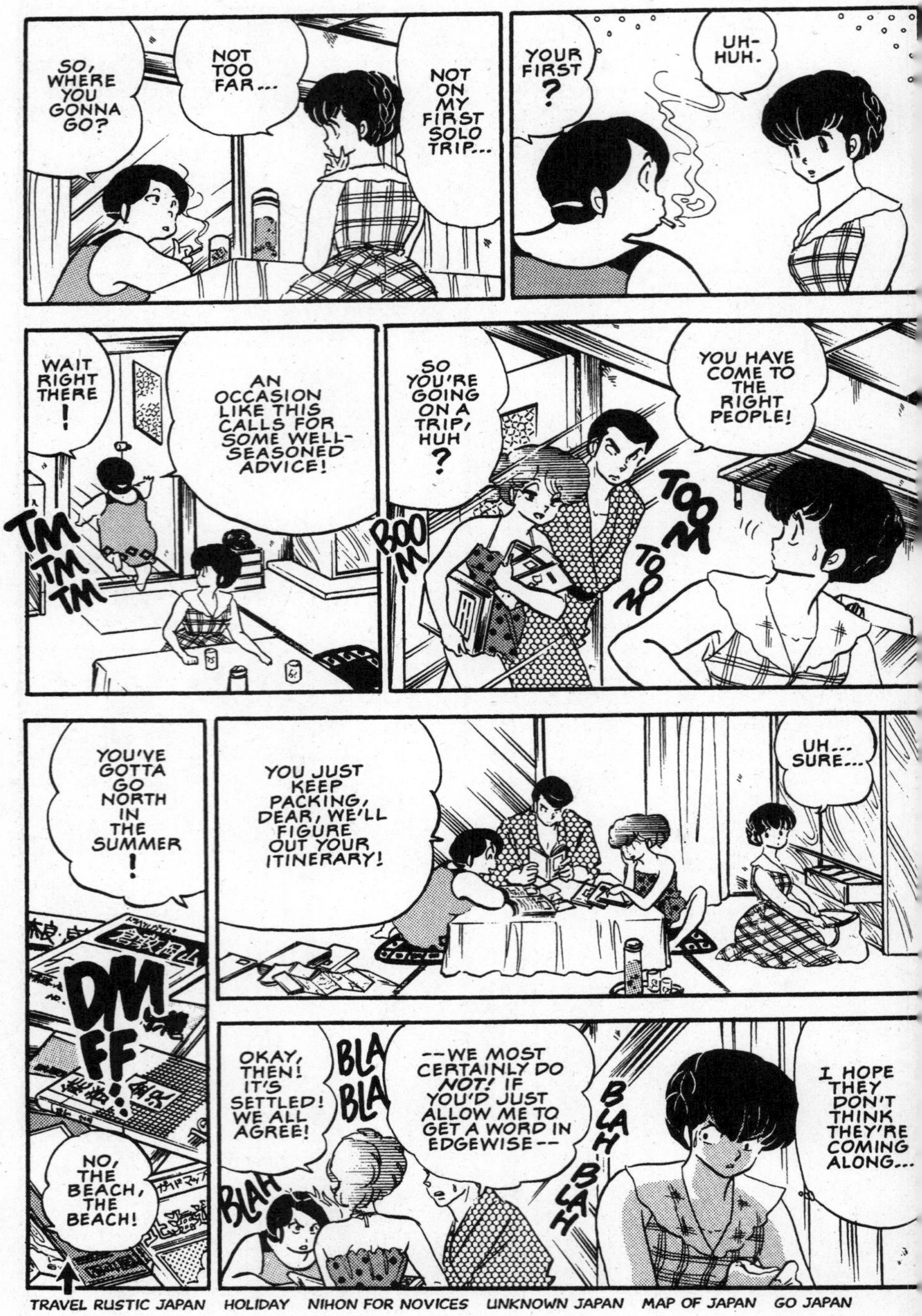
SO, WHERE YOU GONNA GO?
NOT TOO FAR...
NOT ON MY FIRST SOLO TRIP...
YOUR FIRST?
UH-HUH.
WAIT RIGHT THERE!
AN OCCASION LIKE THIS CALLS FOR SOME WELL-SEASONED ADVICE!
TM TM TM
BOOM
SO YOU'RE GOING ON A TRIP, HUH?
YOU HAVE COME TO THE RIGHT PEOPLE!
TOOM TOOM
YOU'VE GOTTA GO NORTH IN THE SUMMER!
DMFF!
NO, THE BEACH, THE BEACH!
YOU JUST KEEP PACKING, DEAR, WE'LL FIGURE OUT YOUR ITINERARY!
UH... SURE...
BLAH
OKAY, THEN! IT'S SETTLED! WE ALL AGREE!
BLA BLA
--WE MOST CERTAINLY DO NOT! IF YOU'D JUST ALLOW ME TO GET A WORD IN EDGEWISE--
BLAH BLAH
I HOPE THEY DON'T THINK THEY'RE COMING ALONG...
TRAVEL RUSTIC JAPAN HOLIDAY NIHON FOR NOVICES UNKNOWN JAPAN MAP OF JAPAN GO JAPAN

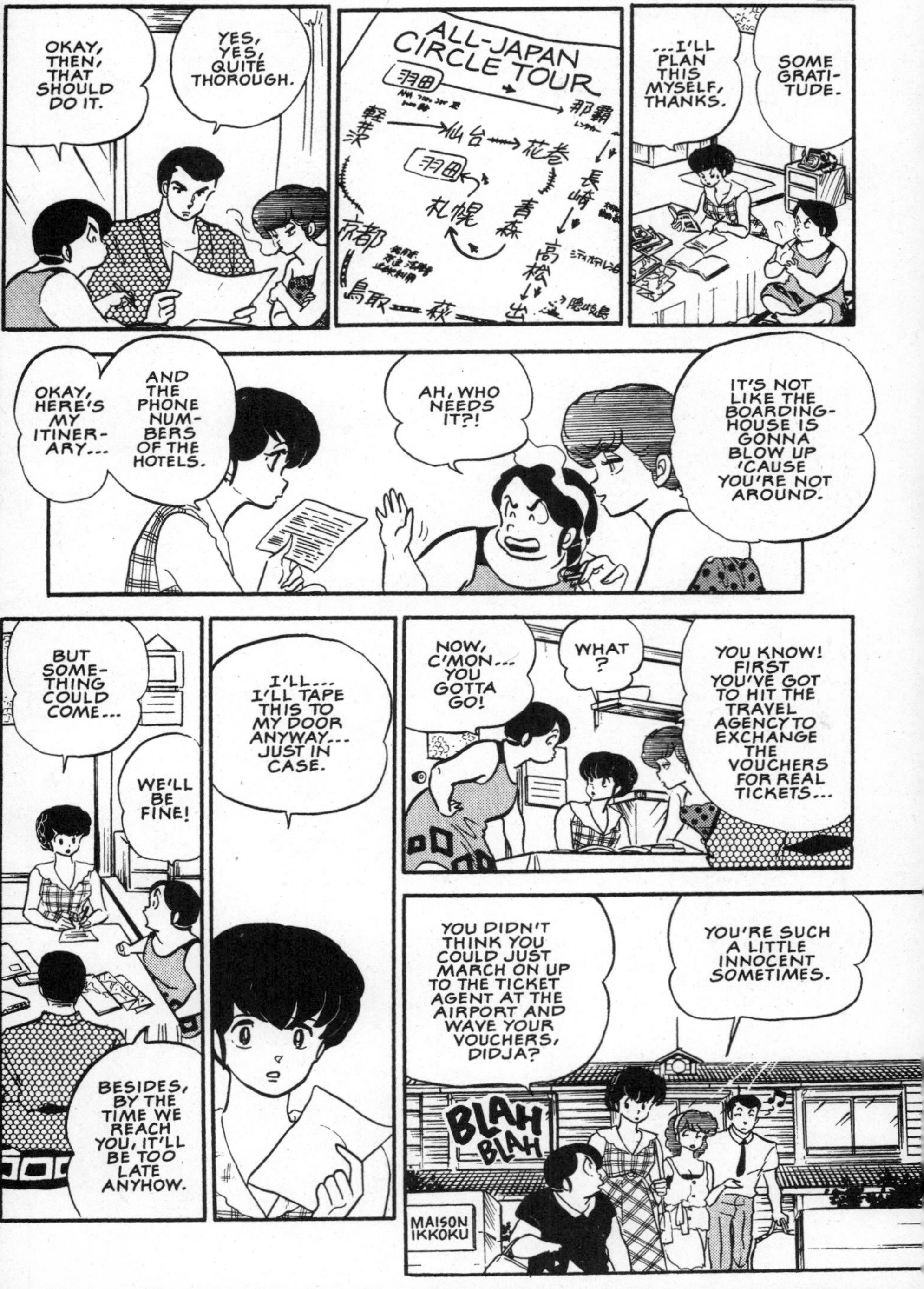
OKAY, THEN, THAT SHOULD DO IT.
YES, YES, QUITE THOROUGH.
ALL-JAPAN CIRCLE TOUR
羽田
那覇
仙台
花巻
長崎
羽田
札幌
青森
京都
高松
鳥取
萩
隠岐島
...I'LL PLAN THIS MYSELF, THANKS.
SOME GRATI-TUDE.
OKAY, HERE'S MY ITINER-ARY...
AND THE PHONE NUM-BERS OF THE HOTELS.
AH, WHO NEEDS IT?!
IT'S NOT LIKE THE BOARDING-HOUSE IS GONNA BLOW UP 'CAUSE YOU'RE NOT AROUND.
BUT SOME-THING COULD COME...
WE'LL BE FINE!
BESIDES, BY THE TIME WE REACH YOU, IT'LL BE TOO LATE ANYHOW.
I'LL... I'LL TAPE THIS TO MY DOOR ANYWAY... JUST IN CASE.
NOW, C'MON... YOU GOTTA GO!
WHAT?
YOU KNOW! FIRST YOU'VE GOT TO HIT THE TRAVEL AGENCY TO EXCHANGE THE VOUCHERS FOR REAL TICKETS...
YOU DIDN'T THINK YOU COULD JUST MARCH ON UP TO THE TICKET AGENT AT THE AIRPORT AND WAVE YOUR VOUCHERS, DIDJA?
YOU'RE SUCH A LITTLE INNOCENT SOMETIMES.
BLAH BLAH
MAISON IKKOKU

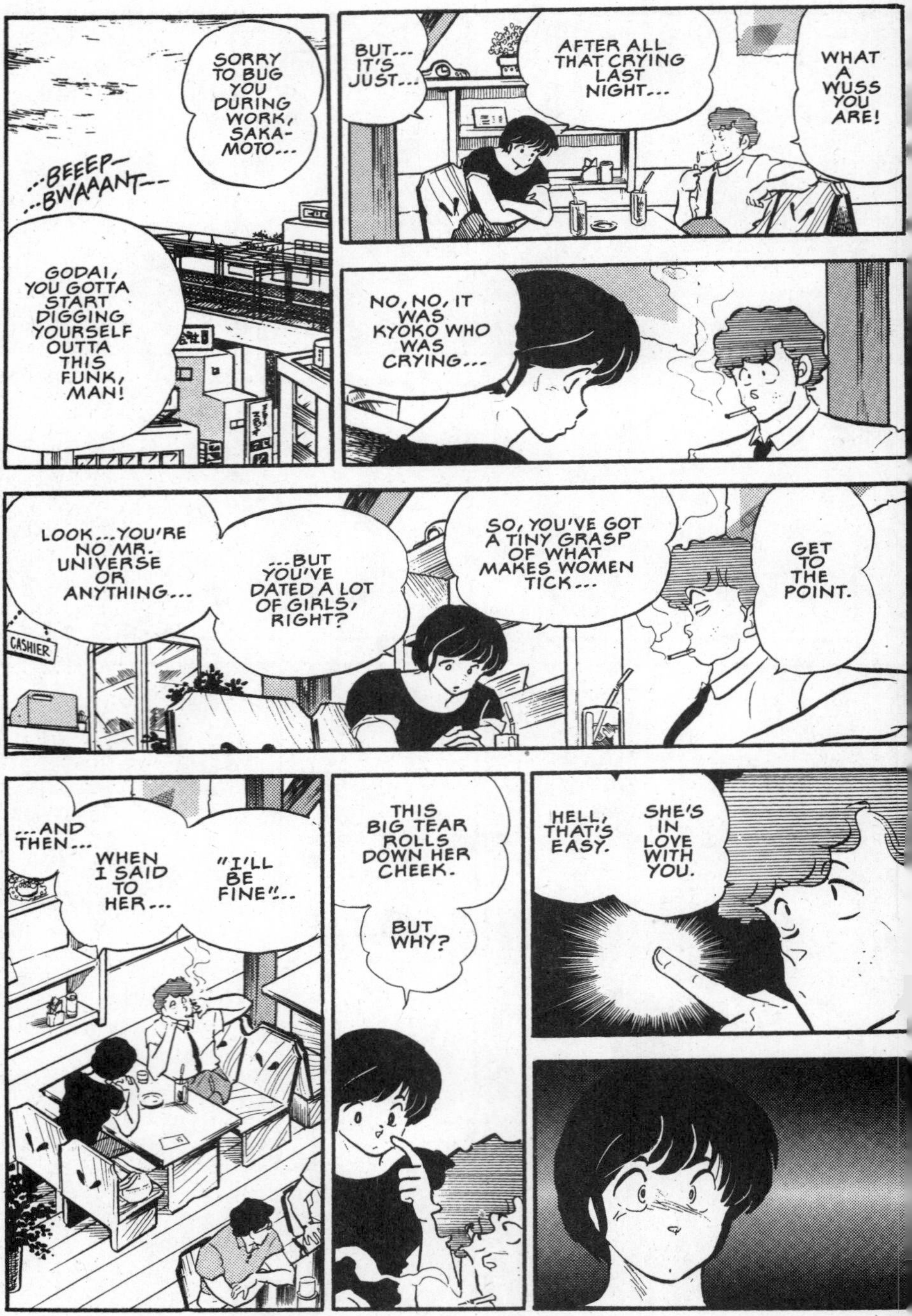
SORRY TO BUG YOU DURING WORK, SAKAMOTO...
...BEEEP— ...BWAAANT—...
GODAI, YOU GOTTA START DIGGING YOURSELF OUTTA THIS FUNK, MAN!
BUT... IT'S JUST...
AFTER ALL THAT CRYING LAST NIGHT...
WHAT A WUSS YOU ARE!
NO, NO, IT WAS KYOKO WHO WAS CRYING...
LOOK...YOU'RE NO MR. UNIVERSE OR ANYTHING...
...BUT YOU'VE DATED A LOT OF GIRLS, RIGHT?
SO, YOU'VE GOT A TINY GRASP OF WHAT MAKES WOMEN TICK...
GET TO THE POINT.
CASHIER
...AND THEN...
WHEN I SAID TO HER...
"I'LL BE FINE"...
THIS BIG TEAR ROLLS DOWN HER CHEEK.
BUT WHY?
HELL, THAT'S EASY.
SHE'S IN LOVE WITH YOU.

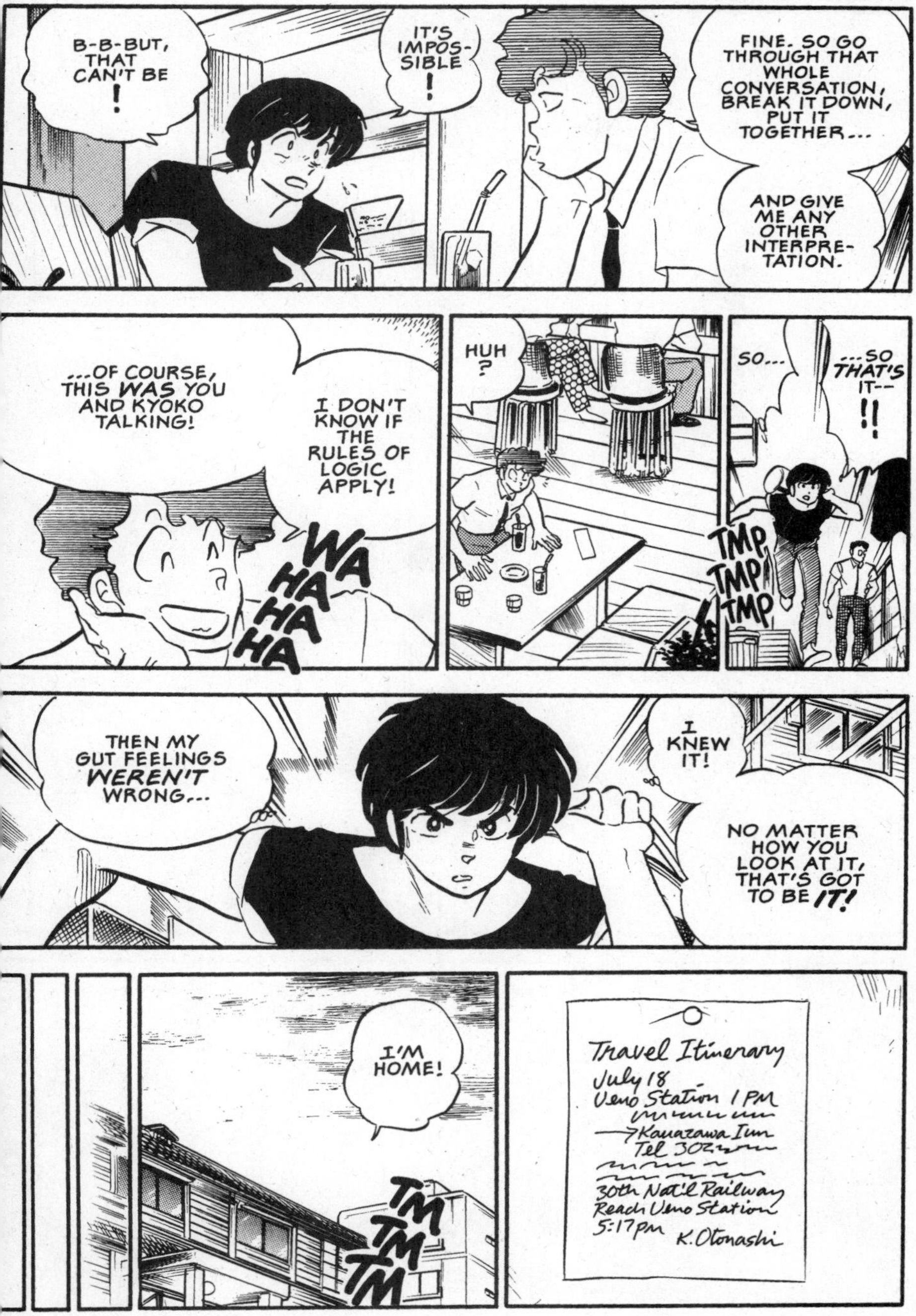
B-B-BUT, THAT CAN'T BE !
IT'S IMPOSSIBLE !
FINE. SO GO THROUGH THAT WHOLE CONVERSATION, BREAK IT DOWN, PUT IT TOGETHER...
AND GIVE ME ANY OTHER INTERPRETATION.
...OF COURSE, THIS WAS YOU AND KYOKO TALKING!
I DON'T KNOW IF THE RULES OF LOGIC APPLY!
WA HA HA HA HA
HUH ?
SO...
...SO THAT'S IT-- !!
TMP TMP TMP
THEN MY GUT FEELINGS WEREN'T WRONG...
I KNEW IT!
NO MATTER HOW YOU LOOK AT IT, THAT'S GOT TO BE IT!
I'M HOME!
TM TM TM
Travel Itinerary
July 18
Ueno Station 1PM
→Kanazawa Inn
Tel 302
30th Nat'l Railway
Reach Ueno Station
5:17pm
K. Otonashi

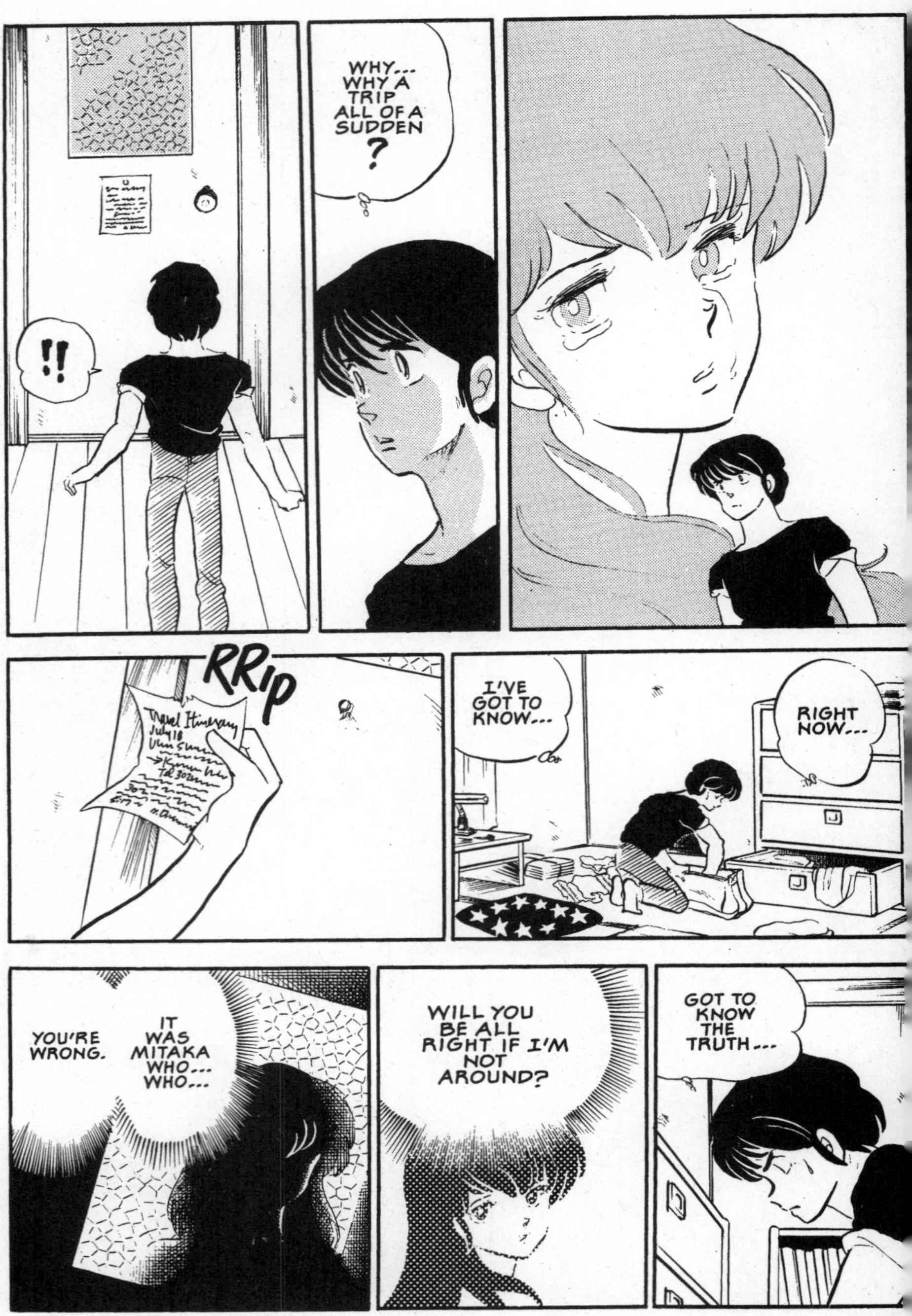
!!
WHY... WHY A TRIP ALL OF A SUDDEN ?
RRip
I'VE GOT TO KNOW...
RIGHT NOW...
YOU'RE WRONG.
IT WAS MITAKA WHO... WHO...
WILL YOU BE ALL RIGHT IF I'M NOT AROUND?
GOT TO KNOW THE TRUTH...

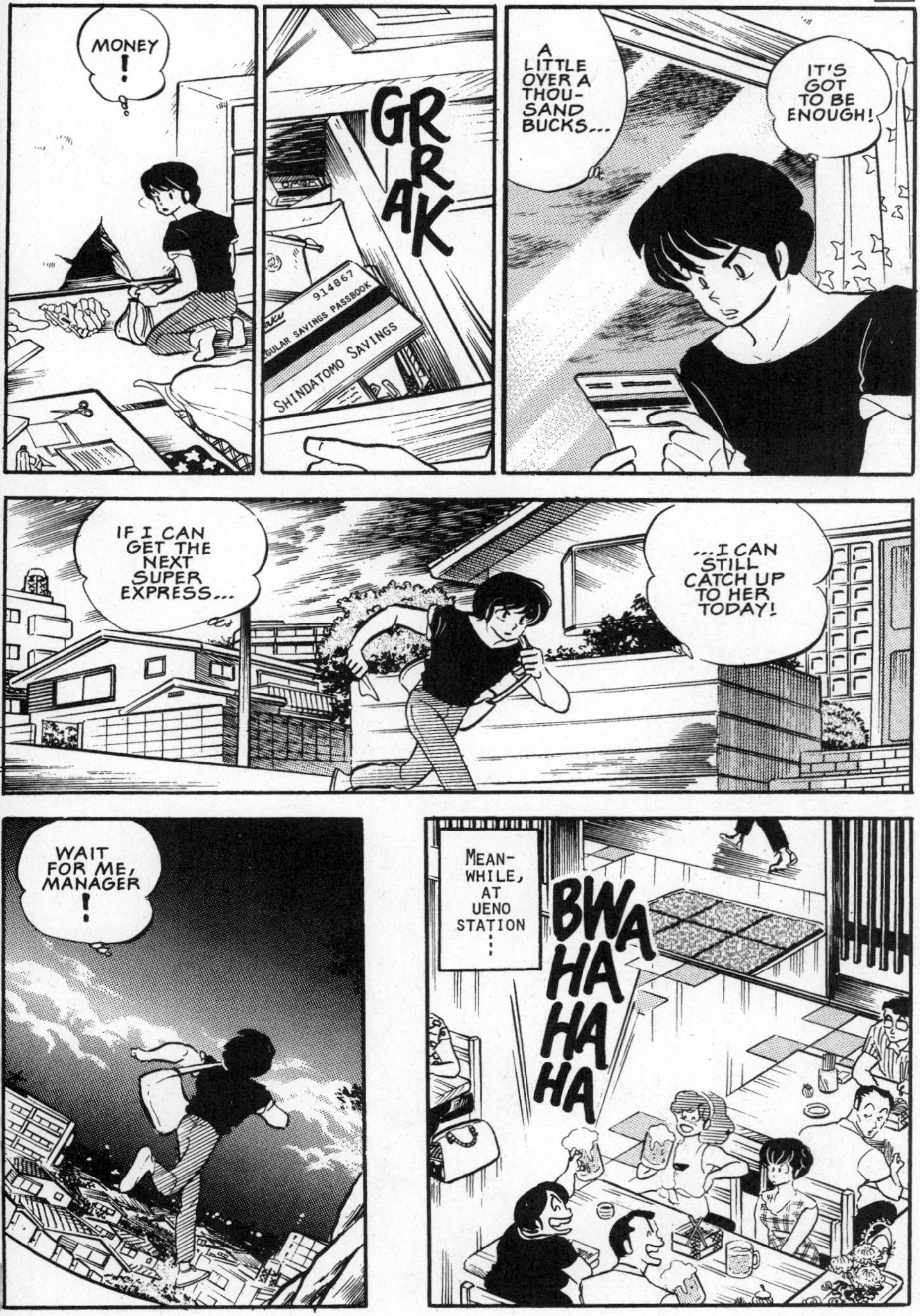
MONEY!
GRRAK
914867
GULAR SAVINGS PASSBOOK
SHINDATOMO SAVINGS
A LITTLE OVER A THOUSAND BUCKS...
IT'S GOT TO BE ENOUGH!
IF I CAN GET THE NEXT SUPER EXPRESS...
...I CAN STILL CATCH UP TO HER TODAY!
WAIT FOR ME, MANAGER!
MEANWHILE, AT UENO STATION...
BWAHAHAHAHAHA

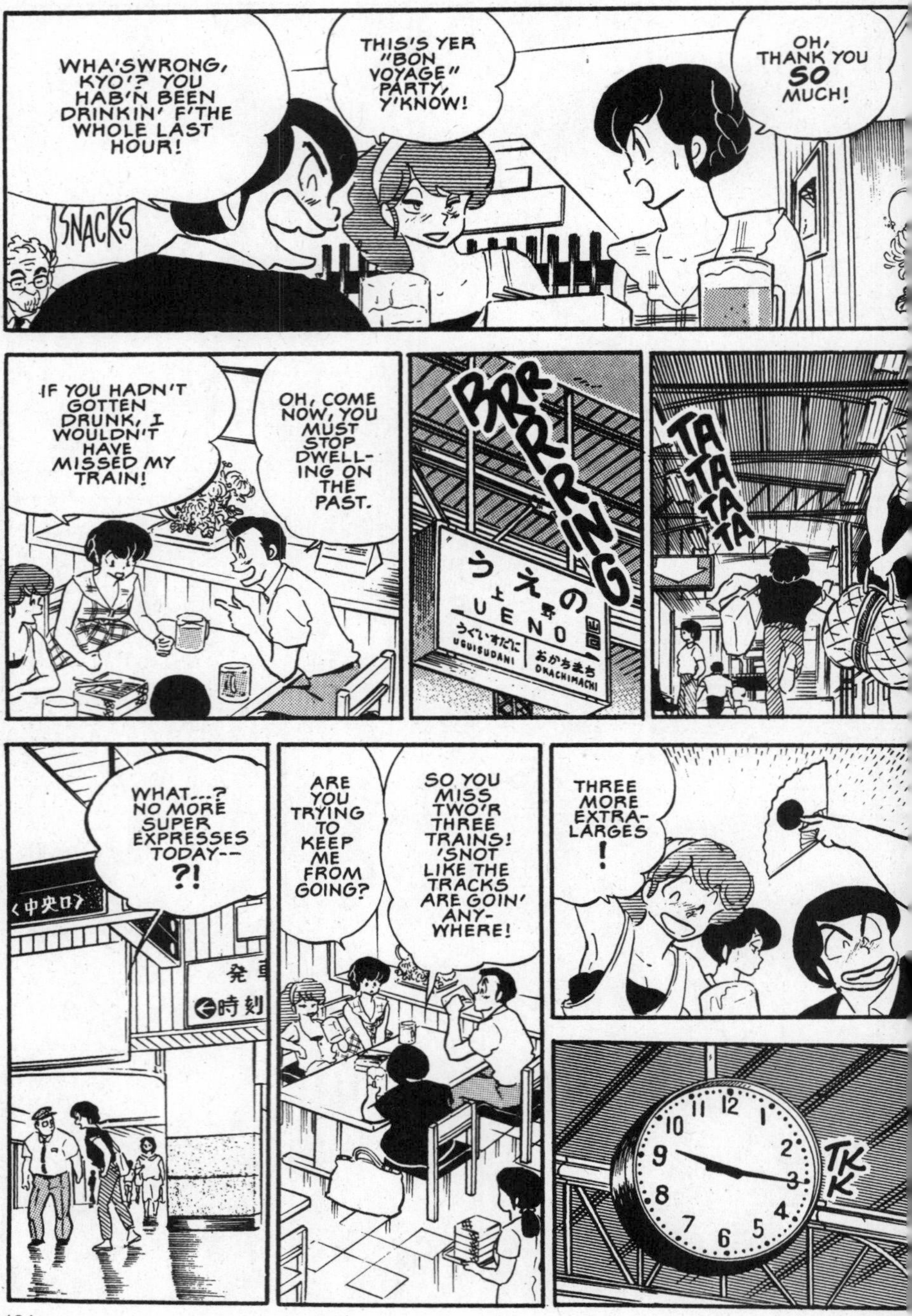

WHA'SWRONG, KYO'? YOU HAB'N BEEN DRINKIN' F'THE WHOLE LAST HOUR!
SNACKS
THIS'S YER "BON VOYAGE" PARTY, Y'KNOW!
OH, THANK YOU SO MUCH!
IF YOU HADN'T GOTTEN DRUNK, I WOULDN'T HAVE MISSED MY TRAIN!
OH, COME NOW, YOU MUST STOP DWELLING ON THE PAST.
BRRRRING
うえの
上野
UENO
うぐいすだに
UGUISUDANI
おかちまち
OKACHIMACHI
TATATATA
〈中央口〉
WHAT...? NO MORE SUPER EXPRESSES TODAY-- ?!
発車
時刻
ARE YOU TRYING TO KEEP ME FROM GOING?
SO YOU MISS TWO'R THREE TRAINS! 'SNOT LIKE THE TRACKS ARE GOIN' ANYWHERE!
THREE MORE EXTRA-LARGES!
TKK

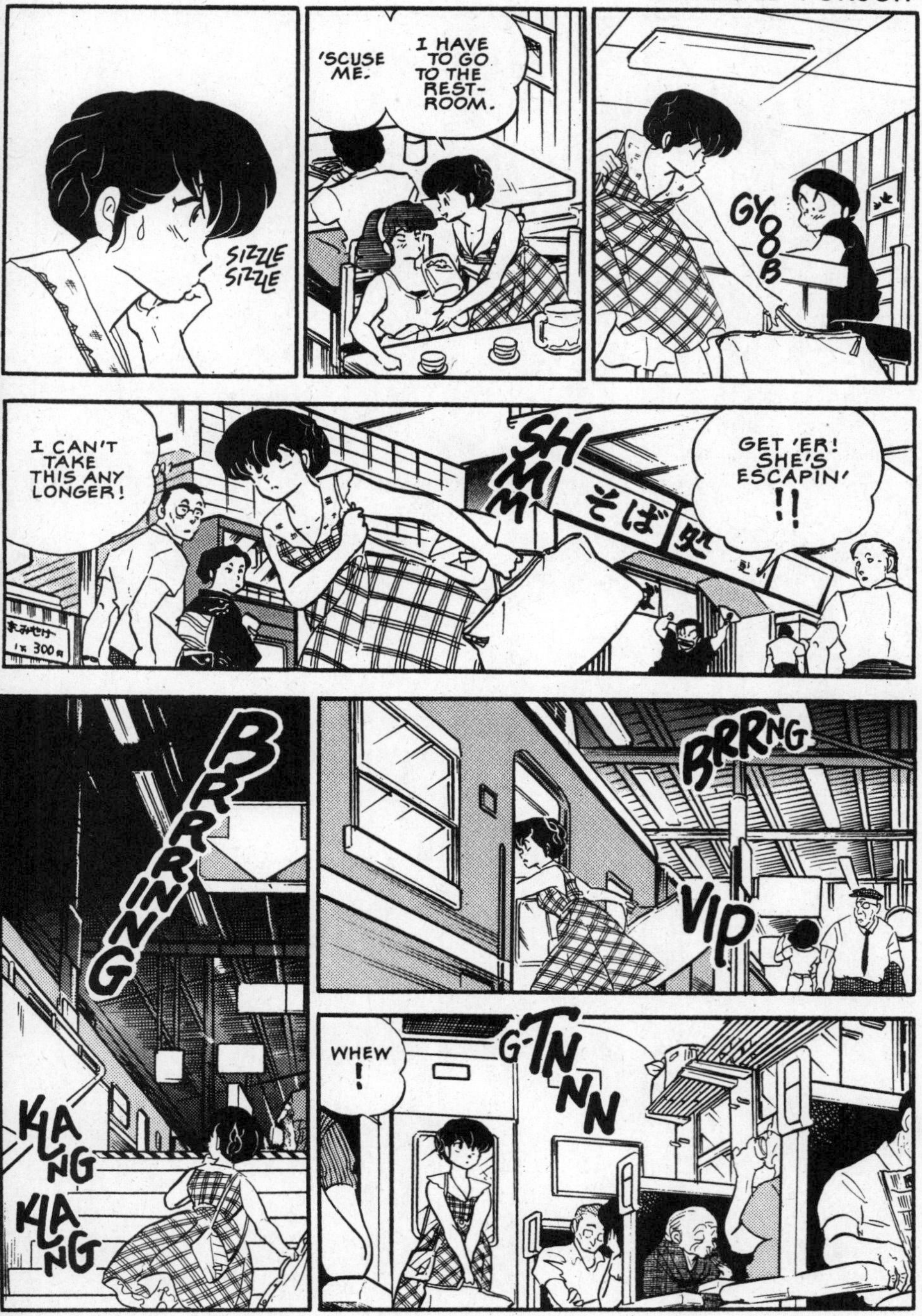
SIZZLE SIZZLE
'SCUSE ME.
I HAVE TO GO TO THE REST-ROOM.
GYOOB
I CAN'T TAKE THIS ANY LONGER!
SHMMM
そば処
GET 'ER! SHE'S ESCAPIN' !!
まみやせけ 1ヶ 300円
BRRRRING
KLANG KLANG
BRRNG
VIP
WHEW!
G-TNNN

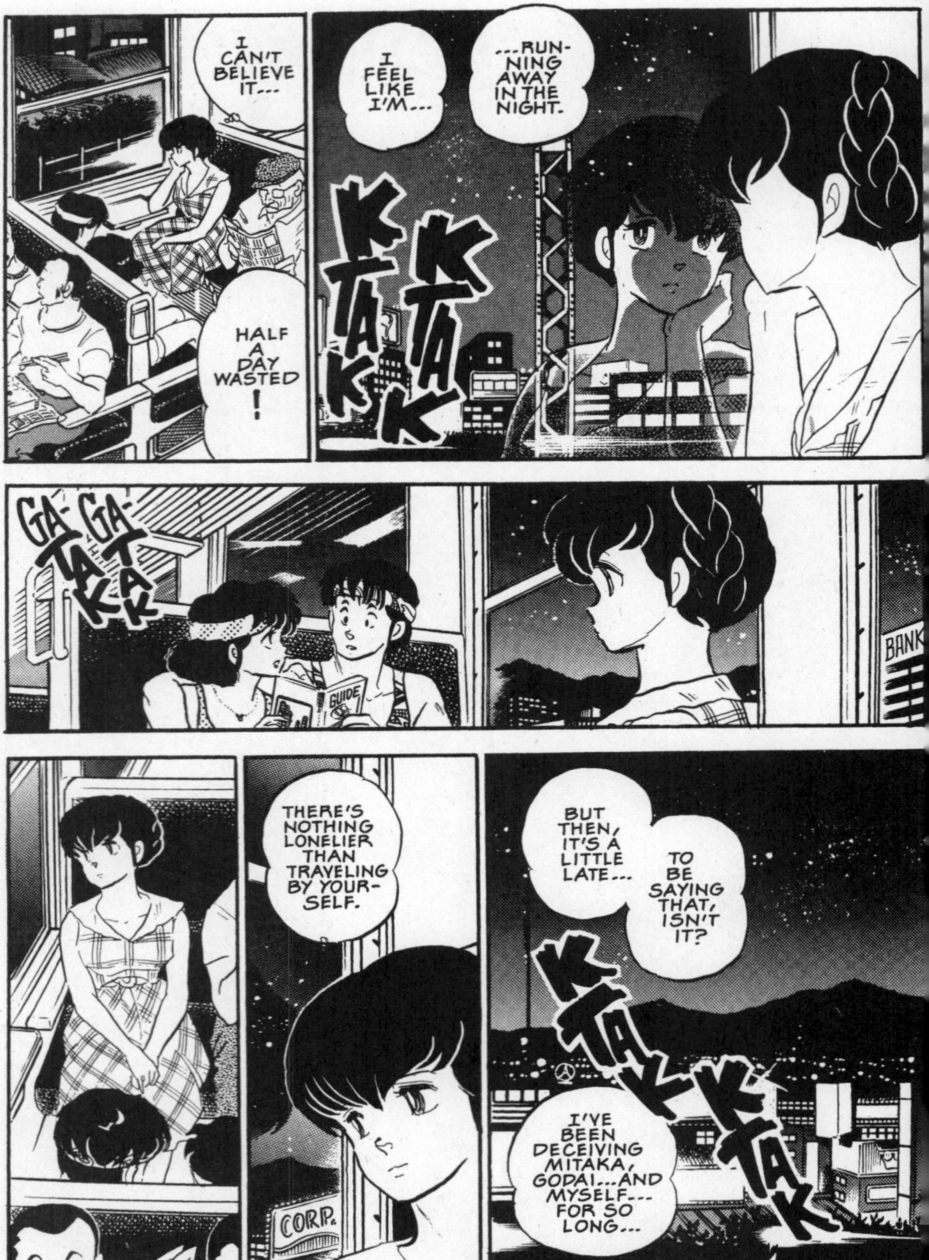
I CAN'T BELIEVE IT...
HALF A DAY WASTED !
I FEEL LIKE I'M...
...RUN-NING AWAY IN THE NIGHT.
K TA K
K TA K
GA-TAK GA-TAK
BANK
GUIDE
THERE'S NOTHING LONELIER THAN TRAVELING BY YOUR-SELF.
CORP.
BUT THEN, IT'S A LITTLE LATE...
TO BE SAYING THAT, ISN'T IT?
K TAK K TAK
I'VE BEEN DECEIVING MITAKA, GODAI... AND MYSELF... FOR SO LONG...

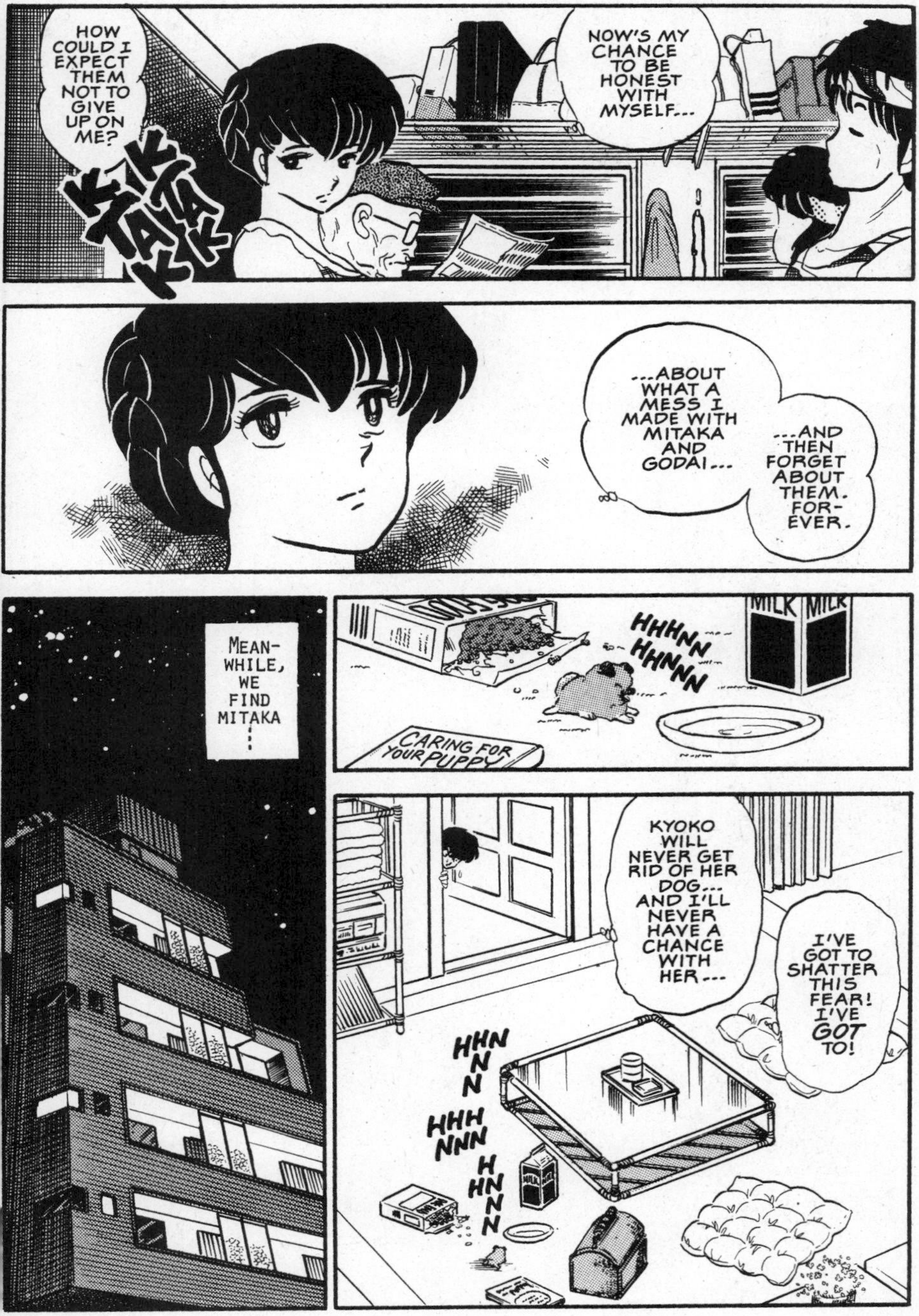
HOW COULD I EXPECT THEM NOT TO GIVE UP ON ME?
KTAK KTAK
NOW'S MY CHANCE TO BE HONEST WITH MYSELF...
...ABOUT WHAT A MESS I MADE WITH MITAKA AND GODAI...
...AND THEN FORGET ABOUT THEM. FOR-EVER.
MEAN-WHILE, WE FIND MITAKA ...
HHHNN HHNNN
MILK MILK
CARING FOR YOUR PUPPY
KYOKO WILL NEVER GET RID OF HER DOG... AND I'LL NEVER HAVE A CHANCE WITH HER...
I'VE GOT TO SHATTER THIS FEAR! I'VE GOT TO!
HHNNN
HHHNNN
HHNNN

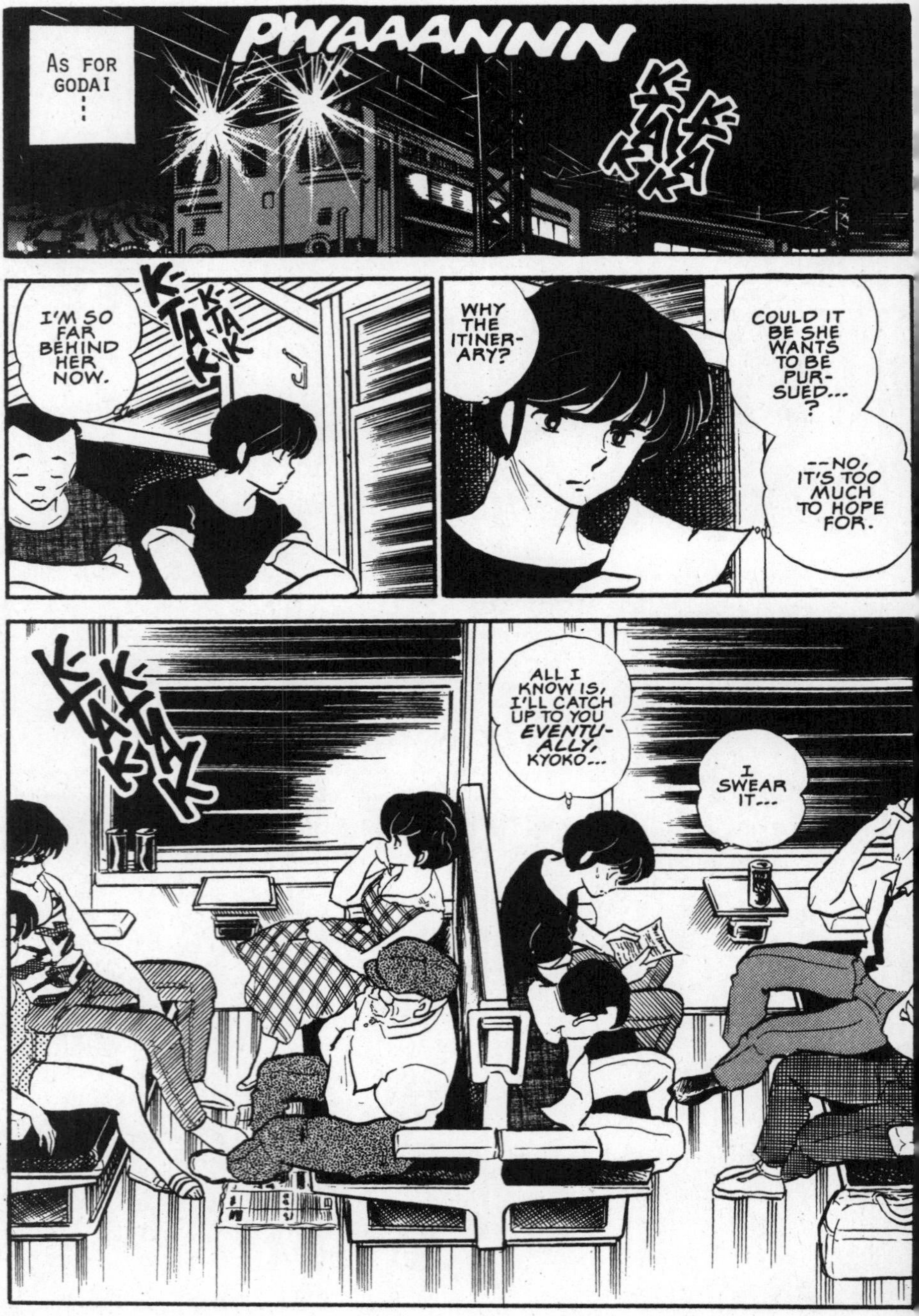
As for Godai ...
PWAAANNN
K-TAK K-TAK
I'M SO FAR BEHIND HER NOW.
K-TAK K-TAK
WHY THE ITINERARY?
COULD IT BE SHE WANTS TO BE PURSUED... ?
--NO, IT'S TOO MUCH TO HOPE FOR.
K-TAK K-TAK
ALL I KNOW IS, I'LL CATCH UP TO YOU *EVENTUALLY*, KYOKO...
I SWEAR IT...

PART 10
PARTY OF TWO

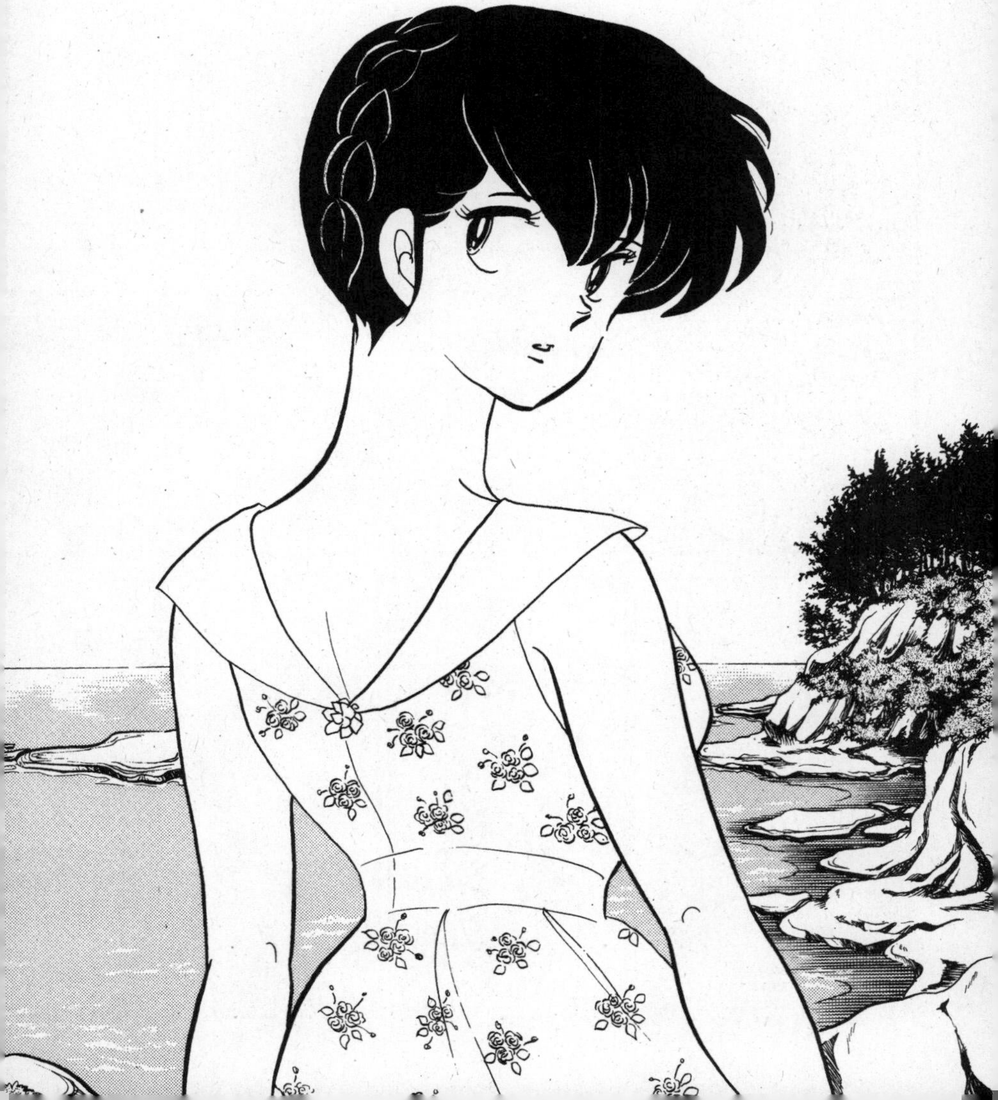

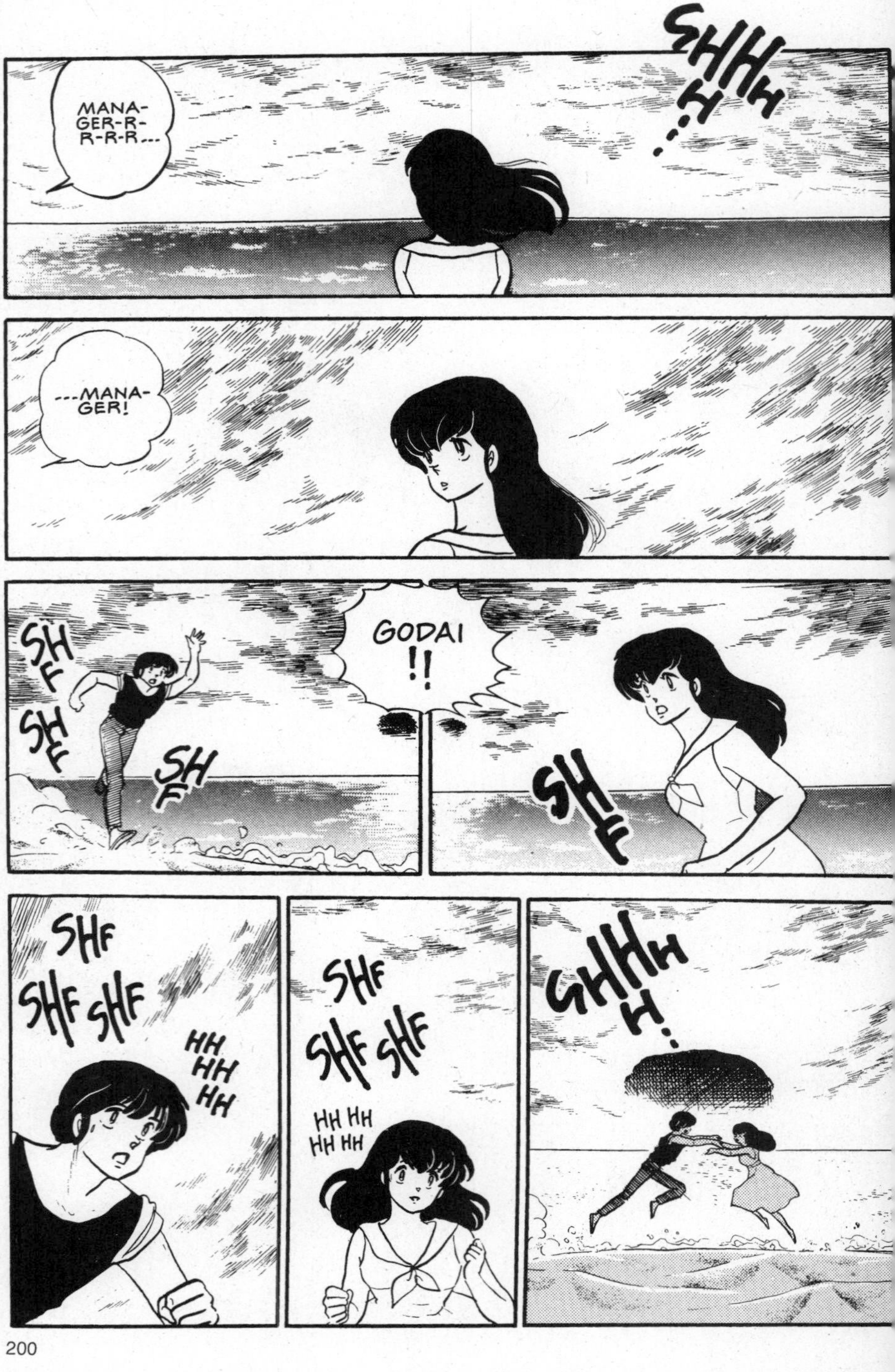
MANA-GER-R-R-R-R...
SHHHH...
---MANA-GER!
SHF
SHF
SHF
GODAI !!
SHF
SHF
SHF SHF
HH HH HH
SHF
SHF SHF
HH HH HH HH
GHHHH..

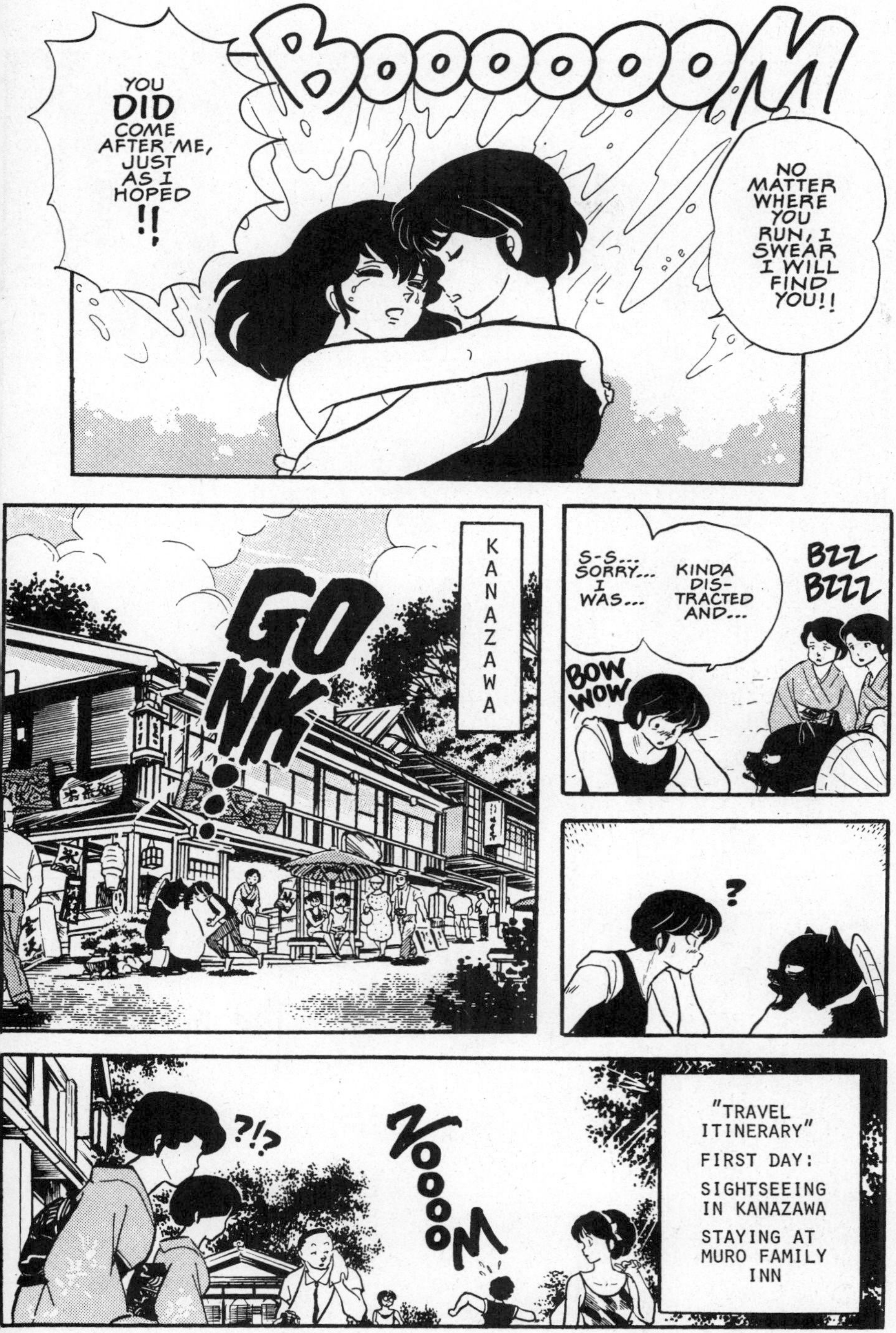
YOU DID COME AFTER ME, JUST AS I HOPED!!
BOOOOOOM
NO MATTER WHERE YOU RUN, I SWEAR I WILL FIND YOU!!
KANAZAWA
GONK
S-S... SORRY... I WAS...
KINDA DIS-TRACTED AND...
BZZ BZZZ
BOW WOW
?
?!?
VOOOOM
"TRAVEL ITINERARY"
FIRST DAY:
SIGHTSEEING IN KANAZAWA
STAYING AT MURO FAMILY INN

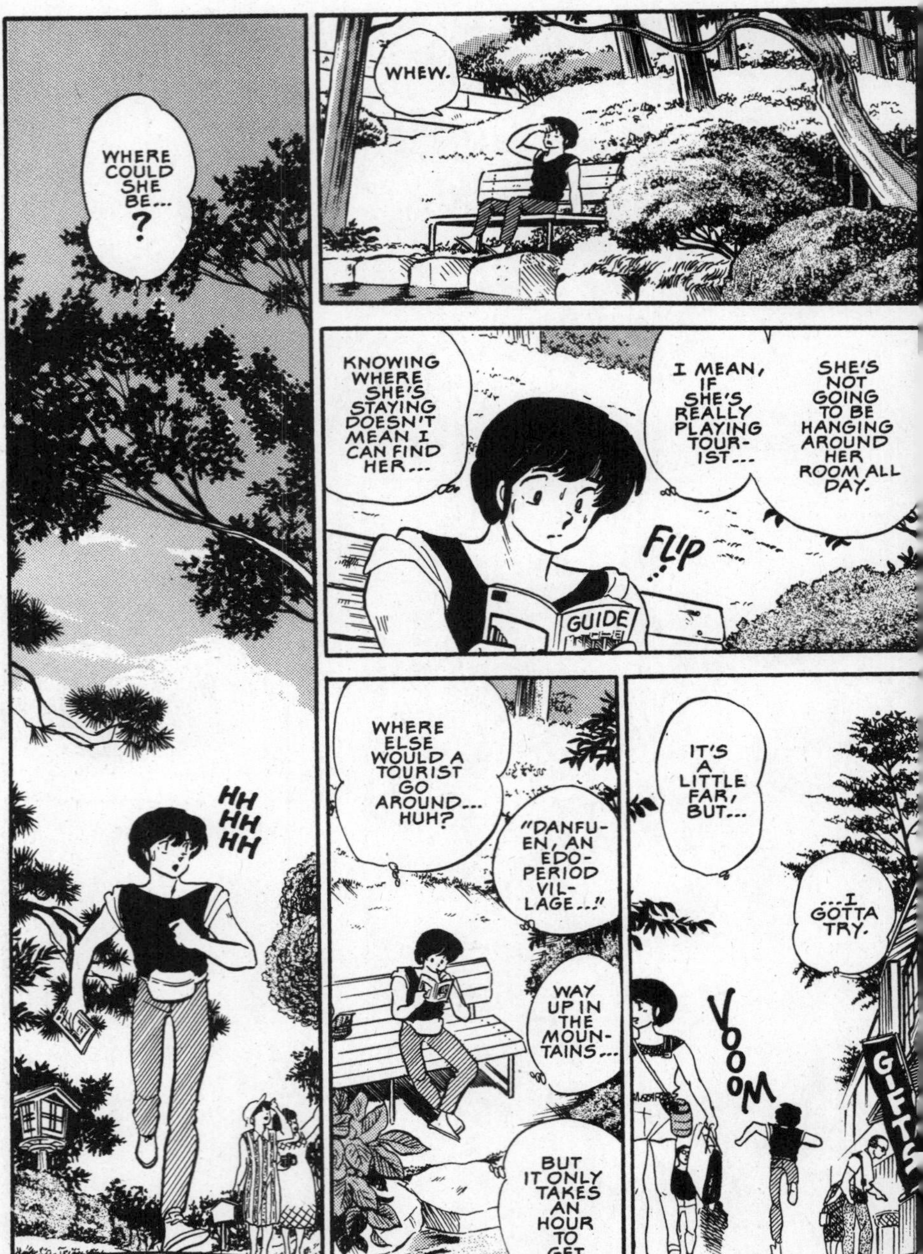
WHERE COULD SHE BE... ?
HH HH HH
WHEW.
KNOWING WHERE SHE'S STAYING DOESN'T MEAN I CAN FIND HER...
I MEAN, IF SHE'S REALLY PLAYING TOUR-IST...
SHE'S NOT GOING TO BE HANGING AROUND HER ROOM ALL DAY.
FLIP
GUIDE
WHERE ELSE WOULD A TOURIST GO AROUND... HUH?
"DANFU-EN, AN EDO-PERIOD VIL-LAGE..."
WAY UP IN THE MOUN-TAINS...
BUT IT ONLY TAKES AN HOUR TO GET THERE.
IT'S A LITTLE FAR, BUT...
...I GOTTA TRY.
VOOOM
GIFTS

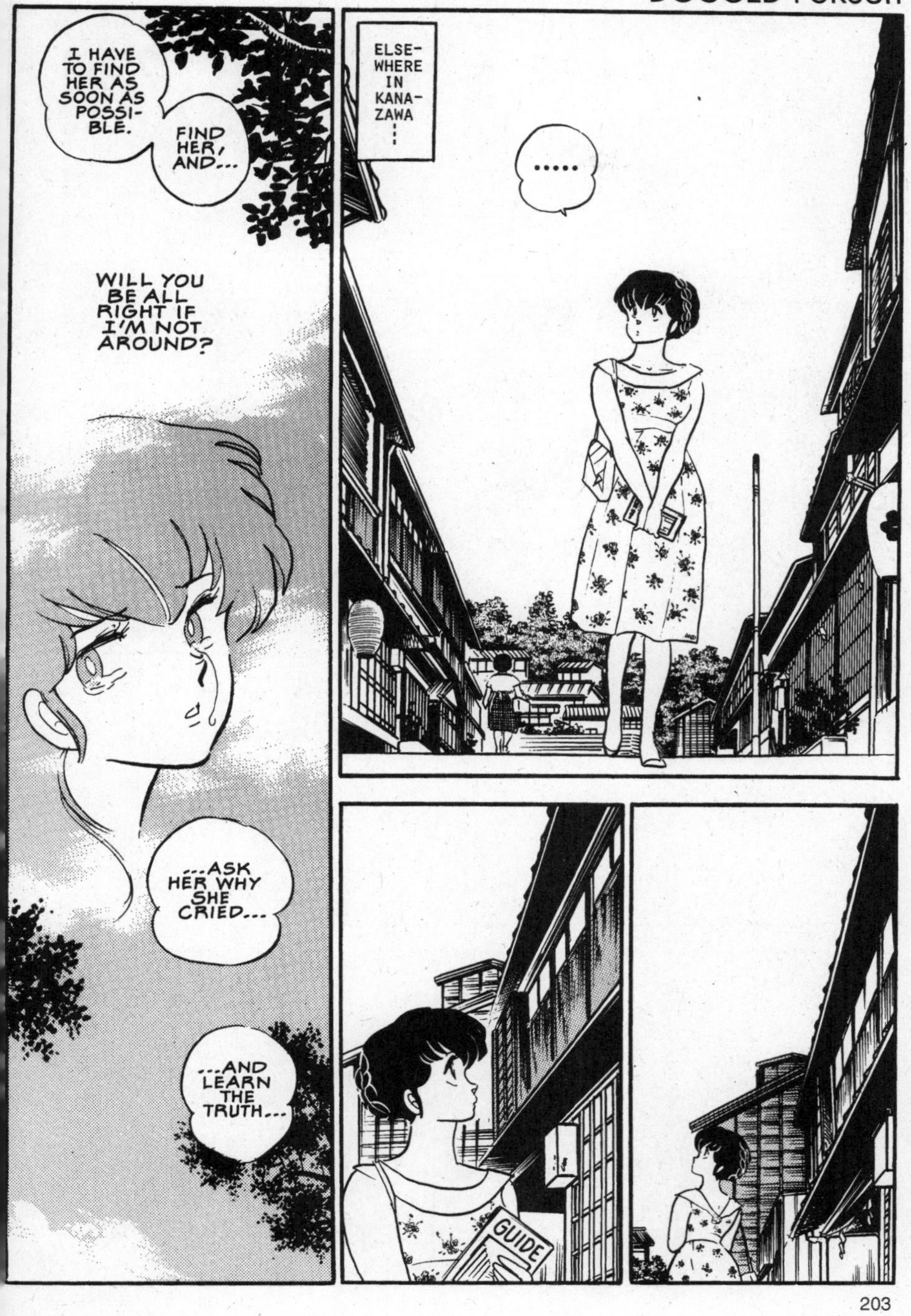
I HAVE TO FIND HER AS SOON AS POSSI-BLE.
FIND HER, AND...
WILL YOU BE ALL RIGHT IF I'M NOT AROUND?
...ASK HER WHY SHE CRIED...
...AND LEARN THE TRUTH...
ELSE-WHERE IN KANA-ZAWA...
.....
GUIDE

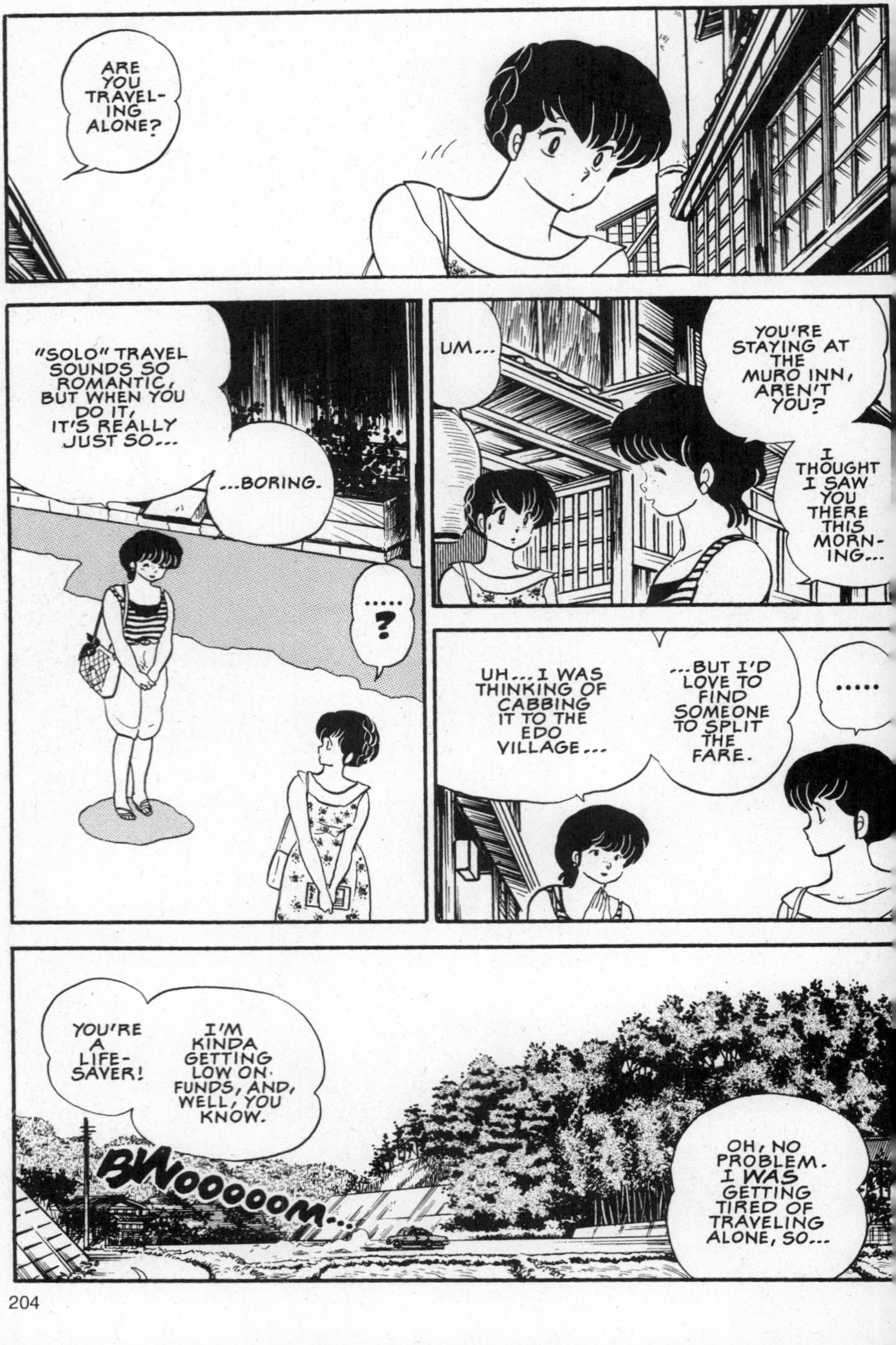
ARE YOU TRAVEL-ING ALONE?
"SOLO" TRAVEL SOUNDS SO ROMANTIC, BUT WHEN YOU DO IT, IT'S REALLY JUST SO...
...BORING.
......?
UM...
YOU'RE STAYING AT THE MURO INN, AREN'T YOU?
I THOUGHT I SAW YOU THERE THIS MORN-ING...
UH... I WAS THINKING OF CABBING IT TO THE EDO VILLAGE...
...BUT I'D LOVE TO FIND SOMEONE TO SPLIT THE FARE.
.....
YOU'RE A LIFE-SAVER!
I'M KINDA GETTING LOW ON FUNDS, AND, WELL, YOU KNOW.
BWOOOOOOM...
OH, NO PROBLEM. I WAS GETTING TIRED OF TRAVELING ALONE, SO...

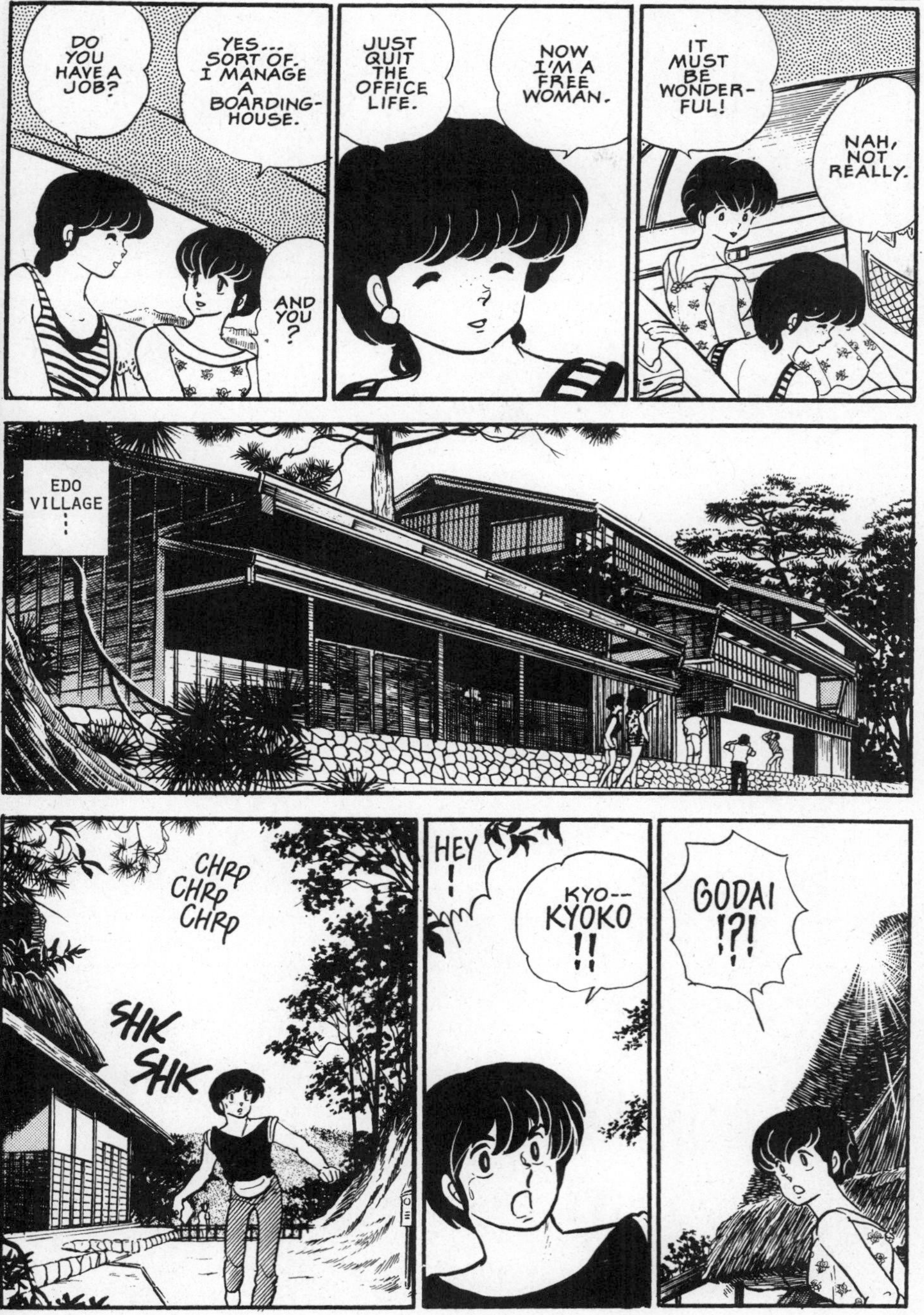
DO YOU HAVE A JOB?
YES... SORT OF. I MANAGE A BOARDING-HOUSE.
AND YOU?
JUST QUIT THE OFFICE LIFE.
NOW I'M A FREE WOMAN.
IT MUST BE WONDER-FUL!
NAH, NOT REALLY.
EDO VILLAGE...
CHRP CHRP CHRP
SHK SHK
HEY!
KYO-- KYOKO!!
GODAI!?!

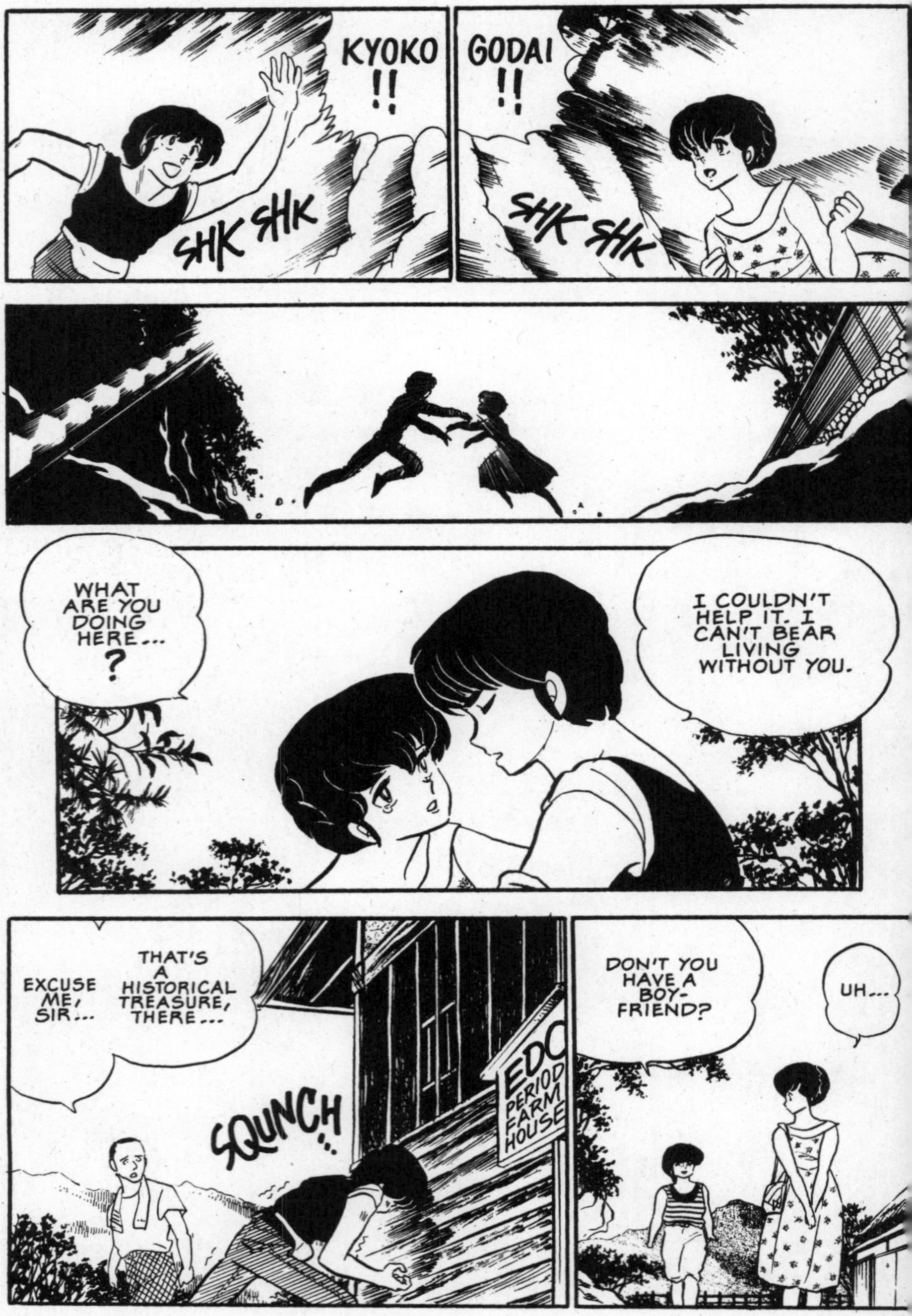
KYOKO !!
SHK SHK
GODAI !!
SHK SHK
WHAT ARE YOU DOING HERE...?
I COULDN'T HELP IT. I CAN'T BEAR LIVING WITHOUT YOU.
EXCUSE ME, SIR...
THAT'S A HISTORICAL TREASURE, THERE...
SQUNCH...
EDO PERIOD FARM HOUSE
DON'T YOU HAVE A BOY-FRIEND?
UH...

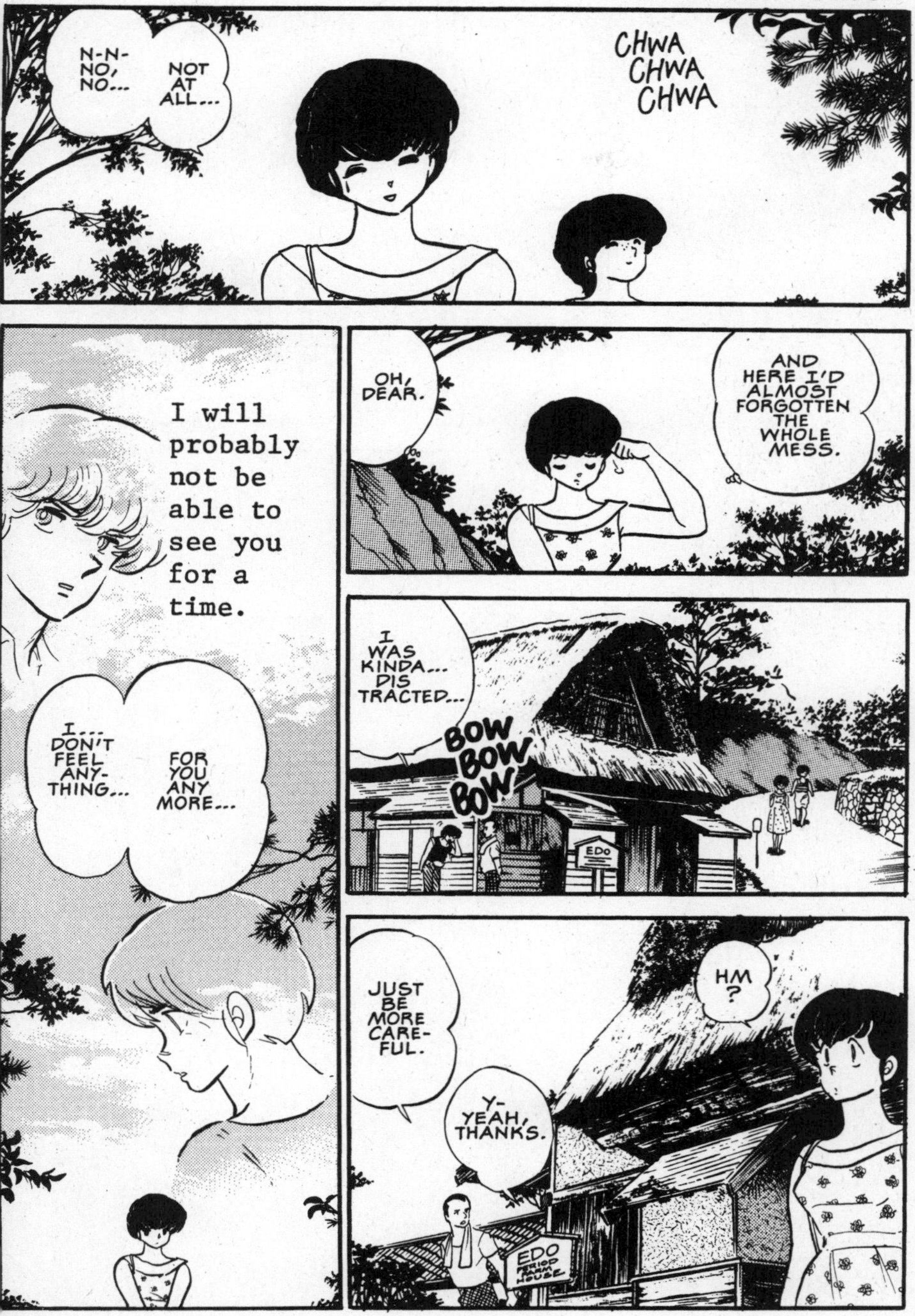
N-N-NO, NO...
NOT AT ALL...
CHWA CHWA CHWA
I will probably not be able to see you for a time.
I... DON'T FEEL ANY-THING...
FOR YOU ANY MORE...
OH, DEAR.
AND HERE I'D ALMOST FORGOTTEN THE WHOLE MESS.
I WAS KINDA... DIS TRACTED...
BOW BOW BOW
EDO
JUST BE MORE CARE-FUL.
HM?
Y-YEAH, THANKS.
EDO PERIOD FARM HOUSE

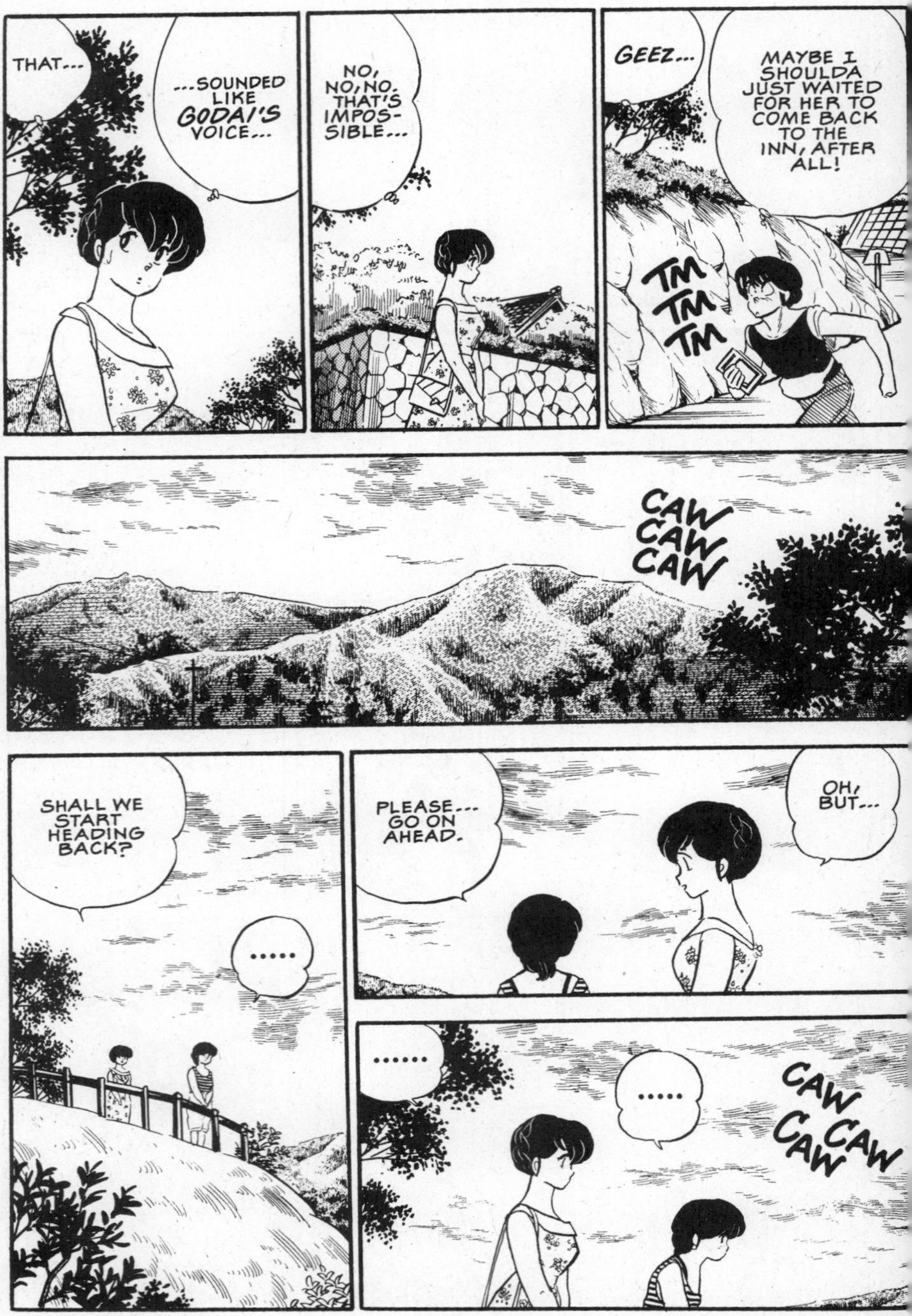
THAT...
...SOUNDED LIKE GODAI'S VOICE...
NO, NO, NO. THAT'S IMPOSSIBLE...
GEEZ...
MAYBE I SHOULDA JUST WAITED FOR HER TO COME BACK TO THE INN, AFTER ALL!
TM TM TM
CAW CAW CAW
SHALL WE START HEADING BACK?
......
PLEASE... GO ON AHEAD.
OH, BUT...
......
......
CAW CAW CAW

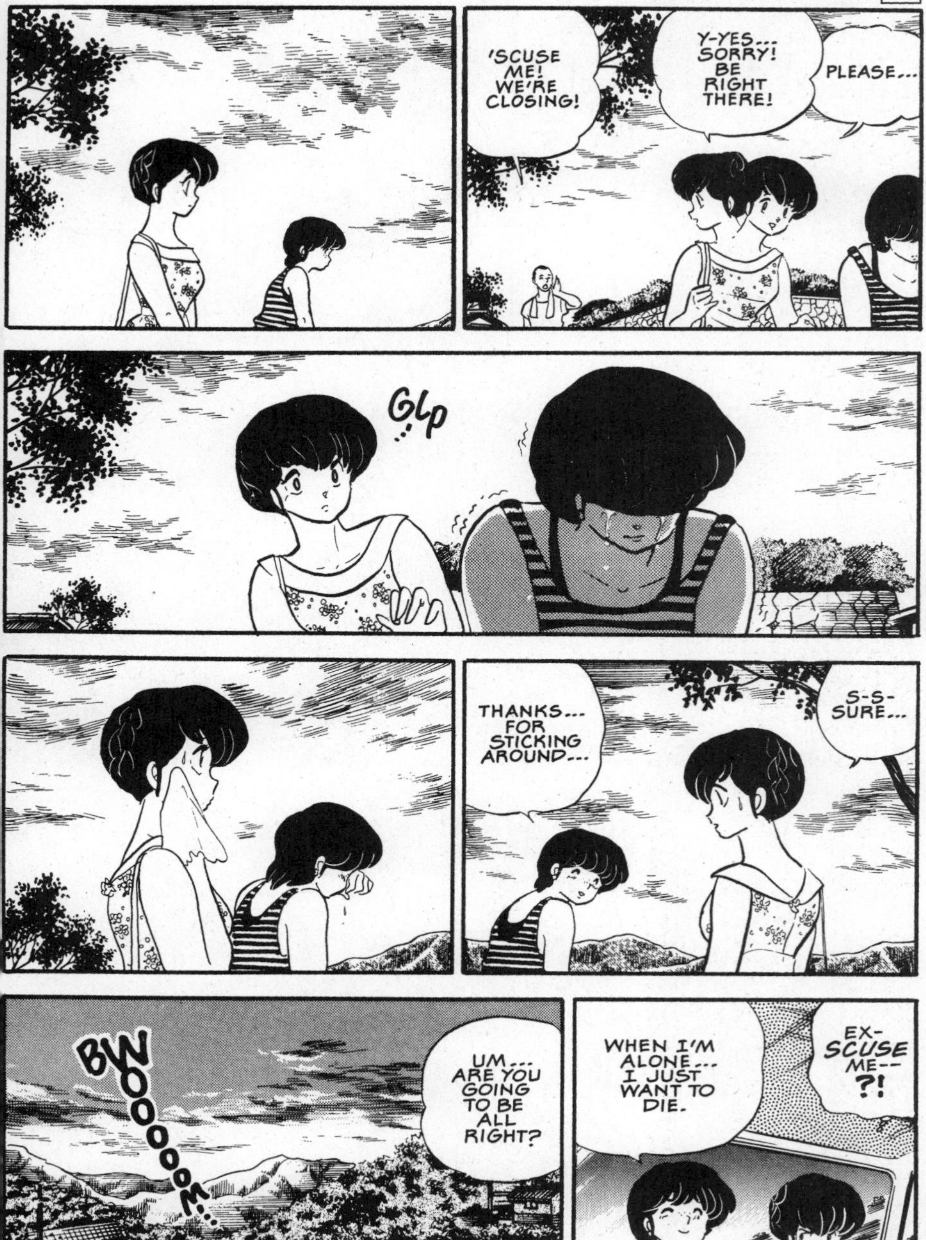
'SCUSE ME! WE'RE CLOSING!
Y-YES... SORRY! BE RIGHT THERE!
PLEASE...
GLP
THANKS... FOR STICKING AROUND...
S-S-SURE...
BWOOOOOOM...
UM... ARE YOU GOING TO BE ALL RIGHT?
WHEN I'M ALONE... I JUST WANT TO DIE.
EX-SCUSE ME--?!

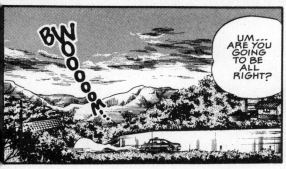

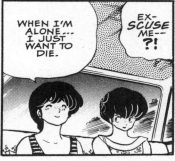

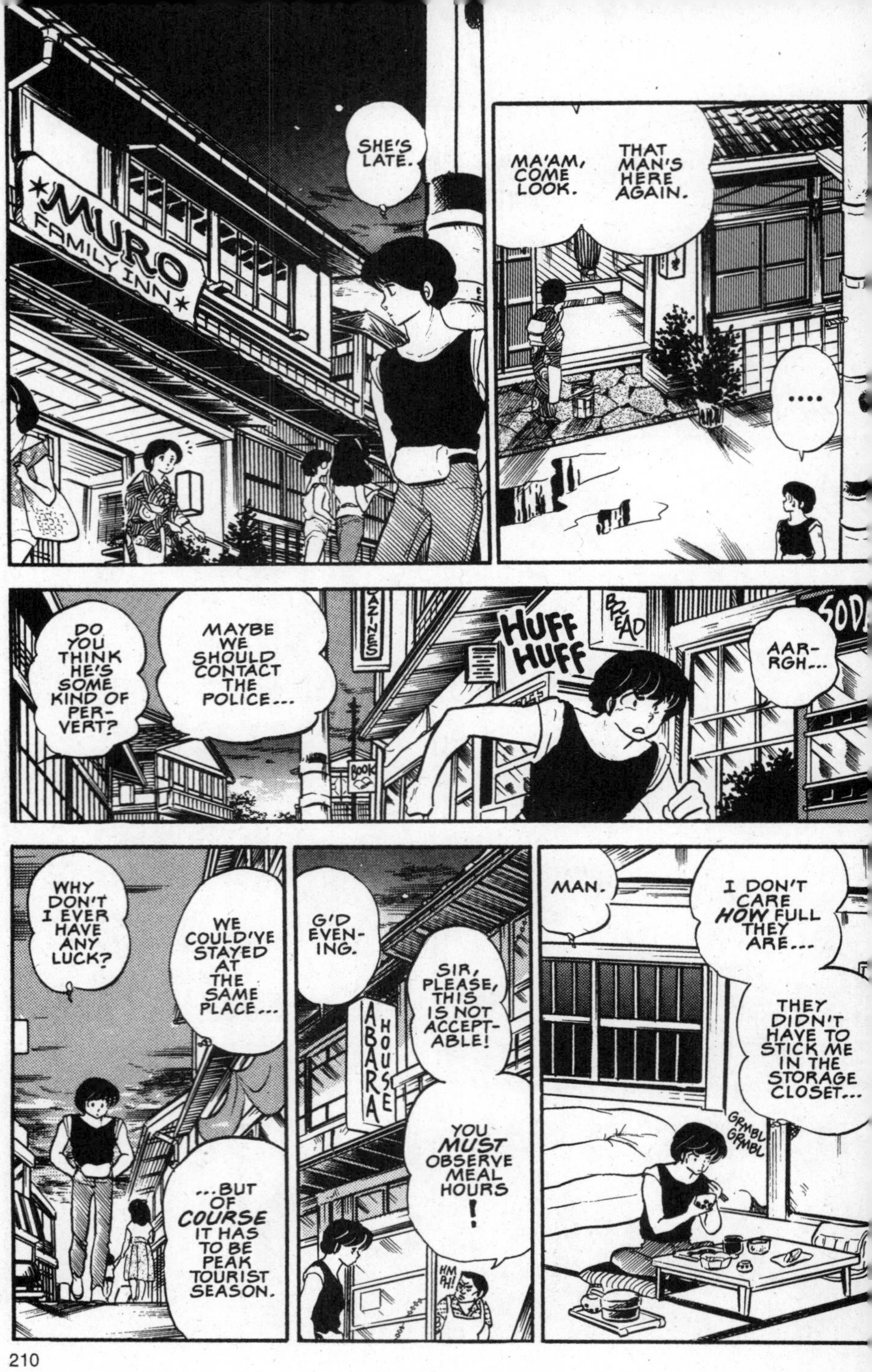
MURO FAMILY INN
SHE'S LATE.
MA'AM, COME LOOK.
THAT MAN'S HERE AGAIN.
....
DO YOU THINK HE'S SOME KIND OF PER-VERT?
MAYBE WE SHOULD CONTACT THE POLICE...
HUFF HUFF
BREAD
BOOK
AARGH...
WHY DON'T I EVER HAVE ANY LUCK?
WE COULD'VE STAYED AT THE SAME PLACE...
...BUT OF *COURSE* IT HAS TO BE PEAK TOURIST SEASON.
G'D EVEN-ING.
ABARA HOUSE
SIR, PLEASE, THIS IS NOT ACCEPT-ABLE!
YOU *MUST* OBSERVE MEAL HOURS!
HMPH!
MAN.
I DON'T CARE *HOW* FULL THEY ARE...
THEY DIDN'T HAVE TO STICK ME IN THE STORAGE CLOSET...
GRMBL GRMBL

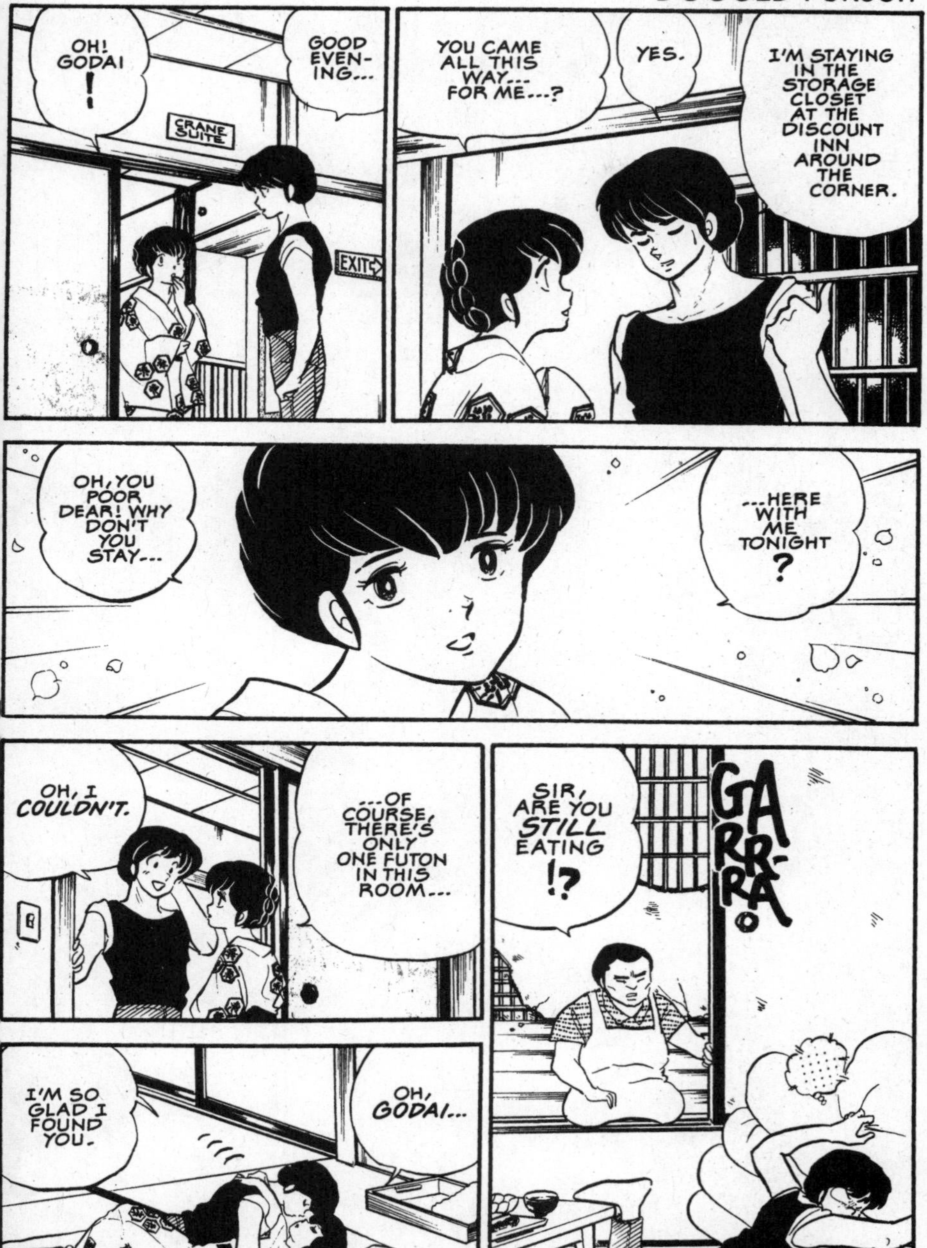
OH! GODAI !
GOOD EVENING...
CRANE SUITE
EXIT
YOU CAME ALL THIS WAY... FOR ME...?
YES.
I'M STAYING IN THE STORAGE CLOSET AT THE DISCOUNT INN AROUND THE CORNER.
OH, YOU POOR DEAR! WHY DON'T YOU STAY...
...HERE WITH ME TONIGHT ?
OH, I COULDN'T.
...OF COURSE, THERE'S ONLY ONE FUTON IN THIS ROOM...
I'M SO GLAD I FOUND YOU.
OH, GODAI...
SIR, ARE YOU STILL EATING !?
GARRRA

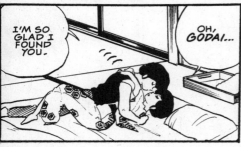

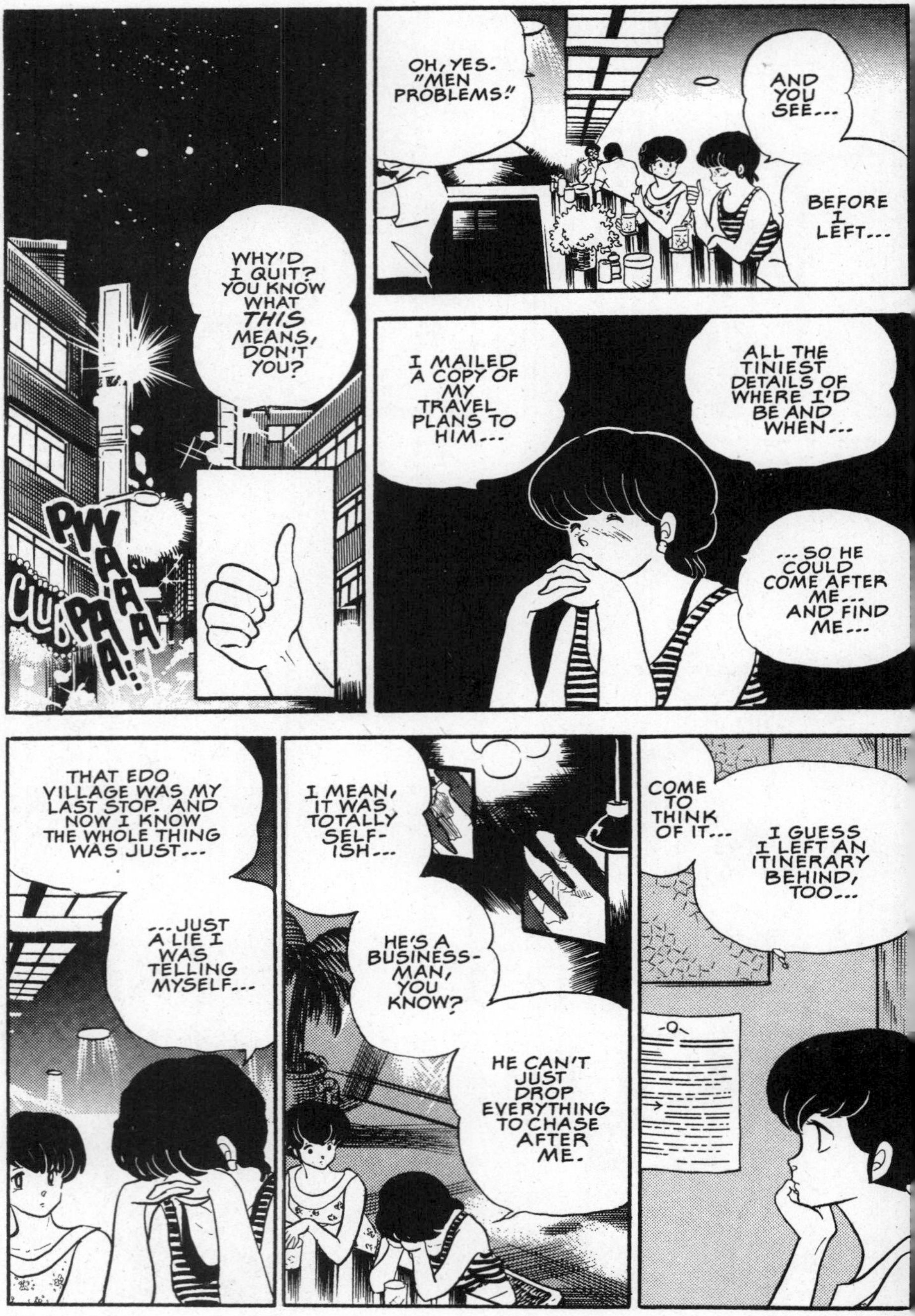
WHY'D I QUIT? YOU KNOW WHAT THIS MEANS, DON'T YOU?
PWAAAA PAAA!
CLUB
OH, YES. "MEN PROBLEMS."
AND YOU SEE...
BEFORE I LEFT...
I MAILED A COPY OF MY TRAVEL PLANS TO HIM...
ALL THE TINIEST DETAILS OF WHERE I'D BE AND WHEN...
...SO HE COULD COME AFTER ME... AND FIND ME...
THAT EDO VILLAGE WAS MY LAST STOP. AND NOW I KNOW THE WHOLE THING WAS JUST...
...JUST A LIE I WAS TELLING MYSELF...
I MEAN, IT WAS TOTALLY SELF-ISH...
HE'S A BUSINESS-MAN, YOU KNOW?
HE CAN'T JUST DROP EVERYTHING TO CHASE AFTER ME.
COME TO THINK OF IT...
I GUESS I LEFT AN ITINERARY BEHIND, TOO...

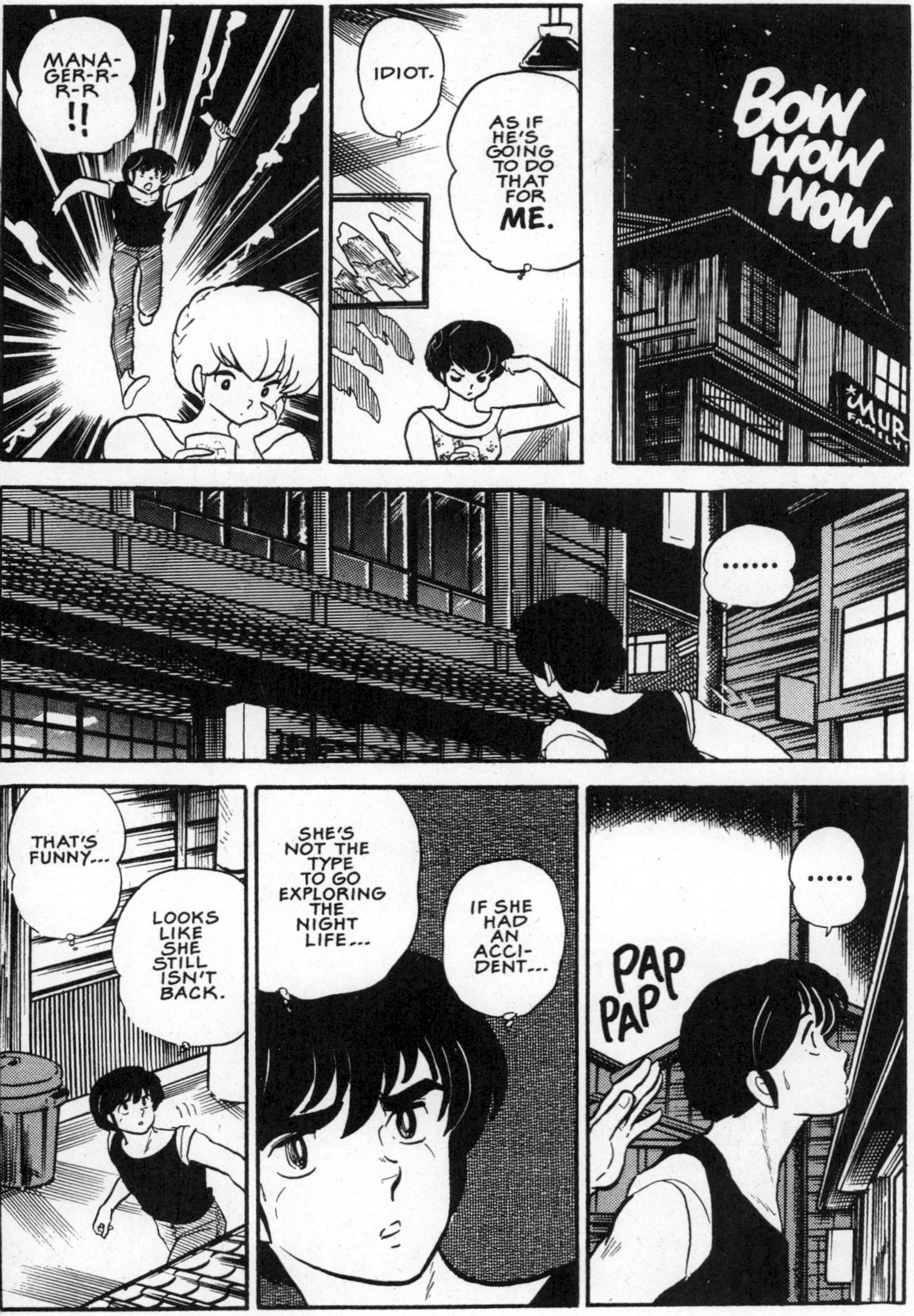
MANA-
GER-R-
R-R
!!
IDIOT.
AS IF HE'S GOING TO DO THAT FOR ME.
BOW WOW WOW
......
THAT'S FUNNY...
LOOKS LIKE SHE STILL ISN'T BACK.
SHE'S NOT THE TYPE TO GO EXPLORING THE NIGHT LIFE...
IF SHE HAD AN ACCI-
DENT...
.....
PAP PAP

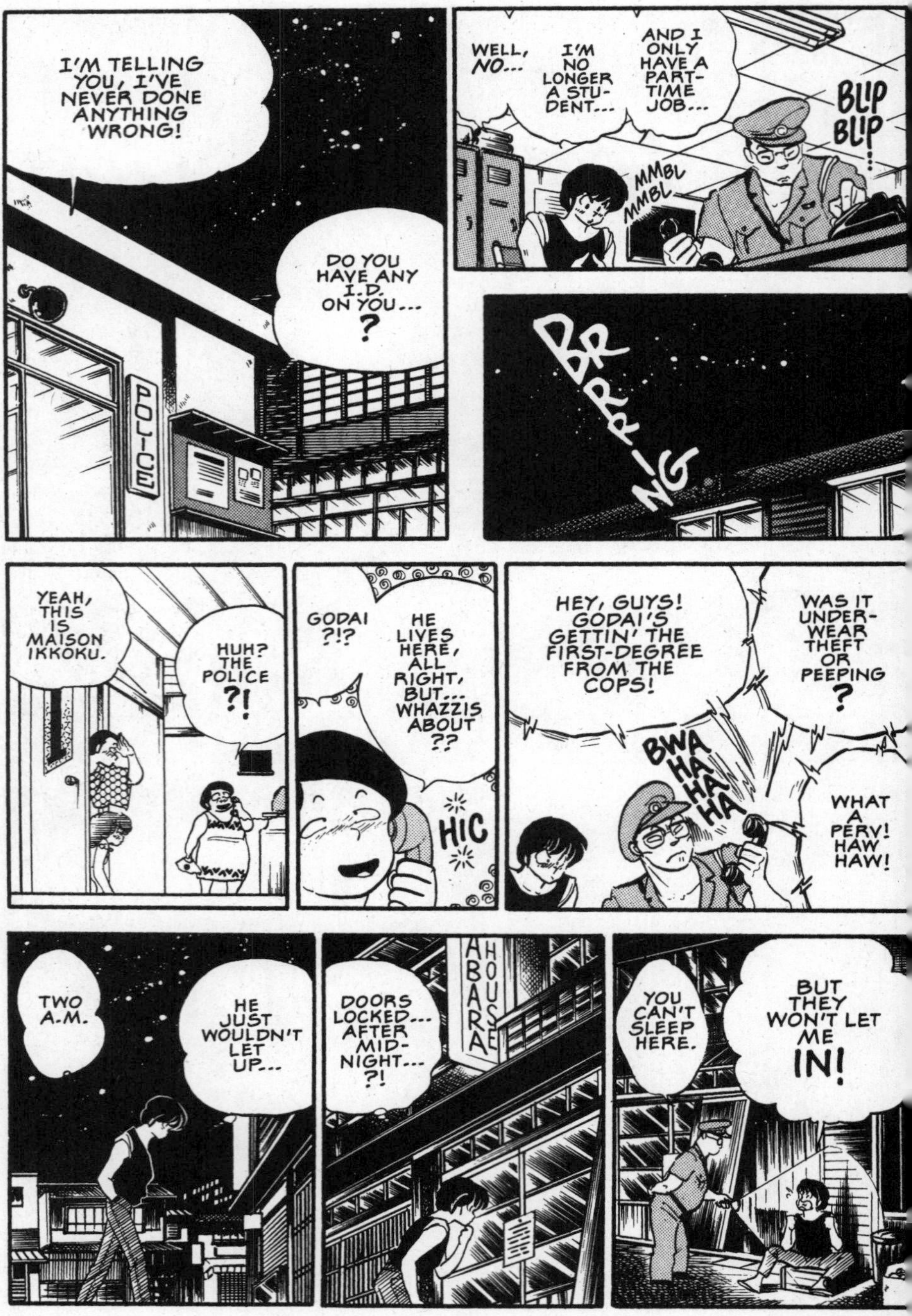

I'M TELLING YOU, I'VE NEVER DONE ANYTHING WRONG!
POLICE
DO YOU HAVE ANY I.D. ON YOU...?
WELL, NO...
I'M NO LONGER A STU-DENT...
AND I ONLY HAVE A PART-TIME JOB...
MMBL MMBL
BLIP BLIP!
BRRRING
YEAH, THIS IS MAISON IKKOKU.
HUH? THE POLICE?!
GODAI?!?
HE LIVES HERE, ALL RIGHT, BUT... WHAZZIS ABOUT??
HIC
HEY, GUYS! GODAI'S GETTIN' THE FIRST-DEGREE FROM THE COPS!
WAS IT UNDER-WEAR THEFT OR PEEPING?
BWA HA HA HA HA
WHAT A PERV! HAW HAW!
TWO A.M.
HE JUST WOULDN'T LET UP...
ABARA HOUSE
DOORS LOCKED... AFTER MID-NIGHT...?!
YOU CAN'T SLEEP HERE.
BUT THEY WON'T LET ME IN!

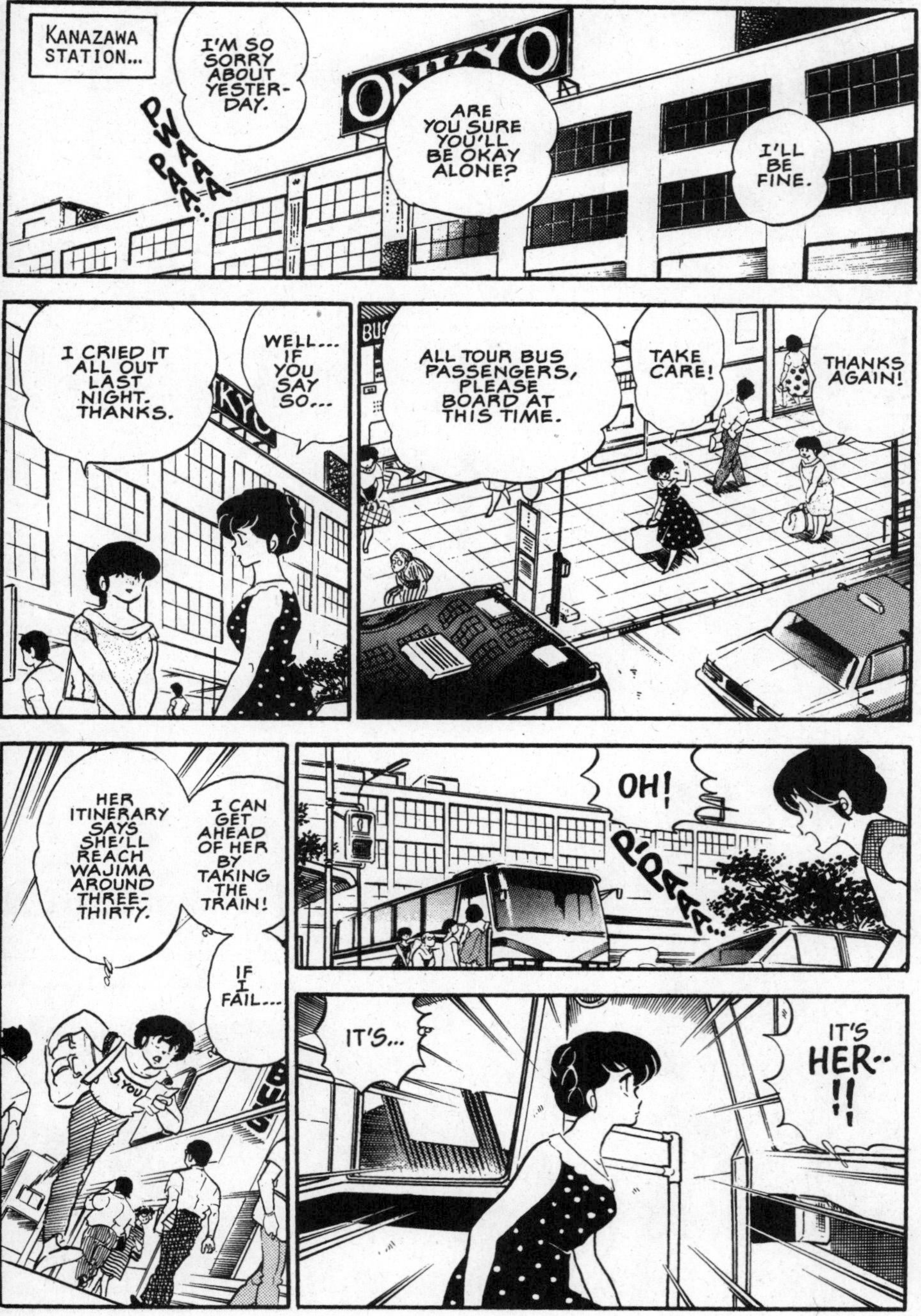
KANAZAWA STATION...
I'M SO SORRY ABOUT YESTER-DAY.
PWAAAA PAAA...
ARE YOU SURE YOU'LL BE OKAY ALONE?
I'LL BE FINE.
I CRIED IT ALL OUT LAST NIGHT. THANKS.
WELL... IF YOU SAY SO...
ALL TOUR BUS PASSENGERS, PLEASE BOARD AT THIS TIME.
TAKE CARE!
THANKS AGAIN!
HER ITINERARY SAYS SHE'LL REACH WAJIMA AROUND THREE-THIRTY.
I CAN GET AHEAD OF HER BY TAKING THE TRAIN!
IF I FAIL...
OH!
P'PAAA...
IT'S...
IT'S HER...!!

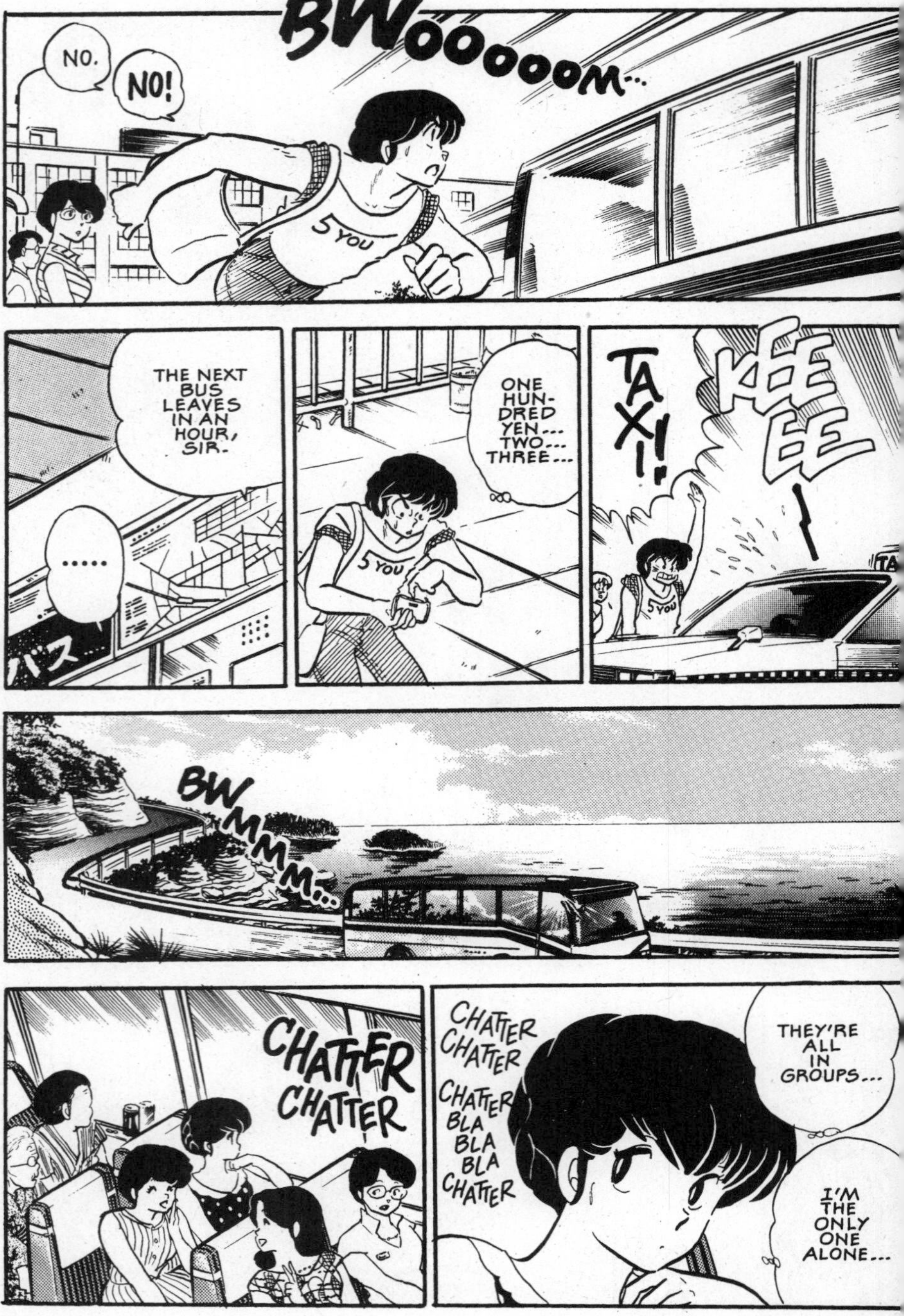

NO.
NO!
BWOOOOOOM...
THE NEXT BUS LEAVES IN AN HOUR, SIR.
......
バス
ONE HUNDRED YEN... TWO... THREE...
TAXI!!
KEEEE!
BWMMMM...
CHATTER CHATTER
CHATTER CHATTER
CHATTER BLA BLA BLA CHATTER
THEY'RE ALL IN GROUPS...
I'M THE ONLY ONE ALONE...

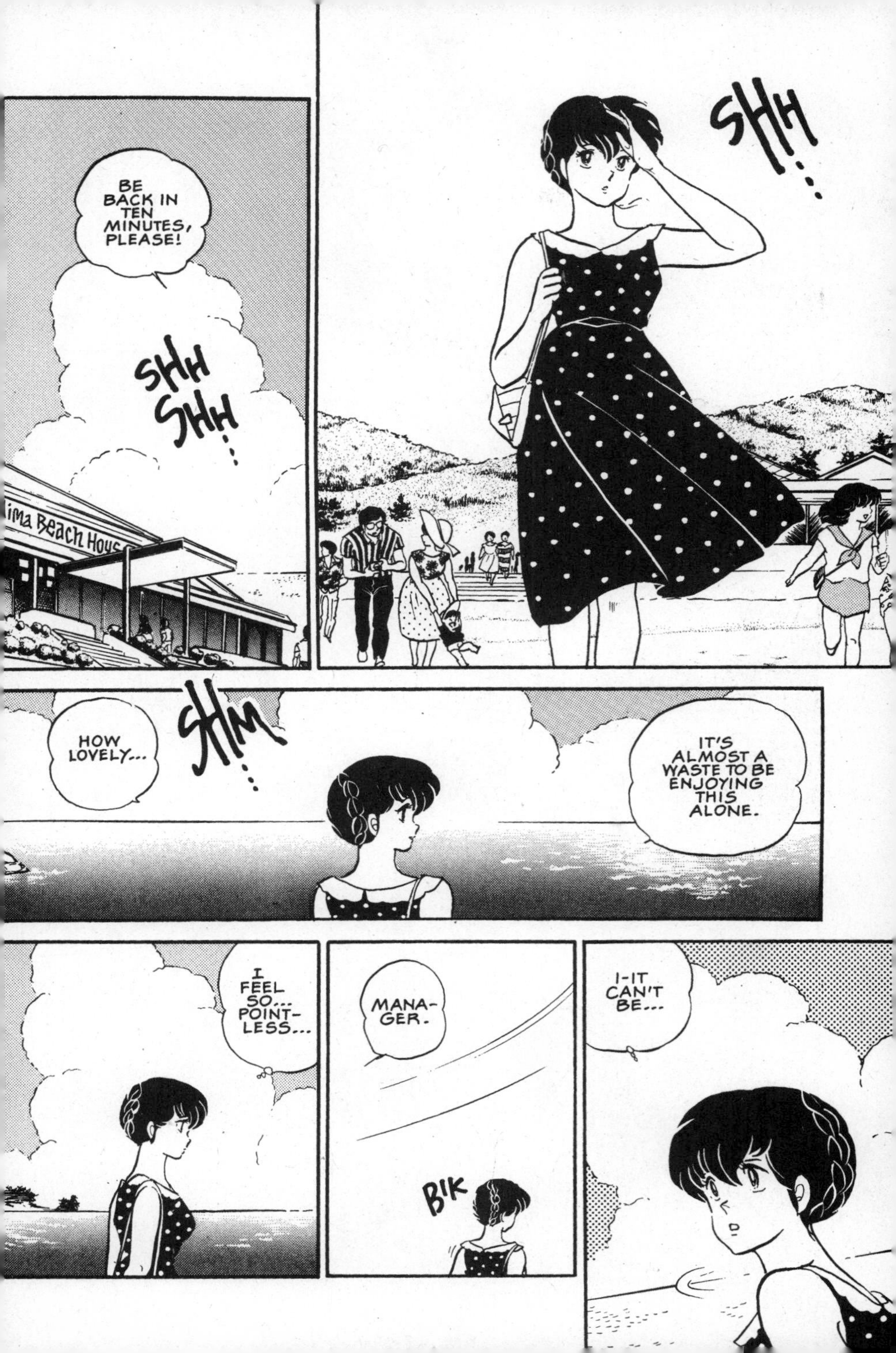
BE BACK IN TEN MINUTES, PLEASE!
SHH SHH...
...ima Beach Hous...
SHH...
HOW LOVELY...
SHM...
IT'S ALMOST A WASTE TO BE ENJOYING THIS ALONE.
I FEEL SO... POINTLESS...
MANAGER.
BIK
I-IT CAN'T BE...

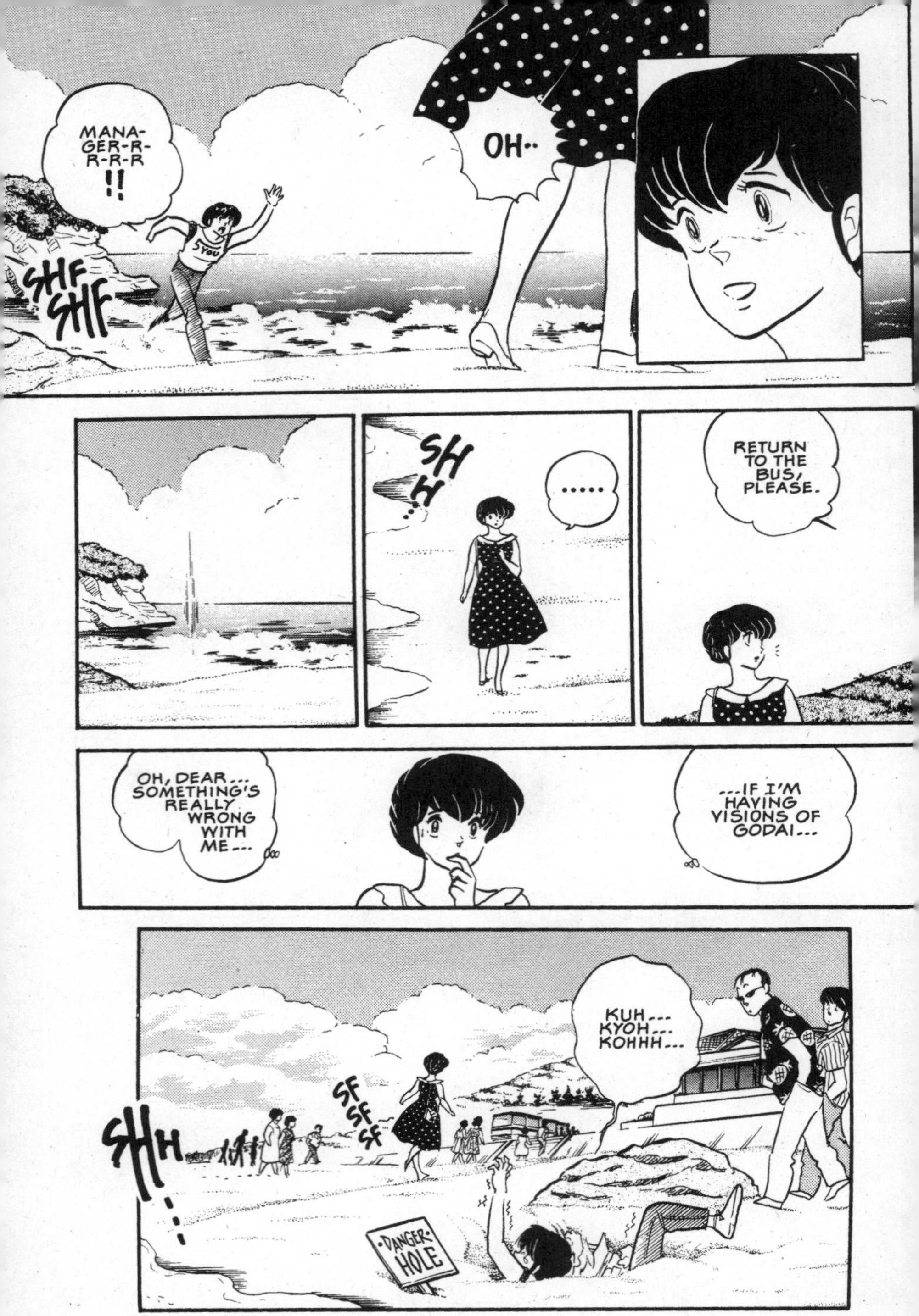
MANA-GER-R-R-R-R !!
SHF SHF
OH..
SHH
.....
RETURN TO THE BUS, PLEASE.
OH, DEAR... SOMETHING'S REALLY WRONG WITH ME...
...IF I'M HAVING VISIONS OF GODAI...
SHH
SF SF SF
KUH... KYOH... KOHHH...
DANGER HOLE

PART 11
STEAMY LOVE

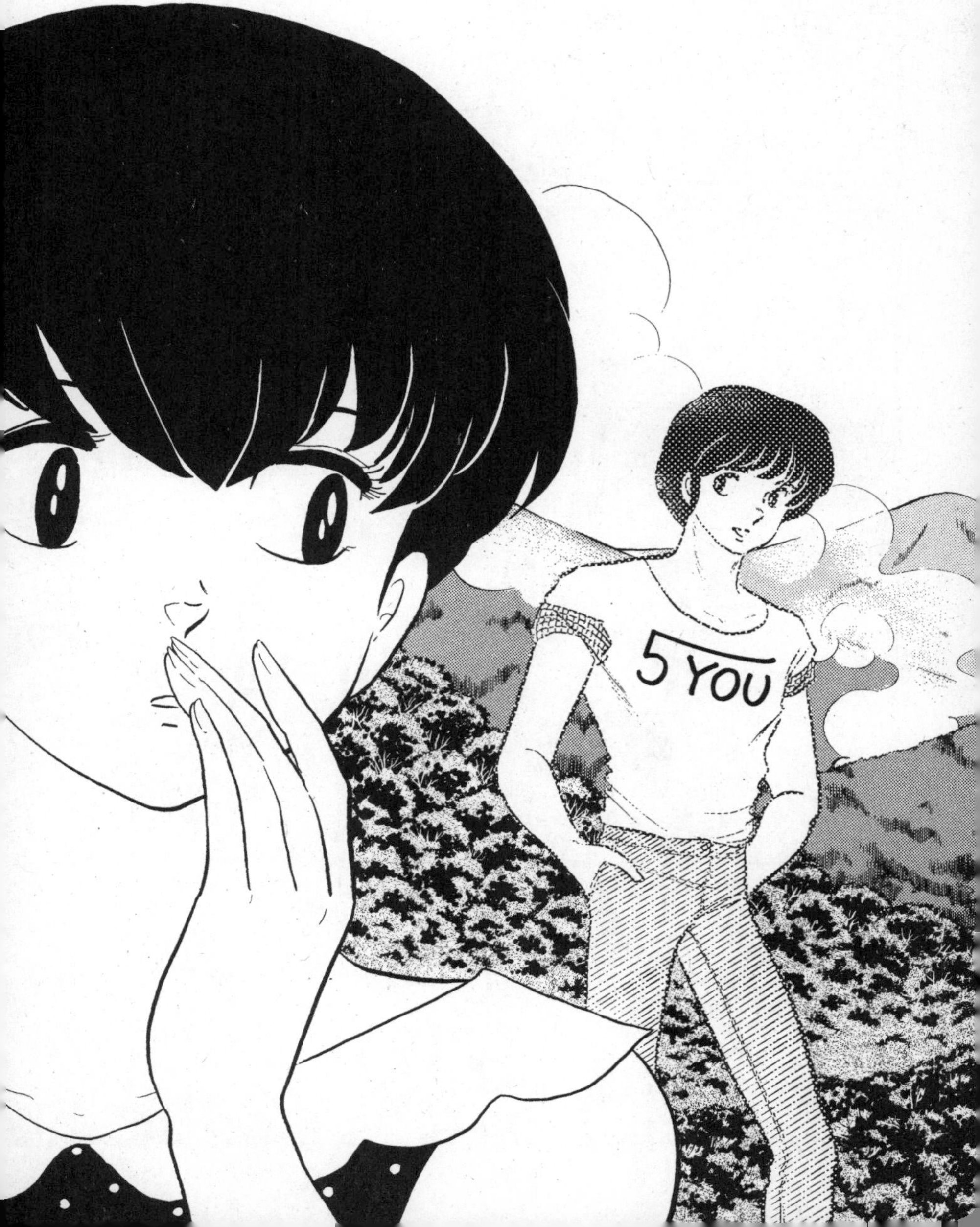
5 YOU

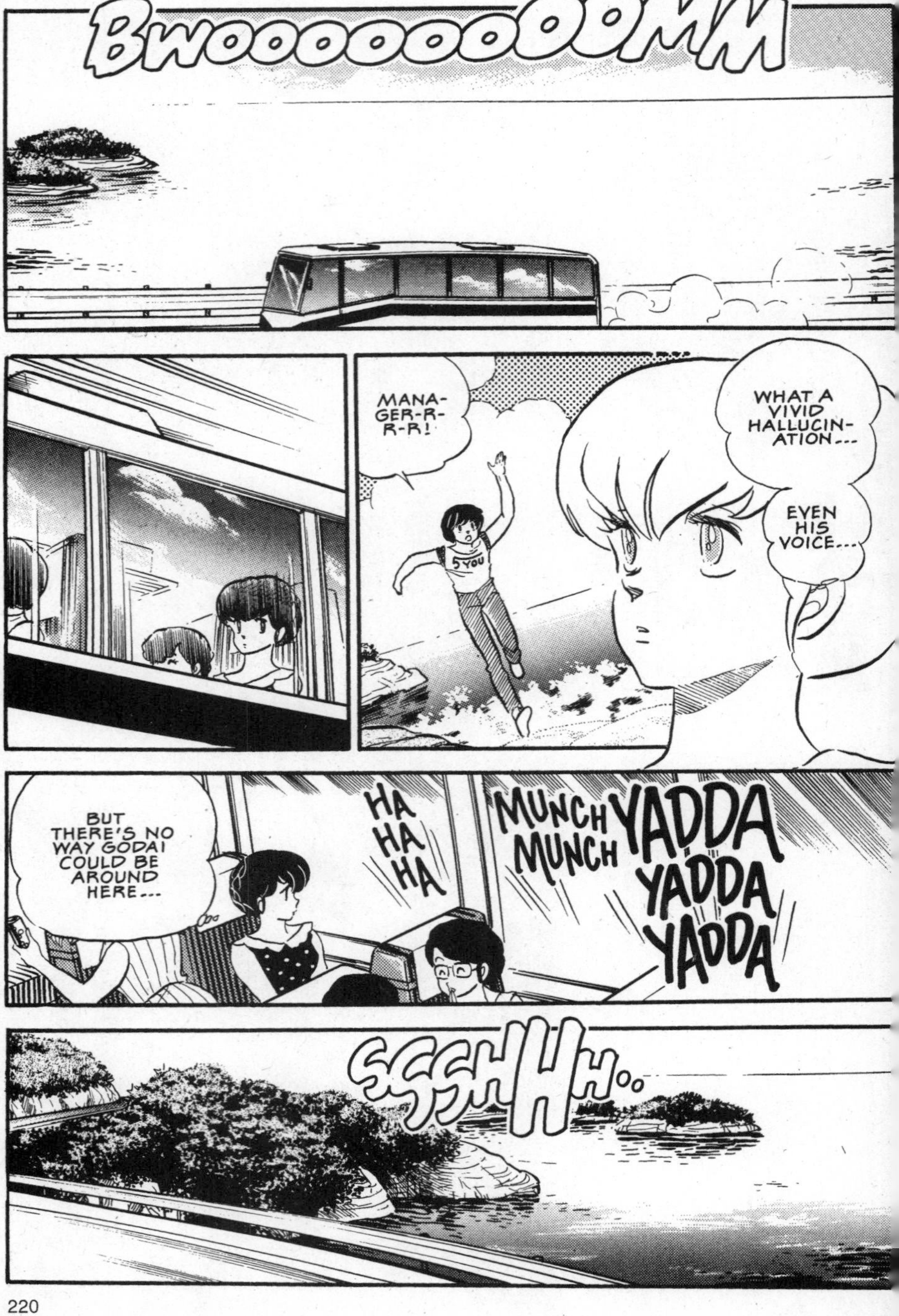
BWOOOOOOOOMM
MANA-GER-R-R-R!
WHAT A VIVID HALLUCIN-ATION...
EVEN HIS VOICE...
BUT THERE'S NO WAY GODAI COULD BE AROUND HERE...
HA HA HA
MUNCH MUNCH
YADDA YADDA YADDA
SSSHHH..

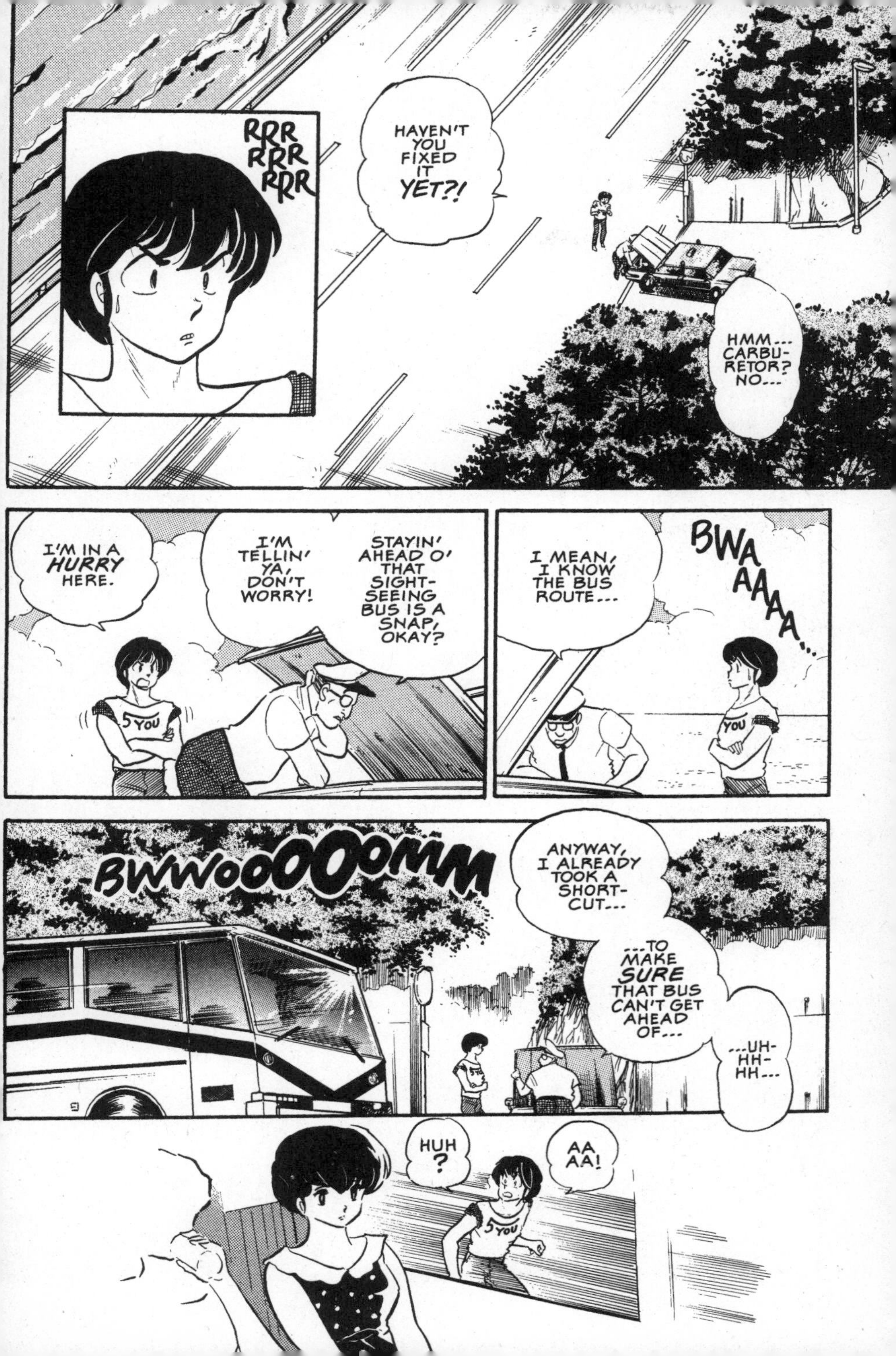
RRR RRR RRR
HAVEN'T YOU FIXED IT YET?!
HMM... CARBURETOR? NO...
I'M IN A HURRY HERE.
I'M TELLIN' YA, DON'T WORRY!
STAYIN' AHEAD O' THAT SIGHT-SEEING BUS IS A SNAP, OKAY?
I MEAN, I KNOW THE BUS ROUTE...
BWAAAAA...
BWWOOOOOOMM
ANYWAY, I ALREADY TOOK A SHORT-CUT...
...TO MAKE SURE THAT BUS CAN'T GET AHEAD OF...
...UH-HH-HH...
HUH?
AA AA!

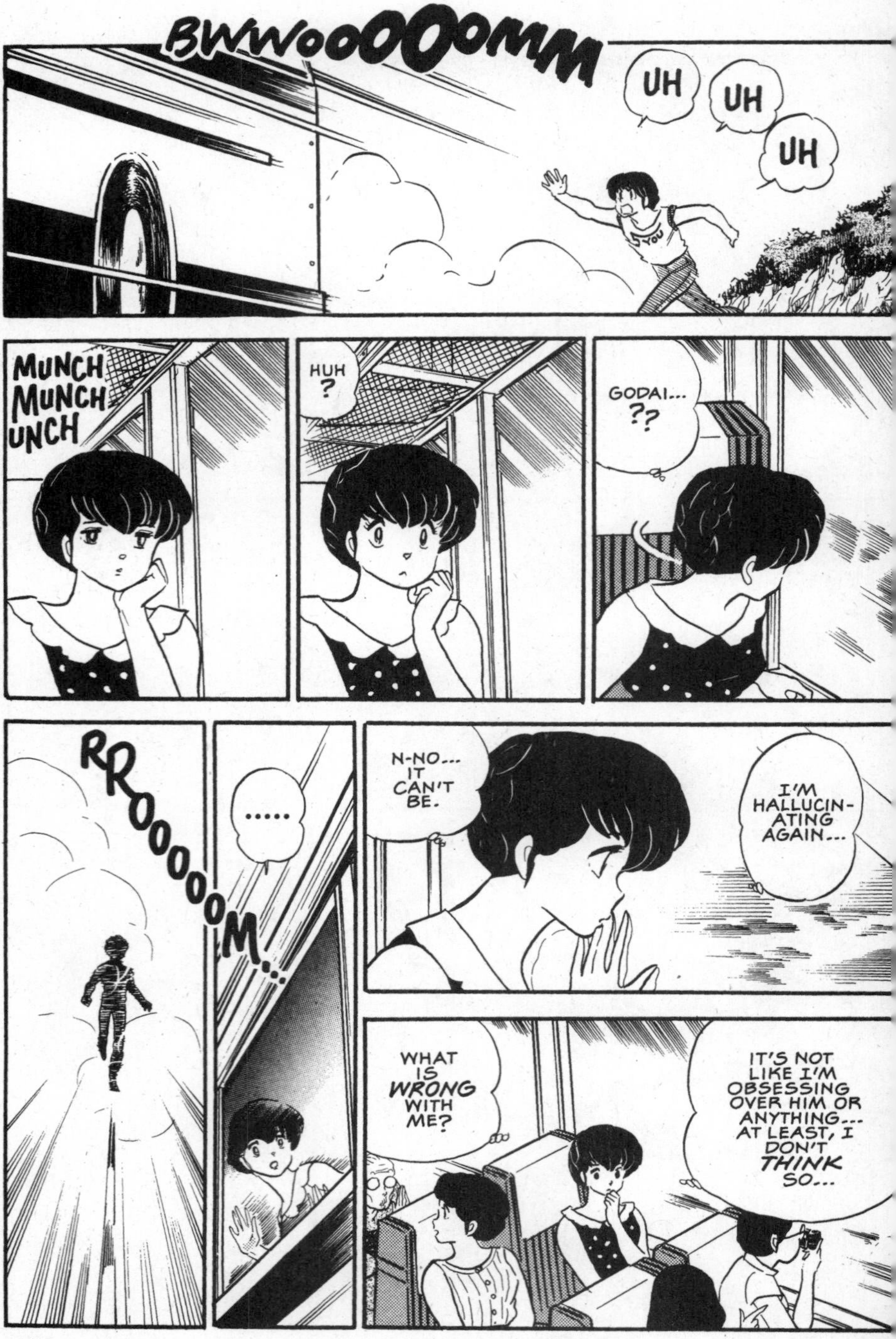
BWWOOOOOOMM
UH
UH
UH
MUNCH MUNCH UNCH
HUH ?
GODAI... ??
RROOOOOOM...
.....
N-NO... IT CAN'T BE.
I'M HALLUCINATING AGAIN...
WHAT IS WRONG WITH ME?
IT'S NOT LIKE I'M OBSESSING OVER HIM OR ANYTHING... AT LEAST, I DON'T THINK SO...

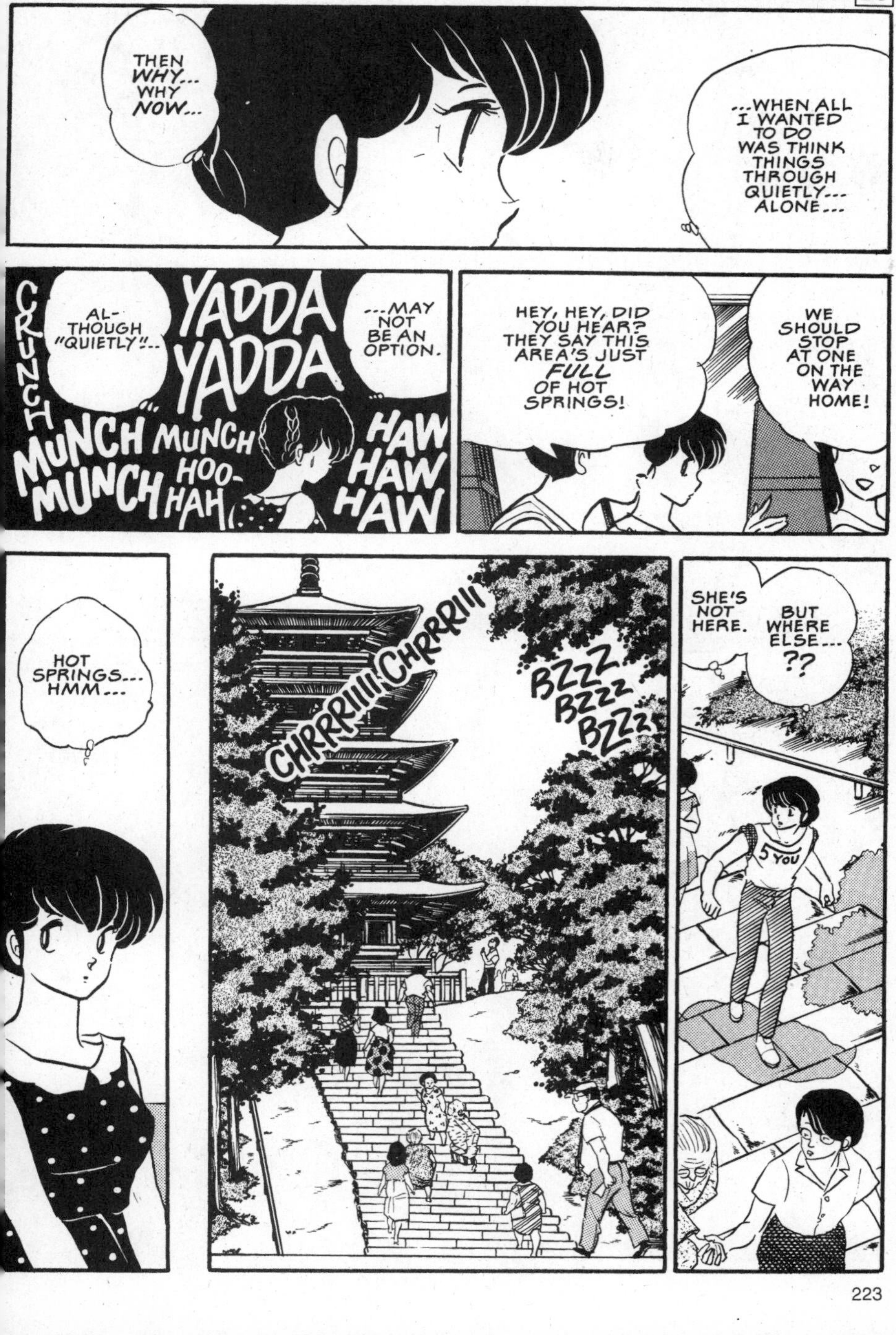
THEN WHY... WHY NOW...
...WHEN ALL I WANTED TO DO WAS THINK THINGS THROUGH QUIETLY... ALONE...
CRUNCH
AL-THOUGH "QUIETLY"...
YADDA YADDA
...MAY NOT BE AN OPTION.
MUNCH MUNCH
MUNCH
HOO-HAH
HAW HAW HAW
HEY, HEY, DID YOU HEAR? THEY SAY THIS AREA'S JUST FULL OF HOT SPRINGS!
WE SHOULD STOP AT ONE ON THE WAY HOME!
HOT SPRINGS... HMM...
CHRRRIIII CHRRRIII
BZZZ BZZZ BZZZ
SHE'S NOT HERE.
BUT WHERE ELSE... ??
5 YOU

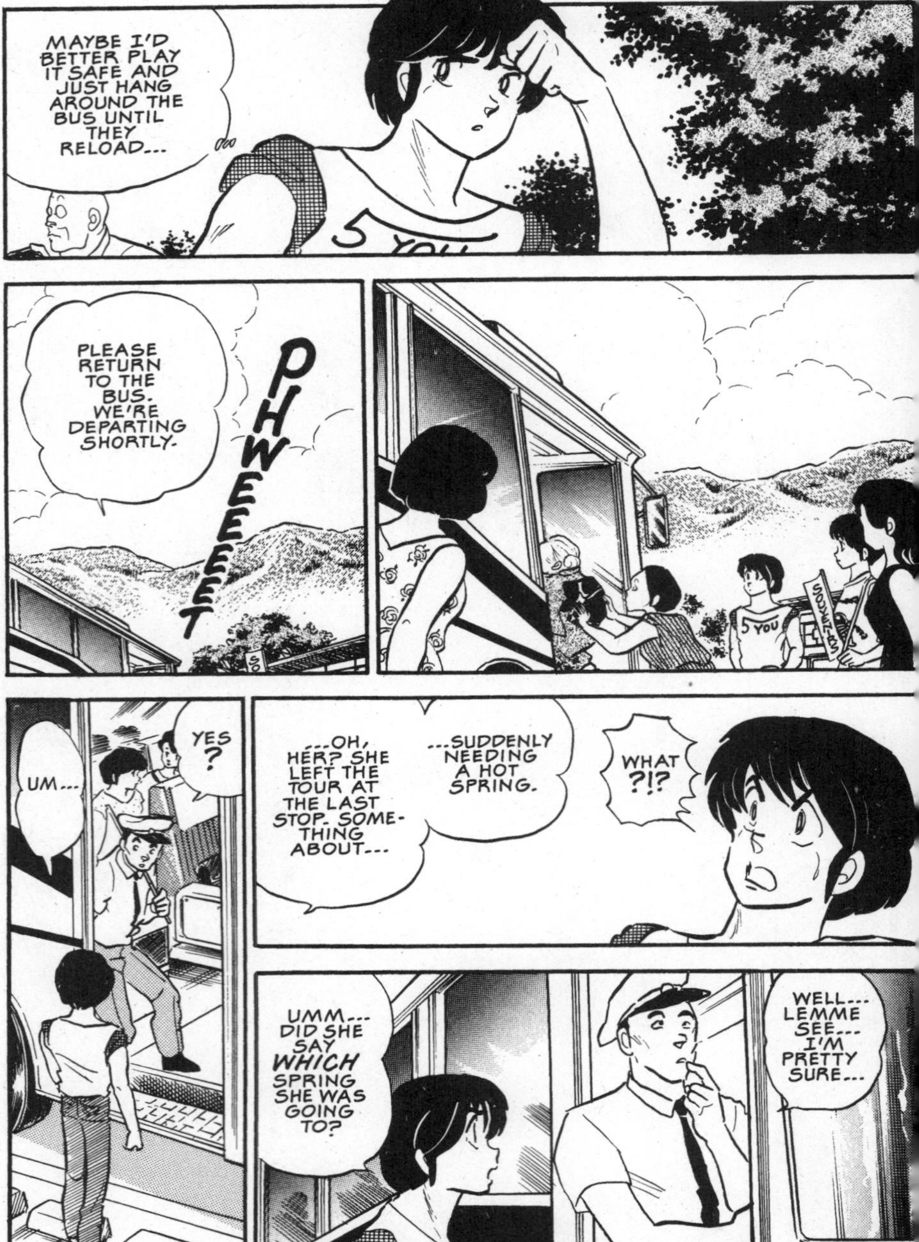
MAYBE I'D BETTER PLAY IT SAFE AND JUST HANG AROUND THE BUS UNTIL THEY RELOAD...
PLEASE RETURN TO THE BUS. WE'RE DEPARTING SHORTLY.
PHWEEEEET
UM...
YES ?
...OH, HER? SHE LEFT THE TOUR AT THE LAST STOP. SOMETHING ABOUT...
...SUDDENLY NEEDING A HOT SPRING.
WHAT ?!?
UMM... DID SHE SAY WHICH SPRING SHE WAS GOING TO?
WELL... LEMME SEE... I'M PRETTY SURE...

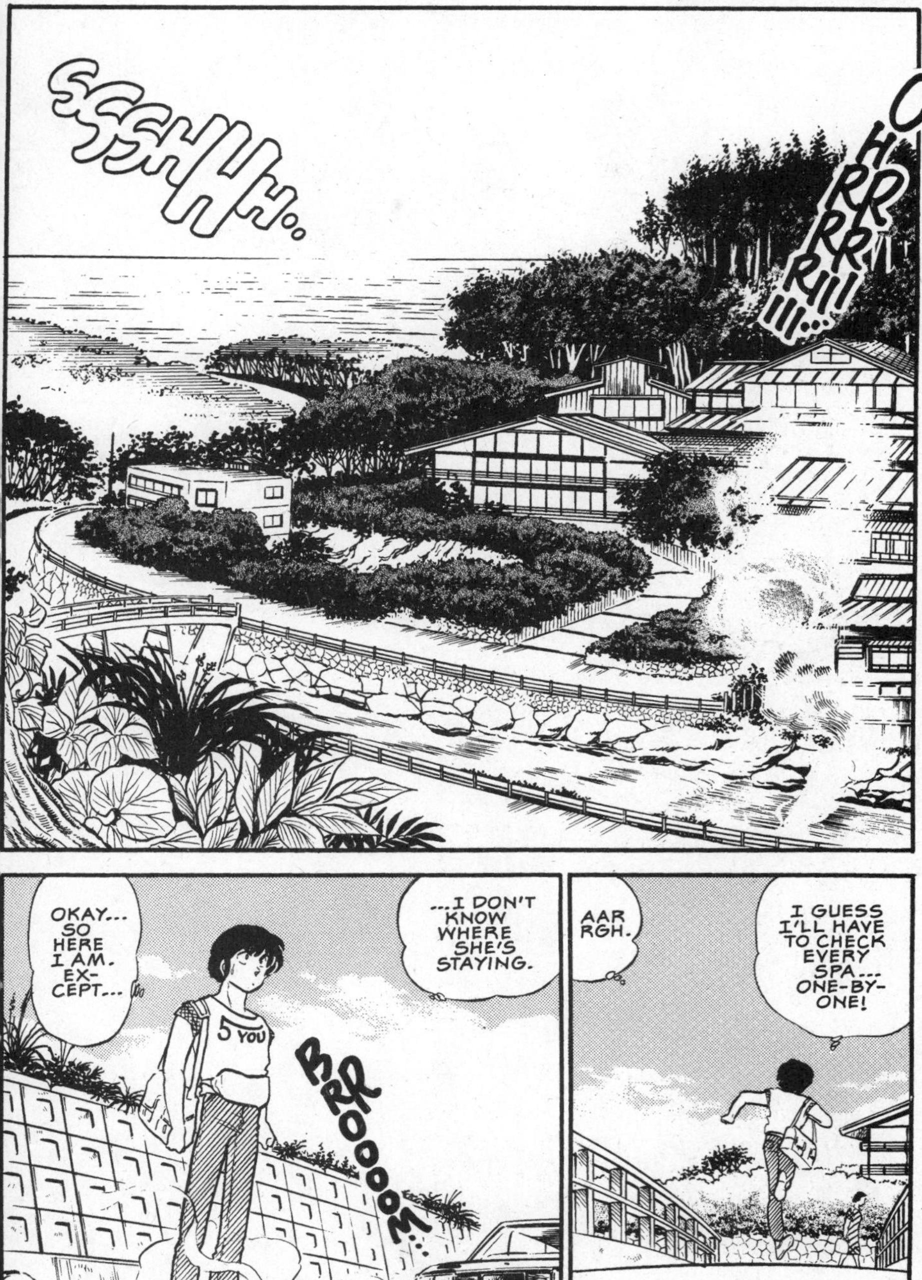
SSSHHHh..
CHRRRRRI!!!...
OKAY... SO HERE I AM. EX-CEPT...
...I DON'T KNOW WHERE SHE'S STAYING.
5 YOU
BRRROOOOOM...
AARRGH.
I GUESS I'LL HAVE TO CHECK EVERY SPA... ONE-BY-ONE!

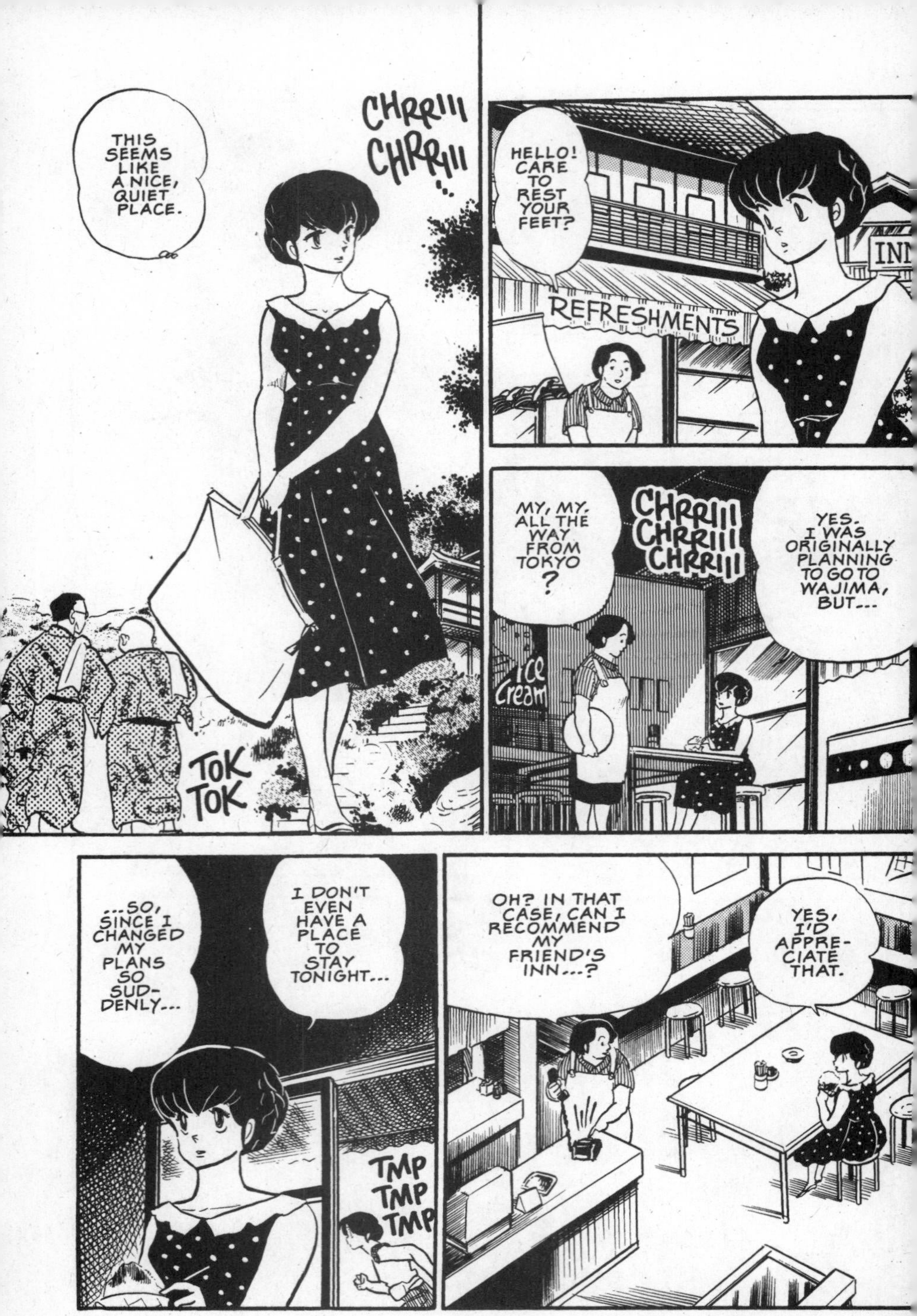
THIS SEEMS LIKE A NICE, QUIET PLACE.
CHRRIII CHRRIII...
TOK TOK
HELLO! CARE TO REST YOUR FEET?
REFRESHMENTS
INN
MY, MY. ALL THE WAY FROM TOKYO?
CHRRIII CHRRIII CHRRIII
YES. I WAS ORIGINALLY PLANNING TO GO TO WAJIMA, BUT...
Ice Cream
...SO, SINCE I CHANGED MY PLANS SO SUDDENLY...
I DON'T EVEN HAVE A PLACE TO STAY TONIGHT...
TMP TMP TMP
OH? IN THAT CASE, CAN I RECOMMEND MY FRIEND'S INN...?
YES, I'D APPRECIATE THAT.

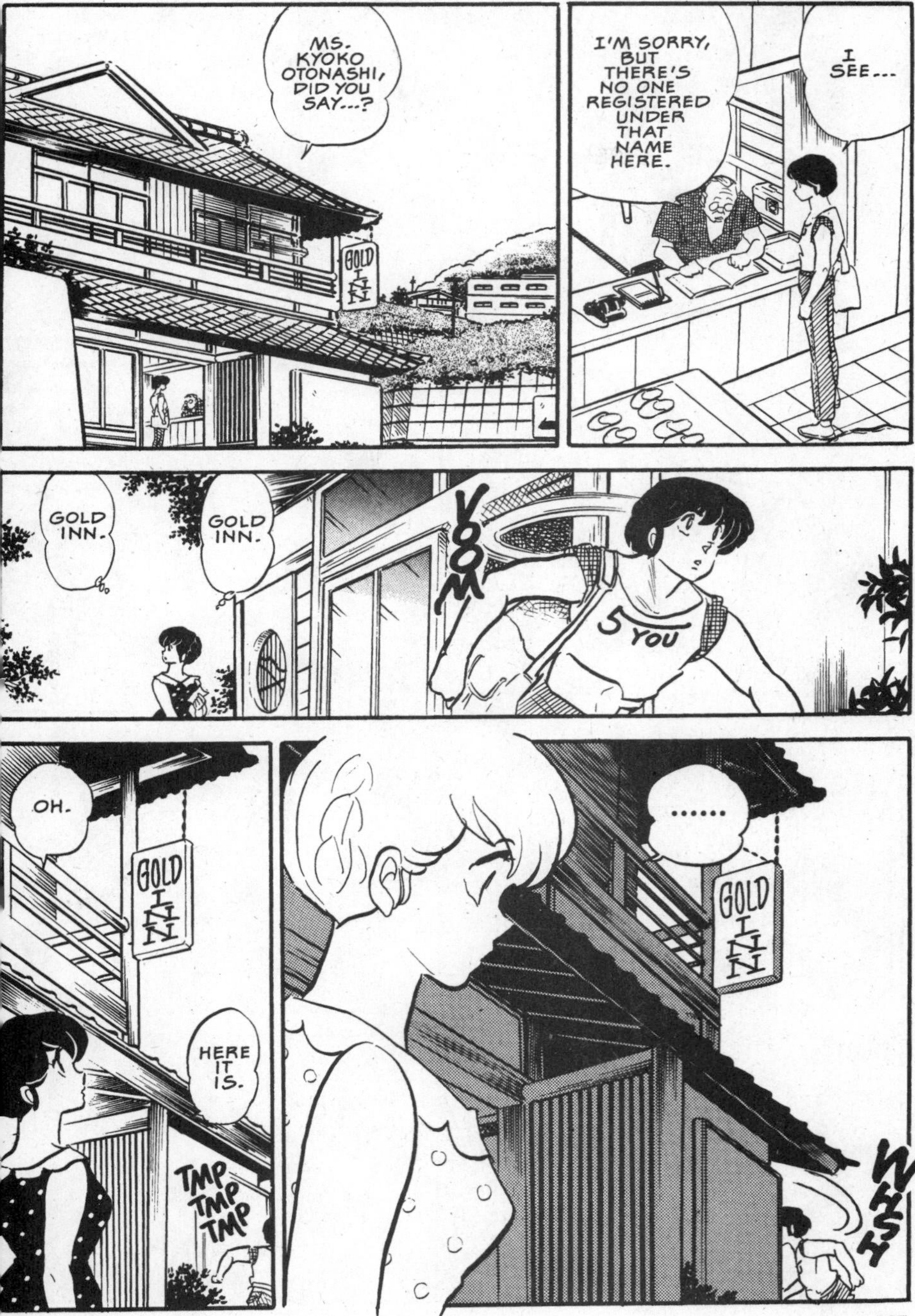
MS. KYOKO OTONASHI, DID YOU SAY...?
GOLD INN
I'M SORRY, BUT THERE'S NO ONE REGISTERED UNDER THAT NAME HERE.
I SEE...
GOLD INN.
GOLD INN.
VOOM
5 YOU
OH.
GOLD INN
HERE IT IS.
TMP TMP TMP
......
GOLD INN
WHSH

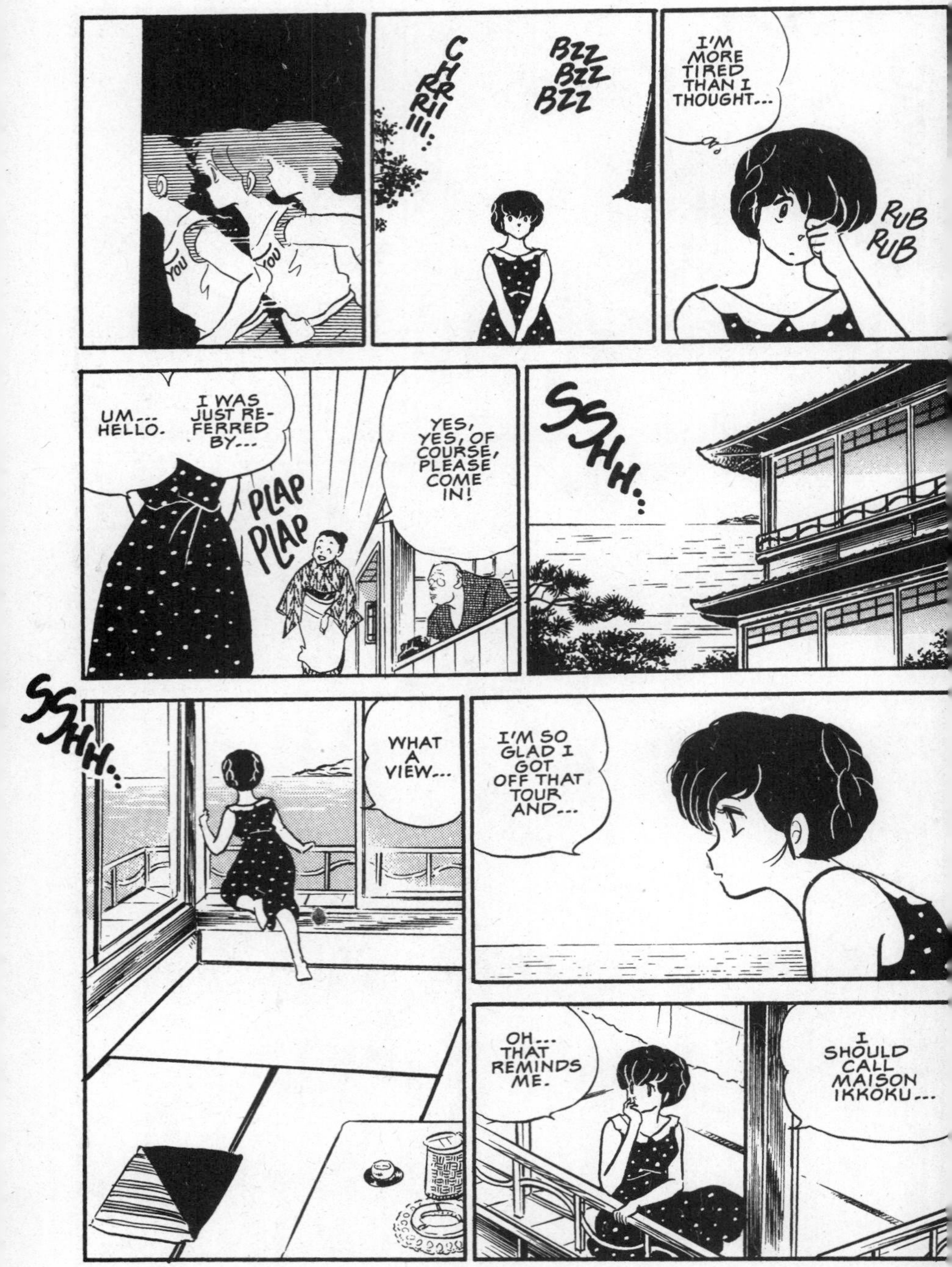
YOU
YOU
CHRRRIIII...
BZZ BZZ BZZ
I'M MORE TIRED THAN I THOUGHT...
RUB RUB
UM... HELLO.
I WAS JUST REFERRED BY...
PLAP PLAP
YES, YES, OF COURSE, PLEASE COME IN!
SSHHH...
SSHHH...
WHAT A VIEW...
I'M SO GLAD I GOT OFF THAT TOUR AND...
OH... THAT REMINDS ME.
I SHOULD CALL MAISON IKKOKU...

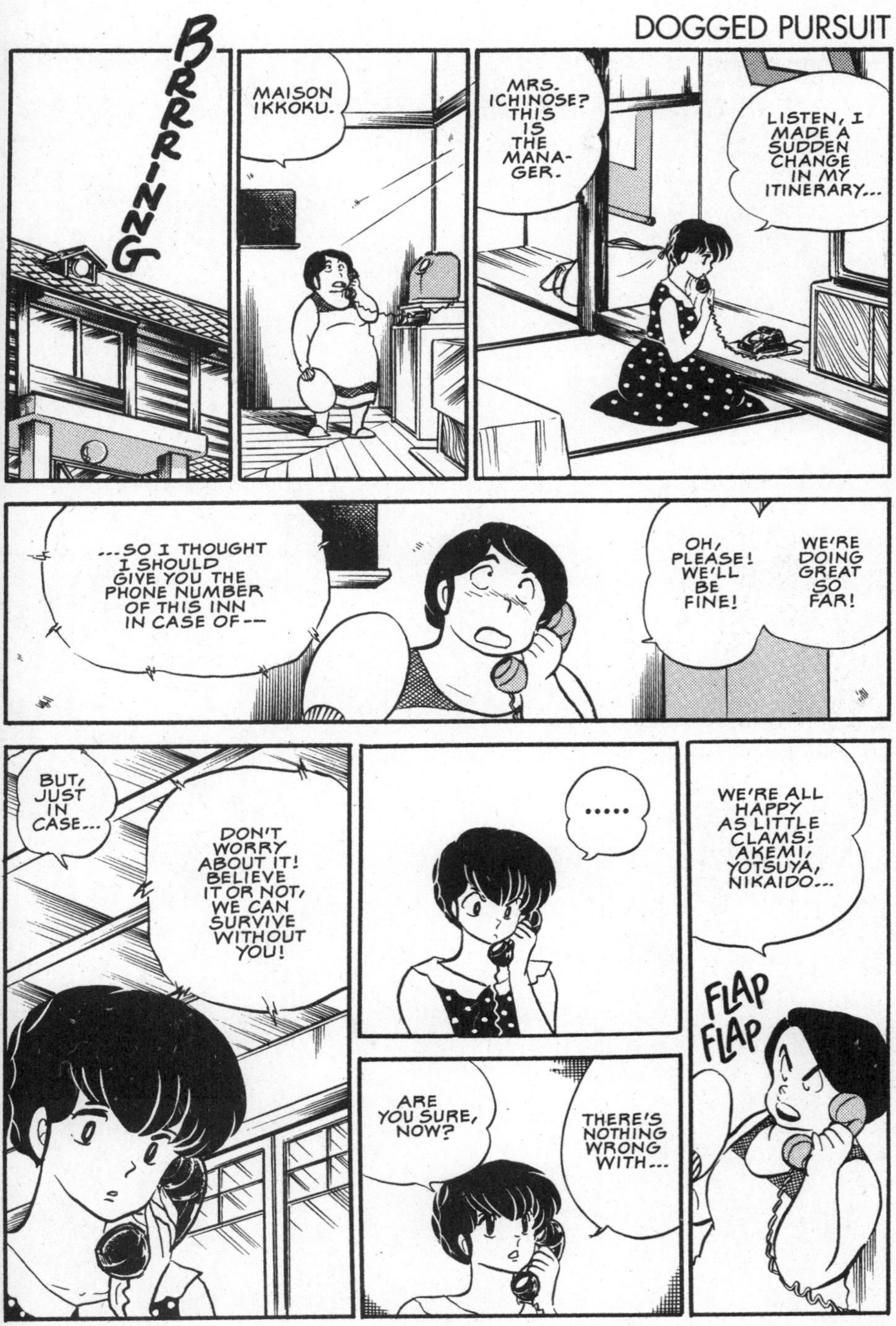
BRRRING
MAISON IKKOKU.
MRS. ICHINOSE? THIS IS THE MANAGER.
LISTEN, I MADE A SUDDEN CHANGE IN MY ITINERARY...
...SO I THOUGHT I SHOULD GIVE YOU THE PHONE NUMBER OF THIS INN IN CASE OF --
OH, PLEASE! WE'LL BE FINE!
WE'RE DOING GREAT SO FAR!
BUT, JUST IN CASE...
DON'T WORRY ABOUT IT! BELIEVE IT OR NOT, WE CAN SURVIVE WITHOUT YOU!
.....
ARE YOU SURE, NOW?
THERE'S NOTHING WRONG WITH...
WE'RE ALL HAPPY AS LITTLE CLAMS! AKEMI, YOTSUYA, NIKAIDO...
FLAP FLAP

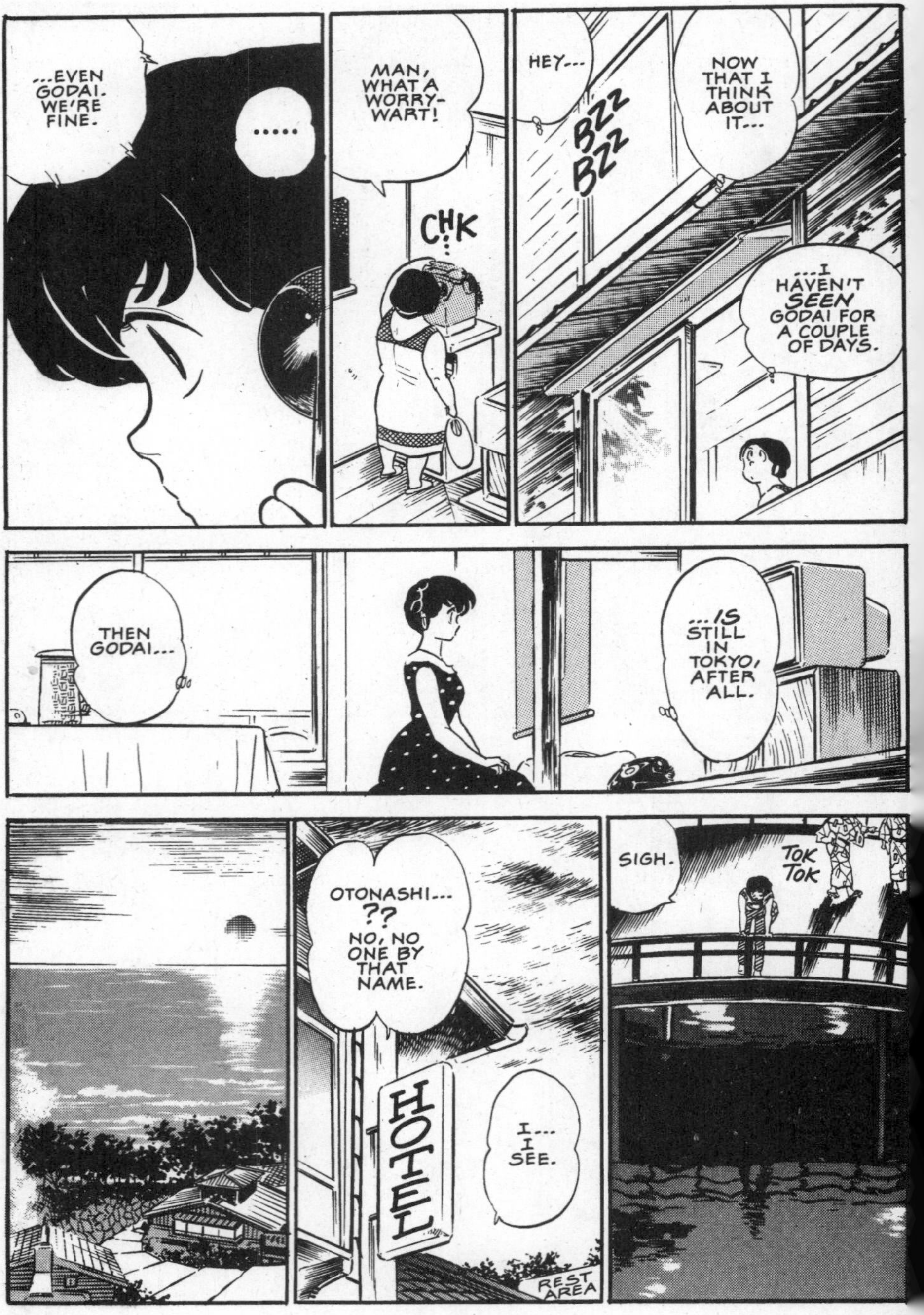
...EVEN GODAI. WE'RE FINE.
......
MAN, WHAT A WORRY-WART!
CHK
HEY...
NOW THAT I THINK ABOUT IT...
BZZ BZZ
...I HAVEN'T *SEEN* GODAI FOR A COUPLE OF DAYS.
THEN GODAI...
...*IS* STILL IN TOKYO, AFTER ALL.
OTONASHI... ?? NO, NO ONE BY THAT NAME.
HOTEL
I... I SEE.
REST AREA
SIGH.
TOK TOK

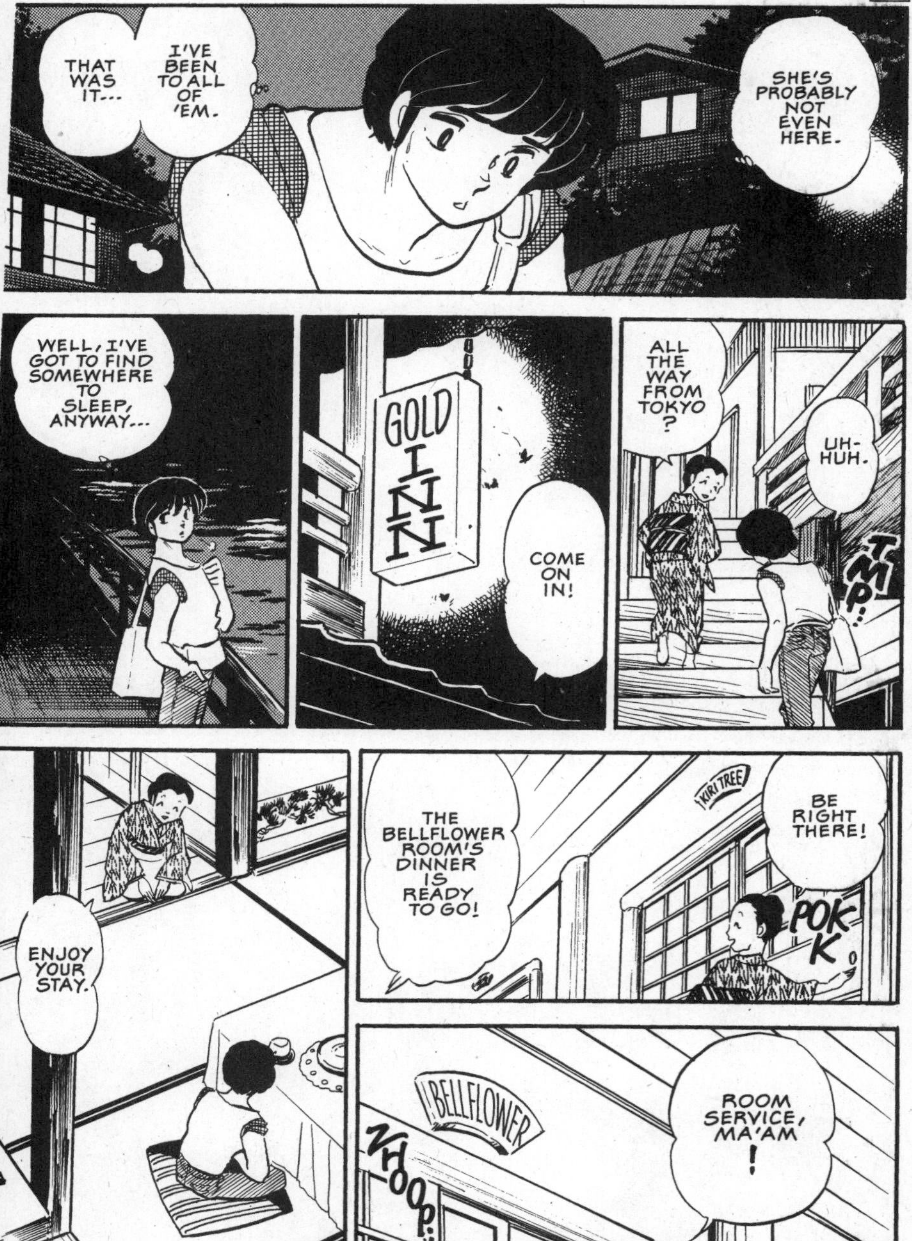
THAT WAS IT...
I'VE BEEN TO ALL OF 'EM.
SHE'S PROBABLY NOT EVEN HERE.
WELL, I'VE GOT TO FIND SOMEWHERE TO SLEEP, ANYWAY...
GOLD INN
COME ON IN!
ALL THE WAY FROM TOKYO?
UH-HUH.
TMP..
ENJOY YOUR STAY.
THE BELLFLOWER ROOM'S DINNER IS READY TO GO!
KIRI TREE
BE RIGHT THERE!
POKK
BELLFLOWER
ZROOP..
ROOM SERVICE, MA'AM!
KIRI TREE

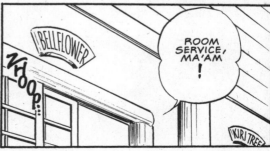

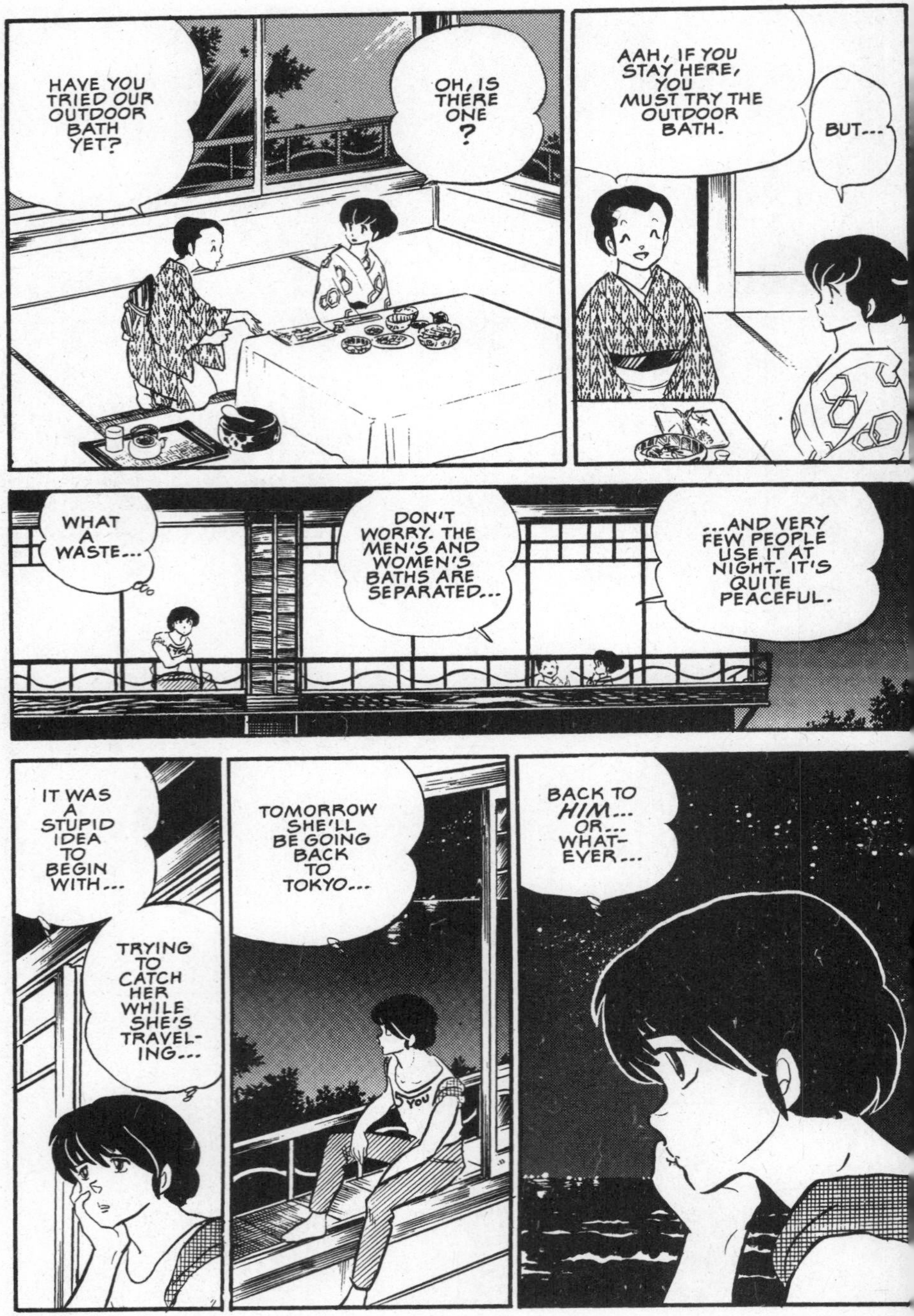
HAVE YOU TRIED OUR OUTDOOR BATH YET?
OH, IS THERE ONE?
AAH, IF YOU STAY HERE, YOU MUST TRY THE OUTDOOR BATH.
BUT...
WHAT A WASTE...
DON'T WORRY. THE MEN'S AND WOMEN'S BATHS ARE SEPARATED...
...AND VERY FEW PEOPLE USE IT AT NIGHT. IT'S QUITE PEACEFUL.
IT WAS A STUPID IDEA TO BEGIN WITH...
TRYING TO CATCH HER WHILE SHE'S TRAVEL-ING...
TOMORROW SHE'LL BE GOING BACK TO TOKYO...
YOU
BACK TO *HIM*... OR... WHAT-EVER...

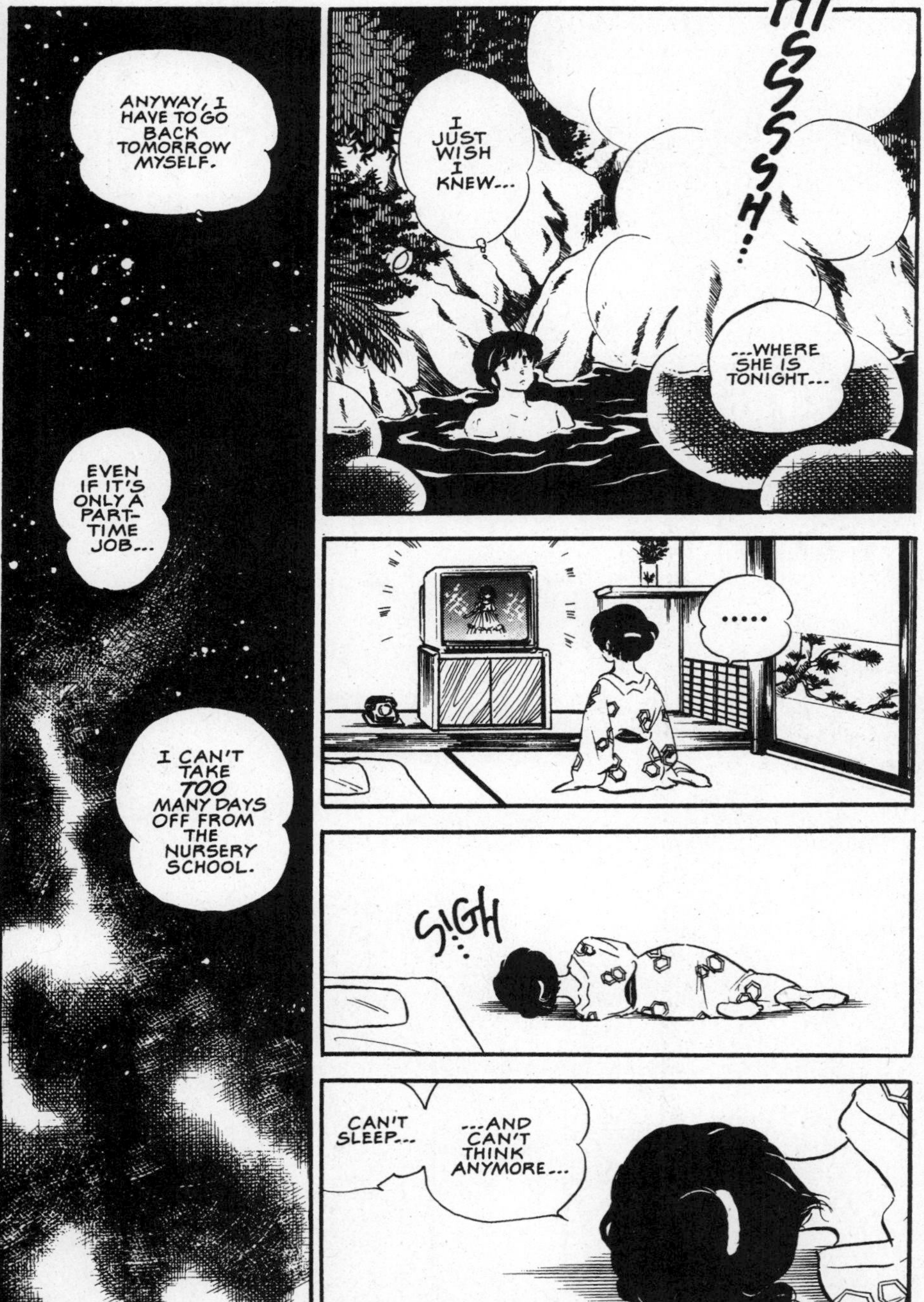
ANYWAY, I HAVE TO GO BACK TOMORROW MYSELF.
EVEN IF IT'S ONLY A PART-TIME JOB...
I CAN'T TAKE *TOO* MANY DAYS OFF FROM THE NURSERY SCHOOL.
I JUST WISH I KNEW...
HISSSSH!!
...WHERE SHE IS TONIGHT...
.....
SIGH...
CAN'T SLEEP...
...AND CAN'T THINK ANYMORE...

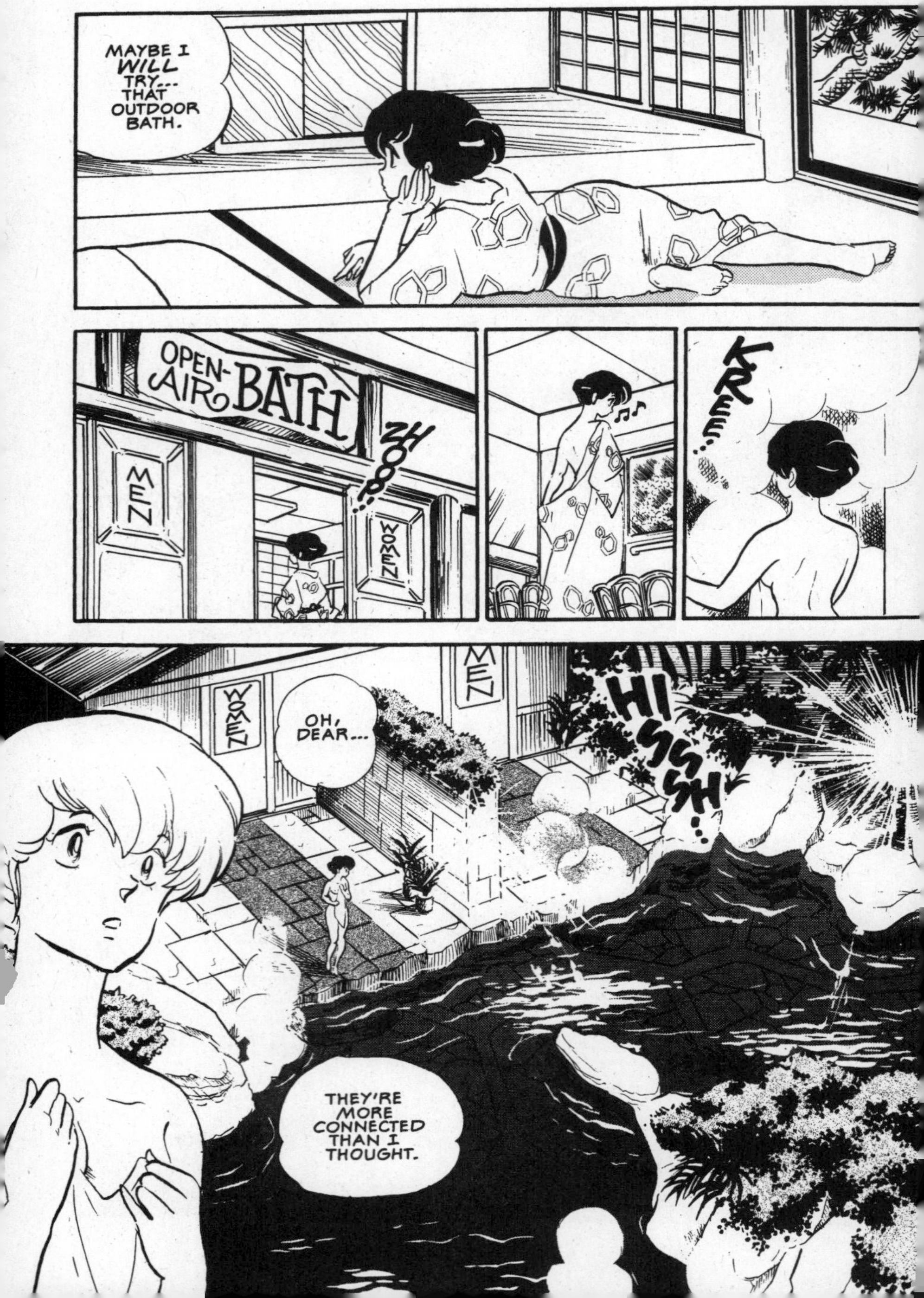
MAYBE I WILL TRY... THAT OUTDOOR BATH.
OPEN-AIR BATH
MEN
WOMEN
ZHOOP!!
KREE...
WOMEN
MEN
OH, DEAR...
HISSSH!!
THEY'RE MORE CONNECTED THAN I THOUGHT.

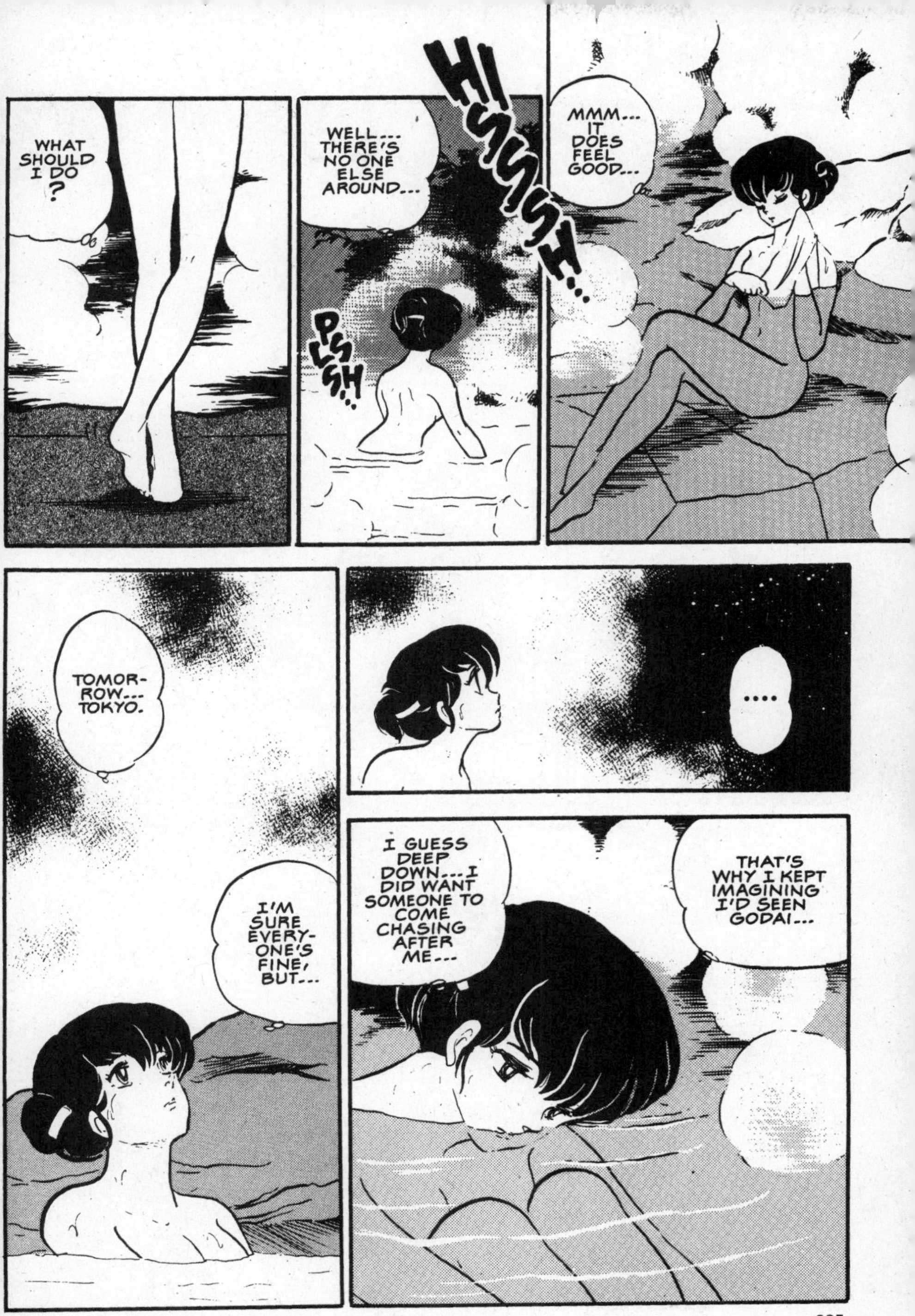

WHAT SHOULD I DO?
WELL... THERE'S NO ONE ELSE AROUND...
HISSSSH...
PSSSH!!
MMM... IT DOES FEEL GOOD...
TOMOR-ROW... TOKYO.
I'M SURE EVERY-ONE'S FINE, BUT...
....
I GUESS DEEP DOWN... I DID WANT SOMEONE TO COME CHASING AFTER ME...
THAT'S WHY I KEPT IMAGINING I'D SEEN GODAI...

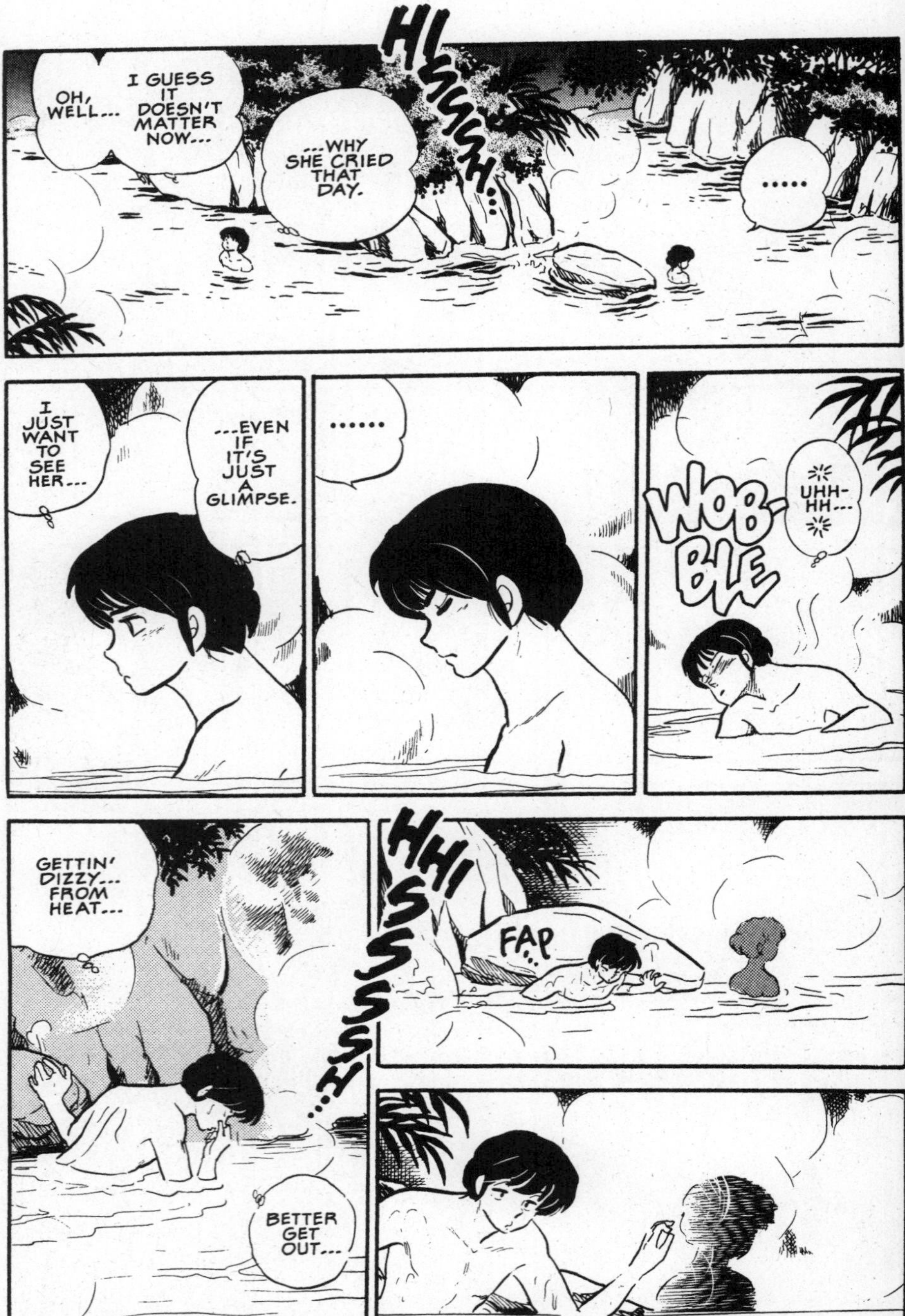
OH, WELL...
I GUESS IT DOESN'T MATTER NOW...
...WHY SHE CRIED THAT DAY.
HISSSSH...
......
I JUST WANT TO SEE HER...
...EVEN IF IT'S JUST A GLIMPSE.
......
WOB-BLE
UHH-HH...
GETTIN' DIZZY... FROM HEAT...
BETTER GET OUT...
HHISSSSSH...
FAP...

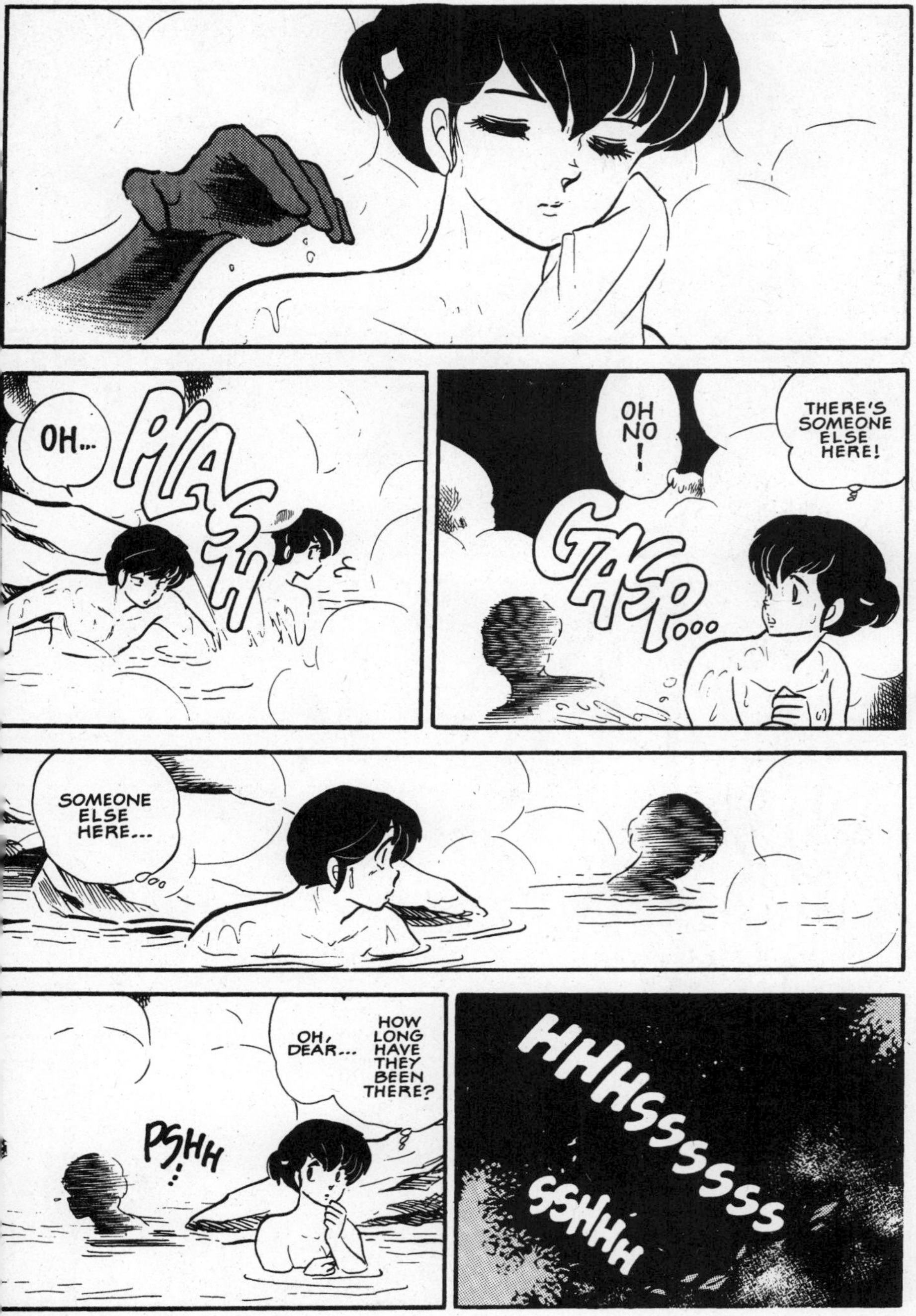
OH...
PLASH
OH NO !
THERE'S SOMEONE ELSE HERE!
GASP...
SOMEONE ELSE HERE...
OH, DEAR...
HOW LONG HAVE THEY BEEN THERE?
PSHH
HHHSSSSSSS
SSHHH

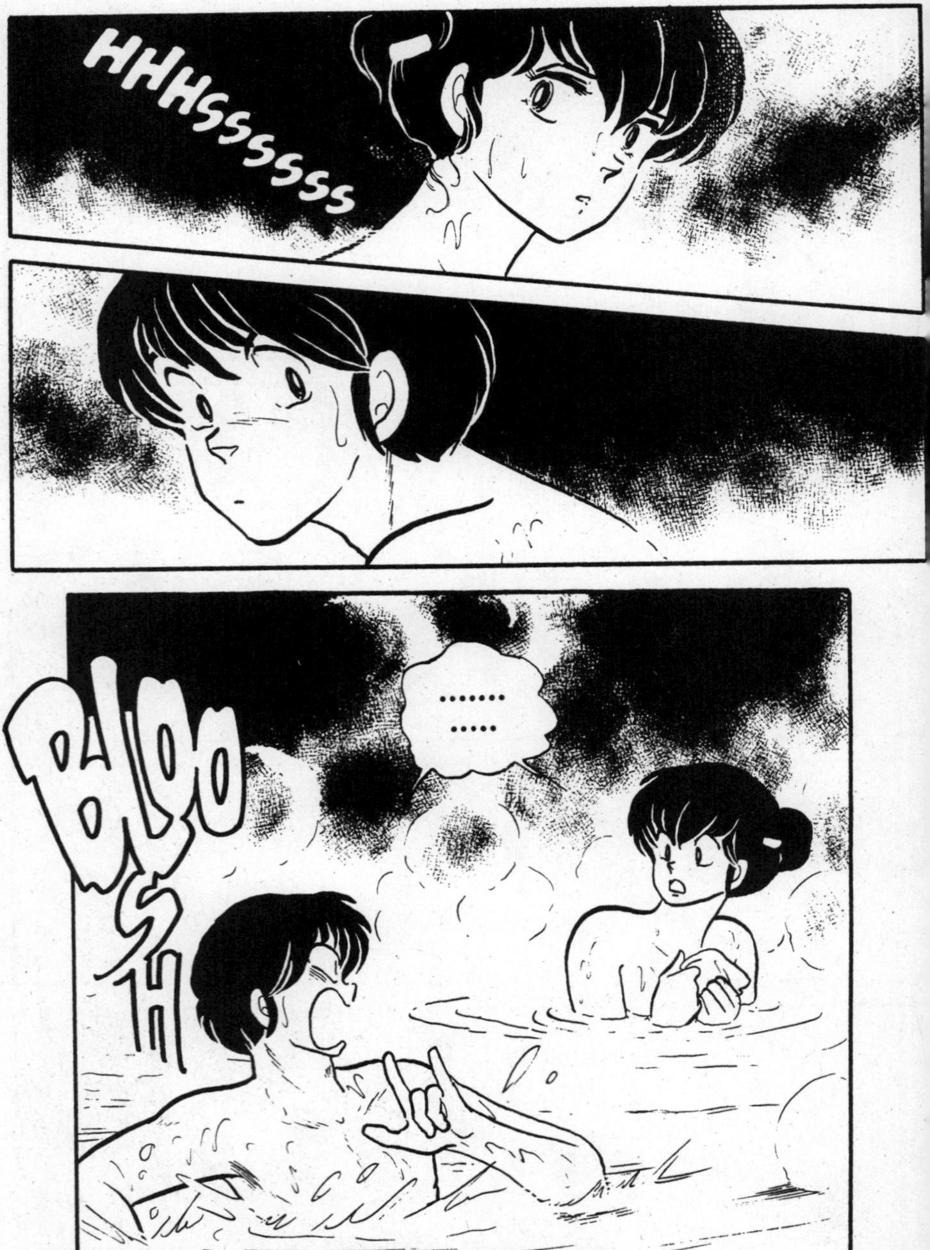
HHHSSSSSSS
......
......
BLOOSH

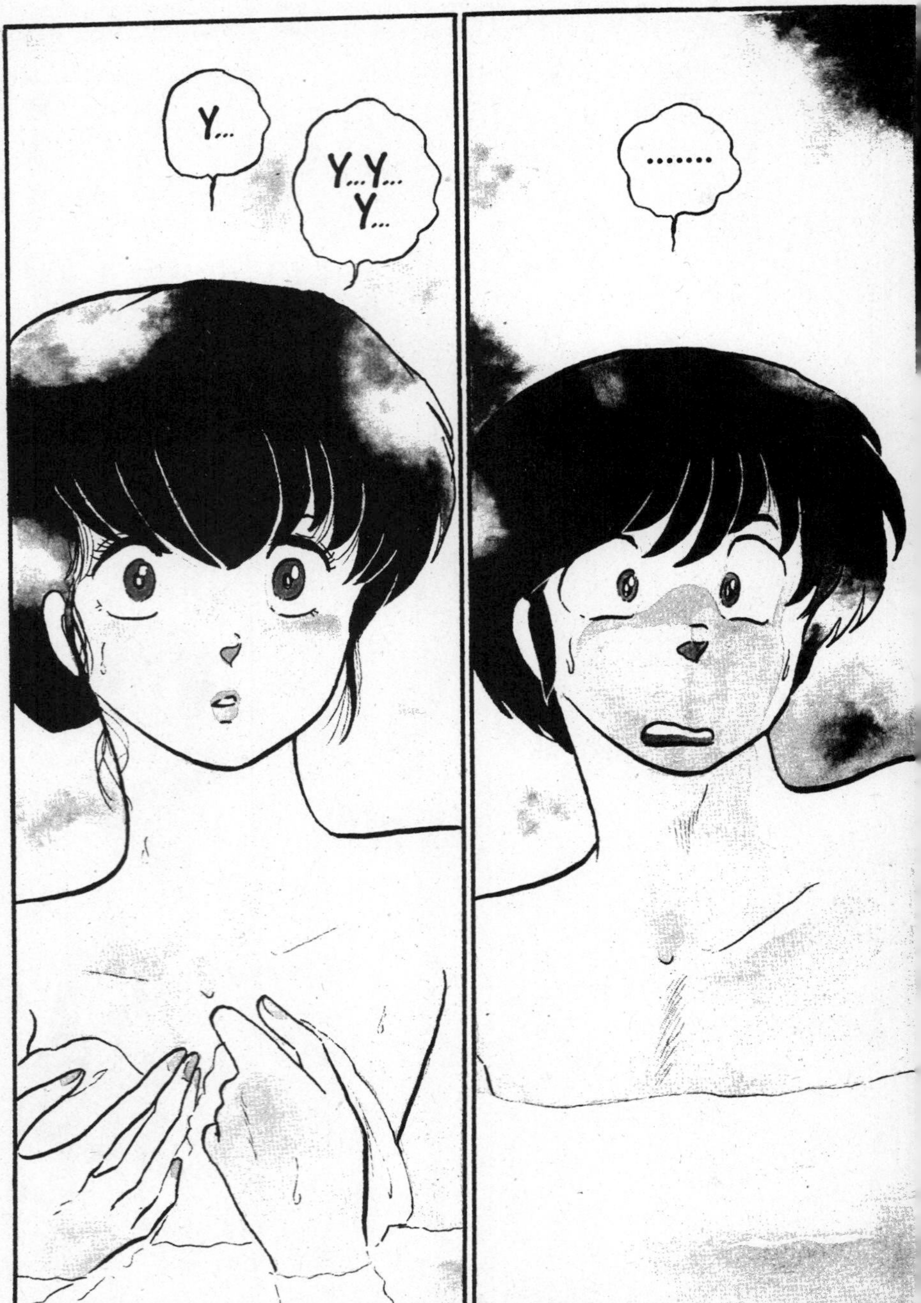
Y...
Y...Y... Y...
....

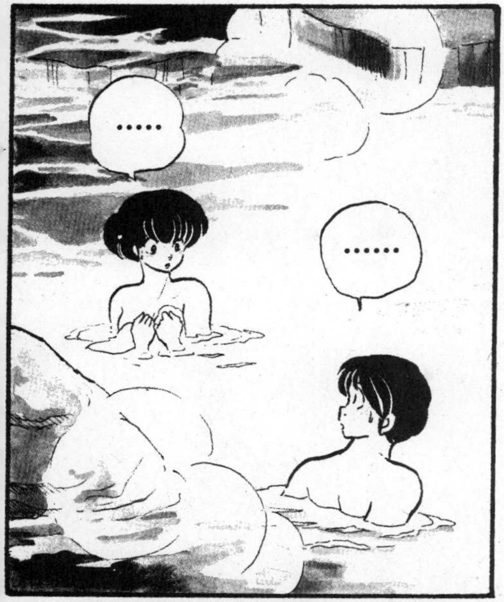
......
....
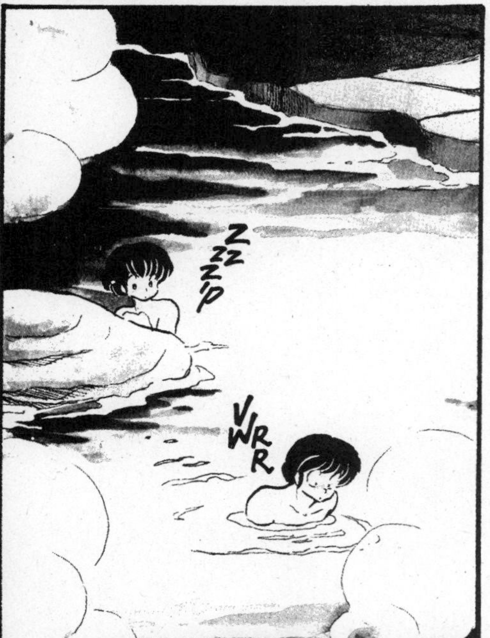
ZZZZIP
VWRR

PART 12

ONE NIGHT DREAM

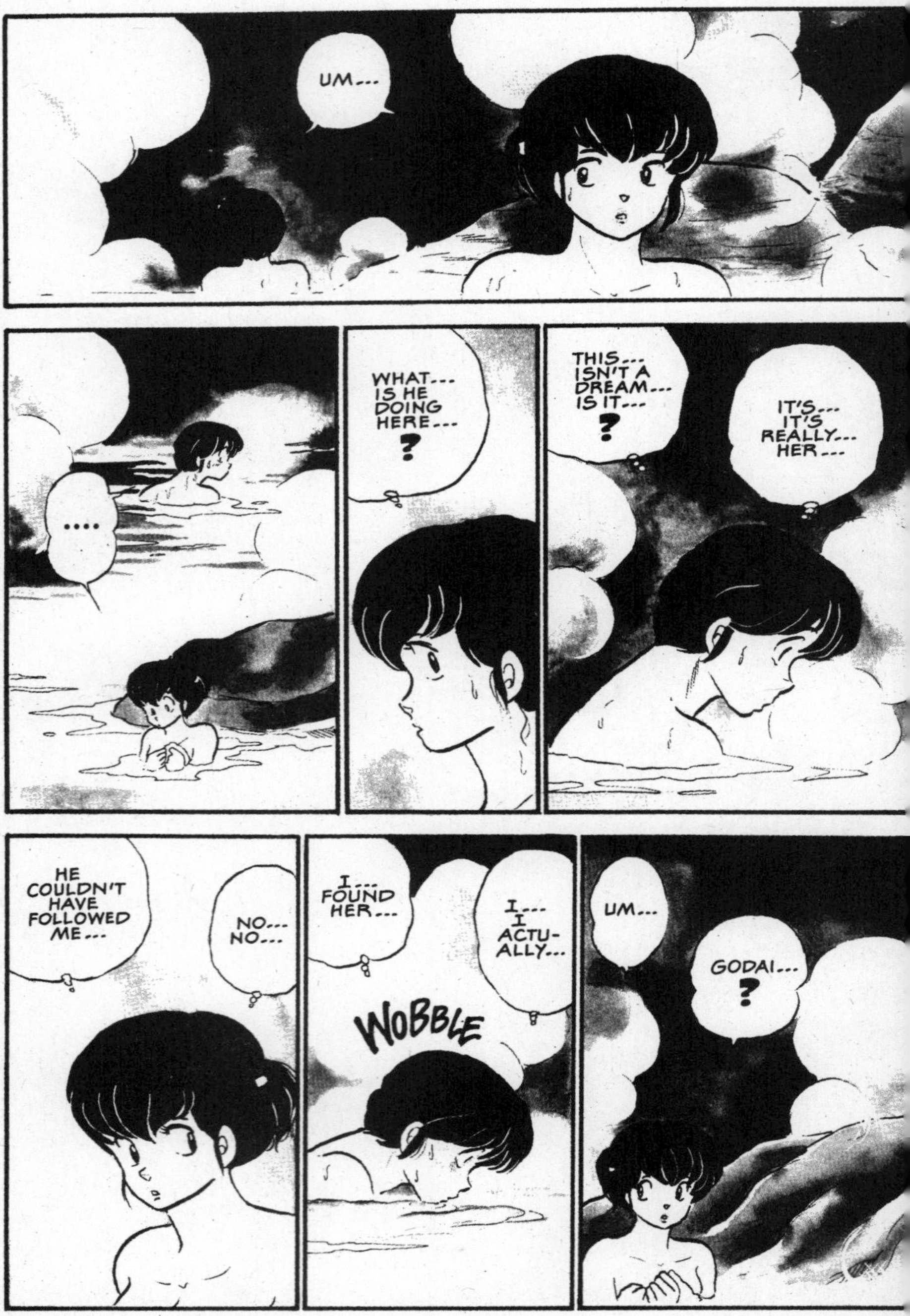
UM...
.....
WHAT... IS HE DOING HERE...?
THIS... ISN'T A DREAM... IS IT...?
IT'S... IT'S REALLY... HER...
HE COULDN'T HAVE FOLLOWED ME...
NO... NO...
I... FOUND HER...
I... I ACTU-ALLY...
WOBBLE
UM...
GODAI...?

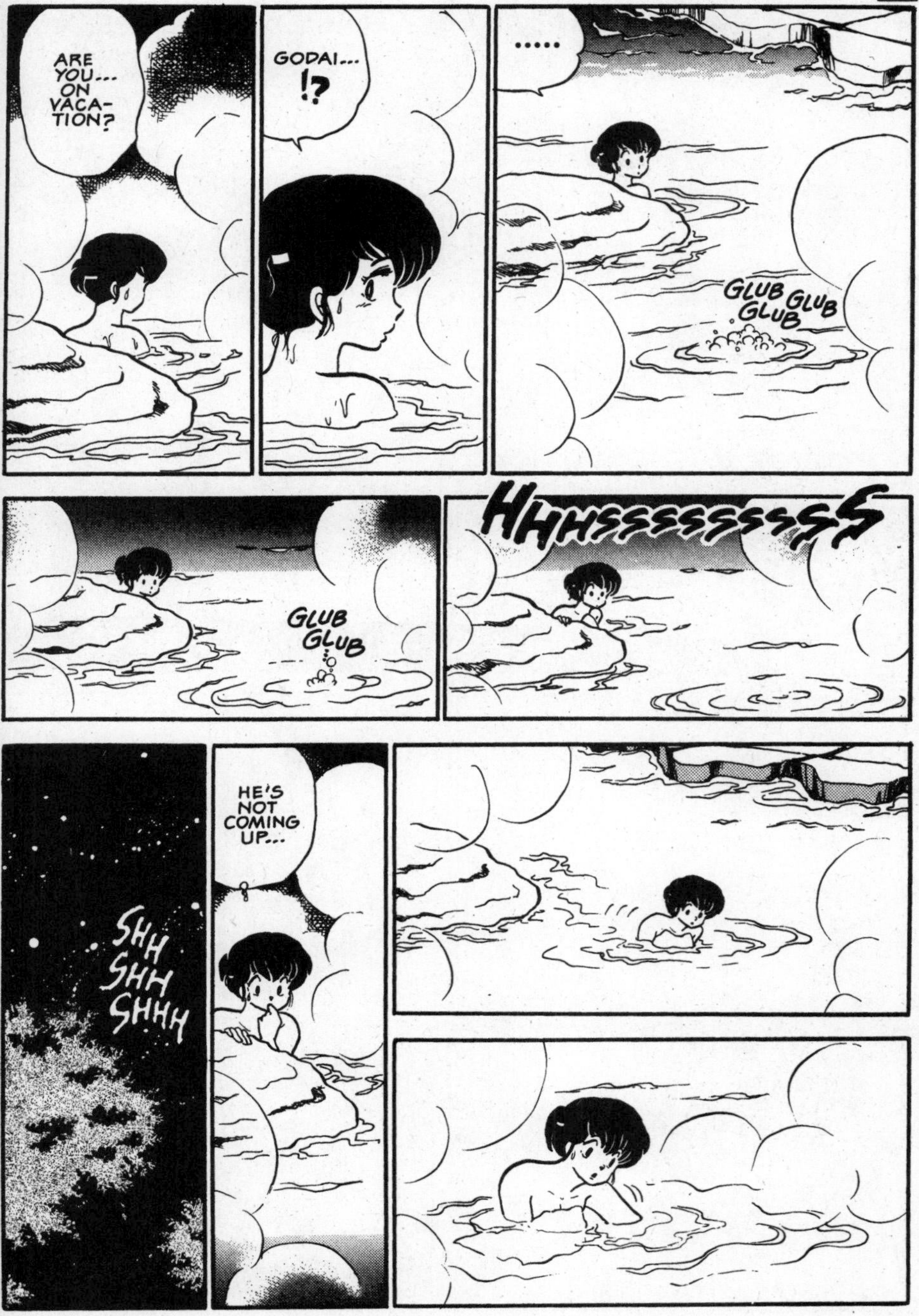
ARE YOU... ON VACATION?
GODAI... !?
.....
GLUB GLUB GLUB
GLUB GLUB
HHHSSSSSSSSSS
SHH SHH SHHH
HE'S NOT COMING UP...

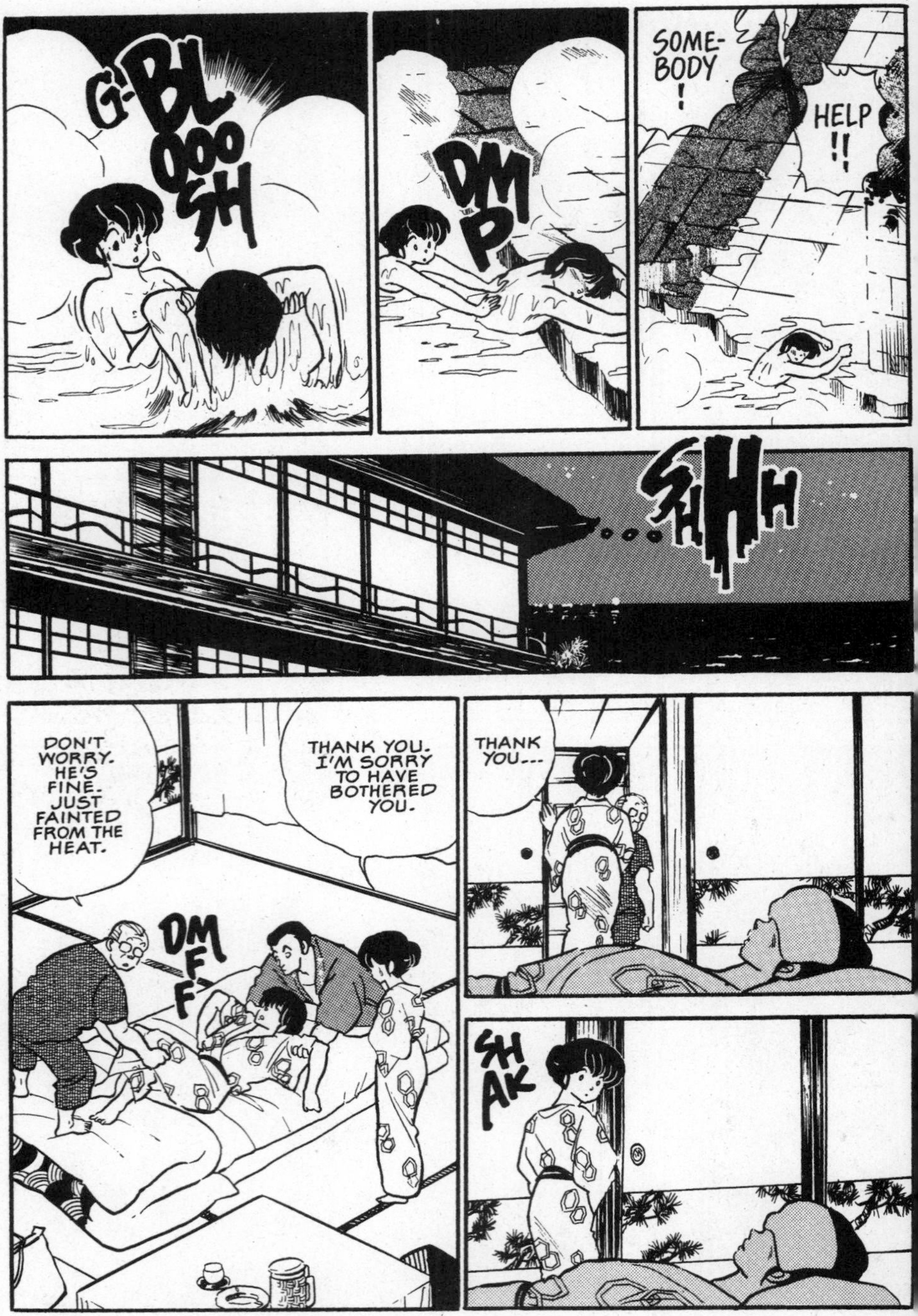
G-BLOOOSH
DMP
SOME-BODY!
HELP!!
SHHH
DON'T WORRY. HE'S FINE. JUST FAINTED FROM THE HEAT.
DMFF
THANK YOU. I'M SORRY TO HAVE BOTHERED YOU.
THANK YOU...
SHAK

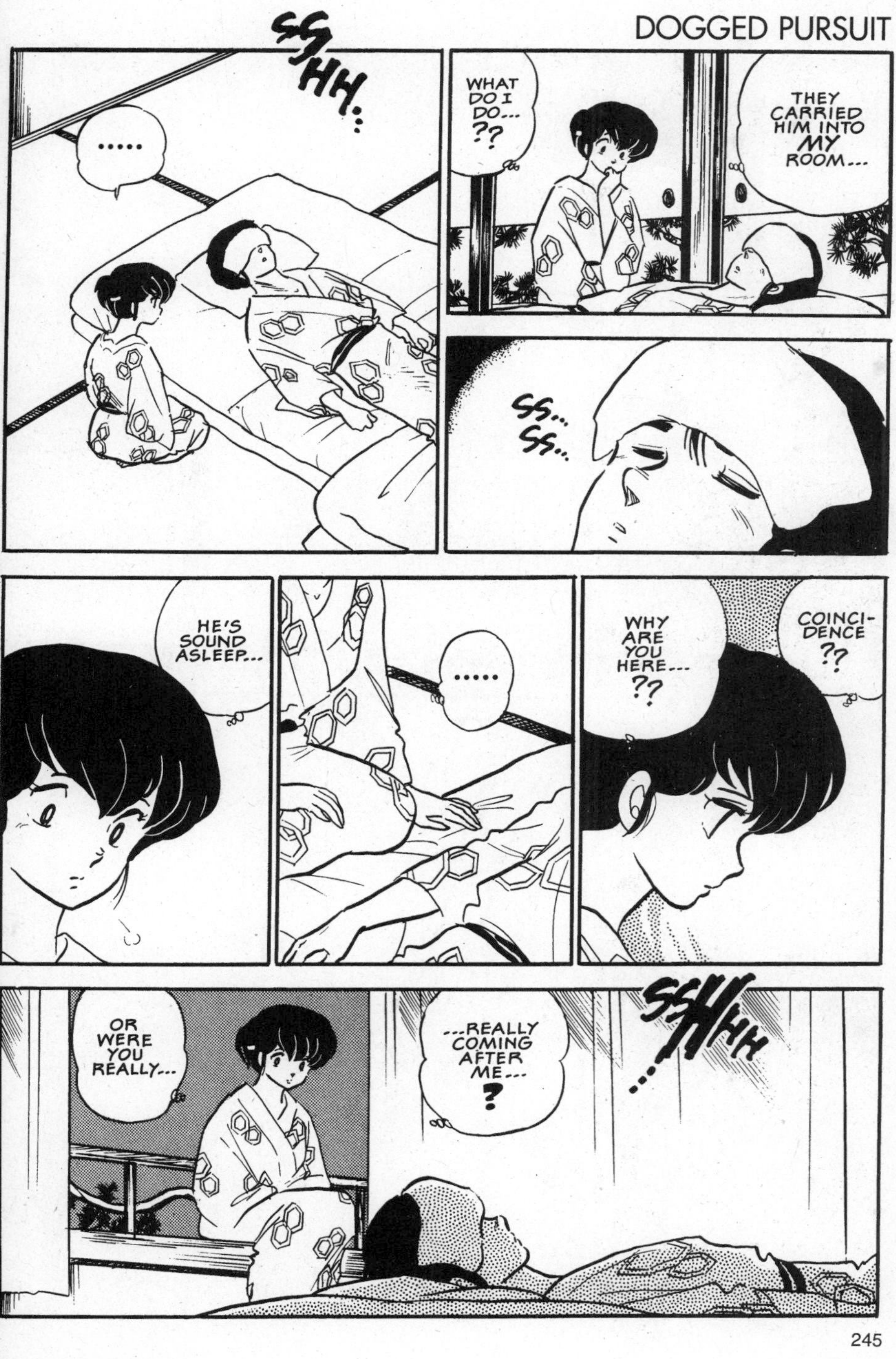
SSHH...
.....
WHAT DO I DO...??
THEY CARRIED HIM INTO MY ROOM...
SS... SS...
HE'S SOUND ASLEEP...
.....
WHY ARE YOU HERE...??
COINCIDENCE??
OR WERE YOU REALLY...
...REALLY COMING AFTER ME...?
SSHHHH...

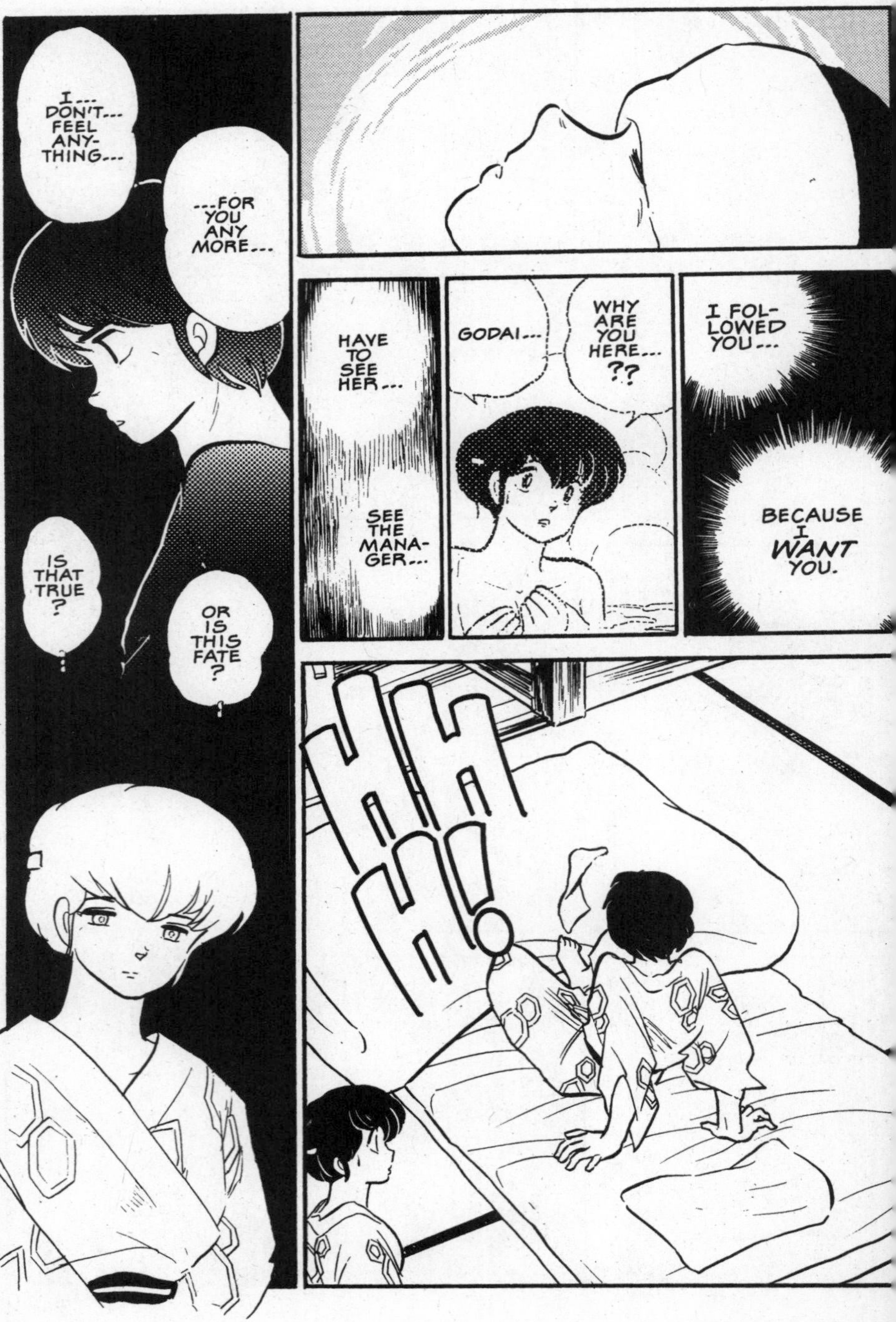
I... DON'T... FEEL ANYTHING...
...FOR YOU ANY MORE...
IS THAT TRUE?
OR IS THIS FATE?
HAVE TO SEE HER...
SEE THE MANAGER...
GODAI...
WHY ARE YOU HERE...??
I FOLLOWED YOU...
BECAUSE I WANT YOU.

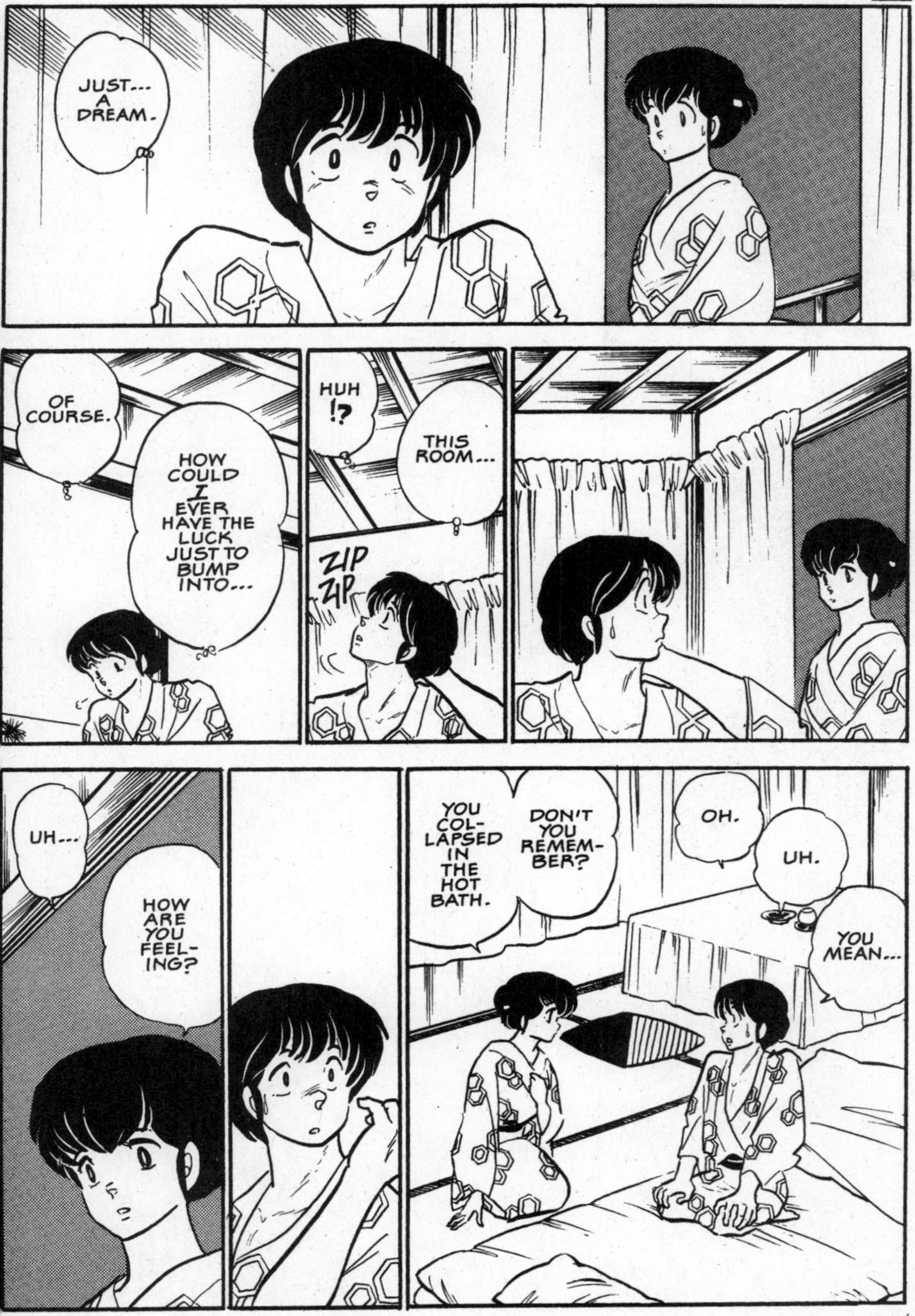
JUST... A DREAM.
OF COURSE.
HOW COULD I EVER HAVE THE LUCK JUST TO BUMP INTO...
HUH!?
THIS ROOM...
ZIP ZIP
UH...
HOW ARE YOU FEEL-ING?
YOU COL-LAPSED IN THE HOT BATH.
DON'T YOU REMEM-BER?
OH.
UH.
YOU MEAN...

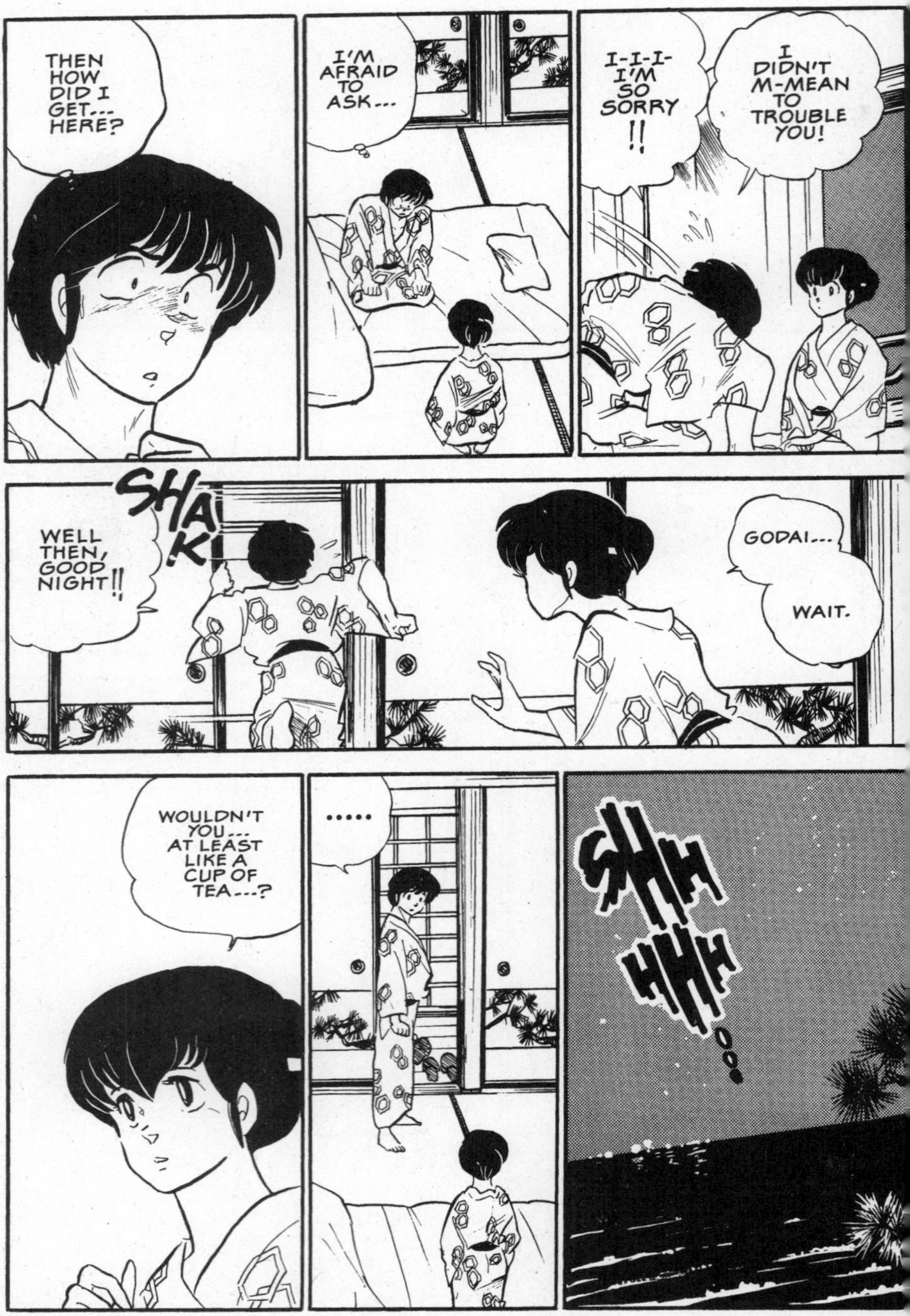
THEN HOW DID I GET... HERE?
I'M AFRAID TO ASK...
I-I-I-I'M SO SORRY!!
I DIDN'T M-MEAN TO TROUBLE YOU!
SHAK
WELL THEN, GOOD NIGHT!!
GODAI...
WAIT.
WOULDN'T YOU... AT LEAST LIKE A CUP OF TEA...?
.....
SHHHHHHH...

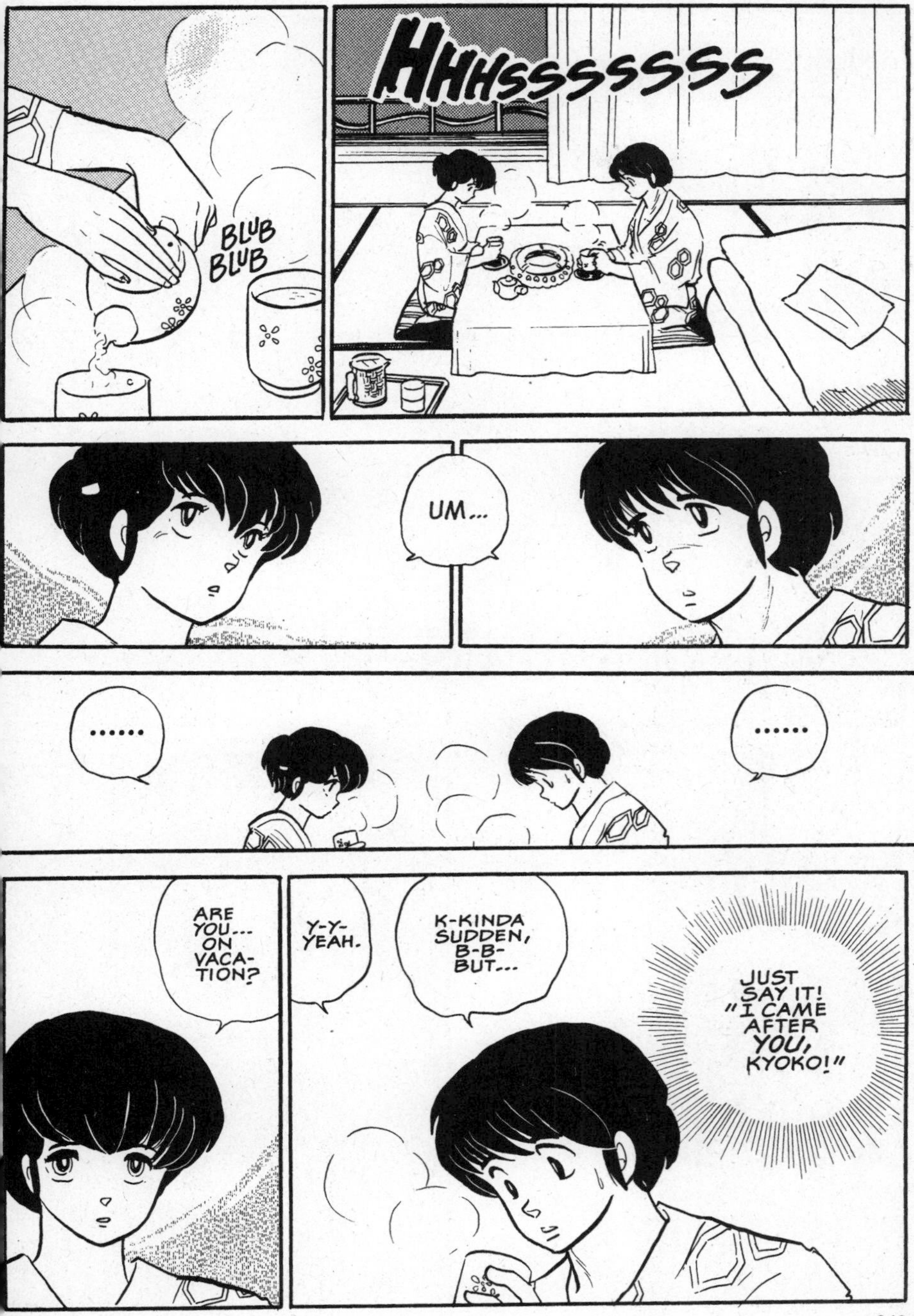
BLUB BLUB
HHHSSSSSSSS
UM...
......
......
ARE YOU... ON VACATION?
Y-Y-YEAH.
K-KINDA SUDDEN, B-B-BUT...
JUST SAY IT! "I CAME AFTER YOU, KYOKO!"

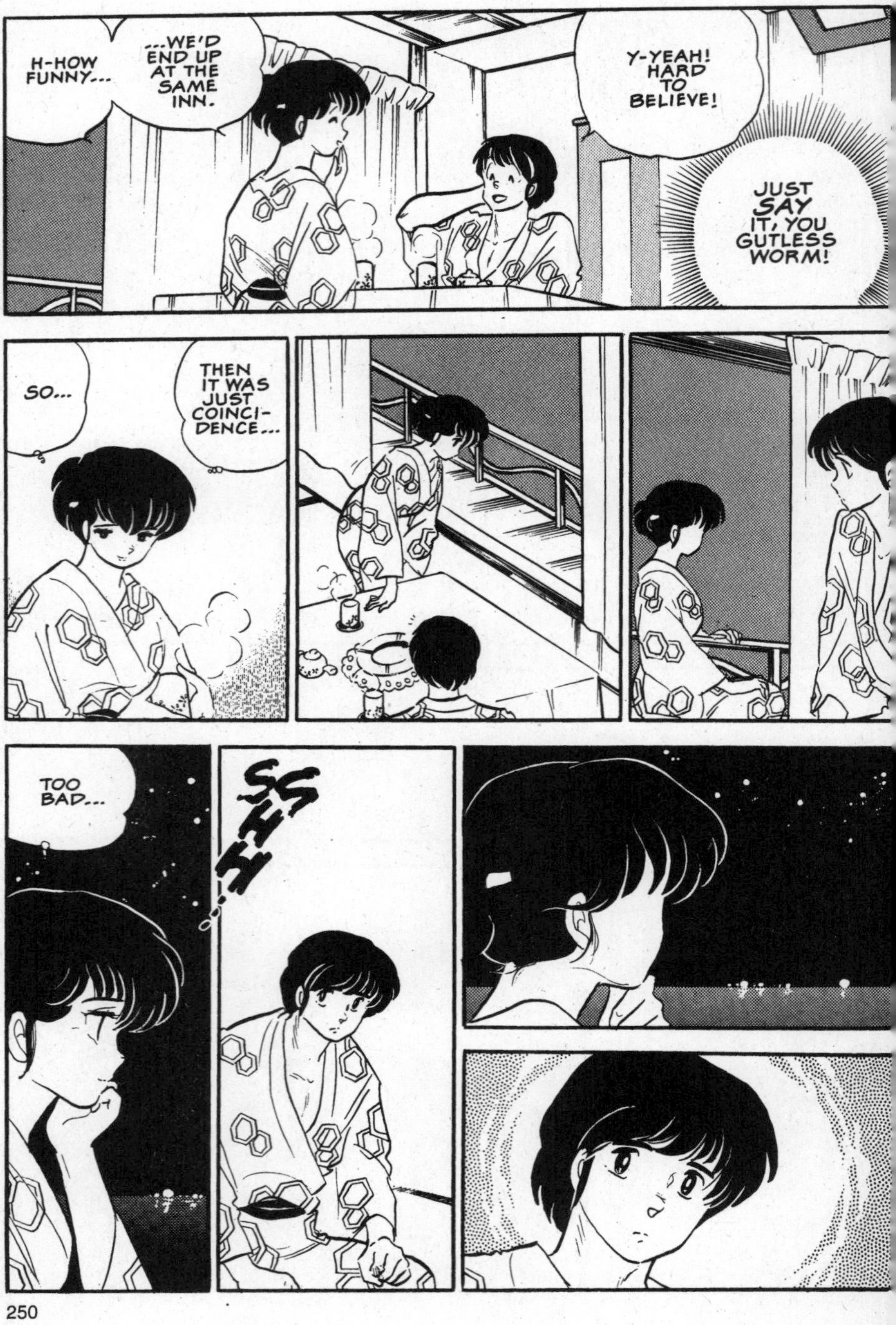
H-HOW FUNNY...
...WE'D END UP AT THE SAME INN.
Y-YEAH! HARD TO BELIEVE!
JUST SAY IT, YOU GUTLESS WORM!
SO...
THEN IT WAS JUST COINCIDENCE...
TOO BAD...
SSHHH...

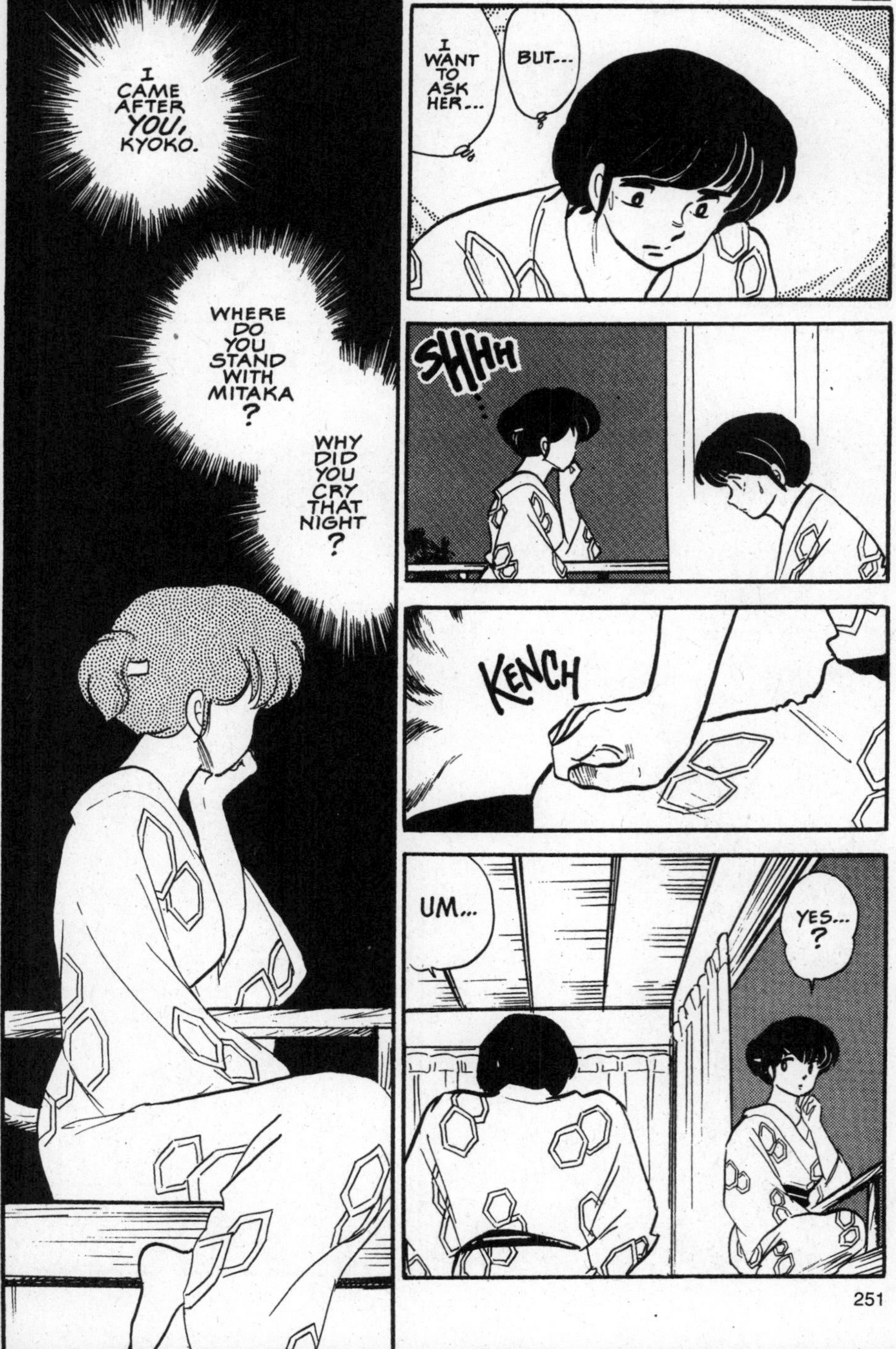
I CAME AFTER YOU, KYOKO.
WHERE DO YOU STAND WITH MITAKA?
WHY DID YOU CRY THAT NIGHT?
I WANT TO ASK HER...
BUT...
SHHH
KENCH
UM...
YES...?

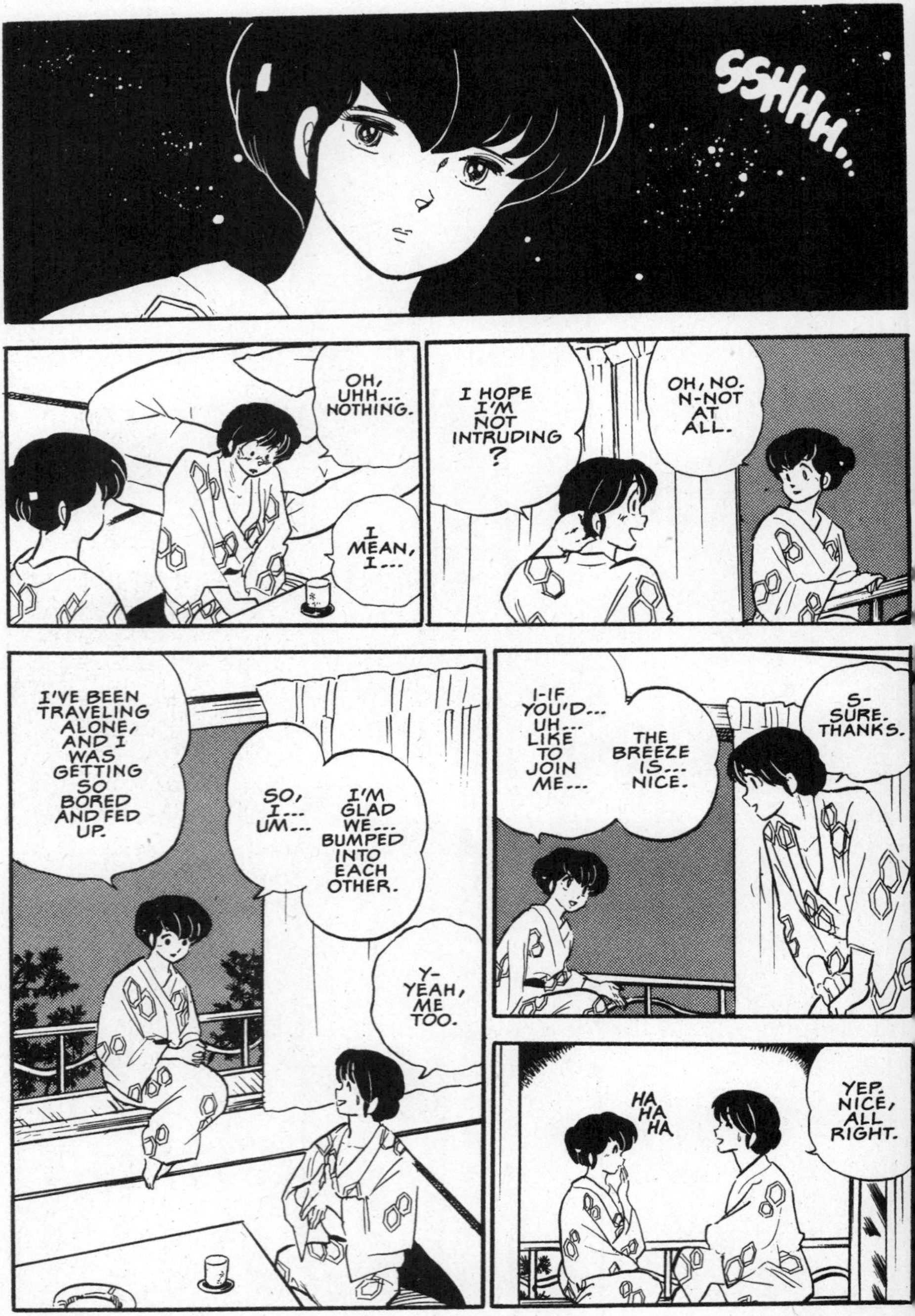
SSHHH...
OH, UHH... NOTHING.
I MEAN, I...
I HOPE I'M NOT INTRUDING?
OH, NO. N-NOT AT ALL.
I'VE BEEN TRAVELING ALONE, AND I WAS GETTING SO BORED AND FED UP.
SO, I... UM...
I'M GLAD WE... BUMPED INTO EACH OTHER.
Y-YEAH, ME TOO.
I-IF YOU'D... UH... LIKE TO JOIN ME...
S-SURE. THANKS.
THE BREEZE IS... NICE.
HA HA HA
YEP. NICE, ALL RIGHT.

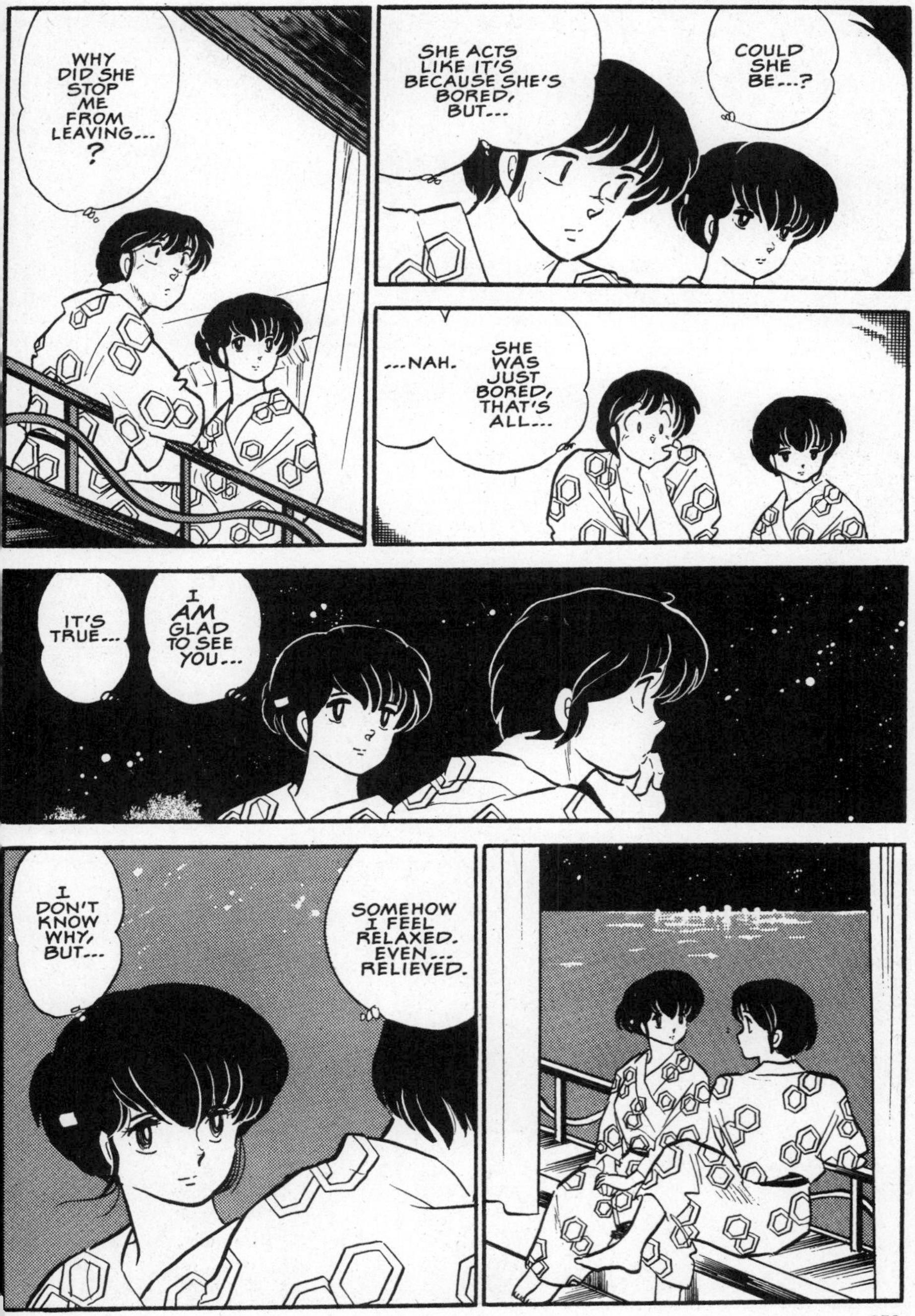
WHY DID SHE STOP ME FROM LEAVING...?
SHE ACTS LIKE IT'S BECAUSE SHE'S BORED, BUT...
COULD SHE BE...?
...NAH.
SHE WAS JUST BORED, THAT'S ALL...
IT'S TRUE...
I AM GLAD TO SEE YOU...
I DON'T KNOW WHY, BUT...
SOMEHOW I FEEL RELAXED. EVEN... RELIEVED.

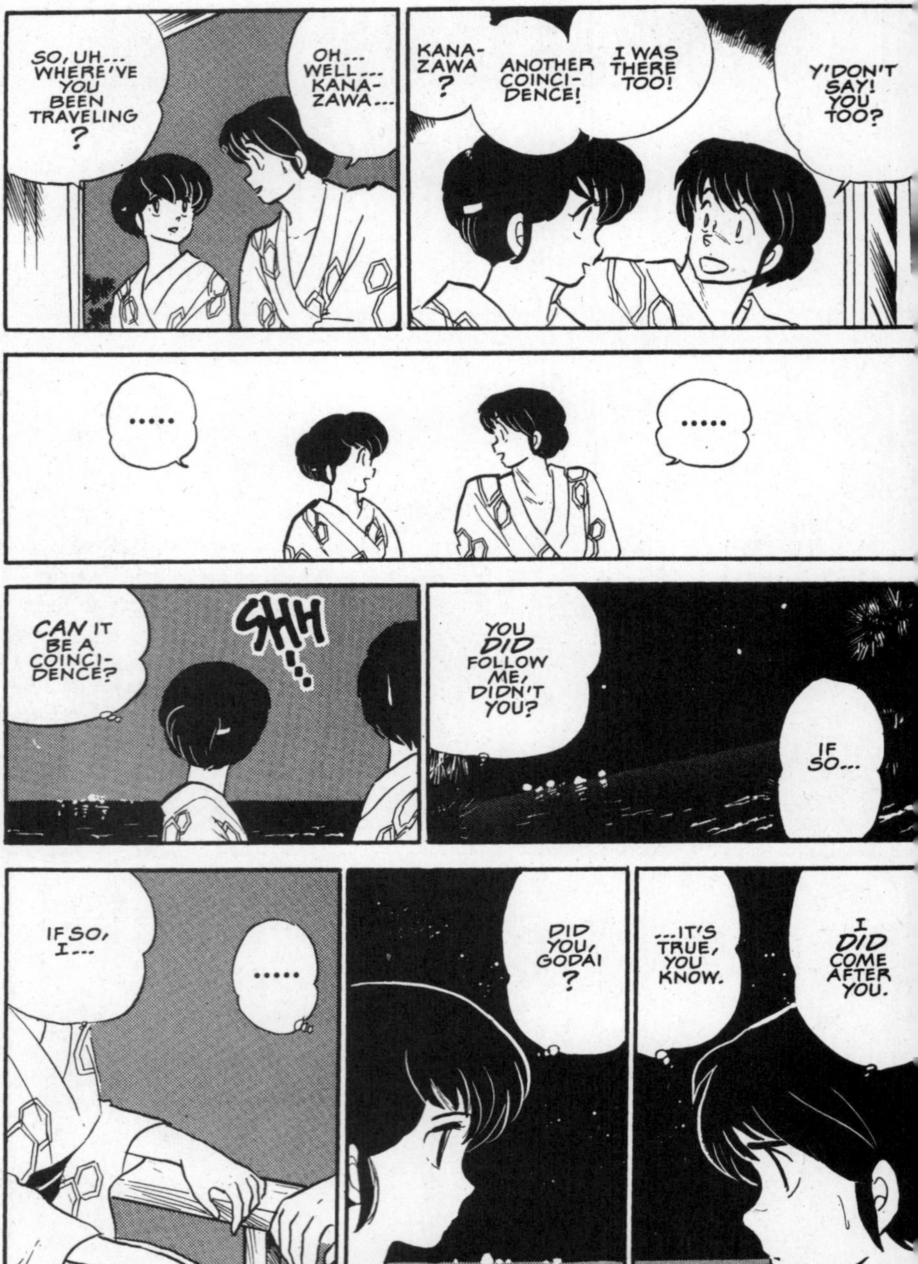

SO, UH... WHERE'VE YOU BEEN TRAVELING?
OH... WELL... KANA-ZAWA...
KANA-ZAWA?
ANOTHER COINCI-DENCE!
I WAS THERE TOO!
Y'DON'T SAY! YOU TOO?
.....
.....
CAN IT BE A COINCI-DENCE?
SHH...
YOU DID FOLLOW ME, DIDN'T YOU?
IF SO...
IF SO, I...
.....
DID YOU, GODAI?
...IT'S TRUE, YOU KNOW.
I DID COME AFTER YOU.

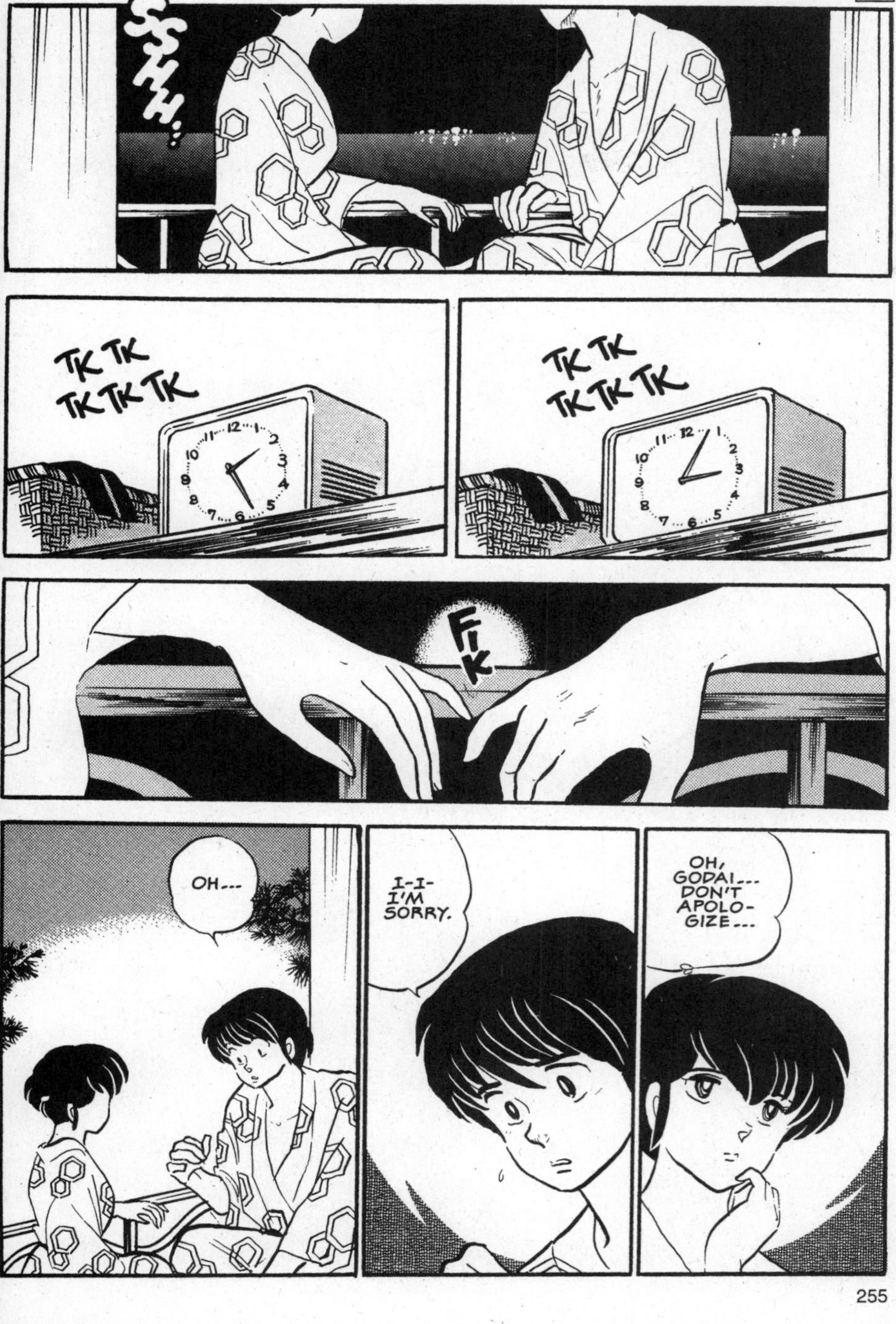
SSHHH...
TK TK
TK TK TK
TK TK
TK TK TK
FIK
OH...
I-I-
I'M
SORRY.
OH,
GODAI...
DON'T
APOLO-
GIZE...

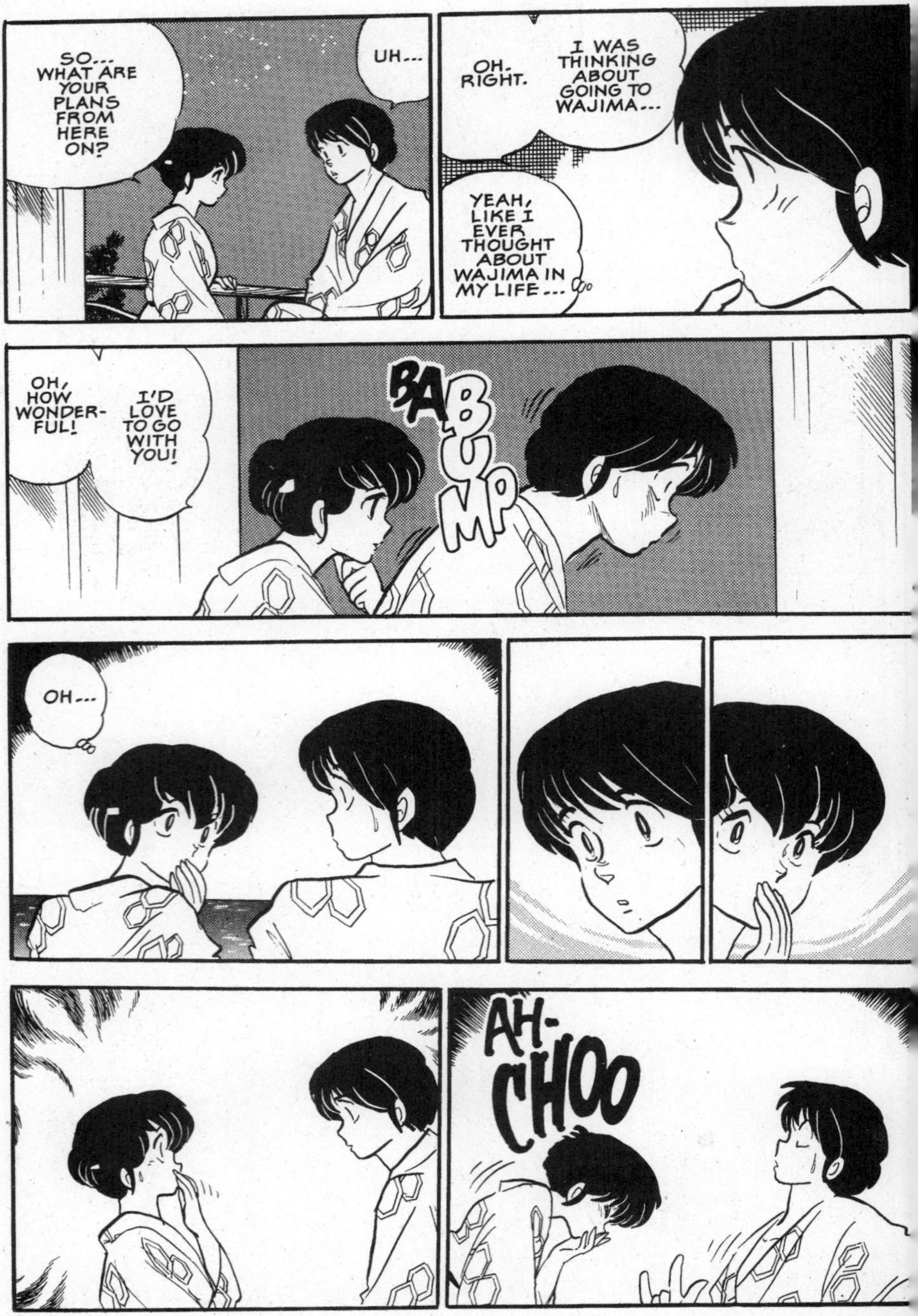

SO... WHAT ARE YOUR PLANS FROM HERE ON?
UH...
OH. RIGHT.
I WAS THINKING ABOUT GOING TO WAJIMA...
YEAH, LIKE I EVER THOUGHT ABOUT WAJIMA IN MY LIFE...
OH, HOW WONDER-FUL!
I'D LOVE TO GO WITH YOU!
BA-BUMP
OH...
AH-CHOO

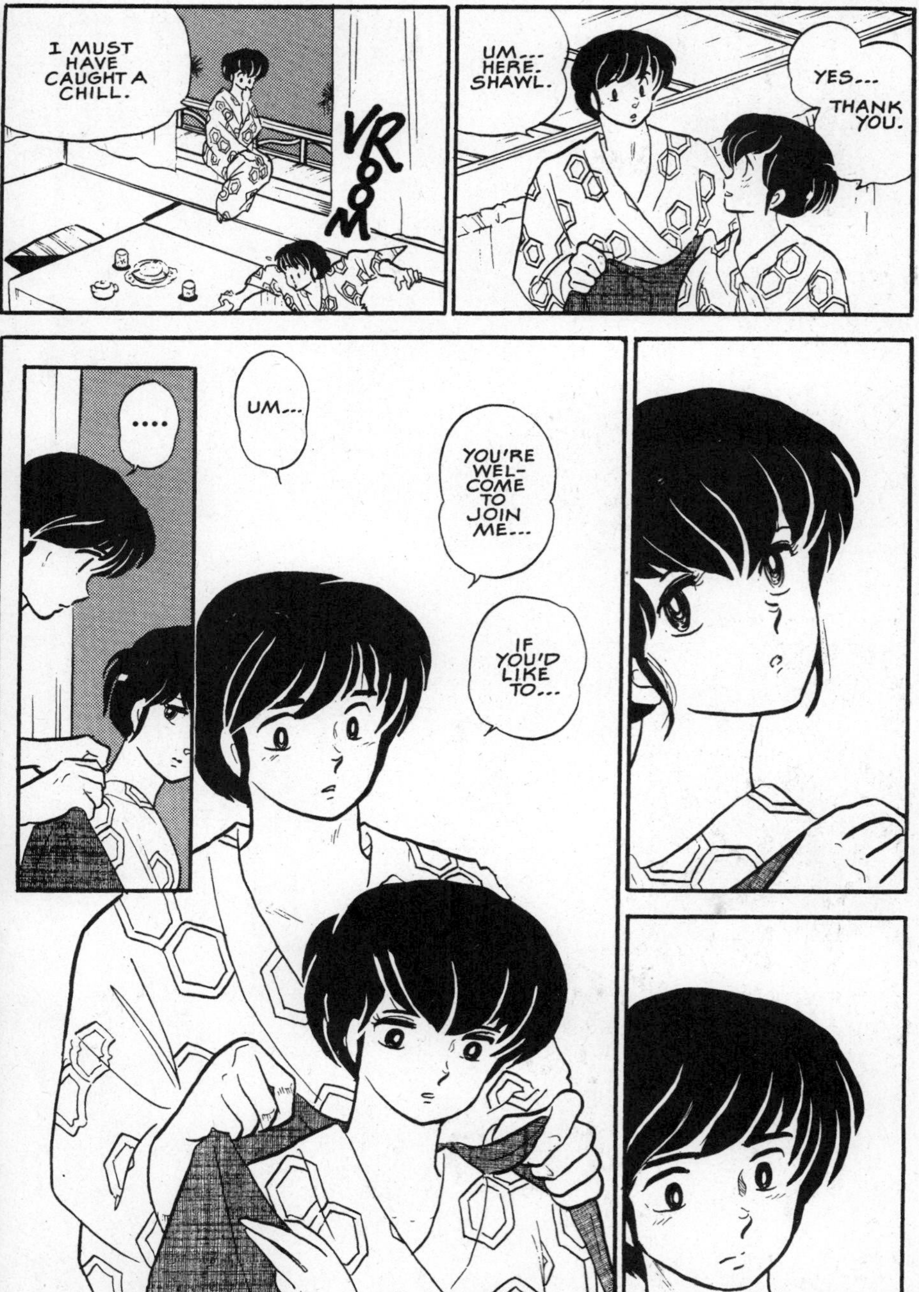
I MUST HAVE CAUGHT A CHILL.
VROOM
UM... HERE. SHAWL.
YES... THANK YOU.
....
UM...
YOU'RE WELCOME TO JOIN ME...
IF YOU'D LIKE TO...

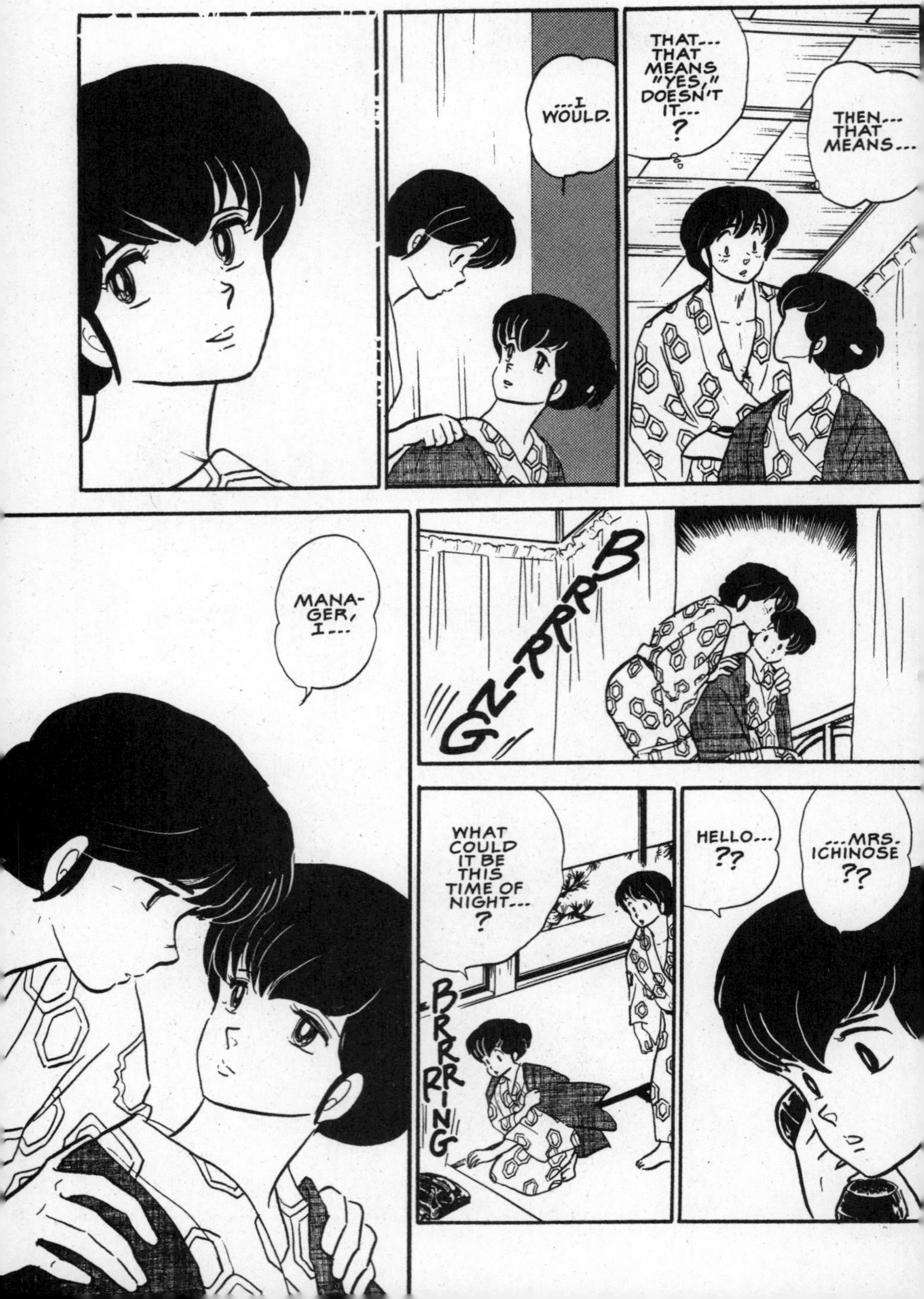
...I WOULD.
THAT... THAT MEANS "YES," DOESN'T IT...?
THEN... THAT MEANS...
MANAGER, I...
GN-RRRB
WHAT COULD IT BE THIS TIME OF NIGHT...?
BRRRRING
HELLO...??
...MRS. ICHINOSE??

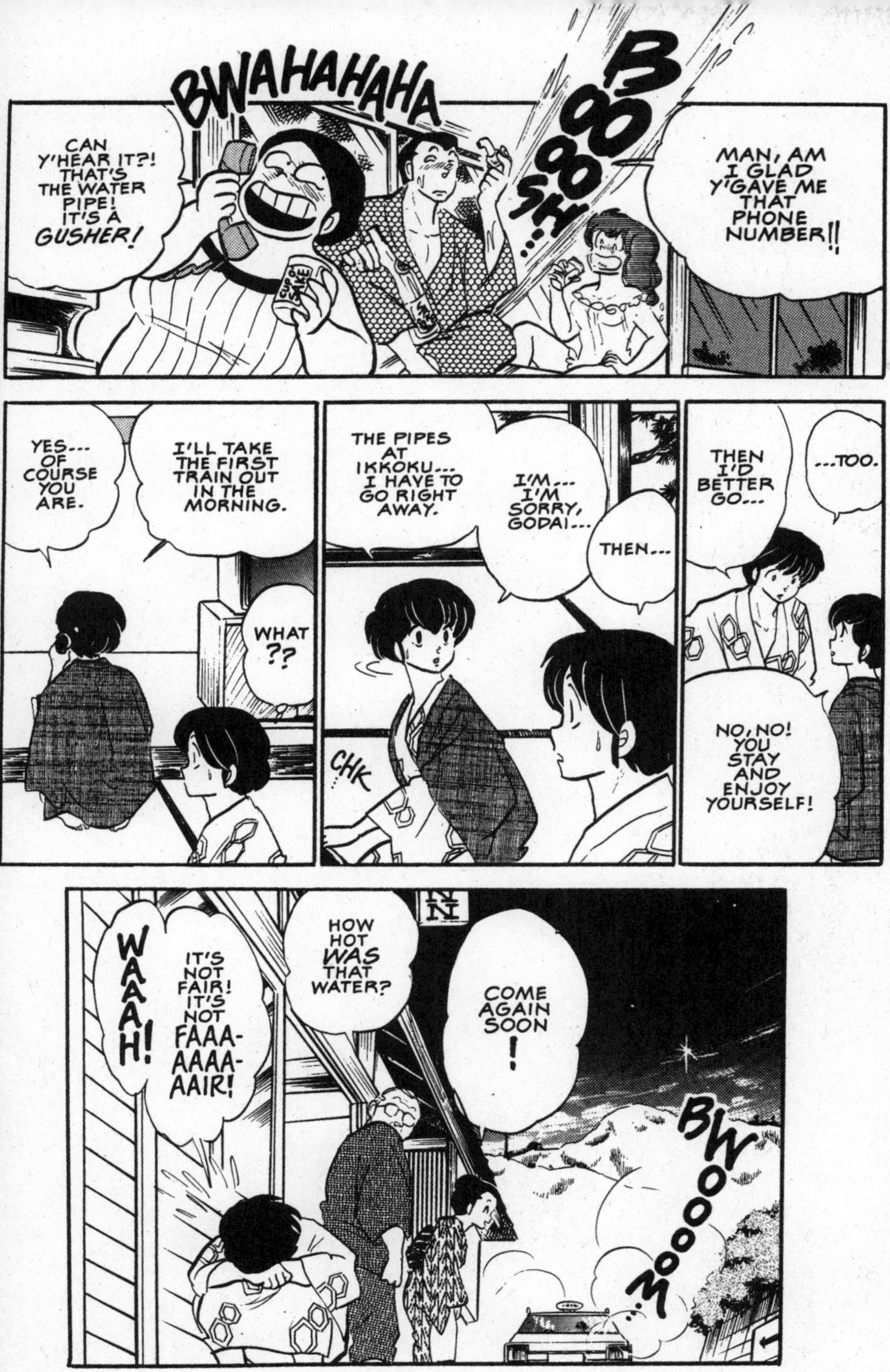
BWAHAHAHA
CAN Y'HEAR IT?! THAT'S THE WATER PIPE! IT'S A GUSHER!
BOOOOSH...
MAN, AM I GLAD Y'GAVE ME THAT PHONE NUMBER!!
YES... OF COURSE YOU ARE.
I'LL TAKE THE FIRST TRAIN OUT IN THE MORNING.
WHAT ??
THE PIPES AT IKKOKU... I HAVE TO GO RIGHT AWAY.
I'M... I'M SORRY, GODAI...
THEN...
CHK
THEN I'D BETTER GO...
...TOO.
NO, NO! YOU STAY AND ENJOY YOURSELF!
WAAAH!
IT'S NOT FAIR! IT'S NOT FAAAAAAAAAAIR!
HOW HOT WAS THAT WATER?
COME AGAIN SOON !
BWOOOOOM...

PART 13
BACK TO...SCHOOL?

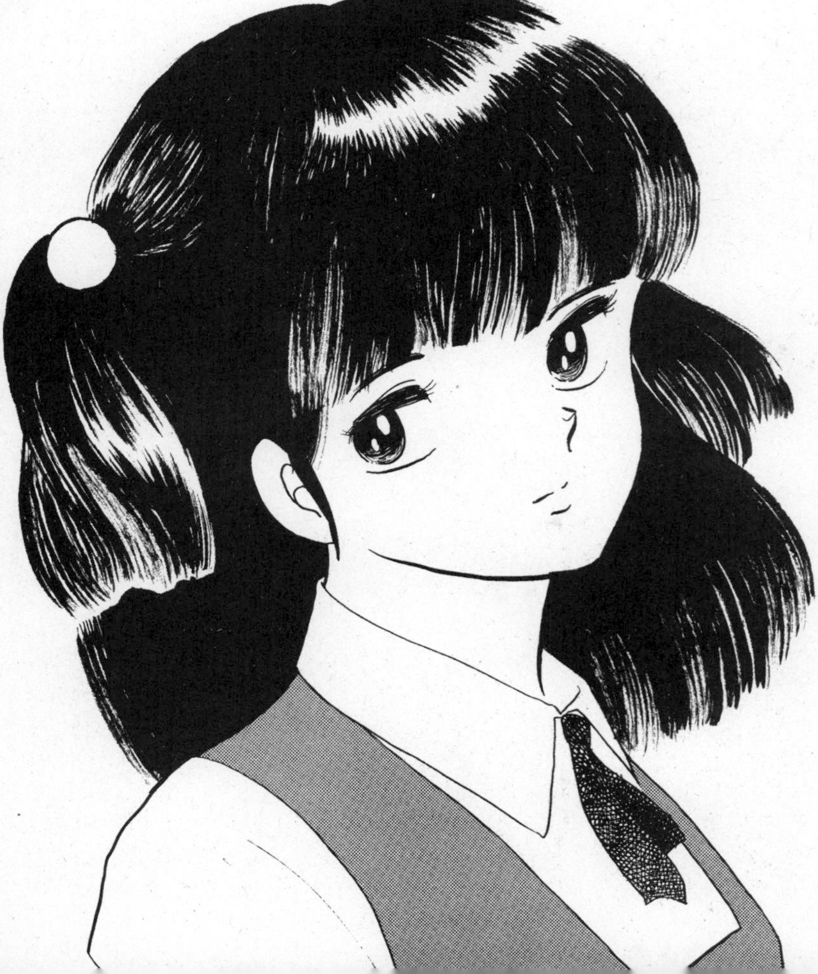

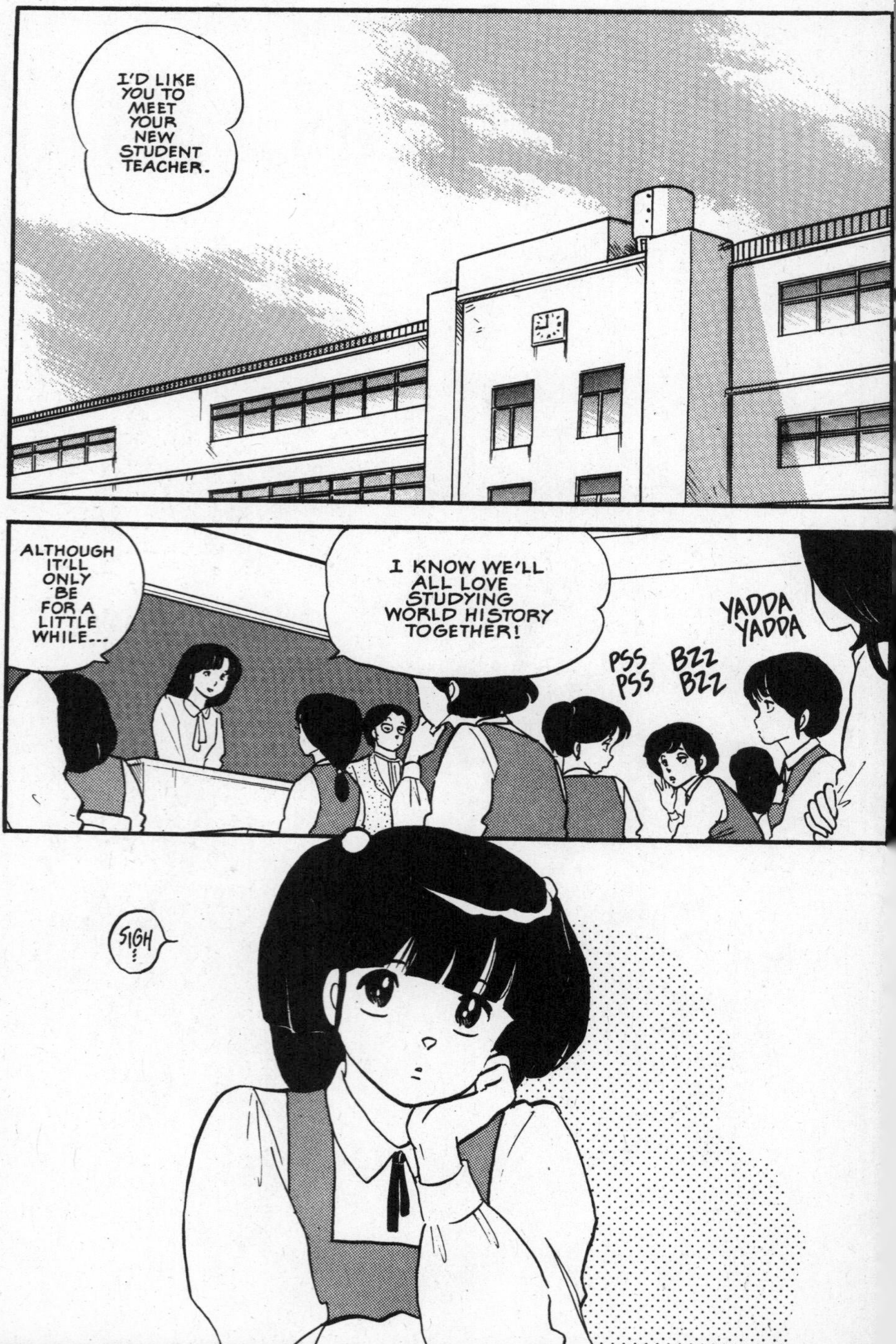
I'D LIKE YOU TO MEET YOUR NEW STUDENT TEACHER.
ALTHOUGH IT'LL ONLY BE FOR A LITTLE WHILE...
I KNOW WE'LL ALL LOVE STUDYING WORLD HISTORY TOGETHER!
PSS PSS
BZZ BZZ
YADDA YADDA
SIGH

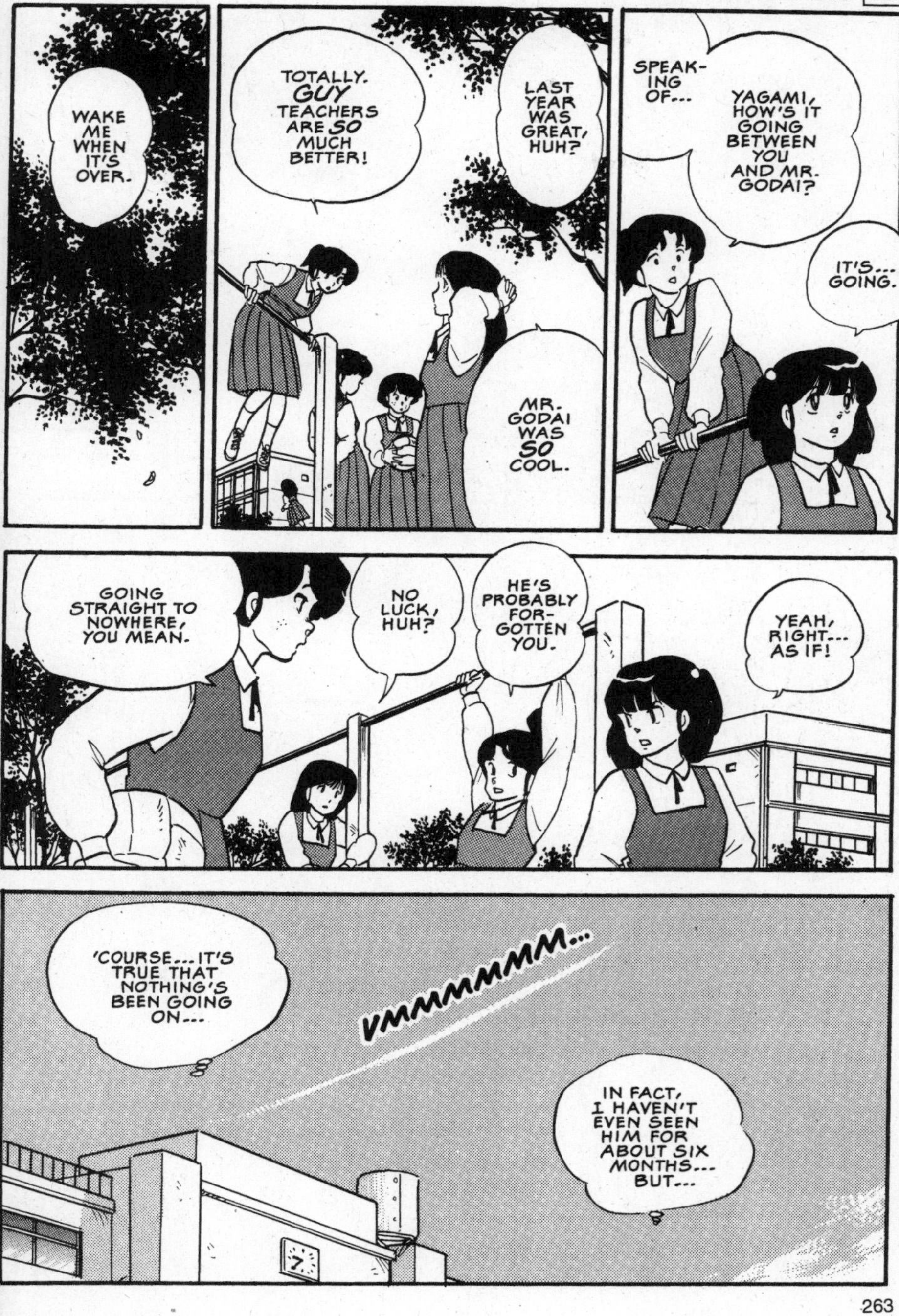
WAKE ME WHEN IT'S OVER.
TOTALLY. GUY TEACHERS ARE SO MUCH BETTER!
LAST YEAR WAS GREAT, HUH?
MR. GODAI WAS SO COOL.
SPEAK-ING OF...
YAGAMI, HOW'S IT GOING BETWEEN YOU AND MR. GODAI?
IT'S... GOING.
GOING STRAIGHT TO NOWHERE, YOU MEAN.
NO LUCK, HUH?
HE'S PROBABLY FOR-GOTTEN YOU.
YEAH, RIGHT... AS IF!
'COURSE... IT'S TRUE THAT NOTHING'S BEEN GOING ON...
VMMMMMMM...
IN FACT, I HAVEN'T EVEN SEEN HIM FOR ABOUT SIX MONTHS... BUT...

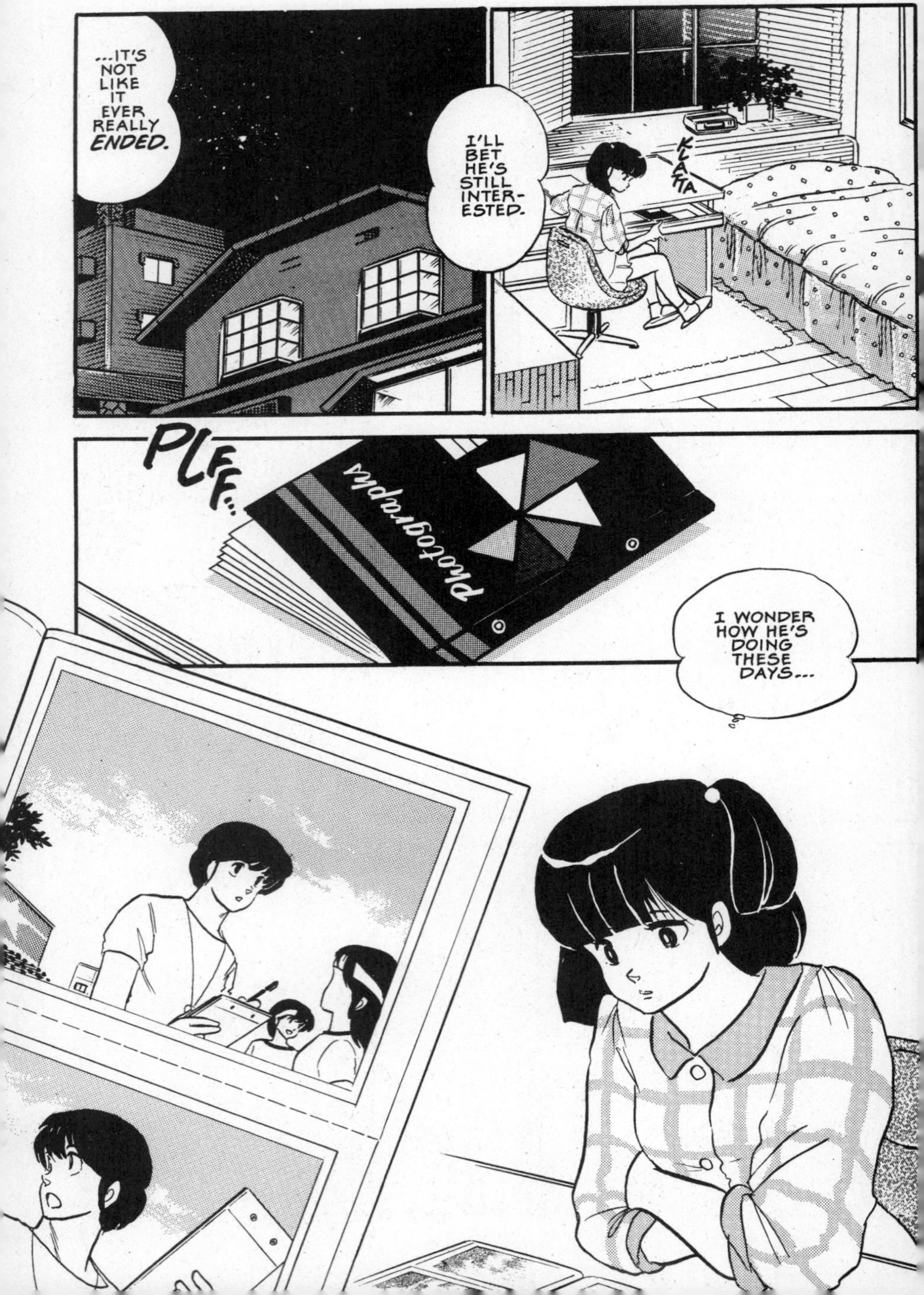
...IT'S NOT LIKE IT EVER REALLY ENDED.
I'LL BET HE'S STILL INTER-ESTED.
KLATTA
PLFF...
Photographs
I WONDER HOW HE'S DOING THESE DAYS...

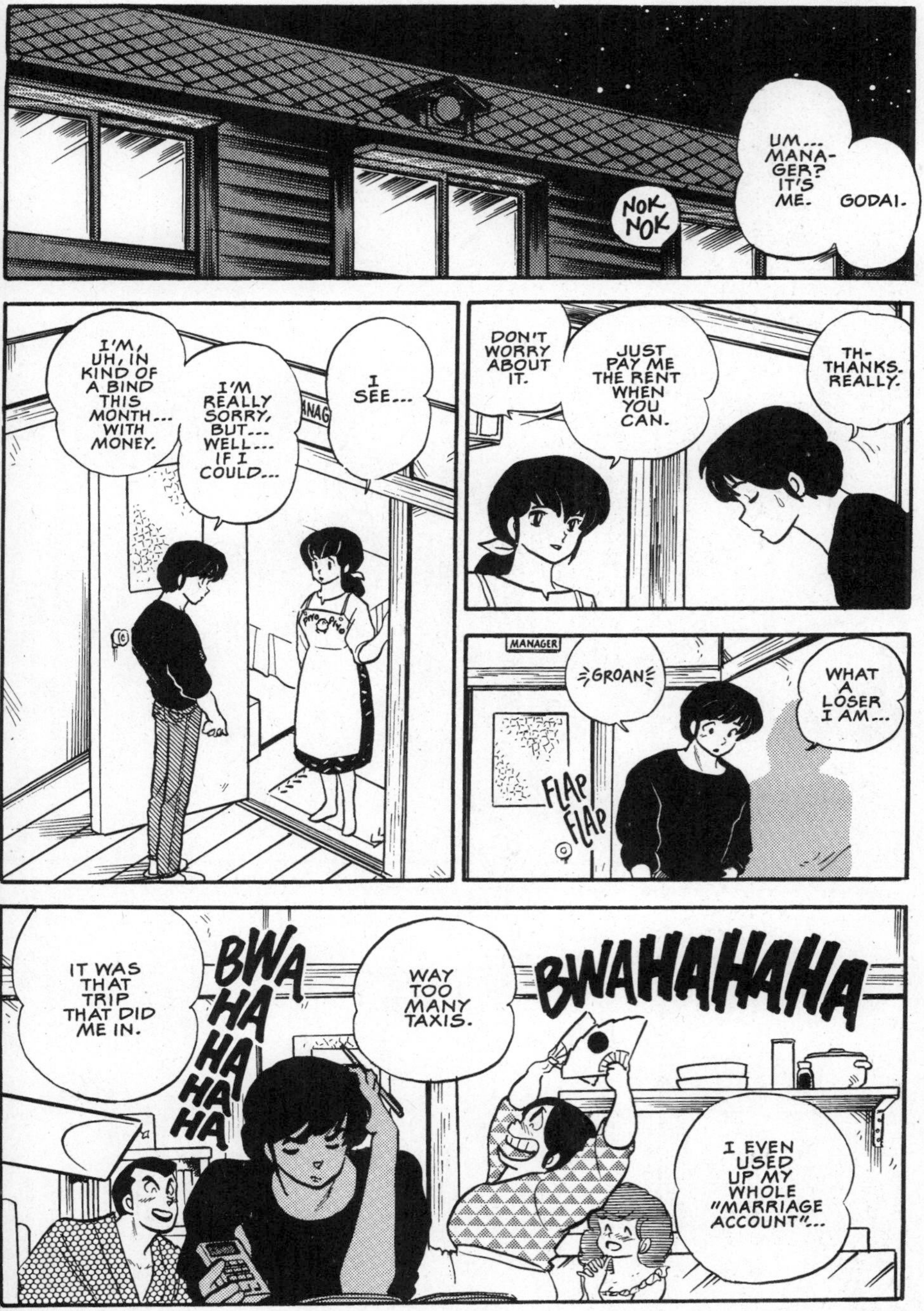
NOK NOK
UM... MANAGER? IT'S ME. GODAI.
I'M, UH, IN KIND OF A BIND THIS MONTH... WITH MONEY.
I'M REALLY SORRY, BUT... WELL... IF I COULD...
I SEE...
DON'T WORRY ABOUT IT.
JUST PAY ME THE RENT WHEN YOU CAN.
TH-THANKS. REALLY.
MANAGER
GROAN
WHAT A LOSER I AM...
FLAP FLAP
IT WAS THAT TRIP THAT DID ME IN.
BWAHAHAHAHAHA
WAY TOO MANY TAXIS.
BWAHAHAHAHA
I EVEN USED UP MY WHOLE "MARRIAGE ACCOUNT"...

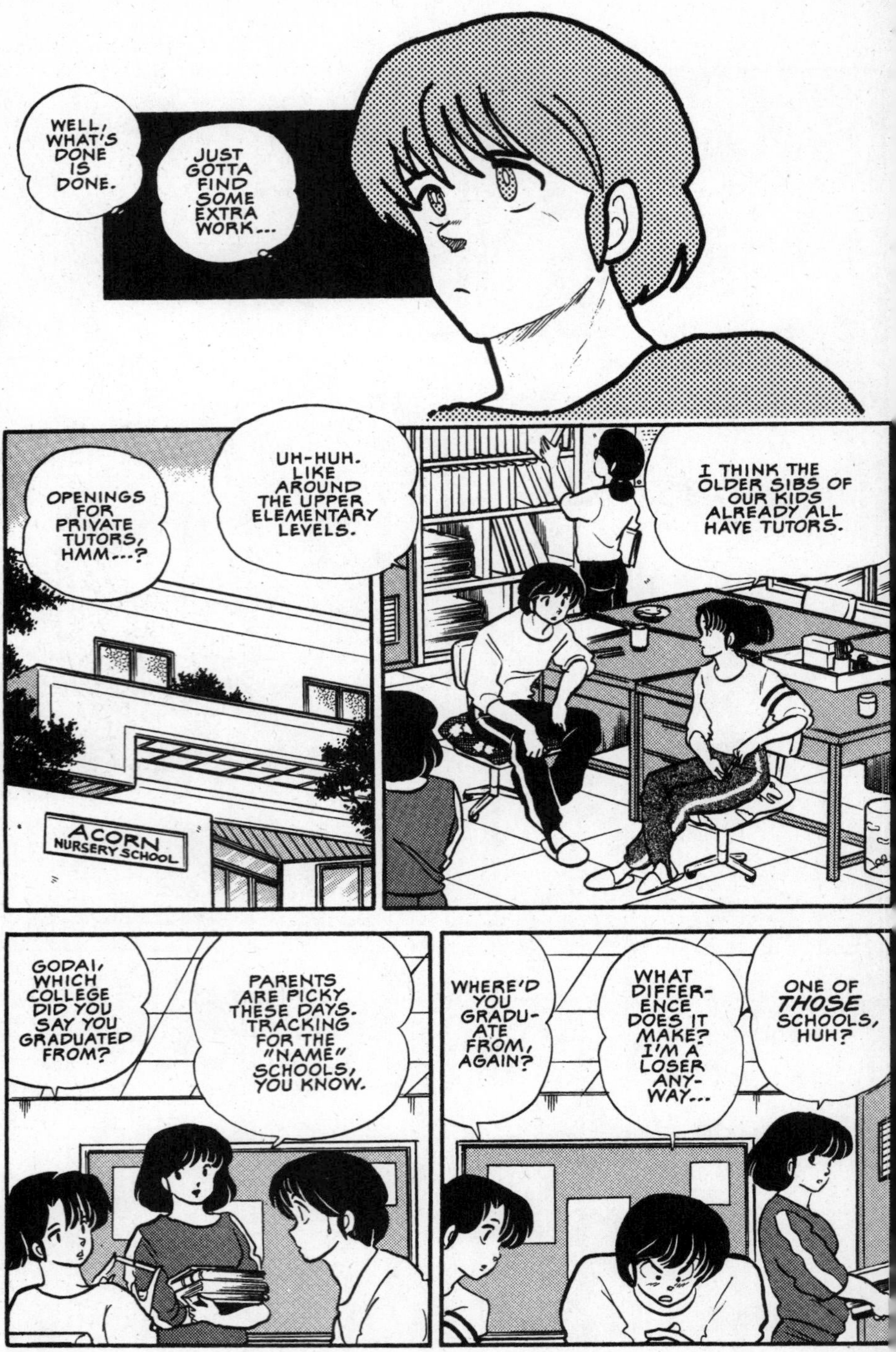

WELL, WHAT'S DONE IS DONE.
JUST GOTTA FIND SOME EXTRA WORK...
OPENINGS FOR PRIVATE TUTORS, HMM...?
UH-HUH. LIKE AROUND THE UPPER ELEMENTARY LEVELS.
ACORN NURSERY SCHOOL
I THINK THE OLDER SIBS OF OUR KIDS ALREADY ALL HAVE TUTORS.
GODAI, WHICH COLLEGE DID YOU SAY YOU GRADUATED FROM?
PARENTS ARE PICKY THESE DAYS. TRACKING FOR THE "NAME" SCHOOLS, YOU KNOW.
WHERE'D YOU GRADUATE FROM, AGAIN?
WHAT DIFFERENCE DOES IT MAKE? I'M A LOSER ANYWAY...
ONE OF *THOSE* SCHOOLS, HUH?

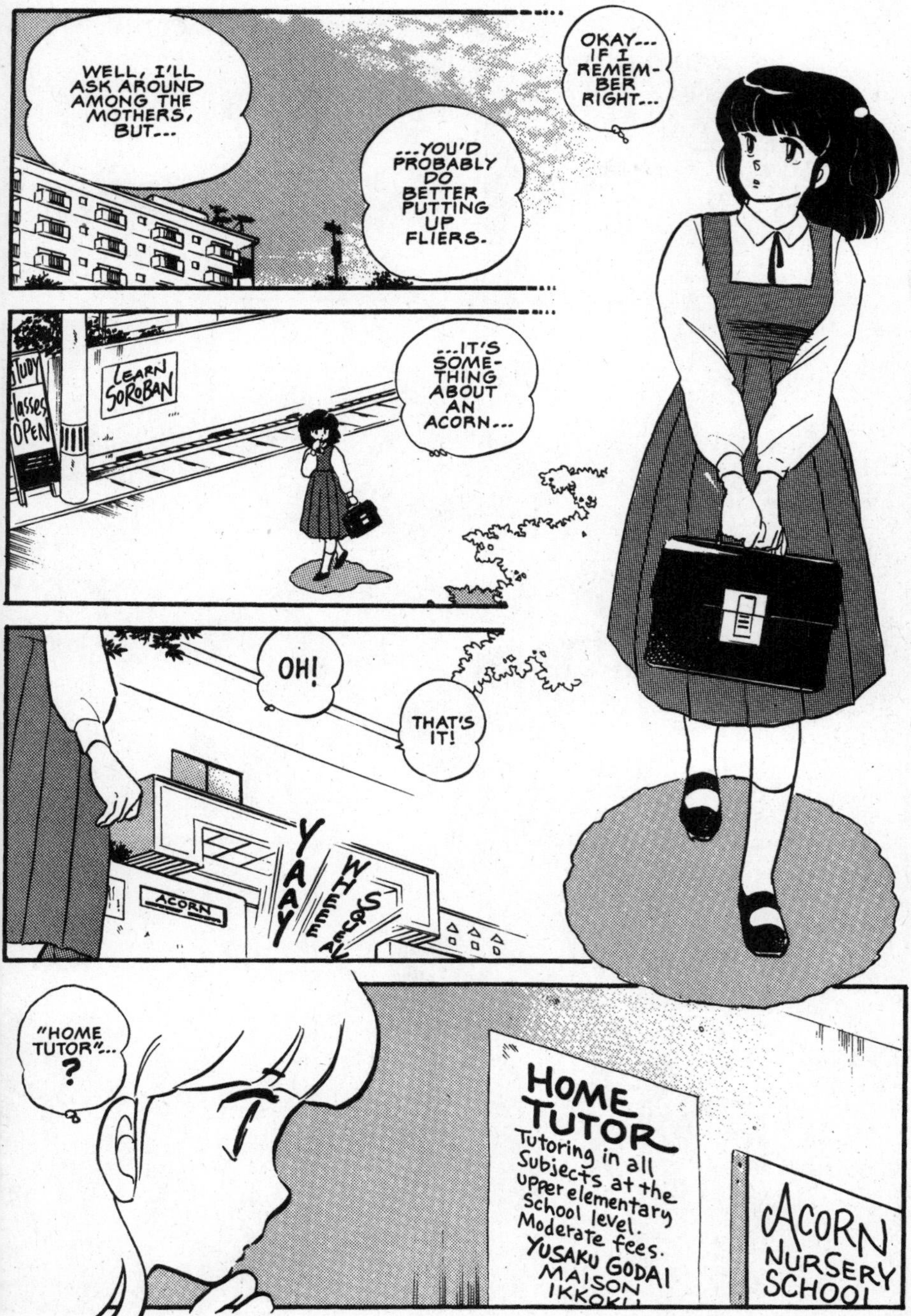
WELL, I'LL ASK AROUND AMONG THE MOTHERS, BUT...
...YOU'D PROBABLY DO BETTER PUTTING UP FLIERS.
STUDY Classes OPEN
LEARN SOROBAN
...IT'S SOMETHING ABOUT AN ACORN...
OH!
THAT'S IT!
ACORN
YAAY
OKAY... IF I REMEMBER RIGHT...
"HOME TUTOR"... ?
HOME TUTOR
Tutoring in all Subjects at the upper elementary School level. Moderate fees.
YUSAKU GODAI
MAISON IKKOKU
ACORN NURSERY SCHOOL

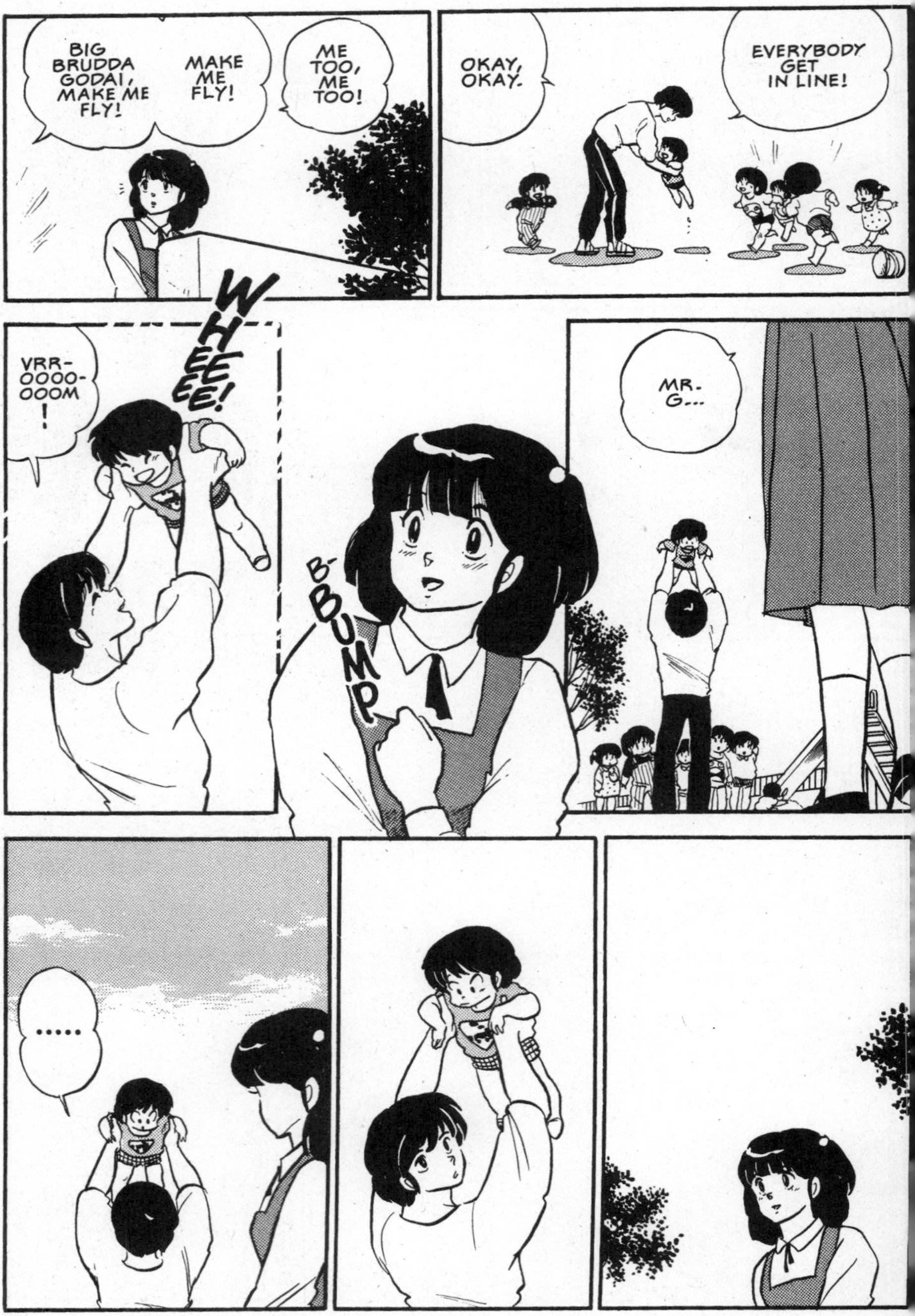
BIG BRUDDA GODAI, MAKE ME FLY!
MAKE ME FLY!
ME TOO, ME TOO!
OKAY, OKAY.
EVERYBODY GET IN LINE!
VRR-OOOO-OOOM!
WHEEEEE!
B-BUMP
MR. G...
......

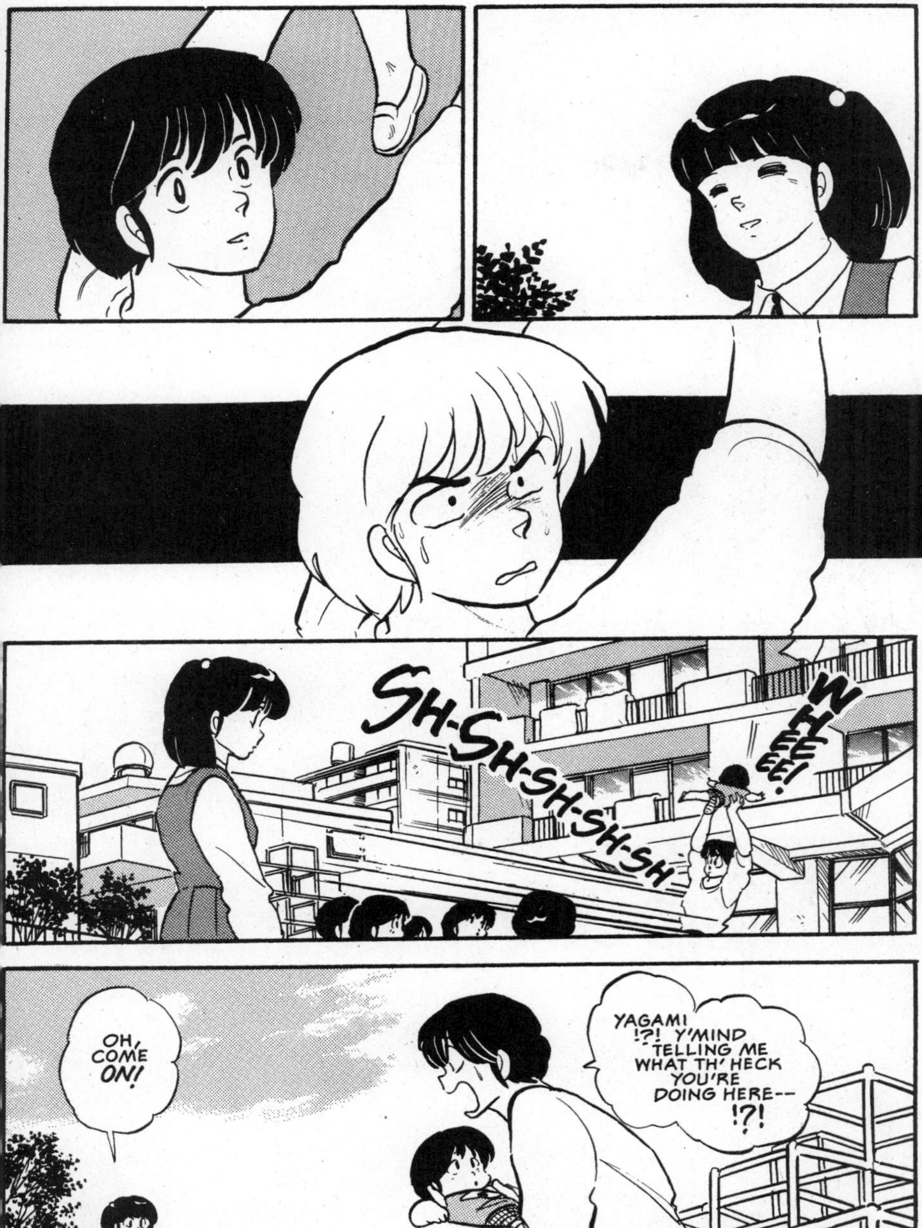
SH-SH-SH-SH-SH-SH
WHEEEE!
OH, COME ON!
YAGAMI !?! Y'MIND TELLING ME WHAT TH' HECK YOU'RE DOING HERE-- !?!

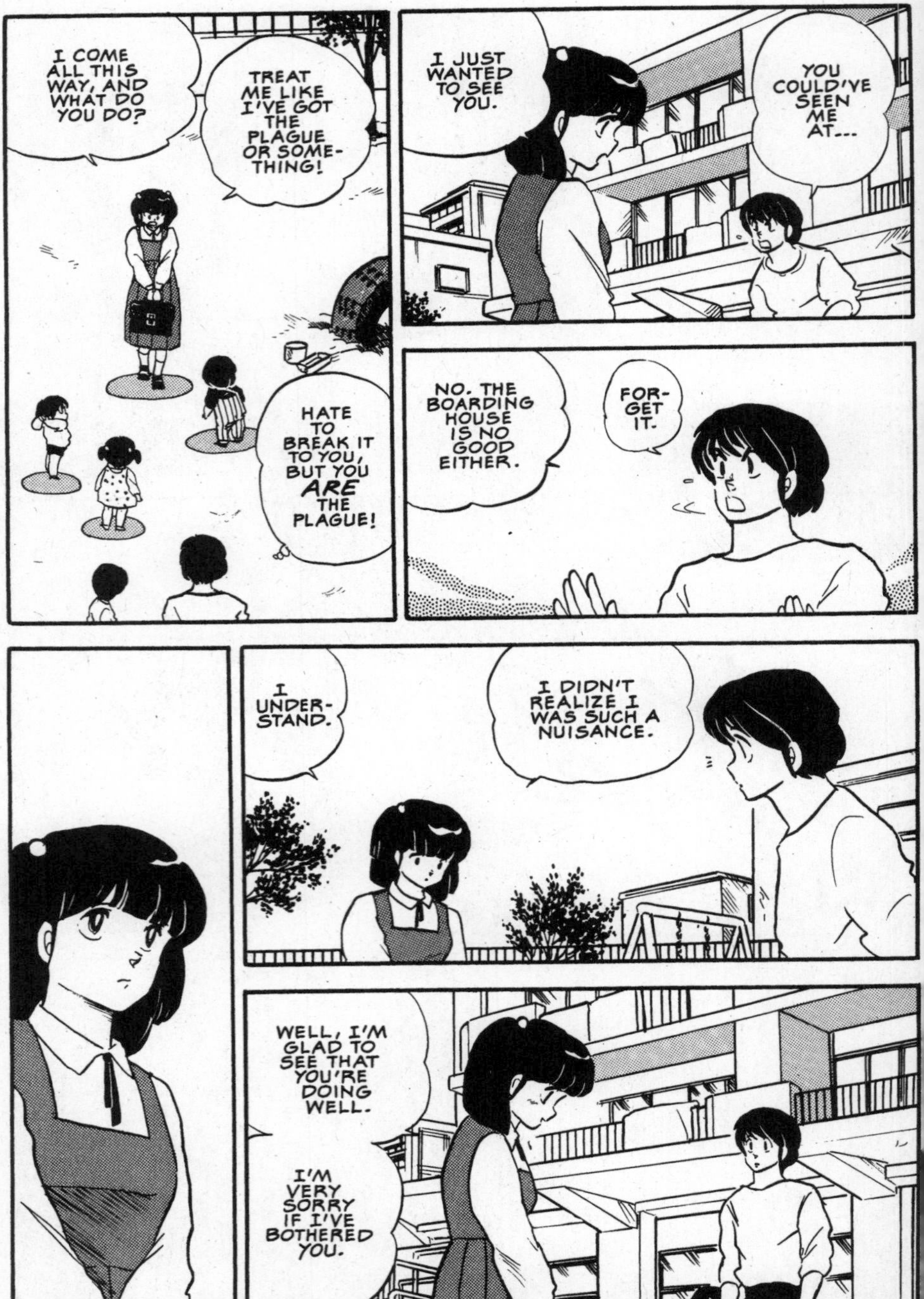
I COME ALL THIS WAY, AND WHAT DO YOU DO?
TREAT ME LIKE I'VE GOT THE PLAGUE OR SOMETHING!
HATE TO BREAK IT TO YOU, BUT YOU *ARE* THE PLAGUE!
I JUST WANTED TO SEE YOU.
YOU COULD'VE SEEN ME AT...
NO. THE BOARDING HOUSE IS NO GOOD EITHER.
FORGET IT.
I UNDERSTAND.
I DIDN'T REALIZE I WAS SUCH A NUISANCE.
WELL, I'M GLAD TO SEE THAT YOU'RE DOING WELL.
I'M VERY SORRY IF I'VE BOTHERED YOU.

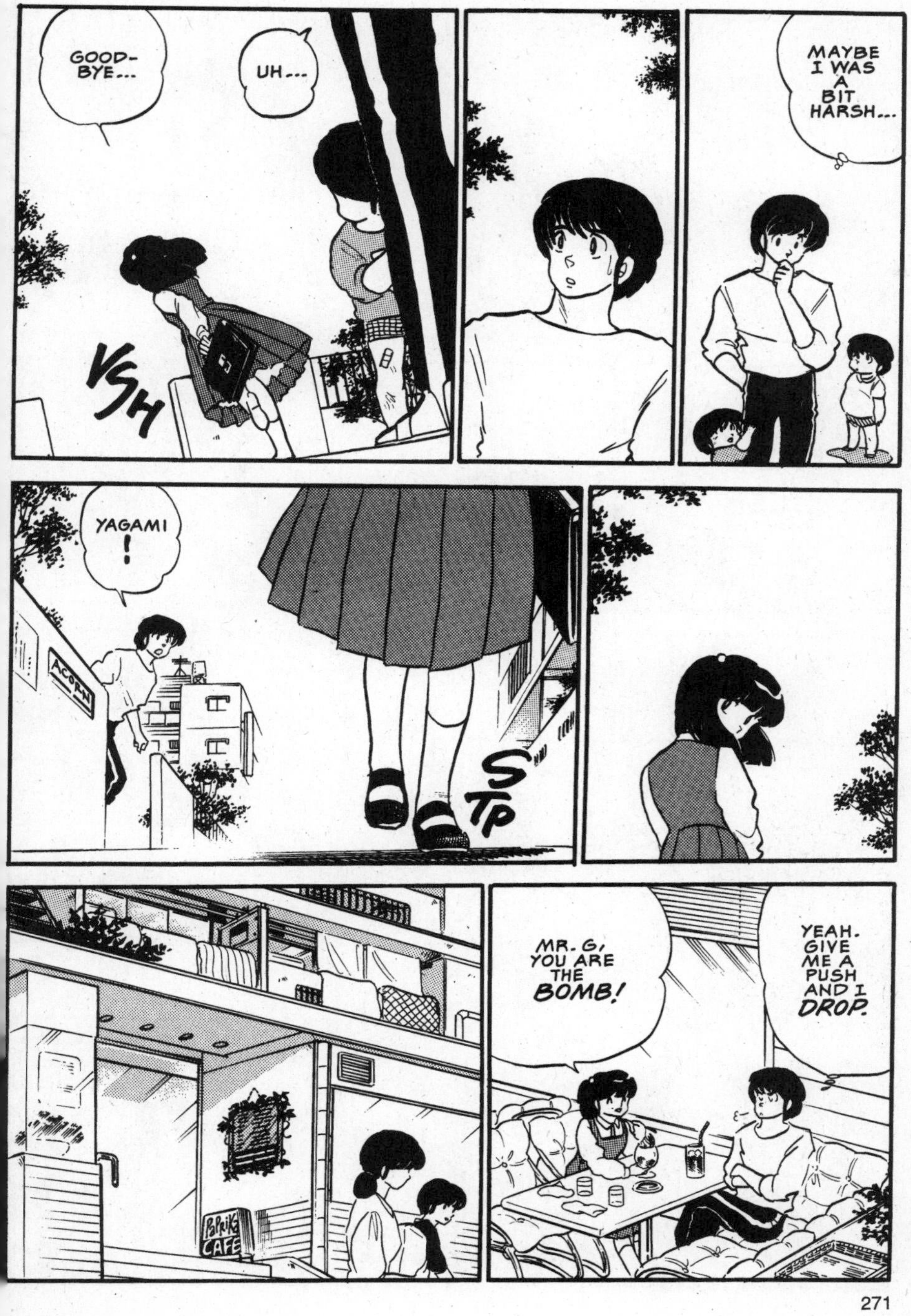
GOOD-BYE...
UH...
VSH
MAYBE I WAS A BIT HARSH...
YAGAMI!
ACORN
STP
PAPRIKA CAFE
MR. G, YOU ARE THE BOMB!
YEAH. GIVE ME A PUSH AND I DROP.

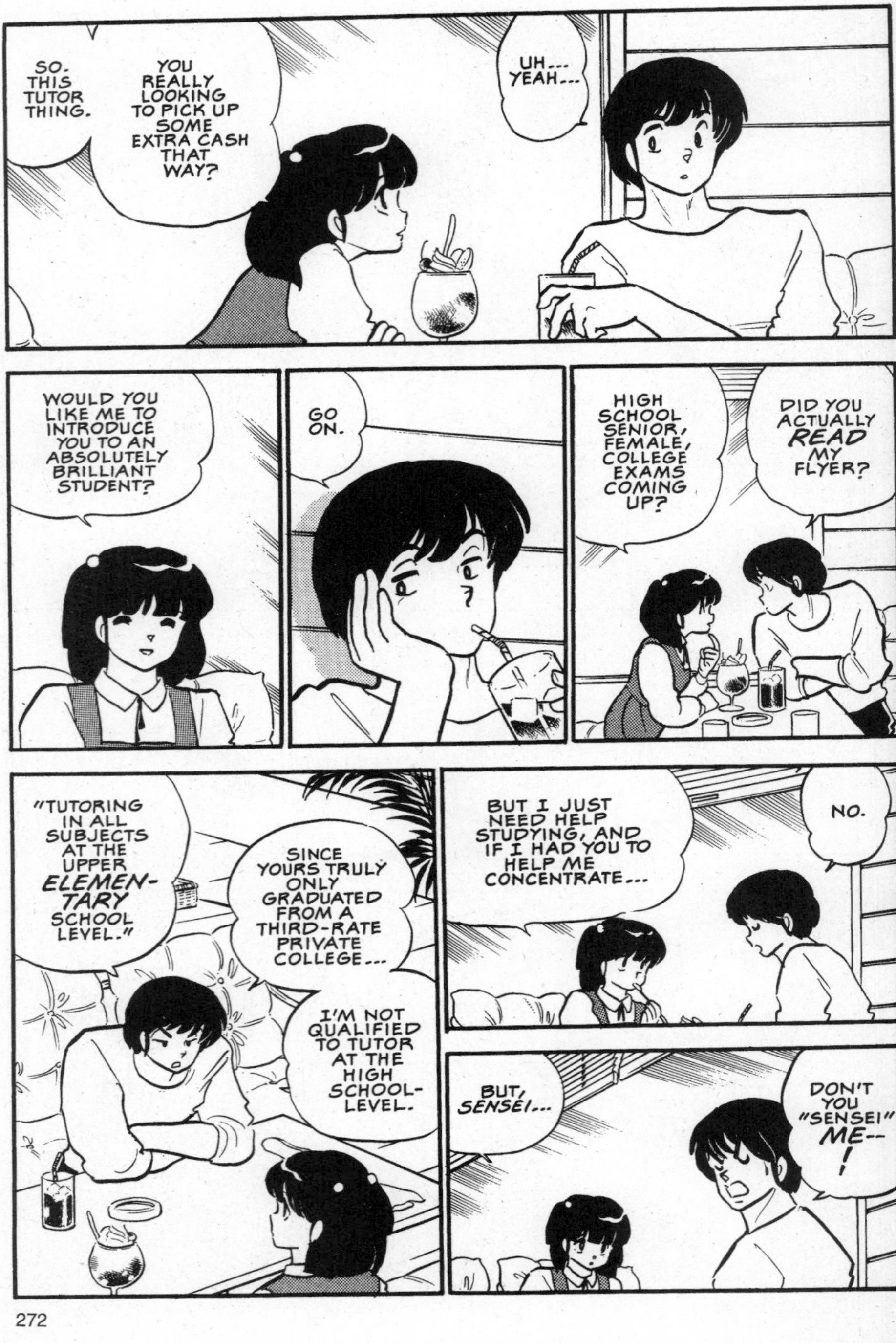
SO- THIS TUTOR THING.
YOU REALLY LOOKING TO PICK UP SOME EXTRA CASH THAT WAY?
UH... YEAH...
WOULD YOU LIKE ME TO INTRODUCE YOU TO AN ABSOLUTELY BRILLIANT STUDENT?
GO ON.
HIGH SCHOOL SENIOR, FEMALE, COLLEGE EXAMS COMING UP?
DID YOU ACTUALLY READ MY FLYER?
"TUTORING IN ALL SUBJECTS AT THE UPPER ELEMENTARY SCHOOL LEVEL."
SINCE YOURS TRULY ONLY GRADUATED FROM A THIRD-RATE PRIVATE COLLEGE...
I'M NOT QUALIFIED TO TUTOR AT THE HIGH SCHOOL-LEVEL.
BUT I JUST NEED HELP STUDYING, AND IF I HAD YOU TO HELP ME CONCENTRATE...
NO.
BUT, SENSEI...
DON'T YOU "SENSEI" ME--!

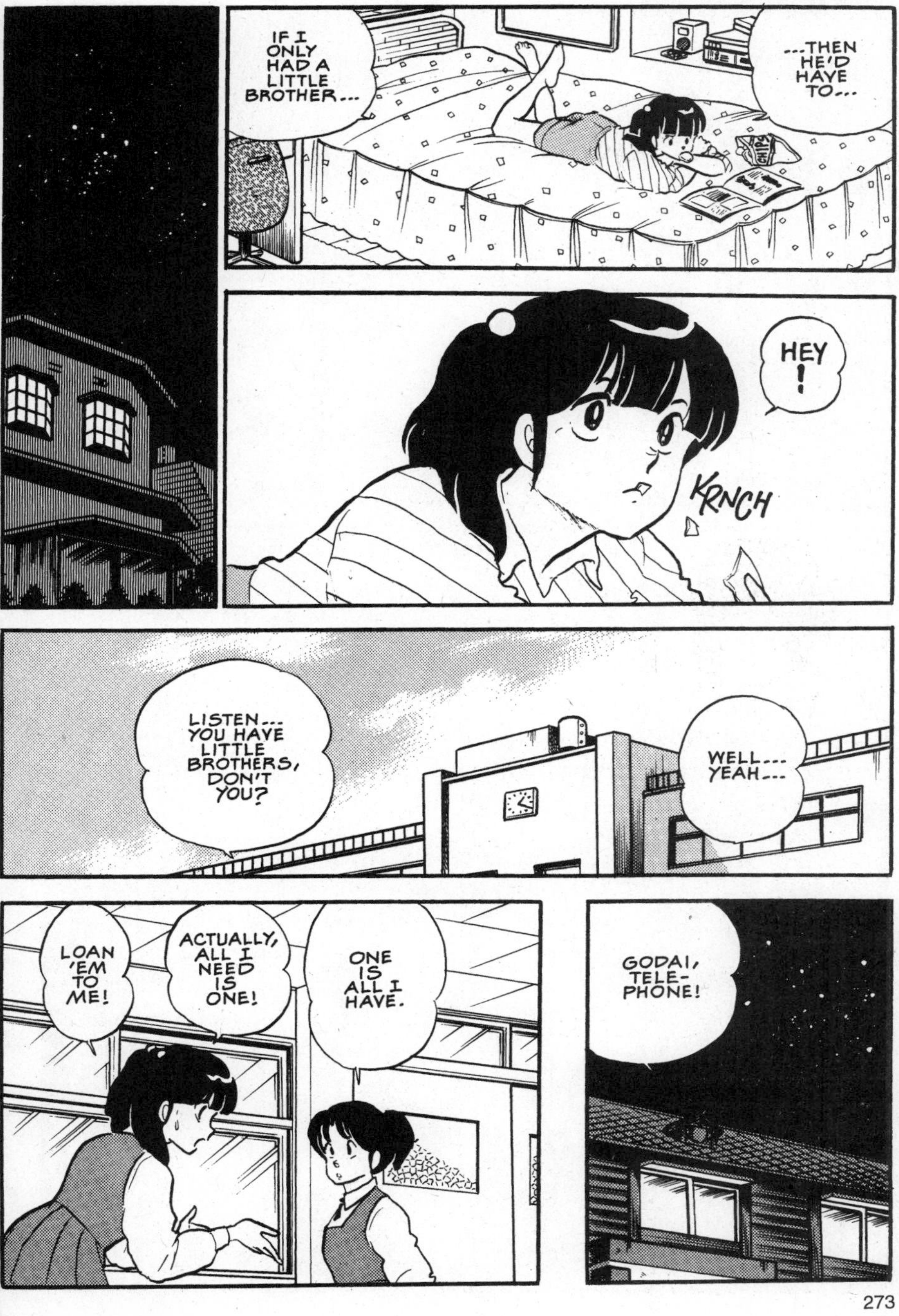
IF I ONLY HAD A LITTLE BROTHER...
...THEN HE'D HAVE TO...
CHIPS
HEY!
KRNCH
LISTEN... YOU HAVE LITTLE BROTHERS, DON'T YOU?
WELL... YEAH...
LOAN 'EM TO ME!
ACTUALLY, ALL I NEED IS ONE!
ONE IS ALL I HAVE.
GODAI, TELE-PHONE!

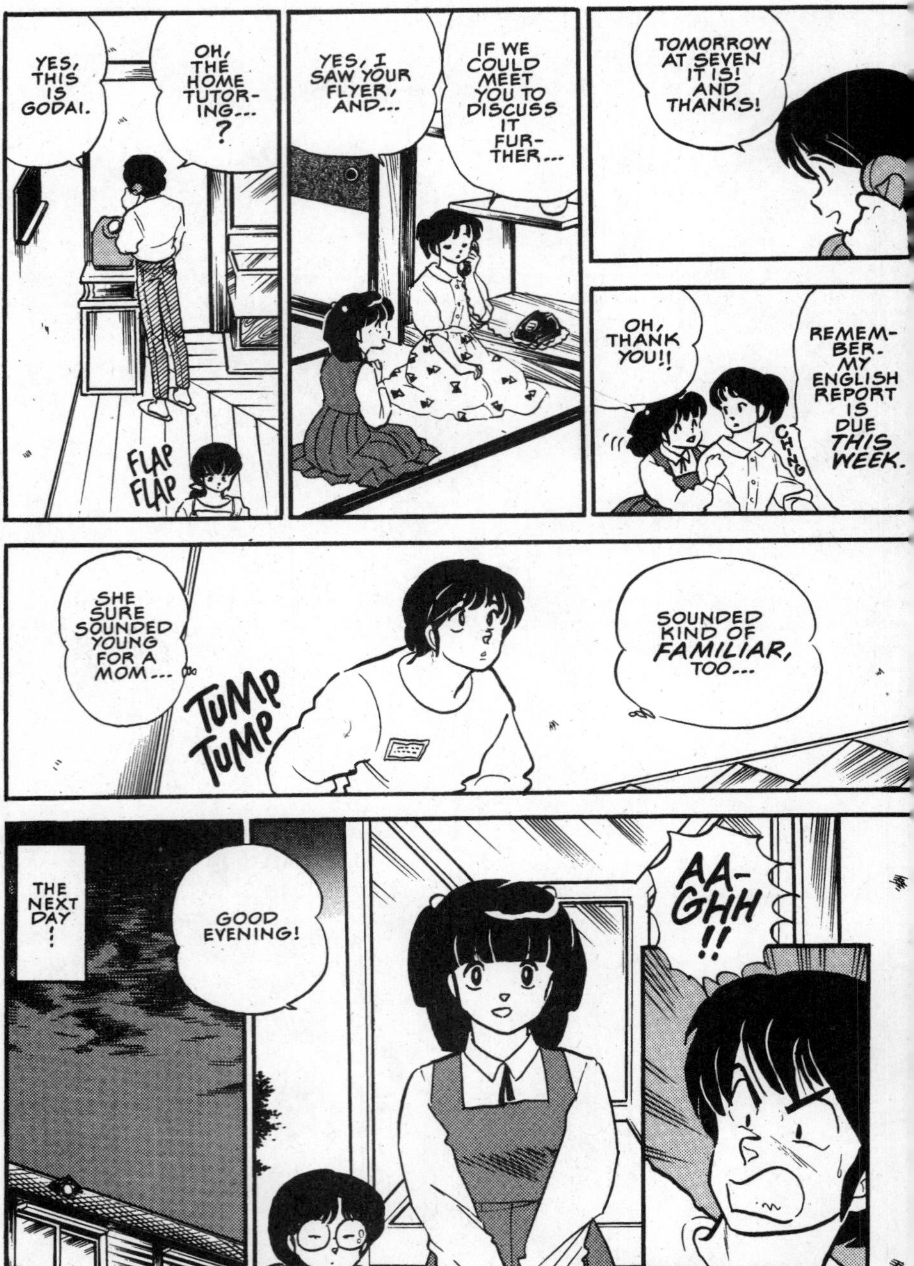
YES, THIS IS GODAI.
OH, THE HOME TUTORING...?
FLAP FLAP
YES, I SAW YOUR FLYER, AND...
IF WE COULD MEET YOU TO DISCUSS IT FURTHER...
TOMORROW AT SEVEN IT IS! AND THANKS!
OH, THANK YOU!!
REMEMBER. MY ENGLISH REPORT IS DUE THIS WEEK.
CHING
SHE SURE SOUNDED YOUNG FOR A MOM...
TUMP TUMP
SOUNDED KIND OF FAMILIAR, TOO...
THE NEXT DAY!!
GOOD EVENING!
AAGHH!!

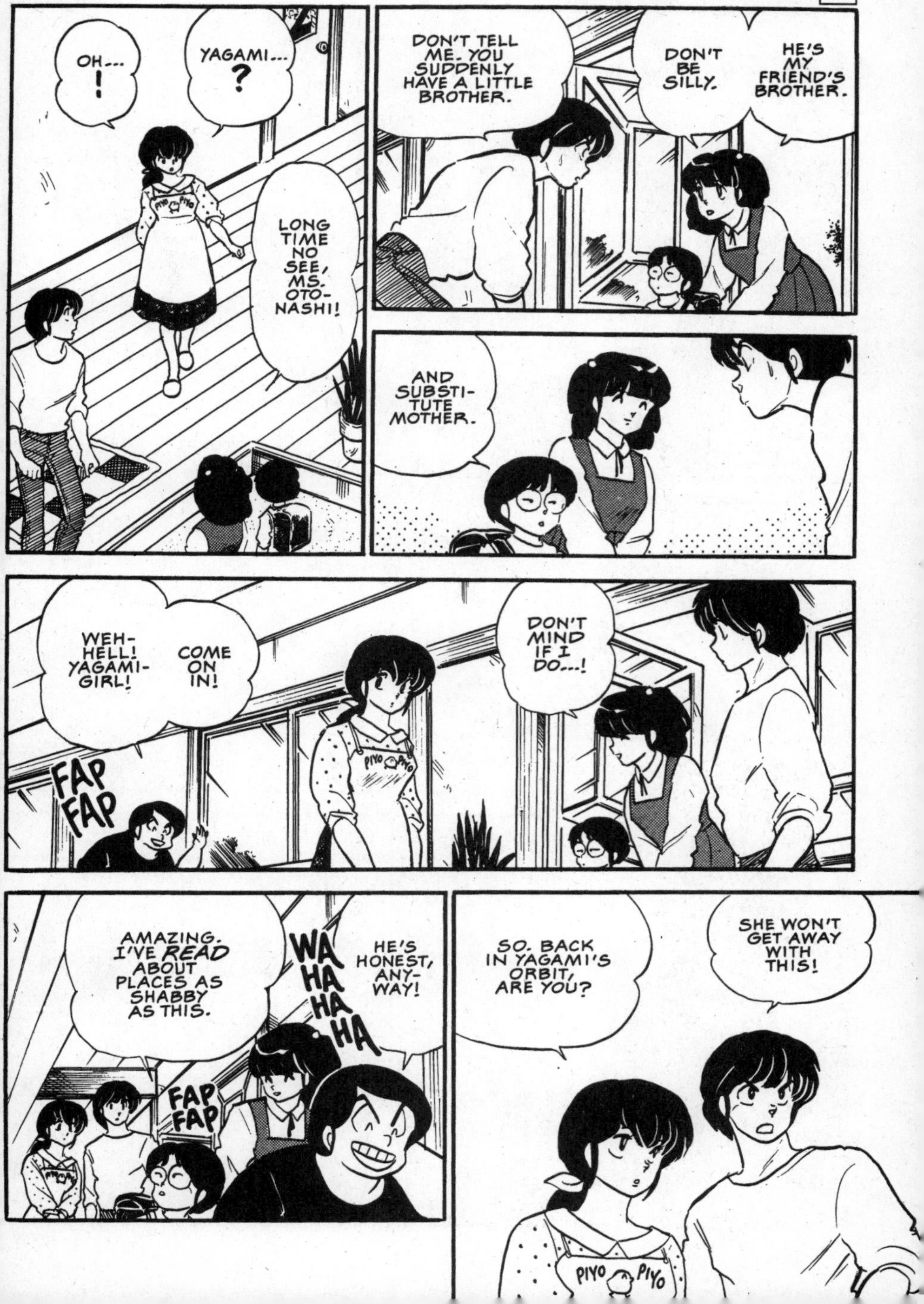
OH... !
YAGAMI... ?
PIYO PIYO
LONG TIME NO SEE, MS. OTONASHI!
DON'T TELL ME. YOU SUDDENLY HAVE A LITTLE BROTHER.
DON'T BE SILLY.
HE'S MY FRIEND'S BROTHER.
AND SUBSTITUTE MOTHER.
WEH-HELL! YAGAMI-GIRL!
COME ON IN!
FAP FAP
PIYO PIYO
DON'T MIND IF I DO...!
AMAZING. I'VE *READ* ABOUT PLACES AS SHABBY AS THIS.
WA HA HA HA HA
HE'S HONEST, ANYWAY!
FAP FAP
SO. BACK IN YAGAMI'S ORBIT, ARE YOU?
SHE WON'T GET AWAY WITH THIS!
PIYO PIYO

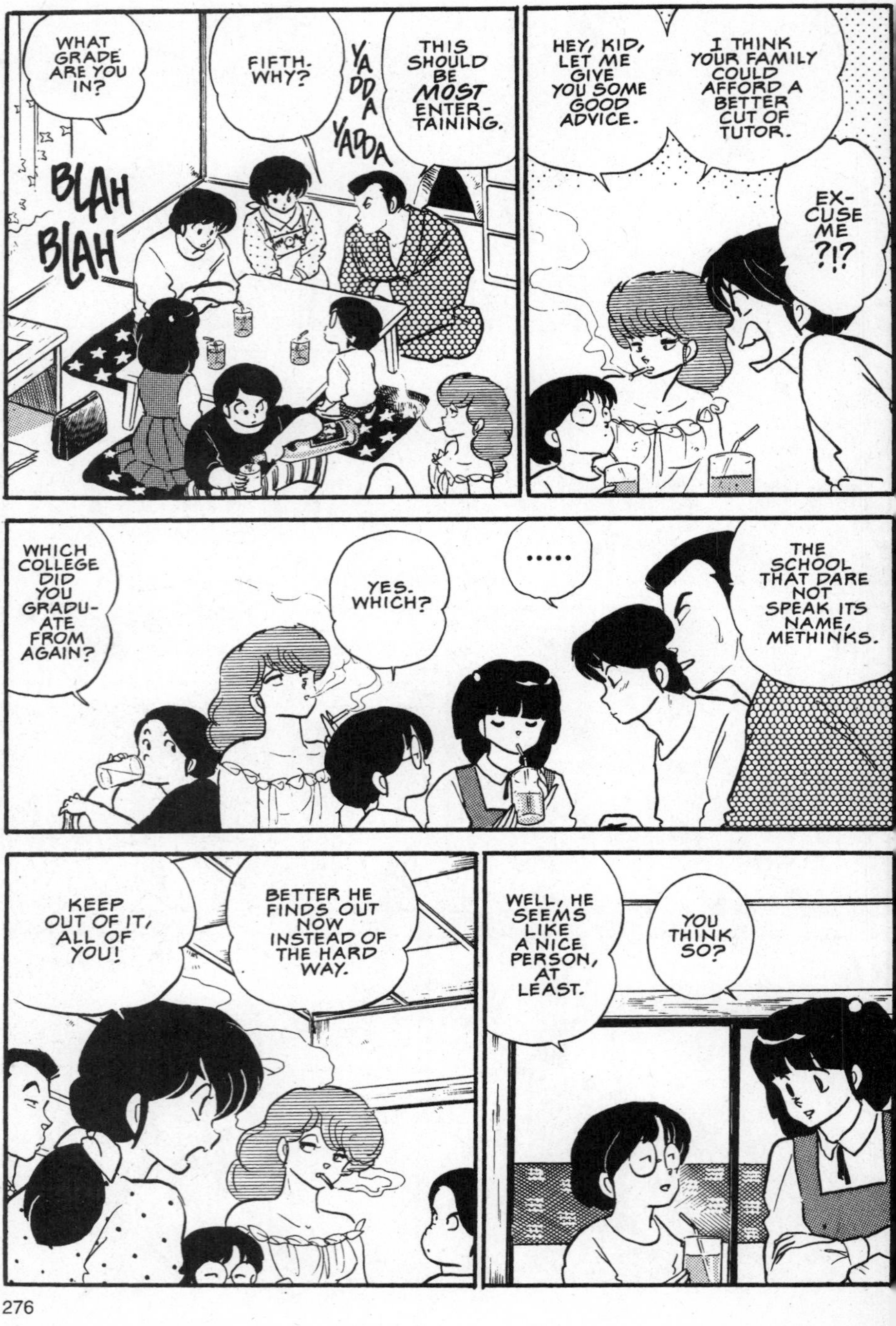
WHAT GRADE ARE YOU IN?
BLAH BLAH
FIFTH. WHY?
YADDA YADDA
THIS SHOULD BE MOST ENTERTAINING.
HEY, KID, LET ME GIVE YOU SOME GOOD ADVICE.
I THINK YOUR FAMILY COULD AFFORD A BETTER CUT OF TUTOR.
EX-CUSE ME ?!?
WHICH COLLEGE DID YOU GRADUATE FROM AGAIN?
YES. WHICH?
.....
THE SCHOOL THAT DARE NOT SPEAK ITS NAME, METHINKS.
KEEP OUT OF IT, ALL OF YOU!
BETTER HE FINDS OUT NOW INSTEAD OF THE HARD WAY.
WELL, HE SEEMS LIKE A NICE PERSON, AT LEAST.
YOU THINK SO?

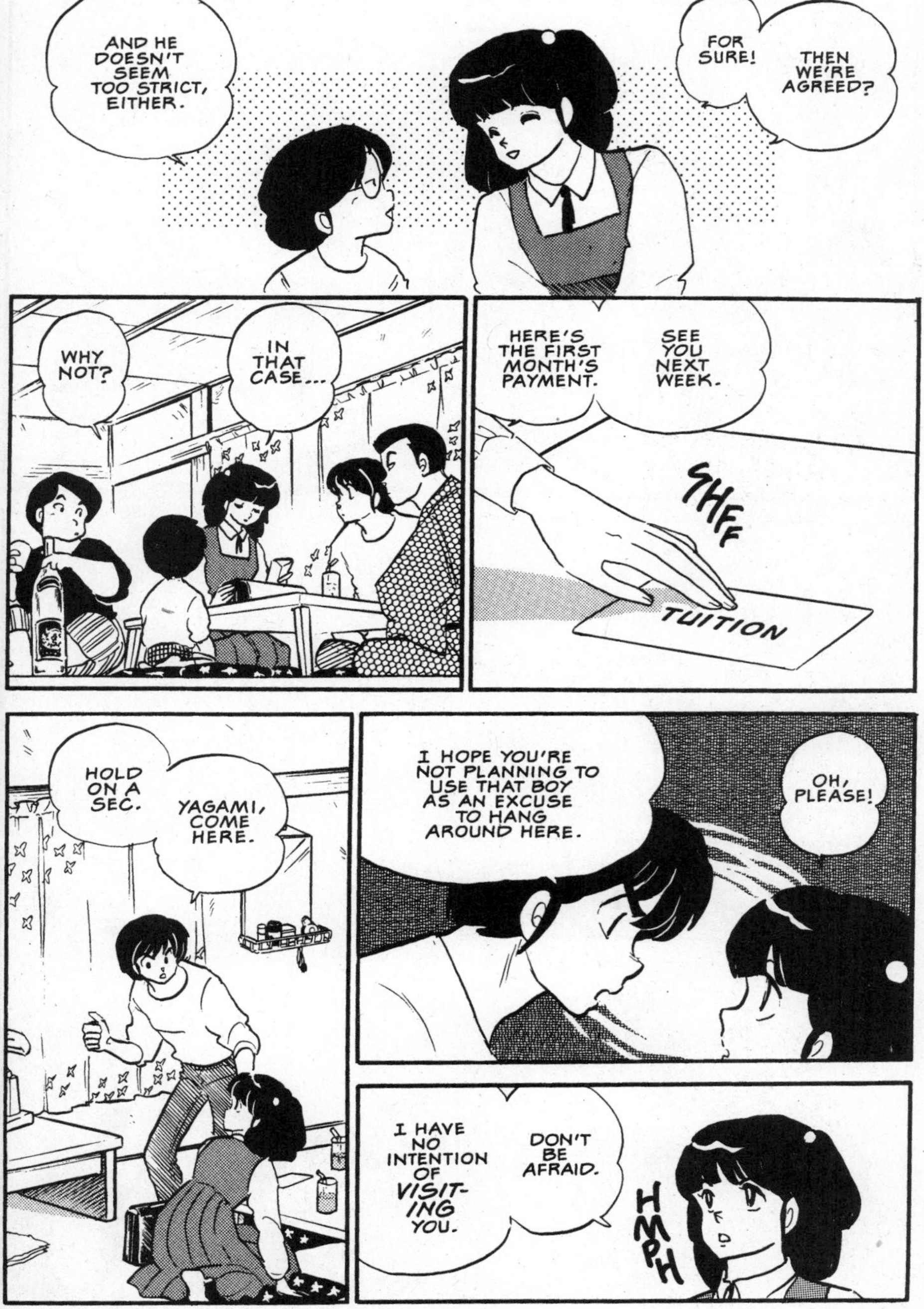
AND HE DOESN'T SEEM TOO STRICT, EITHER.
FOR SURE!
THEN WE'RE AGREED?
WHY NOT?
IN THAT CASE...
HERE'S THE FIRST MONTH'S PAYMENT.
SEE YOU NEXT WEEK.
SHFF
TUITION
HOLD ON A SEC.
YAGAMI, COME HERE.
I HOPE YOU'RE NOT PLANNING TO USE THAT BOY AS AN EXCUSE TO HANG AROUND HERE.
OH, PLEASE!
I HAVE NO INTENTION OF VISITING YOU.
DON'T BE AFRAID.
HMPH

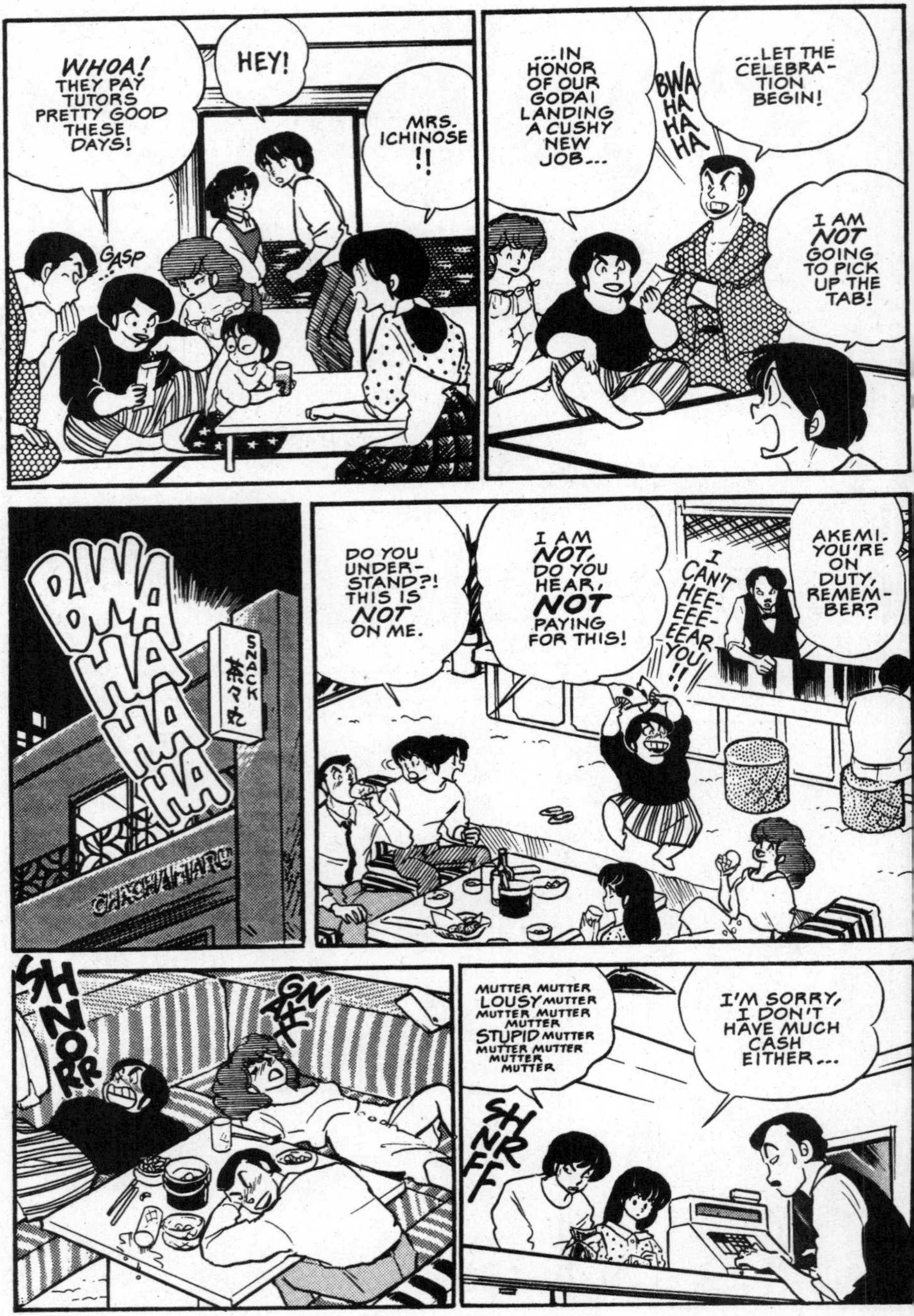
WHOA! THEY PAY TUTORS PRETTY GOOD THESE DAYS!
HEY!
GASP
MRS. ICHINOSE !!
...IN HONOR OF OUR GODAI LANDING A CUSHY NEW JOB...
BWA HA HA HA
...LET THE CELEBRATION BEGIN!
I AM NOT GOING TO PICK UP THE TAB!
BWA HA HA HA HA HA
SNACK 茶々丸
CHACHAMARU
DO YOU UNDERSTAND?! THIS IS NOT ON ME.
I AM NOT, DO YOU HEAR, NOT PAYING FOR THIS!
I CAN'T HEE-EEE-EEAR YOU!!
AKEMI, YOU'RE ON DUTY, REMEMBER?
SHNORR
GNAH
MUTTER MUTTER LOUSY MUTTER MUTTER MUTTER MUTTER STUPID MUTTER MUTTER MUTTER MUTTER MUTTER
SHNRFF
I'M SORRY, I DON'T HAVE MUCH CASH EITHER...

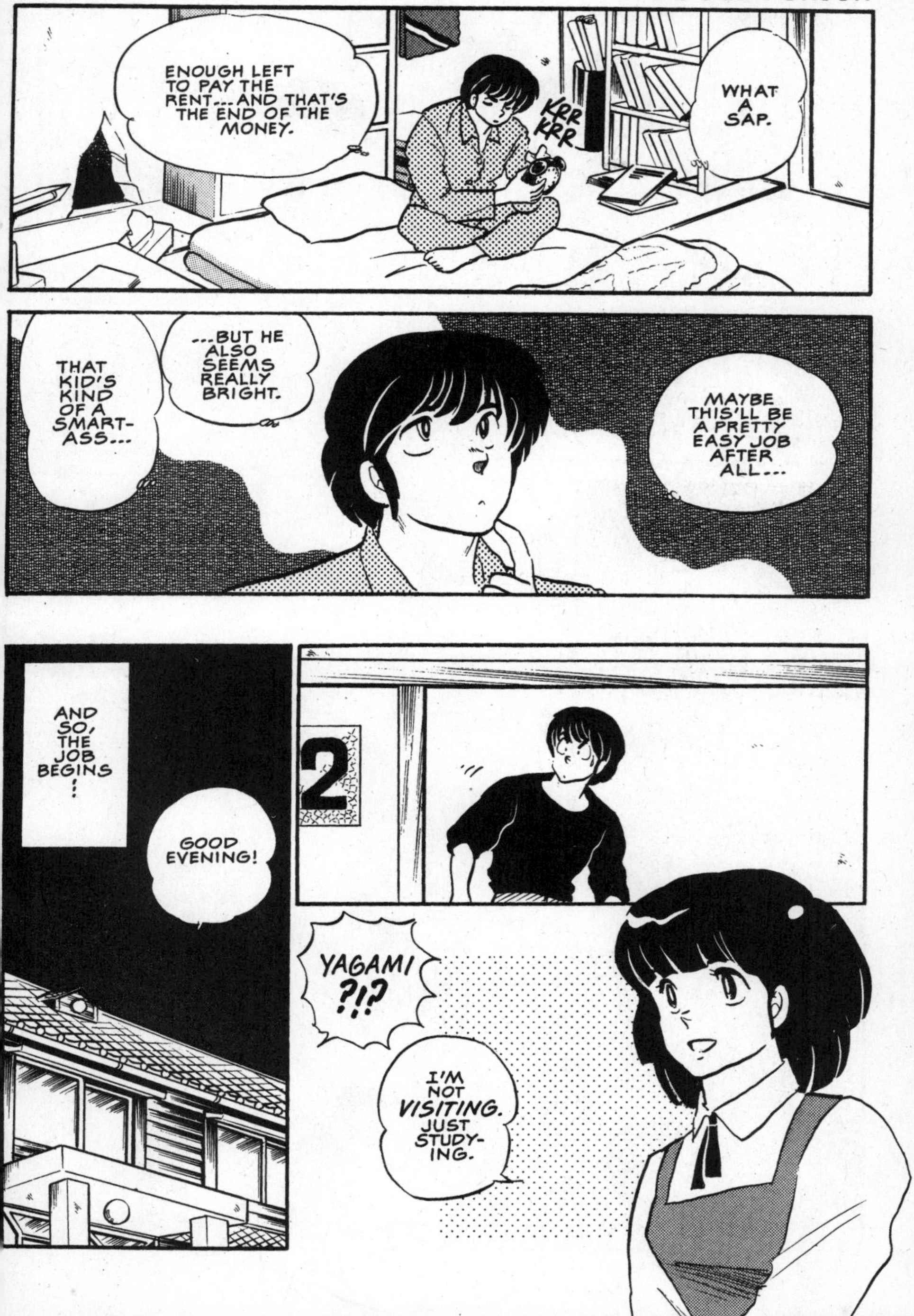
ENOUGH LEFT TO PAY THE RENT... AND THAT'S THE END OF THE MONEY.
KRR KRR
WHAT A SAP.
THAT KID'S KIND OF A SMART-ASS...
...BUT HE ALSO SEEMS REALLY BRIGHT.
MAYBE THIS'LL BE A PRETTY EASY JOB AFTER ALL...
AND SO, THE JOB BEGINS!
GOOD EVENING!
YAGAMI ?!?
I'M NOT VISITING. JUST STUDYING.

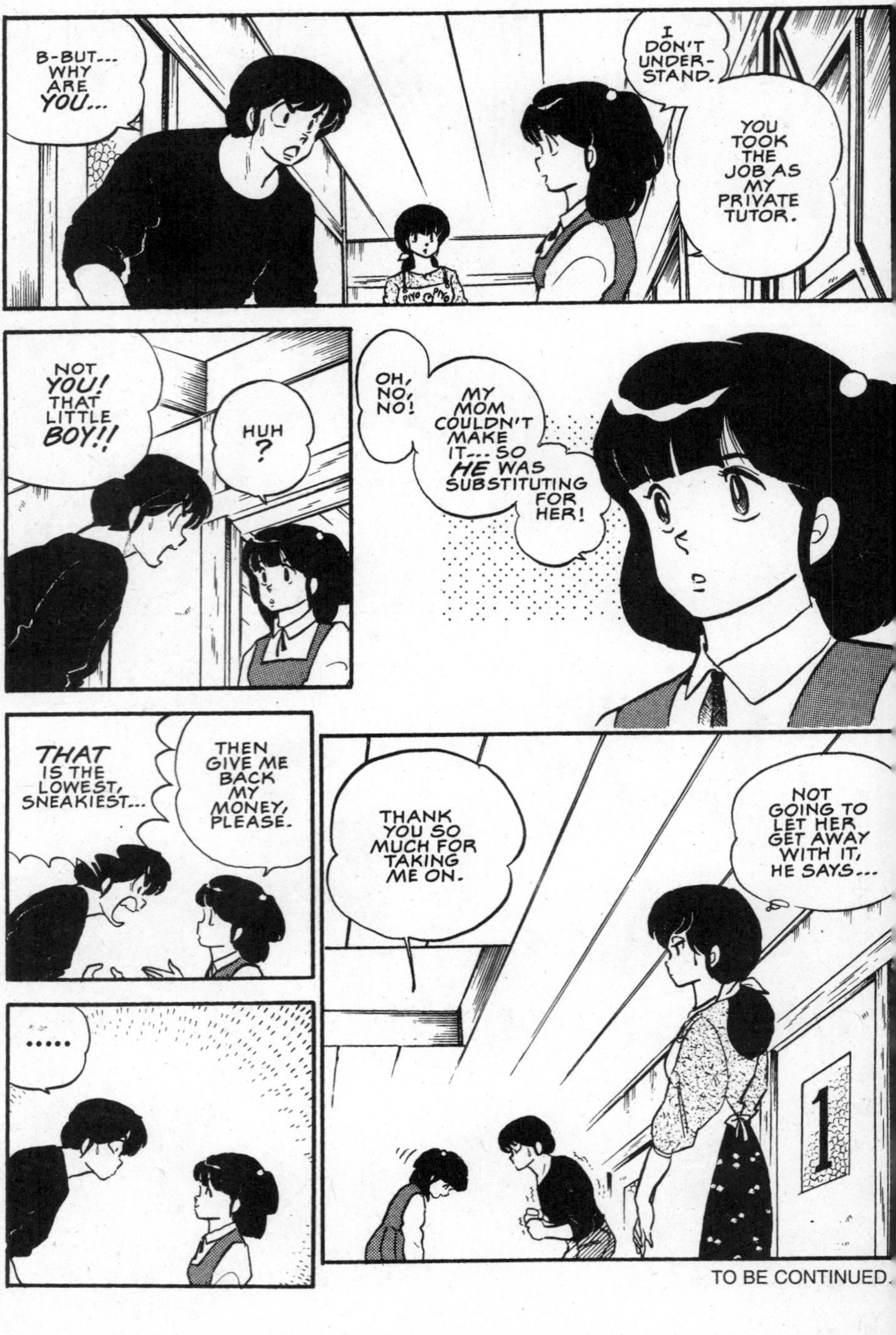
B-BUT... WHY ARE YOU...
I DON'T UNDER-STAND.
YOU TOOK THE JOB AS MY PRIVATE TUTOR.
NOT YOU! THAT LITTLE BOY!!
HUH ?
OH, NO, NO!
MY MOM COULDN'T MAKE IT... SO HE WAS SUBSTITUTING FOR HER!
THAT IS THE LOWEST, SNEAKIEST...
THEN GIVE ME BACK MY MONEY, PLEASE.
.....
THANK YOU SO MUCH FOR TAKING ME ON.
NOT GOING TO LET HER GET AWAY WITH IT, HE SAYS...

TO BE CONTINUED.